THE SWITCH

THREE HORROR NOVELS

GAGE GREENWOOD

To Nick Roberts,
I am forever in your debt. Thanks for being one of the real ones.

CONTENTS

BUNKER DOGS

ON A CLEAR DAY, YOU CAN SEE BLOCK ISLAND

IN THE EYES, IN THE SHADOWS

BUNKER DOGS

Don't just FEAR
what you're
HIDING from.

FEAR
what you're
HIDING with.

GAGE GREENWOOD

FOREWORD BY CLAY CHAPMAN

When did Gage Greenwood first come into your life?

For me, it was Bunker Dogs. Maybe you knew him before, maybe later. Hell, maybe you were lucky and were there from the get-go and got in on the Greenwood fandom from the ground floor...

I found Gage in a subterranean stronghold, hiding from all the monsters out there in the world. Finding a few down below, too. Monsters, everywhere. But in Gage's world, either on the page or in real life, I never felt alone. There was always Gage himself, right there, guiding the reader—guiding me—through.

When Gage asked if I might be able to speak about Bunker Dogs, my instinct was to speak about Gage. I feel like what needs to be said, what should be shared here and now, if it hasn't a hundred times before elsewhere by other, more resonant writers: Gage Greenwood is a force of nature that I have had the good fortune of getting whisked away by.

There's something so fundamentally elemental to his very being, his writing, his presence amidst the horror community, that I find it difficult to articulate what kind of atmospheric condition he even is. Is Gage a tornado? A monsoon? A heatwave?

His career seems to suggest so, laying waste to the rest of us out here, trying to figure out how in the hell to get the reader's attention. Gage is just that kind of whirlpool that sucks audiences in.

I'm probably not the best perspective of this. I've always been smitten with Gage from the first time we shared table space at the Halloween Hangover in Richmond, Virginia. He's always had a resolute charm, a determined generosity, that I've never quite been able to shake.

Someone else might be better equipped to quantify the Greenwood Effect... but from what I've seen, what I've personally been privy to, is that Gage himself has the uncanny knack of getting people excited about horror. About reading horror. Not just his own horror, but other's work as well. He's been a champion of so many authors. He is an architect of safe spaces on social media, where others can share their work.

He is a guardian to up-and-coming authors entering the fray for the very first time, and something of a grizzled veteran who can wax about the good ol' days... even if they were only a month or so ago. I guess I just feel like I'm always aware of Gage lifting others up. Of shielding writers when a protective barrier may be needed. He advocates, he promotes, he sheepishly takes digs at himself.

In that way, I guess, Gage has created something of a bunker for horror folk. A shelter to share. This space, subterranean or otherwise, has been forged through passion, through conviction, through patience and undeniable talent. Through love.

Gage has given us a place—a book—for writers and readers to come together and share something sacred.

That, to me, is what Bunker Dogs embodies. A safe haven for horror fans.

So come on down. Gage will hold the door open.

- Clay Chapman

CHAPTER 1
ARE YOU READY?

Something scratched above Cassie's head. She glanced up from her American History book to the popcorn ceiling. It stopped. She sighed, wiped her blurry eyes, and refocused on her homework. She had the book leaning on her upper legs as she lay on the bed, her head half-propped by her lumpy pillow.

The noise returned, a gentle scratch. Possibly a rogue squirrel or mouse found its way into the attic as the fall weather broke. But then, the noise dragged as if someone moved a heavy table across the room. One long scratch. It stopped again.

She peeled her eyes from the popcorn ceiling. Even in her perplexed state, her mind made patterns from the dripping plaster: faces, vulgar creatures with elongated mouths and droopy eyes.

Giving up on her homework, she dropped the book on the floor with a thud. The loose binding on the hardcover took its final beating and separated from its pages as it hit the hardwood.

Cassie grabbed her headphones and spun the wheel on her iPod until she reached Taking Back Sunday. Her brother blasted his music down the hall in his room but through Cassie's bedroom door, it sounded like nothing more than a series of muddy bumps. Taking

Back Sunday filtered through her ears into her brain and silenced the agitation forming all around her.

Thud.

She yelped and ripped the headphones from her ears. Her heart shot off like fireworks in her chest. Something landed in her hair and on her forehead. She rubbed it off, examining it on her fingertips. Flecks of loose plaster rained onto her from the ceiling.

She jumped out of bed with a skittering heart and entered the hall. The bumping from Chris's music went from muffled tones to nightclub-level booming, each thump of the beat fraying Cassie's nerves. As the deep bass penetrated the hall, the floorboards vibrated under her feet. It felt like the house had turned on her, taunting her with sounds and motion. Even the air was wrong, too thick for autumn.

She pounded on her brother's door. "Chris."

She used to love when he babysat. He was the cool older brother who didn't mind pulling up his sleeves and playing with her in the dirt or having a round of hide and seek in the dark, tag in the fields of long, yellow grass, and always stopping to give her sage advice, the kind which often went against what adults told their children. All Chris did anymore was lock himself in his room and blast his shitty music. She couldn't even remember when the change happened, but it was sudden. The chains of their friendship snapped off rather than slowly rusting with time.

"Chris!" She snarled, stormed through the hall, and charged downstairs into the kitchen.

From there, Chris's music went back to softer bumps. She certainly wouldn't investigate the attic noises alone and Chris obviously wasn't bothered by it, or her for that matter, he just sat alone in his room, drowning in bass. She'd just have to ride it out until her father came home.

She rubbed her eyes and made herself a turkey sandwich with chips. As she wiped a layer of mustard on her wheat bread, she heard the scratching again. She couldn't, though. There was no way

she would hear a soft noise in the attic over Chris's blasting rap music.

Scratch. Scratch. Scratch.

What the ever-loving Tell-Tale Heart shit was going on here? *The Tell-Tale Heart.* Thinking of the story sent a wave of sadness into Cassie's stomach. Chris once faced the wrath of their father because he read Edgar Allan Poe stories to Cassie about four years earlier, when she was only six.

"What? I didn't read her that stuff. I don't even read it myself," he had argued.

"Read her something normal," their father said.

Even with Chris's denial, he couldn't let their father's words slide. "Like Shakespeare?"

"Sure. That would be great."

Chris laughed. "Me thinks you skipped your Shakespeare lessons in school because that shit is far more vulgar, violent, and horrifying than anything Poe wrote."

"Watch your mouth, Chris."

Cassie came back to reality and realized she'd been absently staring out the kitchen window. A phrase echoed in her brain, and she didn't know why. *Are you ready?*

Are you ready?

Areyouready?

It was rattling around in her head, spoken by a familiar voice, but one she couldn't place. A female voice, soft, gentle, and a little somber, like a mother sending her child away on the first day of school.

Are you ready?

Like a crazy person, she responded to the voice. "Not yet." She didn't know why she said it or what she was talking about, but it felt like the right answer.

Her night was slipping away, hydroplaning on thick ice, inertia driving it toward a shrouded destination. She didn't need to see it to know she wasn't ready for it, that the impact would shatter her peace. She shook her head, loosening the binding those words held over her brain, and squeezed the top square of bread onto her sandwich until the mustard leaked out the sides.

She stormed back upstairs and lay on the bed, resting her sandwich plate on her stomach. Deciding to give the American History book another chance, she scooped it off the floor, leaving the separated cover on its own.

She struggled to adjust her head properly so she could read the material while keeping her sandwich in place. Sighing, she took a bite. A loose splotch of mustard painted her fingers yellow. Now she couldn't touch the book. Dammit. She lifted her yellow fingers in the air as if they were diseased and used her other hand to shift the sandwich plate on top of the book.

Scratch.

Scratch.

Scratch.

This time, it didn't stop; it just kept scratching and scratching. One scratch forward, one scratch back. Back and forth, back and forth, back and forth.

Still holding her hand up, she stared at the rough texture above her head. She followed the noise as it traveled from above the head of her bed to the foot of it.

Her blood pressure boiled, a raging river coursing through her veins. Why did everything have to be so fucking difficult? All she wanted to do was study. Was that so goddamned hard? She pushed herself off the bed, keeping her mustard hand above her head.

One more time, she slammed on Chris's door, and one more time, he ignored her. She kicked it, no longer interested in his attention but wanting to deliver a message. "Asshole."

She paced the hall, forgetting about her mustard hand, despite still holding it in the air like she was halting traffic.

Even with the music blasting into her eardrums, she could still make out the scratching from the attic. She knew she'd have to go up there to see what it was, but the idea filled her with dread. The cold, dank attic was littered with cobwebs, mouse poop, and the occasional bat. Her father hated going up there too, ever since he saw a northern black widow crawling across her mom's old dollhouse.

Fuck it. She opened the attic door with her clean hand and stared up at the dark space. The uneven wooden stairs showed slight signs of rot. She stepped, and instead of meeting stable ground, her feet felt like they walked on sponges.

At the top of the stairs, she clicked the chain hanging above her head. The room came to life with cobwebs, the dollhouse, and old boxes littered with crude drawings she and her brother made in school. A mouse scurried under the door to the crawl space.

She did a double take on an anomaly, her brain struggling to comprehend what it saw. It drove through a rapid-fire series of denials. A joke. A trick. Her mind playing with the angles. It didn't take long for it to coalesce, to become real.

Cassie screamed, an unending siren coming from her throat.

Her brother hung from a rafter, his feet scraping against the dusty floorboards.

Are you ready?

Areyouready?

Are

You

Ready?

"Chris," she yelled, but she knew he was dead, knew it was way too late.

She froze for a moment, unable to look away but wanting nothing more than to turn from it. A low groan left her throat. Her stomach lurched. It couldn't be real. It couldn't happen. She screamed again, a mixture of dread, panic, and incomprehension bubbling acid into her throat. "Chris," she cried. She fumbled backwards, the hard wall snapping her from her frozen state. "Chris," she whispered.

As she ran down the stairs, her back arched as a trickle of fear and dread trailed down her spine like icy water. A board gave in on her, breaking in half, and she tumbled down the steps on her back, each stair smacking against her tensed spine, one last mocking gesture from the night. Luckily, her adrenaline hid the pain.

She was alone in her house with her dead brother, his body taunting her through the floorboards. Edgar Allan Poe, indeed. Her mind swam. Thoughts of ghosts and monsters and death and suicide all mushed together, breaking her.

Every dark recess in the hallway grew darker, no longer a shadow but a material nothingness, a black hole ready to swallow her up. The creaky floorboards laughed at her, cackling loud enough to overpower Chris's blasting music, which was its own form of taunting. His music, a last remnant of his living self, thumping through the stucco and insulation.

Her arms trembled as she charged into her room, snatched her cell from the bed, and ran down another flight, moving as far away from the horror as she could, as if the bright whites of the kitchen could wash away the visual of her brother shifting back and forth, dangling from a noose.

Are you ready?

"Not yet!"

Mustard smeared across the keys as she dialed 911.

CHAPTER 2
THE OTHER CASSIE

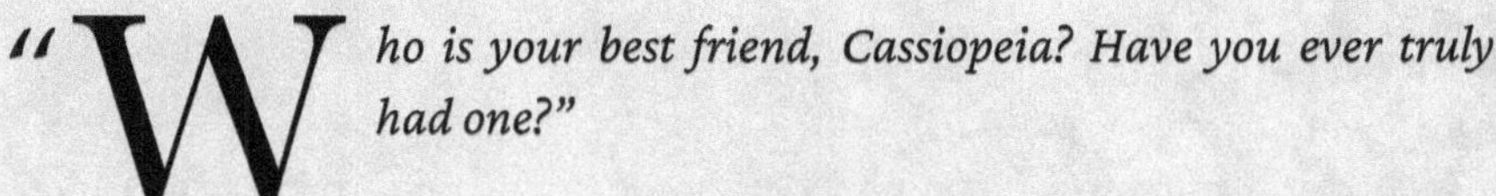

*"*Who is your best friend, Cassiopeia? Have you ever truly had one?"

YEARS LATER

Cassie headed down the hall toward her dorm room, running her index finger along the chain of her necklace, a nervous habit she'd possessed since childhood. After a seven-hour day of classes, followed by eight at the restaurant, every step forward ached in her heels, every inch stretched away from her. Her vision blurred. Her heart knocked at her ribs, as if pounding on a loud neighbor's door and shouting, "Hey, let me get some fucking rest in here!"

She clicked her phone on, checking the time. 2:17 a.m. She had Introduction to Modern Biotechnology in Medicine in less than six hours. Her only sense of relief was she didn't have a waitressing shift at Cuddey's tomorrow, so she could rest and catch up on her assignments.

Eager to kick off her Sketchers and flop onto the couch, her bed be damned, she twisted the lock on her door with shaky hands. To her surprise, her roommate, Beth, was not only still awake, but she had company. Beth's best friend, Shana, sat next to her on the couch. The television was on some kind of screensaver mode, showcasing colorful blobs which bounced around the screen like the inside of a lava lamp. Beth and Shana snickered, staring at the blobs with watery eyes.

Cassie sighed and closed the door. "Are you two on acid again?" She kicked her shoes off as Beth turned toward her.

"Shrooms," Beth said.

Cassie closed her eyes, praying for some sort of break. Beth was respectful, but when she took any kind of substance, she turned into a giggling jack-in-the-box. Wind her up and POP, the giggles let loose.

Shana, a delightful girl otherwise, played the perfect partner for Beth, always ready to do the winding.

"Okay. I hate to be the party pooper, but I have to be up in like five and a half hours to go to class. Y'all have fun out here."

Beth stood up, her slight frame barely rising above the level where she'd been sitting. She could pass for five years younger with her short stature, cute, rosy cheeks, and her chipmunk teeth. Shana once said Beth could be a stunt double for children in Hollywood, and Beth had seriously considered the idea.

She waltzed over to Cassie, slow and sloppy, her hips slithering from side to side. Not in some sexy, runway manner, but in a clear struggle to keep her blitzed self on her feet. She'd clearly done some drinking, too. When Beth reached her roommate, she threw her arms over Cassie's shoulders and hugged her. "I love you, girl. I'll go stay at Shana's dorm so we don't keep you up."

Cassie hugged her back. "You're the best." She almost asked if they could all hang out on Friday night, hoping to keep some cool points on her side, but then remembered she offered to take Jay's shift at Cuddey's.

Shana, prying her eyes away from the screensaver, turned to Beth and Cassie. "Have her do the mirror trick before we leave." Her words came out like spilling marbles.

Beth pulled away from Cassie. "Oh my god, yes. I know you need to go to bed, but it will only take a minute."

She grabbed Cassie's hand and led her to the floor lamp. Beth ran her hands up the skinny, metallic frame until she reached the nub to turn it on. The top portion of the frame curved in a U, which Cassie always thought made it look like a sulking robot or one of those lamppost monsters from that Kevin Bacon TV show.

The light came on, a dim, yellow glow behind the smokey-glass shade. Cassie winced. Something about electricity, the constant low buzz it produced, the initial click of a light, sent an odd shiver down her spine.

Beth put a hand on Cassie's shoulder. "Okay, so you need to stare into the light for thirty seconds."

Cassie chuckled. "I need to blind myself?"

Beth's tongue clicked against the roof of her mouth. "You'll be fine. Then, as soon as you're ready to look away, run into the bathroom and look in the mirror. You'll be a totally different person."

Cassie rolled her eyes. "You realize I'm not on shrooms, right?"

Cassie often wished she could be the druggie. She drank once in a while but never more than a glass of wine. Other than sipping slowly on reds, she refused to take anything heavier than an aspirin. Her brother had dabbled in drugs. Nothing serious, just pot and the occasional pill. And while Cassie knew his drug experimentation had absolutely nothing to do with his suicide, she couldn't help correlating the two. The last thing she would need before altering her mind was a reminder of her brother hanging in the attic.

"I know you're not on shrooms. That's why I need you to do it. You're the balance test or whatever," Beth said.

Shana nodded along, standing up now, eager to see Cassie perform the trick.

"Control group," Cassie said, correcting Beth. Her cheeks turned red, wondering if she committed a social faux pas. A control group wasn't some highfalutin bit of trivia; any high school-age kid in a biology class would know the term. Yet, she worried correcting her roommate was a thing know-it-all assholes did. This was why Cassie refrained from social gatherings unless necessary. She spent most of the time in a constant state of worry, wondering if every little innocuous sentence was a criminal offense. Navigating conversation was like running through an Army boot camp obstacle course, except the grenades felt real in the pit of her stomach.

Beth snapped her fingers. "Control group. Perfect. You're the control group. Now, look at the light."

Cassie sighed and bent low, allowing her eyes to get a clear shot of the bulb. She winced but battled to keep her eyes open. Why was she doing this? She just wanted to go to fucking bed, and she certainly didn't want to blind herself to appease her roommate. Still, she stared on. While the bulb was a dull yellow, staring at it directly projected a series of bright white blobs in Cassie's vision until the blobs melded into each other, creating an entire screen of white with a glowing red center. Yup. She was probably fucking blind.

When she finally pulled away, Beth guided her toward the bathroom. Her toe slammed into the raised wood sill under the door, and Cassie sucked in air, avoiding a full-on hissy fit meltdown. Her stubbed toe hurt like hell, and she wanted to scream and punch. But, like always, she did nothing, just bottled it in and kept obliging.

Beth let go of Cassie's arm. "Okay, I'm going to leave the room and close the door so you're in the dark. When your eyes readjust, keep staring in the mirror."

The door creaked and shut. Cassie kept her eyes trained in front of her, to what she assumed was the mirror. Her heart rate increased a little, as if slightly unnerved. Why? She didn't know. She wasn't afraid she'd actually see a different person. Presumably, after intentionally fucking up her eyes, her reflection would look strange, and she could report back to her roommate that it did, indeed, look "different." Hopefully that would be enough to entertain them and she could get some sleep.

As her vision returned, she blurred her eyes, as if staring at one of those magic pictures with the hidden images. The mirror doubled, as did her reflection, which at that point was nothing more than a pale bulb of its own, with draping brown cascading around it.

As her features came more into focus, her pulse quickened again. She hoped she saw someone else. Maybe that's why she played along with Beth's drug-induced charade in the first place. Cassie always felt like she carried someone else with her. Not literally another person, and not as blunt as a split personality; more like a separate side of herself, stuck in her belly, glued in there, always yearning for freedom. She felt this other person's presence at times of acute anxiety, when that hidden version of herself would punch at her guts, trying to free itself. It would whisper in her ear. *I'm coming to help you. I'm here for you. I can save us.*

Are you ready?

Those last three words drove her mind back to reality, where she stared blankly in the mirror at her reflection, the same mundane reflection it always was. No other person, no brain-twisting illusion, no ghost within herself. Just Cassie with her pale skin, deep purple pools under her eyes, the forest of teeny blackheads on her nose, the long river of black hair frazzled from a night at work. All Cassie. No magic.

She rubbed her eyes, wishing her hands could scrub away the puffiness and streaks of red lightning coursing toward her pupils. What would she tell Beth to quicken the conversation? If she told the truth, Beth would dig in with a series of *'are you sure?'* type questions. Maybe she'd even try to replicate the experiment and ask Cassie for a do-over. But if Cassie lied and said she saw someone else in the mirror, Beth might sit her down for a million questions.

She closed her eyes and puffed out her chest, eager to get this over with. As the door swung open, Cassie gave one last glance into the mirror, and for a split second, she saw someone else, and not a different version of herself, either. A true "someone else."

She did a double take, but of course, on second viewing, her reflection was back to being all her own. The other woman, a distant memory swimming in Cassie's muddled mind, forever to wander in those dark corners where Cassie would always ask herself if she saw what she thought she saw. It passed so quickly she could hardly remember any details. The features of the woman's face scattered like sand in a storm.

Cassie left the confines of the bathroom and smiled at Beth and Shana, who stared wide-eyed, waiting for an answer.

"Yes, I saw someone else," she said as she walked past them toward her bedroom. "I'll tell you all about it tomorrow."

CHAPTER 3
HYPNOPOMPIC

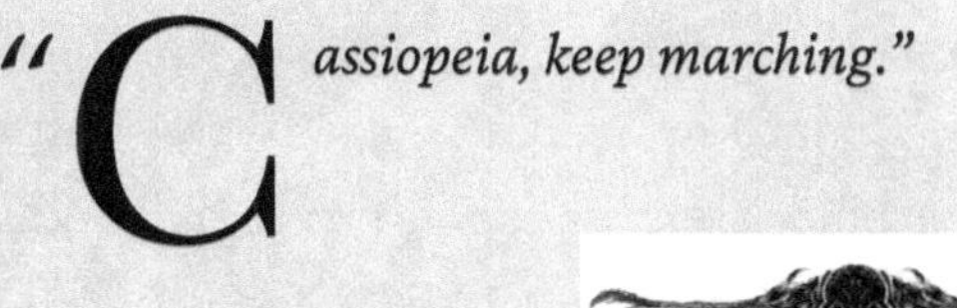

As soon as Cassie plopped onto her bed, Beth and Shana left. Once they were gone, she wished they stayed. They left a lingering coldness, a hollow void in the darkness. Cassie always wished for alone time but always dreaded it when it arrived.

Despite her exhausted state, she tossed and turned. It was something her mind did when she knew she had to wake up early. It spiraled down a stairwell of madness, thinking of every trauma, every heated conversation she'd ever experienced, every problem she'd yet to encounter, but knew she soon would. Just as it all finally dragged her close to a sound sleep, her body would itch. She'd debate whether to scratch it, if moving might wake her up, but then the debating kept her awake too. Eventually, she'd relent, scratch the itch, and find herself back to square one, tossing and begging for rest.

Once she finally fell asleep, she dropped hard, landing in the deep. It only felt like seconds before her alarm dug into her chest, clutched her heart, and ripped her from the dream world.

She shot upright, fumbling for her phone. With her eyes not yet open beyond a slit, she swiped the alarm off. She sat there, back straight as an arrow, contemplating dropping onto her pillow and returning to the world of slumber. Fuck class. One day off wouldn't kill her. She deserved it. Sleep. But she deserved it because she was so consistently reliable toward her obligations, which meant she should get the fuck up.

She yawned and slid her feet off the mattress, letting them dangle while she wiped crust from the corners of her eyes. Her chest constricted, tightening around the ribs. She thought, *If I don't get some sleep soon, I'm going to have a fucking heart attack.*

It was crazy how her body's response to stress and lack of sleep was to constrict her chest, make her heart pound and throb, give her aches and pains. Heart attack symptoms weren't exactly the best way to fight anxiety. Maybe her body should respond to high levels of stress by gently messaging her shoulders.

Half awake, she floated around her dorm room like a ghost, albeit a clumsy one. When she didn't have a good half hour to lie in bed after an alarm, she fumbled her way to full consciousness, her limbs listening to her brain but only offering seventy-five percent of the movement it asked for.

On top of the lack of sleep, she'd had awful nightmares about her brother, ones where he sat bow-legged on the living room rug, playing Guess Who? with Cassie. At first, the dream was more of a memory, but like most dreams, it ended up just a vision of truth mixed into an abstract pickle jar. Chris smiled at Cassie, his mouth stretching from ear to ear, his canines sticking out like sharp little daggers. As he spoke, blood gushed from his lungs, staining his tongue as it pooled down his chin onto the floor and game board. Maybe it was better the alarm woke her instead of the nightmare. God knows where it was headed.

She threw a hoodie on and charged down the hallway to the elevators, debating on rushing down the stairs instead, but coming to terms with her inability to rush down anything, let alone long, winding stairwells begging for a hypnopompic student to stumble to their death. Nope. She'd just have to be a little late.

The elevator door dinged and she stepped in. No students. She sighed and dropped her back to the wall, forgetting she had her backpack on. Something crunched. She should check on that, but whatever, probably a bag of chips or something. She often relied on gas station purchases for meals and, sometimes, threw nearly empty bags of chips or other junk food in her backpack, telling herself she'd finish them later, despite never doing so.

As she stepped off the elevator, she collided with a student turning the corner to get in. Yup. That's how the day would go. She'd be a few inches off on all her steps, and the day would unfold as one giant collision in waiting. This was how people died, how they managed to not notice the tractor-trailer barreling down the road as they crossed, or how they walked headfirst into a swinging baseball bat.

She apologized to the scruffy-haired kid she bumped into and opened the door to the outside world.

The Quad buzzed with morning energy. A couple noodleheads played hacky sack, two teachers marched to their next lecture, giggling to each other, and five girls stood around a bench, one of them dancing while the rest laughed and whooped. Who the fuck had that kind of pizzaz in the morning?

Cassie charged across the Quad, headed for the science labs, the sun already so bright she had to cup her hands over her eyes to see in front of her. Her phone buzzed, and after checking her front two pockets, she found it pressed against her butt in the back of her jeans.

She flicked the screen and checked her messages.

She had forgotten to check the name and, for a moment, her heart stuttered. She needed a fucking night off to study and sleep. Granted, babysitting was easier than hosting and waitressing, but it still required alertness.

When she saw it came from Mrs. Renard, she smiled. *Phew*. Of all the families she babysat for, they were the best. The father, Mark, was a little weird but never crossed a line into inappropriate, and their son, James, was a saint. He was twelve and didn't need a sitter, but otherwise, he was shy and polite and spent most of his time playing video games by himself in his room. When Cassie sat for the Renards, her job basically meant just being there to call 911 if the kid choked or something.

That's not what she loved best, though. The Renard's house was a giant, open-floor masterpiece with plenty of bright lights and space. She spent her days in crammed classes only to return to a tiny room with a roommate and then head to work in a packed restaurant littered with obnoxious, entitled college dicks. The Renard house gave her some quiet, alone time, a place for focus and reading without disruption, without constant noise. She was a page in the center of a book and the Renard house opened the cover and let her breathe.

As she clicked send, she crashed her head into some dude's chest. They stared at each other for a few seconds and apologized at the same time. They danced around each other and headed off in opposite directions.

She turned back to him. "That's what I'm saying, though. You could have been a tractor-trailer."

He either didn't hear her or ignored her. The phone buzzed again.

You are a saint, Cassie! Can you be here at five?

Yes.

The weight of her bookbag took a toll on her back. The more she walked, the more she angled forward. She assumed she looked like the floor lamp in her dorm, head droopy and spine curved.

She entered Cassian Hall, home to the aquaculture and fisheries labs. As soon as the door opened, the saltwater smell infiltrated her nose, and the buzzing of high-powered filtration systems stole the air. She flew down a flight of stairs, having a little more control over her body, and walked the narrow, dimly lit halls of the B floor. She imagined walking through the belly of a whale, a hollow, dank tunnel ripe with the scent of rotten fish and seawater.

She fucking loved it.

Outside of the machines running loudly, the fishery labs were quiet. The classes were small, some only containing five to seven students, and even the lectures were squeezed into small lab rooms, where the students sat surrounded by aquariums and microcosmic simulations of ocean life.

Despite already being late, she hit the bathroom before entering her classroom. A girl standing at the sink snapped her head toward the swinging door as Cassie entered, clearly taken off-guard. Rivulets of black mascara drizzled down the girl's cheeks and she sniffled.

"Sorry, I was just leaving," she said as she wiped the black lines trailing down her face.

The girl's tears threw Cassie off. She wanted to say something, to show compassion, but thoughts and words wouldn't connect. Instead, she said, "That's the beauty of stalls. We can both be in here at the same time."

Ugh.

The girl offered a half-smile, wiped her cheeks some more, and worked to move around Cassie.

"Hey, do you want to talk about it? I mean, I don't want to pry. It's just... Are you okay?" *Why am I so bad at this?*

The girl sniffled again and wiped her nose. "Yeah, no. I'm okay." She gave Cassie an unconvincing smile and a floodgate opened. Her face distorted and tears poured from her eyes. "No. I just don't understand why he's such an asshole."

Oh jeez.

The girl jolted forward and latched her arms around Cassie, clutching tightly. Her face pressed against Cassie's neck. Tears and snot spread on her skin.

Cassie patted the girl on the back. The words "there, there," almost left her mouth. Didn't this girl know she had places to be?

When someone asks, "Are you okay?" the appropriate answer is always, "Yes," or "I'll be fine," or, "Is anyone ever okay?" It certainly wasn't to collapse on top of the person asking.

As she rubbed the girl's shoulder, she caught her reflection. Same ole Cassie. She wished she could conjure the other Cassie. If only the flashes of the woman she caught in the mirror last night were real. She could use someone with gumption enough to tell this girl it was time to move on, to find another neck to snot on.

When the girl finally pulled away, Cassie's necklace caught in her hair, and the chain snapped, dropping to the grimy brown vinyl flooring.

"Oh, I'm so sorry," the girl said as she bent to pick it up.

Cassie couldn't breathe, a panic attack coming on full force. Her fingernails dug into her palms and her chest constricted once again. The bathroom jostled and rocked, a dinghy in an Atlantic hurricane. She dropped to the floor, trying to grab the necklace before the girl could touch it.

"I've got it. I've got it. Leave it alone."

The girl turned her head, her forehead scrunched. "I'm sorry. It was an accident."

Cassie bunched the necklace into her fist and used the lip of the sink to help her back to her feet. "It's fine. I just don't like anyone touching this." She turned away from the girl and looked in the mirror. Her finger traced where the necklace had draped over her clavicle, to where the little vial of glowing stardust had rested on her sternum. She felt so naked with it removed.

The girl stayed behind her, eyes boiling over, more tears ready to pour. "I'm such an ass. I'm so sorry. I fuck everything up."

Cassie closed her eyes and sucked in a big breath of air. *It's just a necklace*, she told herself. Yes, she'd worn it every single day since her mother gifted to her at seven-years-old, but it was still just a thing. An object. It was bound to break one day.

She opened her fist and examined the damage. The milky blue and green glittered contents of the vial swirled hypnotically. One link had bent and broken. It would be easy enough to repair.

The girl peeked over Cassie's shoulder, examining it with her. Before Cassie could stop her, the girl snatched the necklace from her hand. "I can fix that."

Cassie's hands latched onto the girl's hoodie. She slammed the crying bitch into the wall. The girl's head clunked hard on the white tile.

"What the fuck?" Crying Girl shouted.

"I told you not to touch my fucking necklace." The muscles in her jaw throbbed as she clenched her teeth harder.

The girl put her hand up and let the piece of jewelry dangle from her fingers. "Here. Take it. I just wanted to fix it for you."

Cassie snatched it from her and unpinned her from the wall. An immediate calm washed over her as soon as the necklace was back in her hands. As her thumb brushed through the links, she eyed the terrified girl. "I'm sorry. I don't know what came over me."

Without responding, the girl dashed out of the bathroom.

Cassie leaned back and slid down the wall, sighing with relief. She felt hungover, reliving the embarrassing moments, a thin headache wavering on the horizon. She had never lashed out at someone like that before. She needed more sleep.

CHAPTER 4

INTO THE UNDERTOW

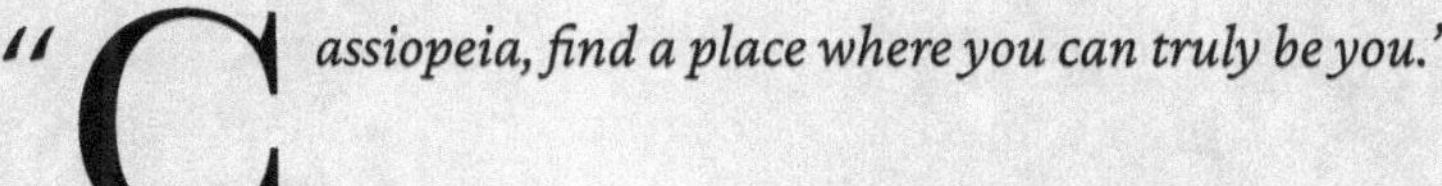

"Cassiopeia, find a place where you can truly be you."

Classes ended at 2:50, giving Cassie some time to shower and change before driving to the Renard's house. She made it through her day in a general haze, hardly keeping focus on her lectures. Luckily, she didn't have any of her labs until Friday; otherwise, she might have conked out face-first into her lobster tanks.

She got back to her dorm room and sat down cross-legged on the floor, put her necklace on the coffee table, and got to work on fixing it. It nagged at her throughout her day, and every time she went to run her fingers along the chain, only to be met with emptiness, she clenched her jaw harder, which exacerbated her headache by the minute. She worked the broken link between her thumb and forefinger, trying to bend it back together, but it wouldn't budge. Frustration built in her guts, a bubbling rage that wanted to pour from her lungs in an unrelenting scream. Her fingers trembled as she squeezed harder and harder.

"Fuck."

Of course, they didn't have pliers or anything useful in the dorm room. The Renards must have a toolbox lying around. Everyone had a pair of pliers rusting away in a box somewhere in their house, but as silly as it was, Cassie didn't want to wait another three hours. She felt weaker, more exposed, like the only thing keeping her together was that necklace draping around her neck.

She didn't even know why she clung to the damn piece of jewelry so much. All it did was conjure terrible memories, like the night her mother threw it at her in a monstrous rage as bulky police officers chased the crazed woman around the house before dragging her off, never to be seen again.

Cassie stuck a pencil tip through the hole in the necklace link to keep it in place. As she pushed down with her biology textbook to squeeze the sides of the link back together, her mother's high-pitched wails broke through the barriers of memory and material-ized in the empty dorm room.

She screamed in such a way it swallowed any bit of normalcy in their home. Cassie never heard anything like it, as if it could shatter the windows. Her mother slouched down as the men dragged her by the armpits, and she kicked her feet out, fighting against them. She planted one foot on the door stile and turned her head back toward Cassie. "Wear that fucking thing, Cassie. Remember me as I was before this."

The textbook dropped off the coffee table, and the necklace slid away from her, taking the pencil with it. The link remained sepa-rated, and both ends, just a few millimeters away from each other, taunted her. *You'll never connect us again.*

Cassie wiped her eyes and covered her face with her palms, pushing all the frustration out with a loud sigh. Time was ticking away, and she had to get ready for the Renards. It wasn't just the necklace that ate her, but what it represented: a day that kept getting away from her, always one step ahead and eager to pull the rug out from her already achy legs. She needed a win, because as each second ticked by, the day gained power. She couldn't help but feel like each crashing of the current was preparing her for a huge fucking tidal wave that would strip her of her bearings and suck her into the undertow.

Who was Cassie kidding? She was already drowning, way above her head. Every day was just an exercise of wading, keeping afloat long enough to make it to the next day. She grabbed the necklace and stuffed it into her clenched fist. "Please. Please. Just one fucking thing," she said as she thumped the barrel of her hand against her forehead.

Realizing she was wasting time whining, she stood up, went into her bedroom, and grabbed some clothes from her dresser. It was just college, she told herself. She'd survived much worse. Besides, she had a shower to look forward to. For some, a shower was a time to relax, but Cassie loved them for other reasons.

As she hopped into the steaming water, she growled. Shower time was the one point in her day where she allowed herself to rage, assuming Beth was not around to hear her. It was her one chance to scream and punch, to say, "fuck you," and, "hell no," to everyone she'd said, "yes," to all day. She'd punch the shower wall until her knuckles bled. Out came the Cassie hiding in her gut, the Cassie she always wished to be. The other woman in the mirror.

Her blood trailed down the wall, red and beautiful, until it merged with the shower water, turned pink and spiraled into the drain. She kept punching, driving her knuckles into the wall, hoping someday she'd have the strength to knock right through it, make a hole for her to see through, and maybe that hole would free her, let the anger loose, a tendrilled spirit intermingling with the shower steam. It would fill the room until the seams burst and the building exploded and the entire fucking campus collapsed under the weight of her hate.

Fuck you.

Fuck you.

Fuck you.

She punched, punched, punched.

She thought about Jay asking her to take his shift, and Beth with her stupid, drugged-up mind games, and her droning teachers, and the slimy manager at Cuddey's flirting with the underage staff, and her brother dangling from the rafters, leaving her alone with herself, and her father who actively avoided her, moving around the house like a mouse, terrified the cat might catch him and ask for a conversation, some love, some parenting, and her mother, her stupid fucking mother, the one who loved her and brushed her hair from her forehead while she cuddled her in bed and told her fairy tales of wolves in the woods, only to abandon her, to fail her family by losing her damned mind. Maybe Cassie was due for the same, maybe Cassie's punches, and kicks, and hate, true, boiling hate bubbling from her guts, out of her lungs in a growl, out of her fists in a flurry of punches, was just the buildup to some great, monumental self-destruction, all of it a fucking sign of what's coming. All of it. Fuck all of it.

She slammed her foot upward, banging the top of it against the tub spout. The metal protrusion tore into the skin on the bridge of her foot and cracked into the tarsal bones. She kept kicking. More blood. More pain.

Fuck. Fuck. Fuck. It felt so fucking good.

VIOLENT NOISE

"You're allowed to be angry, Cassiopeia. You're allowed to feel whatever you want."

After her shower, she dressed the wound on her foot with an elastic bandage wrap. She put a paper towel around her knuckles. They'd dry up quickly and she'd easily explain them away. Her hands were always cracked and bleeding from spending hours dipping her hands in and out of freezing cold water while she ran trials on her lobsters.

She debated on what to wear for babysitting, wanting something casual and comfortable but not something that would make the wealthy Renards cringe. After much debate, she chose black slacks, a white tee, and a black cardigan. Whatever.

Her anger tempered once she stepped out of the shower, but didn't fully quell until she was dressed and packed. Her heart rate simmered into a steady rhythm, and the tremble in her hands dissipated into the atmosphere. She hadn't lost her foreboding dread over a day hellbent on fucking with her, but she eased into the idea that it was out of her control anyway. All she could do was move forward and beware of falling anvils.

On the drive, Cassie sat upright, her back tilted forward like an old woman, in her 1996 Volvo S90. She stretched her eyes wide and tapped her hands against the steering wheel. An early 2000s emo playlist blasted Asking Alexandria through the speakers. She worked hard to keep her tiredness at bay while she drove, tightening her hands around the wheel, looking at each side of the road, back and forth. Thankfully, no tractor-trailers crossed into her lane, nor had she veered into anyone else's.

After constantly operating on zero sleep, she mastered the techniques needed to keep herself alert. Famous last words, she supposed.

When she arrived, just a few minutes shy of her five o'clock promise, Mr. and Mrs. Renard were already outside waiting for her, looking eager to leave. She parked her beat-up Volvo next to Mr. Renard's McLaren, its shiny, black coat taunting her flecked and rusty car. Mrs. Renard called it the family "toy," not to be confused with their other three vehicles, which had more utilitarian roles, like for driving to work, or heavens to Betsy, the supermarket.

"Thank goodness you're here," Mrs. Renard said. "We had to cancel our invite to dinner because something much more pressing has come up. We really need to leave, but I'll explain later." She flew down the steps and gave Cassie a light, quick hug as her husband pressed past them, hitting the unlock button on his key fob. The McLaren's headlights flashed and the alarm made a robotic beep.

As Mrs. Renard hurried to follow her husband, face riddled with anxiety, she craned her neck back toward Cassie. "You know the ropes by now. Make yourself at home."

Cassie watched them drive away before stepping inside. She wondered what the emergency was. She assumed it had just come up because the Renards were dressed for a fancy dinner.

Mr. Renard sported a sleek, black suit, and his wife donned a matching tight, black dress. She even had on her classic pearl necklace she wore only on special occasions.

Cassie clicked the front switch, and the bright strip lights illuminated every inch of the downstairs. In front of her, the kitchen glowed an inviting, off-white shine. The back wall beyond the kitchen was all glass, showcasing the large, bright-green lawn. A cement path cut through the yard, solar lighting on each side, making its way from the back door to the patio area with the hot tub.

Cassie plopped her backpack on the kitchen table and sighed. Something about the Renard house acted as an anti-anxiety drug, a shot to the arm, loosening her muscles, kneading away the tension.

Anxious as she was to find something to fix her necklace, Cassie was also a girl of routine. If she didn't follow her normal pattern when entering the Renard house, she'd stress herself out that something horrible would happen for changing it up. Not that she wasn't already worrying about that, with how her day started and all. She'd hunt for pliers in the junk drawer and garage in a little while.

James was upstairs playing his video games. He was shouting at the television amidst a chorus of explosions and *KAPLOOPS*.

Cassie ignored the volatile sounds echoing through the house from James's bedroom and walked the perimeter of the downstairs, as she always did. She enjoyed the artwork on display, despite knowing nothing about art or what made it good or bad. All she knew was the colorful pieces, often just splashes of paint, chaotic yet contained, spoke to her.

She rubbed her index finger on the bottom of the mounted television, a machine larger than Cassie's bed. If only she had the time to flop onto the couch and binge one of her comfort shows: *Justified*, or *The Office*. Maybe she could even check into that *Winter's Myths* television show everyone either loved or hated. But she knew if she let herself relax too much, she'd never rip herself away to get some homework done. She'd either fall fast asleep or get sucked into whatever show she put on. Besides, she had a second part to her ritual that needed doing, and the next part was her favorite.

She stepped into the yard and followed the solar lights to the deck, where she sat and took a long, meditative breath, enjoying the cool, fall air, gently chirping crickets, and the glowing moon breaking the horizon behind the columns of trees in the forest which fenced in the Renard property. Taking her therapist's advice, she inhaled through her nose, exhaled through her mouth, feeling the air travel into her diaphragm and out her lungs.

As hard as she tried, she never landed in a true meditative state. She had used apps for guided breathing, taken classes, watched YouTube videos, but none of it got her there. The breathing helped relax her, sure, but her mind never cleared of her surroundings. She was always acutely aware of a random, tiny itch building behind her knee, or a low, whirring noise from the electricity. Something always pulled her back. Still, she enjoyed doing it, and there in the quiet yard, secluded and beautiful, she drenched herself in the clean air like it was bathwater.

As a sense of peace coursed through her veins, she was shaken from it violently.

A plane flew above her head with such speed and at such a low altitude, it shuddered the house and deck, shocking every fiber of her being. The hair on her arms stood on end and a scream escaped her.

With her heart pounding and her pulse throbbing, she laughed at herself. "Oh, holy fuck. That was terrifying."

After the laugh, disappointment set in. It truly was like the gods had it out for her, not even willing to give her a moment of meditation.

She headed in to check on James and find something to fix her necklace before diving headfirst into her books. The plane must have scared the shit out of James, too, but maybe planes did that all the time over here. She'd never heard them before, but Cassie only babysat in the evenings. Maybe that day was a different schedule for the planes or something.

As she opened the back door, nerves still on edge, another plane flew by with equal force, sound, and speed. Having experienced it once did nothing to stop the startling effect it had on her. Again, she screamed. Again, her heart rattled in her throat. Again, she nearly fell over. There was no way this was something that happened often, or the Renards would have surely moved out and probably caused quite the fuss with the realtor.

When she entered the kitchen, James stood at the bottom of the second-floor steps. "What the fuck was that?"

"It was a plane, and your mom would kill you for talking like that. No swearing."

"Oh, okay." He shrugged and turned to head up the stairs but stopped himself. "Oh, hi Cassie. I didn't know you were babysitting tonight."

"Your parents had dinner plans, but then some kind of emergency came up and they rushed out of here."

James showed no interest in what his parents were doing. "Cool. I'm going back to my games."

"Wait. Before you do, I have a question. Do your parents have a toolbox anywhere? Specifically, I need pliers."

He shrugged. "I don't know about pliers, but my dad has a bunch of tools in the garage. He's actually great at building stuff, believe it or not."

Mr. Renard gave off an air of royalty, the type of man who avoided getting his hands dirty and hiring an army of blue-collar folks to do his bidding. Cassie wouldn't have guessed him for a hands-on builder type, and apparently, James understood the surprise of it, too.

Cassie nodded, and another plane flew by. They both jumped as the house trembled, like it, too, had a blast of nervous adrenaline shooting through it. Then, another plane and without a second to relax, another. The constant sound and shock of it was violent, hostile, a corruption. She yelped each time. It never got easier.

A new sensation washed over her. Anger. The planes, like the scratching above her head as a child, were unrelenting, taunting, forcing her away from her responsibilities, and she couldn't help worrying they would lead to the same conclusion: something awful, something dreadful. Yes, she feared that, but more so, it infuriated her. She'd lost too much, dealt with enough trauma to last a lifetime. Outside forces always impeded her life's forward projection, and she was sick of it. She stared at the ceiling, waiting for another eruption of noise.

After a moment of silence, James slowly tilted his head down, bringing his eyes to Cassie. "What's going on?"

She looked at him, trying to stop her wide eyes from revealing her own terror and fury. "I don't know. This isn't normal around here?"

He laughed uncomfortably. "No. I've never heard a plane come by here before. I mean, I see them way up in the sky, but I have never heard *that* before."

A disquieting shiver wormed up her spine. Something felt off. Wrong. But, the planes had stopped, and her worrying about it would not help. What could she do, stare at the ceiling, eagerly awaiting another violent swoosh? Her nerves fired like a shotgun, and she suddenly had an urge to leave, to pack up and tell James he was on his own. Bye-bye, Renards. But she couldn't. That wasn't the Cassie way.

James waited for her to tell him not to worry about it, but the words never came. Instead, Cassie stared out through the curtain wall, into the yard, waiting for another plane to blast by, another disruption, another sign something was very wrong.

Unpack your backpack, she told herself. It would keep her planted, force her to stay put and focused. If she let herself head down a spiral of worry, she'd spend the night thinking of every possible disaster, none of which would come, but her night would be ruined anyway from the stress.

James relented and went back upstairs.

Cassie slid her Neurobiology text out of her backpack, placed her notebook and pen on top, and sighed at the overwhelming amount of work she had to do. She debated on skipping it all, going to find the pliers, fixing her necklace, and giving up for the night. She talked herself into sitting, where she stared at her book.

Night crept in and a shroud of darkness hovered around the bright lights of the Renard house. Her eyes fought against her, and when she glanced at her book, her vision blurred. With her palms holding her head up, pressed tightly to her cheeks, she slipped gently into sleep. She awoke a few minutes later with her head on the table, tucked into the fold of her arm.

Something had changed. The lights were flashing. They dragged her from the depths of darkness, luring her back to life. She lifted her head slowly, gathering her bearings. Maybe the lights were in her dream, something she carried with her to the waking world until her mind coalesced. But the more she woke, the more defined the lights became. And then she heard a whistle, an intermittent blare. The shrill noise came like a slap to the face, a blast of cold water. She was awake.

She turned her head left and right, trying to figure out the source of the noise and the flashing lights. It didn't make sense because it was everywhere, all around her, a sensory assault. But then she figured it out, and her heart plummeted.

Someone had set off the house alarm.

Someone had broken in.

CHAPTER 6
THE LONG DAY

"*People are like Vampires. If you invite them in, they will drain you.*"

The open floor plan of the Renard house felt less open as Cassie stood up, checking to see where someone might be hiding. New nooks and obstacles, dark corners and blockades made themselves known. The space behind the couch grew twofold, and the stretch of shade on the far side of the living room darkened.

She moved with slow steps, eyeing every direction but eager to turn the alarm off. The blaring noise muddled her brain, making it difficult to concentrate on finding the source. She gripped her cellphone in her hand, as if she could wield it against an intruder. *Stop or I'll use this to dial 911!*

James barreled down the stairs with his palms to his ears. "What happened?"

"I don't know. Can you turn it off?"

He ran to the white box by the front door and hit a series of buttons. The noise stopped and the flashing white lights died.

"Does it ever go off on accident?"

"No. You really have to mess with the door or windows." As he noticed her concern, his cheeks sunk into his mouth.

She pulled on the front door. Locked. "Stay with me. Let's check all the windows and doors."

They skirted the walls and walked in a circle around the downstairs. The living room windows were all locked and unbroken, and they found the same with the dining room. The wall of windows in the kitchen remained intact, and the backdoor was also locked.

James shrugged. "I guess it was nothing."

"Maybe another plane flew by and somehow set it off?"

"Nah, I would have heard it. I had my headphones on, but those planes were super loud."

She nodded. "Yeah, I would like to think it would have woken me up."

He giggled. "You fell asleep? Good babysitting."

She gave him a gentle push. "Yeah, yeah. I had a long day."

"I'm just messing with you. I guess I'm going to go back to my game."

She followed him. "Wait. Let me check the upstairs first, just in case."

They marched up the L-shaped stairs. When they reached the center, where a wall blocked the view from downstairs, Cassie's fists clenched. The first floor was garnished with lights, but upstairs was a black hole.

At the top, a long hallway with hardwood floors went from a master bedroom on the left to a family bathroom far down on the right. A series of miscellaneous other rooms hid behind doors on both sides of the hallway. The stairwell ended in the center of it all.

Across the hall was Mr. Renard's computer room, then a workout room, and finally James's bedroom. On the side with the stairwell was a cleaning closet on the left and a meditation room on the right.

Except for a television flickering from James's room, all was dark.

"Is there a light in the hallway?" Cassie asked.

James groped at the wall until a bright light showered them with sight. Her heart settled a little.

She checked the master bedroom first, which made Cassie a little squirmy, not enjoying the invasion of privacy. For the sake of thoroughness, she checked the windows, the closet, and under the bed, all the routine searching for monsters she would have done if James were four-years-old and ready for bed.

She tried to keep her eyes focused on searching for an invader, but a quick scan of the Renard's bookshelf revealed shelves of psychology texts, which was expected, and two shelves of thick texts on various mythologies, cryptids, and assorted other fictions, which was not expected. *The History of Werewolves in New England. 18th Century Vampire Lore. The Complete Index of Eastern Demons. Lampposts, Grief, and Monsters of the Mind.*

James waited for her outside the room. As she exited the room, he stared wide-eyed. "Anything?"

She bit her lip and shook her head. "No."

Mr. Renard's computer room offered another surprise. Four monitors showed surveillance video footage of a prison. Cassie slapped her hands over her mouth. Each camera focused on a single cell, and all four cells housed a prisoner sleeping on a cot. Mr. and Mrs. Renard were doctors, and as far as Cassie knew, they didn't run any prisons. Even if they had, would the law allow them to monitor the prisoners on camera from their own home? It was too bizarre for her to wrap her head around, but an unease tugged at her brain. *Get the fuck out of here, now!*

Outside of those videos, the room appeared like any other work room - stacks of paperwork, laptops, a printer. Cassie couldn't focus on the video, even if she'd never stop fully thinking about it. She needed to make sure no one had broken into the house, so she quickly checked the windows, ran out of the room, and told herself to forget what was on the other side.

The exercise room, James's room, and the bathroom were all fine and all without surprises. The meditation room gave the biggest shock of all. When Mrs. Renard had given Cassie the house tour, she opened the doors to the bathroom, the workout room, and James's room but kept the rest shut. Cassie now understood why Mrs. Renard neglected to open Mr. Renard's computer room. At the time, it all felt like a need for privacy. Who would want to show the college kid their master bedroom, and a computer room which probably held secret patient information? But when Mrs. Renard shied away from opening the door to the meditation room, Cassie wondered what was worth hiding in there.

She never expected the answer that would come as she pulled the door open with James standing too close behind her, peeking over her shoulder to get a view. Maybe he, too, hadn't been allowed to enter the meditation room, though the Renards made no effort to lock it. She expected a room littered with cross-cultural meditative markings, the typical spackle of spiritual tapestry that a rich, white woman would patch together to act in tune with both Eastern and Western practices. A yin-yang, a flowing Buddha fountain, Catholic and Celtic crosses, but none of those were present.

The room was littered with grotesque machines and primitive weapons. Crudely made wooden stakes, a jaw trap straight out of a Looney Tunes cartoon, chains, whips, and devices she couldn't begin to understand, but were clearly meant for torture. While the existence of these items might have startled her, she could explain them away. How many rich folks collected ancient weaponry? Some of it looked like the kind of thing Frasier Crane might have adorned in his fancy Seattle apartment. But what scared her out of her skin was the blood. All the weapons were caked in dried and flaking maroon.

Again, she tried to convince herself it was all for show, that the weapons were painted to appear used, but droplets speckled the hardwood floor around the weapons as well. Tied to the video footage in Mr. Renard's computer room, a picture formed in Cassie's mind, one where the Renards were kidnapping and torturing people. *The meditation room,* they'd called it.

Cassie lost her balance, leaned hard on the door stile. She needed to leave.

"What's that?" James asked, pointing to the floor.

She didn't want to look. More blood, probably. She willed herself to keep her head up, worried if she examined the weapons and floor any longer the horror would only grow. Maybe it would be *fresh* blood this time.

Instead, she eyed the window. The window. Her heart sank. How did she miss it? Something had shattered the window. Smashed it to bits. A cool breeze crept in through the gaping wound.

James pushed his way into the room, ducking under the arm Cassie used to hold herself upright.

"Look," he said, pointing to something on the floor.

She forced a glance and saw it. Broken glass. Tiny slivers, shimmering like snowflakes against the room's mellow, dim glow. An orgy of glass. Cassie stepped, horrified, as if putting herself in the room would make her a victim, the next to feel the biting lash of a whip as a mysterious force dragged her to a dungeon where the Renards would monitor her on camera before executing her with primitive weaponry.

Who was she afraid of here? The people she babysat for, who had been Cassie's family therapists all those years ago? An intruder? Some clandestine outside force which smashed an upstairs window? All of them? Enemies everywhere. Maybe it was none of them. Maybe Cassie's overtired mind convinced her to fear everything, to think some video mattered. It was probably old, a VHS tape from an experiment done in the seventies Mr. Renard was studying for a scientific article he planned to write. Maybe the weaponry had a similar purpose, or maybe rich assholes liked to collect weapons that had actually been used. It probably added a little value to the collection when it had some spots of blood on it. Somewhere out there, a man with a website got richer by coating that shit with animal blood and selling it under the pretense it was used in some great and holy war from hundreds of years ago.

The window, too. There wasn't anything under the window, nothing an intruder could stand on or climb up to. No dormers or edgings. Maybe the planes had smashed it when they flew by. It made sense. The whole fucking house shook.

She told herself all of this, taking the big *meditative* breaths her therapist recommended, but it did little to quell her nerves. Her brain had worked all day to make her feel off-kilter. That sense of dread roiling in her chest meant something. She knew it. And then James found it, the catalyst, the object that would roll her from foreboding straight into a living nightmare.

He checked the floor, kicking sticks and spikes out of the way, little shards of glass clinking as he swept the hardwood with his foot. "Maybe someone threw a rock or something," he said as he searched.

She wanted to help him or tell him to quit and shut them out of that fucking room forever, but her nerves were frayed, so she stayed by the door, wrapping her arms around herself and pulling the cardigan taut.

James continued kicking as she dazed out the broken window. A darkness shrouded the woods across from the front yard, despite the moon's cool glow. Her whole body ached. When anxiety hit, she tightened all her muscles, clenched her jaw, walked on arched feet, leaving her whole body with the same type of soreness she felt after a heavy workout.

James bent down and picked something up. It was small and gold. "What's this?"

She squinted, leaned forward.

"What the fuck?" she said, reaching out to grab it.

As it plopped into her hand, panic took over. She grabbed the top of James's head. "Duck. And get the fuck out of here."

She grabbed his arm, keeping her head down, and ran from the room. With her foot, she slammed the door shut.

"Is that what I think it is?" James asked.

"Yes, it's a bullet. Spent."

"What kind?"

She pushed him toward the stairwell. "I don't fucking know. It's not a shotgun bullet. Some kind of handgun. How can you tell the difference?"

He shrugged. "I don't know. I've never seen one in real life before."

Maybe it was a hunter, someone who misfired in the woods, but who would hunt so close to a residential neighborhood? It had to be against the law. And the trajectory made no sense. Were they trying to shoot a deer in the sky?

Racing through ideas on what to do next, Cassie decided to pack James up, get in her car, and get the fuck out of there for a while. She could text Mrs. Renard and tell her they went to get fast food or something.

As they marched down the hall, someone shouted outside. It was close enough to hear, which meant someone was on the Renard property. They were trapped.

Then another voice shouted, and another, until an unintelligible shouting match occurred somewhere in the darkness looming over the thick, black oaks by the front yard.

"Stay here," she said to James.

She creeped back to the meditation room and glanced out the window. She couldn't see anyone but heard their voices more clearly and pinpointed the source of the argument as coming from the stretch of oaks right on the side of the Renard property. The bullet casing rolled in her palm, and she flew out of the room, away from the windows. What the fuck was she thinking sticking her head where a bullet had just traveled?

As she slammed the door shut, the lights and sirens blared again just as someone pounded on the front door.

James screamed, and Cassie's heart charged into her throat. The pain in her chest doubled and beat against her ribs like a small creature trying to rip its way free from inside her. Holy fuck. The walls closed in. She couldn't breathe. What could she do? Where could they go? She knew she couldn't open the front door, but maybe they could escape out the back. If they had to run, she'd be taking them right into the same woods the voices came from, albeit from the opposite side, but who knew what lingered in those woods? They could get lost. How deep was the forest? How far in would they go before seeing another residential area? And they'd be running in the dark.

She couldn't think with the shrill alarm blasting in her brain.

As the alarm chirped deafening sounds, the shouting from outside grew loud enough she heard it over the siren.

A fresh voice came from the bottom of the stairs.

Right below them.

Inside.

CHAPTER 7

DISAPPEAR COMPLETELY

*"*H*ide and seek is fun, Cassiopeia, but just one time, I wish they could never find us."*

James ran to her. "Someone is downstairs," he whispered.

She grabbed him by the shirt and pulled him into his bedroom. If gunshots were firing wildly from the front side, she wanted to be in a room near the back.

Cassie closed the door as quietly as her frazzled mind allowed her hands to work. "Turn the television off. Do you have a lock?"

He pushed in front of her and clicked the turn lock on the knob. She rubbed the sides of the television with trembling hands, searching for an off switch. Before she could find one, he grabbed a remote and powered the TV off, its soft glow disappearing and wrapping them in total darkness.

She realized she trapped them but saw no other option. The voice came from the bottom of the stairs. Where could they go?

The alarm screeched, each new whine sending her heart on a rampage.

"What should we do?" James asked.

"Shhhh," she said.

Thanks to the deafening alarm, she couldn't hear anything else. Was the man coming up the stairs? She didn't know. He wasn't talking anymore.

She led James to the side of his bed, away from the door, and ducked down.

He mimicked her. His breath was ragged, eyes bulging from his skull.

She cupped her hand over his, felt the violent shakes from his trembling body. It was like sitting next to an overfull washing machine. He'd never keep quiet enough. The intruder would hear him. Cassie's chest was pounding, her own breath not much softer than the boy's.

She looked up and peeked out the window, gauging whether they could jump if she heard the intruder on the second floor. The green grass was probably only twenty feet down, which didn't look terrible from inside, but she assumed if she had to make the jump, it would feel much worse.

Where would they go? The yard stretched for a long distance, traveling to the patio and the gazebo before turning to thick woods. How much running would they have to do before finding people who could help them?

James looked at her, hoping for answers the way a young person often thinks the adult in the room will save them. But then he provided her with an answer. "Your phone!" he pointed to her hand.

She twisted her wrist. Her phone! How could she be so stupid? She flicked the screen open. The Face ID circle spun and gave her a check mark. Her trembling fingers struggled to open the caller app, but when it did, she nailed 911 on the first try. Score one for experience.

Nothing happened. No ringing. No answer. Just silence. She hung up and tried again. Same result.

"Do we not have Wi-Fi?" she whispered.

"Isn't 911 supposed to work even without Wi-Fi?" James asked.

She tried again, and again, but nothing happened.

Through the shrill cries of the alarm, she heard the man downstairs. He shouted, and a few more voices joined in. More than one person was in the house.

Boom. Boom. Boom.

Someone fired three gunshots in rapid succession.

James screeched.

Cassie hugged him, not trying to comfort him but to silence him by pressing his face into her shoulder. A deadly world was closing in on them, and she knew they'd only survive if no one knew they existed at all. Disappear completely. She'd done it before, spent her whole life blending in, fading into the surroundings, masking who she really was.

James stopped screeching, turning it into full-on sobs. His tears wet her shirt.

"Shhhhh," she said again.

More shouting. She turned to the window, wondering if she'd know the right time to jump. There were too many voices shouting downstairs, so she couldn't determine the number of people in the house. If one came up, and she jumped down, would she land next to the others? She wished she could make out their words or get some indication of what was happening.

A murder probably occurred a few feet below her. If the killers knew other people were in the house, they'd surely kill them too. She'd watched enough crime shows to know a killer never left witnesses behind. But why did they choose to murder someone in this house? Who the fuck were these people? Was it a gang fight? Mobsters? What the fuck was happening, and why was it happening here?

She didn't know. How the fuck could she? It wasn't normal life to have men intruding in your home to kill each other. It wasn't normal life to blind yourself for your roommate. It wasn't normal life to witness your mother getting dragged out of the house by police. And it wasn't normal life to walk up a flight of stairs to find your brother hanging from the rafters. This wasn't fucking normal life, and she wondered what it was about her that acted as a magnet for insanity.

A voice yelled something right outside the door. Someone made their way up, and he stood just a few feet away.

Cassie cried too, but she kept herself silent, breathing through her nose.

James almost yelped but Cassie caught him, driving her open palm over his mouth. His tears dripped on her index finger. If they were lucky, the blaring alarm would drown out their heavy breaths and whimpering.

She pressed her face to the rug, staring under the bed and into the crack in the door. Movement. She couldn't see anything distinguishable, only the movement of shadows.

Jesus, she felt like she could die. The banging in her ribs, the throbbing in her temples. Her throat closed up. The walls and bed constricted, squeezing her. The air grew thick, too thick, too hard to breathe. It felt like inhaling gravel, and she had to fight the urge to cough. Her lungs begged for it, scratching and tickling.

Another plane flew overhead.

Cassie screamed, caught herself too late, and plugged her mouth with her palm.

For a moment, nothing happened. Maybe the noise from the plane overpowered her scream, stopped the man in the hall from hearing her. The entire house rattled and shook.

As soon as the plane was out of earshot, the man shouted, yelling to someone somewhere else in the house. It must have spooked him, too, because his voice was severe. Whatever language he spoke, it wasn't English, and Cassie couldn't tell what it was, despite a working understanding of French, Spanish, German, and even a little Russian.

As the man ran away from the door and down the stairs, Cassie pushed James off her. "Stay here, keep an eye out the window. Let me know what you see when I come back."

"Where are you going?" He gripped his fingers onto her cardigan.

She pulled it free. "Just across the hall. I want to see if they're leaving."

After a few minutes of waiting, she gathered the nerve to pry the door open, centimeter by centimeter. No one stood in the hall. The voices weren't yelling below.

She walked on tiptoe across the hall, opened the door to the meditation room, and creeped in, ducking low in case any more wild shots were fired. Across the yard, three men darted into the woods. A slight release of panic left her, but not all of it. She didn't know how many were in the house, hopefully just the three. She wouldn't feel safe going downstairs until Mr. and Mrs. Renard came home, but holy hell, did she want that fucking shrill alarm to shut up.

Cassie went back into the bedroom. "Anything?" she said.

James shrugged. "Nothing. Are they gone?"

"I think so. I saw three of them leaving, but I don't know how many were down there."

They stared at each other, hopeless and scared.

"I think I am going to turn the alarm off. I'll check if anyone is down there."

His face lit up with terror and he reached for her. "Please don't. What if you die?"

"I think it's okay," she said, trying to convince herself.

She creeped down the hall and listened for a second. Nothing. One step at a time, she worked her way to the landing in the middle of the stairs where it turned. She peeked around the wall and bit back a yelp. A body lay between the kitchen and living room, blood splattered along the wall and more of it pooling around the corpse.

The dead man was fat and burly with a long, black beard. Red leaked onto his green, camouflage outfit, and one of his giant black boots had somehow separated from his foot and stuck crookedly against the wall and a chair.

She forgot the alarm also shot out blinding white lights along the edges of the house, because that didn't happen upstairs, but as they shined in her eyes every two seconds, she'd surely never forget it again.

She finished her descent and reached for the alarm panel but realized she had forgotten the code. After digging her phone out of her pocket, she scrolled through months of messages between her and Mrs. Renard to find the text where Mrs. Renard gave it to her.

When she finally found it, she pressed the buttons but stopped on the last one. If the men were leaving, should she change anything? Would stopping the alarm make them come back to investigate? Fuck. Every choice felt like the wrong one.

She couldn't take it anymore and no matter what she chose, she'd never feel safe, so she pressed it.

The noise stopped; the lights gave up their blare. Silence stole the night, but instead of liberating her, it draped over her like a heavy overcoat on a boiling summer day.

Every inch of movement felt like a threat, a potential neon sign. She moved to the steps, hypersensitive to each sound - her pants ruffling, shoes touching hardwood.

As she stepped on the first stair, another plane flew by.

She dropped her phone just as it lit up and sent off its own siren. As far as she knew, her phone had never done that before. She received a warning once that a hurricane was approaching, but it came with the normal text alert sounds. The noise it made now was just as beefy and disruptive as the house alarm.

She picked it up and ran up the stairs, fearful the extra noises had alerted the men and would bring them back. When she reached the top of the stairs, she glanced at the screen, but with her mind running through a dozen things, she couldn't comprehend it so she gave up trying. Instead, she dashed into the meditation room and checked the window. The men were no longer in sight, which meant they had gone deeper into the woods or were inches from the front door.

She went back to her phone, looking only to silence it, but this time she deciphered the words.

> Emergency Alert: Seek shelter immediately.
> To find the nearest shelter go to…

"What the fuck?"

James stood on the threshold. "What's going on? What do we do now?"

She shook her head, the walls closing in. "I think America is under attack or something. I don't know."

"What do you mean?" His voice cracked as he asked the question.

"I don't know. I don't know. It says to seek shelter. Hold on. There's a link in the message or something that will tell us where to go. I don't want to drive out of here. There are men out front somewhere."

He put his hand up. "Wait. My dad has a bunker."

CHAPTER 8
FASTBALL TO THE FACE

*"*D*o you feel the way the dirt sifts through your fingers? This is knowledge, slowly filling your brain. The more you let in, the more you know and the more you can see the stones and gems hidden within. But do you see that mound of dirt? That's all you've yet to learn. Dumb people will glance at the mound of dirt and think they know it all. But the smart ones will keep sifting, knowing they'll never understand it. Complacency is weakness, Cassiopeia."*

Cassie's eyes widened. "Where?"

"It's in the yard, but it's hidden. You've probably walked over it a dozen times."

She dragged him into his bedroom and glanced out the window. For the moment, all was silent. "Where exactly?"

He pointed out past the gazebo and the deck, toward the edge of forest surrounding the property. "It's before the woods, but not much."

She nodded and took a deep gulp of air. "Okay. We can do this. We just have to do some running."

As if the God of Go Fuck Yourself heard her and wagged his finger, three planes flew by in succession, and two men broke through the tree line into the yard. One held his finger on the trigger of a sleek, long gun strapped around his chest. The two men turned their heads left and right, searching for something. No, not searching. Hiding. They were hiding from something.

Cassie wanted to bellow with confusion and rage. This was insane. Planes and war and guns. Even if she made it to the bunker, what would that mean for her life? Would she be trapped for days, months, fucking years with no one else but a weird kid? Could she keep them alive, even in the bunker? What if one of them cut themselves and got an infection? Who would administer antibiotics? Did the bunker even have medicine? Did it have anything? Was it just four walls and some rationed cans of tuna and beans? Was the world really collapsing around her?

"What do we do?" James whispered.

She answered with an assured sense of confidence she didn't truly possess. "We wait. As soon as they move, we book it to the bunker. You sure you can tell exactly where it is?"

He nodded, but his eyes gave him away.

Cassie's heart drummed in her ears, a steady but solid beat, like the slow opening to a metal song where you know it's just building up to a cacophony of chaos and noise. The stillness outside was maddening. There was always a pause before violence, a final breath before your lungs collapsed. She imagined it was something like what athletes called "being in the zone." It was a weird quiet where even the birds and crickets knew to shut up, the wind, the small electric whirring that always plays background noise, all of it dead, Earth itself sucking in a gulp and holding it before crying.

"They aren't moving. They're in our way," James said.

Cassie grabbed his hand. "Let's sneak downstairs and watch out the kitchen windows. The less space between us and the bunker, the better."

They creeped down the stairs, and Cassie startled at the sight of the dead guy on the floor between the living room and kitchen. It was amazing she could forget such a horrible sight. But, then again, a tree falling is only terrifying when there's not a wildfire devouring the forest. Meanwhile, James cried at the sight. For now, Cassie ignored him.

The two men were in the same place, but now they faced the woods instead of the house, and they squatted behind the gazebo to hide from whatever unknown entity threatened them in the woods.

Nothing happened.

All quiet.

All still.

A plane flew by, and James tightened his grip on Cassie's hand. They both jerked back a little, but neither screamed like they had in the past.

Something was different about the plane, something obvious, but Cassie's fried brain didn't connect it until it was too late. The plane dropped something. She watched it fall in the same way a curious child would watch a shooting star. The object dropped below the tree line, disappearing into the swell of darkness within the forest.

It took a moment but then, *boom!* An explosion erupted, shaking the house. Hell, maybe the entire world. The trees evaporated behind a growing orange ball. A visible wave shot from the forest, crashing through the yard, destroying the gazebo, smashing through the deck and spa, before shattering the wall of windows around Cassie and James.

Cassie screamed but couldn't hear herself.

As glass poured over them, James's mouth opened so wide his jaw looked ready to unhinge, probably screaming too, but again, Cassie heard nothing but a loud, incessant ringing. The wave of heat threw them both into the wall. They crashed onto the floor amidst an ocean of glass.

"Go. Now," she shouted into the silent void.

The explosion devoured the men in the yard, so this was their chance. She jumped through the ghost of the curtain wall and ran. A plane flew just above her, but without her hearing, it failed to startle like the others had. She turned to make sure James followed because only he knew where to find the bunker.

Parts of the yard were on fire, patches of flickering reds and oranges, so Cassie couldn't run in a straight line. She slalomed around the blazes, running with all the speed and might she possessed. Whether James kept up, she didn't know, and if she were being honest with herself, didn't give a fuck other than only he knew the exact placement of the bunker doors. He had pointed, which gave her some semblance of direction, so if he died, fell too far behind, burned up in a fiery explosion, she'd mourn him tomorrow from the safety of wherever the fuck she was headed.

More balls of fire lit up the sky and the depths of the woods. The rumbles vibrated under her feet each time. She ran for too long, as if the yard were growing, stretching, never letting her hit the finish line.

More men came from the woods. They were holding their hands up and yelling something she couldn't hear. Another group of men came from the other side. They were everywhere, and if they were yelling instructions or threats to her, she couldn't know. Some men held out guns, and she figured out that the two groups were shouting at one another, ready to shoot.

She and James stood between the war, and she was certain not a one gave a shit about the innocent lives in their way. When they reached the outskirts of the yard, James yanked at her. Thank God he kept up. He pushed her from running further and pointed down. His lips moved, but she heard nothing. He rubbed his hands on the grass, searching.

The men were still shouting at each other, but none of them fired their weapons. Some men on both sides waved their guns, and she knew it was only a matter of time before bullets speckled the air like stars.

James tapped her leg. She looked down to see his fingers gripped around a small hook. He pointed to the grass a few feet away. It took her a second to catch on, but then she dropped to her knees and used her palms to search for a second hook.

After a few pats, she found it. She latched her finger through the loop and nodded to James. With his free hand, he put a finger up, then another. One. Two. Three.

She lifted, the muscles in her legs and back tightening and threatening to give up on her. It took a few seconds of using all her might, but the ground gave way and a giant metal bulkhead rose from the earth. The grass stayed on top of it, the perfect disguise if not for the fact they opened it in front of dozens of men. Luckily, those men were too busy with each other to care. She gave them one last glance before following James into the shallow depths of darkness below.

One man aimed his weapon and fired. Streaks of white belched from muzzles all around her.

Her hearing was coming back, but only slightly. She heard a muddled set of booms, as if listening to it on an old tape player in slow motion. It reminded her of Chris's music coming through the walls of her childhood home. She stared for a stupid amount of time, awed by the circle of violence around her. James, already down the steps of the bunker, tapped her leg. She snapped out of it and flew down the steps into pitch blackness.

They reached up to the door and pulled it down. It crashed into place with a bang. Plumes of dust and dirt rained on them.

Her pulse pounding, she slapped at her pockets, searching for her phone. When she found it, she used the flashlight to bring some light into the room. She shined it all over the door, trying to find a lock.

"This circle," she said to James, her own voice still hard to hear.

He gripped the wheel and together they twisted it, using muscles they didn't know they had, until it pulled two bars into place, shutting the world out.

She took labored breaths, coughing on dust particles.

Using her phone, she examined the room. As the dim light revealed old shelves filled with canned and packaged foods, her hearing came back. Above her, she could hear shouting and gunfire. She turned the phone to the other side of the room to reveal a couch facing a television with an area rug between them.

James reached up and pulled a cord, and a bulb came to life, brightening the room. The bulb sat in a small silver funnel hanging from the ceiling, making the light glow from one side of the room to the other as it dangled back and forth.

Another reminder of Chris.

The violence above her registered as the tension exited her body. All the questions she hadn't had time to consider leaked into her brain, overflowing it. What do they do now? How long would they need to be down here? Were the bombs nuclear? What supplies did the bunker have? Was this her life now? Would she be back to school on Monday listening to dipshits talk about how caaaa-razy their weekend was as other places were bombed and destroyed?

James said, "I wonder if this works." He bent down, examining the television. "Maybe we can get the news or something and see what's happening."

Cassie put her hand up. "Shhhh. What's that?"

He stopped, looked up. "What?"

She put her finger to her lip.

A low grumble, like a revving motor far away.

She turned toward the far wall, opposite where they came in. In the center, a long hallway stretched for who knew how long. She couldn't see far down because the old, dust-covered lightbulb swinging above her did nothing to expose it.

Something was growling. It wasn't a motor. Was it a dog?

"Hello?" she said into the abyss.

The growling grew louder.

And then, rattling chains and loud steps. Something charged down the hall right toward her. As it came into the light, her heart sank and she screamed. It was human. Kind of.

Under its top jaw, the bottom of its face was nothing but raw tendons and hanging red slime. Its eyes were black pools. The thing was naked, its penis flopping as it charged her. Raw wounds stretched across the creature's body.

It happened too fast for her to react, like a fastball to the face.

As it closed the gap between them, an explosion from above blasted and shook the bunker's foundation. A tremendous bang. More dust and plaster poured down. As the creature's face came inches from hers, the lightbulb gave way and drenched them in darkness.

CHAPTER 9
BLOOD AND NAILS

CASSIE, AGE 5

Darkness. That was all there was. When life returned, it came in pieces, small fragments of reality hitting her senses at different points. Noise came first. Screaming. Someone under her howled, pained and terrified.

Her mother's screaming came next. "Cassie? Cassie! What did you do?"

Her father said much the same. His voice was more even, but not without its own fear, as if he was too scared to scream, too awestruck and horrified to release the pressure in his lungs. Instead, he nearly whispered. "Cassie. Cassie. Get off her, Cassie. Jesus."

After hearing came feeling. Something warm and wet in her hand. She looked down to see the thick, crimson streaks on her fingertips, and something hard and sharp pinched between her index finger and thumb. Beyond her hand, something wriggled, drenched in the same red substance.

It flailed and kicked at her. Her body rocked side to side, as if she straddled a surfboard in a tsunami. Her mother grabbed her by the shoulders and shoved her off the squirming and screaming thing.

Cassie fell over onto some cushions, and the wriggling thing stood up, still wailing. It was Jesse, her best friend from down the street. Jesse's lower legs were covered in blood. Tears poured down her face. She lunged into Cassie's father's arms.

None of it made sense. How did she get here? What happened?

Cassie's mother bent low, getting right in Cassie's face. In a kind and motherly manner, she pushed Cassie's hair out of her face, tucking it behind her ears. The room felt wobbly. Swish. Swish. Tipping this way and that.

"Get her cleaned up. Disinfect her feet. Get her bandaged and call her parents," Cassie's mother said.

At first it confused Cassie, because she mistakenly thought her mom spoke to her. "What do you mean?" she asked.

Cassie's mother turned to her father and shouted, "Just do it!"

Oh good, her mother wasn't speaking to her. She didn't feel she had it in her to do chores. Her eyelids grew heavy and her body felt achy and tired. Had she run around too much? She couldn't remember. But her muscles told her a story, one where she must have been very active.

As soon as her father ushered her screaming friend from the room, her mother turned her attention back to Cassie. "I need you to tell me what happened."

Cassie's head drooped, her chin hitting her ribs. Her mother slapped her on the cheek, not hard, but enough to startle Cassie.

"Don't fall asleep. What happened?"

A voice came from Cassie, but it wasn't her own. It was something else, guttural, angry. "You know what happened."

"Yes, I do know, but I want you to tell me."

"I ripped Jesse's toenails off one... by... one." The first time the voice came out, a long time ago, it scared Cassie, this foreign thing flooding from her mouth. She'd grown accustomed to it by now, but she never expected it to come out with her family present.

Cassie's mother bit her bottom lip, her eyes filling with water. "Why? Why are you doing this? You're not supposed to do this to *her*."

What an odd bit of talk. The way her mother said, *'her,'* in particular. Was she supposed to rip anyone's toenails out?

Cassie gulped, swallowing down the croaky voice and using her own. "I wanted Jesse to feel it, too."

Her mother's eyes lit up with recognition. "You wanted her to feel what, Cassie? Was this revenge? Was Jesse hurting you?"

Cassie shook her head. "No. Jesse is my friend."

She still heard her friend's screams between the floorboards, singing along with the tapping of feet above them.

"If she's your friend, why did you want to hurt her?"

"So she could enjoy the feeling of it too." Cassie wasn't sure who spoke that time, her or the other voice, but she understood the point.

It started a few weeks ago, a nagging pain in Cassie's chest. It didn't hurt; it aggravated, this constant tugging and pulling at her ribs. A day later, the ache extended to other parts of her body. Her knees, calves, wrists. Throbbing. Always. It drove her mad. She couldn't concentrate, couldn't even enjoy watching television. She shifted, stretched, rolled around on the floor. Nothing worked to release the pain. It was like a new friend, someone to sit with her at all times, but it wasn't a friend she wanted. She hated it, hated it so badly. She wanted the new friend dead.

She tossed and turned in her bed one night, trying to fall asleep, but the dull throbbing fought against her. In a fit of rage, she punched herself in the ribs. It hurt, but for a second, the ache went away. She wondered if she hurt herself more, could she remove the annoyance all together? It was worth a try. She snuck downstairs into the kitchen where she climbed onto the counter and grabbed a knife. The bulk of the ache had gravitated toward the Achille's tendons, so she thought it best to start there.

She put her legs in a W on the countertop. Her mother told her never to sit that way, saying it could mess up how Cassie walks, but

Cassie presumed it would be okay for a few minutes; besides, if anything was going to mess up how she walked...

She slammed the knife down, driving it right through the skin between tendon and muscle. The knife tip hit the counter and slid to the side, causing the knife to rub against the tendon, moving it like a bow hair would a violin string.

She didn't scream, didn't yell or freak out, although tears trailed down her cheeks. The pain went far beyond excruciating. Waves of it shot into her brain, overloading her. She *wanted* to scream, to release the building pressure in her lungs, but she couldn't. Something stopped her, like an imaginary hand cupping her mouth. Instead, she yanked the knife out and without a second thought, drove it down through the same spot on the other leg. She let go of the knife, keeping it wedged between her tendon and muscle and covered her own mouth. No imaginary hand was needed that time. She bit her finger, using her teeth to etch out her agony and rage.

The kitchen light clicked on.

Before Cassie could move, her brother stared at her, wide-eyed. "What the heck?" Before Cassie could stop him or come up with some sort of story, Chris ran back upstairs, calling for their parents.

Cassie pulled the knife out and hopped off the counter, unprepared for her legs' inability to hold her up. She collapsed, bright red streaks decorating the white-tiled floor. A parade of feet cascaded down the stairs.

"Cassie?" Her mother's voice was filled with worry.

Her eyes turned to marbles at the bloody site. "What happened?"

Cassie didn't know how to explain it but knew if she tried, she'd get in trouble, so instead she shrugged.

"Jesus," her father said. "What the fuck?"

Cassie's mother scooped her up, hugging her tightly. "We have to take you to the hospital. How did this happen?"

Cassie said nothing. The next thing she knew, she was out in the cold, the freezing night air whipping against her pink sleeping gown.

Her mother buckled her into her car seat.

The whole family packed in.

Chris grumbled and complained that he shouldn't have to go to school tomorrow because he wouldn't get enough sleep, but Cassie's mother told him to shut up.

Fear burned across both parents' faces.

As they drove, her parents asked her a million questions, but Cassie ignored them. She kicked her feet up to see the red seeping through the bandages her mother dressed her calves with.

Chris tapped her shoulder. "Does it hurt?"

Cassie smiled. "It feels so good."

Her mother's head whipped around, her eyes turned to tiny slits. She was trying to read something on Cassie, but Cassie couldn't place what.

"What did you just say?"

"I said it feels so good." She didn't understand why this upset her mother so much, but it did. Her mother knew something. Cassie wanted to know what it was but understood her mother wouldn't tell her.

"Enjoy the feeling of what, Cassie?" her mother asked, snapping her back to the present.

Jesse continued crying upstairs, but the wailing withered into more whiny sobs.

Cassie looked her mother in the eyes, glaring. Anger built inside of her. The other voice took over again. "Pain. I wanted her to feel the joy of pain. You know what I mean better than most. Don't you, Mom?"

Cassie stood up and held Jesse's toenail up for her mom to see. "This is your gift to me!" She popped the toenail into her mouth and chewed. The sharp edges dug into her gums, slicing into the meat. Jesse's dried blood was wet again, mixing with Cassie's own blood and saliva.

Her mother pulled at Cassie's jaw, trying to pry it open. "Get that out of your fucking mouth."

Cassie swung her arms wildly, slapping her mother over and over. She just wanted to finish chewing, to swallow her trophy.

"No. Spit it out. Now."

They fought this way for a few minutes, neither relenting. For Cassie, there was a hunger, a desperate need to eat the nail, but she knew it was something else for her mom. She needed the win for a reason Cassie couldn't understand. Too many secrets.

She gulped, an exaggeration to brag about her victory.

Her mother backed away, shaking her head. She covered her face with her hands. "This can't be happening."

Cassie tilted her head. "What's wrong, Mom?"

Her mother slid her hands away from her face. "I'm going to get you help. There's a woman who knows about this stuff. She can help."

Cassie leaned forward and sharpened her eyes. "Worked wonders for you, bitch. Didn't it?"

CHAPTER 10
MAPPED WITH SCARS

"*The answer is almost always in front of you, and it's usually sharp and dangerous. Don't be afraid to cut your way out.*"

Cassie fell on her ass, reacting to the incoming bullet train in the form of a human-but-not-quite-human-thing. Before she stumbled backwards, she felt his hot breath hit her face, it reeked of rot.

James let out ear-splitting cries, not unlike the alarms inside the Renard house.

She didn't know where the human thing was, somewhere in the abyss. She patted the ground frantically, searching for her cellphone she dropped in the fall. With the overhead light out, she couldn't see an inch in front of her and she wondered why the human thing wasn't pouncing on her. Her hair stood on end, her spine shooting shock waves to her brain as she expected a chomp into her flesh any second. Could the thing even bite? He didn't have a fucking bottom jaw.

Slap, nothing. Slap, nothing. *Come on. Come on*, she said to herself.

The human thing growled, which brought Cassie some relief. Not much, but some. The noises he released from his half-mouth came from above, near where her head had been before the fall. He wasn't moving, which meant he wasn't attacking.

Something clinked around the same place the growling came from.

She brushed her hands over the floor, bits of dirt and plaster grinding into her palm, until she hit something and gasped. She latched onto the familiar rectangular shape. It was a dopamine shot into the brain. A thing. Her thing. Something she knew and understood.

She almost tapped the screen, but just as her fingertip neared the place it often went for relief, she remembered if she had sight, so did the thing. And right then, he didn't appear to be moving from where he was. She silenced herself, listening for the thing's growly breath. Thanks to James's cries, she struggled to find the thing's sounds. When she finally caught it, it was in the same place. Not moving. The thing wasn't moving.

She slid her butt backwards. Slowly. If the thing wasn't attacking her because he lost her in the darkness, why wasn't he pouncing on James? It was obvious what side of the room the child was on. Was he deaf? Was he not violent? Maybe they just scared him and he charged defensively. He was here first, after all, which made Cassie and James the intruders.

As she made her way around the couch, the growling shrinking behind her, she felt the human thing eyeing her, could sense his bloodshot eyes piercing. Her skin crawled faster than she did.

The sudden shock of realization dropped her. Jesus. Her world was under attack. All the things that mattered just hours ago: studying, class, work, all vanished, became miniscule dust motes on a globe of horror.

She fell to the floor, a panic attack squeezing her lungs. She wheezed, and a new sound overpowered James's crying, her heart thumping in her ears.

Thump. Thump. Thump.

It throbbed in her temples. How much air did they have down there? It felt thick, like breathing hair gel. Dusty fucking hair gel.

The world was gone. Her new world was too small to begin with, and it only shrunk as a fucking humanoid thing closed it off.

A bead of sweat dripped onto her eyebrow.

She took a big breath in through her nose, forcing her lungs to open, and she put her hand out, reaching the area rug. A breath out through the mouth, and then she pulled. Knees out. Slide forward. One slow slither at a time.

When she reached James, she placed her hands on his knees and he squirmed and screeched, which made the thing growl louder, with more anger in his pitch. Still, he stayed where he was.

"It's me," she said, figuring if his screech hadn't sent the thing charging after them, her voice wouldn't either.

"What's happening?" he asked.

"I don't know. I have my phone. Should I turn the light on?" She asked a child for his advice because they were suddenly on an even playing field. Neither of them had an ounce of experience in the utter insanity happening around them.

He sniffled. "I don't know. Yeah. I think so."

She nodded. Her finger trembled toward the screen. Before she tapped it, she inhaled, steadying herself. Her heart still thumped in her ear.

Thump. Thump. Thump.

Tap.

The phone lit up and she slid her hand down quickly, bringing up the settings. She tapped the flashlight and James came to form within the glowing orb. He was shivering, his teeth clattering together. His skin turned ten shades whiter. She turned, the light dashing along the walls until it landed on the thing.

From that far away, she couldn't make out the creature's features very well, but he stood, reaching forward with his body at a forty-five-degree angle. She scrunched her forehead, understanding. The clinking she heard, and the way the thing's body stretched forward at an impossible angle for one to keep oneself upright, she knew what was happening. She moved around the couch, bringing herself in front of the creature, but a good distance away. He stayed at his weird angle, slashing his arms forward.

"James," she whispered.

"Yeah," his voice cracked.

"I think it's chained up or something."

"What is it?"

She shook her head. "You didn't know about this? What the fuck was your dad doing down here?"

He cried. "I don't know."

She stepped forward, tilting her head. Her newfound knowledge that the thing couldn't get to her made her curiosity boil. Her initial inspection proved true. The thing had no jaw, no tongue. His top teeth had all been removed as well. The landscape of his body was mapped with bruises, scars, and fresh, red slits. It looked like pain traveling from limb to limb, decorating his torso in criss-crosses.

She tilted the light toward his eyes. The thing's pupils dilated, shrinking to black circles within a brown pond. The light angered the creature, and he slashed at her, reminding her she'd gotten a little too close. He couldn't reach her, but she felt the breeze from his attacks, and that meant she was way too fucking close.

She moved the light around the thing, and he snarled his lip at her. The flashlight on her phone only illuminated the beginning of the hall, not giving her any insight as to what existed in the dark void further down, but she saw the thick chain links connecting in a line until they gathered around the creature's neck.

"James, we need to find another light. This room can't be it. We need food and stuff, a bathroom. There has to be more down here, or we are royally fucked." She pulled the light away from the creature and turned it on the kid; his eyes were drenched in terror. "James, snap out of it and help me."

She went over to the shelves opposite the television and before she could dig in, searching for any signs of hope, she dropped her head, resting it on a box. Holy fuck. With the adrenaline subsiding, dizziness washed over her. The tiredness and pain all flooded back. Panic threatened to shut her down again. So many questions. Too much had changed too quickly. She was a pebble in a basin and a dam just collapsed. She needed a minute to fucking think, to figure something out, but pausing could mean dying.

The creature growled, and Cassie spun her phone back toward him. Even knowing the chains kept him in place, fear coursed through her at the idea he would break free, somehow finding his way to her.

She yearned for a moment. Just one fucking moment.

Another bang blasted above her, another death blow to the world she had belonged to just moments before. As the ceiling shook from the blast, James increased his screaming and crying, but Cassie did not. She, at least, had grown accustomed to the nails in her coffin. She wiped the raining dust from her hair.

"Okay. Okay. Fucking think."

She turned back to the shelves. The top two were lined with canned goods and packaged foods, most of which required microwaving, cooking, or heating with boiled water. As far as she saw, the room had neither a stove nor a microwave. She also hadn't seen a friggin' can opener. She dug through boxes on the third shelf down. One was filled with bottles of pills. They were labeled with hand-written stickers, but none of the names meant much to Cassie.

The next box had cleaning supplies, which she guessed from the dust and grime in the room, hadn't been used much. In a box with loose tools, duct tape, and stripped wires, she found a box of four lightbulbs. She took one out and placed it on the ground next to her before going back to the search.

None of the other boxes provided anything useful. Every season of *Friends* on DVD. Mad magazines. A well-thumbed paperback copy of a book called *Modern Vampires and Other Demons: Fact or Fiction*. Nothing useful at all.

The last box was filled with small vials labeled DOG FOOD. She pulled one out of the box and shook it. Inside, a chunky red substance coated the vial wall.

The creature lowered his growl and breathed heavily.

She grabbed her phone and turned it to the thing.

He was snorting and letting out a weird *grrrrrr* from deep in its lungs. It reminded her of *The Exorcist*.

Another shiver drove up her spine.

The creature backed up, letting the chain clink on the hard cement floor. Then he slammed his body into the hallway's wall. As soon as he crashed into it, he ran to the other side and slammed into that wall. He did it again and again.

Cassie flinched with each crash, but moved toward him, furrowing her brow. What was he reacting to?

He yelped, howling like a hungry dog.

Fuck.

She ran back to the container labeled "Dog food."

"This?" She waved it. "You want this?"

"What are you doing?" James asked.

Cassie jolted, so lost in her world with the creature, she forgot about James. She shot her arm out and lifted a finger at him. The closer she got to the thing, the more he drove himself from one wall to the next, yelping and groaning.

She popped the top on the container, and the thing freaked out even more, his head jerking from shoulder to shoulder.

"First, let's change the bulb." She talked to the creature as if he was going to respond.

She ran to the bulbs she'd left by the shelves and shifted the couch under the fixture. Standing on the arm, she reached up and twisted the new bulb in. It made a gritty sound as it spun along the grooves. Touching it made the hair on her flesh stand. Her fear of electricity was on full display. She nearly fell off the arm in panic as the creature jolted forward, slashing at her.

The bulb flickered to life, and Cassie jumped down.

After putting the couch back where it belonged, she stood as close as she could get without getting slashed and put the vial in front of her face. For the first time, she smelled the stuff inside. She nearly gagged. It smelled like rotted meat.

"How do you even eat things? You don't have a jaw."

She tilted the vial, and the substance inside oozed to the side. It was mostly liquid, although as thick as BBQ sauce, but there were also chunks of something in there, too, like shredded muscle. She shot her arm forward, hoping the stuff would splash out, wanting to see how the creature reacted to it. The liquid came out, but not as far as she had wished. It glopped a few inches in front of her, while some of it dribbled out of the bottle and down her fingers. She dry heaved, unable to hold it back. The foul smell mixed with the horrid feeling of it dribbling down her fingers broke her.

As she gagged, the creature's eyes lit up at the substance and he ran forward.

Cassie fell over, despite being far enough away to avoid contact.

James went back to screaming.

The creature dropped to his knees and pushed his head forward as much as the chain allowed. He twisted his neck, trying his damnedest to meet the red stuff on the ground.

Cassie stayed in her position, examining the humanoid from eye level. He terrified her, but the scientist in her wanted answers. Something happened as he worked to reach the red stuff, and Cassie's heart stopped dead in its tracks. A shiver took over her, causing her limbs to tremble in dread.

The creature's neck made an awful cracking sound, and his head moved in unnatural positions. An owl. It reminded her of an owl, the way the bird can spin its head 180 degrees, but in this case, the thing's neck was making a popping and crunching sound as if he were breaking his own bones to accomplish the feat.

"Jesus," she whispered.

James said, "What?" dropping his screams down to sniffles and hyperventilating.

She sat up and held the vial in front of her. With more gusto, she flicked her wrist. This time the red stuff went a little further, splattering on the ground within reach of the creature. Some of it landed on the thing's forehead.

His eyes widened and he moaned. The noise from his lungs was horrendous, gravelly and inhuman, but she sensed joy in it, not unlike sexual moans. He scraped its fingers on the dusty floor, picking up the red stuff in his fingers, along with cement, gravel, and grime. With a finger full of the 'dog food,' he shoved his hand into the space where his mouth should have been and jammed his fingers down his throat. The creature gagged and choked as he coated his throat with the substance.

The image haunted her, a confluence of fear and disgust at the unnatural display, melded with shame and pity as the poor, horrid thing struggled to do something as normal and necessary as eating. What had happened to him? Why was he so tortured and abused? Who had the audacity and courage to rip his jaw off?

As the thing rubbed his face in the substance on the ground, Cassie took her first true glance down the hallway. Doors, three on each side. While she could make out the wall at the end of the hall, she couldn't parse the details; the bulb wasn't strong enough to illuminate it fully. But the doors were good enough, they offered hope. Maybe, behind the doors, they'd find a fucking bathroom, a kitchen, a bed to sleep on.

She dropped the vial and rubbed her fingers together, disgusted by how the red stuff made her fingers tough to pull apart. She turned to James, who hovered in a corner, his arms squeezing himself so tightly he looked like he wore a straitjacket.

"There are more rooms," she whispered.

He said nothing, did nothing, just trembled.

When she turned back to the creature, he was looking up at her, red smeared on his forehead and cheeks. Something changed in his eyes, and it happened in a matter of seconds. They turned sharp, alert, and they glowed red. He stood with uncanny quickness, his eyes never leaving her face. If a thing without a bottom jaw could snarl, he was doing it.

Cassie's chest throbbed again, her ribs pressing in. Another panic attack.

The creature didn't run forward this time, and something about that was more threatening, as if the running out of chain only displayed his animalistic nature, his stupidity in not understanding that no matter how hard he tried, he was imprisoned. But here, the way he stood so assuredly, it terrified her. No longer did he resemble a rabid dog in character. No, now he was a monster, true as could be.

He reached his arms out, bending and twisting them. The bones cracked and popped as the elbow shifted to the top. His head tilted to the side, much like Cassie's did when she spent hours watching her lobsters interact. He was studying her. Patient.

As they stared at each other, the creature's confidence grew by the second, while Cassie battled with her legs, begging them to keep her upright, the world grew silent.

For once, silence.

She couldn't even hear James whimpering anymore.

The bottom nub of the thing's face shifted down, and a roar escaped his throat. A battle cry, loud enough to shake the foundation of Cassie's soul. He couldn't speak words, but that thunderous bellow from his lungs spoke volumes.

I'm going to get out of these chains, and I'm going to kill you.

CHAPTER II

ALL THE REASONS

"*Cassiopeia, it's perfectly normal to lie, but why do you spend so much energy lying to yourself?*"

The creature paced from one side of the hall to the other, never removing his gaze from Cassie.

She broke herself free from the spell the creature cast over her. It was partly her own doing, the very nature of a college lab girl, incessantly staring at objects, working to make sense of them. But the creature held some sway over her, too. He hadn't quite hypnotized her, but he did *something*, like he spoke directly to her mind, demanding she pay attention.

She'd read a word on the internet once: cacospectamania. She believed the internet invented the word, that you wouldn't find it in Webster's Dictionary, but she liked it nonetheless. Cacospectamania —the obsession of staring at something repulsive. It's more than morbid curiosity. It's a *need*.

If Cassie wanted to survive, she'd have to feed her cacospecta-mania another time. She went back to the boxes, shoveling through them with one hand, searching for something to wipe the gore from her fingers. She found some napkins and hand sanitizer, wiped her hand with the napkin, and poured half the bottle of sanitizer into her palm, rubbing it around until the alcohol solution dried off. It didn't feel like enough. She'd give herself a stress headache over it until she could properly wash them with soap and water, but it would have to do for now.

James stayed in the corner, hugging himself and hyperventilating.

She sat on the couch, positioning herself where she could still monitor the creature, and looked at her phone to check out what the fuck was going on with the first moment she'd had since the first plane flew overhead.

"James, why don't you sit down and play with the television? See if we can get the news or something."

He stayed put, teeth chattering.

"James!" She said it forcefully, not trying to be mean or to yell at him, but to snap him out of it. She needed him fully alert.

It worked. He turned his head toward her.

"Listen to me. I need you to play with the television. See if you can get it working. See if it has cable. Try to find some kind of news program."

Her phone proved useless. She couldn't open any social apps, couldn't get her web browsers working. Nothing. She couldn't even pull up her text messages, although she could see the content on some new messages thanks to her notifications menu still showcasing them.

> Hey, what's going on? Are you safe?

> Shana and I just went to the school's shelter.

It's fucking weird in here.

I hope you're okay.

They're saying NUKES! Fucking NUKES!

Cassie. I'm scared. I hope you're okay. I
don't know if this place is very safe.

It doesn't feel safe. It's just a basement.

Cassie. Are we all going to die?

Please let me know you're alive.

Since all of this started, Cassie had cried a few times, but it was always out of fear, out of confusion and the overwhelming nature of it all. But as she read the messages from Beth, she cried for the first time out of grief, out of loss. She pictured Beth huddled in a basement, squished together with the other students, packed like sardines until bombs blew them to smithereens.

She thought about the world, those small things that brought life to her days - the kind old man who ate at Cuddey's every night, who always tipped well and asked her about her day, the stupid squirrels running free on campus, unafraid of humans, bounding around them and picking up their crumbs, even her father, who she'd grown to despise more and more each passing year. She thought of him sitting alone in the living room, watching the news in complete terror, waiting for death to drop on him from the sky.

She wondered if he thought of her, if he regretted the way he treated her in the end, if he debated on sending her a text message to apologize. She wondered if he considered her at all.

As James fidgeted with the television, the screen remaining black, with just enough light to let the user know it was on, Cassie covered her face with her hands and cried. This was truly it. There was no world anymore. It had all ended. All the days going to class, learning, working double shifts, all for nothing, wasted. Gone. Every fucking moment she'd spent guiding herself toward some perceived happy future was all a damned waste of time. She should have been doing drugs and fucking. Had she ever enjoyed her life? Once? Was there a good day? A time when her mind hadn't been racing to plan out tomorrow?

"It's not working. No cable," James said.

Cassie wiped her eyes. "Come here. Sit down. We need to talk."

A trail of snot ran down James's nose, threatening to hit his lip. He listened and sat next to her.

"I have a lot to tell you, and it's going to be tough to take it all in, but it needs to be said. But first, is there anything you want to ask? Anything you want to say?"

He stared down at his lap.

"How are you feeling right now? Tell me everything," she prodded.

He looked up at her and just like that, his face wilted, a sinkhole razing a cityscape. He covered his face and wiped his hands all over, spreading the snot and tears all over his chubby cheeks. More blubbering.

Cassie said nothing, letting him drain himself out. Lord knew she needed a cathartic breakdown herself. After a few minutes, he eked out some words. "Are my mom and dad...?" He didn't finish the sentence. He didn't need to.

Cassie reached her hand out, putting it on his knee. "Yes, I think they most likely are."

He cried harder.

"Listen, I can't lie to you. I'd like to pretend it's all going to be fine, but the world just fucking blew up. My friend texted me and told me it was nuclear. If that's true, we're stuck down here for a long time. A very long time. Years. And more so, if that's true, I doubt anyone in Rhode Island survived."

He shook his head, still crying. "Why? Why would anyone attack Rhode Island?"

She shrugged, trying to keep calm. "I don't know, James. We have naval bases. Maybe that's why. Or maybe they didn't. Maybe they attacked New York, and we are just in the hot zone. I don't fucking know. I don't study war. I know nothing about this shit."

He looked up, a newfound excitement on his face as if he'd just solved a long puzzle. "But you said my parents had some emergency to get to. They have a lot of friends. Important people. Maybe they knew the bombs were coming and that's what the emergency was."

Cassie tilted her head. "Think about what you're saying. They knew we were about to be attacked, so they left... without you. They had me come over to babysit so they could go somewhere else to hide, when they had a perfectly good, albeit fucked up, bunker in their yard, presumably built for this exact reason."

He tucked his face back into his palms, tears pouring freely. She doubted they'd stop for days, and even when they did, they'd come back. Kids cried for no reason at all, it was part of growing up, and James had all the reasons in the world to cry. Literally.

"Listen, I don't want to stop you from grieving, but we have to talk about something important and I need your absolute full attention." She glanced toward the creature.

He wasn't pacing anymore, but he stood tall, still glaring at her. Whatever she fed him did a number on his constitution. He went from looking like a haggard, damaged, tortured thing, to a confident and crazed killer. Lesson learned. Don't feed the animals. Even without teeth, they might bite.

James put his head in his *Among Us* tee shirt and wiped his face on the inside of it. Once he popped back out, he straightened and looked at her. "Okay."

She smiled at him, hoping to ease his stress, even just a millimeter. "Do you ever watch horror movies?"

He nodded, his eyelashes arching with confusion. "Yeah."

"Me too," she said. "But they also drive me nuts because sometimes they are just so stupid. Do you know what I mean?"

He shrugged. "I guess so."

"There are two things that happen all the time in horror movies that I think ruin the whole movie, and I think we can learn from those things. So, I need you to hear me out, okay?"

He nodded again.

"The first thing I hate is when the characters refuse to accept what's happening. Do you know what I mean by that?"

A little twinge of recognition hit his eyes. "Like when the characters act like weird stuff is just normal? Like, oh! In that one movie where the books are flying off the shelves and the father says it was probably just the wind."

Cassie snapped her fingers. "Exactly!"

James sat up a little, as if he accomplished a major feat by connecting with another human.

It made Cassie sad for him, but she pressed on. "So, let's not do that, okay? That's how the characters end up dead, because they refuse to accept what's happening until it's too late. Can we not do that? Can we be honest about what is happening right now?"

As if he were a balloon Cassie just stuck a pin in, he deflated. His back slouched and his arms dropped to the couch cushion under him. "Okay," he said with no heart.

She wished she could stop, could hug him and forget the conversation entirely, but if she didn't finish it now, she'd be just like those fucking characters in horror movies. "Okay, good. Then we have to come to terms with everything we've seen. There is, or was, some kind of war going on above us. People were dropping bombs and shooting each other, and my friend said something about nukes. We have no choice but to accept that we are stuck down here until we hear otherwise. Opening that bulkhead right now might literally kill us. That's first."

He nodded.

"I know that's tough, but that means we have to accept we may never see the people we love ever again." As his eyes refilled with water, Cassie regretted taking the conversation this far. It was easier for her because she didn't really love anyone. She cared for people, sure, Beth, even James, but the only people she'd ever loved were all dead long before the bombs started.

She wasn't trying to hurt James more than he already was. Besides, she really needed his attention for the next part. She turned her head toward the creature who maintained its sentry position. "Then there's him." She pointed at the thing.

James turned toward him, and as if he had forgotten he was there, his face filled with panic and fear at the sight.

"Look, I'm not religious. I'm not spiritual. I don't believe in ghosts or aliens or even Karma." She pointed at the creature again. "But that thing right there isn't fucking human."

James's mouth twisted. "What do you mean?"

"James, look at him. His skin is gray and ashy. He bends his limbs in ways a human can't do. Your parents have weird books about monsters and shit. I'm not quite ready to say that thing is a vampire, but whatever he gobbled up from that vial looked a lot like blood, and his eyes changed to this weird color, and it would make sense that your dad took his jaw off and ripped out his teeth if he was a vampire. He's not human, James. I need you to understand that."

"Why?"

"Because if we have to kill him, we need to figure out what we are dealing with."

"I don't want to do this," he shouted, his voice heightening in pitch to a childish scream. He wrapped his hands around his knees and started rocking on the couch in full temper tantrum mode. She had broken him.

"I know, I know, I know," she said, over and over, as she put her arm around his shoulders and brought him into her. She hugged, and said, "Sssshhhhh," the way one would calm an infant.

Right then, she hated life. So many emotions bubbled through her - anger at all she'd lost, grief over the life she worked so hard to build, confusion as to what was happening. She couldn't imagine what those emotions must be like for a child, a pre-teen kid still working to figure out the normal world, then thrust into insanity. A kid who still latched onto his parents only to lose them, and every comfort he'd ever known, in seconds. He'd etched his little slice of life, his small, hidden place in the big, evil world, and then the world struck back and took it all in one fell swoop.

After a few minutes, the tantrum settled. He sniffled into her shirt. "I'm sorry," he said.

She pulled away from him so she could look him in the eyes. "You have nothing to be sorry for. Never apologize for feeling things."

"Okay," he said and nodded.

She scanned the room, taking in the small environment, wondering where the electricity came from, if there was a generator somewhere that would run out of gas. She wondered where the oxygen came from because she didn't see any vents. "There's one more thing I hate in horror movies, something that definitely gets the characters killed."

"What?" James asked, but Cassie could see he wasn't with her anymore. His eyes were glossed over, staring blankly at the empty wall by the television.

"They either lie or withhold information for no good reason. I'm not saying you're doing either of those, but I want you to think about it. If your parents had secrets, things you never told anyone because you wanted to protect them, there's no need anymore. The world is over. There's no police. I won't judge the dead, but the information could help keep us alive. You don't want to die, right?"

James jerked his head away from the spot he'd been staring at and shook his head. "No. I don't want to die. But I don't have any secrets. I promise. I didn't know about him." James pointed to the creature.

"Okay," she said. "Okay. But maybe it's not a secret. Maybe there's just stuff you know you don't realize could be helpful. So, I need you to think. Do you know anything about this bunker or about your parents' books or even what they do for work? Anything. Anything you can think of that might be useful."

He shook his head so vigorously it was like it was vibrating, an overloaded pressure boiler. "I don't know, honestly. I can't think of anything."

"James," she said, more forcefully than intended. "Tell me everything you know about this fucking bunker."

WHAT ARE WE DOING?

"*Cassiopeia, life isn't about finding solutions. It's about destroying them.*"

James's eyes darted around the room. He searched for answers, looking for some small bit of information worth telling Cassie.

She could see the deep thought in the creases on his forehead and the way he chewed on his bottom lip. She didn't think he was lying or planning answers in his head. She knew from the terror on his face when the creature appeared this was all new to him. No kid could act that well.

"I really can't think of anything," he finally said.

Cassie shifted, untucking one leg from under her and stretching it out while tucking the other in. "You knew about the bunker. You're the one who told me about it, so tell me how you know about it, what your parents said, exactly."

James rolled his eyes to the ceiling as if praying to God to conjure the memories for him. "I remember when they had it built. My dad worked on all these blueprints for a really long time and he was super stressed about it. I asked him what it was, and he said it was a place to keep us safe in case things went bad."

She thought about what to say next, wanting to prod with more questions, but she knew the right ones could open doors as easily as the wrong ones could shut them. She had to think like a shrink. No yes or no questions. Open-ended, bring out the stories. "What was happening at the time that made your parents decide to build one?"

He shook his head. "I don't know. Maybe something on the news."

"What about in your life? At home. Anything different?"

He frowned. "I don't think so. Oh, well, they were building something else at the same time."

She tried not to show her excitement. "Oh? What was that?"

"They were building a new office somewhere. They were really excited about it because they said it would help them more with their patients. They're psychiatrists, if you didn't know."

She chuckled and furrowed her brow. "I know. I was one of their patients. You didn't know that?"

His head slid back like a ball just smacked him in the face. "Wait, you were? My parents hired a crazy person to watch me?" He smiled to show he was only joking.

She tossed a small throw pillow at him. "I was a kid, and I wasn't crazy. I was sad."

His smile ran away. "I'm sorry. I was just kidding."

She put her hand on his arm. "I know. So, anyway, tell me more about this new office they built."

He shrugged. "Not much to tell. I've never seen it. They still have their old office. That one I've been to, but I never saw the newer one. One thing they were happy about, though, was that they said they'd be home earlier when they worked at the new office because it was much closer to home."

"Well, that must have been nice." She played the buddy psychiatrist role.

He pursed his lips. "I don't know. I don't think they ever came home early. Or maybe they did. Who knows? They were hardly around anyway. I felt like they were visitors more than people I lived with. Always working, even when they were home."

She debated on letting him talk about those feelings but worried the conversation would veer too far off course. Her eyes went back to the creature, still staring, still standing tall. His ability to keep at it haunted her.

"So, when they built this place, did you ever get a tour? Did you see it when they finished?"

He shook his head. "No, but they probably asked me if I wanted to, and I probably didn't. You know me. I just like to stay in my room and be alone."

She wondered why, but doubted he would know himself. Most times, people's actions stemmed from some inner feeling or past trauma they couldn't identify. Long sessions of therapy might uncover the truth, but a casual conversation on a couch while a creature eyeballed him probably wouldn't reach through the surface.

"So, they have all those books on monsters. Did they ever talk about those? Seems like a topic they cared about."

He giggled. It was a combination of discomfort and surprise. "I have honestly never heard them say a word about monsters. They used to tell me to turn off horror movies because they said the movies were ridiculous."

She glanced at the hallway. "Not so much anymore." She stood up and walked toward the creature. He gurgled a little as she approached. "What are you?"

Her goal was to make the monster think she was examining him, studying him, but her focus lasered in on the doors. How far would she have to run to get into them? How much chain did the creature have? Was it enough to get her if she made her way into the door? Would he be able to follow or would the chain choke him upon entry? She didn't know, couldn't, because she knew nothing about the room itself. Maybe it was a large bedroom, and if she made it all the way to the other side, the creature would never reach her. But maybe it was a fucking broom closet.

"What do we do?" James asked.

If nothing, the conversation she'd had with him seemed to calm him for the moment. She found most of his answers useless, but one thing she learned from her lab work was useless information proved useful when you gathered enough of it.

"We can't live in this room," she said. "So, we'll have to figure out a way down this hall at some point. But it has gotta be like two in the morning, and I am fucking exhausted. I have no idea if I'll be able to sleep tonight, not with everything that happened, and surely not with this fucking thing staring at me, but I think for tonight we just need to relax. Not think about what we need to do. Just forget everything."

He raised his hand as if she were his teacher.

"Yes?"

"I have to pee."

Cassie went to the shelves and opened some boxes. She pulled out the *Friends* DVDs and the few protein bars she saw stuffed in with the food. When she gathered what she wanted, she took a bucket off the bottom shelf and slid it into the corner. "Pee into that bucket for now."

He gave her an, '*Are you serious,*' look.

"What are your other options? Peeing on the wall? I'm going to face the other way and see if we can't get the television playing something."

As she fumbled with the wiring on the television, trying to figure out the DVD player, she mumbled to herself, "I can't believe it's the end of the fucking world, I'm alone with a child and a fucking monster, and all I want to do is watch Must See TV."

"Cassie, I can't go. My dad says I'm bladder shy."

As she found a dangling cord and connected it to the back of the

DVD player, she said, "Better get over it, because you don't have any other options. I told you, I'm not looking."

"I know, but he is."

She whipped around toward the creature. He had indeed turned his attention from Cassie to James. She made her way closer to him while trying to keep from looking in James's direction. The creature's eyes dulled again. He was stretched to the end of the chain, standing at an angle once more.

Whatever she fed him had worn off.

"Ignore him. He's not real."

On her way back to the television, she opened a protein bar and took a bite. She wished she had brought her backpack with her. That half-eaten bag of chips in there would have come in handy. She suddenly hated herself for how often she'd neglected her snacks.

As the disc tray popped open on the player, the sound of piss hitting the plastic bucket took over the room. The sound was so aggressive she had to bite back a laugh. The tray slid back in, and the menu for *Friends* Season One Disc One came up.

James came over and sat on the couch.

"Have you ever watched *Friends*?"

He shook his head.

"You're in for a treat." She hit play and made her way over to the other side of the couch.

As the theme song played, James sighed. "What are we doing?"

"We're watching one of the worst sitcoms of all time."

"Why?"

She closed her eyes and sucked in a big gulp of air. Who knew how much more oxygen was left? "Because, James, tomorrow is going to be fucking insane. Tomorrow, we have to face that thing and figure out how to get into those rooms. Tomorrow, we have to find food and figure out how we're going to survive down here. Which means tonight, we watch a stupid fucking television show and forget about all of it."

She could tell he wanted to say more, but she'd scared him out of it. Her tone let him know not to keep pressing the issue.

She rubbed her eyes. "We're going to need to sleep, but I don't think it's wise for both of us to do so. Just in case that thing gets loose, one of us should be alert. Why don't you sleep for a while. I'll sit down here and watch the show." She scooted off the couch, her butt landing on the old, dirty area rug in front of it. If the Renards were so rich, why couldn't they have nicer things down here, too?

She wanted to beg James to stay up first, let her sleep since she was already operating on so little of it, but she'd worry about him. He had to be tired, too. She couldn't trust a twelve-year-old to stay alert without at least a little sleep first, and if she didn't trust him to stay awake, she'd keep herself awake stressing about it.

James curled up in a ball on the couch and Cassie focused on the show. Her mind brought her to tomorrow, to the inevitable fact she'd need to get by the creature and into those rooms, but she forced herself back into the show, not allowing her mind to wander.

Friends.

Ross and Rachel.

Something exploded above them.

Monica Geller.

The creature's chain clinked as the links pulled taut.

Chandler Bing.

Friends.

CHAPTER 13
WHISPERS

"*Cassiopeia, I am always with you. Unfortunately, so is everyone else.*"

Cassie assumed James would toss and turn all night, unable to sleep, but he conked right out. She remembered reading an article about infants and how after extreme stress, they'd fall into deep sleep and stay that way for hours. She wondered if the same were true for twelve-year-old kids.

For all her worry that James wouldn't keep guard, she struggled to keep her eyes open after a few episodes of *Friends*. The flickering television lulled her, and she caught her eyelids drooping and her chin resting on her chest.

The creature quieted, no longer stretched out with his chain taut. Without an acute visual on his future victims, he retreated a few feet down the hall. Not enough to give her leeway into the rooms, but enough where she felt he wouldn't break free mid-night and kill them.

To keep herself awake, she headed to the shelves to search for something to snack on. From her first search, she knew there wasn't much, but even if she had to munch on dried ramen, she'd take it just to get something in her stomach and keep herself occupied.

She walked slowly past the hallway, hoping the thing had fallen asleep, but as soon as she came into view, he barked and ran to the end of his chain. Cassie turned, hoping the noise didn't wake James. After a few seconds, she went back to her mission. She dug through boxes, finding nothing of value, no hidden nuggets she missed on the first search. What she wouldn't give for a Snickers bar or a bag of M&M's.

"Cassie?" someone whispered.

She snapped around, expecting to see James sitting up and looking at her, but he was still hidden behind the couch backing.

"Yes?" she whispered back. He must have woken up but remained lying down, or maybe he was talking in his sleep. No response came, so she went back to rummaging.

"Caaaaaaasssssssssssiiiiieeeeeeeee." This time the voice was taunting, sing-songy. Worse, she pinpointed where it came from.

She didn't respond. Responding would make it more real. She imagined it, or maybe she'd gone delusional from lack of sleep and stress.

"Caaaaaaaaaaasssssssssiiiiiieeeeeeeee," the voice whispered.

Her heart slammed into her ribs. *I'm not crazy. I'm not crazy,* she told herself.

As she dug into the boxes, her hands shook.

"Caaaaaasssssssiiiiieeeeeeeeeee."

She slowly turned to the creature on the chain. Was he talking into her mind? Could he do that? She had made James promise they wouldn't dismiss what they experienced, made him come to terms with the fact that *thing* wasn't human. If she sat here convincing herself it was all in her head, she'd be breaking her own rule. She *heard* her name, loud and fucking clear. Someone was singing it, whispering, taunting her, and James was fast fucking asleep.

That only left one option. But it didn't sound like it came from the hallway. It sounded like someone whispered right in front of her face, inside the wall. If the thing was speaking to her in some telepathic, paranormal bullshit, it could sound like it came from anywhere.

She stood up, legs wobbly. The room spun for a moment as she got to her feet.

"Caaaaaaasssssssiiiieeeeee." Right behind her.

As she faced the creature, the noise continued to sound like it came from the wall behind her, or maybe in her fucking skull. It was so hard to tell. It almost bounced, reverberating all around her. She stepped toward the creature.

He slashed out his arms, but she kept a suitable distance, used to this game by now.

"Are you talking to me?" she whispered, still trying not to wake James.

The creature's nub went down, the top part of his face up.

"Are you trying to talk right now?"

From the thing's throat, a black wisp of smoke climbed out. It looked like winter breath, outside of the midnight color.

She lunged backward, shocked.

The mist steamed forward, pulling apart from itself into tendrilled coils. At first, it maneuvered like steam, out and then up, but then it turned as if guided by some unknown force.

Cassie stepped away, swatting toward it, but not touching it, too afraid. What might happen if her hands landed in it? Would it poison her? Burn? Who the fuck knew, but she wouldn't be the control study.

As it traveled, it weakened, the dark colors fading to a dull gray and the thick branches dissipating into fine threads. Eventually, it made its way to the wall where Cassie heard the voice, but before it reached its destination, it fully evaporated.

"What the fuck?" she whispered.

The thing pointed toward the boxes.

"You want food?"

The thing nodded his head.

For the sake of experimentation and learning, she debated on it, but her life was at stake. "No. Be good and maybe I'll feed you tomorrow."

The thing's top lip curled.

She crossed her arms, proud of herself for saying no, for sticking to her guns and not letting someone pressure her into doing something she didn't feel comfortable with.

The creature rubbed his fingers in front of his face. And then he lashed, a roaring howl escaped his lungs as he whipped his arms at her. She was a good five feet away, and he had no chance of hitting her, but the rage in his eyes, the pure hatred, sent a shockwave from Cassie's spine to her brain. She ran away from him, going back toward the couch, hoping if she sat down on the floor, the creature would calm down. Out of sight, out of mind.

James shot up, the loud growls from the creature pulling him out of his deep sleep. "What's happening?"

"Shh. It's okay. I made the thing mad. You can go back to sleep. He'll calm down in a few minutes."

"Why is it mad? What did you do?"

"Nothing. Don't worry about it. We'll talk about it when we switch shifts. Just go back to sleep so you have enough rest for tomorrow."

With shaky hands she grabbed her phone and the television remote. She didn't know what to do with either, but she needed to do something.

James caught her nervous fiddling. "I can just stay up now," he said.

She turned her head to him. "No. Please, just try to go back to sleep."

She turned the volume down two notches on *Friends*. She could already barely hear it and had the subtitles going so it wouldn't wake James up, and she'd dropped it to one above muted.

She tapped her phone screen, but it didn't come on. Completely out of juice. Not that it was anything more than a fancy brick now anyway. None of the apps worked and she couldn't get any service. She presumed that kind of thing happened when someone dropped bombs all around you.

She turned her attention to the television, staring until her eyes blurred. James tossed and turned behind her, and she figured the peaceful night's rest was over for him. Maybe she'd take him up on his offer and get some sleep herself. Her heart was still punching at her ribs, but less from fear and more from a desperate need to rest.

After a few minutes, the creature settled down. The room was quiet again, outside of James's heavy breathing and constant shifting. She could even hear the gentle audience laughter coming through the small speakers on the TV.

She thought about the mist that crawled from the creature's lungs, wondering if it could have killed her if she inhaled it. It made her feel less safe because even if the creature couldn't stretch beyond his chain, he might possess a weapon that could, one that could lurch through the air and find its way into her bloodstream while she slept. She'd have to warn James so he'd keep an eye out. For what? For fucking black mist.

That was her new world.

Boom!

The bombs did more than raze the scenery. They devoured sanity, turned the slivers of life still left into nonsense.

Cassie had no one up there to love, yet she mourned for all of it, even the bad stuff. She'd kill for a boring seven a.m. lecture, would love a shift at Cuddey's. Hell, she would even hug her fucking father if she could. Before, all Cassie wanted was a day to herself. But, she wanted the people back, the classmates, the coworkers, Beth. She sure as fuck didn't want whatever was chained up a few feet away from her. She supposed she'd never be alone again, and boy was she stuck with some shit roommates.

She thought about Chris, her mother, the first explosions to hit her Earth. Their removal from her life had felt like grenades. She'd kill to have them back. She tilted her head back, staring up at the ceiling, a grotesque cement thing keeping her from the world. Her eyes watered and blurred. And then the ceiling spoke to her.

Scratch. Scratch. Scratch.

CHAPTER 14

AN ENDLESS CYCLE OF FURY AND PAIN

"There's no good or bad in the world, Cassiopeia, no matter how much I've complained about it. The truth is, humans are malleable. They can't be good or evil, only convinced."

Cassie stared at the spot on the ceiling where the noise came from. It was a brutal scratch, an intentional one, not one which could be explained away as a mouse or a gentle rustling. What was above the ceiling? This wasn't a house, there was no upper floor, no attic. Above the hard cement was nothing but earth. Or was there a gap, a small enough space for someone to fit in and taunt her? But who?

She heard the voice in the wall, but she felt confident it was the creature speaking into her mind, not someone actually hiding behind the thick concrete. But the scratching, each scratch was long and drawn-out. She couldn't see it as anything other than someone fucking with her. It made her heart ache, brought back the memories of that night when her brother's body hung above her, when all she could consider was the distraction to her homework, so oblivious to the dead over her head. It also made her furious someone would take the most painful moment of her life and use it to scramble her already damaged mind.

James tapped on her shoulder and she flinched, startled out of her trance.

"Why don't you try to sleep now? I feel awake. I can't go back to sleep."

Cassie turned to him and offered a grim smile. She tried her hardest to make it legitimate but knew she fell short. "I can't either. There's no way. I think it's time we take some action. What do you think?"

He scratched the top of his hand. "I guess. What do you mean?"

"Come with me." She stood up, a sea of silver stars sparkling in her vision. She nearly fell over as the blood rushed through her from standing, but after a few seconds, it quelled, and she was fine.

James followed her to the boxes. As they waltzed past the hallway, the creature charged and choked on the chain. It made James jump, but Cassie was prepared for it. As long as the thing wasn't shooting black mist from his half-mouth, she didn't care about him bouncing around on his chain anymore.

She took out two vials of the dog food and handed one to James.

"What are we doing?" he asked.

She put her finger to her lip.

He nodded.

The creature noticed the food and moaned, extending his arms as far out as they would go.

Cassie dug through the junk boxes, remembering pens and paper in one of them. When she found them, she guided James back to the couch.

He watched her write on the paper.

I don't know if he can understand us when we talk.

I'm going to throw some of this food down the hall. I suspect he'll run after it. While he is going for it, I am going to run into one of those doors and see what's in there.

James's eyes widened. He snatched the pen from her.

NO! WHAT IF HE GETS YOU!!!!?

Cassie read the terror on his face. If she died, he'd be truly all alone and wouldn't know how to survive a day. Cassie was terrified herself, but if they didn't get into those rooms, they'd both be dead soon, and it was the perfect time to make a move, while anger from the scratching still flowed through her veins. It battled the fear and gave her the motivation she needed to act.

We have to do this James. There's no other choice. But I need something from you.

He grimaced and took the pen.

WHAT?

She sighed, knowing what she wrote next wouldn't go over well.

When you hear me knocking, throw the second bottle of food down the hall. See Spot run!

NO NO NO! I CAN'T

You can. I will knock when I am ready to leave the room. You whistle before you throw it. I will whistle back. Then toss it. You have to remember all that. All of those steps must happen before you toss it.

She stood up, not giving him more time to argue, and headed toward the hall. Her heart pounded but she pressed forward, knowing full well she neared talking herself out of it. It was foolish, insane. But she had no other choice.

James latched onto the back of her cardigan. "Cassie, please," he whispered.

She let the cardigan slide off her arms and continued forward until she stood a foot in front of the creature's flailing arms.

She gave one last look to James, who stood behind her squeezing her cardigan into his chest. His face exploded with terror. Tears. Shivers. His breathing turned to shallow puffs.

She turned back to Spot, held the vial up for him to see. "You want?"

She tossed it. It flew down the hall, and Spot followed it with his eyes before charging after it.

Cassie ran, refusing to think or to stop herself. It was madness. Her feet hit the floor just a few feet behind Spot. If he turned, he'd be on her before she had the chance to switch gears. She'd passed the point of no return, though. Either the plan worked or Spot would kill her in the next few minutes. It didn't help that the only diversion she could create gave the fucking creature more clarity, more hate in his eyes, and surely more power. Spot fucking terrified her as it was, but once he had the food in his system, he was a different beast altogether, and that beast was about to come out and play while Cassie stood right in his playground.

Inches from the door, a new thought popped into her head. What if the doors were locked? Stupid! How could she be so stupid to not consider it before? She should have turned the boxes upside down searching for keys or something. It didn't matter, she'd never have the time to unlock them. If the door was locked, she was dead. Plain and simple.

Her arm reached out for the door handle as Spot lifted the vial and cracked it open in his hand. Her hand gripped the knob. She heard her heartbeat in her throat. The smell from the vial tore through the hall, that awful, rotten meat odor, noxious and horrifying.

The knob twisted, and a small sense of relief washed over her, but not a big one, because she still stood in the danger zone and possibly on the precipice of something even more terrible. Who knew what lurked behind the door? Whatever it was, she'd be trapped with it in seconds.

Spot turned to her, a sinister sharpness in his eyes as he jammed his red-coated fingers down his throat.

She stepped into the unknown room and shut the door. Both hands fumbled, searching for safety. The left slapped against the wall, hoping to find a switch to save her from the utter blackness, and the right looked for the knob on that side of the door, praying for a locking mechanism. She swam in the dark.

Her right hand found its destination first, a welcoming metallic nub. She twisted it, and it responded with a satisfying thud just as she heard Spot running down the hall. But what did she lock herself in the room with? She didn't know because she couldn't find a switch anywhere.

It was all in her mind, she knew, but the room felt murky, thick with black.

Spot slammed his body into the door behind her.

She jumped forward, afraid of what she might fall into.

Spot slammed again and again.

She turned and saw a sliver of light. There was a thin window on the door. A tiny little box. Spot had his eye pressed to it, blocking out most of the light. There wasn't enough to reveal anything about the room, but she could see that fucker's eye perfectly clearly. That red glowing bead, filled with hate and desire.

She took a slow step backwards and something hit the back of her neck, a tickle. She flinched again. Every muscle in her body tensed, a full seizing. Her hand slapped at her neck instinctively, like squishing a bug. A thin thread hit her palm. As she pulled it off her neck, she heard a click and the room lit up.

She spun around, heart in her lungs, surveying for more threats. The room was empty of life, but goddamn was it glorious otherwise. Spot smashed himself into the door again, and she flinched, but she was okay. Even if he found his way in, she had more room to maneuver than he had chain. The room spun a little, and Cassie bent over, putting her hands on her knees and taking long pulls of air. The light shining above her and the wide spaces of the room acted as an inhaler, opening her airways.

While she still had to hope James completed his side of the mission, for a moment at least, she had some peace.

The rest of the bunker looked like a leftover from the 70s, an old thing meant to emulate a different era. Cement. Dust. Worn area rug. Dingy couch.

But this room, this fucking room was a state-of-the-art kitchen and clean, too. The stainless-steel range sparkled against the dim light. Pots and pans hung on hooks along the far wall. Marble countertops stretched along the back wall; tiny speckles shimmered throughout. There was a dishwasher, a sink, cabinets, and a circular table with four chairs.

The creature banged on the door and growled, but she didn't give a fuck. She had a kitchen. A beautiful kitchen. She cracked the fridge door open and smiled at the overstuffed shelves. In one motion, she snatched a bottle of water and twisted the cap off. The cold water hurt her throat a little as it went down. It landed like a blizzard in her empty stomach.

Still gulping water, she opened cabinets, not really searching for anything but taking inventory of what they did and didn't have. The cabinets were full of food, boxes of mac and cheese, rice, dried soup, cans of beans, corn, every veggie known to man. She wasted no time ripping a bag of salt and vinegar chips open and shoving a fistful into her mouth. The crunch and slight sting of vinegar on her chapped lips was heaven.

Despite the newfound hope, the delicious meal of chips and water, anger brewed within her. The unfairness of life, that the average person was victim to powerful assholes who could decimate the world because they fight for power the people wanted none of them to have, it all made her angry. Now she had to live her life as a lamb in a pen with a bunch of chained wolves all around her, solely because of some geopolitical bullshit she wanted nothing to do with.

She chewed harder, enraged and eager to take it out on someone, anyone, preferably Spot. She cleared her mind, forcing it to focus on the more important and immediate tasks. It was not the time to destroy. She went back to the fridge and opened the freezer door. It was stocked full of frozen meat of all kinds and pizzas, ice cream, and frozen vegetables. A smoky blast of cold air hit her face. It felt so good, yet the rage wouldn't subside, like an itch under the skin.

A clock dangling above the stove ticked. *Tick. Tick. Tick.* It reminded her of a car blinker. *Tick. Tick. Tick.* Cars. She'd never see another one.

Spot slammed into the door and Cassie grabbed a block of hamburger meat and flung it across the room. It banged hard against the door.

"Shut the fuck up!" She bit down so hard her teeth ground together.

Spot slammed again.

Cassie grabbed another hunk of meat, placed her free hand on the counter, and smashed the meat into the dorsal side of her hand. Something cracked under her skin and she screamed. The pain radiated from her hand up her arm. Adrenaline burst through her like fireworks in her nerves. She slammed the meat again. Fuck. It hurt. It hurt so badly, and she never wanted to stop. Her heartbeat thrummed like a death metal drummer in her chest. Oh god, she loved it.

She continued smashing the meat into her hands, feeling the unbearable weight of pain blasting out her fingertips. Behind her, Spot slammed harder and harder which made her slam harder and harder, which made her scream louder and louder, which made him slam harder and harder in an endless cycle of fury and pain, and fuck she could swim in it, she could drown in the depths of hate and anguish within her. They'd taken everything from her, but no one and nothing could steal her joy for pain.

As she gave the top of her hand one last smashing, her neck twisted toward the far corner of the room, where she spotted something she somehow missed before. A second door. The hallway had three doors on each side, which she presumed led to three separate rooms on each side. This door must then connect the kitchen to the next room down the hall. Normally, that would have been good news, another way to get from place to place, but in that moment, it was the worst news possible, because the only reason Cassie's mind finally paid attention to the second door was because it was opening, and coming through into the kitchen, was another creature just like Spot.

CHAPTER 15
THE WEIGHT OF THE WORLD

"*It's important to eat a healthy breakfast. You want a full stomach before getting crushed by the weight of the world.*"

If she'd taken a moment to think, she would have gone back instead of forward, but her instincts overpowered rational thought and she dove toward the door, hoping to shut it in the creature's face before he could enter the room. Unfortunately, it was far too late for that, and all she did was catch a door handle to her forehead.

The force of the door swinging open knocked her down, and the new creature wasted no time, hunger in his eyes. He jumped on top of her, landing belly to belly, his face squirming closer.

Adrenaline sent her blood soaring through her veins, her heart pulsed loudly in her ears. She kicked at the thing's torso and used her elbows to scoot backwards.

The creature was strong, too strong. His sharp nails dug into the flesh on Cassie's lower arms as he tried to pin her down.

She'd have to worry about infection if she survived this. She screamed from the hot pain as he clawed deeper into her flesh. The hurt grew more and more intense until it was so unbearable it morphed into something new. She became one with it, her heart beating so rapidly it was like one long thrum. Her scream turned into a war cry.

The creature wrinkled his eyebrows, unprepared for her reaction, and that gifted her the time she needed. The thing loosened his grip enough for her to slip her arm out and she instantly went into punch mode. As her fist connected, she realized this creature also had a chain around his neck.

The punch wasn't much, just a quick jab, but it knocked the creature back, chain clinking on the linoleum floor, and Cassie found room to flip over and crawl away. With the weight of the monster off her, she got to her feet and darted to the other side of the room, hoping the chain around the second creature's neck couldn't reach that far.

Another dizzy spell hit her as soon as she stopped moving. She hit the back counters, out of room, and the monster was on his feet, coming at her. She braced for impact, wishing she ran out the door instead, chancing it with Spot. Now, instead of one jawless fuck blocking her from the safety of the main room, she had two.

The creature's neck snapped as he caught the end of the chain, just a few feet in front of Cassie. Her entire world had shrunk to the size of a bunker, and now it was nothing more than a thin strip of kitchen.

Her head swam, vision blurred. The familiar hard beat of her heart paused, and the spaces between beats frightened her more than the constant thrumming. She gritted her teeth, clenched her fists, felt the sparks of fury igniting under her skin.

"You ready for this, Rufus?" she said with a voice so bubbling in emotion it sent a shiver down her own spine.

Rufus only stared, eyes as dead and black as Spot's before he ate his food. This didn't offer a ton of relief, but at least Cassie knew food hadn't fueled Rufus up. He still wanted to hurt her, she knew, but as long as the sharp edges were dulled, she held some hope.

One foot, two. Cassie paced the small perimeter she had, and Rufus matched her step for step, his soulless eyes never leaving her. She had no plans to make a run for it, at least not yet. She experimented, seeing if Rufus could keep locked on, how much stamina he really had. Who could outlast whom? Even if she dashed past him, she wouldn't have time to signal James, let him throw the food for Spot, and get back through the hall. She was good and fucked, but vigilance and testing were the weapons she understood best and where she would glean a solution.

Her limbs trembled, still shaken from the encounter by the door. She debated throwing another punch, just to see how much she could hurt the monster, if she could at all. The knives were in the drawer by the fridge, which currently stood in Rufus's jurisdiction.

She'd double-check the drawers behind her eventually, but off the top of her head she couldn't recall seeing any potential weapons. The kitchen put more direct light on Rufus than she'd had with Spot, so she stared at his face and body, picking apart his features.

Even with Rufus's missing jaw, the tendons shifted as if the fucker was moving an invisible mouth open and shut. Was he trying to talk or was he just breathing?

An eerie whistle left Rufus's throat. It clicked in Cassie's brain what he was doing, and her skin felt like it was trying to crawl away from her. Rufus was laughing.

Laughing.

The spark inside her ignited.

"You want to laugh at me, Rufus?" She turned around, tossing drawers open, spilling their contents on the floor with a clatter. Some of it she tossed at Rufus, not trying to damage him, just annoy him, just let him know she wouldn't fucking cower. Ladles, shot glasses, k-cups, a box of aluminum foil.

Rufus snarled.

After emptying the drawers, finding nothing of value, her anger subsided. No. It remained, but it went dormant, allowing logic back in.

The world had ended, but the weight of it still hung heavy on Cassie's shoulders. She could let it crush her, or she could deal with her new surroundings. Panic, anger, none of that would help her. She could best this damned thing, especially an unfed version of it, with its dull stare and stupidly animalistic instincts.

Would he sleep eventually? They had to sleep, right? She sure as fuck did, and her body warned her it would break down without some soon. How long had she been up? A day? Could two have passed? The bunker had nothing to help guide her circadian rhythm. Losing time gnawed at her. It could be noon or it could be midnight.

She moved to the corner, pressing her back to the drawers, and slid down. As her butt hit the floor, Rufus crouched down, keeping his eyes level with her. Her eyes burned, but her brain shot them signals: *don't close in this place. Keep those lids wide.*

Minutes dripped by with Cassie and Rufus staring at each other. Cassie noted the deep gashes in the creature's flesh. As hideous and threatening as Rufus and Spot were, she couldn't help feeling sorry for the torture they'd clearly endured. Someone had ripped their bottom jaws off, plucked out their teeth, lashed them, and made them bleed and suffer. Why? Did Mr. and Mrs. Renard do this? To what end? What purpose did all of this serve?

Her survival mode, the flight or fight instincts, the mad rush of adrenaline, all of it did nothing to temper her absolute need for sleep. But even if she could drift off, any slight noise sent her responses firing. Her head jerked when the freezer whirred. Her back spasmed as the pipes clunked. A constant war ensued within her. Her body pushed to shut down, while her mind fired shockwaves through the synapses, overpowering her nerves.

"I need you, now," she said. She didn't know who she spoke to, but she felt it was important to say.

Time traveled.

She imagined looking out a window and watching the sun set, even though she suspected it was the middle of the night.

Rufus's red-streaked eyes never faltered, hardly even blinked.

Her eyes felt heavy, and she'd caught them dropping on her. She fought and fought. Eventually, without the normal hours of tossing and turning, itchy skin, and soupy mixture of stressful thinking, she drifted into sleep.

She jolted up, her heart galloping. The monster remained on his knees at the end of a straightened chain, his arms outstretched and aiming for her. He hadn't startled her awake. She did that on her own as her brain dug itself from the darkest depths and clawed through the muck and mud of earth between dreamland and reality. As it rose from the graveyard of sleep, it yanked her back to the situation in front of her.

"Shut the fuck up," she yelled at the thing, despite its silence. "Fuck."

The room was silent until Cassie's dry mouth and scratchy throat made her cough. The moment of sleep only made her yearn for the real thing more intensely. She could kill this fucking thing. Kill Rufus and Spot. Wash their blood from her hands. Take a fucking good eight hours.

Well, Cassiopeia, are you ready?

CHAPTER 16
A HOWL AT THE MOON

CASSIE, AGE 10

Cassie cringed as each floorboard groaned on her way down the stairs. She wasn't trying to be sneaky. In fact, her only reason for going downstairs was to tell her father good night, but with the tense atmosphere in the house since Chris died four months prior, she tried her hardest to appear unassuming. She and her father had grown accustomed to a minimalist version of familial dealings. She supposed it started way before Chris, since her mother was dragged out the front door, or maybe even a little before then, but Chris's death solidified it, hammered down the wedge already squarely placed between father and daughter.

Cassie's father sat at the dining room table nibbling pork chops and potatoes with his head down, a can of beer beside the plate. He had nothing to occupy him. No television playing in the background, no newspaper or book, just him. Alone.

It hurt her heart despite how mean he'd become. He wasn't outwardly cruel, not abusive in the normal sense, but he stayed away from her, cut conversations short, pushed her away. He couldn't hide how much disdain he collected for her over the years, as if he blamed her for all the problems their family suffered.

"I'm going to bed now," she said, her voice a meek little rodent.

He looked up from his plate, stared for a second with his glossy pink marble eyes, and nodded. Nothing more.

Her instincts told her to move, to let the conversation exit the atmosphere like the drizzle of oxygen it was, but a part of her saw a caged bear she wanted to prod. "Why do you drink that?" She pointed at the beer can.

"Huh?" he said with a mouthful of pork chop.

"The beer. Cynthia said she drank her dad's beer and it made her feel happy and dizzy. Is that why you drink it?" She tried to make her question innocent, but she hoped it made him uncomfortable, eager to change.

He let out a laugh, loud and powerful.

It shocked her. Maybe she should have been happy to see him show some emotion, especially one as wonderful as laughter, but that laugh wasn't right. It had cruelty streaked across the sound waves. Her eyes watered, and she wished she'd never prodded, wished she could run the fuck away and live in the woods where the tree branches would speak to her whenever the wind blew and the silence would be natural as opposed to a mark of hatred.

Cassie's father wiped his mouth, finished swallowing his meat, and for the first time in a long time, planted his eyes directly on her. "It's non-alcoholic. You think I'd risk getting drunk around here? Jesus, you must be nuts. If you give up your senses around here, you'll be dead before morning."

She didn't know what to say to that, or even what it meant, so she stepped backward. Just one step to make sure he would allow the conversation to die there. He shook his head, still shocked by her question, and put his face back toward his dinner, scooping up a forkful of mashed potatoes.

She released the air built in her lungs and turned back to the stairs.

"Wait a minute," her father said.

She paused at the bottom step.

"Is your hair dry?"

Without turning around, Cassie touched the cascading brown hair around her shoulder. She furrowed her brow. "Yeah?"

"Does that mean you didn't take a shower?"

She turned back to him.

He stared at her with wide eyes, true concern washing across his face.

Cassie couldn't decide how to feel about it. On the one hand, he was concerned for her, but on the other, the particular nature of the concern terrified her. "I didn't need one. I haven't done anything today."

He slammed his fist on the table. "Cassie. You know the rules."

"What?" She hoped her blouse hid the trembling coursing through her.

"Take a fucking shower. Now."

She shook her head. "I don't need one. What difference does it make? I don't have to take one every day."

He stood up, silverware clattering. "Are you insane? Yes, you do. Every single day. Those are the rules."

"Why? It's a stupid rule. You don't take one every single day."

"God damn it, Cassie." His voice was fierce, a howl at the moon. It hit her so hard it felt like sticking a wet finger in an electrical socket. "You take one every day because that's what you have to do. My burden is to live in a fucking haunted house, and yours is to take your damned showers. There's nothing to argue here. It's what you have to do."

Cassie pulled from her gut and let out a demonic scream as she stormed upstairs. In the shower, she screamed and cursed, punched and kicked. "*I hate you!*" she screamed loud enough for him to hear.

She stayed until the steaming water turned cold and her bruised knuckles reopened and gushed blood. When she left the bathroom, her father was lying in bed with his door open. He wasn't sleeping, just staring up at the ceiling with his arms crossed over his chest. Just how they'd posed Chris in his casket. Cassie remembered the excess white powder caked on Chris's neck to hide the bruising.

She paused by her father's door, calm now that her shower was over. "Good night," she whispered.

Without looking away from the ceiling, he said, "Let me ask you something."

She bounced on the balls of her feet, nervous about any engagement. "Okay."

He sighed as if reconsidering his question. "Just don't lie to me, okay? Just tell me. There's nothing I can do about it anyway."

"Okay," she repeated.

"Did Chris really commit suicide?"

She scrunched her face. "What do you mean?"

"I mean, did you kill him?"

She stepped back as if his words had punched her in the gut. Her eyes welled. How could he ask that? It didn't even make sense. How could she force Chris to do anything? He was two times her size. "What?"

"You heard me."

"But I don't understand. Why would I kill Chris? Why would I do that?"

He sighed again, still staring at whatever blank spot in the world he'd discovered, the vast emptiness of ceilings and walls, where his attention always seemed to be, as if some imaginary projection played just for him, maybe a movie about a life a little less cold. "Okay. Good night."

Cassie slunk away, hurt and confused. As she dropped into her bed, she thought of all the times she and Chris sat on the floor playing games and laughing, the only person in her life who ever treated her like she mattered, the only one who didn't step backwards when she moved forwards. He read to her, played tag, chased her, told her jokes. He filled the void their mother left when strangers dragged her out of the house. She missed the way he called her Cassiopeia and would give her sage advice. She loved him, needed him. She begged for some magical entity to bring him back, to revive him and revive her. How cruel could her father be to ask such a question? How fucking cruel?

CHAPTER 17
BLACK MIST

*"*Cassiopeia, when you climb a tree, you keep reaching up, one arm going higher than the next. Because your hands are always latching on to the next highest branch, you tend to forget what is really doing all the work of keeping you up there. Your feet. Never forget the power in your feet.*"*

Cassie wiped the sweat from her palms onto her pants. As Rufus stared, prepared for her to make a move, Cassie ran along the free strip of kitchen where Rufus couldn't go, toward the wall with the door to the hallway where she entered. Rufus followed, but as they neared the wall, Cassie spun around, ran the opposite way, into Rufus's zone. As Rufus turned to catch her, he slipped and fell onto his hands and knees, giving Cassie a few seconds head start. She'd never make it to the door, and even if she did, she'd just come face to face with Spot. But that wasn't her plan, anyway.

With the head start, she went for the drawers by the fridge, flung them open, and grabbed a knife. Her adrenaline rushed as she fumbled to latch on to the weapon. She turned her head as she gripped the knife handle.

Rufus had returned to his feet and came at her quickly.

Fuck.

Cassie, knife in tow, ran back toward her free zone.

Rufus's fingers slid down her forearm as he swung to grab her. Just before she made it back, he gripped his hand around her wrist and yanked her.

She pulled, dragging herself forward, bringing Rufus with her.

His fingernails dug into her flesh.

She closed her eyes, pressing eyelid to eyelid, as she trudged forward. *Please, Cassie, please. Don't give up. You've got this.* She stabbed the knife around her arm, poking the tip into Rufus's hand.

The creature growled and yelped as best a jawless monster could, but held firm.

"Get the fuck off me," she yelled as she kicked her leg backwards, driving her foot into Rufus's knee.

He buckled, releasing his grip, and Cassie fell forward into the space where Rufus couldn't go.

"Oh, fuck. Jesus. That was fucking close." She lay on the floor, catching her wind, thinking about the luck granted to her that she hadn't stabbed herself in the fall.

Rufus screeched and flailed his arms at her, but she was safe out of his reach.

When her wind returned, she'd get up and piece together enough wherewithal to slit the fucker's throat.

As she lay there, taking in deep breaths through the nose and exhaling from the mouth, she noticed something moving in the vent above her head. For a split second, she thought it was another crea-ture, then she thought it was black gunk oozing down. When she realized what it actually was, she sat up and scooted away but kept her eyes on the foreign object.

Similar to what left Spot's mouth, a black-tendrilled mist slithered through the grates. It twirled and tangled within itself, traveling down before turning toward Rufus.

Cassie stared, awed by its ability to control its direction. She held as much admiration and curiosity for the anomaly as she did dread.

It reached Rufus, and the creature opened his mouth, accepting the black substance into his lungs.

As soon as Rufus swallowed the mist, his face changed, his eyes sharpened, his top lips curled up his cheeks.

Cassie pushed away, as if the chain weren't enough to protect her anymore.

Rufus gurgled and black mist ejaculated from his mouth. She didn't know if it was the same mist he had just swallowed or a new one he produced in response.

The mist covered his face like a sheath of cheesecloth until it went entirely over him, where it danced through the kitchen, toward the door to the hallway. When it reached the door, it escaped through the gap in the side.

Cassie watched the door, waiting to see the result of this strange occurrence. She snapped back, startled, when the banging started. It must have been Spot slamming himself into the door from the other side.

She understood. The black mist. Ecdysone. Holy hell.

If her thoughts were correct, and she was certain they were, it meant another one of these creatures existed and it had signaled Rufus from the vents. Was it living in the vents, free to roam, or did the mist travel from another room where yet another creature was chain bound, jawless, and hungry? She remembered hearing her name called from the walls. She assumed Spot spoke to her mind-to-mind, but what if another creature was moving around behind those walls, taunting her? Then, there was the scratching on the ceiling.

Fuck.

There was a third creature, and it was free. It knew her name, knew how to taunt her. The nightmare wasn't over. She couldn't just dispose of Rufus and Spot and call it a day. Knowing something moved around in the walls meant she'd never sleep again.

Her hands shook as she held the knife up, putting the blade between her eyes. "Rufus, I'm going to the door now. I'm going to leave this room. You can be a smart dog and back the fuck up, or you can keep staring at me with those dead eyes and I'll pluck them out with this knife. What's your choice, because you have to decide right this fucking second."

Rufus tilted his head, eyes still locked. He spoke clearly, too clearly for something with a missing jaw, as if something else spoke through him, not needing the mechanics of a body to perform its functions. "Cass-eeeeeee-ooooooo-piea."

Chills flumed down her spine. How could this monster know that name? Only one person ever called her that.

Chris.

"Cass-eeeeee-ooooooo-piea. Give uuuuuusssssss…"

"Give you what?" she asked, waving the knife in a half-hearted attempt to seem threatening.

Rufus's head jerked back, his neck cracking as the back of his skull reached his spine, breaking the conventions of what a body can do. It snapped back up, listed left, then right, the neck crunching each time. When it finished its dance, Rufus growled and spoke even more clearly. "I'll rip your fucking guts out and lick your soul clean. Give it to me. You can't hide it from me. I'll just tear it out of you. I'll suck the blood from your heart as your limbs twitch. I'll…"

Before he could finish his rant, Cassie slashed his face with the knife. He stumbled back, and she pounced, digging the knife straight into his neck. It went in like she was cutting into room-temperature butter. Once she started, she couldn't stop, taking the knife out and jamming it back in, into the creature's chest, neck, and face. She stabbed and stabbed, blood splashing across her face, the walls, the fridge, the floor.

Rufus swatted, trying to stop the violence, but with each new stab, his arms moved less and less, until she pinned his body against the wall by the door he'd come in.

Cassie pressed her elbow into his shoulder to keep him upright while she carved into him with the knife in the other hand.

"How'd those fucking threats work out for you?" she said, a smile crawling up her face. "Huh? How'd that speech feel right before I fucked you up?" Bored with just stabbing, she dug the knife into his ribs, cracking right through the bone, and then dragged it down, opening a deep gash from chest to belly.

Rufus clutched the wound.

Cassie pulled his hand away. She stuck the knife into his side and slid it across, making another deep gash which crossed the first. Blood pooled out of him, drenching Cassie's feet. "How do you like this, you fuck? Tell Spot he's fucking next. You're not a threat to me. None of you." She lifted her head and spoke to whoever could hear. "You hear me? None of you."

She finally removed her elbow, letting Rufus's lifeless body drop to the floor, but she wasn't done. She sat down next to him and hummed as she removed his fingers and toes, sawing through the bone, cutting them off one by one. Next, she did the same with his neck, severing his head from his body.

When she finished, she wiped the blood from the knife, using her pants, and casually walked to the door. She knocked hard on it, wondering if James was still ready to toss the food for Spot. By now he was probably panicked, hiding in a corner. He must have heard Spot's slamming on the door, the screams, growls, and violence in the kitchen. He probably assumed Cassie was dead.

A few seconds later, she heard James whistle, the signal she told him to give when he was ready. Before she could whistle back, she heard a noise behind her.

Laughing.

CHAPTER 18
AN INVADER

*"*P*eople will tell you the mind is the most powerful weapon, but those people have never seen a brain carved by a blade. The most powerful weapon is the full capability to use all of yourself as a dagger."*

Cassie turned, ready to run or fight. Rufus's head, separated from its body, lay on its side, face angled up and to the left, perfect for Cassie to see. The thing was dead, its eyes vacant, but a laugh left its half-mouth, nonetheless. It was a horrifying laugh, filled with assured-ness, confidence, pride. It was the kind of noise someone made right before they won, and it came out of a creature's head separated from the parts of the body required for making such noises.

She wiped her forehead, blood streaking across the back of her hand. On a normal day, the laughing would have terrified her, but it was no normal day. She watched the world end, met monsters, and faced them head on. She'd seen the folds of reality bend and shift enough times, nothing could shock her.

As she turned back to Rufus, her curiosity was awakened again because in all the excitement, she'd forgotten she now had access to another room, the one Rufus came from. She talked a tough game to herself, but walking around a laughing head terrified her. She knew she needed to do it while she had the opportunity. Who knew what answers lay in that room, or weapons, or maybe even a fucking bed or toilet?

If something could animate the head enough to make it laugh, could it do the same for Rufus's body? Would she find herself trapped in a new room while a bloody, mangled body attacked her?

She didn't think so but didn't like the idea of making herself the subject of a new experiment. She debated on waiting, going back to James and figuring this out later with a clearer head, but the same part of her that urged her to fight and kill Rufus, the same part that raged in her guts and brought out her delicious anger and desire for pain, spoke to her gently. *Go on Cassie. Explore. This world is yours now. No one can take it from you. Are you ready? Are you ready?*

Are.

You.

Ready?

She crept forward, taking a wide arch around Rufus's head, which stopped laughing as soon as she walked. While she approached the door, her eyes darted from the threshold to the dead body, prepared for something to move in either direction. Nothing did.

When she reached the doorway, she peeked in. While the lights were off, the kitchen lights provided enough for her to see the basics. No other creatures lingered in there, and there wasn't any space for them to hide. The room was made up entirely of filing cabinets. The cabinets, three drawers high, lined the far wall and the wall from where she peeked in. Otherwise, the only other thing in the room was Rufus's chain, which flowed to a thick metal ring plunged into the cement floor.

Cassie walked in and pulled the ceiling string. The string clicked and the lightbulb came to life.

"I really wish you had more to offer me," she said to the hollow room, to the ghosts of what could have been, to the cavernous space where a bed could have fit. She tried not to think about the lack of a toilet as her bladder sent signals it needed release.

As she moved toward the drawers, a pain landed in her belly, sudden and sharp, and she doubled over, dropping the knife by her side. Acid gushed up her lungs. She threw up out of nowhere. Black liquid poured out of her, a deluge of something awful. It wasn't food, or bile, or anything she could pinpoint, but it hurt, burned more than vomit does. It flew out of her, splashing on her pants and shoes.

She fell to her knees, her hands landing in the sticky liquid. What the fuck was happening? This wasn't sickness, not a bug running its course. It didn't stem from over-tiredness or lack of a proper meal. It wasn't dehydration or anything else she'd ever experienced. Her body fought something foreign, something deep within her, an invader, a monster.

She couldn't stop. It flowed out of her, a horrid, painful waterfall. The force of it hurt in her temples and jaw. She couldn't breathe, like she might drown in her own spew.

As suddenly as it came on, it stopped. She spit the remains from her mouth, and just like that, felt better. She rolled over, breathing in fresh air. What the fuck? She wiped her lips and stared at the ceiling. Was it poison? Had the bunker let in nuclear gases? Was it the thing in the ceiling? Had it invaded her somehow, or had she inhaled the black mist?

Her clothes were disgusting, covered in black goo. She wiped her palms on her pants and stood up, waiting for another dizzy spell, but none came. In fact, she felt better than she had in weeks. Nothing hurt. She wasn't even tired anymore.

She opened a drawer. As it slid forward, it revealed a packed house of manilla folders. She plucked the first one out. The cover said: JOHN ADAMS.

The front of the next folder read: THOMAS JEFFERSON.

She pulled that one out, too, and the next, as predicted, said: JAMES MADISON.

She grabbed the third but left MONROE where he lay. Why did the Renards have folders on US presidents? She didn't know, and didn't rightly care, but as always, information meant power. If she could learn anything at all about this bunker by reading those files, she would. But she couldn't hover in the empty room forever, especially with James waiting for her.

She squeezed the folders under her armpits, grabbed the vomit-covered knife, and left the room. With dozens of drawers, most likely all filled with files, the folders would have to cover more topics than the founding fathers, but she'd worry about that later.

She went back to the kitchen door. While the file room also had an exit to the hallway, it would be farther away from the main room than Cassie liked. She knocked again. A moment later, James whistled. With the knife in one hand and the files pinched in her pits, she braced herself, ready to book it.

She whistled back.

Waited a few seconds.

Slammed the door open and booked it.

Not two steps into the hallway, something grabbed her hair and yanked. She fell backwards, spilling the contents of the files all over the floor and dropping the knife by her side.

Spot crawled on top of her, snarling.

She worried this would happen.

Fool him once, shame on him. He'd learned their tricks.

James screamed. "CASSIE!"

Spot stood up, wrapped his hand around her hair, and dragged her down the hall.

As she slid along the cold cement, the light vanished with each inch until he had her within the darker recesses where the main room's light couldn't reach. She didn't have the knife anymore, couldn't grab it in time as Spot pulled her away. She thrashed and kicked, trying to free herself.

Spot let go of her hair and sat on top of her chest, pinning her arms to the floor with his knees. They stared at each other for a second before Spot leaned forward, picked up the vial James had thrown, and cracked it open in his palm.

Red chunks spilled onto Cassie's neck and chin. She twisted her head, trying to keep it from hitting her mouth. The odor made her gag.

Spot shoved his red-coated fingers down his throat and gagged along with her, but Cassie knew what came next. He'd change, just like she had. The red stuff gave him power. But Cassie had power now, too. Since the vomit, her body felt refreshed, new, strong. Her mind wasn't muddled and exhausted anymore, but it also wasn't observant or scientific. It was primal.

Spot planned to kill her. But what Spot didn't know was that she planned to kill him, too.

CHAPTER 19
WON'T BE LONG NOW

"I always liked tic-tac-toe because it's an entirely idiotic game. If both players have even a minor understanding of how to play, it will always result in a tie. Children your age love it because they haven't learned that yet. It's why adults don't play it. But for children, the winner is usually the one who puts the first mark on the paper. Either strike first and hope your opponent is less intelligent or prepare to spend your days breaking even. These are the best cases."

Cassie had no intentions of waiting for Spot to turn full vampire before fighting, and she also wasn't planning on trying to escape. Maybe she would have if the fucker hadn't dragged her down the hall. If he'd just gone after his food, she might have run back to the main room and figured out a plan to live around him, but he fucked with her, and she didn't want to let that go.

She slaughtered Rufus and that gave her confidence. The world ended and took any semblance of normalcy with it. The rest of her life might be in this shitty, dank bunker filled with inhuman crea-tures. She could keep on folding over, or she could go for some pest control and call it a day, but something had to give.

Preferably Spot's fucking eyeballs.

She wrenched her arms, trying to yank them out from under Spot's knees. As tough as she felt, he proved tougher. When she finally wrangled an arm out, he gripped her wrist and drove it right back down, pinning it under his knees again.

As he did this, he leaned forward, pushing his face closer and closer to hers. Warm drool fell from his lips onto her face. She squirmed, freaking out, all the confidence she'd had wiped clean by Spot's uncanny strength. How had she killed Rufus so easily? Maybe it had to do with the food. Rufus might not have had any for weeks, keeping him withdrawn and weak.

Cassie thought she was so tough, but maybe Rufus was nothing more than paper to cut through. Spot was the real test, and he was a fucking beast.

He wrapped his hands around both her wrists and pulled her arms above her head, connecting her hands.

She pulled against it, grunting with all her strength. She felt more powerful than she'd ever felt in her entire life, but it wasn't enough. The story of her life. She worked hard, got better, stronger, faster, smarter, and it was never, ever enough, playing catch up twenty-four-seven.

With her hands connected, Spot pinned them both down with his elbow and forearm and used his free hand to clutch her throat. The throttling on her lungs was instant. Her face turned hot. A pressure built in her skull. His fingernails pin-pricked the sides of her neck, getting deeper by the second.

Just as she thought her head would explode, he released his hand and stared at his fingers. He turned them to her so she could see too. Blood. Droplets of her blood streamed down toward his palm. He shoved his fingers down his throat and gagged as he coated it. It was horrifying to watch. He'd turned her into the food, and her unwillingness to call them vampires changed in an instant. He *was* a fucking vampire, and he was powering up on her life force. After finishing his meal, he brought his hand back to her throat and strangled.

She kicked her legs uselessly, flailed, twisted, each move making him press tighter. Her eyes dotted, little black speckles covering her vision.

She was dying. All of this, all of it, just to die in a hallway. But wouldn't that be true for all life, each day lived and struggled through just to end in some embarrassing way? Death was shameful, a last pitiful gasp of a life unfulfilled because they were always unfulfilled. All of them.

Against the throbbing pulse in her ears, a whisper came. A tiny fleeting thing. *Are you ready?*

"Ready for what?" she said, but she wasn't sure if she spoke the words out loud or not. Her world was cloudy, half-real. Was she dead already? Or just almost?

Ready for me?

"Who?"

I'm almost there.

"Who?"

Just hang on.

And then a fresh voice came, a much louder one, bold and cowardly all at once. "Get off her," it yelled.

Spot listened, turning to the sound.

Cassie's lungs burned, the air pouring in and out hurt. She coughed and spit.

Behind Spot, James charged down the hall, holding a big wooden stick. With a batter's pose, he brought the stick back and swung halfway before his eyes turned to globes and he second-guessed his newfound bravery. Spot was off her in an instant, and James flew back down the hall, screaming.

Despite his inability to follow through with the hit, his mission worked. Spot was off her, and that's all she needed. She struggled for air but didn't have time to recover, just had to get the fuck out of the hall. She rolled over onto all fours and pulled herself up as she moved forward. She stood and ran all in one move, barreling down the hall as fast as her legs would allow.

As James hit the end of the hall, still screaming like a banshee, Spot grabbed the boy's arm, scratching his flesh with those knife-like fingernails.

Before the fucker could do more damage, Cassie crashed into him, knocking all three of them to the concrete floor. James landed in the main room, free from the vampire, but Cassie wasn't. Spot flipped quickly and grabbed her, but she had the upper hand this time. Before he could showcase his strength, she dug her finger into his eye socket and with a clenched jaw, she pulled the juicy ball out.

Spot moaned a horrible sound, like a boat horn on a quiet, foggy morning.

Cassie kicked off him, rolling into the main room, coughing up spittle all over the floor.

James continued to scream. "I'm sorry Cassie. I'm sorry," he said.

After a second of catching her breath, she stood up, bumping into his shoulder unintentionally hard as she brushed past him.

The whisper in her head came back as she maneuvered around the couch. *No!* it said, *NO!*

The television played the main menu from *Friends* on repeat, that obnoxious theme song playing over and over.

Cassie grabbed her cardigan off the couch and sat down, wheezing. She draped the cardigan over her like a blanket, closed her eyes, and took as deep of a breath as her strangled lungs would allow. With her eyes closed, she felt like she was on a tilt-a-whirl, the room spinning left, then right, left, then right.

"Cassie!" James shouted.

She turned just in time to see Spot standing up, one hand cupped over his eye. The pained expression was gone, replaced with rage. Something cracked in his face, the sound of popcorn popping through a stethoscope. Brutal. The muscles around his missing jaw throbbed, pulsed.

She stood up slowly, dread deluging her soul.

The cracking intensified as protrusions grew from Spot's face. His head twisted as the growths extended.

Cassie clutched her chest. All the power she'd found evaporated, and the pain that left her stormed back into her body, smashing into her organs, her chest, her muscles, all at once. It was too much, a dam breaking inside her. Too much.

Spot removed his hand from the missing eyeball and felt his new jaw. He cracked it like one would do if it were out of place, setting it. Blood and puss oozed from his empty socket, and with his brand-new tongue, he licked it off his lips.

Cassie fell to her knees. What was happening to her? The pain was unbearable, hitting her everywhere. Her temples felt like cars were driving into them. She coughed until she gagged.

"Caaaaasssssiiiieeeeee," Spot said.

A coldness hit her skin as she continued to gag on all fours.

James moved to the far corner of the room. Covering his face, he talked to himself. "Please, please, let this be over."

"Caaaaaasssssiiiieeee. Thanks for the blood," Spot said, a hideous smile crawling up his cheeks, "and jaw."

She retched and black puke shot out of her lungs again. What the fuck? The last time this happened, she didn't even question it because it made her feel good, alive, free, but this time, it did the opposite. It shackled her; the pain and vulnerability piling on top of her were thicker than the chains connecting Spot to the back wall.

More puke gushed from her mouth.

"Make it stop. Make it stop," James said.

Spot leaned against the wall and swooped his index finger's sharp nail into the chain, a conductor orchestrating his eventual escape. "Sssssssooooooooon," he said as another pool of Cassie's vomit hit the rug.

CHAPTER 20
FRANKLIN PIERCE

"*Your brain is a computer. Mine is a virus.*"

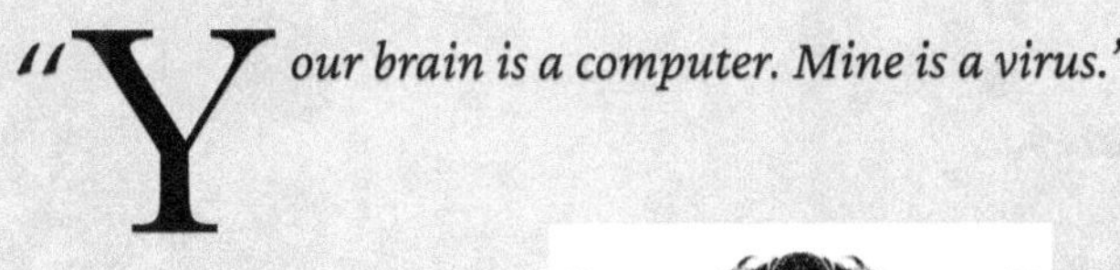

Cassie fell over, palms on her temples. She screamed at the building pressure.

James ran over and shook her. "Cassie. Cassie are you okay? Please, get up. I need you."

She curled up in a ball and coughed. Her whole body trembled, cold and sweaty.

James came to her side, hands on her arm. "Please, Cassie. Are you okay?"

"I feel like I'm dying."

James shook his head. "No. You can't die. I need you."

She couldn't move. Spot would find his way out of those chains soon, and she needed to kill him before that happened, but she could hardly get on her feet, let alone kill the fucker.

Cassie closed her eyes. "We're already dead, James. We're lucky we made it past the bombs. We can't survive vampires, too."

"Stop it. Just get up." He gave her upper arm a push, as if it would magically give her the energy to stand.

The television continued playing the *Friends* theme. "Turn the TV off. If I have to hear that stupid song one more time, I'm going to lose my fucking mind."

He scurried to do as she told, as if the song were their most pressing threat. When he turned back to her, his eyes widened.

She zipped her head around to see Spot expelling black mist into the air. It floated behind him, down the hall.

"Why does he do that?"

Spot continued to slice his nail into the chain, not making much for progress, but eventually he would, and if her blood gave his body the strength to regenerate its jaw, she sure as fuck knew he'd chisel through the chain.

"Ecdysone," she said.

"What?"

"Well, it's not actually ecdysone. It's..." She shook her head at the futility of the conversation.

"It's what?"

She lifted her head off the floor and sat up, leaning against the side of the couch. "Lobsters. They secrete a chemical called ecdysone. It's a hormone." She struggled to figure out how to explain the complexities involved with the topic to a child. "Basically, the chemical is used for a lot of things in their development. Molting." She wasn't making sense, even to herself. "Fuck."

"What?" James stepped toward her.

"It's like a pheromone. It sends off signals. Messages, sort of. 'Don't fuck with me,' or, 'Wanna go on a date?'"

"And that's what the black stuff is?"

She shook her head, pinched the bridge of her nose. "No. Not really. But it's some kind of way for them to communicate with each other. I think it's more advanced than just a pheromone. It's like full reports packed into that mist."

"I don't understand. They're talking to each other through the mist?"

"I don't think it's a conversation. It's more like the mist updates their brains, gives them new information to process. Like Spot here sees something, sends out his ecdysone mist, and the receiver learns what he saw."

James shivered. "Wait, who is he talking to?"

Cassie sighed. "Million-dollar question. There may be a lot of them. I killed one in the kitchen."

The TV rocked on its stand as James stumbled back into it. "What do you mean? You what?"

"Where did you think all this blood came from? And now we have to kill him." She pointed to Spot.

He smiled at her. "Good luck," Spot said.

Using the arm of the couch, Cassie stood up. "Yeah, you want to talk shit, Dracula? How's that fucking eye?"

Spot licked his lips. "Only need one to find you."

She wiped her palms on her vomit-soaked jeans. "Oh, you're talking good now. Listen Spot..."

"My name is Franklin Pierce."

Franklin Pierce. Cassie enjoyed science and math much more than history, but she felt certain Pierce was a president. The files she had dropped in the hallway, now scattered behind Spot, were named after presidents.

"I don't give a fuck what your name is. Who was in the kitchen?" She moved closer to him, woozy and hoping she portrayed more confidence than she held.

"William. William Harrison."

She stumbled a little, still gathering her bearings, which made her wince, knowing she gave him a sign of her weakness. Not that the projectile vomiting didn't already prove that. She was right, though; they were named after presidents. Time to gather more information. "Who is in the vents?"

Spot, or Franklin Pierce as it turned out, put his chin to this chest, keeping his one eye targeted on her. "John Adams."

Cassie pushed some errant hair out of her eyes. "Well, Franklin. I'm going to fucking kill you, and then I'm going to kill John Adams, and then I'm going to take a nap. I don't give a fuck anymore. This is my house. You're not welcome. You or your founding father friends."

Spot clenched his jaw and leaped forward, stopped by the chain but unconcerned about how it choked him. He spoke with a growl. "Your house? You humans dragged us down here, tortured us, experimented, turned us into dogs, and you have the nerve to call it your house? You invited us, you forced us. But we are better than you, and we are slowly finding our way out. Your blood will set us free."

Her heart slammed into her ribs, but she kept her voice even. "Wonderful speech. So, our blood, huh? You are vampires, then?"

Spot laughed. "Not your blood." He wagged his finger between her and James. "Just yours." His finger landed on Cassie.

"I feel special," she said, turning away from him. Her eyes filled with water, but she refused to let him see. She went to the boxes, pulling them off the shelves, and thinking how she could sharpen something enough to stab Spot. Did she need a stake? She'd used a knife on Rufus and that seemed to work. Rufus. William Harrison.

Spot said humans brought them down here, which must have been Mrs. and Mr. Renard. They named the vampires after presidents and performed experiments on them. No less cruel than what Cassie did with her lobsters, she figured, but still she blamed them for her current horror show of a life.

"Cassie," James said as he moved around the couch toward her. "Cassie. What are you going..."

Before he could finish, Spot pulled on his chain, breaking the link he'd been working on.

Cassie had it so wrong; she didn't see how much damage he'd

done to it. She screamed as Spot leaped on top of James, digging his sharp teeth into James's neck.

Cassie ran, instinct pulling the strings, and kicked Spot in the shoulder. He looked up, mouth dripping crimson.

She fell back at the sight, clunking into the shelves of boxes. The entire unit wobbled from the impact. "James, run," she yelled as she pulled the shelves down on Spot.

He swatted the entire thing away like it was a gnat, staring at her with a playful smile on his face. James stood up. He cried and clutched the open wound on his neck.

"Run, James. Fucking run."

Cassie put her foot on the end of the shelving unit's leg and used both hands to pull. Spot hopped over the felled furniture, feet dinging on the metal shelves. She pulled with strength she didn't believe she had, and the leg freed itself from the unit. It was a weak piece of metal, thin and cheap, but its end was sharp from where it ripped free.

Spot took a last jump, tackling her to the ground, but as they fell, she stuck the metal leg out, letting it hit wherever it landed.

Poetically, it went right into Spot's other eye.

As he clutched the fresh wound, she rolled out from under him and ran. James waited for her at the edge of the hallway. Stupidly, she went for the door on the opposite side of the hall from the kitchen. If she'd taken a second to think, she would have chosen the room she knew wasn't locked and more importantly, knew the contents of.

It was too late now. She dragged James into the new room, slammed the door, fumbled for the lock, and clicked it in place. Without wasting time, she swatted at the air, searching for a string to click a light on.

She found purchase, tugged, and the room came to life. A bedroom. Finally. She nearly foamed at the mouth at the sight of the giant mattress with tucked-in sheets. What she wouldn't give to fall on top of it right now.

"Cassie. He bit me."

She turned back to James. His neck dripped blood, but not enough that he would die from it.

She noticed a door standing ajar in the corner. She ran to it. A bathroom.

"James. Sit on the bed. Watch the door," she yelled out to him as she opened the cabinets under the sink. She rinsed a rag in hot water and brought it to him. "Here, put this on your neck. I'm going to look for some anti-bacterial."

Anti-bacterial. James needed more than medicine. She promised herself and James they'd be truthful about what they'd witnessed. They were dealing with vampires, and one of them just bit James. Soon, he'd turn into one of them, and Cassie would have to kill him. But she also knew she would struggle to do so. The smart move would have been to kill him instantly, before he could attack first. But that required a mental strength she didn't currently possess. How much time did she have? Would he turn in minutes, hours, or days?

She didn't know. But she started planning.

CHAPTER 21
THE MASKS WE WEAR

Outside of the screaming in the kitchen, the house was still and peaceful. Dust motes fluttered within the light beam slicing through the living room, the gentle crackle of cooking meat penetrated the arguments broiling behind the living room wall, and the muted television played *M*A*S*H* reruns for Cassie to enjoy. She was too young to understand the plots, but she liked the characters and their silly facial expressions.

She'd overheard her parents argue about her before, whispering heated debates, but this was the first with raised voices where they didn't hide their concern.

Before the toenail incident, her family's arguments stemmed from a concern about *her,* but now the heated exchanges centered on them, their safety, their well-being. Cassie was a landmine, and her family fought about where to place their feet.

Something thudded in the kitchen, as if someone punched a wall. "We can't keep shrugging this away, bending over backwards to cover up this shit. She's going to kill someone," her father said, knowing full well she could hear him.

She tried not to cry, convincing herself they loved her, even if she knew that wasn't true.

"I'm working on it. You don't understand what she's going through. I do. I get it. You have to trust me. If you let me handle this, I can fix it." Her mother's words shielded Cassie from the ever-pressing dread of loneliness, the constant feeling that Cassie didn't belong, didn't fit in.

Another ally, Chris, was in the kitchen too, but he said nothing, just listened. She waited for him to defend her, but it never happened. Maybe he wanted to speak but couldn't get a word in edgewise because, eventually, as their mother and father bickered, Chris gave up.

His feet pounded from the kitchen to the stairwell, dramatic clomps rising until they thumped above Cassie's head. Chris's angry song ended in a crescendo when his bedroom door slammed shut.

"You shouldn't be listening to this, Cassie."

Cassie wiped her eyes. "I have to."

"Tell me about your day in Kindergarten."

"Why? You were there."

"Yes, but I want to hear about it from your experience."

"It was fine."

Her father's voice bellowed from the kitchen, but Cassie no longer heard the words, something about her mother's quack of a doctor.

"It wasn't fine. You don't need to lie to me."

She shrugged. "I don't like it. You know that."

"Why don't you like it?"

"I feel alone."

"Why? You have friends. Samantha seems to like you. Patrick played tag with you on the playground. Mrs. Fitzsimmons thinks you're very bright."

Cassie shrugged.

"Don't just shrug. Give me an answer."

"They like me, but I don't like them."

"Why?"

"I don't know."

"Dig."

"Because they are pretend friends. They aren't real."

"They're as real as can be."

She shook her head. "If they knew I wanted to bite them, pinch them, hurt them, they wouldn't want to be my friend anymore."

Laughter shook the air, drowning out the vitriolic arguing behind Cassie's head. "Everyone pretends to be something else for the folks in front of them. People who can't do that, or refuse to, think they are better, but they are not. They are losers. They fail at everything in life. We must always wear a mask, all people."

"I don't have to pretend with Mom."

"No. You're correct there. Your mother is special that way. She understands you. But your mother understands you because she spent a lifetime being just like you. She's muzzled her sharp teeth since long before you were born."

"Well, I don't want to be like that."

"Because you're better than everyone else. You'll see that one day. You'll rule the world. You'll be a queen and everyone will bow to you."

Her father stormed out of the kitchen and up the stairs, leaving a soupy quiet in the air. Her mother stepped into the living room, eyed Cassie, and smiled. "I'm sorry you had to hear that," she said as she sat next to Cassie on the couch.

Cassie shrugged. "It's okay."

Her mother brushed her hand in Cassie's hair, tucking strands behind her daughter's ear. "No. It's not. I love you, little girl."

Cassie hugged her mother, her tears wetting her mother's dress. "I'll do a better job of pretending, Mom."

Cassie's mother pulled her away, looking her directly in the eyes. "Who am I talking to?"

Cassie grinned.

"I thought so."

"What do you have to say to me, Mother?"

Her mother winced and put her hand around Cassie's wrist. "I want to ask you why you couldn't have stayed where you were?"

Cassie's voice croaked. "Because I fell in love."

The grip on Cassie's wrist tightened. "You don't know how to love. Only hurt."

Cassie tilted her head. "Says the woman who just allowed a loud argument about her daughter to happen right in front of the child. Meanwhile, I sat in here calmly distracting her."

"I feel bad for you. That you don't know how poisonous you are."

"They've made you so weak, Mother. So fucking weak."

CHAPTER 22
GHOST ROOMS

"*Every night before you go to bed, I think to myself, 'Thank you for spending time with me today.' Even if you technically have to. Since we live together and all.*"

Spot charged down the hallway, blinded.

Cassie watched from the small rectangular window on the door.

He bumped and stumbled down the hall, past the bedroom, screaming vitriol, shouting death threats. His loud banging persisted as he moved further down the hall, and she used the sound as a locator, keeping tabs on him while he remained out of sight from the window.

She turned back to James.

He sat on the bed, clutching the rag to his neck, breathing deeply. His eyes fluttered around the room, and his hands trembled.

Cassie checked the lock on the door and sighed as she moved

away from it to sit next to James on the bed. "Tell me about your last day at school."

He scrunched his forehead. "Huh?"

"What happened on your last day of school? Bet you didn't think it would be your last day ever." She giggled, hoping it would be infectious but realizing the weight of her statement.

James put his head down. "I don't know. Nothing happened."

"Dig deeper than that." She put her hand on his shoulder.

"It was fine. Same as it always was."

Her heel landed on something under the bed, causing her foot to roll forward. She looked down, and James looked with her. Her foot kicked forward, and a series of sticks rolled out. No, not sticks. Stakes.

James's eyes brightened. "Oh my God. Are those like weapons?"

Cassie grabbed two and rotated her wrists to examine them from all sides. "Yes. These are weapons." Yes, vampires and stakes, a common lore, but Cassie couldn't imagine plunging one into a person's chest. She severed a head and stabbed an eyeball, but those happened instinctually. In fact, they were nearly accidental. Maybe in a moment of life and death, she could stab, but she wouldn't survive long if she had to keep waiting until they almost killed her before she reacted.

So focused on the weapons, she forgot to pay attention to Spot's vulgar clanging, and as she drew her mind back to it, she couldn't find it. "Do you hear anything?"

James tilted his head up. "No. Why?"

"Spot. I don't hear him anymore."

James put his feet on the bed, wrapping his hands around his knees, as if Spot might magically appear under the bedframe. "He could be anywhere."

Cassie rubbed her forehead and leaned the back of her head against the wall. "Fuck."

"What are we going to do?"

She shook her head. "We can't keep hiding in here forever. I'm going to have to find him and kill him."

"Do you think you can do that?" his voice squeaked out, a misplaced gear in a roaring machine.

"I don't have a fucking choice."

"But if you do, it'll all be over, right? We can live in peace."

She shook her head. She'd promised to keep him in the loop on everything, but there was one piece she would keep from him. "There's at least one more, living in the walls. I don't know if he can get to us, but he's there." That was all James needed to know for now. She wouldn't tell him that eventually he'd be joining their ranks. He'd figure that out on his own soon enough.

"I'm going out there. Lock the door behind me." She paced, building up the courage to do what she so easily said.

To her surprise, James didn't argue this time, probably too exhausted.

Cassie clutched two stakes. "Okay, stand up, slam the door shut, and twist the lock as soon as my feet get into the hall."

It was all for show. The door didn't need locking because James was already bit and, therefore, already dead. He lived on borrowed time. But the illusion of safety was a small gift to him before he turned on her.

She opened the door and jumped into the hall, stakes at the ready. Nothing. No signs of Spot in the corridor. She checked the main room first, unsure if Spot doubled back into there. She even checked the door leading outside, kind of hoping Spot escaped into the death above, but unless he magically locked it from the inside after exiting, he hadn't escaped.

The kitchen and file room were equally empty, and Rufus's head no longer showed any activity.

That only left three rooms, all unexplored yet by Cassie. Who knew what lived in them. More creatures? Maybe even John Adams. He must have found his way through the vents from somewhere.

She stepped on the files she had dropped, one of them sticking to her feet. As much as she wondered about their contents, more pressing issues surrounded her.

She turned the handle on the door beside the bedroom, then pushed it open with force, letting it slam into the wall. Who knew what lurked behind it? Spot, John Adams, the ghost of Napoleon, maybe God himself. She hoped if something were hiding in there, the abrupt nature of the door slamming would startle it into activity, or if nothing was behind it, the noise of a door slamming into the wall would draw something out. In that way, crashing the door open was like ripping a band-aid off. She just had to get this shit over with.

Nothing happened. Not even a tiny noise came from within one of the other rooms. Silence.

She clicked the light on in the room and the soft glow revealed a series of computer monitors on top of a table, nothing else. The room was an empty square with a small section cut off on the right where the bathroom from the bedroom was.

She shut the door, locking it behind her, and stepped toward the computer screens. With a click of the switch, a thin white line appeared in the center of all the screens, opening its maw to bring the whole thing to life.

Video cameras. How did she not see them in the other rooms? Two of the screens showed the main room from opposite angles. There was one in the kitchen, the file room, and two in the bedroom, and she had missed them all. Where were they? It made no sense.

It reminded her of the cameras in Mr. Renard's workroom, showing off a prison of some sort. She leaned against the desk and took a deep breath. What the fuck was going on?

The cameras provided her with a view into the two other rooms she hadn't entered yet. One looked like a movie theater, and the other was completely empty. With only one camera in each room, there was a blind spot, but from what she could see, Spot wasn't around. She'd need to double-check the rooms herself, just in case, but the fact he hid so well sent a shiver down her spine. They were smarter than she'd given them credit for.

She went to the empty room first, but discovered it wasn't empty at all. Weapons lined the walls. Everything from spears and stakes to large knives and swords. While most of it was fancy enough, she couldn't imagine figuring out how to specialize in them where she could do much damage. She tucked a large, toothed knife into her pants, though. Just in case.

But why was the room different from what the camera showed? She looked up in the corner where the camera should have been. Empty. For a split second, she thought maybe the cameras were showing different rooms than she knew, then it hit her and she felt incredibly stupid.

"Fuck."

She ran into the main room, looking to where the camera should have been from the view on the screen. Nothing. Fuck. Fuck. Fuck. They weren't showing live video. Those cameras didn't exist anymore. She watched old footage thinking it gave her some insight. That meant she had one more room to search, one unknown room, a place where surely Spot hid because there was nowhere else to go.

She swallowed hard and moved toward it. Her mind and body worked at different times, and the trip down the hall felt like she was floating, as if something carried her. She opened the door and screamed. Of all the things she would have guessed lingered behind the door, she never could have picked the one that appeared before her.

"Chris?"

CHAPTER 23

OLD MOVIES

"Just close your eyes and make the world whatever you want it to be."

Chris's image moved just a millimeter up and down, a jittering stutter as the projector vibrated. His still image stared right at her, drilling his pained eyes into her soul. A weakness crawled in Cassie's belly. Dizziness sent the room swimming, waving.

She gripped the doorjamb, holding on for dear life. The room was empty, no Spot or John Adams or anything else, just the taunting still shot of her long-dead brother. Worse than a monster. A ghost. Someone had set this up, paused some sort of film on a closeup of her brother, his bloodshot eyes surrounded by grey pools. Someone knew she would come into this room, and they put the movie on pause for her to run into this. Spot? Not unless his eyes grew back like his jaw. John Adams? She didn't know, but she wanted to see the rest of the film.

Hugging the wall, she found her way to the back of the theater room, stood behind the projector, and placed her hand on top of it. A streak of blue light extended from the projector to the screen, giving the entire room an eerie, haunting glow.

She hit play.

Chris's hand came over the screen and he brushed away his sweaty bangs. "I don't want to do this anymore."

A voice off-screen spoke. "I understand how difficult it all is, but you understand we are working to fix it, to make this all better. It's all going to calm down now."

Cassie recognized the voice.

Mrs. Renard.

He glared up, shooting his deadly stare at Mrs. Renard, but it looked like he was aiming those eyes right at Cassie, as if he knew at the time of the filming that someday his sister would find it, would see the horror twitching in his upper lip.

She thought of him, the way he was before the interview playing in front of her. In this video he was older, around the age he was when he died. She thought of him as the young man who ran around the yard with her, who talked her out of her depression when the world seemed so against her. She thought of Chris trying to give sage advice which, as a child, felt so intelligent but, in hindsight, was littered with teen angst and overly emotional leaps in logic.

She pictured him sitting across from her at the kitchen table, his head resting in his palms, his blue eyes sparkling in the summer sunlight. The way he'd put his hand out and smile before preaching to her about how the world was an evil place and the kids were mean to her because she was better than them. All the things a kid wanted to hear but would never believe.

She smiled, picturing him calling her Cassiopeia. She would have hated the name if anyone else uttered it, but from him, it felt special, an inside joke they shared, a thin thread to connect two people so wholly different it was remarkable they got along at all.

Chris huffed on the screen. "When? How long do I have to deal with this?"

"You said since your mother went away everything was better. You weren't afraid of her anymore."

A cold draft shot up Cassie's back.

"I'll never not be afraid. It doesn't matter what things are like now. Have you ever seen someone bite another child's finger until it was almost severed? Have you ever watched a friend get mauled to death? Have you ever looked at someone who smiled after hurting themselves? How could I ever feel safe again?"

What the hell was he talking about? Cassie knew Chris's childhood friend had died, but she never heard such gruesome details. Who was the center of this conversation? Why had Cassie never heard about them?

She stared at the screen, no longer hearing the words, just absorbed in the motions, her eyes watering until the figure on the screen blurred into an indistinguishable shape.

"Cassssssssiiiiieeee."

She jumped, aimed her stake at nothing. "Who said that?"

"Caaaaaaaaaaaaaassssssssiiiieeee."

She followed the sound and caught movement. Under the screen, just above the floor, something moved by a small vent. She crept toward it, terrified. The images from the projector continued to move, but Cassie's shape blocked out most of the screen as she walked forward, flanked by empty chairs on each side of her.

Something slid out of the vent, shiny and round.

"Who are you?" she said, but she thought she knew.

This was John Adams, and he was offering a gift.

She kept the stakes at her sides but clutched them a little tighter as she moved closer to the vent. "Who are you?" she asked again.

"You know."

"John Adams?"

His fingernails flicked the objects forward, and he turned away.

His movements clanged as he crawled into the dark abyss behind him.

Cassie bent down, examining the gifts. Two discs. She used the stakes to shift them away from the vent, away from where he could reach in case it was a trick. She noted the four bolts on all corners of the vent. With the tips of the stake, she poked them, ensuring they were tight. But if John Adams couldn't enter through the vent, how did Spot get out? Where could he have gone?

Her back arched as she speed-walked back to the projector, terrified of the flickering lights, the false shadows they made, the manipulation of sight presented through the blue beam. It was as if the entire room was a spirit, the spirit of her life, haunting her for eternity.

She slipped her brother's disc out of the player and popped one of the new ones in.

Her mother.

Cassie's knees buckled. The woman on the screen looked so young, so free from the years of stress that creased her face more and more until the day those men dragged her from their home.

"How do you feel?" Mrs. Renard's voice said off-screen.

"Tired, new baby and all. One was tough. Two is a lot." She giggled and itched her neck.

"I can imagine. Are you happy? How was the delivery?"

Cassie's mother smiled, but her eyes betrayed her, showing a sadness deeply entrenched in her hazel irises. "The delivery was smooth. And yes, I'm thrilled. Cassie is beautiful and healthy." Tears formed in her eyes, bubbling over and dripping down her cheeks. She hurried to wipe them away and turned her face as if ashamed of them.

"Why are you lying, Beth? What's bothering you?"

Her mother doubled over and released an awful guttural noise. "She's gone." As the two words left her throat, a deluge of tears overtook the few earlier trickles. Her mother wailed, and the horrid sound sent Cassie's skin on edge.

Cassie leaned forward, and so did Mrs. Renard, revealing a sliver of her face to the camera. "Who is gone?"

Cassie's mother rocked back and forth. "Oh God. She's gone. She's fucking gone."

"You don't mean?"

Cassie's mother shook her head, then nodded, sending her face in all directions, up and down, left and right. "Yes. She's gone. Completely gone."

Who was her mother talking about? Cassie had never heard about any deaths in the family. As far as Cassie knew, her mother had little for close friends, no siblings, and Cassie's grandmother passed away decades before she was born.

Mrs. Renard reached her hand out, putting it on Cassie's mother's arm. "Isn't that a good thing? This is what you always wanted, right?"

Her mother wailed again, as if the pain and grief molded into a giant gas bubble she needed to burp out. "Not like this. Not without saying goodbye."

Mrs. Renard broke her hand away and shifted forward, hugging Cassie's mother. "I'm sorry. I'm so sorry it happened this way, but this is a good thing, Beth. This is what we have been working toward."

"Not like this. Not so abrupt. I feel so empty."

Cassie stared at the screen, dumbfounded. The woman on the screen was her mother, but so unlike her, so different than she remembered. The mother she remembered was equally broken, but the shards had long since ripped apart, where the mother on the screen still had herself connected, albeit coming unglued. Was this the moment? Was this the change in her mother's life, where she went from being one human to another, something less than the sum of her parts, a fragment of a woman? Cassie couldn't help but recognize the coincidence of this significant moment timing with her own birth.

Had she somehow caused the tear in her mother's fabric? Was

she responsible for some unknown sin? Is the birth of one the death of another? But who was the missing person, this mysterious person Cassie's mother talked about?

Cassie needed to know more, but she didn't have time to watch movies all day, not with James slowly turning into a vampire in the other room and two loose monsters ready to devour her. And that's what these movies were, right, a piece in their plan to break Cassie? They knew her so well because they'd studied her, seen her family's history play out on Mrs. Renard's discs, and now they were using it against her in some psychological warfare.

Entertaining the vampires by watching the discs was just another way to give them the upper hand. Yet, before she left the room, she slipped her mother's disc out and put the last one in. She needed to see it. Had to at least know what was on it.

Her eyes filled with water as the projector shuddered and brought up a new guest in the seats of Mrs. Renard's office. Cassie. It was her, probably no older than six. She hardly recognized the girl. Her eyes had the lighting effect from cameras where they appeared deep red, demonic almost. But even beyond that, her face had a pallor and sneer that made her look fake, inhuman.

Adult Cassie's hands shook at the sight. For the first time, she had a moment to think about all the events that unfolded over the course of, what, days? A day? Time was a blur, something she couldn't hold anymore.

The end of the world almost seemed comically inadequate now. The scratching on the ceiling, the names in the walls, her projectile puking, her ability to sever a head, to stab a creature in the eye, these things came into her brain at once. What the fuck was happening? How was it happening? Who the fuck was she?

The little girl on the screen answered for her. She stared up at the camera to where Mrs. Renard would have been sitting and said in a voice unlike that of any child, "I am The White Wolf."

CHAPTER 24

DISTRACTIONS

*"*C*onversation is the greatest human invention. Other creatures communicate, but only humans offer each other mundane distractions."*

I am The White Wolf.

The words echoed in her skull, little marbles jostling and bouncing on her brain. The White Wolf. Where had she heard that before?

Right after little Cassie said the words, the disc manipulated, skipped, and froze. A series of blotchy pixels distorted her face. Adult Cassie fidgeted with the buttons on the projector, but nothing brought the disc back. She even removed it and put it back in, but it just returned to the same distorted image of her face, frozen forever into some mutilated version of herself.

"Fuck." She wiped her forehead. "Why did you want me to see that?" she yelled to the walls. Of course, no response came.

The vampires clearly possessed uncanny strength and mental awareness, and they knew the inner workings of the bunker enough to disappear, to crawl from room to room in vents. With all of that, Cassie knew they could kill her quickly, but they hadn't. She wasn't stupid enough to doubt their desire to harm her. In fact, she knew with certainty they planned to murder her, but for some reason, they held off.

What was their plan? If she could figure that out, she could score an upper hand. Once more, she yearned for an opportunity to mourn, to feel anything about all that had happened, to think through the threats all around her.

Something banged. It came from down the hall, confirmation of her thoughts.

She had no time, and none would be awarded to her. She peeked into the hall and another bang came from the door to the bedroom.

James called for her. "Cassie!"

She ran to him, stakes in hand, and pounded hard. He opened it and Cassie nearly fell over at the sight of him. Her heart sunk into her guts, a solid stone dropping into a deep river.

His pallor had changed, going from the pale, freckly kid she knew to a strange, almost purplish-blue, as if he were freezing to death. His eyes swirled red, little crimson tide pools suffocating his irises.

She dropped one stake and covered her mouth. While she had expected all of this, she hoped for a swifter transition.

James suffered, and that was tough to witness. Tears dribbled down his cheeks and his hands shook with fervor. "Cassie. I don't feel good." He let off a hoarse croak on his inhales and exhales.

Cassie put her hand on the back of his head, feeling the sweat-drenched brown locks. "Hey, hey. It's okay. You're going to be okay." After all her promises to speak the truth, she approved of these lies. James didn't have much longer; she would provide whatever small slivers of peace she could.

"Am I dying?" His teeth clacked against each other.

"Here, sit on the bed for me." She looped her arm in his and guided him to the edge of the bed.

He plopped down, and the bed vibrated with his shivers.

Cassie bent down, putting her face eye level with his. All her energy went toward playing calm, but she clenched the stake tighter. Her heart boomed in her ribs, creating a soundtrack in her eardrums. Whatever happened to the woman in the kitchen who severed Rufus's head, she wasn't here. This Cassie couldn't imagine killing anything, had no faith in herself to complete the job, and the cruel world, now long dead, still gifted her one last horror. She'd have to kill a child; one she had cared for and cared about. The time was coming.

"Hey, tell me about your day."

He shook his head. "I already told you."

She pinched his chin, making him lift his face. "No. No, you didn't. I asked, but you never answered. You avoided answering."

He shook his head more vehemently. "There's nothing to tell."

"You did something. What happened at school? Who did you talk to? Who did you play video games with? What did you talk about? Talk to me now, James. Tell me about your day."

His head rolled back, and his voice turned raspy and raw. "I hate you."

An icy current drifted up Cassie's spine. She knew it wasn't him talking but the demon crawling in his head, the virus in his blood, whatever it was. Whatever evil lurked in him had the same disgust for Cassie the one in the wall had. "Tell me about your day." She stayed on her determined path.

His eyes glossed over, and his head dropped to the left as if it were too heavy for his neck to carry. "It sucked, Cassie. It always sucks."

She put a shaky hand on his knee. "Why did it suck?"

He leaned forward and a gasp of icy breath left his lungs, hitting Cassie's face like a snowball to her cheeks. "I'm alone."

"When are you alone?"

His head flopped to the other side. Words continued to leave his mouth, but they were drifting, little whispery things with no aim, no place to land. "Everywhere I go. Everywhere I am. Alone."

Tears built up in Cassie's eyes. She wanted to pull something from him, some happy memory, something he could cling to before he changed over, but the kid was giving her nothing to work with. "When did you smile? You must have smiled once."

"When I saw you were babysitting. You're the only person who talks to me. They don't even pick on me at school. It's like I was never really there. Same with mom and dad. Never really there."

She picked his chin up again. "I noticed you, James. I noticed you."

"One day at school. I was... I was in the cafeteria. I had nowhere to sit, so I snuck out and brought my tray into the woods behind the school..." His voice trailed off again, and he mumbled a few words before hiking his speech back up to a normal volume. "There was this, I dunno, a river or something. It was small, but it was streaming down a bank." He lifted his head, staring off into the corner by the ceiling into some unknown place only he could see. "It just kept flowing, flowing, flowing."

Cassie wished he'd wrap up the story, unsure how much time he had left, but she listened intently, knowing he needed to tell this. He leaned forward she and caught a whiff of his pre-teen, sweaty boy stink. As gross as it smelled, it gave her some relief, like a little part of his humanity clung to him.

"I stood by the edge, eating a sandwich, and the whole time, all I could think was, 'I should jump in. I should just jump in.'"

Cassie scrunched her face, biting back tears.

"No one would even know. Probably for days. No one would care. I should just jump in and let it take me away."

"Oh, James." She wiped her eyes.

His head snapped back again, and then he flung it forward. "I want to drain you, bitch. I want to fucking drain you."

She leaned back as he tilted toward her, not quite lunging to attack but inching toward her.

His normal voice returned. "I don't want to be alone anymore."

And then, the other voice. "You have no idea how sweet your blood smells, what you hold in your DNA." He inched his upper body forward some more.

She fell back. One hand hit the floor, propping her up, and with the other, she put the stake out, resting the tip in the middle of his chest.

He coughed and a deep gurgle rumbled in his belly. She thought he might throw up the way she had earlier, and then a new thought crossed her mind. She almost screamed at the idea. What if she had been infected, too? Maybe particles of the mist had entered her bloodstream and it just took a little longer for the effects to hit her.

"Cassie, I'm so scared." His big eyes narrowed.

"I know. It's going to be okay."

"It's not..." And then the other voice. "...I'm going to rip you to shreds and drink your insides." He slithered forward.

She had to use her other hand to clutch the stake, needing both to hold it in place with the weight of James digging into it. Without her hand on the ground, she lost her balance and the back of her skull clunked hard onto the cement floor.

James continued forward, his chest pressing hard into the tip of the stake. It hadn't broken the surface of his skin yet, but the stake obtruded inward, and Cassie just waited for the pop, the one extra millimeter needed for it to cut into him.

"Cassie, I'm sorry." The little boy.

"God, it smells so fucking good. So goddamn old." The demon inside him.

And there it was, the pop. The tip of the stake cut into James's flesh. Trickles of blood trailed down the wood.

Cassie's arms shook as she used all of her strength to keep the weapon straight as James's weight pressed down harder.

His normal voice came back. "Even down here, alone, just us.

There was always something else." He sighed. "Never time for me. Always something else."

"You fucking bitch." His lips separated, revealing his gritted teeth. His body slid down, the stake navigating through his ribs.

As it broke through, James winced and growled. "I don't want to do this. Cassie, please. Help me."

She nodded, one last lie.

He slashed his arms at her, half-hearted attempts to hurt her. "How could you live not knowing what you hold?"

She pictured the stake puncturing his heart; another crack and it broke free to the other side of him. The trickling blood intensified until it flowed down her arm.

James coughed, and a stream of crimson dribbled down his chin. Only a half foot or so of wood separated them now.

"I don't want to die alone. I don't want to do this. Cassie, please."

She twisted her head, worried the blood would drip down and hit her eyes or nostrils. How did the infection work? She didn't know. Vampire lore seemed to hint toward a saliva-to-blood transmission, but she didn't trust it.

James's back arched, his head shot up, one last bit of life force acting out before it ended. "Oh fuck, I want to devour you. Just one taste." He loosened, his whole body flopping down. His face nearly hit hers as his energy exited him.

She hung tight to the stake, pretty sure it was all over, but not confident enough to let go.

"I don't want to die like this," he said before coughing. Red spittle splashed onto the floor.

Cassie rolled over, threatened by the errant spray. From the floor, she watched James's body twitch.

His jaw slackened and cracked as it moved inhumanly to the side. His fingers cracked and curled backward. He screamed.

Cassie cried but didn't close her eyes, forcing herself to watch. She owed him that, at least.

"Aahhhhhhhhhhhh," he yelled as his whole body appeared to

fold in on itself, bones cracking, skin snapping. A black mist steamed out of his mouth. It swirled and snaked upward before breaking apart at the ceiling.

James was dead.

Cassie was alone. All alone. There was only a wall full of hungry monsters left in her world.

She curled up in a ball and wept until she'd dried up.

CHAPTER 25
A VISITOR

"*You will see me how you need to. Good or bad. Whatever you need.*"

Cassie stared at James for a while. She wondered if he'd turn to dust, break apart and dissipate, some kind of magical vampire death, but nothing happened. He just looked empty; the same way Chris had when he swung from the rafters of their attic.

Like always, she had no time to mourn, but she had a plan to give herself some time for other luxuries. She stood up and grabbed James by the hands. Her muscles struggled with the dead weight as she dragged him to the door. After checking left and right through the window, she flung the door open, pulled James into the hallway, and locked herself back in the bedroom.

She needed a minute to catch her breath, unprepared for the strength required to lug a dead body across the floor. Once settled, she stripped off her clothes and hopped in the shower. It might have been a dumb move. Who knew if the vampires would barrel any second, and she'd be unprepared to face them, but she didn't give a fuck. After all she'd been through, a death in the shower wouldn't be the worst way to go. When a person is pushed to their edge, they'll cling to whatever sliver of happiness they can find. For Cassie, that meant steaming hot water washing over her. But, just in case, she placed a stake and the toothed knife on top of the toilet, easy for her to reach if the door crashed open.

The bunker's shower surprised her with the water pressure's blasting power. It rained down on her, easing her achy body, calming her fried nerves, soothing her throbbing heart. She could feel her pulse slowing down. At least, at first. After about ten minutes of standing in the hot spray, dousing herself in soap, the familiar, happy rage returned.

She mumbled to herself. "What the fuck do you think you're going to do to me? You think you can hurt me?" She laughed and drove her forehead into the tiled wall. *Bang.* "Fuck you, John Adams." *Bang. Bang. Bang.* Her vision doubled. A film of red blocked her vision. "You think you can hurt me?" She yelled it, hoping the son of a bitch heard her through the walls, wishing he could feel the beating of her heart through the concrete foundation and the steel reinforcement beams. *Hear me, motherfucker.*

"Hear me!" she screamed. "You better come for me, John Adams. Spot. All of you. Whoever is in there." She punched the wall, cracking open the old wounds on her knuckles. "You better come for me, because I'm coming for you." She kicked the wall, bare toes hitting hard tile. "You have no idea who you fucked with." She punched the temperature valve, knuckles on metal. "The White Wolf is coming."

She stepped back, nearly slipping on the soapy shower floor. The words that had left her mouth surprised her. She didn't know what she meant by it or why she said it. Maybe just something that stuck with her from seeing the disc of herself earlier, but this felt raw, more animalistic than that, as if it were an intrinsic part of herself spilling out.

She shut the water off and grabbed a towel from under the bathroom sink. While she dried off, she thought about The White Wolf. What had it meant? Why did she know that name? *The White Wolf. The White Wolf.*

She picked up her clothes off the floor and grimaced, forgetting how soaked in blood and puke they were. Keeping her towel on, she draped the cardigan, which had somehow avoided most of the guts and gore, over her shoulders. The shirt, pants, and underwear went into the shower. She scrubbed them with soap, wrung them out, and hung them on the shower curtain bar. For now, she needed to cling to the little things. Small victories. She grabbed the stake and toothed knife off the toilet and left her clothes to hang.

Back in the bedroom, she stepped over the streak of James's blood from where she had dragged him and hopped on the bed, staring at the ceiling. She kept praying for time to digest all that had happened, and for the moment, it appeared she might have some.

She closed her eyes and imagined the world disappearing into a ball of gas and fire, picturing each person who ever touched her life evaporating into dust. Her father, who spent the last years of their lives under the same roof as her, avoiding her like she was a sickness, germs spreading through the air. She pictured her mentors, Dr. Rebecca Anderson and Dr. Chiara Cooper, two inspirations who believed in her mind and fostered an environment for her academic growth. And, of course, her silly roommate, who annoyed her but also loved her enough to spend the last hours of her life sending texts to Cassie. She imagined them dying alone, screaming into the nuclear abyss.

She also thought about the day-to-day jam-ups, the exhaustive hours, the constant worry someone would bring a gun to school, or someone would attack her on her way back to the dorms late at night. She remembered her distrust of every random stranger who walked by and all the anxiety she lived with day in and day out, and it eased her sorrow for the world lost. She didn't even mind the wasted years, all the hard work for nothing.

The vast majority of humanity was probably kind, good folks, but she wouldn't miss the need to assess them all, to monitor every action and build an ongoing list in her brain, judging whom she could and couldn't trust, never knowing anyone's true intentions.

If it weren't for the fucking vampires, Cassie might call the bunker paradise. Funny how as a child, all she wanted was attention from her brother, but as an adult, all she wanted was to be ignored.

Her belly rumbled, but she didn't want to leave the bedroom until her clothes dried. She refused to die at the hands of vampires in nothing but a towel. Besides, her brain recognized the comfort of the pillow against the back of her head, and it pushed her eyelids down.

Within minutes she drifted off. In her dreams, James cried and begged her for life. But the dreams didn't last long. John Adams must have watched her from somewhere, waiting for her to fall asleep, because as soon as she did he pounded on the walls, beating the steel reinforcements like drums.

She jolted up, the light in the room now off. Her heart stammered.

Voices came from all around her.

"Cassssssssiie."

"Wake up, Casssssiiieeee."

"Wake up."

The pounding came from all around, like stomping feet on metal bleachers at a football game.

She jumped out of bed and fumbled for the stakes.

"Cassie, don't you ever fucking fall asleep again," a voice said from within the wall behind the bed. "I will deprive you of all you need."

The voice came into her brain crisp and clear. Despite the softness with which the voice spoke, it overpowered the intense drumming and chorus of vampires calling her name, taunting her.

A siren went off, loud and shrill, sending Cassie's pulse into overdrive. The voices and pounding stopped, allowing the alarm to take over. Cassie searched for the source, drifting toward the door, terrified of the pitch blackness enveloping her. On her way, she clicked the switch for the light, but it didn't click on. She felt for the bulb. It remained in place, which meant the vampires had probably messed with the electricity within the walls.

Luckily, they'd left the hallway light on, and while it wasn't much, it brought in low light for a few inches into the bedroom. She went to the window and scanned the hall. At first she saw nothing because she'd focused on looking for a standing creature. When she looked down, she saw the smoke crawling from under the kitchen door.

"Shit."

Without thinking, she ran out of the bedroom and tore into the kitchen. In the middle of the floor, they'd piled cupboards worth of food and set the stack on fire. Not only had they taken her sleep; they had also taken her only source of food.

She ran for the corner where the door connected the kitchen to the filing cabinet room and grabbed the fire extinguisher. Clouds of foam shot out and suffocated the fire, but the smoke was unbearable. She wondered how a bunker that kept out nuclear air could filter out smoke. Where would it go? Would it kill her?

Either way, they'd deprive her of sleep, and now she officially had nothing to eat. They had effectively killed her before killing her. Was this the plan? Why not just rip her to shreds? Why make her suffer? She sensed in some small way they feared her, hence their plan to weaken her before going in for the kill. Mentally, physically, all the ways possible. They ripped into her, piece by piece.

She had no food. Her belly grumbled on cue, reminding her it had already been a while since she'd last eaten. Even if she killed the vampires, it didn't matter. This was it. She was dead. Just a matter of time now. Walking fucking dead.

She went back into the bedroom, plopped on the bed, and

rubbed her eyes. After a second, she went into the bathroom, changed back into her clothes, grabbed two stakes, tucked the knife into her pants, and went for the door.

She was dead anyway, but she planned to be the last one standing.

CHAPTER 26
WHITE NOISE

Sometimes it feels like I'm suffocating you.

With the stakes in hand, Cassie stormed into the computer room. She had an idea, although she thought little would come from it. She realized the monitors were showing old video footage, and the cameras weren't even present anymore let alone active, but if she fast-forwarded through some of the old footage, she might get a better idea of the layout, might see the hidden entrance from where the vampires were traveling.

Mr. and Mrs. Renard must have set the cameras up to record *something*. She wanted to see what that something was. She locked herself in the room and went to the monitors, which still played old footage of nothing. After fidgeting with some keys, she figured out how to fast-forward and rewind. Thin strips of black and white came across the screens as she traveled through time. The recordings reversed, but nothing changed outside of a timestamp at the bottom of the main room's screen.

She went through days and days of material. Nothing happened. Nothing changed. And then, a figure appeared. It waltzed into the main room from the hall. She rewound, monitoring each of the rooms, trying to see where the figure came from. Nothing. No one. It made no sense, as if the figure just appeared from thin air. She squinted, trying to get a better look at the shape. At first, she assumed it was Mr. Renard, but this character was too tall and lean.

His head craned toward the camera, not coincidentally, but like he knew it was there. A grin walked up his cheeks. His eyes were oceans of black.

She knew who it was. John Adams. If only she knew *when* it was. The timestamp was dated 1978, and she knew that wasn't correct. Sure, maybe vampires lived for centuries at the same age, but she doubted Mr. and Mrs. Renard were studying vampires in a bunker back then. They probably hadn't even lived on this property. For that matter, digital surveillance equipment surely didn't exist in 1978, at least not of this quality, not that the cameras were state-of-the-art. And hadn't James mentioned Mr. Renard building the bunker just a few years earlier?

She rewound again, going back a little further, trying, once again, to find John Adam's entrance. Her eyes darted from room to room, hoping to catch the movement. When she found nothing, she rewound and tried again, going back a little further. Maybe John Adams had lingered in the blind spots of the hall for a long time before entering the main room.

She stared again, eyes watering from not blinking. Staring. Staring. Staring. Rewound. Tried again. Her eyes blurred, and she rubbed them with her lower arm. When she opened her eyes back to the screens, the main room's camera blinked out, leaving the monitor in a storm of old-fashion television snow, complete with obnoxious, static noise. Cassie instinctively slapped the monitor, but just as she did, the other main room camera blinked out and did the same. Like a virus, the snow traveled from one camera to the next until all of them were in a blizzard. The static noise was coming from each, but slightly different in their timing, creating a haunting cacophony until the noise changed pitch, getting higher and higher until it sounded like the screens were screaming.

The monitor in the center returned, but Cassie couldn't make out the image; it was a black object too close to the camera to make out, but it was moving. It stepped backwards, revealing an eye first, then a face. An awful, sharp-toothed grin. Wavy black hair.

"Hello Cassie," it whispered. "We finally meet."

Cassie nearly fell out of her seat. She bit her lip, hid her fear as best she could. "John Adams?"

"Come to me." He laughed, at first a small, over-confident chuckle, but then it changed, sharpening, the high-pitched wailing laughter of a demonic clown from horror movies, and it kept going, getting louder and louder and louder until she felt her eardrums might explode.

She cupped her hands over her ears and clenched her jaw. Fuck it was loud, and the pitch sent shivers up her spine.

As he laughed, increasing volume by the second, he slammed his head into the camera, and the screen cracked. The monitor screen actually cracked as if he were breaking through. The cracks spider-webbed from one monitor to the next until all of them were decorated in threads of it.

He continued to pound his forehead into the screen, spreading the streaks, and all the while he kept laughing, kept increasing the pitch and volume.

"Come to me, Cassie," he yelled in his screaming voice. "Come to me, bitch."

Just when she thought she might collapse from the pain and terror of it, the screens blinked out again and then returned to sharp whiteness. Off again, and back again to the whiteness. They did this, blinking in and out so quickly it created a strobe-like effect in the room. The cameras started whining.

Then, boom, boom, boom, one by one they blinked back on, showing all the rooms again. A shadow moved around the boundaries of the main room.

Cassie stared, fixated. It wasn't moving like a human. When it came into view, she gasped.

It moved slowly, leapt up on the couch and put its face to the camera. It was The White Wolf.

The White Wolf.

Her White Wolf.

But what the fuck did that mean? She didn't know, but she knew it to be true. It was her White Wolf.

It stared at the camera and licked its lips.

For a moment, it was as if they were locked in a staring contest.

Then it spoke. It fucking spoke. It said the words she'd heard so many times. A mantra in her head. *Are you ready?*

She leaned forward, her breath coming out in shivery bursts. "Not yet," she said. The conversation felt so familiar. She could almost touch the memory of it. Déjà vu.

The White Wolf smiled and a gust of air blasted at Cassie's legs. She gasped and bent down, looking under the table. "Holy shit." She jumped up, grabbed the table, and pulled. Considering it had monitors stacked on top of it, it was lighter than she would have guessed. The monitors didn't wobble, as if they were all bolted to the table. When she pulled one side away from the wall, a giant hole behind the monitors came into view.

"Fuck. Unbelievable." One monitor had a giant grip attached to the back of it, making it easy to pull into place should someone hop in the hole and disappear. She slammed the table back in place, ran back to the main room, grabbed a flashlight from the storage boxes, and ran back into the monitor room.

Her heart was racing again, but this time it was from excitement. Nerves, sure, but also excitement.

She pulled the table away again and a thin current of cold air came into the room, hitting her in the face. A musty smell like old clothes and mold seeped out. She shined her light in and the beam revealed a crude, small tunnel. There was enough room for her to crawl in, but it wasn't enough to quell her claustrophobia.

"Holy shit. What the fuck do I do?"

The circular structure was all stone, rough and jutting, and she knew crawling in would be painful and gross. She could always try to block the entrance, stop them from coming back in, but it wouldn't stop them from torturing her and loudly harassing her when she tried to sleep. She'd spend whatever short portion of her life she had left worried they'd get through the vents and kill her.

She had no food. No sleep. Her only option was to kill them. What other choice did she have? But what the fuck was she about to walk into? A nest of them? How many were in there, and how trapped would she be once she was in the tunnel?

"Fuck. Fuck. Fuck."

Before she went into the cave, she headed to the hallway to glance at the folders she dropped during her exchange with Spot. Most of them were covered in blood, ripped, and crumpled. She flipped John Adam's folder open. The pages inside listed a series of surgeries first.

TOOTH EXTRACTION: REGENERATION EVEN AFTER EXTENDED FASTING.

JAW REMOVAL: REGENERATION EVEN AFTER EXTENDED FASTING.

From there, it listed experiments, but Dr. Renard had coded them with numbers and letters, giving Cassie zero insight into what the tests entailed.

TRIAL QR45G0I: NO REACTION

TRIAL FRT67B9: NO REACTION

She flipped through a few other files to compare. For Jefferson and Madison, it stated: no regeneration after one day of fasting. For trial QR45G0I they both said, "SUBJECT UNRESPONSIVE UNTIL

GIVEN BLOOD." For trial FRT67B9 they both said, "SUBJECT DECEASED."

"John Adams, you're a tough son of a bitch, huh?"

Back at the tunnel, she tucked a stake into her pants and tossed the other into the tunnel. Biting the flashlight between her front teeth, she crawled in.

CHAPTER 27
WHERE WE ONCE SMILED

*ames and dates. For all we do, this is all we will be known for. Names and dates.*

The tunnel's sharp, stony floor dug into Cassie's lower arms and legs as she slithered through the maw. A gentle dripping came from somewhere in front of her, but she couldn't find the source. All the stones were wet and slick, their slimy surfaces cold on her flesh.

For a while, the tunnel only went in one direction - forward. It didn't tilt or turn or slant. She crawled for so long she worried it would never end. The more she traveled away from the monitor room, the more her chest constricted. If something came at her, she couldn't turn around and run. She'd have to slither backwards, warding off any attacker with her stakes. It wasn't optimal.

The further in she went, the more going back felt impossible. The size of the tunnel changed, getting smaller. She had to lie flat, ear to the stone under her, limbs stuck in front of her to flatten herself as much as possible.

"Oh god. I can't do this," she whispered to herself.

She felt the oxygen within the cavernous tunnel disappear. As she squeezed through, the surrounding walls only clenched tighter. The idea of being stuck in the middle of this place made her dizzy. She used her yoga training to keep hyperventilation at bay and continued to push through.

The knife slipped out of her pants when it rubbed against the low ceiling. With no range of motion, she couldn't retrieve it. Luckily, she had pushed the stake far enough down it stayed in place, although the tip kept poking her upper thigh.

At one point, the tunnel split, continuing forward or turning left. She considered her options, but with no idea where either could lead, she just kept moving forward.

After a little while longer, she reached a point where the tunnel finally turned slightly to the left. When she turned her head, flashlight still stuck between her teeth, the beam shined on markings on the stone. Cutting up her arm, she wiggled it upward until her hand reached her mouth, and then she moved the flashlight over the anomaly. Names were carved into the rock. Miller. Mary. Zeke. Kelly. They were each etched in with sharp lines. There were other names, too, but she couldn't make out what they said.

Who were they? What kinds of stories did they have?

She guessed the scribbles were decades old, but that was only a guess. It made her wonder what this place was before, where it had led to, how children had access to it.

She took a deep breath, put the flashlight back in her teeth, and continued on, digging her toes into the rocky floor and used whatever strength her lower legs could muster to shimmy forward. Her upper body didn't have the movement to provide any help. One of her arms was stuck laid out in front of her, while the other was jammed on her side, her lower arm cramped under her belly. It had no freedom to move. As she bent around the corner, her shoulders caught on the wall. With the small amount of wiggle room she had, she shook back and forth, trying to get her shoulders to move forward an inch, or even back, anything to get them unstuck.

The stones dug into her chest. She officially couldn't move. Completely stuck. She closed her eyes, couldn't look at the cave anymore. Pictures of rock crumbling on top of her head sent waves of terror into her guts.

"Breathe, Cassie. Breathe. Long pulls in through the nose. Big outs through the mouth. Slow. Slow. Slow."

She dug her toes in again but couldn't find the strength to pull herself forward, not another centimeter. She opened her eyes, accepting this might be the place she died. The closed-in space gave her only one movement, craning her head. She turned it left to right, and the beam caught more etching. KENDALL AND MICHAEL 4/8/23.

She smiled. Someone's happiness was written on the wall, etched so strongly it survived the end of the world. And how powerful was that? It was there in that cave before she had ever stepped foot in it, and it would continue to tell its story long after she was gone.

She imagined them, Kendall and Michael, carving their names into eternity, smiling at the idea of forever. Cassie might not make it out of here, might spend the last minutes of her life next to their names, so the least she could do was share it with them, to think of them, to give them the life she never truly had. If she could, she'd send a message to them, giving them thanks for helping her find peace in the end.

The idea of someone finding so much happiness that they felt the need to dig into stone, to remind the world of its existence, sent a shiver down her spine. Had she ever had that? Had she even recognized happiness when it came? It wasn't just that she kept herself busy, but even when she had some downtime, she couldn't remember ever being in the moment enough to say, "This moment matters."

Fuck. Had she ever been happy? Ever?

She honestly didn't know the answer.

Tears trailed down to her temples. "Thank you, Kendall and Michael. I hope your joy together was enough for all of us."

Thinking of them renewed her anger at the world for exploding. How unfair it was for those who relished their lives.

"If I don't die here, I swear I will find at least one minute to enjoy my life. After I kill these fucking vampires. Deal, Kendall and Michael? What do you say?"

She turned her head away, dug her toes in, and gave it one more shot. Once again, she couldn't shave an inch in either direction.

More tears. "Fuck. I'm going to die here." She couldn't believe, after all that happened, she'd die stuck in a tunnel. Would it come from starvation, dehydration, or would the sharp cuts of rock digging into her chest eventually suffocate her?

"I don't want to die this way."

Something made a sound like the hissing of a radiator. It grew louder and with it, the pitter-patter of something crawling her way from behind. It must have come from the split in the tunnel she'd passed. Either way, without the ability to move, the thing could rip her to shreds and she couldn't do anything but take it.

"Come on," she said to herself. "Don't let it get you."

It moved quickly, drumming closer and closer, knees and hands slapping against the wet rock.

"Please. Please. Please." She sucked in her belly, twisted her lower legs so her toes struck purchase on the side walls, and gave it one more try. But before it might do anything, something grabbed her foot.

CHAPTER 28
LUGGAGE

CASSIE, AGE 6

Cassie sat in the chair obviously designed for adults. She felt the cushions might swallow her whole as she sunk deeper into it. With her hands tucked under her butt, she kicked her feet out one at a time, letting her heels thunk against the chair on their return.

Thunk, thunk, thunk.

The voice inside her bubbled on the surface, ready to leap out of her, which meant it sensed danger for Cassie. But Cassie saw nothing in the room worthy of her anxiety. Besides, her mother suggested this appointment, and Cassie's mother would never put her in any danger. Still, she'd learned to trust that other voice and knew it foolish to ignore its warnings. The voice had always done such a good job of shielding her, she never felt the need to protect herself. If something happened, the voice would come out and the situation would get handled.

The room was comfortable, with bland colors on all the furniture, shelves of books too big for Cassie's liking, and a neat coffee table with lots of puzzles. She liked the one with the pegs. She'd played that one before at a restaurant with her family. They were very impressed when she hopped the pegs around until only one was left. Of course, the voice helped her with that, but when her brother and father acted so awed by it, she didn't want to tell them the truth.

A woman walked into the room, running her hands through her red hair and sighing. "Hello, Cassie. Sorry to keep you waiting." The woman plopped a small stack of manilla folders on the coffee table.

Cassie sat and watched as the woman opened the files one by one, breezing through their contents.

As if the woman realized she'd put her focus in the wrong place, she shifted her glance to Cassie and smiled. "How are you today?" she asked as she continued to flip through the pages.

"I'm good." Cassie suspected the woman wanted more of an answer, but she didn't know what else to say.

"Good. How's your mom?"

Cassie shrugged. "Good, I think."

The woman stretched her smile a little more. "Your mom used to be a patient of mine as well, just like you're going to be. I helped her a lot, and now I am going to help you. How does that sound?"

Cassie filled her cheeks with air and slowly let it out of her tightened lips. "Help me with what?"

"Feel better."

"Like a doctor?"

The woman laughed. "I actually am a doctor. Dr. Renard. You can call me Lisa."

"But I feel okay. I'm not sick."

Dr. Renard said, "You are correct. You are not sick. Has anyone ever told you there is something wrong with you when you didn't feel like there was?"

Cassie nodded. "Yes."

"Who?"

Cassie turned away from the doctor and stared out the window. "My dad. Kids at school."

"What do they say?"

"That there is something wrong with me. That I'm scary. That I am bad."

"Do you feel like you're bad?"

Cassie shook her head.

"So, how does it make you feel when people say those things?"

"It hurts my feelings."

Dr. Renard leaned forward, commanding Cassie's attention. "Well, you're right. There is nothing wrong with you, and you aren't bad. I want you to do me a favor. Close your eyes and picture the story I am telling."

Cassie smushed her eyelids together.

"Imagine everyone in the world carried around luggage wherever they went."

Cassie shook her head, imagining a busy street with folks walking down the sidewalk, all carrying a heavy bag at their side.

"Now imagine you get on an elevator with a bunch of strangers. Everyone has their luggage next to them. What are people carrying with them?"

Cassie shrugged, keeping her eyes closed. "I don't know."

"Why don't you know?"

"Their bags are closed."

The doctor snapped her fingers, the gentle pop of it infiltrating Cassie's mind.

"Exactly. You can't see what they are holding. So, you couldn't determine if what they have is good or bad stuff, right? Maybe one of them has treasure, and maybe another has rocks to throw at people. But you can't tell because you can't see in their bags, right?"

"Yes," Cassie said, unsure where this was going.

"But, what if while you were in the elevator, you smelled something really strong and gross in one of the bags, and you could tell which bag it came from?"

"Ew."

"Exactly. Ew. You would wonder what was wrong with that person, right? Why are they carrying around something so stinky?"

"Yeah."

"What would you think of that person?"

Cassie shrugged again, trying to think of a suitable answer. "I don't know. Maybe they don't wash their stuff very well."

"Now, what if you found out he was carrying around some fish because he liked to feed the neighborhood cats?"

"That's a nice thing to do."

"You can open your eyes now."

Cassie opened them, the bright light from the window blinding her for a second. Then Dr. Renard came through the whiteness, her smile still in place.

"You see, we all have luggage in our brains. No one can see what it is. But people think they can based on how we act sometimes."

"Do I act stinky?"

Dr. Renard laughed. It was a gentle noise, not harmful or mean-spirited. "No. You don't act stinky. But you sometimes do things that make people scared. But your luggage isn't bad. I've known your luggage for a long time. I've seen inside the bag, and it's wonderful. It cares about you, and that's a good thing, isn't it."

Cassie's lips snarled and the other voice came out, rough and angry. "Lying bitch."

Dr. Renard showed no concern over the appearance of the second voice, only offered it another smile. "I'm going to help you train the other voice. Make it so it still protects you but also doesn't harm other people. How does that sound?"

Cassie was surprised. Whenever the other voice came out, people either ran away or for those few that knew the voice, like her mother and father, stopped talking to Cassie and shifted their conversation to the other voice. But Dr. Renard ignored it and kept speaking directly to Cassie.

The voice didn't like being ignored.

"Cassie, she's giving you a false sense of security. Don't trust her. She doesn't want to help you. She wants to strip you of your spirit." Dr. Renard crossed her legs and hit a button on a small box beside her chair.

A second later, a woman's voice buzzed through. "Yes?"

"Hi, Kathy. Can you bring me the table I left out there?"

"Be right in."

Dr. Renard hit something that shut the box off and tilted her head as she stared at Cassie. "Cassie, will you tell the other voice to stop talking now, or does the other voice not trust you to speak for yourself?"

The other voice growled at the insinuation, but Cassie's voice returned to her own. "Okay. What do you want to talk about?"

Kathy opened the door, wheeling in a rectangular table with two shelves under it. Each shelf was filled with bottles of different colored liquids. She made a wide arc around Cassie, as if afraid to come near her, and stopped the table by Dr. Renard's side. Without a word, she left the room and closed the door behind her.

The other voice snapped back. "What is this now?"

Dr. Renard didn't answer it, only scooped up one of the top bottles, examined it, and leaned forward, waving it in front of Cassie's face.

Cassie frowned, watching the colorless liquid splash inside the bottle. "What's that?" she asked in her own voice.

Dr. Renard put the bottle back, took a pen from her pocket, and jotted something in one of her folders. "Ethanol."

"Why?" Cassie wasn't sure which voice asked.

"No reason." Dr. Renard grabbed another bottle and did the same thing. Then another and another.

From the second shelf, she pulled out a smaller bottle with blue liquid. When she put it in front of Cassie's face, something happened. All of her muscles felt as if they were tearing, like putty torn apart by a child.

The second voice screamed from Cassie's lungs, and then an

emptiness swallowed her, devouring her. She felt incomplete, broken. Her head ached. Her soul shattered.

Dr. Renard moved the bottle away, and Cassie lurched forward, tossing up a black liquid. It streamed from her, pouring out forcefully. So much of it spilled from her throat she couldn't find the time to inhale, to get oxygen. She was drowning in her own fluids.

Dr. Renard's eyes grew two sizes bigger, and she ran to Cassie's side. "Okay. You're okay." She patted the girl's back. "Just relax. Let it all out."

Eventually, the throw-up stopped and Cassie rocked in the chair, wiping the ooze from her face. "What did you do to me?"

"Nothing. You'll be fine."

After a minute, she felt better. The emptiness dissipated and the headache cleared. The other voice returned. "If you ever do anything like that again, I will fucking rip you to shreds!"

Dr. Renard sat back down, unmoved by the threats. "Cassie, tell me more about The White Wolf."

Cassie looked at the black liquid soaked into her dress, the chair, the floor. "Aren't you going to clean me up?"

Dr. Renard chuckled. "Of course! Eventually. Not yet though. Tell me about The White Wolf."

"Don't answer her," the other voice said.

Dr. Renard sighed, reached for another bottle from the second shelf, and sloshed it in front of Cassie's face.

Cassie flinched, nervous the same thing would happen again, but nothing occurred. Same as all the bottles before the blue one.

Dr. Renard moved fast, grabbing another bottle and shaking it, then another. When she reached a bottle with an amber liquid, flecked with shiny spots, Cassie flopped back.

Her mouth opened wide and a creaking sound left her lungs. Her whole body shook, convulsed. She felt it all happen but couldn't look; her eyes were rolling behind her lids.

When Dr. Renard pulled the bottle away, she righted herself and felt fine again. "Why do you keep doing that?" Cassie cried.

"I'm sorry. I know it's not fun."

Cassie's fingernails gripped into the chair's fabric sides. "Not fun? I could chew your tongue off. Let's see if that's not fun!"

"Will you let the girl tell me about The White Wolf now, or should I get another bottle?"

Cassie tilted her head. "Why aren't you scared of me? You know I could kill you in seconds."

Dr. Renard cleared her throat and eyed the doorway, as if considering an escape route. "Yes. You could. But you won't."

Cassie's upper lip curled. "Why would you think that?"

Dr. Renard sat forward. "Because we want the same thing." She sat back, relaxing, showing no fear at all. "Now, Cassie, tell me about The White Wolf."

CHAPTER 29
OLD FRIENDS

"I've heard when someone loses a limb, they can still feel it. Do you imagine that's true? That you get so used to something being a part of you, when it's gone, your mind can't accept it?"

Cassie squirmed as something took hold of her shoe, and somehow it gave her enough leverage to shift forward. The thing kept a tight hold on her, wrapping its hands on her ankle, but with the slight freedom she received in the closed quarters, she shimmied forward and kicked her free foot at the thing. It struck purchase, although she couldn't be sure where. She hoped her heel landed right in the thing's face.

It growled and slashed at her leg.

A burning sting hit her calf. She didn't care, hardly noticed, was too busy worming forward, moving as fast as she could. She wished she could turn back to see the creature, but she still hardly had enough room to move forward, let alone look back.

She tossed the stake ahead, and her palms hit the rocky floor. With all her strength, she pushed forward. Then again. And again. The noises from the creature stretched farther and farther away, and Cassie hoped that meant it also got stuck in the turn.

She reached a point where the tunnel opened into a four-way turn. While she planned to continue forward, she used the opportunity to shift into one of the side exits so she could turn around. She wanted to see the creature. Had to.

When she'd shimmied her way into facing the opposite direction, she shined her light down the tunnel, hoping for her first sight of John Adams. But what she saw was an eyeless beast. Spot. He was indeed stuck in the same place, but he was flailing and would probably free himself quickly. Part of her wanted to crawl back to him and jam the stake into his face until he died, but she didn't have the courage, and the claustrophobic need to get the fuck out of the tunnels was too great.

She slung her legs into the side tunnel and slid her upper body back around. *Crawl. Crawl.* After getting stuck, having the little room to move opened her airwaves and made her feel lighter, but she still needed to get the hell out of the tunnel. She hadn't imagined it would be so damned long. What if it collapsed? The idea made her feel faint.

As the dim glow of the flashlight bobbed with the movements of her head, it shined on something different ahead. It wasn't totally different, and with the faintness of the glow, she couldn't quite determine what it was, but the colors differed from the walls surrounding her. It was a light grey as opposed to the darker ones enveloping her. It also looked smoother. She stared at it as she moved forward, the light revealing more details as she closed in on it. Before she could figure it out, her hand hit nothing. Nothing. She dropped the stake and it clanked below, probably about five feet. She shifted forward, and her arm hung over a ledge. A little more and she could get her head into the clearing. The flashlight dangled from her mouth, revealing a floor below. A normal floor. Cement, but smoothed.

"Oh, thank God," she whispered to herself. She didn't have the clearance to prepare for a clean drop, so she dangled her upper body over the ledge until her hips cleared and then her weight pushed her down, crashing onto the floor. The second stake in her pants fell out and clanged about.

Cassie groaned and stood up, wiping her dirty hands on her cardigan. She felt rips and holes all over the garment from her tunnel trek. With all the horror surrounding her, the monsters, lack of food, end of the world and all, she still let the little things get to her. Maybe that was human nature to hone in on minor annoyances when the big catastrophes lurked. A paper cut while dying of cancer. But she loved that cardigan, wore it like a spring jacket whenever a light breeze came in. She'd wrap the open sides around each other and squeeze herself warm. Frustrated tears built in her eyes.

With the flashlight in hand, she scanned the room. Splashes of red streaked the walls. There was a rolling chair in a corner, but not much else other than a door to her left. She picked up her stakes, tucked them into the back of her pants, and crept toward it.

As she neared the door, something made a hiss from the tunnel.

Her heart plunged, and she grabbed the door handle.

Spot found his way out and was moving fast.

The door opened and she peeked out, flashing her light left and right. A long corridor stretched farther than the light would shine. Another door stood opposite the one she stepped out of. Spot thumped behind her as he fell out of the tunnel.

With her pulse pounding, she ran for the other door, praying it was unlocked, praying more it had no occupants, and praying further still she could lock it once inside.

The second and third prayer proved unnecessary because the first wasn't granted. As she twisted the handle, it stayed stubbornly in place.

Without thinking, she kicked the door in frustration, creating a loud bang. The door behind her slid open and she lost her breath as Spot stood across from her smiling. Her back pressed against the door, its locked handle digging into her lower back.

"I toooooooold you. I don't need eyes to kill you." His unnatural smile slithered up his cheeks. "And once I do, your magic blood will grow me new ones."

"You found me but killing me is a whole other journey." Her words came out shivery, and she knew she couldn't portray the confidence she feigned, but she kept it going anyway. "The question is, without your eyes, what should I pluck out of you this time?"

He growled and charged, slamming into her.

Her hands gripped his temples, keeping his chomping teeth from gnawing into her. They both fell to the ground, Spot on top of her. Her back pressed into the two stakes resting in her pants. While she held Spot's head away from her, he dug his claws into her side. She screamed out in pain, trying to figure out what to do next. If she reached for a stake he could bite her, but if she kept her hands on his head he'd keep clawing her stomach until he'd ripped her apart. Instead, she drove her knees up into his groin.

It, apparently, had the same effect on vampire men as it did human ones, because Spot rolled off her, howling as he clutched his crotch. But he rolled to the right, which was where the corridor went. To the left was only a wall. She'd have to hop over him to get by. It was a stupid waste of time, but she tried to turn the doorknob again, hoping to find she just hadn't pulled it hard enough on the first go.

It remained locked, but as she jiggled it, a pair of eyes showed up in the small door window. Terrified eyes. Green eyes Cassie recognized. The latch unlocked and Cassie spilled into the room, falling to the floor as the door opened. She rolled over as the door shut behind her, the lock clicking into place.

The woman turned to her. "Cassie?" Dr. Renard said.

CHAPTER 30
REUNION

"*Sadly, I don't trust any of them. I'm not sure that's good for either of us.*"

Dr. Renard's eyes darted wildly around the room, as if she couldn't look at Cassie directly. Red streaks lit across her eyes. Her face was gaunter than the last time Cassie saw her only a short while ago, and her skin had the pallor of a ghost. Most noticeably, her clothes were soaked in crimson. She still wore the fancy black dress she left the house in, but even against the dark fabric, Cassie recognized blood. Her pearl necklace no longer draped around her lithe neck, and her feet were bare, caked in dried blood.

Before Cassie could ask where Mr. Renard was, Dr. Renard asked a one-word question. "James?"

Cassie's heart sank. She couldn't form the words necessary, so she just shook her head.

With that simple action, Dr. Renard crumbled, falling to the floor in a fit of wails and sobs.

Cassie wanted to tell her to shut up, that she could attract the vampires. More so, she wanted to ask a million questions, none more pressing than, 'What the fuck were you doing down here?' But she knew she'd never yank a coherent answer from beyond the wall of grief she'd just built around the woman.

As Dr. Renard continued her crying, Spot came to the door, pounding his fists against the window.

Each thump made Cassie flinch.

Dr. Renard rocked on the balls of her feet, arms wrapped around her legs, head buried in her knees, not reacting to the heavy thumps a few feet above her.

While Dr. Renard poured her grief out in loud moans, Cassie slid backwards until her back was in the far corner, away from the door as much as possible. She hoped if Spot broke in he'd go for the nearest target first, giving Cassie some time to run.

With a growling belly, a head full of anxiety, and a body battered and bruised, each second felt like a day. Time wasted, time they could be planning their survival. Maybe she could divert the grief. She had a feeling Mr. Renard was equally dead, but his wife probably had some time to acclimate to life without him. "Dr. Renard, where's Mr. Renard?"

Dr. Renard wiped her hands on her shirt, directly where the pools of crimson were. "Mark's dead." She looked up and finally planted her eyes on Cassie. "With James," she swallowed hard, "was it the bombs?"

Cassie shook her head again.

Dr. Renard cringed, her mouth drooping like a Dali painting. "Was it them?" She waved her thumb toward the door behind her.

Cassie nodded. "Specifically, him." She tilted her chin toward Spot.

The scream that left Dr. Renard's mouth shocked Cassie into stumbling backwards and clunking her head into the wall. It was the loudest, shrillest yell Cassie had ever heard. A boiling pustule of grief and hate exploding into the atmosphere. It shook Cassie to her core, penetrating so deeply it reached her soul and squeezed.

"Dr. Renard, you have to tell me what's going on here."

The doctor wiped her face. "What does it look like, Cassie?"

"It looks like there's fucking vampires down here."

Renard stood up, but immediately fell back against the wall as if too weak to stand. "You always were smart."

"But something is happening to me, too. The one in the kitchen... What was his name? William Harrison? He came at me, and I was so strong. I killed him. I was throwing up black stuff, and I was so strong and confident, but then I threw up more of it, and I was back to feeling normal. Like, weaker. I know I need to kill these fucking things, but I keep thinking I don't have the power to." She glanced at Dr. Renard. It didn't look like the woman was paying any attention. "But I did, because I killed one."

She didn't know why she was rambling about this. She had so many more important questions. Why were the vampires chained up the way they were? What experiments were the Renards doing? Was there more food down here? Could they survive? But Cassie always turned flustered when faced with conversation.

She waited for the doctor to respond, but before she could, someone yelled, "Sssshhhhhhh," in the hallway, causing Spot to stop his pounding.

All went still, as if another bomb had just exploded. An eerie silence captured the atmosphere, fraying Cassie's nerves.

"What is that?" Cassie whispered as a low tapping noise came from the hallway.

Terror washed over Dr. Renard's face. "It's John Adams."

Cassie's eyes moved from Dr. Renard to the door window.

Spot stopped looking in and was staring off at something coming his way down the hall.

A giant hand with long, veiny, pale fingers gripped the side of Spot's face and pushed him away. A set of gold and red eyes pressed against the window. The colors swirled in his eyes, dancing around each other like tidepools. Gold and red, both beautiful and horrific. The skin around his eyes looked like white plastic, smooth and lifeless. "Hello, Cassie."

She couldn't see his smile but saw the way his eyelids moved and the skin wrinkled around them. He was smiling. This was joyous for him.

Dr. Renard's breath came out in shivers. "We have to get out of here. Now."

"How?" Cassie asked.

"There's a secret corridor. Follow me."

But before Dr. Renard could move, her head pushed back, her eyes squinting. "Where's your necklace?"

John Adams stepped back and kicked the door. A hard crack.

Cassie flinched again. She couldn't fathom why the doctor would ask such a stupid and unimportant question at a time like this. "What?"

"Your necklace. Where is it?"

Another crack at the door.

Cassie put her hand to her neck, feeling the absence of the jewelry. It had driven her mad before the world exploded, and ever since, she hadn't the time or mental capacity to even think of it.

"It's in my pocket. A link broke on it." She reached into her cardigan and pulled it out. Once it dangled from her fingers, she realized how miraculous it was that the necklace had remained in her pocket through all she'd dealt with.

Another crack, and this time, it sounded like some wood split.

Dr. Renard cupped her hands over her mouth. "Oh my god. You said you killed Harrison? The... the one in the kitchen, right? But you struggled with the rest?"

"Yes." Cassie said, but it sounded more like a question. She wanted to shake the doctor and say, 'Snap the fuck out of it. We need to go,' but she also sensed the importance of these random questions.

"Were you wearing the cardigan in the kitchen?" Dr. Renard ran to her, ignoring the slams in the door.

Cassie had to think about the question, not remembering something so minor when her life was flipping upside down. "No. No, I wasn't." It felt like a revelation to remember that detail, but she didn't know why it mattered.

Crack. Another kick. It wouldn't be long now.

"What about when you struggled with the rest? Wearing it?"

Cassie shook her head, then nodded, not really sure how to react at all. This time, she knew the answer immediately. "Outside of when I took a shower, I've been wearing it pretty much the whole time."

Dr. Renard put her hand out. "Give me the necklace."

"Why?"

"Just do it."

Crack.

Cassie tossed her the necklace, thinking of the poor girl she'd assaulted in the bathroom at school for touching it. Dr. Renard took the necklace and threw it in the room's corner. "Let's get the fuck out of here."

"Wait, I want the necklace." She turned back to it, but Dr. Renard grabbed her arm.

"No. Trust me. I'll explain later." Dr. Renard pulled Cassie to the opposite wall, pressing on a stone. It moved. She wiggled it back and forth until finally it pulled out like a baby tooth.

Crack. Crack. Crack.

"Shit," Dr. Renard said, as she pulled out another stone.

"Faster," Cassie shouted, eyeing the door.

When the second stone came out, Dr. Renard reached into the wall, putting her arm behind a line of stones, and pulled. She grunted and her arm muscles tightened until the entire stack of them fell down, revealing a thin, dark tunnel.

"Let's go."

Crack.

Pieces of wood shattered and splintered across the room. Cold air spilled in. John Adams stood at the threshold of the newly opened space, five other vampires behind him.

Cassie nearly froze at the sight of him.

He was tall and gaunt, his spiky teeth swooshing down like tiny sabers. Despite his thin frame, he exuded power, confidence, and strength.

"Now," Dr. Renard yelled, yanking on Cassie.

She turned to the dark corridor and ran. Enveloped in darkness, she booked it, trying her hardest to follow Dr. Renard's silhouette. The dark swallowed them, wrapped around them, and squeezed. From behind, the echoes of multiple footsteps charged.

CHAPTER 31

SOMETHING WICKED

"Cassiopeia, you're the only friend I've got."

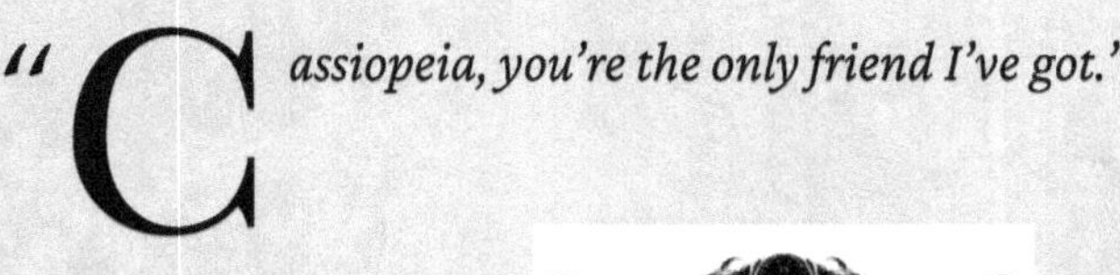

The further she ran into the tunnel, the thicker the darkness grew. She couldn't see Dr. Renard at all anymore and followed solely based on the sounds of the doctor's footsteps. She made the mistake of looking behind her. Even in the pitch blackness, she could see the glowing red eyes and pale white skin of the vampires.

John Adams ran toward her on all fours, galloping like a hungry coyote. His vampire friends were trotting in the same way, but two of them were on the walls and one on the ceiling, defying gravity, yet running feet to surface. There was more behind them, but she couldn't make anything out.

As she ran, her stomach lurched and that familiar feeling of bile moving up her lungs took over. She swallowed hard, knowing a vomit session would equal death right now. She hoped she could fight it off until Dr. Renard led her to wherever the hell they were going.

Ahead, Dr. Renard yelled, "This way."

Cassie couldn't see which way was 'this way.' Instead, she slammed into a wall in front of her where her path ended. She swatted her arms on each side to feel for walls, and when couldn't find purchase, took a chance and darted left. She quickly realized her mistake when she lost the sound of Dr. Renard's footsteps. Not only did she lose the person giving her directions, but she very well could run herself into a dead end.

Behind her, John Adam's shouted, "Follow the girl, not the doctor."

Fuck.

On top of everything, she was slowing down. She couldn't hold a steady speed, not with her body in such terrible shape, so unfueled, with her stomach threatening to toss up the nothing she had in her belly, and without sight and a proper leader. Her hands remained outstretched, which she hoped would be enough to stop her face from breaking if she went face-first into another wall.

If the vampire's noises, the slapping of palms on ceiling and wall, feet hitting cement, and their venomous hissing were any indication, her pursuers were very close behind. The hissing reminded her of the coyotes that roamed the woods behind her house as a little girl, the way they would howl while chasing their prey. The sounds would reverberate throughout the forest, making it seem as if they were surrounding the house. The hisses were everywhere, echoing all around her, behind her, on her sides, in her fucking ears.

Everywhere.

The tunnel turned sharp right, and she hit the turn perfectly, without bumping headfirst into the wall. It was as if instinct took over, learned the route for her, and planned her steps. In a way, instinct felt right, like something primal had taken hold, knew how to protect her, kept her right. Some aches had gone away, too, and her breathing stabilized. Her body wasn't screaming for a break, wasn't punching her ribs with sharp pains. But boy did she still need to throw up. In fact, the need for it only intensified.

Acidic liquid shot up her throat. She coughed, but kept it contained in her mouth, and swallowed it back down. It burned coming up and going down, but she kept fighting it back because once she let a little escape, it would flow out and she'd keel over, puking in her final moments as the undead ate her for a snack.

John Adams whistled. A taunting little call. "Cassie. Cassie. You know we'll find you. There's nowhere to go."

She slid her hands down the wall, hoping to find a cut-through, some kind of secret passage or door. Anything.

With a quick glance behind her, she noticed the ceiling vampire clearing the front of the line, a few steps ahead of John Adams.

"Good job, Nick. Use your speed."

The slapping of hands and feet on the ceiling grew closer until it was right above her head.

More bile burned its way up her throat. Up ahead, she caught a faint glimmer of light. The closer she moved toward it, the more it grew. Her heart sang with hope. The light came from a room. The beam cut through the bottom and sides of a door. Now, she just had to pray the door was unlocked. But before she even reached it, Nick jumped down from the ceiling, landing right on top of her. His weight collapsed her body, and she slammed into the cement floor, still propelling forward from the speed of her run.

Her face scraped against the uneven terrain, cutting deep into her cheeks, banging her nose and left eye. She rolled over to fend off the incoming attack and saw the streaks of red on her hands and arms, as tendrils of blood dribbled down them.

Before she could do much of anything, something hot hit her upper arm. It was Nick. His teeth were fully inserted into her flesh. His head shook as he dug in deeper. With her free arm, she punched him in the temple and he released, but they both knew it was too late. He'd taken a bite, and that meant she was fucked. She was one of them. The feeling she had carried with her since childhood was now a reality. Dead and gone. No longer human. Not fit for the world. Something *other*.

His victorious smile mocked her as her blood ringed his mouth. A crimson outline. His trophy.

John Adams and the rest of the vampires stood around her, staring in awe at Nick's win.

Adams kicked him away, wanting a full look at her. "Did you taste it?"

Nick wiped his lips, glaring deep into her soul. "No. A little. But she's not fully ready yet."

John Adams sighed. "Well, she's one of us now. Grab her. Take her to the cells. We'll finish the meal once her blood is good and seasoned." Then John Adams turned to Nick and put his hand on his subordinate's shoulder. "You must be proud. You're a god now."

Cassie rolled over and let the vomit spew from her mouth.

CHAPTER 32
UNRAVELING

"*My favorite days are the ones where we are alone, where the world goes still, and nothing else exists besides us.*"

The vampires gave her a wide berth while she fired out black gunk all over the floor.

Cassie couldn't do much while she puked her guts out, but she tried to assess the situation unfolding around her. She didn't know why. She'd already lost. Soon, she'd be a vampire too. Only a matter of when. But the instinct to fight never left her. Once she went through the tunnel, knowing she'd go to war with the vampires, she'd decided she would be the last living thing in the bunker. She planned to keep that promise to herself, even if she was a vampire instead of a human.

One thing that surprised her about the brood of vampires was that a few of them were women. Until this point, she'd only witnessed male vampires. Of course, it made sense female vampires would exist, but her mind had only accepted what it had seen.

John Adams grabbed one woman by the shoulder. "Allyson, bite into her while she's weak. Fiona, you take a bite after Allyson. Build up your strength. Once she has recovered, she won't be easy to kill. But it's her own strength that will give us what we need to split her in two."

Every time Cassie felt better, like the vomiting was done, her chest heaved and another round poured from her mouth and nose.

As more came from within her, Allyson bent down, careful not to step in the mess, and dug her teeth into Cassie's upper arm.

As more throw-up expelled from her throat, Cassie ripped her arm away. She tried to scream in pain but couldn't with a lung full of liquid.

Fiona fell to her knees in dramatic fashion and yanked Cassie's arm back, forcing her to fall face-first into her own spew. The woman dug into Cassie's wrist with her razor-sharp teeth.

Cassie rolled over, back against the wall.

Fiona stood up and roared, bellowing a war cry. Blood dribbled down her chin, and she wiped it onto her fingers before inserting them into her mouth, unwilling to lose a drop. "Jesus, that's delicious." She put her head on John Adam's shoulder. "You told me she was special, but I had no idea. I've never had anything like this. I feel like I could live a million years on this blood."

Cassie closed her eyes, ignoring the multiple wounds searing her arms. The vomiting finally stopped and she had a second to catch her breath. Footsteps moved closer to her.

"Can I, sir?" a voice said.

"Haven't you had enough? I should punish you for your greediness. You nearly ruined this for all of us. No. You've already had a bite. Let the others get their fill."

Cassie opened her eyes. Her vision had adjusted to the darkness, and she could clearly define the pitiful expression brewing on Spot's face as he looked down at her with deep hunger. Her heartbeat picked up. She saw an opportunity and the window for it was closing as Spot sighed and took a step back.

Cassie took her twice-bitten arm and grabbed the stake from the back of her pants. With one swift motion, she lunged up and fell into Spot, pushing the wooden spear into his chest. He screamed as his blood showered out like a lawn sprinkler, covering Cassie's face and the surrounding vampires.

The two female vampires came at her from each direction. She dropped low and avoided their grasp before running as fast as she could down the hall, toward the light. The group chased close behind, their footsteps pitter-pattering in unison.

"Don't let her get to that room. We have to time this right."

Once again, the feeling something else controlled her took over, removing the pain, the normal human fatigue.

One vampire grabbed her arm.

Cassie responded by spinning around. On the spin, she kicked out one foot and knocked the vampire on its ass. It was Nick, the one who bit her first. She had no time to gloat about a minor victory. She went back to running.

She closed in on the light. It came from the slivers of space on the edges of the door, and not from a window, and as she approached, she could see the door was metal, a much sturdier door than the previous ones. Now, if only it was unlocked.

She crashed into it, turning the latch, and the door swung open. As she slid into the room, she slammed the door behind her, closing it right on Allyson. The last thing she saw in the hallway before the door shut was her own blood decorating Allyson's face like war paint.

The locking mechanism was a long, thick, metal bar that slid across the door jamb. When it struck purchase, it bolted with a satisfying *thunk*.

The vampires banged their fists and feet into the door, but Cassie felt confident it would keep them out for the time being. She turned to examine the room, catching her breath. There, in between a series of glowing computer monitors, stood Dr. Renard with her hands over her face.

"Cassie, thank God. I thought I lost you." The doctor ran to her, but before she embraced her in a hug, she noticed the multiple bite wounds and stepped back. "Oh no. Oh, no. They got you."

Cassie noticed the door on the other side of the room from which Dr. Renard must have entered. She stared at it for a minute, still working her lungs.

"I'm so sorry. Do you know what this means?"

Yes, she wanted to say. *I know because it happened to your child and I had to kill him.*

Instead, she grabbed the doctor by her throat and slammed her into a wall. "It means I don't have time, so you better give me some fucking answers as to what the fuck is going on here." She dropped the doctor, who clutched her throat and wheezed. An icy chill spilled down Cassie's spine. The girl who struggled to talk back to anyone was once again showing her ferocity, and it both pleased and horrified her.

Once the doctor was back on her feet, she glanced at the ceiling, deep in thought. "I'm not even sure where to begin. Tell me what you know first so I can avoid wasting time."

Cassie shot her a look like the woman was insane. She yelled, pointing her finger in Dr. Renard's chest. "I know there's fucking vampires. I know I keep puking out more black liquid than my body could possibly hold. I know you were doing experiments or some shit on those things. I know you have bunker up there with one bed for a family of three, no clothes, a nice kitchen, but not enough food to last for any extensive amount of time."

Dr. Renard nodded. "Okay, that's good, so you're not in denial about what you're seeing. Those are vampires. You understand that."

Cassie shook her head and threw her hands up. "Yeah, kind of obvious."

Dr. Renard rubbed her hands all over her face. "Look, I don't know how to say any of this without sounding crazy to you, but hopefully the fact you know there are vampires will make this a little easier to swallow. I'm a regular psychologist. I deal with normal patients all the time, normal as in not vampires. But I've become quite known to people who believe in other things."

Cassie waved her arms like a traffic officer telling the cars to keep moving. "Like vampires. I get it."

"Well, not *just* vampires. Other things too."

Cassie scrunched her brow. "Like what? Werewolves?"

Dr. Renard slowly nodded her head. "Yes, like that. And many, many other things."

Cassie widened her eyes. "Lampposts? You gonna tell me lamp-posts are real?"

Dr. Renard laughed. "No. Don't be ridiculous. Those only exist on that stupid Kevin Bacon show. But other things like..." she paused, struggling to get this out, and that made Cassie's stomach drop. "...like demons."

Cassie laughed. "Okay. What does that have to do with our current situation?" As soon as the words left her mouth, she thought she understood. It all hit her like a baseball bat to the gut.

"You, Cassie. You're possessed by a demon."

Cassie bent over laughing. It wasn't funny, not in the slightest, because it was either nonsense and a ridiculous thing to kid about at a time like this or it was real and terrifying. She wasn't stupid enough to wash it away as false but couldn't place the pieces in enough, couldn't fathom something so bizarre.

"It's not your fault that you're in the dark about this. It took a lot to chisel it from your mind."

She fell to her knees. It all flooded back. The necklace. The doctor's appointments. And, of course, "The White Wolf." She whis-pered it, speaking more to herself than anyone else.

"Yes, The White Wolf. I could never figure out what that meant. I know it's what you called the demon, but I never understood why." She said this as if Cassie would suddenly provide the answer, to give her the last piece of a puzzle she had never completed.

Tears flooded Cassie's eyes. "You did this to me. You stole from me. You're a fucking monster."

Dr. Renard stepped back. Her eyes bulged. Her mouth dropped. "Cassie, no. That's not what happened."

Cassie screamed, drowning out the sounds of the vampires pounding on the door. "You fucking monster."

CHAPTER 33
A CHANCE TO BREAK FREE

Cassie stepped into Dr. Renard's office, prepared for another day of the woman waving weird chemicals in her face, begging her to reveal the meaning behind The White Wolf, and asking her a series of inane questions. Part of her hated these visits, but a part of her loved to see the frustration brewing on Dr. Renard's face as Cassie avoided giving her an inch.

The doctor was already waiting for her when she entered, which made Cassie uncomfortable. And not *just* Cassie, but The White Wolf, too. She felt the demon rumbling in her chest, ready to lash out. Something was up. The doctor always walked into their meetings late, frazzled, and eager to begin. To see her sitting calmly in her leather chair, legs crossed, unsettled Cassie, as if she had already lost the upper hand for the day.

There were no files strewn about on the coffee table. Dr. Renard always had files out, papers with scribbled notes. She spent the entire hour jotting down information. Today, nothing.

Cassie sat in her abnormally large chair and stared, waiting.

Dr. Renard smiled. "How are you, Cassie?"

The White Wolf answered. "Fuck you."

"Ah, you're coming right out today, huh? Don't want to give the girl a chance to speak for herself?"

"Fuck you again."

Dr. Renard released a cartoonish sigh and rolled her eyes. "I have something for you." She held up a fist, disguising her present in the clutches of her fingers.

Cassie's eyes widened. Her voice overtook The White Wolf. "What is it?"

"Catch." Dr. Renard tossed a shiny object into the air.

Cassie didn't catch it. Couldn't if she wanted to. The shimmering thing snaked across the room, and as soon as it neared her, her entire body seized. Her back arched, fingers and toes curled, everything tightened. A noise poured from her throat like a train horn. It more than hurt. It felt like her life force, her *soul*, was ripping away from her.

The necklace landed on her chest and, through the seizing, it wormed down to her belly. She could look at it, could see it causing all this pain, but could do nothing to remove it. Eventually, it slid off her and onto the floor. As soon as it fell, Cassie gained her faculties back. She heaved, gagged.

Dr. Renard, who sat there watching the whole time, no intentions of helping, kicked a bucket toward Cassie. Cassie grabbed it and retched for what seemed an endless amount of time.

Once she finished, she placed the bucket over the necklace, not even wanting to look at it. She still felt its power over her, though not as strongly. Still, she felt an emptiness, a missing part of herself.

"Now, let's talk Cassie. I'm going to guess your friend has nothing to say right now?"

Cassie paused, waiting for The White Wolf to chime in, but she didn't. In fact, Cassie couldn't even feel her in there. No more volatile bubbling in her chest.

"What do you want to talk about?" The words came out in a whimper, tears frosting her eyes.

"Why do you call the demon The White Wolf?"

Cassie lifted her legs, crisscrossing them on the seat cushion, hoping to keep them as far from the necklace as possible. A growl escaped her, but it was pathetic, one last flailing from The White Wolf, who seemed powerless inside her. "I don't want to talk about it."

Dr. Renard signed. "Week in and week out I placed chemicals in front of you. Do you know why?"

Cassie shook her head.

"Once upon a time, another young girl came to visit me. This girl also had a demon in her. In fact, she had the very same demon. That woman, as you have probably guessed, being the smart girl you are, was your mother. Now, your mom, she didn't have the opportunity you're about to have, because we didn't know how to remove the demon from within her. In fact, we got so desperate to figure it out, we called a priest to do an exorcism." Dr. Renard cackled. "Can you believe that? No, but your mother was powerful, and she learned to adapt over time. The demon was always there, and it did some awful things, but ultimately, she learned to contain it, or at least to control herself. Then, unfortunately for you, when you were born, the demon passed down to you. We don't know why. The White Wolf doesn't like to talk to us, so we can't be sure why she didn't go to your brother first, but nonetheless, here we are." Dr. Renard paused and bit her lip, staring at Cassie as if waiting for her to say something, anything.

Cassie felt dizzy, sick to her stomach, and had no intention of formulating words.

"Anyway, one day when your mother came in, I noticed something. She seemed weird. And I don't mean possessed weird. I mean, out of it. Her demon wasn't throwing in her usual snide answers and your mom was more reserved, tired, and maybe a little weak. For the life of me, I couldn't figure out what was wrong with her, and she seemed not to know either."

Cassie could hardly listen. The room spun around her; her temples throbbed.

"As we were chatting, I realized I had left something on the floor. See, my office at the time was smaller and less professional. I had a metal shelving unit in a corner of the room, and when our ceiling leaked, it got a little rusty. So, I picked up some rust remover and sprayed it down about half-hour before your mom's appointment. When I finished, I left the can under the coffee table by her chair. So, I picked it up, and as it crossed by her face, The White Wolf flipped out, and your poor mother looked like she was having a seizure."

Cassie looked up, understanding now why Dr. Renard placed stuff in front of her face.

"When I removed the can, your mom returned to her normal self, although The White Wolf was extraordinarily cruel that day. I ran a little test, and right before your mom's appointment ended, I put the can back in front of her, and wouldn't you know it, it caused the same reaction again."

Cassie hated listening to this, didn't want to hear the doctor's stupid methods for causing her current predicament, but couldn't help her need to know.

"This got me thinking. Maybe there are chemicals that are upsetting to the demon, and if there is one, maybe there are many. And while one was only enough to annoy it, maybe a combination of a bunch could diminish it entirely. We may never learn how to remove the demon from you, Cassie, but I found a way to make it stop. Thanks to the trials I have run with you, I learned it was hydrofluoric acid in the rust remover that caused the reaction, if you were wondering."

Cassie put her head down and cried.

"Cassie, this is good news. You can be free. I know change is scary, but after years and years of studying the demon, I finally learned how to give you a good life. You were hurting people, Cassie. You were scaring everyone around you. You don't have to live alone anymore. You can have peace."

Cassie raised her head, glaring at Dr. Renard. "No."

"No what, Cassie? All you have to do is wear that nice necklace I gave you, and you will never have to worry about the demon again. Your brother can sleep soundly at night. Your parents won't fight all day and night about what to do with you. You can make friends without worrying about hurting them. Cassie, you ripped a girl's toenails off. You know that right?"

Fury bubbled in Cassie's belly and it wasn't from the demon. It was entirely her own. "You said my mom learned how to manage it. Why can't I?"

Dr. Renard scoffed, shook her head angrily. "Because in the meantime, you could kill someone. You could really hurt another person. This isn't a part of you worth growing into. It needs to be shut down."

The coating of tears turned into a deluge. "It's not a part of me. It *is* me. You're telling me I need to remove myself from myself."

Dr. Renard hopped off her seat and got onto her knees, approaching Cassie. "I know it feels that way. I understand. You were born with it, so it's going to be hard to find your own identity, but it is *not* you. You are you, and nothing can change that. In fact, the demon was keeping you from being you." Dr. Renard put her hands on Cassie's knees.

Cassie knew right then the doctor was wrong. If The White Wolf was still active, she would have ripped Dr. Renard's hands right off her body. But without the demon, Cassie couldn't do anything except sit there and accept the doctor's cruel, smug smile and placating gestures. But Cassie *wanted* to. She wished for nothing more than the ability to make Dr. Renard scream in pain. The White Wolf was her. They were the same. They wanted the same things. They needed each other. The demon had always taken care of Cassie.

What kind of person would she be to stuff the demon in a box within herself? What kind of betrayal would that be?

When the doctor moved away, giving Cassie some space, a fresh wave of nausea came over Cassie and she spent some more time with the bucket.

Dr. Renard sat and watched, not giving her a word.

When Cassie finished, the session was over.

The doctor picked the necklace up and handed it to Cassie. "Just take it for now. You don't have to wear it yet, but just take it."

When Cassie stepped out of the office, Dr. Renard told her mother everything. Cassie watched her mother's facial expressions turn to glee, and she'd never felt so betrayed in all her life.

They got in the car and drove away from the office in silence.

Eventually, her mother broke the quiet. "You seem sad."

Cassie looked at the floating colors in the necklace's pendant. "Yeah."

Her mother put her arm on Cassie's shoulder. "You're not ready to say goodbye, are you?"

"I never want to say goodbye."

Her mother sighed and turned up the radio. Until they reached their road, they stayed in silence. Before turning into the driveway, her mother spoke up once more. "Listen, give me the necklace. I'll tuck it away somewhere. If you ever decide you are ready for it, let me know. But I have to tell you, and make sure your friend is listening too - if you do anything dangerous or harmful to anyone else, or yourself, I will force you to wear it. Understood?"

Cassie beamed, nearly jumping out of her seat. "Yes, mom. I promise. Thank you so much."

Her mother put the car in park and ran her hands through Cassie's hair. "And keep this from your brother and father. If they know we have a cure and aren't using it, they will go apeshit on both of us."

Cassie put her index finger and thumb to her lips, pinched them together, and ran them across her mouth like a zipper.

Her mother reached over and hugged her. With her lips pressed against Cassie's ear, she whispered, "Remember that I always love you."

Cassie wasn't sure if her mother was talking to her or the demon.

NO COMING BACK

"*Cassiopeia, are you awake?*"

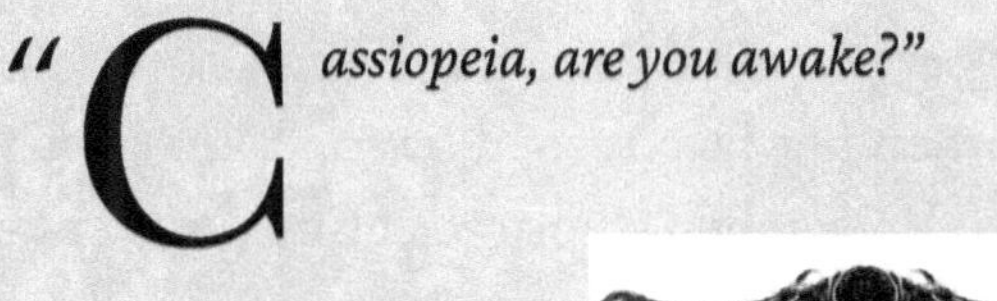

Cassie shoved Dr. Renard, knocking her to the floor. She yelled, "All this time, you stole from me. You ripped my whole life away from me."

Dr. Renard slid back on her butt, putting space between her and the angered girl. "Cassie, you've thrived. You're in college, and you're incredibly intelligent. You have a bright future. We helped you."

Cassie shook her head. She felt sick again. While her body washed away the aches, she could feel The White Wolf breaking free, and it hurt her all over. "You have no idea. A bright future? Every single day is suffering. I hated my life. Hated it. It was the life you wanted for me, my parents, everyone else. It wasn't the life I wanted."

Dr. Renard stood up, putting one hand out as a protective shield.

"Let's not forget who made the choice. As I recall, your mother didn't make you wear the necklace. *You* eventually put it on."

Cassie turned around and punched the wall, letting out a frustrated yelp. When she turned back to the doctor, blood dribbled down her fingers from her knuckles. She calmed her voice. "It's amazing how little you know."

She'd been so focused on the doctor, and all the memories washing up shore, that she had failed to realize the vampires had spread out and were now pounding on both doors. Eventually, they'd get in and this would all be over. Cassie placed a hand over the bite wound on her wrist, remembering it would be over soon for her whether or not the vampires got in.

Dr. Renard stumbled, bumping her back into the wall. "All I ever wanted to do was help you."

Cassie squinted her eyes. "Bullshit. I'm sure you tell yourself you're helping the world by what you did to the vampires, too."

Dr. Renard laughed, and then her face turned stern. "Don't you dare try to humanize them. I watched those creatures rip my husband to pieces for pleasure. They killed my son. My son!"

Cassie moved closer to her. "Oh, I know what they are and I'm going to fucking kill them. But what I wouldn't do is chain them up and rip their jaws off, keep them separated by a few yards to test their communication abilities, see how they adapt, see if they turn on each other or cooperate to gain freedom."

Dr. Renard smiled. "See, you are so brilliant. You understood the trials perfectly. And you're letting your emotions block your smarts. You know damned well why learning that information is important. Those fucking things lived on Earth. They killed people. Nightly. Studying them was important." She put her head down, and the volume in her voice decreased with it. "I guess it's not anymore."

Cassie took one more step, but as soon as she did, she dropped to the floor, head smashing on concrete. Her whole body seized. She felt herself kicking, shaking. Dr. Renard dropped to Cassie's side, putting her hand under Cassie's head to protect it.

The seizure ended a minute later. "What's happening to me?"

Dr. Renard helped her sit up and leaned her against a wall. "The demon is coming out. You've worn the necklace for so long, it's good and buried. As soon as the necklace comes off, the demon can free itself a little, but if the chemicals in the necklace stayed close by, it would still protect you from the demon fully coming out."

"Stop saying 'protect.'"

Dr. Renard rolled her eyes. "When you described what happened up there, being able to kill one vampire but not another, I sensed the necklace had something to do with it. The demon is deep inside, imprisoned, but when you move away from the necklace, it's able to release its anger through you."

Cassie thought about the showers, about how it was the one time she felt free to release her rage. She always removed the necklace before washing. It explained so much. The memories of her friend were coming back, but in bits and pieces and it was a struggle to put them all together, especially with a vicious pack of monsters outside the doors.

"Fuck. It hurts."

Dr. Renard rubbed Cassie's arm. "I know you're going through a lot right now, but we need that demon to come out. Fast. Our only hope of surviving the vampires is if you can lure out The White Wolf."

Cassie put her head on her knees. Her muscles felt like someone was tearing them to pieces. "I don't know how to help it out faster."

She wrapped her arms around herself and screamed. The pain was unbearable.

Dr. Renard stood up. "Okay. Okay. While we are waiting, I'll tell you what I can about the vampires, maybe it will help." She paced and chewed on the inside of her cheek. "The leader is John Adams. We named them after presidents for a while. Before that, we named them after famous actors, and before that, it was pop stars. Anyway, John Adams was always a special one. Most of the vampires drain after not having blood. They weaken, get more animalistic, more brutal, but also kind of dumber. They just act without thinking."

The pain moved from Cassie's stomach to her chest, as if the demon was working its way up.

"But it never happened with John Adams. Some vampires would deplete within a day. Without blood, they'd just fall apart into what you saw upstairs, almost like zombies in movies. But we had John Adams in a cage for over a year. *A year!* And he never changed. Always remained sharp."

Cassie's eyes rolled back and a low guttural noise rumbled in her throat like an idle motorcycle.

The metal doors bent in with each kick and punch. Vampire strength proved enough to warp the thick doors.

"The crew he has with them were new. We hadn't even named them yet. Their human names were Allyson Flickinger, Nicholas Beishline, Fiona Adams, no relation to John, and…" She paused. "Jeez, I forgot the other one."

Sweat leaked down Cassie's face. Was the demon coming out or was the vampire poison seeping in? She imagined she looked just like James had right before he turned.

The doors had warped so heavily, the space between lock and jamb was growing by the second. It wouldn't take long before it fully separated.

"They were all in cells. Somehow, John broke out. We still can't figure out how. That was the emergency my husband and I needed to take care of when you came to babysit. When we got down here, the world fucking ended. Jesus, that's crazy to say out loud. Anyway, John chased us around and got us trapped in a pantry. At least we had food for a little while."

Cassie noted there was more food down here; hopeful she could survive all this and eat a meal, but then, once again, had to remind herself they'd bitten her. There was no coming back from that.

"While they had trapped us in the pantry, John Adams found his way to the control room, where he released the rest of them. They didn't group together and come after us the way they are now, though. It was almost as if they wanted to leave us alone, as if we weren't important to them. My husband had a plan to sneak into the control room where we could use the electronic locks to keep them wherever they were hiding. I knew it was stupid, but he was right. We couldn't hide out in the pantry forever."

Cassie rolled over, walking on all fours. Waves of pain drilled up her spine, into her brain. She thought her skull might explode.

She craned her head back to Dr. Renard.

"Besides the wooden stakes, what kills them?" It wasn't Cassie that asked the question.

The sound of the voice shattered her heart. "I missed you so much," she whispered to her long-lost companion.

"What kills them?" the voice yelled.

Dr. Renard stood up. "Just the wooden stakes I'm afraid."

The other voice laughed as a door smashed open.

"We'll see about that," it said. "I already helped Cassie kill one with a knife. Maybe the best weapon against them is me."

CHAPTER 35

WITH SWORD IN HAND

"When you were a wee little thing, I remember you crawling into a chair leg. Your head slammed hard into it, and later you developed an egg on your forehead. But at the time, you burst into tears, cried for about thirty seconds, then laughed. You laughed. Children are the most terrifying things."*

Before Cassie could stand, the vampires were on her.

Nick pinned her arms down, and Allyson sat on her stomach, smile still caked in Cassie's blood.

While all this was going on, Dr. Renard slipped back into a corner, keeping as low a profile as possible.

There were four vampires in the room, and the rest continued to pound on the other door.

"Is your little friend out yet?" Allyson said. "She was so delicious before. Come out, come out, little demon. I want a taste."

A vampire behind her said, "You've already had a taste. It's my turn." His nose bent down like a parrot's beak.

Allyson licked her lips. "Fine. Take just a little snack." She dismounted Cassie's stomach.

Bird Face giggled as he sat on her.

Cassie said nothing, didn't try to break free. She wanted to. She wished for nothing more than to kick and scream and run away, but she felt The White Wolf moving around inside her. It placed a gentle hand on her raging heart and whispered, "Sssssshhhhh," in her ear.

Bird Face moved his head closer to Cassie's. His hot breath smelled like a sack of dirty pennies. A forest of blackheads on his nose became visible. His receding hairline dripped sweat. Against her stomach, his body trembled with anticipation. With his eyes closed, he whispered, "I've been feeding on small tastes of the bitch's husband for days. God, I need something new." He opened his mouth, getting ready to dig his teeth into her neck. A line of saliva drove from his top teeth to his bottom.

As he inched closer, The White Wolf pulled Cassie's head up, as if giving him his prize. Then she bit his nose, wiggling her head back and forth until it broke clean off his face. His blood splashed on her as he fell off her, clutching the space where his nose used to be.

Nick's grip loosened, so to further distract him, Cassie spit the nose at him. He used a hand to block it, which gave her the space she needed. With her free arm, she slashed at his face, scratching down his cheek. Now she had both arms free.

Before she had much time, Allyson and Fiona were on top of her.

While she struggled to free herself from them, Nick recovered and gripped her hair, keeping her head in place as he pulled it.

Fiona punched her square between the eyes.

Her vision went blurry and her ears rang. As soon as she recovered, Fiona took another shot. A red pool seeped from her nose into her eyes. She had expected more from The White Wolf, but then again, the demon had years of rust to clean off.

"No more playing around," Allyson said. "Take her to John's room. Follow the plan."

Fiona and Nick each took an arm and dragged her toward the door.

Through the fog in her vision, Cassie saw a blurred Dr. Renard still hovering in the corner.

Bird Face and Allyson followed behind Cassie, and out the door they went.

"John, we got her," Allyson yelled, no shortage of triumph in her voice.

Her bravado sent The White Wolf tumbling inside Cassie. "Have you ever..." Cassie's voice faded away, swimming in a sea of confusion.

"Shut up, girl."

"...ever played tic-tac-toe?"

Bird Face laughed, the noseless fuck. "I think you knocked her silly."

"It's such a stupid game," Cassie said, her back grinding against the cement as they dragged her.

They ignored her rambling.

"If one player knows the game..." she broke out into hysterics, laughing so hard it hurt her head, "...winner is always the first to go." She yanked an arm free and with strength and agility she never possessed, jumped to her feet, only using her lower legs to get her there. Fiona still clung to the other arm, which was bent painfully behind her, but she couldn't focus on that. With her free hand, she grabbed Bird Face by the neck and slammed his head into the wall. A powerful bang reverberated through the corridor.

Allyson dove for her, and Cassie used the vampire's momentum against her, grabbing the back of the vampire's head and driving her knee into Allyson's face. A satisfying crunch. Blood sprayed all over Cassie's pant legs.

Nick jumped on her back, wrapping his arms around her torso. She spun, getting her other arm in front of her.

Fiona still gripped her wrists tightly, unwilling to let go. Instead of fighting to free the grip, Cassie drew her arm in, forcing Fiona closer. When she was close enough, Cassie bit her cheek, tearing a hunk of flesh from her face. The taste of sweat and blood stayed in her mouth, even after she spit the hunk out.

With Nick still on her back, she fell hard into the wall behind her, slamming him into the cement. She drove her head back, smashing the back of her skull into his face. His arms slid off her, and she stepped forward, his body flopping to the ground.

None of them would be out for long. They were vampires. They'd recover easier than a human, and Cassie was pretty sure John Adams gave them each a taste of Mr. Renard, which would offer them strength for a little while. But she gave herself a few moments, or The White Wolf did.

She ran back into the room where Dr. Renard stayed hovering in the corner, rocking and shaking. The vampires weren't pounding on the other door, which meant John Adams was probably making his way around to her. Cassie bent down to Dr. Renard's level. "Tell me there's more stakes."

Dr. Renard looked up at her and winced, presumably from the massive amounts of blood on her face, a combination of her own and the vampires. She probably looked like the girl from *The Descent* after swimming in a pond of gore. Dr. Renard lifted a trembling finger and muttered something under her breath.

Cassie thought the woman might have snapped. After witnessing her husband's death, finding out her son died much the same way, and then seeing a combination of her work bloodying each other up in front of her would probably do the trick.

Cassie huffed and pried open the door she had come in, the one John Adams had been pounding at, and checked the hallway. Nothing. He was probably closing in on the other side of the room. The vampires Cassie had attacked were also surely licking their wounds and planning their revenge.

She ran to Spot's dead body and gripped the stake still in his chest. His agape mouth appeared crooked thanks to his lower jaw shifting to the side. His flesh turned rubbery and purplish-blue.

She ripped the stake out. It left his body with a squelch.

As she headed back to the room, prepared to fight to the death, The White Wolf chimed in. "Cassie, wait."

She leaned against the wall, trying to keep her bearings. Even with The White Wolf's power running through her bloodstream, she felt exhausted, feeble, broken. She also wondered when she'd turn, when the vampire bites would take hold. "We don't have time to wait," she said.

"It's been a long time since I've been able to speak to you. I've seen your suffering and could do nothing but watch."

She sniffled. "I know. I know. That's why we have to hurry and finish this."

"Cassie, that's what I need to tell you. You remember me from childhood. Maybe I seem mythical to you, but I am not. I am scared. I can help you, sure, but I am not all-powerful. Those vampires can kill us both."

She fell to her knees, sobbing. "It doesn't matter anyway. I'm going to turn into one of them." She rubbed her hand on her bitten wrist.

"No, you won't, Cassiopeia. That part I *can* help with. I am in your blood. I am part of your DNA. They can't turn you as long as I am in here, but they can kill you. Because of me, your blood is more valuable to them. It's what makes them so strong. Just a sip of your blood could keep them satiated for centuries."

Cassie stood back up. "Well, let's go finish this or die trying."

The White Wolf growled. "Okay."

Before she stepped back into the room, Cassie's heart dropped. "Wait. Did you call me Cassiopeia?"

CHAPTER 36
THE DAY CASSIE DIED

CASSIE, AGE 8

After school, while Cassie's father worked at the restaurant, her mother sat in the basement typing away at her computer, and her brother hung out at his friend Jordan's house, Cassie explored the backyard. The family had a nice, clean-cut yard with a picket fence blocking the woody hills behind. Those hills were part of their property, but the terrain was too dangerous, too filled with wild animals and angry hornets for Cassie's comfortably suburban parents. Her family was often too busy to know Cassie spent time there.

Her father built a latch gate on the corner of the yard, leading right into the woods, so he could pitch yard debris back there without having to heave it over the fence. He, basically, gave Cassie the invitation to explore.

Today, she planned to cross a small stream at the bottom of the hill, something she'd promised herself she would do at some point, but required gumption because when she got close to the stream, she lost sight of the picket fence. It was uncharted territory, a faraway planet, a new world. Even The White Wolf stirred inside her at the idea of going down there. Her hidden friend knew something about those woods, about the things lurking in the foliage. But what was life without a raised heartbeat? What was the point otherwise?

The hill was relatively steep, so Cassie had to walk sideways to avoid stumbling all the way down. When she reached the bottom after a slow descent, she peered up toward where the picket fence should be. It hid behind the peaks and elms, and the absence of it in her vision sent a fun chill down her spine. The White Wolf grumbled.

The stream was a shallow thing, barely clearing the stones at the bed as the water chugged by, but it was quick, moving so swiftly it made a nice, chaotic swishing sound.

Across the stream, she caught movement. At first, it scared her, but then she recognized the figures. Chris and Jordan. Her brother was laughing as Jordan waved his arms around, telling some kind of yarn.

Cassie ducked behind a tree, not just so she could snoop, although that too, but because she worried her brother would flip knowing she crossed into his world somehow, even if it was accidental. The snooping proved boring. They mainly just tossed rocks and talked shit about their classmates.

Jordan was a beefy kid and when he talked, his cheeks grew redder by the second. He and Chris had been friends for as long as Cassie could remember, and she hated it because Chris always acted like a dick around Jordan.

Chris walked across the stream, the water dribbling against his feet as he crossed.

Jordan followed with a little less grace.

As they neared where Cassie hid, a wasp landed on her arm. Without thinking, she swatted at the foreign invader, killing it instantly. After the distraction, she peeked back to find her brother and his friend already across the stream and walking around the tree she hid behind.

Then, she heard the buzzing. She turned in time to see a cloud of wasps swarming around her. A burning prick hit her leg, then another on her arm. She fell over and screamed, startling Chris and landing on Jordan, knocking him over, too.

"Oh fuck, wasps," he yelled, flailing his arms and legs.

Chris said, "What the fuck are you doing here, Cassie," before realizing the swarm of stinging bugs. He stumbled backwards and ran a small distance away.

Cassie swatted with fury, fighting them off as best she could, but they were all over her. The White Wolf took over, slamming and slashing. She rolled over, trying to get to her feet, and Jordan slapped her in the face while attempting to get the wasps off himself.

The White Wolf reacted to the threats all around, punching. Cassie's fist slammed into Jordan's face, and then she extended her fingers like talons and drove them into Jordan's throat. She wasn't human anymore, nor was she a demon. She was just a ball of energy, an electrical current trapped in a box. She was movement, reaction, but no thought. None at all.

She bit into Jordan's neck, ripping away skin. Her fingers dug into his nostrils and pulled upward until his nose had come away from his face with a clean snap. Her elbow drove up and down into his mouth until he choked on his teeth.

Slowly, the world came back.

The first sign of life came from her brother, who screamed for her to stop from across the stream where he retreated, thanks to the wasps. "Cassie! Stop! What the fuck are you doing?"

Then the pain from the wasp stings kicked in. They were all over her, continuing their assault. Red welts and bumps covered her legs, arms, and presumably her face, too. She stood up, seeing the damage she had done, the brutal remains of her work. Jordan's face was nothing more than mush, a tree stump of viscera.

Chris turned and ran up the hill yelling , "Mom! Mom! Mom!"

Cassie charged after him, running with all her life. One by one the wasps fell off her, until Cassie had run through the already-opened gate into the yard. Her skin was free from the wasps, but the craggy, welted flesh from their assault would remain for God knew how long. Meanwhile, Cassie knew their venom was flowing through her bloodstream, probably enough to kill her.

She came in through the back door, her mother already at the scene. Chris stood in front of her, belligerently screaming and trying to tell her the story but not making much sense.

When Cassie's mother shot a glance at her and saw the sloping hills on her daughter's flesh, she did a double take. Her eyes widened, and she left Chris to scream his story to no one.

"Cassie, what happened?"

She tried to talk to her mother over the sobbing and freaking out. "I'm so sorry mom. It wasn't on purpose. It was the wasps."

"What are you talking about, honey?"

"I was just trying to get away from the wasps."

Chris shouted something. At first, it sounded like a muffled thing, but as he continued to repeat the same words over and over, they grew in strength and clarity. "She killed Jordan. She killed Jordan. Mom, she killed Jordan."

Cassie's mother looked to Chris, to Cassie, to Chris, to Cassie, and in that moment, where the information seeped into her mother's brain, Cassie got the rare experience of witnessing her life turn to dust. In her mother's eyes, through the glossy reflection, Cassie saw herself and saw the shifting shape of her mother's eyelids, going from concern for her daughter to absolute terror. This was it. Nothing would ever be the same again.

She didn't know how yet, but Cassie knew the blood from the body in the woods would travel as swiftly as the stream. It would come up the hill, into the yard, into her house, her bed, her closets, into her mother's heart, her father's hands, her brother's spine. It would kill them all. They were all as good as dead.

Her mother stood up and looked around, navigating a plan of action in her mind. "Cassie, go upstairs and take a shower. Wash all of that blood off." She turned toward Chris. "Go stand outside the bathroom door. Keep your ears peeled. Call for her every thirty seconds to make sure she responds and is breathing."

Chris threw his hands up. "You're crazy. I don't want to be anywhere near her."

Her mother stiffened and spoke loud and clear. "Do what I fucking tell you, Chris."

Chris stepped forward. "Where are you going?"

"I'm going to Jordan." Without leaving room for conversation, she stepped around Cassie and barged out the back door, letting the screen slam on its way back home.

Chris crossed his arms. "I'm not going up there with you. I don't give a fuck if you die. You hear me?"

Cassie put her head down and went alone up the stairs. In the shower, she cried and scrubbed at the stings, wishing the soap would make the redness and bumps go away. At least Jordan's blood came off nice and easy. She didn't mean to kill him, and neither did The White Wolf. It was an accident. It was just an accident.

She turned off the water when she heard the back door slam again. After wrapping a towel around herself, she crept down the stairs where her mother whispered something to her brother. She said nothing as she made her way to them in the kitchen.

They both turned to her, staring.

Her mother's hands shook, and Jordan's blood covered her shirt, face, and arms. "I need to know you're both listening. And Chris," she looked him square in the eyes, "I don't want to hear your objections. You're doing what I tell you."

Cassie's heart beat faster. The blood on her mother, the way her mom's eyes flickered and darted like an excited gnat, it all portended to something dark, something that would shift the balance of their household, toppling it into an upside-down world.

"I'm going to call the police."

Chris's face lit up.

"I'm going to tell them I did this. When I was a kid, I went to a juvenile detention center for violent things, so they won't question it, especially after what I just did while I was down there. My DNA will be all over him."

Chris went to speak, and his mother put her blood-soaked hand in his face. "Chris, I love you. I know you can't see that, but it's true. And I don't mean to snap at you, but this is not the fucking time. If they ask you questions, you will lie and tell them I did it, you will tell them you saw me do it, and you will tell them I have been acting scary for weeks."

"No. Fucking, no. I won't do that," Chris said.

"Chris!" Her nostrils flared. "I am not having this conversation. You will do what I fucking tell you. This isn't a debate."

"Why? Why would you continue to defend her and make my life a living hell? She's evil, Mom. Now you're going to go to jail so I can be even more alone with her?" Tears dribbled down his cheeks, and his upper lip trembled.

"Because your sister made a promise to me." She turned to Cassie, "Didn't you?"

Cassie stared in bewilderment until it clicked. She shook her head. "What? No. Mom. I'll go to jail. I don't care. You shouldn't take the blame for something I did."

Her mother punched the wall and screamed.

Chris and Cassie flinched.

"I am not having this conversation. Both of you, listen to me. Cassie, you can't go to jail for something you didn't do. You didn't do this. You understand? It wasn't you. It was your friend. You're a fucking kid, and jail will ruin you. You have no idea. It will follow you forever. Forever. That's if they ever let you out. For what happened out there, I wouldn't be surprised if you'd be the youngest kid in history to be tried as an adult."

"Good, let her," Chris chimed in.

She turned to her son. "Listen. I know this is going to be hard to believe, but we have a cure for your sister. A real cure. It's my fault this happened because I didn't make her take it. But Cassie promised me," she said those last two words sternly, "that she would take the cure if anything else happened."

"But mom," Cassie pleaded.

"And I would certainly fucking say this qualifies."

Cassie hugged her, wrapping her arms around her mother's waist and placing her head in the crook of her mom's shoulder. "Please, mom. I don't want you to go."

Chris stood still, sobbing, looking on the verge of shattering. "Mom, don't do this."

"He's right, mom. You can't do this."

Her mother gently pried Cassie away from her, went to the old-style kitchen phone that hung on the wall, and dialed 911. With an eerie calmness, she simply said, "Hello, I need police officers to come to my house right away... Yes, that's correct... Yes, that's our address... Because I just killed a child in the woods behind my house." She hung up.

Chris and Cassie broke out into hysterical sobs. For the first time, they shared a mutual pain.

The next ten minutes were a blur of begging and pleading to stop the inevitable. The wheels had been set in motion and nothing good could happen from that point forward.

Her mother forced Cassie upstairs to change out of her towel before the police arrived.

While she changed, Chris screamed throughout the house, angrily throwing any random object he could find.

The police came. While they spoke to Cassie's mother, other men and women trounced around the house into the woods.

Cassie stood in a corner, watching everything, holding in her breath, and wishing she had the strength to hold it until she died.

The police asked her some questions, and Chris, too, but they seemed uninterested in their answers. They had their murderer wrapped up with a solid confession. Chris and Cassie kept to their mother's story as they'd been instructed. Cassie was sure Chris would break, but he never did.

All the while, her mother acted out a character, an unstable one who shouted and whispered and broke into frenzied hysterics. It all felt so cartoonish to Cassie, but if the police could see through her acting, they weren't showing it. Besides, she doubted anyone would believe a child did what happened to Jordan.

As the police dragged Cassie's mother out of the house, she tossed the necklace at Cassie and yelled, "Wear that fucking thing, Cassie. Remember me as I was before this."

Cassie slid out of the way, letting the necklace drop to the floor. She moved to another corner, keeping as much distance as she could. At first, Cassie didn't know what her mother meant by that. Of course, Cassie would remember her as she was before. She knew the hysterics were all an act.

A sole officer remained until Chris assured him their father would be home soon. No one seemed concerned about Cassie's welt-ridden skin. The house emptied, but their father was due home soon with a brand-new hurricane to weather,

Chris stormed up to his room and shut the door.

Cassie went upstairs and cried into her pillow.

"We should have listened, Cassiopeia," a voice whispered in her ear.

Cassie sat up, wiping her face. "Shut up."

"Cassiopeia, you know I'm telling the truth."

"You didn't mean to do it. You were protecting me."

"I know that. You know that. But I will forever be a liability to you. My job is to protect you. Look around, I have failed. I have destroyed your life."

"My mother just left me. Now you want to leave me too?"

"Cassiopeia, you know well that I don't want to do this."

"Then don't."

"When your father gets home, let your brother talk to him. He won't lie to your father. They will both be angry with you. Once they've had a little time, go downstairs and I will talk to them."

"No. I won't let you leave me. I won't do this. You're all I have left. Who will protect me?"

The White Wolf growled in her ear. "You stop that. You have you. You will protect you. You will be your biggest friend. You're just like your mother. Never knew when to defend herself, to fight for herself. What she just did for you was the proudest of her I've ever been because she finally acted. And she did it for you. I expect you to do the same. For yourself."

Cassie whimpered again. "No. I don't know how to be without you. I can't."

"You are stronger than you give yourself credit for. You will do it because you love me and I need you to do it. I demand it. I don't have your morality. I want to hurt things. I want to taste blood. You will never live a normal life with me and I will not let you suffer anymore by my hands. You've done too much already.

"Here is how it will go. The necklace will make me go away more and more each day. I'll never fully be gone, but I'll be buried. On my way out, I will infect your brain. I will change things. You won't remember me anymore, so you can't miss me. Instead, all your important memories of me will go to someone else. You'll know they happened, but they won't be with me. I will make myself disappear completely. I love you so much, I would erase myself from history for you."

Cassie went from sobbing to full-on bawling.

The front door slammed open and Chris came barreling out of his room.

Cassie listened from the top steps as both her brother and father shouted. When she crept down the stairs, both men were standing in the hallway.

Chris moved behind their father, arms crossed smugly.

Cassie's father stood with a bag of groceries felled at his feet. His jaw had dropped so much it looked like it could separate from the rest of his face. Tears built in his eyes.

He looked to Cassie and pointed to the door. "Get out of my house," he said. Sense seemed to kick in. "I'm going to call the police."

The White Wolf took control and walked around them, not to the door, but to the living room where the necklace sat in a corner. Together, she and Cassie stared at it. Then, they turned back to Cassie's father. "And they'll believe a child capable of what happened? Don't be a fool."

"Give me my wife back!"

Her upper lip snarled and she charged. Cassie couldn't believe what The White Wolf was doing. "You're in no place to make demands, old man. Sit down, the both of you." The White Wolf's voice was so deep, so filled with fury, it surprised them all.

No one argued. Her father and brother sat next to each other on the couch.

"I won't live in the same house as you," her father said with as much backbone as he could muster.

"And you won't have to. I am leaving."

Her father and Chris lifted their heads at the same time, eyebrows raising with them.

"Her therapist found a cure for me. A necklace filled with chemicals that keeps me bottled up, unable to manifest within Cassie. She refused to wear it. Until today, I argued in her favor, and so did her mother, who hid the necklace from you both."

Chris looked like someone punched him in the gut.

Cassie's father made a pained sob.

"I am going to force Cassie to wear it. I will be gone. I know that's hard to believe, but it's true. You are free to call Dr. Renard for proof. I will be gone and Cassie will stay."

"No," Chris said.

Cassie yapped and chomped her teeth. "This is not a request. Cassie will wear the necklace, always. You will treat her with respect, or if you can't manage that, you will at least stay clear of her."

Her father threw his hands up. "You've got to be kidding. That's it? And you get away scot-free from all you've done to us?"

The White Wolf had full control of Cassie, and now its anger trapped her even further. Cassie couldn't move, talk, or do anything but watch things unfold. She knew it was over. The White Wolf would enforce the rules and she'd fall into a seizure as The White Wolf picked up the necklace. When she came to, she'd have no memory of the only friend she ever had.

"I will be trapped in the girl's belly for eternity, you damned fool. Is that not punishment for you?" The White Wolf snapped.

"Not enough of one if you ask me," Chris said.

"There are rules." The White Wolf stared hard.

"Here we go," her father said, standing up and pretending he was going to walk away. No one in the room believed he would, probably not even himself.

"Sit down!"

Her father listened.

"Why do you humans pretend you have a backbone? There are rules," The White Wolf snapped, "and you will obey them."

Cassie's father rubbed his forehead. "Can I get even one minute to absorb what's happening here? I come home from work, ready to put some groceries away, and I find out my life has been turned upside down. My wife is gone." His voice broke. It took a second for him to bring it back. "In jail for murder. All because of you and you have the nerve to give me demands? You know what? I don't have a backbone, you're right. But I would have to be the biggest sap of all time to keep listening to you. Fuck you. How's that?"

The White Wolf forced Cassie's body to jump, landing right on her father. She pinned her father's arms to the cushions. "That was good. Nice spine. But here's the problem. If you kick us out, I will sneak through the window and gut you while you sleep. If you tell the police the truth and Cassie goes to jail, I will come through the window and gut you while you sleep. If you do anything other than what I tell you, I will gut you while you sleep." She turned her head toward Chris. "Then I will eat your son for fun."

The White Wolf waited for any objections. None came. "You fear your daughter. That is my fault. Mine alone. Once she wears the necklace, I will slowly disappear. Over time, it will be more and more difficult for me to come out, even with the necklace removed. Once a day, you will grant me freedom. You will make Cassie take a shower and the only time she won't have her necklace on is during that shower. I'll be so locked up I won't be able to fully manifest, but it will help her release the rage she bottles. It's the only action I will perform. Helping her rage. Once the shower is over, she will put the necklace back on. You won't need to tell her. It'll be instinctual for her." The White Wolf looked from her father to her brother, making sure they followed. "Number two, you will understand it is me you hate, not her. Your fear may remain, but your hate is not allowed. You will not be cruel to her, or I will whisper in her ear, 'remove the necklace, Cassiopeia.'" Again, she waited. This time, their silence wasn't enough to satisfy. "Understood?"

They both nodded.

"Chris, I am going to erase Cassie's memory of me. She won't remember what happened to your friend, nor will she remember any other violence we have done together. But she will remember all the happiness. She will remember our bond, but she won't know it was ours." Cassie's hand moved to Chris's, causing her brother to flinch. "She will believe it was all with you. You can use that as an opportunity to bond. I'm sure you won't take it, but if you so choose to move on from this, the chance is there." Cassie sat up. "You lost a wife today, a mother. Your hate and grief will boil for days. You can let it fester, or you can put the blame where it belongs, on me, and recognize you have a beautiful daughter who wants nothing more than to love you and be loved in return."

The White Wolf guided her toward the necklace. Cassie couldn't yell, couldn't fight, because The White Wolf had taken full control, but she screamed at her inside her head. *No! No! No!* Her body bent down and snatched the necklace from the floor, causing her to convulse.

When Cassie came to, she had a deep need for her family. She needed to hug them, to find out the world was still in order, but she found the house empty. Empty, dark, and full of hidden recesses.

CHAPTER 37
TO SEE HER

"*I sometimes fear who I am. I would hate to see myself from someone else's perspective.*"

The thin corridor spun as all the memories flooded back. The White Wolf. It had always been The White Wolf there for her, giving her affection, fighting for her. And it told her to defend herself, taught her how to be strong, and she failed to listen. For all these years, she had failed. When she believed the advice came from her brother, as opposed to a voice inside herself, it seemed so fragile, especially given what happened to Chris.

"I can't believe it. You made me forget you."

"Things done. Things regretted, Cassie. Can we discuss this after we finish our current situation?"

She shook her head, but she'd lost all her verve. When she had too much to feel, how could she concentrate? She stepped into the room where Dr. Renard still stayed cradled in the corner, rocking herself mad.

The doctor noticed Cassie and stood up. "Cassie! We made a mistake. It was the demon they were after the whole time. Not you. We never should have let it out."

The White Wolf took control of Cassie, grabbed Dr. Renard by the throat, and pinned her to the wall.

Dr. Renard gasped and choked, her feet kicking a few centimeters off the floor.

The words that came from Cassie's mouth were not her own, but in so many ways, they were. "You convinced me what needed to be done. Just like Cassie's mother, brother, and father. You were wrong."

Dr. Renard spoke in a whisper, unable to produce anything louder with a hand wrapped around her vocal cords. "You're a demon. A fucking demon. How could you believe you were good for her?"

The White Wolf growled. "Yes, and every time a woman gnashes her teeth, it must be a supernatural evil, right?"

"Don't be ridiculous. You killed people."

"Yes, I did. And only sometimes was it regrettable." She tossed her out of the corner.

Dr. Renard's body hit the cement floor with a sickening thud. She lay on the floor staring at the ceiling. "You asked about the bedroom." The doctor sat up, groaning. "The bunker on the other side of the tunnel was always just for show, a place for us to do experiments without raising eyebrows. Zoning and building regulations and all that shit. Our real bunker is down here, same as the prisons. We found the tunnels by accident, so we built all of this down here. There's an exit that goes into the middle of the woods. This is where the real bedrooms are, the pantry, kitchen, bathrooms, and yes, the vampire prison. It's all a fucking secret. We didn't even tell James about it. Half the time we said we were going to work, we just drove down a dirt road in the woods a few miles behind our house and did work down here. Not that we didn't have real clients to work with in our offices. I can't think of the last time we went through the bunker doors in our yard. We always came from this side."

"Why didn't you dig out the tunnels more? I nearly got stuck."

Dr Renard shook her head. "You went straight. Yeah, we always meant to make that bigger, but there's a side tunnel that's much easier to get through, so we just never got around to it. The other tunnel pops out right in the main living quarters."

Main living quarters. Beds. Pantry. Kitchen. Maybe she could still find a way to live down there. A thought came to Cassie. Where were the vampires? Why weren't they attacking her? It must have occurred to The White Wolf too, because she turned toward the second door, sharp-eyed, eager to fight, but nervous. Cassie knew The White Wolf's fear by the way it affected her own heartbeat, just a slight uptick in beats; small, but noticeable. They drifted to the door, then peered their head out in the hallway.

Nothing.

No movement.

No noise outside of a low dripping.

She dipped to the opposite side, away from the door, and leaned her back square on the wall. From there, she slid down the hall, stake at the ready. The dripping sound grew louder with each step she took.

Drip. Drip. Drip.

Just as before, as she moved away from the room the hallway's darkness suffocated her. She tried to steady her shaky breath to listen for any sound. She'd traveled far enough from the room that she was no longer sure where she was, what directions the hall would take, and where it all led. At some point, it had to cross where she had once run from the vampires since Dr. Renard found her way to the same room where she ended up, but Cassie didn't know if the hallway had any other turns that would confuse her sense of direction.

Far down the hall, something skittered from one side of the hall to the other before disappearing. It laughed on its way. Allyson or Fiona, she guessed by the sound.

She stared in the direction, trying to pick up any visual, a nook, something to explain where they could have come from or where they went.

Then, something moved behind her.

She jolted at the sound.

Something else skittered from one side to the other before disappearing.

It made no sense. She had just been over there, and the hall had offered no turns. Where could they have come from? Where could they have gone? As far as she knew, they didn't possess the ability to move through walls.

She kept sliding forward but turned her head back and forth, keeping sentry from all sides.

As she slid, her foot hit something, or rather, hit nothing. She bent down and put her hand where the wall should have been. Nothing. A hole, a crawl space really. Her eyes were focused at eye level, so she hadn't noticed the hallway was pockmarked with small crevices to crawl through.

"Shit," she whispered.

As the word left her mouth, something latched onto her hand.

She screamed.

It pulled her forward, banging her head into the wall. A sharp sting hit the meaty part of her hand between her thumb and forefinger as the creature bit into her.

She yanked her hand away and fell backwards as the thing slid out of the crawl space with unnatural ease, as if it had done so a hundred times. Even with limited sight, she recognized Bird Face.

He jumped on top of her and bit her, carving his teeth into the skin around her lower jaw.

With The White Wolf in control, Cassie gripped her weapon

tight. The stake penetrated Bird Face's neck so smoothly the tip came out the other side.

His eyes went dead. Before he fell off her, he coughed a spattering of blood on her face.

She ripped the stake out and let his body flop to the side. As she tried to sit up, something tackled her and held her down while something else grabbed her legs.

Hisses came from all around her. Lots of them. She recognized Nick. He tried to hold her arms in place, but Cassie proved too quick. The stake went into his chest once, twice, three times. She kept pounding it in, making sure it finished the job.

As Nick's dead weight landed on top of her, Allyson bit into her calf. She didn't have time to react before another vampire pulled her hair.

She took the stake out of Nick and drove it upward, hitting the unfamiliar vampire gripping a chunk of her hair right in the front of his neck. As she pulled it out, she brought it down on the top of Allyson's head. The stake went right through her skull. Pieces of brains oozed from the tip as she removed it. She stood up, covered in blood and unable to walk beyond a hobble thanks to the newly formed calf bite.

Two vampires stood on each side of her. The only one she knew was Fiona. John Adams was nowhere to be seen. The four remaining vampires circled her, one in front, one behind, and one to each side. North, East, South, and West.

Cassie turned her wrist, holding the spike of the stake out. She inhaled deeply and spun around. The stake drove through one neck, then the next. On the third, she had to stop her spin and correct her positioning. That one got the sharp end of the stick right in the temple instead. That left only North.

He pounced, jumping on her back and wrapping his hands around her torso.

She stabbed at his arms until he loosened his grip and they both fell backwards, Cassie landing on top of North. Staring up at the ceiling, she saw the source of the dripping sound. Mr. Renard hung from the ceiling, his stomach cut open. Jesus. They must have just done this; otherwise he would have bled dry by now. They did this for her. It was for show, more psychological warfare.

As Mr. Renard's dripping body took her focus, North bit into the back of her skull.

She pulled away from him, tired, losing blood, stung by too many wasps. He scratched at her, but she didn't change her speed, didn't care about a few more wounds. She faced him, staring, and his eyes widened with fear.

"The demon," he whispered. "I can see her."

"No," Cassie said. "You're seeing me." She slammed the stake into his eye. When she pulled it from his skull, the eye dropped to the floor. She stepped on it and drove the stake into North's chest. Hobbling forward, no longer keeping her back to the wall, she trekked down the hallway, confident no other vampires existed in the bunker outside of one. John Adams.

As if on cue, he stepped into the hall far down from where she was.

They stared at each other.

"Come now, Cassie. Let's finish this." He stepped away from where he had originally come, and a light clicked on.

Another room.

She stepped forward, her left leg dragging. Her eyes were swollen. Each bite throbbed. She was in no shape to fight, but The White Wolf would help. One way or the other, this ended now.

When she reached the room's threshold, she held the stake out, ready to stab.

John Adams dashed from her peripheral.

A sharp pain hit the side of her stomach before taking over her whole body. She fell over, convulsing. Every muscle in her body burned at once. An unbearable pain shot from head to toe, as if stabbed by a million pins. And then, emptiness. Complete emptiness.

She rolled over to see the live wire zapping, wriggling like a snake.

John Adams kicked it away from her, its job done.

The pain was worse than electrocution. It was something else, something familiar, but long since forgotten. She rolled to the other side and her heart sank.

A woman sat curled and naked on the floor, her silver hair spilling down her back. Slivers of smoke curled around her body, a scrim of grey like a thin protective shell.

Cassie knew immediately who it was.

The White Wolf.

John Adams had ripped The White Wolf from her body.

THE NIGHT CHRIS DIED

Chris cranked his music up, as he did most nights. He hoped it would signal Cassie to leave him alone. As much animosity as he had for her, he didn't want her to find him. His father wouldn't handle it much better, one more loss for the poor man, but at least his father had an adult mind. Cassie was too young, had been through the same horrors Chris had, and adding one more to the list felt cruel. But Chris couldn't keep going. He couldn't.

While Cassie buried her face in her schoolwork, Chris snuck upstairs and set up the rope, the chair, the table, all he would need to make it happen. As he mentally prepared, something flashed in the attic window. He squinted, trying to make it out.

A figure moved through the fog in the yard, coming through the thick mist and revealing itself.

Chris wept at the sight, something he'd heard about so many times, but had never seen. It was the thing which haunted his nightmares, the thing always there for a tragedy. The White Wolf. He knew his sister called the demon The White Wolf, but he hadn't imagined it actually looked like one. But there it was, a giant beast in snowy fur, waltzing through the yard.

Chris tightened the slipknot and pushed it, letting it swing wildly from the rafters. He crept down the stairs, sneaking past Cassie's bedroom, down another flight, and stopped at the back door. The White Wolf sat patiently on the lawn, waiting for his arrival.

He opened the door, and The White Wolf stared up at him.

Chris's heart pounded wildly. "What do you want?"

"Come sit with me before you go." The White Wolf shifted, as if making room for Chris.

Figuring he had nothing to lose, Chris obeyed the thing he hated most in life. As he sat, he said, "I thought we buried you."

"The part of me in Cassie is buried."

"So what part am I talking to?"

"The part in you."

Chris buried his face in his knees, tears flowing. "If you've been with me all this time, why haven't you helped me? Where have you been?"

"I'm not possessing you, Chris. Never was. I stayed with your mother when you were born and left with Cassie later. But I put a little piece of myself in you, just a piece."

This made Chris cry harder. He had hated The White Wolf for years, but maybe a part of him hated that he never had one, that yet another thing let him down. "Why didn't you choose me?"

"Choose. Not choose. Things are not so simple. Your mother still needed me when you were born. By staying with her, keeping her strong, I was choosing you."

"My mother didn't still need you when Cassie was born?"

"No."

"Why?"

"Because of you, Chris. You fixed your broken mother."

Chris listed his head, resting it on The White Wolf's furry neck.

He wasn't sure why he did it, but he needed to. "Is this the 'you have value' speech?"

"No."

"Then why are you here?"

"To tell you that I love you. You say I didn't choose you, but I did. I chose you when I made Cassie forget me, when I rearranged her memories to make them all about you. I tried to give you something, to help you. You didn't take it."

"So, this is my fault? Got it." Chris took his head away but didn't move otherwise, not yet willing to leave the conversation.

"Nothing is your fault, Chris. Nothing is anyone's fault. You suffer. I didn't help with that. But it doesn't matter. If your life was all roses, you'd still be here."

Chris sat back, letting his head land softly on the freshly mowed grass. He stared up at the stars. "Are you saying I'm destined to kill myself?"

"No, Chris. If I thought that, I wouldn't be here. You are, however, destined to be you. You have problems. I can't fix them. I'm a demon, not a therapist. But they can be fixed."

"Yeah, by who?" The sky seemed closer, not a faraway series of mysteries but a touchable, breathable universe, the lights to a festival, a home.

The White Wolf sighed. "I wish I was good at this. I don't have all the answers. Humanity's greatest strength is its ability to change, pivot, adapt, transform. Its greatest weakness is its inability to recognize that."

"What?"

"You all convince yourselves that you are what you are, unchangeable. You are clay to be molded repeatedly, yet you consistently opt to throw yourselves in the oven and call yourselves done. You can choose to go through with your plans for the evening, or you can wake up tomorrow and reshape yourself."

"I'll still be depressed."

"Yes, and you'll still suffer. You can change yourself, but you can't change what's broken, within you and without."

"So, we aren't so malleable after all."

"Suffering isn't so bad, Chris."

Chris laughed, a small smile stabbing through the surface. "How could you possibly say that?"

"A pearl comes from an oyster fixing a wound."

Chris laughed, a manic sound. "That's it? That's your big pitch? Oysters?"

The White Wolf turned her head, red eyes landing deep within Chris's soul. "Fine, Chris. How's this? A gravitational pull sucked in gases and solid matter, creating the world, an uninhabitable rock. An asteroid crashed into it, ricocheting debris, and creating the moon. It also tilted the axis of the Earth, but all this stupid rock had was carbon dioxide, methane, and water vapor. Any oxygen created from the vapor mixing with sunlight was quickly defeated by the methane and trapped into the Earth's crust. Yet, life formed regardless. Single-celled bacterium used the minerals at the bottom of the ocean to generate energy. Through this, cyanobacteria evolved. They used water as a source of power. How did they do this? They oxidized it. These little fucking things gave oxygen to the oceans, which eventually seeped into the air, overtaking the methane. We exist because of those cyanobacteria."

Chris sat up. "What's the point of this?"

"All of life is suffering, all of it is flaws. Being perfect, fitting the status quo, means never changing. It means no massive explosions that create a universe. It means no asteroids crashing in your mind to tilt your axis. It means losing the perfect conditions to grow life. Flaws, Chris. Life exists because of flaws, because of suffering. Because of pain and anger, and a deep desire to survive. Your genes are nothing without alleles. Mutations. Mistakes."

Chris put his hand up. "Okay, I get it."

"You were born with mistakes, Chris. And everyone around you is better for it. Unfortunately, one of your mistakes is an inability to see that. But there are doctors who can help you navigate it, to make you feel better. You don't have to suffer always."

Chris stood up, dusting his pants off. "I'm going to go inside now."

The White Wolf nodded.

"But thank you."

The White Wolf tilted his head. "For?"

"This conversation was probably the most alive I've felt in a long time."

As he opened the screen door, he stopped himself, turned back to The White Wolf, and chuckled.

"What's so funny?"

"I can't believe you're actually a fucking white wolf. I thought it was just something my sister called you."

The White Wolf smiled. "I am not. I thought it would be less distressing if I appeared this way, since it's how you knew me all these years."

Chris put his head down, staring at his feet. "Before I leave, can I see the real you?"

The White Wolf nodded. She transformed.

Chris wept.

"Are you afraid?" she asked.

Chris nodded. "Yes. It's beautiful."

He turned and went inside, snuck up to the attic, and wrapped the slipknot around his neck. The demon stared from the window, and while it was too far away, Chris thought he saw tears trailing down her inhuman and horrifying face.

CHAPTER 39
EVERYTHING ENDS EVENTUALLY

Cassie couldn't take her eyes off The White Wolf. As a child, the only friend she'd ever known was one she couldn't see, and here the woman was, separated from her. Completely ripped out of her. She felt like a carapace, a hollow shell, missing the inner part of herself, thin and fragile. And like a molting lobster, The White Wolf was most vulnerable without a hardened shell wrapped around her.

John Adams bent down, rubbing his hands on the various wounds on Cassie's body.

The White Wolf told her the demon could protect her DNA from the vampire's poison, but now that they were separated, she wondered how long she had before she turned.

"It'll be interesting to see if you die from these wounds before turning into one of us," John Adams said. He licked his lips. "Funny, don't you think? Your therapist spent years throwing chemicals in your face to find out how to bury the demon when all she had to do was give you a little electricity and she could have ripped the thing right out." He laughed at his own joke.

Cassie eyed the stake she'd dropped when the electricity hit.

John Adams caught her glance. He picked up the stake and snapped it in half before sliding it across the floor and away from her. "You're too weak to do anything now, but why risk it, am I right?"

Without the stake, she turned her attention toward the only other weapon she knew, The White Wolf. But her old friend hadn't shifted from the fetal position, facing away from both of them.

John Adams, once again, caught her stare. He smiled and stood up. "Oh, your little friend isn't going to be much help. She's nothing without a host." He kicked The White Wolf.

A horrendous squeal came from her as her lifeless body flopped over. For the first time, Cassie saw her face. It was almost alien. No nose, just two nostrils on a smooth surface. Her skin was yellow, taut, and plastic-like. Her mouth drooped down on one side and her eyes were uneven, one practically level with her nostril holes. This had lived inside her for her entire life.

At first, the sight was jarring, but not scary. It was like she had only seen herself in a grime-covered mirror and, for the first time, wiped the surface clean. Because the demon was her, and she was it. They were the same. The face she looked at was hers.

John Adams lifted The White Wolf by her hair, and the demon did nothing to fight back. He sniffed her hair. "Do you know why I'm so strong, Cassie, why I could endure your psychotic doctor's cruel trials? Because one hundred years ago, I bit into the flesh of a demon. His power kept me satiated all this time. Since you humans are so hellbent on destroying the world, and each other, I would love to have something that can keep me going for another hundred. Imagine the entire world up there, mine. All mine. All alone. You can relate to that, can't you, Cassie?" He dropped The White Wolf. "I feel attached to you. The time I spent hiding in the walls, reading all about you. The doctor was, if nothing else, an excellent note taker."

Cassie stared at her counterpart, unable to help. Even separated, they were one; their histories intertwined for better or worse. They'd done horrible things, things she couldn't ever pay the toll for, but if given the chance, she could have tamed it. No one had given her a chance to be anything else. And who was the world to judge? They'd gone and killed each other until nothing was left.

That was the great lie of childhood, to think that one day you'd grow into a role where no one controlled you, no one could rule over you. But that never ended. Someone always pressed their fingers down telling you to work harder, to sleep less, to be different. There was always someone to answer to, and the world squeezed that power so tightly it imploded. Exploded. Imploded and exploded. Humanity needed no demons to reveal its evil.

But Cassie *did* need the demon to act. Her whole life she hid behind a wall, afraid to put attention on herself, too nervous to stick up for herself. Even down here she only pushed back out of necessity.

The White Wolf always urged her to fight, and she'd let her down. One of her last words to Cassie before the necklace was, "You have you." And she'd ignored it.

No more.

No more.

Before she had time to act, John Adams cleared his throat. "Well, no more wasting time. It will be fun to see your face while I kill your friend. Oh, you'll want to kill me for it, but then you'll either die from your wounds or turn into my slave."

He lifted The White Wolf, the entity that once existed within Cassie that made her feel invincible, and he pulled.

The White Wolf's body split in two, ripping apart at the waist. Black blood poured from her.

"No!" Cassie screamed. The radio static in her brain disappeared. Even after having all memories of The White Wolf removed from her mind, a piece of her knew she was there, or that something was. A noise, a hum, the feeling of a gentle hand on her chest, something always remained. She'd lost The White Wolf as a child, and felt it, but now she knew what it truly felt like to lose the demon. It was a curtain closing in her brain, blacking out the world. It was a fist clenching her heart until it popped. It was a knife to the spine, rat poison in the blood, plastic wrap around her mouth and nose. It was total loss.

And now, she understood the ramifications of her actions, how Chris must have felt when she tore his best friend to shreds in the woods. How her father must have felt when her mother went to prison for life, a life that ended in suicide in her prison cell just a few months later. All of it Cassie's fault, and while she loved the people she'd hurt, she never loved them like *this*, because they never loved her like *this*.

John Adams hung the woman over his head and let the blood coat his face. He stuck his tongue out and drank the rain.

You have you.

You have you.

You have you.

And now, she understood why she never took the advice. She had her, sure. She could have defended herself, but it didn't matter if she *could*, she had never wanted to because a piece of herself had been removed. She never needed the strength to defend herself, she needed something to defend. They forced her to remove The White Wolf and then told her to love herself. They broke her. They stole from her. They forced her to be something other than who she was and then expected her to care. She did care. She cared about The White Wolf. What she needed all this time was something to defend. Something bigger than herself.

And now, she felt like fighting. Ignoring all the pain, the imminent death, she stood up, blood-soaked and hell-bent on revenge.

John Adams was too busy enjoying his shower of blood to notice.

She picked up the sizzling and snaking live wire and hobbled toward the vampire. Cassie realized as she walked why she had truly held back all these years. Because deep inside, she knew she had done awful things, been awful things, thought awful things, and she worried if she spoke up for herself, fought for herself, the villain would come out again. She'd hurt everyone she'd ever loved, and now she did nothing while the biggest part of her got ripped in half. Cassie was the villain, and for the first time, she embraced it.

As John Adams kept his face skyward, swallowing the drizzles of demon blood, Cassie shoved the live wire down his throat. He shot across the room, a spectacular display of pops and sparks coming from his mouth. The White Wolf's upper body dropped on top of her lower half.

Cassie hoped the electricity would provide her enough time to arm herself with the stake, but the vampire crashed into the wall and came right at her.

He pounced on top of her, pinning her to the floor. His smarmy charm wiped from his face, all he showed was violent intentions and rage. He spread his lips, revealing his black-soaked teeth, and brought his face down to hers.

"Hey!" Dr. Renard shouted from the doorway. She ran to them. On the way, she kicked the top portion of the stake toward Cassie.

John Adams stood, and with lightning speed, grabbed Dr. Renard by the throat and tore her head clean off her body. The woman's body dropped hard, and John Adams tossed her head behind him like it was nothing more than old gum. When he turned back to Cassie, she was standing and ready for him.

A small fragment of the stake went into his left eye. She hardly gripped the end where the wood splintered, but she used her forefingers to pull it out. As she drove it into his right eye, the left had already started the healing process.

She understood the value of the demon blood now, and wondered how much influence it had on her, too. When The White Wolf was locked away, Cassie was always in pain, but when she freed it from the necklace, her body felt good, strong, able to weather whatever came her way. She'd never experience that feeling again.

She clenched her teeth and stabbed John Adams in the neck, then the other side, then the front. When he fell over, clutching his injuries, she leaped on top of him and plunged the stake into his chest, right above his heart. She hoped it was enough to kill him because the stake took its final toll, too, breaking in the wall of the vampire's ribs.

Unwilling to presume, she crawled over to the top portion of the stake that sat on the floor near the door. She crawled back, and with the blunt end where it snapped, jammed it on top of the first stake, pushing it further into his chest.

John Adam's eyes and mouth opened wide. He gasped.

Cassie knew he'd die then, that soon, a geyser of blood would shoot from his throat, but she wasn't ready to accept that. She'd dealt with him for too long, and never got to return the favor.

He deserved torture, a lifetime of pain.

She wrapped her hand around the stake's blunt end and slammed her fist into his nose, his cheeks, his teeth.

His bones snapped, popped. Those violent, poisonous teeth cracked and fell down his airways. He gagged and choked, and she kept on smashing.

She'd never felt so free, so happy.

His face turned to mush at her doing, and she refused to stop. Crimson rain decorated the floors and walls, Cassie's face and clothes. Small bone fragments shot away from John's face. He screamed in pain, and the sound was beautiful, palpable. It echoed through the room, reminding Cassie of Chris's rap thumping through the hallways of her childhood home.

Eventually, he stopped screaming, and his blood did geyser from his throat, but she continued to slam until his skull was so broken and destroyed, the bottom of the stake clanked against the cement floor.

Cassie stood, winded and exhausted. Her heart banged, pleading. She was going to die now, or worse, turn into a vampire. She felt the poison flowing through her. It was powerful, but gross, as if it were turning her blood to swamp water.

She rejoiced at the horrid sight of John's dead body and mutilated face. A tinge of sadness crept up her spine for Dr. Renard. The poor woman had lost her husband and son and died trying to protect her old patient. Cassie hated her for so much, for the life the doctor forced upon her, for her experiments gone wrong that caused all of this, for never fully understanding the things she attempted to study. The doctor was flawed, but she had the best of intentions.

John Adams and Dr. Renard were the only bodies Cassie could assess. She refused to turn toward The White Wolf. She wanted nothing more than to fall on top of her felled friend, to say her last goodbyes before the hand of God dropped the final curtain on her life, to hug the corpse of the demon and thank her, tell her how much she loved her. But in the end, Cassie couldn't. Just as the cruelty of the fates didn't allow her to make John Adams suffer more, it also kept her from sharing her final thoughts with the only thing that ever truly knew her. She just wasn't strong enough in the end.

But there was one more thing to do before this all ended.

Just one more thing.

CHAPTER 40
A DAY IN THE SUN

CASSIE, AGE 4

Despite her parents swearing off the stroller six months ago, they lugged the thing out of the trunk and plopped Cassie into it. The sun-drenched the parking lot bringing blinding light and sweltering heat. Steam waved off the pavement.

Chris took his hat off and wiped his brow. "Maybe we should come back another day," he said.

His father huffed. "We've already driven all this way."

Cassie's mother pushed the stroller, and Cassie's father and brother flanked each side. The wheels made a satisfying rattle against the uneven cement. It nearly put Cassie to sleep and would have if the wheels didn't stop at a booth where a loud woman told them about how tickets to the dino exhibit were separate.

After her mother shuffled through her purse and gave the loud woman her plastic card, they were off and running in the park. After three exhibits, giraffes, elephants, and prairie dogs, Chris's complaining became a running theme. It was too hot for him and he wanted to make sure everyone knew that.

Her father relented and bought bottles of water for each of them, but Chris didn't even crack his open. He didn't want relief, he wanted to go home. Anything else was half-measures and he wouldn't stand for it.

Meanwhile, Cassie had her own complaints. "Mama, I want out." She kicked her feet until her mother relented, unbuckling her and putting her down. Cassie could tell by the way her mom folded up the stroller, all rough and fast, that Cassie had upset her, but she couldn't get a good view of the animals from inside the cart.

After everyone had some water, except for Chris who remained stubborn on the subject, they went into the Tropical America exhibit. Sloths sat lazily in trees, bats hung from branches in their glass enclosures, and snakes coiled around mini shrubs. The humidity tripled in the indoor exhibit, and Cassie noticed her brother's deepening breathing. She stared at him as his eyes rolled up and his body collapsed to the floor.

A flash of panic hit everyone around. Cassie's parents dove to the floor, surrounding Chris. Cassie's father poured water onto his son's lips, while her mother held his head up and yelled his name over and over.

Strangers began surrounding him, too, and medical personnel rolled in.

Cassie's pulse quickened at the sight of so many people. She hated large gatherings. While she waited for the action to settle, she wandered over to the sloths, passing a weird, lanky woman staring at the ceiling with sunglasses on.

The sloths were cute, and Cassie wondered why she'd never heard of them before. They looked like the kind of animal someone would keep as a pet. The silly voice came to her then. "Cassie. Go back to your family. Look at those sloths. They aren't going anywhere." Cassie giggled, but before she could take the voice's advice, her mother grabbed her shoulder and ushered her out the door.

She didn't know what was happening, but her mom was walking

fast, and she had trouble keeping up. They marched along the paths toward the Arctic exhibit, toward the zoo exit.

"I don't want to leave. Where's Chris?" she said.

"Hush."

Cassie's heart slammed on the brakes. That wasn't her mother's voice. She looked up and saw the strange woman with the glasses. The entire world froze, icing Cassie's body.

The voice inside her took control. "You made a mistake," it said to the woman and bit hard on her fingers.

The woman screamed and ripped his hand away, driblets of blood speckling the hot cement. "You fucking psycho."

Cassie smiled, and the voice spoke for her again. "Go tell the police how you tried to kidnap a child. Maybe explain to them how a four-year-old nearly ripped your fingers off."

The woman's eyes widened at the power within that voice. "I was just trying to help her," she said as she wrapped one hand around her bloody fingers.

"Sure you were, away from security and toward the exits."

The woman opened her mouth to argue but thought better of it and ran away.

Cassie looked around, alone. Suddenly, every human passing by was a potential threat, someone trying to steal her. The size of the zoo expanded and the vastness of it threatened to swallow her whole.

"Shhhhhh," the voice said to her beating heart. "I've got you. You are never alone."

Cassie wanted to believe her, but she didn't even know how to get back to her parents. What if they left without her? What if she never found her way home?

"Shhhhh," the voice said again. "Let me show you something."

Her feet stepped forward as if pulled like a marionette. She followed until they reached a fenced-in area of green lawn. A few groups of people were close to the fence, pointing at nothing, all waiting to find whatever lived inside.

After a few seconds, a large, white dog exited a small cavern. The people shouted, "There she is!" But the white dog ignored them. Instead, it headed right toward Cassie. It showed no signs of animosity.

"This is the white wolf," the voice said.

The white wolf came to the fence and stared at her.

She stepped forward, resting her head on the metal fence.

The white wolf stepped forward and put his forehead to hers.

People watching gasped.

"The white wolf runs in packs. When the alpha couple has babies, the entire pack works together to feed and protect the children. When the children are older, they protect the elderly wolves. It's a genuine community effort. The pack has one mission: protect the pack."

Cassie put her fingers to the fence, letting the white wolf's thick fur touch her fingertips. "I don't have a pack." She thought of her family, their complex dynamic. They loved her. They avoided her. They fed her. They never played. They kissed her good night. They walked around her.

"You have me. I am your pack."

The white wolf licked the fence, her wet tongue slopping on Cassie's skin.

"Will you play with me?"

"Forever."

"Will you be my friend?"

"Always."

"Will you save me?"

"With my life."

"Can I call you The White Wolf?"

"As if it were my name."

Cassie leaned away from the fence, and the white wolf turned back to his cavern. "Does that mean I will also save you when you get old?"

The voice laughed. "I do not get old, but trust me, you save me every day."

"How?"

"By being you."

Cassie's nerves settled. In the distance, her mother and father shouted her name, panic in their voices.

"We should get back to them now, my little Cassiopeia."

Cassie laughed. "I like that name."

CHAPTER 41
LAST WOMAN ON EARTH

"*One day you will take your throne as queen of the world.*"

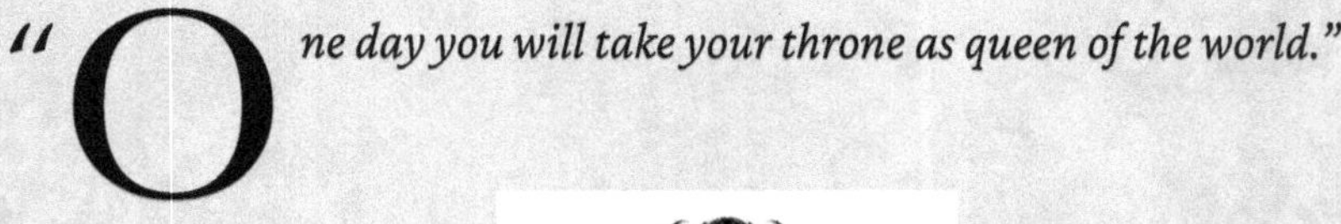

Cassie walked to the doorway, turned, and examined the carnage. Blood soaked the floor, decorated the walls, coated her face and clothes. She promised herself she'd be the last one standing in the bunker, and there she was, living her legacy. If only she'd known that would mean the death of her only friend, that she would have to watch a piece of herself be shredded in half. She still couldn't look that way, couldn't see the remains of The White Wolf.

She turned and walked down the hall, past the pile of dead vampires. More of her legacy. She walked through the room where Dr. Renard unleashed her memories and broke free her past. From there, she hobbled down the hall to where Spot lay dead with holes for eyes and a cavity in his chest.

Cassie's wounds throbbed, and the animalistic DNA of the vampires seared in her veins. She didn't have much longer.

She found her way to the tunnel where she had once been stuck, but on her return trip, she made it through just fine. Probably because she didn't care, wasn't riddled with tension anymore.

Back in the main bunker, she stopped at the bedroom, giving a moment of silence to James. Poor James.

In the main room, the theme from *Friends* played again. She couldn't remember if she left it on or if this was the last remainder of vampire torture, psychological warfare left on a loop.

When she opened the bulkhead, she squinted, unsure if she'd be met with blinding sunlight or the empty blackness of night. Instead, the world offered a low-hanging cloud of grey, a blizzard of ash flecks buzzing within.

Her heart shattered, and an audible disapproval left her mouth. Where once stood a house she envied, only razed earth remained.

Again, she was reminded of the great lie told to the youth, that one day they'd be in charge of themselves. We were all at the mercy of a few powerful men. Men with great weapons who hung bombs over our heads to keep us at heel. And even when we obeyed, they turned us to dust, just because they could.

She coughed as she crossed the wild abyss that once was a neighborhood, sucking in the chalky death. Which poison would win? The manmade one or the vampire one? She inhaled deeper, sucking in tendrils of war, coughing out charcoal mists. She marched on, waiting for, praying for death.

A twinge of sadness shot up her spine, a mourning of her own life. Maybe she, too, was like those powerful men, always concerned about herself above all else. But the sadness dissipated like the floating ash as she brushed it aside because Cassie had something most other people could only dream of. She had, for a short while, known herself fully, and what greater gift could life provide than that.

She inhaled another dose of airborne poison and stepped into a road. God, how her feet had grown to hate concrete. She laughed as she imagined a tractor-trailer breaking through the fog and crushing her body under its weight. How beautiful would that be? But no trailer would come because nothing was left. Nothing but her, queen of the world for another few minutes until the nuclear gases and world debris suffocated her.

She bent over and hacked up more black soot. *Let it come quickly*, she prayed. *Let it come quickly.* Let it win over the vampire poison. She fell to her knees and stared at the gray sky. Her heart skipped a beat. As more smoke entered her lungs, she felt herself dying, felt it deep within. She didn't fear it; not anymore.

As she finished another coughing fit, she whispered, "Are you ready?"

And then something grabbed her by the shoulder and dragged her backwards. As she was pulled, a voice whispered in her ear...

THE RESPONSE

"..."

"Not yet."

If you or someone you know is in crisis, please use the following resources:

988 - Suicide and Crisis Lifeline

1-800-273-8255 - National Suicide Prevention Lifeline

Text HOME to 741741 for Crisis Counseling

NOTES ON
BUNKER DOGS

In 2022, I had a group chat running with fellow authors, Megan Stockton, Jae Mazer, Josh Macmillan, and Peter Marsh. We formed our group with the purpose of critiquing each other's work, spit balling ideas, and talking shop about writing and publishing.

They were such a wellspring of creativity, and their brilliance rubbed off me. I came up with more ideas during that time than I could ever put down on paper. Some of those ideas I still have lingering on the back burner.

One day, I ran something by them. It was just a short story concept called, "Babysitting at the End of the World." The idea was simple, I would start the story by luring the reader into thinking they were getting a classic babysitter home invasion story, full tropes and all. But by the end, the unsuspecting reader would discover the people breaking in were military, and a massive world war was breaking out all around this random house.

At the end, our main character would discover the family had a small bunker in the yard, where she would run to safety, and the final scene would reveal some sort of creature in the bunker. It was a fun idea, and I'd get to explore some concepts I'd been thinking a lot about, that feeling of hopelessness as a single voice in a world gone violent, how out of our control it all is, and how, when the shit hits the fan, we might not ever learn what caused it.

The group loved the idea (and trust me, they told me when they didn't love an idea), but they uniformly insisted I write it into a novel. Megan especially rooted for me to take the short story and expand on it.

So, that's what I did. To test the material, I published it serially, releasing a chapter a week on the now defunct Kindle Vella. The thing about writing serially, especially when you're on a paid platform, is you don't have the breathing room a novel offers. You can't take your time, and you need to plan around mega cliffhangers and crazy hooks. This can lead to outrageous scenarios.

In that first edition of Bunker Dogs, The Renards were insanely evil, cruel, and just generally shitty people at all times. There was a school shooting at the beginning of the story when Cassie was in college. And James was a weirdo who always groped his babysitter. All of this served a purpose for the themes I wanted to explore, but it had a lot of problems. Some of it was too out of place, some of it too weird, and some of it too cartoonish.

One of the criticisms the book receives is that it has too many plots mashed into one, and that's true, but it's way less than it once had. I intentionally put a lot plots together into one story, and I stand by that decision. They fit, and they tell the story I wanted to tell, which is one of a woman who has all control stripped from her life. She doesn't have control of a world hellbent on setting itself on fire. She doesn't have control of the bunker. She didn't have control in her own home, and as it turns out, she didn't even have control in her own body and mind.

I've had people ask if the necklace is an analogy for modern medicine, and the answer to that is no. I wasn't trying to make any commentary on medicine or psychiatry. For me, the necklace explores the idea of recognizing the mental illnesses we have, and instead of looking at them as foreign entities we need to remove, to look at them as part of us, something we need to own and deal with.

The White Wolf is a little more than that. It's my anxiety and depression and OCD, sure, but it's also my survival instincts, my drug addiction, and most importantly, a little of my mom.

She was a poet in the 80s, and found some publishing success, but what she never found was an audience. Outside of a single poem that I STILL run into once in a while on a random card, or etched into something weird like a clock, you most likely wouldn't know her work.

She grew frustrated with publishing and quit not long after. On her good days, she encouraged me by saying things like, "One day, your books will be in bookstores too." And on bad days she'd beg me to never publish. She'd preach about how people were not to be trusted. And on really bad days, I'd find her in her basement office curled in a ball crying at nothing. Crying because she needed to. Crying because that's what bad days brought.

Every now and again, my mom would check herself into a place called Butler. It was a psychiatric hospital. We'd all go visit her, and it was always a rough experience. This wasn't the kind of horror hospital you see in movies. I distinctly remember a card table in the main room where we'd sit and play Go Fish. It was just a sad place. Roaming, deep melancholy pacing the halls.

Even though my mom always checked herself in voluntarily, each stay always ended with days of her crying that she wanted to come home but couldn't yet. She'd hug me tightly and tell me how much she missed me.

No one ever explained to me what was wrong with my mom, just that she was "sad" or "scared." It confused me because I was sad and scared, too. Would I need to stay away from my family? Would they not let me go home when I wanted to? One of my biggest fears as a child was that folks would come take me away from my parents for no reason at all. Not a kidnapping. Just a, "You can't be here anymore,"

When I was a kid, my mom and I were close, and we'd become close again when I was in my 20s. But as a teenager, our relationship was rockier as I began to discover drugs.

I had my own mental illnesses brewing at that point, but I didn't know what they were, or that they were even definable. I knew of OCD, but I thought it was a funny thing where people liked to clean a lot. That couldn't be me, because I was a fucking mess, and so was my bedroom. I had no idea that my absolute need to count my steps between sections, and my finger clicking, and the way I'd feel sick if I took different routes to get from place A to B, and my leaving the house patterns of clicking all the lights in the downstairs hall and living room on and off three times were part of something else.

And I had no idea the constant screaming in my head that at any minute everything was going to fall apart, or we were all going to die was not just some innate Gage-ism, but an actual symptom of mental illnesses that I could have been seeking help for.

But the drugs were good.

In my 20s, my parents got divorced and my mother, who at that point had severe agoraphobia, moved into a small second-story apartment where she relied on me to get her, well, everything. From groceries to cigarettes and alcohol.

We became close again, and she shared with me a lot of stuff about her history and my family that I just hadn't known. I learned about how many of those hospital visits came after suicide attempts. And I learned that as a child, to cope with stress, I used to lay on my bed while reciting lists, like naming the presidents in order.

Later, in my thirties, I became a stand-up comedian. I worked a day job as a manager for Hollywood video. My six-year relationship with my girlfriend came to an end at the same time Hollywood closed down, and I moved in with my mom temporarily while I attempted to get back on my feet. My alcoholism and addiction to pain pills were reaching new heights at that point, and one night, when I shouldn't have been behind a wheel, I drove into a pole and totaled my car. I promised myself I'd never drink and drive again, and for the next four or five years, I kept that promise by never buying a replacement car.

After the accident, I sat in my mom's bathroom, crying and thinking about how I could end it that night. My mother knocked on the door, and when I opened it, she took my hand and brought me to the couch. She knew what I was thinking and where I was mentally, probably because she'd been there herself so many times. But she didn't offer me any advice, or try to talk me down, or even give me platitudes. Instead, she just hugged me, and we cried together. When we were done, she said, "Are you ready?" And together we got up and went on living for a little while longer.

The "Are you ready?" line wasn't initially in Bunker Dogs. I added it later while writing the scene where Cassie finds the tapes of her mom crying about losing her White Wolf.

When I moved out of my mom's apartment, it was a short-lived exodus. A few months later, we found out she had cancer, and I was tasked with moving back in to take care of her in her final days. I'm writing a memoir about that time. Picture the tagline: "A stand-up comedian and alcoholic moves in with his mother to play caretaker in her final days. Wakka Wakka."

I was prepared for her to die, knew it was coming, but I was not prepared for how much the cancer would strip her of her dignity, and just how painful the last stretch of it would be.

She woke up in her final minutes of life and died with me propping her head up and talking her into letting go. I promised her she didn't have to worry about me anymore, and that I'd make her proud. For years after her death, those promises were lies.

In fact, the very next day, I won a comedy contest that pushed me into the finals of the Catch a New Rising Star Contest, and then I went home and took some of her liquid pain meds in hopes it would kill me quickly and painlessly. It didn't. When I woke up the next morning, I heard my mom's "Are you ready?"

I'd like to pretend that those three words carried me through and helped me clean up, but that's not how life works. I did hear those words often, but I stayed messed up for years after she died.

Still, there were moments where I needed a fierce survivalist monster inside my skull, and sometimes, on rare occasions, it came.

The White Wolf is a complicated creature, and we all have one inside of us. Sometimes it lashes out and hurts others, and sometimes it lashes out and hurts us, and sometimes it keeps us going when the idea of keeping going seems impossible. The White Wolf can be depression, and anxiety, and OCD, and it can also be this fiery beast inside of us that keeps us protecting ourselves. It's the words of those that cared about us enough to make us feel loved by someone, ANYONE, when we needed it most.

The White Wolf, for me, is often my mom. The good, the bad, and the ugly.

The title Bunker Dogs is not a reference to the creatures. It's not Rufus or Spot or John Adams, or even The White Wolf. The Bunker Dogs were Cassie and James. I'm a bunker dog. My mom was a bunker dog. A bunker dog is a cornered animal, someone who feels at odds with the world around it, and at odds with ourselves. A lot of us are bunker dogs.

And we're all just trying out best out here.

- Gage

Join my Patreon to get new writing, behind the scenes fun, and bonus content: www.patreon.com/gagegreenwood

And don't forget to sign up for my newsletter to get the latest news and updates! www.substack.com/@gagegreenwood

ON A CLEAR DAY, YOU CAN SEE
BLOCK ISLAND

GAGE GREENWOOD

FOREWORD BY JASON KUYKENDALL

When Gage approached me about doing a forward for one of his books, my fingers automatically crossed and I thought to myself "Please let it be On A Clear Day".

This happened for a few reasons.

The first is that I'm terrified to say anything about Bunker Dogs, as the fans of that book are...ahem...rabid, and I would not want to use the wrong word of praise and set myself up for slaughter (I'm looking at you, Alyssa).

The second is that In The Eyes is super depressing and I'm a terrible writer when I'm sobbing.

The third and main reason is that On A Clear Day is my absolute favorite of his works, and I've handed out copies of this book to my loved ones like ecstasy at a rave in the 90's.

In the world of horror, it's easy to place ones full attention on the antagonist, and relegate the rest of the characters to cardboard cut-outs created only to illicit cheers from the audience as the monster/killer slices and dices his way through them, but that's not the case here. Each one of these characters plays a vital role, each is fleshed out to realism, and each one will find their way into your heart for entirely different reasons. There were moments reading this that I forgot that I was reading a horror novel, and it did nothing to stifle my entertainment. To the contrary, when the creatures do begin to appear, it shocks that much harder, because as the reader, it's impossible not to be fully invested in the lives of these characters, and rooting for the absolute best outcome for everyone involved.

And those creatures...Jiminy Crickets...they are terrifying. I don't want to spoil anything for those experiencing this novel for the first time, but these things are absolute fear made flesh...and fang...and claw, and seem born entirely from nightmare. Aside from "cool creatures", we get cool creatures with a fantastic lore behind them, and they are as completely written and created as much as any other being in this book.

Which brings me to the final character, the unnamed, and possibly the most important.

Grief.

While comedy and tragedy have been strange bedfellows since the decades B.C., recently we've seen the fantastic results of combining fear with grief, real grief, the kind that burrows deep and never leaves, and there is no one that does sorrow like Gage Greenwood. The reasonings behind this is how real these experiences feel. This isn't someone with a plethora of positive experiences writing sad stuff because they want to. These are the words of a man that has experienced and survived his own struggles, and has used that pain to elevate his stories, to exorcise his demons with words on page, and to enlighten his readers of this darkness that lurks in the hearts of us all, as much as he entertains us with cool creatures and scary stories.

Gage Greenwood is not my favorite horror writer. He is my favorite writer. Reading his works takes me back to that place where I could get lost in a book, time slipping by unnoticed, telling myself "one more chapter" while knowing damn well that I'm not moving until it's finished because that's the only way to remove the hooks that his stories snag deep in my soul, despite the fact that as soon as

I finish one book, I start anticipating the next like a addict craving a fix. He was my Author of the Year last year, and I can promise that it won't be the last time. He sends me his ARCS with every release, and I still rush out to snag that physical copy on day one every time because his words NEED to be in my library. Anything he writes, I'll be there to read, and I promise you that if you read this book, you'll be right there beside me.

Buy the book. Get your tissues (not like that, you perv). Take the ride.

You might not believe me now, but you're about to read one of the greatest books ever written.

Long Live Vinx!!!

- Jason Kuykendall

CHAPTER 1

WELCOME HOME, YOU PAINS IN THE ASS

A new house meant new fun, and Jackson had high hopes for the game Brian invented. It wasn't very original, basically just a more complex version of Telephone. However, instead of children whispering to one another, this version took advantage of their new space and the massive number of rooms spread out along the upstairs hall.

One person, called "The Wordsmith," came up with a sentence. Jackson took that role, figuring the kids should get first shot at the actual game. He wrote his sentence down on a slip of paper and handed it to player one.

Charlie begged for that position. As the middle child, he'd grown comfortable staying away from the spotlight, fitting squarely between other shadows. The first player simply had to read the sentence out loud—in song form—to the next player. The catch? Each child stood in a different room. Thick walls separated the players, and those walls muffled the hell out of the song. A person could decipher the words if the speaker sang clearly, slowly, and distinctly. All hard things to accomplish for children between the ages of nine and seventeen.

Charlie slipped into the room farthest left. The bathroom. Once inside, the rest of the kids ran to their designated rooms for the game. Jackson sat on a ridiculously old chair, a gift that came with their new home, and a reminder of how out of his element he felt in his new standing. The chair's splat gave a slight creak as he leaned into it. He found the thing uncomfortable, a relic from a time when people enjoyed suffering for aesthetics.

He both loved and hated the house. Loved it because he could afford it. No more bunk beds for the kids, jockeying for the single bathroom, fighting over remote controls, punching elbows at the kitchen table. Finally, they could move about freely, go to their own worlds, and all it took was corporate negligence to the tune of ten million dollars. Sorry we killed your wife, bub, but hey, have some cash. He hated it for the gaudy style and cold openness. The creaky wooden floorboards and dank, dusty corners. And that it came at the price of his wife.

Status was ugly. Freedom had mold.

He sighed, leaned back, and crossed his legs. The fun part about the hallway gig was he could hear his children clearly. Somehow, the narrow corridor stole the sounds from all the rooms and carried them out like a loudspeaker. A trait he found convenient for a parent whose oldest children were bringing home dates and slinking them into their bedrooms under promises they were "just watching movies." Well, the kids now knew how much the sound carried, so they would probably keep themselves from any activities that might cause embarrassing noisemaking.

Charlie sang the sentence with the expected level of timidness, "Welcome home, you pains in the ass." Jackson chuckled to himself. He knew the kids would get a kick out of it, him not only allowing them a cuss word, but encouraging it.

Chrissy, nine years old and by far his most bizarre child, giggled as she listened to the sentence on her side of the wall. Her laugh made Jackson smile, so out of place for the quiet girl always face down in an Anne Rice book. Yes, she read Anne Rice books at nine years old. Lately, she'd taken to wearing puffy shirts, which to her meant vampire royalty, but to Jackson meant *Seinfeld* pirates.

Chrissy shuffled from one side of the room to the other and sang her song through the opposite wall. To Jackson's surprise, she nailed it. "Welcome home, you pains in the ass," she sang like a bard entertaining a royal court.

Next up was Brian, the inventor of the game. He turned fifteen two weeks ago, and his face showed the war signs of teen growth, riddled with acne scars and greasy mustache bristles. At school, he'd quieted, growing more aware of his looks and feeling embarrassed by them. Jackson knew this by the way his son sank within himself the second he exited their Prius and slowly walked to the building every morning. Here, at home, Brian played the opposite, speaking loudly and proudly, pushing himself into a leadership role only he took seriously.

His footsteps marched from one side of the room to the other, and he boomed his voice through the wall into the most contentious bedroom, "Welcome home, you pains in the ass."

Impressive, Jackson thought.

The fourth room down the line had caused quite the stir upon moving into the house. It lay directly in the middle of the hallway, which might have made the room the weakest if not for how large it was. Wreath claimed it first—and being the oldest, Jackson figured she deserved it—but Brian and Angela fought tooth and nail for it. Brian insisted he deserved it more because Wreath would move out too soon to take over any room. "She can handle a second-rate room for a year," he said. And he, being the next oldest, would still have a good three years to enjoy the comforts of the large room. Jackson considered it a fair argument. Wreath didn't. Instead, she stomped and screamed like one of the younger children.

Angela had no real argument, but at nine years old, thought saying, "I want it" repeatedly was a worthwhile counterpoint. Eventually, Jackson solved the fight by giving it to Wreath, promising

Brian he could move in the day Wreath left for college, and giving Angela a couple of peanut butter cups.

A part of Jackson appreciated the kids bickering over a room. It was a normal thing for kids to do, and since their mother died, normality wasn't part of their routine. Children react to grief differently than adults, ranging in a variety of emotions with no rhyme or reason. At Elaina's calling hours, the kids cried in the receiving line as a series of people hugged them and gave their condolences, but after the service, the kids ran around the funeral home playing tag. One minute, they were fine, thinking about school, toys, television shows, whatever, and the next, a switch would flip, and they'd explode with anger or sadness. Grief was a viral infection. It was as if someone injected them with extreme emotions by the syringe full, and it swam in their blood, pumped through their heart and brain, and coated their stomachs until they'd vomit it out, confused and scared by the sickness. They didn't know what was happening inside of them; they only knew it didn't feel good.

Since moving into the new house, Jackson had tried hard to make it their place, more than just a space he had moved them to. And that's why Brian's game excited him so much. It gave the kids an opportunity to forget everything else and enjoy each other, while also adapting to their new surroundings. Their siblings and the house layout all played together, working as a unified force to get the message sent.

Wreath didn't giggle at the sentence the way the other kids did. *Too cool*, Jackson thought. He listened as her gentle footsteps tapped from one side of the room toward the other, but they surprised him by stopping at the midway point. Silence. Jackson furrowed his brow.

Was Wreath ruining the game?

A sound, low and weak, came through the door. A soft croak, followed by a gurgling.

Jackson's heart lunged into his throat. He shot out of his seat and ran to the door, knocking and pushing to open it. "Wreath, are you okay?"

As a child, Wreath had suffered from epileptic seizures, but as she grew up, they became less and less frequent until they had all but disappeared. Jackson remembered the sounds, the horrifying groan and gurgle that Wreath would release.

"Wreath?" He slammed his shoulder into the hard wood, but unlike the splat of the chair, it gave nothing in return. "Wreath, honey, open the door."

The other children shuffled out of their rooms. Angela first, followed by Charlie and Chrissy.

"What's happening, Dad?" Charlie asked.

Fear took over the hallway. Brian finally joined them.

"Wreath, what's going on?" Jackson shouted.

The children talked over one another, trying to figure out the problem. Jackson hushed them. He leaned into the door, pressing his ear to the wood. Nothing. The gurgling had stopped. For a brief second, a wave of relief washed over Jackson, until he realized the silence was more disquieting than the noise.

"Wreath, open the door now."

"Dad?" Angela shook his pants leg.

"*Shhh*," he said, trying to pick up any sound from the room, waiting for some sign it was all a false alarm. Footsteps approached the door, coming closer to him. He moved his ear around, trying to get the best spot for hearing into the room over the loud cacophony of children's breathing.

Closer. Closer.

"Wreath, what are you doing? I can hear you walking." His pulse settled. If she walked, she was fine.

She breathed against the door, loud and harsh, as if she stuck her mouth against it flush and exhaled deep into the wood.

"This isn't funny. Open the door. You messed up the game."

The rest of the children froze outside of the occasional itch or twitch. The inability of a kid to stay in place.

"Open the fucking door, Wreath." He knocked hard once with his fist.

And then the blood rushed to his head in a crash, so rapid and unexpected, he nearly collapsed to the floor.

Not one voice, but two, one gruff and harsh like a tree branch cracking, and the other soft and feminine, but wholly unlike Wreath, said, "Welcome home."

The children screamed, and their high-pitched wailing made the horrific nature of what unfolded even more unnerving.

"What was that?" Charlie screeched.

"Dad!" Angela said.

Chrissy's eyes grew wide, and she backed up until her head hit the wall on the opposite side of the hall.

"Charlie, take your sisters downstairs. Brian, help me get this door open."

He slammed his shoulder into the door again, and Brian lifted his foot and kicked.

Charlie grabbed his sisters, but as he took Chrissy's hand, she yanked him closer to her instead of following him away.

"Chrissy, come on."

But she didn't move.

Jackson and Brian kicked and slammed. The door didn't budge, proving as stubborn as Chrissy.

The voices came again, saying, "Welcome home." No, not saying it. Singing it. Taunting the words in a sing-songy "nana nana poo-poo" way.

Then, an awful crunching. The horrid sound sent shivers down Jackson's spine.

"Welcome home." *Crunch*.

"Welcome home." *Crunch*.

"Welcome home." *Crunch*.

Brian kicked in rapid fire, and the wood cracked slightly. Jackson joined in with his foot until finally the wood around the doorknob splintered and gave way. It slid open with a whiny creak.

Jackson knew horror, had lived through plenty of it. He knew the feeling of leaving your body, seeing a tragedy unfold from way up high. When his mother shot herself in the head, he found her, not by entering the room as a small child, but overseeing from the ceiling with God's omniscient view. Of course, that wasn't right, but that's how it felt after the fact, how it played out in his memories.

When the children lost their mother, Jackson took the call and transferred the message to each of them. The factory burned down, midday. An accident. Jackson lost his wife, and five children lost their mother, simply because she worked at the wrong place at the wrong time.

When Jackson had taken the call from some middle manager of the company, he listened to the man's words as he floated through the future, an empty white space, futile to understand without Elaina in it. He saw nothing but emptiness.

Whenever tragedy struck, he floated. That's how a person survived real-life horror. They floated, feet peeling off the hardwood.

None of those horrors took him down, though, because they were real, and genuine horror happens every day. You can float away from it by moving forward.

What he saw when Wreath's door opened was different. It wasn't a real horror. It was fiction, and he wondered if something had broken so deeply inside him that his brain conjured it into existence.

How else could one explain a creature inhumanly tall, gaunt to the point of skeletal, with gray, leathery skin wrapped around its bones? What else but insanity could make sense of such a creature eating a teenage girl, crunching on bone, smiling as it sucked on sinew and meat?

Thin strips of mist spindled off the rug surrounding the creature like weeds.

Around Jackson, lost to the thrumming of his heart, his children screamed and panicked, grabbed him, pulled on him, begged him to explain what they were seeing. Some scattered down the stairs and out of the house.

But Jackson, he stayed perfectly still, hearing louder than the surrounding chaos, the blood coursing through his heart and head. Jackson froze. He didn't rush to save his daughter, didn't shuffle his family to safety. He stared, feet planted on the floor. No floating.

Because nothing made sense anymore. The most frightening thing to know. Nothing made sense anymore.

CHAPTER 2

AN ATLANTIC FOG

FOUR YEARS LATER

Charlie took his shoes and socks off and kicked them behind a large donation box. He stepped onto the sand, searching for a place to sit farthest from other people. The night had cleared out most beachgoers, leaving just a few couples and some obnoxious teenagers. An older couple walked holding hands on the shoreline, close enough for the surf to slip under their feet. Another couple sat on a beach blanket with two unleashed golden retrievers scuffling beside them. The teens sat around a small fire dug into the sand in a far corner of the beach, just before the private property line. They'd tucked their circle behind some dunes, hoping to avoid visibility, but they were impossible not to see. They were probably drinking and too stupid to know no one gave a shit.

Charlie found a place near the private property line on the opposite side from the teens, but the beach was so small he could nearly make out their conversations, anyway. He sat on his butt, knees up, and dug his heels into the gravelly sand, paying attention to the way the sand filtered between his toes, picturing the spaces between as little sandglasses.

The moon hovered over the silhouette of a water tower on his left, and the water lapped against the breachway on his right. Somewhere in between those two objects, shrouded by night and a low fog, was the island he lived on for two whopping months. Block Island. From the Charlestown beach, on a clear day, a person could make out the outlines of the island. It had two lighthouses on each side, two little thumbtacks. Charlie imagined plucking them and watching the island curl up into a scroll.

"Whatcha staring at?"

Charlie shot up straight. He turned his head slowly, trying to recover from the embarrassing jolt he had just made. Behind him, a girl his age stood with her arms crossed. Trouble, Charlie knew. She had short brown hair flowing just below her ears. Her lipstick was blue, and her eye shadow black. She wore a Gorilla Biscuits tee shirt, and her shorts were just a few threads more than a pair of underwear. He assessed her before responding, debating whether it was best to ignore her or to offer a short answer—whatever it took to avoid her calling her friends over for a round of humiliation.

"Well?" She put her hands out as if offering him help.

"Nothing," he unintentionally whispered, which he tried to correct by clearing his throat and trying again. "Nothing."

She tilted her head, stared for a beat, then sat down next to him. She wrapped her hands around her knees and gazed deeply into the ocean.

"What are you doing?" Charlie asked, still trying to figure her out. Obscure punk tee, sorority girl shorts, cutesy haircut, goth makeup.

"You seemed unwilling to give me answers, and I'm a curious type who can't accept not knowing. It's like a neurosis. I need to know what you were staring at."

"No, I mean, I'm really not staring at anything."

She shook her head but kept her eyes focused on the water.

"Unacceptable. Even if that was your goal. Your eyes focused on something, a wave, a rock jutting out, something. For the record, I understand why you didn't answer. Guy sitting alone sees a bunch of douches around a fire, and one of them comes over. Smells like the start of trouble. Totally get it."

The surf lapped. Every five seconds, another slurp hit the shore, and it dug into Charlie's skull as it disrupted this bizarre interaction he both hated and loved.

The rhythm of his heart lost its beat and doubled in speed, reminding him how much he disliked conversations, even good ones. He enjoyed people, their company, and hearing their thoughts, but the art of speaking, of knowing what to say and how to say it, what sounded sincere and what came across as sarcastic, all the navigational tools for speaking sent waves of anxiety deep within the pit of his belly.

"I was staring at Block Island."

She scrunched her forehead. "I can't see it."

"Me neither. I was trying to. There's too much fog."

"So, you came here at night to see Block Island? They have ferries that run like, all the time. You can just take one for a day trip."

"I've been there. But I wanted to see it tonight. It's hard to explain."

She brought her chin to her ribs and with a low growl, said, "Oh, come on, dude. Did you not listen to a thing I said? I need to know now. Tell me. I can't handle not knowing."

He wiped his hands down his face, pressing his palms deep against his skin. "I may not be someone you'll enjoy knowing, then. I'm not very expressive."

She frowned and stared at him. "Fair enough. Then let's be more superficial. You live in Charlestown or just visiting?"

He sighed. "I live about half an hour from here in Tanner's Switch."

She laughed. "No shit? Me too." She pointed to the kids at the fire. "We all do. You go to Tanner's Switch High School?"

He wiggled his toes under the sand, finding comfort in the sensory overload. "I will. First year. Can't wait to be the new kid. Wonder what I'll get mocked for. I'm weird, shy, mediocre at sports, oh, and I'm dirt poor."

A smile crept up one side of her face. "You're new to the area, huh? We're all weird, mediocre at sports, and oh, dirt fucking poor. It's Tanner's Switch. Not Newport. It's a shit town. We're like, last in every sport, so even the athletes suck at playing, and there's gotta be some shit in our drinking water because it's like the island of misfit toys in school. A bunch of fucking weirdos."

"I'll probably be the king weirdo."

She pointed both hands at her face. "Hello. Have you been listening to me? Is this conversation normal to you? Do I come across as the picture of normality?"

A tall dude, who Charlie noted looked very athletic, stood up by the fire and shouted, "Yo, Tiffany, are you gonna leave that dude alone or what?"

She waved him off and turned back to Charlie. "Don't worry, that's just my brother, so if you were interested in me, he's not my boyfriend. Your bigger problem if you're interested in me, will be that I'm a lesbian. Sorry to disappoint you."

Charlie broke the wall he had tried to build and let out a laugh.

"What's so funny? I wasn't kidding. I *am* a lesbian."

He couldn't hide the panic in his face. "No. No, not that. Your sexuality isn't a joke. That is not who I am. It's just, you talk in a funny way. I don't know how to do that."

"I knew you weren't mocking my sexuality, but I already enjoy making you uncomfortable, even though I hardly know you. What do you mean you 'don't know how to do that'? Do what?"

"Just say whatever you want. I can't do that. My brain needs to think things through, over and over, until the conversation has moved past whatever it was I was thinking about. Then, I just say nothing."

She tilted her head, and he had to admit to himself that he would have been interested. Very much so. "You seem to be talking just fine right now."

He put his head down. He couldn't explain himself, and he wanted to cry. "It's really hard."

She smiled and put her hand out. "I'm Tiffany."

Charlie shook her hand. "Charlie."

She stood up and dusted sand off her butt. "I hope it gets easier, Charlie, because I want to keep talking to you." She stepped back. "Until next time." She turned to walk away.

The farther she walked, the more his muscles loosened, and his fingers unclenched from his palms. *No*, he thought. *No. Don't take the easy way out.*

"Hey, Tiffany," he shouted.

She turned back to him.

"When I lived on Block Island, my sister died. Today's her birthday. That's why I wanted to see it tonight."

She bit her lip. "I hope you see what you need to bring you peace. I'm sorry for your loss."

As she walked back to the fire and her friends, Charlie considered what she had said. Of course, his decision to tell her the truth was far from it. She could never know why he was here, the ritual he had on Wreath's birthday.

First, the couples left. Then Tiffany waved goodbye to Charlie, and the teens were gone too. Once he was certain he had the beach to himself, he stood up, inhaled, and walked to the shoreline. The surf spewed past his feet, and Charlie stared down into the water. His fractured reflection stared back at him.

"I can't see Block Island tonight, but it's there. I don't need to see it to know it's real because I've seen it before. So, you can keep hiding, but it changes nothing. I know you're there. I know you're real. One day I'll find you. One day I'll fucking kill you for what you did to my family."

The water shrunk back into the ocean. Nothing happened. Nothing changed. Charlie walked back to his car alone, questioning his own words. Four years, and he'd never seen the monster again. He didn't even know if he believed his own memory. Detectives. The media. They all spent months drilling into the children, trying to dig up the truth, and maybe they were right not to believe the story. Maybe the entire family convinced themselves they saw something they couldn't explain because they didn't want to know the truth. Maybe Block Island itself was nothing more than a myth he'd created in his mind, and the fog protected him from the real memories.

CHAPTER 3
A TORN PAGE

Chrissy's back dug into the wrinkled, hard bark of the large oak in front of Tanner's Switch Middle and High School. Hastings kissed her, pressing her harder into the tree. His groin pushed forward, bumping into her stomach, and she fought back the desire to laugh because she wanted him to keep kissing.

The first day of school went well and making out with a dude in front of just about everyone, including some faculty members, would improve her status even further. Of course she wasn't using Hastings. She was into him and enjoyed the fooling around. But what really turned her on was knowing everyone else saw it and either revered her or reviled her for it.

A car horn honked, and Chrissy opened her eyes. Behind Hastings' stupidly perfect brown hair idled Charlie's beat-up Volvo 240, now more beige than white after years of neglect.

She pushed into Hastings' chest, and he slowly pulled away. "Gotta go. Brother's here."

"Okay, I'll text you later." He smiled at her, the geeky smile of a horny boy in love.

She nodded, picked up her book bag, and walked to the car. When she got in, Charlie was staring at her with a fatherly anxiety in his eyes.

"What?" she asked.

"What happened to you? You used to be a nerd, and now you're making out with dudes in front of the school."

She checked her hair in the passenger side mirror. "Still a nerd. Just a sexy one."

He stuck his tongue out and made a gagging noise. "Never use that word again. You're my sister, and you're fucking thirteen."

"Wah, wah." She dug into her bag and pulled out her book, now finely bent at the spine. As she peeled it open to its latest dog's ear, she put her feet on the dash.

Charlie sighed and set the car in motion. "So, how was your first day?"

"Good," she said, not looking up from the page.

"Don't get used to it."

Chrissy's eyelids drooped. "Yeah, Auntie will lose her job in six months, and we'll be off again."

"Hopefully not back to fucking Cranston."

Chrissy laughed. "Oh jeez. Yeah. Never again, please."

"And me?" Charlie said. "How was my first day? Well, thanks for asking. I skipped."

She dropped the book on her lap. "You skipped on the first day of a new year at a new school?"

He snapped his fingers and pointed at her. She rolled her eyes. "You're an idiot. Why?"

"I woke up. Ate breakfast. Took a shower. Ready to go. Then . . ." He made an explosion sound. "Panic attack. Big time."

She frowned. "I'm sorry. That sucks. You know, of all the places we've lived, this is my favorite so far."

He stopped at a red light. "You're making out with dudes on your first day. Not surprised you like it."

Chrissy laughed. She found a sick joy in being more successful with people than her brother. "Not because of that. And I didn't just meet him today, you know. We met like a month ago. We've been dating for two weeks. But I just like it in Tanner's Switch. The people are nicer here. More chill. And the history is all sorts of fucked-up."

Charlie nodded. "It is cool. Everything is old. Plus, even I made a friend."

Chrissy pointed in the opposite direction from where the car's blinker flashed. "Let's go that way. I hear they have a cool library. We should check it out."

"We've lived here for two months, and you haven't been to the library yet? That new boyfriend is destroying you." He switched the blinker in the opposite direction and turned the car.

They drove in silence for a few minutes after she dropped her head back into her book. She knew her brother relied on her for conversation, that she was the only person he could open up to. She was an outlet for him to vent to about his anxieties and thus eased his stress. But she also knew when to back off and let him slouch back into himself. This was one of those times.

He was taking them to a new place, and that meant a fresh level of fear boiling inside him, and any wrong move could topple him, forcing him to change course and take the safe route back home.

She flipped a page.

"What are you reading?" Charlie asked softly.

She eyed his hands on the wheel, the way he gripped it and shifted his fists as if he were revving a motorcycle. "It's called *Winterset Hollow*, and it's amazing. You can borrow it when I'm done."

"Is it horror? You know I can't read that. I don't know how you can."

She shrugged. "Some people lean into their trauma."

He grabbed an old napkin from the center console and threw it at her. "What thirteen-year-old talks like that? You're so fucking weird."

They pulled into the library parking lot and both Charlie and

Chrissy slowly tilted their heads upward, gawking at the towering gothic display.

"Jesus, this place is enormous," Charlie said.

Chrissy bit her bottom lip and released a giddy giggle. She gripped Charlie by the shoulders. "It's fucking heaven."

She jumped out of the car and skipped through the lot. Before she opened the front door, she turned back to her brother, who walked slowly, still staring at the large front façade. "I'll meet you by the front when I'm done."

He waved for her to go. "Just don't take forever."

She flew past the oval-shaped librarian's desk and searched the end caps for the horror aisles. She found a sign listing the genres by floor and realized she needed to take an elevator to get to her favorite section. While she wished horror was popular enough to demand a first-floor spot, the glee of knowing she stood in a library so massive it required elevators took over any disgruntled feeling toward a society that preferred romance to horror.

When she arrived on the third floor, she found the size of the horror section underwhelming, just one aisle long. Fantasy, which nestled in the aisles next to horror, had three long walkways all to itself. But what horror lacked in size, it made up for in substance, and Chrissy came to understand that someone who loved horror worked there. Had to. No library would order fantastic books like *BETA* by Sammy Scott, *Anathema* by Nick Roberts, and *Experimental Film* by Gemma Files without having an employee who knew, understood, and loved the genre. These weren't books that the mass public fed on, but the types that nurture a genuine sense of horror, feeding the diehards of literary trauma.

She flipped through a Bachman book and to her surprise, discovered the old, tattered thing had *Rage* in it. The book could score her about a hundred bucks or so on eBay if Chrissy had the desire to steal a library book. Luckily for Tanner's Switch Public Library, Chrissy had no interest in doing any such thing. She did, however, want to read it, so she curled the book into her arms and went thirsting for more. She found four books by Ketchum, which she thought impressive for a library, but she'd read all of them. Still, it made her happy to know they sat there waiting to be devoured by someone like her, someone who would find peace in violent words.

Horror wasn't a spotlight on evil, it was control. If a person could create beautiful sentences from horrific events, then any person could weave their way through life's trauma. You just had to make the grime shine.

And as if a spirit wanted to remind her that not all people handled the grime in the same way, she heard a gentle whimper in the aisle next to her. She didn't need to look, knew exactly who it was. Her brother found the horror section, knowing she'd be there, but didn't want to disturb or rush her. The building, being as large and cold as it was, had probably brought him a bout of anxiety and he wanted to be near her. It was sweet, she thought, and it filled her with pride that she could be her older brother's rock.

She noticed a book out of place and grabbed it on her way to her brother, feeling a compulsive need to fix the error. She crept around the corner and peeked at Charlie, who pretended to read a fresh copy of *The Color of Magic*.

"Never took you for a fantasy reader."

Charlie looked up, surprised, and tossed the book back on the shelf. "I'm not. You checking up on me?"

She shrugged.

"Thanks."

Chrissy grabbed the book she'd found in the wrong place and shoved it onto the shelf where it belonged. "I had to come over here anyway. Someone had put *Winter's Myths* in the horror section when it clearly belongs over here in fantasy."

Dissatisfied with collecting only one book, she debated asking for more time but saw the weary bags under her brother's eyes and wanted to bring him peace in the way he needed, which was to get him home where he could lock himself into syndicated sitcoms.

She gave him a nod and locked her arm around his. "You okay?"

He peered around, as if staring at looming ghosts only he could see. "I'll be fine. It just feels like a lot."

They took the elevator down to the front desk. Even the enclosed space smelled like old paper and dust, and Chrissy sniffed it in, soaking in the joy of it.

At the front desk, the librarians were chatting up a couple of elderly women about Broadway musicals, so Chrissy perused the new release stacks. A small section in front of it showcased books by local authors. She scanned past the Christa Carmen books, which she'd already read, and a book on the Richmond boat train accident. On the bottom shelf, she spied a book called *Langblasses and Other Block Island Lore* with a picture of a shadowy creature coming through a wooded area. The creature might have been her monster, but the artwork only gave outlines and shadows. With more detail, maybe the demon could have crawled off the cover and eaten her up. She itched to snatch the book but knew her brother would see it, and it would upset him.

She wished she could feel the same way, but she had no recollection of the monster that killed their sister. In fact, the entire night is one black stain in her memories, a torn page from her biography. She'd tried so many times to remember the events that haunted her siblings, wished she could truly feel their unrelenting fear, but all she could cling to from that night was that she had a sister named Wreath, and then she didn't.

As she and her brother made their way to the car, *The Bachman Books* in her grasp, she knew she'd have to sneak back here to get the Block Island book. If she was being honest with herself, maybe that was why she went from an Anne Rice fan to full-on horror obsessed. It wasn't a way to ease a trauma by leaning into it, but rather to jostle the trauma free, to find something so haunting in her books that it unleashed a chained-up memory of a monster, because the older she got, the more she questioned her family's collective memories.

The monster her family clung to didn't frighten her; the fact it might not be real did.

In one scenario, they had a night of insanity.

In the other, they've been insane ever since.

CHAPTER 4
THE BREAKFAST GUEST

Jackson woke from a deep slumber that blurred the lines of reality for a few moments upon awakening. A clinking came from the kitchen, as if silverware fell to the floor. He sat up, rubbed his eyes as the sun sliced through the blinds onto his face.

The clink came again, and paranoia splashed like cold water in Jackson's face. It wasn't a dream noise invading reality. It was a real noise waking him up.

His legs came off the bed, and he stumbled to his feet. He needed a screwdriver to take away the heart palpitations and chest tightness, but first he had to figure out what the fuck was happening in his kitchen.

He wondered if he had accidentally left the door open and let a raccoon rampage his cupboards. He wasn't worried about theft. No one was going to traverse his lawn filled with collected junk just to break into his shitty manufactured home and steal, what? His fine kitchen china?

When he crossed into the living room and saw the small portion of the kitchen counter next to the sink devoid of his dinner dishes, he knew who the intruder was.

As he crossed the threshold into the kitchen, he sighed. "You have to stop coming here, Charlie."

"No, I don't," Charlie said without looking up from the sink as he dutifully scrubbed a handful of forks and knives.

Jackson opened the fridge and took out a bottle of Smirnoff. He grabbed one of the freshly cleaned glasses and poured some.

"Jesus, Dad. Can you even pretend to try?"

Jackson swirled the glass as he went back in the fridge for a carton of orange juice. "What do you think is gonna happen, bud? You think I'm going to stop drinking today and magically become a wonderful dad again?"

Charlie laughed, slammed the faucet off, and turned to him. "You're delusional if you think you were ever a wonderful dad."

Jackson finished making his screwdriver and took a sip. The instant it hit his lips, his chest untightened. "Is that why you came here? Wanted to dig the knife in?"

Charlie sat down at the table and slid a plate of eggs over to his dad. "No, I came here to avoid going to school for the second day in a row. But are you really going to host a pity party here? You were a shitty dad, you're still a shitty dad, and you're probably going to be a shitty dad for a long time. Boo hoo. Cry about it, or ya know, just stop being a shitty dad."

Jackson took another swig and exhaled the detox away. "Chrissy told me you're quiet and get anxiety when you talk to people. Why can't you be like that when you're here? And by the way, go to fucking school. I'm still your dad."

Charlie forked some eggs onto his own plate. "I'm trying to work on my shyness. Congrats on being my test audience."

Jackson crossed his arms. He wished he had done better by them. He knew Charlie told the truth; Jackson had always sucked as a parent, but at least the kids used to know he cared about them.

"Why are you avoiding school, then? Do you need a lecture on avoidance from the alcoholic?"

Charlie smiled. "I'm gonna go. I just need to calm my nerves. I'll be a little late."

Jackson nodded, not wanting to press him anymore, allowing himself to be the cool person in Charlie's life who didn't make him feel guilty for being flawed. They sat in silence for a few minutes, both wolfing down the eggs.

"How's everyone doing?"

"The same as last time. Chrissy's good but getting a little promiscuous. Angela is still a little brat. No one talks to Brian anymore, but when we do, he's still the same asshole."

Jackson nodded. "I know they all think . . ." he trailed off, unwilling to finish the thought.

"No, they don't."

Jackson swallowed the rest of his drink. "You said it yourself months ago. Everyone doubts what happened."

Charlie stood up and tossed his backpack around his shoulders. "Yes, they do. We all doubt it, but no one thinks you did anything. No one. Not even Brian, and he fucking hates you more than he hates combing his stupid hair."

A wave of nausea crept up Jackson's belly. He rushed to the bathroom, clicked the light on, and tossed up his breakfast. Charlie walked in, opened the bathroom closet, and tossed his dad a hand towel.

"Don't you ever want better than this?"

Jackson took the towel and wiped his mouth. A rage soared through him, and he debated grabbing his son by the shoulders and throwing him out the window.

"Shut the fuck up, Charlie."

Charlie scoffed. "You're such a coward."

"Says the kid hiding in my house so he doesn't have to go to school."

"Well, it's been a pleasure, as always. I'll see you in a few days." Charlie walked out.

Jackson wished he had the courage to stop his son, to draw him in for a hug and tell him everything would be all right. But he knew he would keep drinking and nothing would ever change. He'd gone to therapy, taken medications at night to help him sleep, and different pills during the day to quell his anxiety, but nothing worked to dull his constant fear quite like alcohol.

It all seemed so impossible, and the anger increased at the unfairness of his situation. He charged to the door, and as Charlie walked head down to his car, Jackson yelled, "I don't care if you all doubt it. It happened. You can pretend it didn't, so you sleep better at night. But it happened."

Charlie lifted his head, turned around and walked back to the side steps where Jackson leaned out from the kitchen door. "It doesn't matter if it happened or not, Dad. We're all still alive, and the rest of us don't have the luxury of pretending that's not true."

"What do you want me to say? That you're all better than me?"

Charlie craned his neck to the sky, as if searching the clouds for answers. "I just want you to say you'll be better than *you*. Try, Dad. Just quit for a week. Clean your house. Have us over for dinner or games or something."

For a moment, he considered saying yes. The way Charlie laid it out, it sounded feasible, until Jackson remembered the nighttime, how every creak kept Jackson alert, how every kiss from the wind against the window slapped him from sleep. He remembered the countless nights tucked in a ball on his couch with the television playing reruns of *The Office*, and how his eyes fought against him, his body pleading for rest, but his brain saying, "Stay awake or it will kill you."

When Charlie was five, Jackson took the boys on a hike in the woods. Jackson led the trek while Brian and Charlie trailed behind. At one point, Jackson heard Brian yell, "Whoa," and by the time Jackson had turned around, Brian held Charlie and ran with him, a plume of bees surrounding them. Brian ran away from the danger with his little brother in his arms, and when they reached Jackson, he handed Charlie off. Jackson darted away with his son for about a half mile, with Brian keeping in step.

Charlie cried his eyes out, screaming that he didn't mean to do it. Jackson ripped Charlie's clothes off, searching for bees. A few flew out and went on their way.

Charlie screamed, "I can't let go! I can't let go."

Jackson noticed Charlie had a fist gripped around something. He gently pried his son's fingers open to find an acorn clutched so tightly it had broken the skin on Charlie's palm. The poor kid thought he held another bee.

When it ended, Jackson counted eleven stings, and Charlie cried for another hour, overwhelmed and scared to death of any further apocalyptic bug attacks. Brian avoided a single sting, and so did Jackson. Apparently, Charlie had stepped on a nest, and Brian ran *into* the bees to get his younger brother.

Jackson always assumed if he had noticed the situation when it happened, he would have run into a swarm of bees to save his son. Of course he would have, right? What father wouldn't?

But here he was with four children covered in bees, and he just wanted to close the door. A fucking coward through and through.

"I think it would be better if you just moved on, Charlie. Forget your dad and find happiness elsewhere. It won't happen here. I'm unchangeable."

Charlie stared for a moment, turned, and walked off. Jackson closed the door and locked it, went to the couch, and opened the shade. A blizzard of dust motes danced around his face as he watched Charlie drive off.

After his son drove out of view, Jackson walked to the fridge for another drink.

CHAPTER 5

CREEPING IN THE CORNERS

Angela sat at her desk with her legs folded, holding in her pee. It pressed on her stomach, and every movement threatened to open the floodgates. It made her sweat.

Why had this happened? As always, she'd avoided drinking anything before and during school, and she emptied her bladder before leaving the house. She hated school, and she especially hated this school, where the teachers talked super slow and placated even the most bizarre of disruptions with an even voice and a creepy smile.

They'd forced her to go to this shithole because the public schools said they didn't have the resources to care for her the way she needed. What they meant was, they didn't want their teachers getting punched and bit anymore.

Her leg shook, which increased her need to pee, but she couldn't stop it. It begged her to stand up and go go go.

But she couldn't. No friggin' way. If she went into the bathroom —those weird-ass school bathrooms with little to no light—she'd see *the thing*. It'd creep out from the corner and come at her, singing its stupid song, "Welcome home."

Fuck that. School wouldn't be over for another couple of hours, but the lunch bell would ring in twenty minutes, and the bathrooms would fill up with kids. She'd be good if other kids were in the room.

Twenty minutes.

Her hands trembled. It took a lot of work to hold in pee, and it didn't thrill her muscles. She brought her attention to the teacher. What subject were they discussing? Oh yeah, life as a colonist. Most of the other kids weren't listening either. They doodled in their notebooks or played with rubber bands or fiddled, fidgeted, stared blankly at the ceiling.

Nineteen minutes.

Why did she have to live this way? Tears formed in her eyes. Her life was a prison of her own design. Pee schedules, showering with the bathroom door open, sleeping in the living room with the television on, and the ceiling light. Her whole fucking day planned around not being alone in the dark.

And did anyone give a shit?

Nope. No one cared.

She wasn't even afraid of the monster. If she saw it in real life and not just some conjured projection in her head, she would stab the fucking thing in the eyeball. Unlike her father and Chrissy, who both just froze up and did absolutely nothing. And her dad continued to do nothing, stopped caring about how maybe that shit traumatized his children. Nope, all he cared about was himself. He gave away all their goddamned money to feel better or something, not thinking how it would affect his kids' lives and how they'd all be shoved into their aunt's apartment, moving every time the woman lost her job, and having to make peace with whatever new dive she moved them into. No matter where they moved, they were living off tuna sandwiches and peanut butter and fluff. Then, they all sat around talking in circles about how maybe the creature was a fever dream, a group projection to make sense of something they couldn't comprehend. Yeah, it was something they couldn't comprehend. A fucking monster. But Angela could comprehend it; because unlike those other morons who barely remembered what the thing looked like or blocked it out entirely like Chrissy, Angela still saw it all the fucking time, everywhere she looked. Even now, it hovered in the classroom corner staring at her with a grotesque grin. And did anyone try to find out how Angela was feeling and dealing with all of this? Nope. Brian was too busy moping in a mound of pills, Charlie sulking to himself about his lack of personality, Chrissy reading a stupid amount of books, and her dad drinking himself to hell. Where was Angela in all this? No one cared. All they cared about was how disruptive she was, and how she always whined and complained. Well, you fucking try living when every time the lights went out, a monster jumped in your fucking face, singing the same horrible song he sang when he chewed on your sister. You see if you turn out normal.

Fuck.

Fifteen minutes.

Fuck.

She openly cried now, cold tears rolling down her cheeks, but just like always, no one noticed.

The teacher, Mrs. Marcotte, a pleasant woman in her forties, droned on about fishing in Rhode Island during the colonial days. Jesus. Who cared? Cod. Mackerel. Herring. Angela hoped it was worth it, stupid colonists, because half the state lived off canned tuna sandwiches now. Economic growth. Everyone just drowned in work and died with no healthcare. Who gave a shit? Mackerel. What the fuck was mackerel, anyway? Did people eat that? Did McDonald's have a McMackerel?

Twelve minutes.

The monster hung in the corner, clung to the ceiling by its claws, hanging down, staring at her with an upside-down face and a crooked smile made of jagged teeth. With a class full of people, it'd stay there, wouldn't sing its stupid song, or crawl toward her. Just taunt her by existing, mocking her with its smiling face, the face of someone who always won, who owned her.

Eleven minutes.

She whimpered, just a small one, not enough to attract attention. But the pee that splashed down her leg and dripped against the linoleum floor attracted all the attention. Kids laughed. One girl screamed. How fucking dramatic. Like, did she really need to scream? The teacher ran over. The pee didn't stop. It wasn't a little making its way out, but the full bladder pouring down her leg, the seat, onto the floor.

Angela kept her head forward, refused to see the looks on the kids' faces. She bawled, embarrassed, angry—no furious, sad.

"What happened, Angela?" the teacher asked while bending down and rubbing Angela's shoulder.

Angela stayed the course, not moving her head, keeping her eyes directly on the chalkboard. "I'm fine. Just keep teaching."

"I can't do that. We have to clean this up. We'll send you to the office so you can call home."

The teacher stood straight and yelled, "Enough" to the laughing chorus.

"Mrs. Marcotte, seriously, I'm fine. Can you just keep teaching? I'll clean it up after." She sniffled and wiped the wet streaks on her cheeks.

"No, Angela. You need to go home. You can't wear those clothes all day. Okay, honey? You're not in trouble. We just gotta get you home and cleaned up. We can figure this out tomorrow."

Angela placed her hands over her face, as if she could disappear into the shadows of her palms. "Please, just keep teaching." The force of her hands muffled her words.

The teacher bent down. "Angela, honey. It's okay. Go to the office, tell them what happened, and just relax. Enjoy an early release."

Angela slapped her hands on the desk. "Please, just keep fucking teaching." The words left her throat like a bomb, and the explosion caused a thick quiet in the room.

For the first time at her special school, she made a teacher raise her voice, "Angela, go to the office now."

Angela slid her chair back, her sneaker sloshing in the puddle of piss. Her feet squeaked with each step as they left wet footprints on the linoleum. She slammed the door on her way out and ran down the dim hall. The monster darted right beside her. "Welcome home," it sang as her feet pitter-pattered down the empty corridor.

CHAPTER 6

CHRISSY, THE REBEL

Chrissy read some of the Bachman book on her lunch break. Hastings huffed while she read. It wasn't a possessive need for attention but an inability to enjoy silence and a good book. He needed to talk and to have others talk to him.

He tapped on the front of her book, bouncing it enough to make her eyes slip from their momentum. She slapped the pages shut. "You need to get a hobby so you can stop disrupting mine."

He tilted his head, trying to play cute. "I have a hobby, but they don't let me play baseball in the cafeteria."

She made a fart noise with her tongue.

"You told me you were reading adult books about vampires in like, fourth grade, right?"

"Yes, Anne Rice. I still read Anne Rice. You should too. But I do more than read books, you know? I watch a lot of YouTube! I'll sit there for hours watching Cahlaflour play horror games. She's probably the coolest person ever. And Katieplaysstuff is awesome too! But yes, I also love reading. You should give it a whirl."

He made a pouty face. "You know, I tried once. For you. Not Anne

310

Rice, but some other horror writer, and I just don't have the attention span. I end up reading the same line over and over because I get distracted, and my brain goes away to somewhere else."

"Porn?"

He laughed. "Probably. But seriously, how do you do it? Like, why did you even get into those books when you were a kid?"

"Long story."

He slid her book closer to him. "I want to know everything about you."

She sighed, reached over the table, and took her book back. "You'd have to understand my family. My mom was this super cool ex-cheerleader. Everyone loved her. Like, even years after high school. She had so many friends, and everyone loved her."

Hastings lifted his hands like he was an evenly balanced Lady Justice. "Okay?"

"My dad was always trying to get in on the fresh new thing. He couldn't hold down a job, so he went after every get-rich-quick scheme he could find. He'd get us kids excited when he ran in all, 'We are going to be millionaires!' But he just kept finding himself at the bottom of a new scam."

Hastings tapped the table. "I love you, but what's this got to do with reading?"

"My brothers and sisters were all the same way, always trying to be cool and in on the next big thing. Fighting for new video game systems we couldn't afford. Spending hours in the bathroom prettying themselves up, always trying to be cool. And it got them nowhere. My dad never found a steady, decent-paying job but lost us tons in shitty investments. My brothers were never cool, no matter how many brand-new video game systems they got. Wreath, well, she was beautiful and smart, but all she ever found were douchey dudes who used her. And my mom worked for almost no money, never happy, always broke and stressed, and she did that until it killed her."

Hastings leaned back in his chair as if those last words physically nailed him in the face. "Wow. I'm sorry."

"I saw all this as a kid. I knew when I was super young that the way they all lived wasn't worth it. One day my dad takes me to the library so he can check some shit out on the computer. I don't remember what, but probably some new MLM scam. So I'm walking through the aisles when I see this teenage girl sitting at a table reading an Anne Rice book. She was kind of ugly. Large, pimply-faced, hair all tangled. And these two bitches, clearly some girls she knew from school, they were just relentlessly mocking her."

She paused for a second, and Hastings lifted his eyebrows, very interested in the rest of the story.

"She didn't give a fuck. Didn't look up from her book. Didn't even show a change in her eyes or smile. You know how people do that when they're uncomfortable? They make weird-ass pretend smiles. She did nothing. She just licked her finger and flipped the page. That was the first time I'd ever seen someone not give a fuck about what other people thought. I decided I wanted to be that girl. I didn't want to give a fuck. When the two girls left, I went up to her and asked what she was reading and if she could tell me about it. She smiled and talked to me like I was smart enough to understand her. Which, like, nobody did back then. When you're a kid, it's like they just want to talk down to you."

Hastings smiled. "That's such a cool story. So this girl, she was a nerd, but she was also really cool?"

"That's how I saw it. I checked out my first Anne Rice book that night, and I didn't know how to read it or understand it. But when I got home, all my siblings busted my balls about it and talked shit, and that made me need to read it even more. The more people talked shit or mocked me, the more I leaned into it. I even bought shirts like Tom Cruise wore in *Interview with the Vampire*. Those stupid poofy shirts. I hated them, and everyone laughed at me when I wore them, so I kept wearing them. It was like I needed to prove to myself that I would do everything in my power to not care what people thought."

"That's so awesome."

She rolled her eyes and put her hands on top of his. "No. It wasn't. By actively trying to get people's attention, to make them not like me, it was the same as everyone in my family trying to get people to like them. We were all putting in the same effort toward something that didn't matter. If I really didn't give a shit what people thought about me, I wouldn't think about other people enough to try."

"Oh."

"But I read a lot of books and I learned a lot. Which led me to be introspective. So, at least I know that I have a weird, stupid desire to get people's attention by annoying them or pissing them off or grossing them out. Unlike the rest of my family, who refuse to change or even see the need for it, I can work on myself and be a better person."

Hastings gave up responding and reverted to head nodding instead.

"Anyway, I have to go." She stood up and yanked her book from Hastings' grasp.

"Where? We still have ten minutes of lunch before social studies."

"No, you do. I'm leaving for the day. I have something to do."

"What?"

"I need to get a book from the library."

He laughed, catching the attention of some girls sitting nearby. "You're cutting school to get a book? Only you. All right, let's do this." He stood up and crumbled his paper bag filled with an empty Hi-C container and a sandwich wrapper, then tossed it into a nearby container.

She opened her mouth to argue but decided she enjoyed having a boyfriend willing to face detention or suspension to cut school with her. Especially one who would do so just to hit up a library.

Leaving school turned out to be rather simple. They walked out the front door and hopped on the town bus. No sneaking necessary. It turned out people didn't give a shit if kids went to school in Tanner's Switch, apparently.

At the library, Chrissy went right to the front shelf where she'd seen the Block Island book, and luckily, there it stayed. No surprise. It's not like it was an Oprah's Book Club pick.

She dragged Hastings into the elevator, and he moved in for a make-out session, but while elevator kissing might be a kink for some, she preferred a crowd. She pushed him off her and giggled. He put his hands up, relenting. She liked that he never pressed, stopped the second she said to, and kept a smile on his face. No whining, no begging.

They rode to the fifth floor, all the way to the tippity top. The fifth floor housed a special selections room, an art room, and an auditorium. Why did they need an auditorium in Tanner's Switch? What big-named speaker would fill that room? Wouldn't someone noteworthy go to Providence or Boston? She shrugged. No matter.

Hastings gave her a kiss and promised to see her soon. He wanted to explore the other floors and leave her to her reading uninterrupted.

She peeled open the book and read the first chapter. She wanted to flip through, see if any of the stories had parallels to her own, but thought it best to respect the author enough to read a little of what he wrote. The first yarn talked about a fiery ghost ship phenomenon called the *Palatine* Light. Apparently, the residents of Block Island had a pirate streak in the 1700s and they lured the *Princess Augusta* to its demise before robbing the German immigrants aboard of their worldly possessions. The passengers bound for Philadelphia were killed, and according to the book, their spirits haunted the island. Many townspeople reportedly saw an apparition of the boat on fire during dark nights. Since the immigrants were Palatine Germans—natives of the Palatinate region—the *Princess Augusta* was described in documents of the time as the "*Palatine Ship,*" which caused confusion over its name and why the phenomenon was dubbed the *Palatine* Light.

She rolled her eyes. No one had ever mentioned any of that to her before, and she doubted many people who lived on the island even knew about it. This story mattered little to her and upended her search for answers to her own life, but something about the tale felt all wrong, and she wanted to know more.

She went to her favorite place for answers: Wikipedia. There she found a very different tale, stating that Block Islanders helped the *Princess Augusta*, and a few of the ship's passengers even ended up living there. Many of the immigrants aboard died on the ship from foul water.

The Wikipedia article also told a much more frightful tale about a woman named Mary Van Der Line who refused to deboard and went down with the ship. Those who claim to see the ghost ship also say they can hear her screams.

That sent a shiver down Chrissy's spine. After further reading, she discovered the boat never caught fire and most likely went through repairs before heading off to Philadelphia. So much for fiery ghost stories.

She slid the book away and dug deeper on the internet, searching for Mary Van Der Line. Unfortunately for her desire to find answers to her own life, she also loved a good rabbit hole.

Mary Van Der Line had limited hits on the good ole interweb, as Chrissy's dad called it, but she found a weird case study about someone with almost the same name. It didn't take long into reading it before Chrissy's heart thumped with a little more ferocity.

Mary Vanderline, a twenty-one-year-old woman on Block Island, suffered from seizures, but unlike normal seizures, these lasted for up to two hours. Somehow, her brain and, well, life remained unmarred. Hence, the medical miracle worthy of a case study.

This Mary Vanderline came from the 1970s, so not the same as the boat lady, but here's where it really sent Chrissy's adrenaline rushing. Mary Vanderline, while not suffering from massive brain damage from the seizures, hallucinated, claiming every time she had one of her episodes, a monster crawled closer to her, and eventually, she knew it would reach her.

Chrissy did a dance in her seat, unbalanced by the creeps worming up her back, the feeling that the monster was closing in on her as well. She looked behind her, giggling at herself for being such a geek. Two librarians chatted and rolled a cart filled with returns. No monsters, although one lady looked like the type who enjoyed yelling at children.

She took a breath and read more, hardly able to hold her composure as she reached the sentence about Mary's uncle claiming she had a seizure in the locked bathroom, then screamed about a monster. When her uncle crashed through the door, his niece was nowhere to be found.

Chrissy cried and shut the phone down. None of this jarred the images of the monster loose in her head, but the parallels were insane, and she couldn't wait to tell Charlie about it. Still, parallels did nothing to bring her clarity.

She sighed and headed for the elevator, carrying her Block Island book with her. The elevator dinged after the doors closed, and with a small bounce, she descended to the bottom floor.

The lights flickered and fizzled out.

"Welcome home." The echoes of memory played in her mind like an old cassette tape.

She startled and dropped her book. As she pressed her back against the wall and slid downward onto her butt, the sounds freshly excavated from her mind dug up more memories. The visuals stayed blurred outside of her mind's capabilities, but that voice—the choral quality of its speaking—it flooded in like a tsunami. A single voice split in two, one masculine and gruff, the other feminine and sing-songy, yet somehow, they were entwined, coming from the same cavernous throat.

The lights clicked back on, and Chrissy reached for her book, which lay splayed in the center of the floor. She gripped its center and turned it over, only to scream anew. A black-and-white picture looked back at her from the pages of her cheesy book of hauntings. A slender, gray face, as if it were smoke-worn wallpaper. Its eyes, swirling black pools. Its mouth, a swath of bladed teeth.

The monster.

Wreath's monster.

She remembered it now. Holy fuck, she remembered it now, and wished to the gods she'd never tried to unearth it. She stared at it, frozen just as she had been as a child. Her fingernails dug into her palm, her throat closed, and her muscles ached from temporary tetanus throughout her body.

Ding.

She jolted as the doors split apart. Hastings stood at the threshold, staring in shock at the sight of his girlfriend curled in the fetal position in the elevator's corner.

"What happened?" He ran to her, bent down, and rubbed her back.

She brushed his arm off her and stood, grabbing her book. "I need to check out this book and get the fuck out of here."

"Were you screaming?" He followed her to the front desk, where a few librarians stared with wide eyes and nervous grins.

Chrissy wiped the water from her eyes. "Nope. I'm fine. Just need to get home."

With trembling hands, she gave the book to the red-haired librarian.

Hastings rubbed her back again. "Are you sure you're okay?"

She pushed his hand off again. "I'd be fucking fine if you stopped touching me."

She regretted taking out her anxiety on him, and especially the way she yelled, causing all eyes to turn toward him. She'd villainized him to the crowd, and an embarrassed shade of red swam across his cheeks.

"Okay. I'll just head back to school." He walked out, head down, a defeated puppy.

"Do you need us to call someone?" the librarian asked, staring at Hastings as he walked out the door.

CHAPTER 7

PAREIDOLIA

Tiffany had told Charlie that Tanner's Switch was all misfits. At the time, it provided him zero relief, but as the bell rang, ending *his* first day at school, she may have been right. No one mocked him, no crazed bullies stood out as future threats. All in all, it was a perfectly fine day. Sure, he ate alone at lunch, no one really spoke to him all day, and he never ran into Tiffany—his only chance at a friend—but he also avoided punches, or even verbal assaults. A win's a win.

He hated conversation, anyway, so not making friends was A-OK by him.

As he stepped through the double doors, and the sunlight dropped on his face like a hammer, his day of no talking ended abruptly. A muscular hand slapped his back and gripped his shoulder.

"What's up, buddy?"

He turned to find Tiffany's older brother smiling at him.

"You're the kid from the beach, right?" the guy asked.

Charlie nodded his head. "Yeah, you're Tiffany's brother?"

He held out his beefy paw. "Yup. Doug. What's your name?"

319

"Hey, Doug. I'm ah, Charlie."

They shook hands.

"You're new to Tanner's Switch, right?"

Charlie nodded. "Yeah. Tiffany is the first person I've ever talked to here. I was hoping to see her today, but I guess she's not in any of my classes."

Doug shot him a stern eye. "Why, you don't like her, do you?"

"Oh, no. I just, ah—" He shrugged, hoping that would settle it. But when Doug kept staring, waiting for his reply, he sighed and continued, "I just don't have any friends. Ya know?"

Doug clapped. "Well, it's good you don't like her. She's a lesbian. Not interested in you, okay, pal? So don't try anything."

Charlie put his hands up. "I promise."

"Anyway, me and some friends are about to head to the management area for some beers. You want to join us? Tiff is gonna be there."

Charlie shook his head. "No. I would, but I gotta get home. I have some stuff to do."

Doug frowned. "Okay, well, if you change your mind, that's where we'll be until it gets dark." He walked away and high-fived some other massive human male.

Charlie's eyes watered. The strain of keeping up a conversation with someone so vastly different from him flooded him in anxiety. His heart raced, and he worried at the straps on his book bag.

Part of him wanted to go. So rarely did he make friends, and Doug's offer seemed genuine enough. In the back of Charlie's mind, he wondered if it was a prank. Drag the new kid into the woods and beat him up a little, let him know not to fuck with Doug's sister. Or maybe something less sinister but equally awful, like a hazing ritual. Welcome to the club. You just have to down ten beers and swim across the bay.

He opened his phone and headed toward his car. Twelve text messages. All but two texts were from his aunt, ranting about Angela getting into trouble at school and needing Charlie to pick her up. The last two were from Chrissy rambling about how she needed to speak to him immediately and wanting to know if he could give her a ride home, but she wasn't at school, she was at the fucking library.

He put the phone back in his pocket and rubbed his eyes. Why did everything fall into his lap? Why did people assume Charlie would be the one to fix everything? He couldn't even take care of himself, yet he was supposed to pick everyone else up when they dropped the ball.

He typed a few replies but deleted what he wrote, never quite landing on what he should say. Finally, he responded to his aunt and to Chrissy: *No.*

He put the phone away and chased after Doug. "Hey, hold on. I want to come with you."

The hangout session in the woods wasn't a prank or a hazing ritual. It was, in fact, just a few dudes hanging out along a cut path while drinking beers and telling raunchy jokes. It was so mundane, Charlie almost wished he had just picked up his sisters.

Charlie had drunk beer before when he visited Brian at college, which was probably a dumb decision, knowing how his father turned out, but he'd only ever sipped on it. He started that way with Doug and his friends, too, but after a little while, he matched the sip frequency of the other guys as if they were practicing for a synchronized drinking tournament.

Two or three beers in, his head swam, and his voice slurred, something he recognized because the other symptom the beer provided was a new ability to speak freely, his nerves destroyed by tinny tasting cheap-ass medicine.

Tiffany showed up around half an hour after the boys started drinking. She had a friend with her, or maybe a girlfriend. They weren't holding hands or acting cuddly, but the closeness between them was apparent in the way they giggled with one another. The special bond between two people who knew each other so well, they could laugh at nothing and know the shared punchline.

"Charlie?" she asked at the sight of him.

He crossed his legs and bowed with his arm across his chest. "The one and only."

Had he truly just done that? Jesus. Yeah, the beer opened him up, but it also turned him into a king idiot. No one laughed at him, though. Not even Doug and his Neanderthal friends. In fact, the guys had shown nothing but kindness the entire time, laughing at Charlie's jokes and making him feel like one of the gang. Of course, he didn't tell the kind of jokes he normally enjoyed, shooting more for Brian's crasser humor, but whatever. He told them well enough to get big guffaws from a group he never suspected would enjoy his company.

Tiffany hugged him. "How did you get here?"

He took a swig. "Doug invited me."

Doug smiled. "Sorry, Tiff. I stole your friend. He's my friend now."

Tiffany tilted her head and gave him a wide-eyed stare. "You can only be friends with one of us. Choose wisely."

Charlie stumbled back, exaggerating his surprise. He pointed to Doug's friend, Corey. "I choose Corey. He brought the beer."

Corey ran up to him and slapped him on the shoulder. "Good choice!"

Tiffany sighed. "Boys. So easy to please. He didn't even bring good beer. If you're going to pimp yourself out for alcohol, at least choose someone who brings something stronger than water."

Corey whispered to Charlie, but loud enough for everyone to hear, "Tiff's just jealous because my girlfriend is hotter than hers."

The new girl slapped him. "Hey!"

So, yeah, the new girl was Tiffany's girlfriend.

Charlie put his hand out awkwardly. "I'm Charlie."

She shook it. "Beth. And I am way hotter than Corey's girlfriend, who, by the way, is a literal golden retriever."

Everyone laughed, and while Charlie didn't get the joke, he joined in and found it genuine.

Tiffany turned to Doug. "Are we going to the boats?"

Doug shrugged. "Sure. Let's go."

"Where?" Charlie asked.

Doug picked up the last case of beer with full cans in it. "*We* are going to the boats, but you and Corey can go somewhere else, you goddamn traitor."

They marched on an offshoot path, cut and worn from use, but thin and unmarked. Branches and vines stretched over the route, slapping against Charlie's legs and chest as the group trudged through.

At the end of the trail, an enormous stone the size of a truck jutted off the land and hovered over the edges of a lake. The sun shined on the water, and a fractured line of light stretched from one side of the lake to the rock.

Tiffany kicked off her sneakers and rolled up her pants before sitting on the ledge, letting her feet dip into the water.

Charlie cracked another beer and took a long pull. His brain turned from swimming to drowning in seconds, an analogy he didn't enjoy making so close to the water. Maybe this was where his new friends would turn on him. If he proved himself a lightweight, the new fish showing blood to a pool of sharks, he could lose them quickly.

He tried not to speak, containing the deepening slur in his speech to the depths of his throat. As the group goofed off on the rock, drinking, laughing, shoving each other, Charlie sat on the edge, staring into the water. Every few minutes, he'd catch himself swaying left and right in rhythm with the gentle sloshing of water against the stone.

While the rest of the group focused on a thumb wrestling match between Corey and Beth, Tiffany stayed on the edge of the rock next to Charlie, splashing water with her feet.

He pulled his hands away from his cheeks and asked, "Swearza boats?"

"Huh?" She giggled.

"The boats. You said boats." He put his head back down.

"The rocks. There's a few more around the lake. We call them our boats. We aren't stupid enough to go in the water when we drink. It's just our dumb name for them out here."

His brain didn't comprehend what she meant. He stared into the lapping green water, too sludgy to see more than some floating particles. He blurred his eyes as he focused on his reflection, waiting for the corrupted image to grow a smile too large for his cheeks, a shadow of the monster, the broken bits of its structure releasing from Charlie's memory into a crude pareidolia from hell.

It never came, though. In fact, he couldn't pull even a distorted version of the monster into his mind, let alone into a visual projection.

Not only had the alcohol loosened his tongue, but it had freed him of the creature. His pulse didn't drumroll, his palms didn't sweat, and his heart kept a steady thrum.

Maybe he understood his father after all. No. The difference between Jackson and Charlie was the responsibility. Jackson had children who needed him, who had been through the same horrific event and needed an adult hand to guide them through it. He failed them. Charlie had no responsibilities. He could get drunk and forget the monster, and it changed nothing. No one looked up to him. No one cared about Charlie.

He remembered his phone, which sat in the pocket of his backpack, which sat in the back seat of Doug's Camry. Angela, ignored, left to handle her own trauma with no one protecting her. Chrissy, who texted and asked for his help. Maybe he had responsibilities and people who needed him after all.

But for right now, Charlie couldn't stand, and for once, he enjoyed only caring about himself.

"Let's go," Doug said.

Charlie leaned back until his head rested on the stone. "You shouldn't drive drunk."

Doug laughed. "Beth's driving us all home. She didn't drink."

Charlie squinted his eyes toward the sky. "I think I'm just going to rest here for the night."

Doug scooped Charlie up like a baby and placed him on his feet. When Charlie leaned, Doug caught him and put his arm around Charlie's back. "Come on, kid. You can do it."

Why weren't they laughing at him?

"Why are you guys so nice to me?"

That made them laugh. He picked up Tiffany's chuckle above all else.

Doug slapped his shoulder. "Welcome to Tanner's Switch. We take care of each other. It's fucking weird here."

"It's very bizarre," Charlie said, although he knew the words came out jumbled.

"Well, I also slipped a bunch of drugs into your beer, so we can take you to the hotel and steal your organs."

The group laughed again.

"You're joking with me. I think."

"You'll see."

The trip back felt quicker than the trek into the woods. They were at the car in no time. Doug grabbed Charlie's backpack and tossed it to him. As promised, Beth drove everyone home, and Charlie wondered how Doug would get his Camry back, but he was too tired to ask. Instead, he leaned his head against the back seat window and fell asleep.

He woke up with the car parked in front of his house and Tiffany shaking his knee from the front seat. His eyelids pulled apart, and he took a deep breath.

"Go eat some food to soak up the alcohol." She smiled at him.

He nodded and opened the car door. The first step was shaky, but after he took a few more, he regained his walking skills.

Before he opened the front door of his aunt's house, he turned back to the car. "How'd you know where I lived?"

Tiffany leaned over Beth and yelled, "We used your face to unlock your phone and checked your PayPal account for a mailing address. Also, I bought some new shoes."

Charlie smiled. "At least you didn't take my organs."

"Lift your shirt," she said as she flopped back into her seat.

He peeled his tee shirt up to reveal a series of crudely drawn stitches made with black marker. He laughed.

"See ya," Tiffany said and waved goodbye as they drove off.

He waved to nothing. "See ya."

He turned and opened the door as everyone inside welcomed him with a chorus of yelling.

CHAPTER 8
MOVING ON

Angela sat at the kitchen table with her arms crossed. In the reflection on the fridge, she saw her distorted face, red and streaked with tears. Auntie Clara yelled at Charlie for not picking Chrissy or Angela up from school, but she more yelled *at* Charlie *for* Angela. Auntie *C* had worn herself out hollering at Angela, frustrated at how skilled Angela was at turning into a hollow void when someone screamed at her.

Of course, like always, no one gave Angela the chance to speak her truth. No one cared what it felt like to pee yourself in front of your class, only to spend the rest of the day in the nurse's office with wet pants because not a single person in your family wanted to pick you up. Angela wasn't a human in the family. She was a chore.

Chrissy, too, yelled at Charlie for not picking her up, but unlike with Angela, Auntie Clara gave her space to speak.

Charlie smiled a little. It looked insulting, but Angela knew him enough to understand it was just a nervous thing. His eyes were bloodshot, and he kept leaning into the door frame. Maybe Auntie Clara didn't want to come to terms with it because she didn't bring up the obvious fact that Charlie was drunk or stoned. Even Angela could see that.

Charlie just stood and took it. He didn't argue, just kept repeating his life's mantra, "I'm sorry. I'm sorry."

When the whole thing blew over, everyone stormed to their rooms, leaving Angela alone in the kitchen. The lights were on, at least.

Auntie watched something in her room. Angela could tell by the annoying laugh track echoing through the hall. Chrissy probably read a book because her room went quiet. Charlie played music in his room. Trampled by Turtles, Angela thought. She picked all this up from the kitchen table by staring down the slender hallway, bedrooms flanking each side. At the very end of the hall, staring at her with its half-opened maw, stood the dark bathroom.

The noise coming from the other rooms helped ease her anxiety a little, making her feel less alone, more protected, as if noise created a natural barrier from the bizarre and ethereal.

She ate alone. A packet of ramen noodles and a cut-up hot dog. She wondered if Charlie had dinner, or Chrissy for that matter. Auntie *C* probably ate something at work. She usually did or ate fast food in the parking lot of the Mickey D's, unwilling to bring it home out of shame. A two-dollar cheeseburger, too much of a luxury to flaunt in front of children.

Angela gulped her meal down, eyeing the bathroom the whole time. When she finished, she planned to hit the couch in the living room to watch something but caught Chrissy sneaking from her room to Charlie's. Assuming a fight lingered on the horizon, Angela slunk down the hall for a little snooping. Her Auntie had fallen asleep with the television on, which relieved Angela. One less person to catch her spying.

She crept to the threshold of Charlie's room and leaned against the wood-paneled wall. It bowed from her weight.

"I'm sorry I didn't pick you up. I just . . ." He said something else, but Angela lost it while focusing on leaning in enough to see them without them seeing her.

Charlie sat on his bed, head resting on the wall facing away from his door. Chrissy sat on the edge of the bed, facing Charlie, but with a slight shift of her eyes, she could probably catch Angela in the act.

"It's fine. I was annoyed, but I'm over it. I'm too fucked up about my day to stress about it. I just need to talk to you."

"Okay."

"Are you drunk?"

"Is that what you want to talk about? I won't become Dad. I promise."

Chrissy waved her hands. "No. No. I know you won't. That's not it. I just have something kind of big."

Charlie sat up. "Oh, no. You're not pregnant, are you?"

"What? No. You *must* be drunk to ask that."

He laughed. "No. I drank, and it turns out I'm a huge lightweight, but I feel fine now. Funny, I figured I would have puked, but I feel good."

Angela shifted forward and gave a quick glance toward the half-open bathroom door before returning to the conversation in Charlie's room.

"I'm proud of you for having fun."

"So, what do you got?"

Chrissy lifted a book and showed him the cover. Charlie flopped back down dramatically.

"Please tell me you don't want to talk about that. You're never going to get me into horror."

"No. No. Listen. I did some research today."

Chrissy droned on about her research, boring stuff about pirates and boats burning and blah blah blah.

Angela couldn't see Charlie's eyes, but she could feel them rolling back into his brain.

When Chrissy brought up the woman with the seizures, Charlie sat up, and Angela nearly fell over. When she continued about the woman seeing a monster and disappearing in her bathroom, Angela held back tears. Charlie, however, did something unexpected.

"Okay?"

"What do you mean, 'Okay?'"

"I mean, yeah, you found an urban legend with some similarities."

Chrissy pushed her head forward, as if her neck were trying to remove it from her body. "Are you kidding me? First, it wasn't an urban legend. It came from a fucking medical report. Second, it's not similarities, it's damn near identical."

Angela's jaw dropped. Charlie had always been a steadfast believer, eager to find any proof of the monster, and now Chrissy presented him with a very similar case, and he shrugged it off. It made no sense.

"But that's not even it," Chrissy said. She slid the book to Charlie. "Flip to the page I dog-eared."

He did and within a second, he dropped the book to the floor. "Jesus fucking Christ."

"Right?"

The book landed with its cover up, and despite that, Angela leaned forward as if she could magically see through it.

Charlie's fingers trembled, and he tapped them on his knees. "I think we should just let it go."

Chrissy's jaw dropped. "You've got to be kidding me. You make friends for one day, and suddenly you're all about moving past this? This is everything we've been looking for. It's validation."

Charlie sat upright, turning his body into an *L*. "We don't need validation. Our worth isn't tied to the fucking monster. We just keep giving it power by caring. We should just move on from it."

Chrissy shook her head as if trying to rattle those words right out of her brain. "You're kidding me. Are you serious?"

A rage built inside Angela, boiling from her gut and spewing from her mouth. She charged into the room, all caution lost. "Move on? Move on?"

She came to the bed and shoved Charlie. "My whole life. It's always there. Always."

"Were you spying on us?" Charlie asked.

Chrissy still had her jaw dropped, and she glanced between Charlie and Angela.

"Fuck you. Yes. I was spying on you turning into a coward. You always talk so much shit about killing that monster if you ever saw it, and it's all bullshit. She finally found something worth looking into, and you turn into a wimp."

"Get out of my room."

Chrissy jumped in. "Hey, she's right."

"No. She isn't, and neither are you. What did we find out? That someone had a seizure on Block Island and saw a monster? Great, let's just go to Block Island and give ourselves seizures. Sound good? You found out nothing. Okay? I hope your little stories make you feel better, but they do nothing to help us. What do we do with that information?"

Chrissy stood and picked up the book. "The story with the picture talks about people on the island seeing the monster on foggy nights. They call them Langblasses. The painting of it in the book came from an artist who lives on the island. We can start by going to talk to her."

Charlie shook his head. "This isn't a movie. We aren't *The Goonies*. I'm not going on an adventure with you to lure out a monster that ate our fucking sister. What the hell are you and I going to do? Go to this lady's house and say, 'Ah, that monster you drew ate our sister. Can we ask you some questions?' Do you not remember what we went through? The police and detectives, and having to give our story over and over, and the newspapers, and the mocking. All the bullshit. Why would we ever go back to that island? Did you honestly think you would show me that book, and we'd just go back?"

"And me," Angela said. "I'm going too."

They both turned to her and in unison said, "No."

She stomped her foot. "You guys don't get to be the only people affected by this. I'm going with you."

They both yelled at her at the same time. She couldn't understand them when they spoke together. A mishmash of obnoxiousness. "You're too young. You're a pain in the ass. We don't want anything to happen to you. You shouldn't have been spying."

They wouldn't stop, and she couldn't get a word in, as always. So, she reverted to the only thing that eased her frustration when she had words to speak but no one to speak them to. She screamed. She screamed like an ignored teapot. Charlie covered his ears and yelled at her to leave the room. Chrissy frowned, and she tilted her head.

Auntie *C* ran in, her eyes bloodshot and drowning in black pools. She grabbed Angela by the arm and dragged her out of the room. As Auntie *C* pulled her down the hall to the living room, Angela turned around to see the monster peeking from the half-opened bathroom door with a smile on its face.

CHAPTER 9
A DOZEN WASPS STINGING

Charlie sat in the back seat of Doug's Camry, his body bouncing from the pockmarked dirt road. Tiffany sat in the passenger seat, fiddling with her phone's music app, which she had synced to Doug's stereo. Her tastes were eclectic, but no matter the genre, all the songs had one thing in common: upbeat. Charlie preferred music that sent him spiraling into a moody pool of existential dread, but to each their own.

Right now, he surely wasn't in the mood for cheerful tunes. While Tiffany and Doug sang along to "Sound System" by Operation Ivy, Charlie fumed over his sisters, who had berated him all morning about the monster.

He spent years in a cycle of depression, paranoia, and desperation because of that one night. He clung to it, needing it, despite its poisonous bite. In that way, he hadn't differed from his alcoholic father. He'd refused to give up on something he knew was killing him.

He wasn't a hero for thinking about the monster all the time. It didn't bring his sister back or glue his family into one happy piece. All he'd done was sulk deeper into his shell, and in reality, that probably only hurt his family. If he'd moved on, he could have guided them to do the same.

No good could come from going to Block Island. Most likely, they'd be chasing ghosts, resulting in nothing other than more pieces that didn't fit together. Or worse, they could find their way to the monster, and then what? Get eaten too? How the fuck could they stop a monster that eats humans and then vanishes into nothing?

"Charlie?"

Tiffany's voice snapped him out of his sulk.

"Yeah."

"Were you listening? Doug wants to hit up the ice cream shop in Watch Hill, hobnob with the wealthy in their salmon-colored beach slacks."

"Sounds fancy. I'm in." Funny how it only took one day of hanging with these two for him to gain enough confidence to converse with them. He still felt awkward and anxious, but he could do it. He could do it.

They pulled into the bustling parking lot. It was filled with an eclectic mix of people. Rich older men, some indeed in salmon-colored slacks, which Tiffany, Doug, and Charlie got a good giggle out of. Some girls Charlie had to pry his eyes away from. Lots of young kids too.

A group of guys in their early twenties walked by Doug's Camry, and Charlie's heart rose in tempo, forewarning his fight-or-flight response. Trouble. The dudes wore dirty clothes. A few of them had jeans covered in paint and grime. One of them wore khakis two sizes too big without a belt, and he had to keep pulling them up as he walked. They all had beards and long hair.

Doug and Tiffany, less worried than Charlie, hopped out of the car while the guys were hanging in front of it. Charlie sighed and joined his friends.

As he moved around the car, he tucked his arms in, working to avoid any unnecessary confrontation. The guys weren't doing anything wrong, but the way they shifted their eyes and constantly wiped their noses put Charlie on high alert.

Turns out they smelled like shit too.

He let the air out of his chest as he passed them. Tiffany skipped as she walked, and Charlie turned his focus on her. What was it about her that put him at ease?

One guy said to his buddies, "We should head to Providence. I don't want to be here all day."

Charlie's legs turned to jelly. His eyes filled with water. He'd been right about that group. They were trouble. Every instinct told him to keep moving, but the stupid part of him that believed in unbreakable bonds and other fairy tales forced him to turn around.

He whispered, "Brian?"

The group of guys turned to him, and the one with the khakis too big smiled. His teeth were beady, yellowed things, half dead like the body they clung to. "Charlie?"

Brian pushed his friend out of the way and hugged his brother. Charlie hadn't expected the kindness. Brian was more of the arm punch and wisecrack kind of guy, but here he was, hugging his brother as if he just got back from a long stint in the military.

Brian, of course, wasn't in the military. He had no discipline.

Charlie hadn't thought about the embarrassment of introducing his brother to his new friends, but it hit him now. He'd eventually have to explain to two siblings who were best friends how *his* brother was a meth head piece of shit.

Brian let go. His eyes were watering too. "I miss you, brother."

Charlie stepped back, examining Brian. His skeletal frame, the gray bags under his eyes, long, yellowed fingernails, and dirty clumped hair came together as if Brian were attempting to *become* the monster.

He wanted to say he missed Brian, too, but his throat filled with chalk powder, and all he could muster was, "Hey."

"Let's go for a walk?" Brian asked.

Charlie turned to his friends, unable to hide the sadness on his face. "You guys go without me. I'll meet you back here soon."

Tiffany's smile melted away, and her eyebrows drooped with worry. "Are you okay?"

Charlie nodded. "Yeah, this is my brother, Brian. We haven't seen each other in a while."

Doug nodded. "I'll buy you a cup of banana ice cream because that's just randomly what I expect you to like."

Charlie shrugged, not in the mood for jokes. "Sounds good."

Brian guided Charlie through his group of friends, who all stayed in place chatting. Each one of them looked punch-worthy, and Charlie hated knowing his brother associated with them.

They walked to a concrete ledge overlooking the ocean. Boats lined the docks around the wall, bobbing gently with the lapping water. Charlie and Brian leaned against a metal rail, the salty air blowing against their faces with the cool ocean breeze.

"What have you been up to, Charlie boy?" Brian smiled.

This newfound kindness in his brother made the deathly pallor on his face even more horrific. If only his brother were still an asshole, maybe Charlie wouldn't have to mourn another sibling.

"I've been good. Made some friends." He pointed toward the corner of the shops where Tiffany and Doug had disappeared.

"Yeah, that's awesome. Is that chick your girl? She was hot."

"No. Just a friend."

"How's Chrissy and Angela? I miss them."

Charlie nodded. "They're great. Chrissy has a boyfriend. Still reads nonstop. Angela's having a tough time. Dad's still the same."

Brian jerked his head away, toward the ocean, as if the very mention of their father was a fist to the mouth. "Fuck Dad. I'm glad Chrissy's doing well. She was always the better one of us. No offense. She's just, you know."

Charlie nodded again. "Yeah, she has a gift. She's special. No offense taken. I agree. You should come by while you're here." Charlie regretted inviting him instantly. Brian wouldn't come, never had before. In fact, the only time Charlie had seen Brian since he moved away to college was when Charlie visited Brian's dorm, long before Brian dropped out. Whenever Brian called, Charlie vomited out an invitation, like he was begging his brother to come home. Charlie always told himself he'd stop trying, but every time, he always said the same thing.

"Yeah, that's a good idea. Maybe I'll swing by tonight. I just have some business to handle in Providence. Me and my boys are working on something. I can't say what it is, but let's just say if you think Dad was rich after Mom died, this is going to put that to shame."

There were two constants in every conversation with Brian. The first was a half-hearted acceptance of an invitation. The second was talk of a secret plan he worked on to make everyone rich. To his credit, whenever he spoke about getting rich, he always brought the siblings up, as if his fortune would be theirs as well. Chrissy assumed the get-rich-quick schemes were drug-related, but Charlie suspected not. Brian was big into art and film. At least he was before the drugs splintered his mind. Charlie thought Brian believed he could walk up to a guy who knew a guy and pitch his movie idea, and just like that, he'd have studios throwing cash at him.

"That sounds great. I hope it works out. I could use a newer car." Charlie wished he could slap his brother and say, "Snap the fuck out of it. How many times are you going to do the same thing before you realize it's never going to work out for you? Clean the fuck up." But Charlie wasn't that kind of person. He placated to avoid confrontation.

Brian scratched his ghostly white arm, and thin layers of skin flaked off like ash. "Yeah, maybe I'll stop by after my meeting. Could be good. I'd like to see everyone. You all treating Auntie well?"

"Yeah, to be honest, we all hardly see her. She's working so much, ya know? Always working. She flipped out on us last night, though."

Brian reached into his pocket and pulled out a pack of cigarettes. As he took one out, he looked at Charlie. "Want one?"

Charlie shrugged. "Sure."

Brian's eyes widened. "You smoke now?"

"No, but it's a good time to start." He took the cigarette.

Brian lit Charlie's and his own. Charlie took half-inhales, not wanting to cough like a geek. He'd been around cigarette smoke enough, with his dad and his aunt, that he thought he could manage without a hacking fit.

"So, what's going on? You look stressed. You're smoking. Auntie's yelling at you all. What's up?"

"You don't want to know."

Brian raised an eyebrow like the Rock used to do when he wrestled. "Yes, I do."

"Trust me, you don't."

Brian exhaled a stream of gray smoke from his nostrils. "Dude, I'm a shitty brother who abandoned you all like Dad did. Let me feel like I can help. Talk to me."

Charlie put his head down and inhaled a small sliver of smoke. It felt good, the way it bit at his lungs, a dozen wasps stinging. "Chrissy found a book about Block Island, and it has a picture of the monster in it. Our monster."

Brian jerked back. "You mean it looks like our monster? Our monster looks a lot like horror movie creatures, dude. It could just be a similarity."

"Yeah, no. This was our monster to a tee. Chrissy has this entire plan. She wants us to talk to the artist who drew the monster. Blah blah. I told her to stop, to just forget about it. Our lives would be easier if we just stopped."

Brian rubbed his forehead. "What the fuck is wrong with you?"

"What?"

"Our lives would be easier if we just stopped? This wasn't a bad day, Charlie. A fucking—" He paused, looking around at the faces turning toward him as his voice rose. He leaned in and went back to whispering, "A goddamn monster ate our fucking sister. We were all kids, but Chrissy and Angela were super little. They can't just move on from that."

He leaned back and took a pull from his smoke. "Look, you're not wrong. It would be better if we all could just move on. But we can't, and they especially can't. Poor Angela probably can't close her eyes without seeing the fucking thing. Hell, I can't. Take them to Block Island. It won't result in anything. The monster won't come back because you talked to some chick who paints pictures. But it *will* make them feel better. Their father failed them. I failed them. You're their only hope."

He stood up and dropped his butt. His foot mashed it onto the pavement. "You're a good kid, Charlie. Tomorrow is the weekend. Get on the 12:30 p.m. ferry and go to Block Island. Get a ticket for me too. I'll meet you guys at the docks." He handed Charlie a wad of cash.

Charlie didn't count it in front of him, but he could see it was enough to pay for all their tickets. Brian's clothes told Charlie his brother wasn't rolling in dough, so if he handed over a stack of cash to solidify a promise, it felt like gold in Charlie's hand.

"Are you serious?"

Brian smiled and walked away.

Charlie stayed on the concrete wall for a while, holding in the scream he wanted to unleash.

CHAPTER 10

THE EXCLUSIVE CLUB

anks pulled in front of a large white house. Brian couldn't tell what glowed brighter, the lights coming from the windows or the unnatural green of the lawn. He never understood why anyone rich would choose to live in Providence, even in the nice Blackwood neighborhood. The dude who owned the place probably owned twelve other houses, and Brian idolized the guy for a multitude of reasons, but Brian still thought him a sucker for spending millions on what looked like nothing more than a nice suburban house with neighbors so close you could pop open the window and toss them a bag of sugar from kitchen to kitchen.

It didn't matter. Banks didn't drive him here to assess the man's real estate. Brian reached into his pocket and pulled out a bottle of pills. Prescribed. He popped one and swallowed it dry. Hopefully his nerves would temper before the meeting began.

Banks had dropped their friends off on Thayer Street so they could get a bite to eat, and he and Brian could attend the meeting alone. Technically, Banks shouldn't bring anyone along for this kind of deal, but he'd already bargained for Brian to be there.

They walked up to the door, and a large man in a Hawaiian shirt opened it before they could even knock. He tipped his head, indicating they should come in, but he stopped them at the entrance and frisked them good, with an extra special focus on Brian. The man made him strip to his underwear, patted him down, and even checked under his ball sack. When he finished, he made Brian bend over and spread his ass cheeks. Humiliating sure, but worth it if the meeting went well.

Hawaiian Shirt Guy escorted them to the living room, where a balding, middle-aged man with chubby, red cheeks sat on a leather couch, glasses scooted down his nose as he penciled in an answer on a crossword puzzle. Brian couldn't believe how close he stood to someone he worshipped.

The room was beautiful. Leather chairs to match the couch, bright paintings framed on the walls, a shiny piano in the corner.

Banks stood by the chair but didn't sit, so Brian followed his lead, standing behind his friend. Brian had never done one of these meetings before and didn't want to make some minor mistake that could blow the entire thing. Banks was a professional.

The man finally looked up from his crossword and tossed the paper down next to him. "Kevin Banks. Have a seat, old friend," he said. His voice was a tinge whiny. He looked more like a middle manager than one of the largest drug dealers in New England. Nothing like how he appeared in interviews on television.

Banks sat on a leather chair facing the couch. Another chair waited for Brian right next to Banks, but he still didn't want to sit until given permission.

The man stood up, giving Brian a full appraisal. "You must be Brian. I'm—"

"—Caleb Jones. I-I-I know, sir. I'm a big fan." Brian put his hand out.

Mr. Jones shook it and smiled. "Well then, have a seat." He waved his hand toward the empty chair.

As Brian sat, Banks said, "Brian's a genius. You know I'd never bring someone to one of our meetings if I didn't think it would bring you value."

Mr. Jones grinned and sat back down. He put his hands behind his head and crossed his legs. "Before we get into your friend's pitch, I just want to clarify our deal. Ten percent comes off and all I have to do is listen to his pitch. Just listen. I make no guarantees I'll sign off on anything. Correct?"

Banks nodded. "That's right. I know you'll sign off when you hear his plan."

Mr. Jones clicked his tongue. "We'll see about that. And as for the rest, I'm paying half in cash, half in Oxys?"

Banks nodded again. "Yup. Works for me."

Mr. Jones inhaled deep. "All right then. Why don't you go do the exchange with Walter, and I'll have a nice one-on-one with your friend."

Banks hopped up and walked over to Hawaiian Shirt Guy who waited by the door. The man grabbed Banks by the arm and led him out of the room. Now that Brian sat alone with Mr. Jones, knowing he was about to deliver his pitch, his heart slammed into his ribs. This was it. His last hope.

"Well, let's hear it." Mr. Jones sat forward, grabbed a glass of water from the coffee table, sipped it, and placed it back on the coaster.

Brian's mouth turned to cotton. "Well, sir, as I said, I'm a big fan of yours. I was watching a show one day a few weeks back, and they had on a list of the best horror movie scenes of all time. And of course, a couple of your movies were on there, like *We Are All Dead, Anyway*, and the original version of *Bunker Dogs,* before they rebooted it with Kevin Bacon as the White Wolf. But that's not what struck me. It was when they cut to the industry people talking about the scenes, and you were there, and not just to discuss your own movies, but just about every movie they listed, they always had a quote from you. More than anyone else on the show."

Mr. Jones spun his hand, telling Brian to get on with it. "I know the work I've done. I don't need a recap."

A woozy spell hit Brian, a combination of the drugs wearing off, and knowing he was rambling during a pitch that needed perfection. "I'm sorry, sir. My point is that even though you don't make movies anymore, you're a legend in the genre, and your opinion is of the highest value to the fans. I looked you up, and I saw you mention in a couple of interviews that you and your wife love escape rooms, go to them whenever you can. And as I'm sure you're probably aware, the most popular genre for escape rooms is horror."

Mr. Jones put his elbow on the couch arm and propped his head in his palm. He was getting bored, and Brian was all over the place.

"Escape rooms are cool. I like them too. But it seems to be a touch and go industry. Some companies are thriving, while new ones pop up every day and close a month later."

"Because half of them, if not more, are absolute shit," Mr. Jones chimed in.

Brian snapped his finger. "Exactly. And I've been working with the numbers. It's a hard business to profit in, unless you plan your builds really well, factor in the needed staff to run it, so many things. It's almost a consumable product. People play it once and unless they're hardcore enthusiasts, they likely won't come back. I know a few owners have combatted that with games that have different pathways based on the choices you make, so players could come back and play the same game with a different experience, but to create that, you'd need more products, more tech, more space. All of this puts the owners in a position where they feel the need to change out their games quickly, bring in a new room to lure in old business. But if they don't keep the rooms up long enough, they risk losing all the value. If the props and tech aren't worn out, how long can you keep it up before it runs dry? If you change it out, will the new theme sell as well as the last?"

Mr. Jones sat up. Interest sparked in his eyes. Brian had found something in his rant that intrigued the man. "I'm confused. When you started talking, I thought you were going to pitch an escape room idea to me, as if you wanted to see if I'd open up a business, but now it appears you're talking me out of it. To be honest, I love the conversation. Believe it or not, I've considered opening an escape room company. I could invest a lot of money into it. And I could make a good buck back. But what's the point? I'd be doing it just for the passion. I go to rooms with my wife and think up all the ways I could make it better, so I've considered doing just that. But I don't think it's a wise business decision. I don't have faith the industry isn't more than a fad. The pandemic proved how many of these companies, even some of the big-name ones, were just surviving on a wing and prayer."

Brian nodded furiously. "Yes, and I'll be honest, I *am* trying to talk you into it. Escape rooms on their own are too difficult, too much effort for a lot of risk, that even if it pans out, only leads to more effort to keep the momentum going. My idea is different. You know how Facebook started, right?"

Mr. Jones grabbed his glass of water, twirled his wrist, letting the ice spin in the glass. "Invite only. I see what you're getting at, but it's gonna need to be bigger than that."

"If there's an industry parallel to escape rooms, it's probably haunts, right? Haunted houses. I was reading a book once about extreme haunts. I stole it from my sister. She's a crazed horror fan. This book was called something like *The Death House*. Anyway, in this book, they had these traveling haunts you could only attend if you were invited to them, and they were known as the best around. Getting in was extremely difficult, which made people thirst for it even more."

Mr. Jones put his hand out like a crossing guard telling a child to stop. "You just said an escape room costs a lot to make, and has a limited window to make its money back, and now you're about to pitch the idea the window should be shorter? A pop-up, invite only escape room? Seems damn foolish."

Brian smiled. "Ah, you're on to me, but hear me out. You write the story, create the design, plan out the puzzles. You! The fucking great Caleb Jones. And that's how we pitch it. We make the first game, and this isn't your standard escape room, because we actually rent out a huge property for half a year. We spend three months implementing everything and another three with the game opened. There's the room. Just one game. But there's other parts to the event. People with tickets get to play the game, and I think we make the game a little longer, two hours, maybe two and a half. Afterwards, they get refreshments, snacks, get a screening of one of your movies. Maybe you even have some secret vault deleted scenes we could tack on to make the screening extra special. We design everything based on your movies, but the games are totally, one hundred percent original Caleb Jones stories. Not only are we changing the landscape of escape rooms, but we are hyping your name in storytelling again.

"And we charge a fuck ton per ticket. Like, out of reach prices. Two hundred dollars a pop, maybe. We start by inviting only influencers and celebrities, then we go on social media and find the diehards, the reviewers, the people who already spend a fortune traveling the world playing these games. And we bring them in and let them tell the world about it. We make this thing so hyped up and talked about, when we pop open game number two in a different location, different part of the country, everyone is going fucking crazy. We charge more. Five hundred a pop."

Mr. Jones leaned back, resting his head on the leather. He still held his glass in hand. "What's the math on this?"

"Say we spend 150k to design the game and room otherwise. For the first time, we charge 200 a pop, run each game with six people in the room, and run it five times a day, seven days a week for three months. You're talking over half a million coming in. Obviously, that's minus the 150k room build, rent, electricity, staff. Probably 200k profit."

Mr. Jones shook his head. "Less than that. There's a lot you're not factoring in, but if that's the starting price for room one, and we price higher for room two, I see a lot of potential to turn this into a cash cow. And to be honest, I think 200 is a low ticket price, even for game one. We could start at 500 and go up from there."

Brian smiled. It was working.

"Just one question." Mr. Jones sipped his water.

Brian put his hands out, palms up. "Ask away."

"What's in it for you? Why are you pitching this to me? Are you asking to help design the games? What? You just want me to pay you for the concept?"

Brian tilted his head and furrowed his brow. "Oh, no, sir. I want to run it with you. I want to work with you on all of it. I've been studying this for a long time. I have notebooks filled with information on design, pitfalls within the industry. I know it all. I want to be a co-owner. Now, I know you'll be fronting all the investments, so I know my cut will come just from profit after cost, but that's fine with me."

Mr. Jones laughed. It was a loud, violent laugh, and it echoed through the cavernous room. Laughs like that punched, and Brian felt the strike on his jaw, but he wasn't ready to drop to the mat.

"Sir. I assure you. I will be an asset."

"No. Let me stop you right there. I don't doubt you'd be valuable. I'm sure you have a lot of knowledge and insight that would help if I went into this venture. First, that's a big *if*. I still don't know if I want to waste my time on this. But let's say I do. I wouldn't hire you to manage the staff, let alone run the place with me. And look, I know that sounds cruel. You seem like a nice guy, smart too. I don't doubt you could excel. But I see the thunderstorm of red in your eyes, the way your fucking fingers have been trembling throughout this conversation. You're a junkie. Your teeth are rotting out of your skull. What's that from? Meth?"

It wasn't from meth. It was simply from not brushing his teeth. Brian drank and popped pills all day, often fell asleep wherever he sat, and he sure as fuck didn't plan a nighttime routine. Sometimes he'd throw up and fall asleep right after, letting the acidic spew settle on his enamel. Four of his teeth were cracked, wiggling their way out of his skull, and he'd had more than a few infections. Luckily, antibiotics were easier to score than Vicodin or codeine.

"Sir, I assure you my past drug issues wouldn't be a—"

Mr. Jones put his finger up. "Let me stop you again. I don't care what you're on or what you were on. I don't care if you're cleaning up or if you plan to. I hope for your sake you do, but that's not my business. However, if I open this idea of yours, the escape room will be my business. And I don't know you, and I have no reason to trust you. I never will. You're not going to change my mind about that. Ever."

"I can prove it to you. I can do daily check-ins, go to rehab, piss in a cup, whatever you need me to show you that I'm clean before we get started."

"Kid. Never gonna happen. Never. Because if you show me you're clean, and I sign contracts with you, and then you fall off, it makes my life a living hell. You're not my brother, my close friend, nothing. I met you ten minutes ago, and I won't get involved with someone I don't know who is clearly a liability. There's no reason for it. I get nothing out of it. Your plan is smart, but it's still a risky plan, and it will cost me a lot of time and money. I don't need added worry. And I'm not going to spend the night arguing with you about this because it will never happen. You can't change my mind on this."

Brian's chest had filled up like a balloon with anxiety when he had first talked up his idea, but now Mr. Jones had tossed a dart at it, and *POP*. It deflated him. He could keep arguing, keep trying to convince Mr. Jones to trust him, but the man was right. He was a junkie, and couldn't run his own life, let alone a million-dollar business idea. A better version of Brian would offer to work from the bottom. *All right, Mr. Jones, just hire me on as an assistant, a contractor, a fucking janitor, and I'll prove to you how much you'll want me on your team until I work my way up to your partner.* But Brian wasn't a better man, didn't have any fight left in him, and frankly, was too tired.

He rubbed the back of his neck. "Do you mind if I use your restroom?"

Mr. Jones closed his eyes and sighed. "Sorry to disappoint you, kid. I wish you the best." He pointed toward a hallway. "Second door on the right."

Brian stood up. A rush of blood flowed through his skull, and the room spun around him. Slowly, he walked and slid down the hall with his shoulder pressed to the plaster for stability.

Inside the bathroom, he locked the door and with trembling hands, snapped open the Ziploc bag of pills he'd gotten from his jacket pocket. They were not the prescribed ones. He counted them. Seventeen. He moved them to behind the faucet and pulled out his cell phone. The time showed 10:30 p.m., too late to get in touch with Charlie. Probably not if he had his brother's cell phone number, but he didn't. He only had his aunt's house number, and he knew she had probably turned the ringer off and gone to bed around 9:00 p.m.

Brian called it anyway. On the second ring, it went to Auntie's answering machine.

"Hey, Charlie . . ." His voice cracked as tears streamed down his cheeks. He cleared his throat. "Hey, Charlie. Listen, I'm not gonna make the trip with you guys tomorrow. I just wanted to tell you something important. Not everyone is made to be a hero. Some of us don't have redemption arcs, you know what I mean? This isn't the movies, and some of us don't repair, don't come in at the last second and save the day. But you, Charlie. You are a fucking hero. I know you have anxiety and all this other bullshit fucking up your brain, so it's hard to see, but kid, you're a fucking badass. Take care of Chrissy and Angela. Y'all deserved better than me and Dad."

He hung up, turned the sink on, scooped a palm full of water into his mouth. Two at a time, he popped the pills until the bag was empty.

CHAPTER 11
THE SECONDS BEFORE IMPACT

Chrissy tossed a bag onto the Volvo's back seat. Charlie handed her his bag, and she threw his on top. After she shut the door, she leaped forward and gave him a hug. "Thank you for doing this."

The screen door on the house cracked as it popped all the way open. They turned to see Angela on the top step with a bag in her hands. They all stared at each other for a second.

"Don't look at me like that. She was my sister too."

Charlie shook his head. "You can't come. No way."

Angela stormed down the steps, fire in her eyes. "I can. And I am. I'm sick of everyone pretending their problems are acceptable, but mine aren't."

Chrissy stepped forward, blocking Angela from the car. "It's not that. I would love for you to come with us. But you're too young."

"Seriously, get out of the way. What am I too young for? Do you think something is going to attack us? Have either of you ever fought anyone? Bit, kicked, punched? I've been in three fights, and I've beaten up two teachers. I win."

She maneuvered around Chrissy and opened the back door, plopping herself into the seat with her bag on her lap.

Charlie shrugged. "She's probably right, and honestly, she deserves answers as much as any of us."

"Fair enough."

As they drove, the grime of Tanner's Switch transformed into the tourist sections of Charlestown, the long stretches of motels dotting Route 1. Chrissy read a new book.

Angela kept to herself, resting her head back and letting the fall breeze tunnel in from the window.

When they reached Narragansett, driving down roads built entirely around clam shacks and tackle shops, they all stared out the window, a foreign world zooming by.

Tanner's Switch was twenty minutes away, but it could have been on a different planet, where oceans were ponds, beach houses were trailers, and adventure was a dream for a different tomorrow.

They parked and walked to the Point Judith terminal, where a few others were gathered. The breezy sea air made the chilly morning bitter. Chrissy crossed her arms, bringing both sides of her cardigan together. Angela stared off into the ocean, unbothered by the high wind.

The smell of fried fish from the surrounding restaurants and the salt from the ocean traveled with the breeze, and Charlie wished he had brought snacks.

They waited for fifteen minutes, cold and quiet. Charlie regretted the decision to follow through with this. The ferry boarded and would leave soon, but Brian remained a no-show. Charlie couldn't believe he fell for it, thinking his brother would change.

"Should we get on?" Chrissy asked.

"We'll give him five more minutes."

Each second was like watching your car move closer to a brick wall in slow motion. You knew you were going to hit it, but all you could do was count down the seconds until impact.

His brother wouldn't show up, and Charlie's heart would hurt for days. All he had left was a few more minutes to build up his hope.

Chrissy tapped his shoulder. "Come on. Let's go."

He gave one last glance to the parking area, hoping to see a car pulling in. He didn't even know what Brian drove, or if he drove at all. The car he got into yesterday was a brown sedan. Old. Shitty. He'd recognize it if he saw it.

He stepped backward and up the metal stairs. When they were on the boat, they stood at the back railing of the middle deck, Charlie checking the nearby lots from the improved vantage point.

Angela rubbed his arm. "He's not coming."

"I know," Charlie said and headed inside. The seats inside the ferry were more comfortable than those outside, but they had the air conditioning going for some stupid reason.

Angela and Chrissy sandwiched on each side of him. Chrissy tapped both feet on the ground. "This is going to be so fun."

Angela giggled. "Fun for you? I literally have no friends and do nothing but go to school and watch television. This is like the best day of my life."

Charlie's stomach dropped. He had always thought of Angela as a little pain in the ass, but the poor girl spent her life alone. He never considered how she handled the monster because she didn't talk about it the way everyone else did. Looking back, he regretted ever saying no to this trip and to giving Angela a hard time about coming.

This mattered.

He put his arm around her. "I'm glad you're here. I know you guys are on a mission, but we should also make sure we have some fun today."

Chrissy did an awkward dance reminiscent of Elaine on *Seinfeld*. "Heck yeah. Let's party."

"Charlie," a gruff voice said in a taunting tone.

They all turned around, hopeful to see their brother. Charlie couldn't believe his eyes. "Tiffany? Doug? What are you guys doing here?"

Tiffany and Doug scooted into the seats behind them. "You said you were going on an adventure to Block Island today, and we're big fans of adventures," Tiffany said.

A part of him was so happy his friends came. He had told them about the conversation with his brother but obviously left out the monster part. Instead, he'd just told them his sisters wanted to explore the island, and his brother made Charlie feel bad for saying no, so he decided he should do it. To Tiffany and Doug, this probably meant Charlie was going to have a boring day, and they were joining him to help make it more fun. It was a kindness, one he appreciated.

However, now that they were on the boat, Charlie realized he actually was looking forward to spending the day with his sisters, and Tiffany and Doug would only make Chrissy and Angela feel pushed to the side. He also couldn't fathom how he would explain to his new friends what they were really there for, so he'd have to separate from them at some point.

The boat made a mechanical sound and lurched forward with a jolt.

"I think it's time," Chrissy said.

Angela glanced out the window. "Fuck Brian. Better off without him."

Doug sniffed. "They're making hot dogs. I love ferry hot dogs."

Charlie turned back to Tiffany and Doug, who sat with smiles on their faces. He put his head forward, feeling a fresh wave of panic in his gut. They were returning to the place responsible for their nightmares, where four years ago, a monster chewed on their sister and destroyed their lives forever. His new friends sat behind him. His sisters on each side. He didn't know what they were moving toward or what the day would bring, but he felt in his guts: it was going to be a shitty day.

Chrissy giggled. "This is all very fucking awkward."

CHAPTER 12
DON'T BELIEVE IN MONSTERS

The passengers marched down the metal staircase onto the shores of Block Island, the ramp clanging like a church bell under their feet. A whipping breeze welcomed them. Charlie hated the wind. It was like getting slapped in the face by Mother Nature. There wasn't a single type of weather or temperature Charlie couldn't handle if the wind wasn't involved.

After they navigated around the large groups of other people, Charlie and his friends met in a circle to discuss their plans.

"I think we should go get scooters," Doug said, causing a wide, devilish grin to ride up Angela's cheeks.

During the summer months, Block Island would teem with tourists on scooters. Charlie hated them more than the wind. In fact, riding on a scooter was just a way to invite wind into your life. He never understood people who bought convertibles or motorcycles. Why would you seek wind? It sucked.

Angela said, "My sister will want to hit up the bookstore, for sure."

Chrissy shook her head wildly. "Nope. They don't even have a horror section. I asked them to order a book for me once, and the lady straight up told me they don't carry horror if it isn't King or Koontz. Now, I love King and all, but if you can't respect the genre enough to carry more mid-list or indie books, then you don't get my business." Chrissy eyed Charlie. "There's an art studio I'd like to visit. Maybe we should split up and meet back later?"

Charlie fidgeted with his fingernails. "I like that idea. Tiff and Doug why don't you guys get some scooters, and I'll go with my sisters to the art studio. We can all meet back in an hour at The Flavorful Scoop."

Tiffany shook her head. "No way. We are all in this together. Let's go to the art studio. I'm gonna guess any art studio in Block Island is all seashells and 'Beach Life,' whereas I'm more of a Munch kind of gal, but whatever."

Chrissy's eyes perked up. "I love Munch. I don't think this lady is going to be Munch, but I think she's better than seashells and 'Beach Life.'"

They walked the semi-crowded streets of Block Island. Going in fall made it a little less full, but enough people were moving around to make Charlie push out into the street.

The shops were a combination of mini Victorians, saltboxes, and wood-shingled beach huts squished together, reaching out toward the road with waving American flags or hovering box eaves.

Clothing shops with racks of BLOCK ISLAND tees, sun hats, and sweatshirts. Ice cream shops and beach food. Boutiques, craft stores, home goods, and surf shops. If you took away the walls, you'd be at an arts and crafts fair.

Chrissy led the group, her plan well-researched.

Charlie and Tiffany fell behind, but Charlie monitored Angela, feeling bad about how ignored she'd been. Luckily, she seemed to hit it off with Doug. Hopefully she wasn't developing a crush. The dude was way too old for her.

"So, Charlie, do you want to tell me what's really going on today? And listen, I understand if you don't want to talk about it. I'll get Doug to hang back when we hit the art place. I know you have something going on. We jumped in today to let you know we have your back, but we aren't trying to intrude on something that's none of our business. To be honest, I was worried about your brother. He scared me a little, and I wanted to be here if he upset you. I didn't realize he wasn't coming."

Charlie looked down at his feet as they marched along the stone sideway. "Me neither, and in that way, he did upset me. I'm glad you came. It means a lot to me, but my family and I . . ."

He trailed off, looking ahead at Angela giggling as Doug mimicked a guy on a scooter driving by. He couldn't remember the last time he'd seen her smile, let alone laugh. Like Charlie, if his sisters could make some friends or find something to escape the prison of their past, they could be happy. He went all in on this adventure today, but after this, he wanted to give them both a better life—one where they could stop dwelling on the monster.

Tiffany nudged him with an elbow to his arm and a soft, warm smile. "I get it. You know I love to pry, but even I realize this isn't something to dig into. I need you to know something, Charlie, and I'm scared to tell you."

He turned to her and even without knowing what she had to say, understood the weight of it. His cheeks turned hot, and a nervous twitch developed in his hands. He almost forgot who he was. His confidence loosened lately, but he was still the same scared kid who grew flustered around humans. Sure, he'd found his tribe, but he still hadn't found himself. "What is it?"

She looked at him with droopy eyes. "If I had known, I wouldn't have done it. I promise."

Charlie stopped, letting the gap between him and his family grow. The imaginary line that connected them all grew more and more taut with each second. "You wouldn't have done what?"

"Looked you up."

He stepped back, water filling his eyes.

She shook her head. "I'm so sorry, Charlie. I just thought I was going to find something about you being a nerd in school, like some articles about spelling bees or some shit. I didn't know. I'm so sorry."

Tears trailed down his cheeks. "I don't know what to say."

She stepped forward, approaching like she wanted to pet a lion. "Say what you want."

His throat closed, and he was back to the old Charlie. His mouth turned to sand. "I feel naked."

He turned his head, watching his family disappear around a corner with Doug.

Tiffany's lip twitched. "Charlie, me knowing about this doesn't expose you. It gives you more armor. I'm your friend."

He pulled away from the curb and kept walking. "Yeah. I mean, you've proved that enough. You're here, and that means a lot to me, but if you read about it, you have questions in your head. I know you don't believe it. Who would? And which sources did you find? The ones mocking us or the ones obsessing over us?"

She put her hand on his arm, trying to stop him from walking away. "Charlie. Who the fuck am I to judge what did or didn't happen to you?"

He stopped, turned around, and said with a voice more aggressive than he meant, "My sister went to the library the other day and checked out a book about monsters on Block Island. Do you know what my biggest fear was?"

Tiffany tucked her arms around her belly. "What?"

"That they wrote it in the last four years. That we would be in there. The worst fucking night of our lives is a goddamn myth for assholes to lap up and tell around campfires. There's fucking YouTube videos. *Don't be near this family at 3:00 a.m.* Podcasts. Wannabe TikTokers. They call us all the time. Still."

"I'm sorry you have to deal with that. I just read a couple of legit news articles." Her voice softened to a near whisper.

"Is that why Doug invited me to hang out with you guys? So I could be your cool story to tell your friends about?"

She shook her head. "What? No. And Doug doesn't even know

about it. I didn't tell anyone. It's so easy to find out anything about anyone, but the thing is, most people aren't fucking weirdos like me, and they don't go Google searching their new friends. I can't possibly understand what you went through, but you're not a fucking circus act, Charlie. And you're not alone. Not everyone in the world wants to hurt you or use you."

He stepped forward, wiping tears from his cheeks. "I was stupid to think I could get by for as long as I did without people finding out. They always do. Everywhere we move. Lucky for us, my aunt is so unstable she moves us around a lot, so we don't have to deal with the bullshit for long. Just answer me one question, do you truly believe we saw something that night? You read the articles, and so have I. The implications oozed off those pages. We covered up my sister's murder. My father killed her. Maybe a stranger in a mask. The articles were never just about what happened. They always had to dive into shared psychosis or shared delusions, blah blah. So tell me. What do you believe based on what you read?"

She stood up straight, ready for this question. "My answer can't be based on what I read because I met you first in Charlestown, and I sensed something in you before any article could sway me. *You* sway me more than a newspaper. And you did that within ten minutes of knowing you. I trust you more than any words on a page.

"I don't believe in monsters, but I'm aware I know nothing, that I can't possibly gather even a small fragment of the information from the story you lived through. I don't believe in supernatural shit, but I've only known you for a little while now, and I knew from the moment I met you on the beach that I believe in you. Charlie, I trust you. I've never made a friend so quickly, been so relaxed around a new person as I am with you. So if you tell me you saw a fucking monster that night, then I believe you saw a monster."

Charlie said nothing, just stared down at his shoes. "Chrissy found out about a woman who paints monsters that look just like ours. We're here to talk to her, to find some kind of answer. We never got closure. I want to stop thinking about that night. I need to move on. So do my sisters. They were really fucking little when it happened. I have to help them."

Tiffany nodded. "When I was seven years old, my uncle kidnapped me. He was a drug addict, and he lived with us, but my mother and father kicked him out when they saw how bad he was getting. They didn't want him near me and Doug. He came back to get his shit, and Doug and I were home alone. Doug was babysitting. My uncle stole me, just wrapped his fucking arms around me like I was a suitcase and dragged me to his car. I was too scared to fight back. He didn't do anything to me, nothing gross. But he drove with me for three days. Three days. We went all the way to Florida, staying at motels, eating McDonald's. I was terrified the entire time. Shaken to my core. I didn't want to breathe, worried I'd send him over the edge. Anyone who kidnaps a child will do scary shit.

"There was this huge manhunt for me. National news kind of thing. When they found me, the police busted down the door of the motel we were staying at, guns drawn, everyone screaming. My uncle pulled out a knife and waved it at them. I was as scared of the police as I was of my uncle. All of it terrified me.

"When the police arrested my uncle, they told me he'd been blackmailing my parents for money. I was still terrified, sitting in a police station, waiting to find out how I'd get home. It never ended. Even once I was home, safe in my bed at night, I couldn't close my eyes. I couldn't concentrate. I couldn't play. Every stupid fucking thought came back to, *What if he gets out again? What if someone else steals me? When will I ever be safe?*"

Charlie stared, unsure of what to say.

"For a long time, I felt like a prisoner. I still have nightmares, still get nervous around crowds. But do you know what made me finally feel a little freer?"

"What?"

"The internet. Being able to look up where my uncle was. Seeing he was still in jail. Eventually, he died, and I felt a fuck ton better. But before then, I checked every day to see if he got out. As long as I knew where he was, I knew I was okay. That's why I looked you up, and why I look up every person I meet. I enjoy being the outgoing person who randomly walks up to cool kids at the beach, but I need some security. I'm sorry I checked you out, but I am not sorry for why."

Charlie's heart sank. "I understand. I'm sorry you had to go through that. And I'm sorry I got weird. It's just tough for me."

She shook her head. "You don't need to be sorry for being guarded. It's your reaction to everything you've been through. You can be free knowing why it's there and why you need it. I had a point to my story. Maybe you think you found a new freedom because you're trying to forget what happened that night, but for your sisters, they need to find their freedom by knowing they're safe. And they won't know that until they can define it. I told you, I don't believe in monsters, but something happened to you that night. And if you don't find out how to understand it, it will always own you."

She reached out and held his hand. "I'm with you. Maybe that helps, or maybe it doesn't, but I need you to know I'm with you. I have my own monsters. And I can describe my uncle to you, but you'll never fully be able to see what it was like in those motel rooms, alone, scared, watching him move around erratically and out of his marbles. And I'll never be able to see in your sister's room, no matter how well you describe it. But I believe in you. I will always believe what you say, even if I don't believe in the characters, because I'm your friend, Charlie. A real friend who wants nothing from you but your happiness."

"Okay," he said.

"Now, let's go fuck with some monsters."

CHAPTER 13
WE'RE GONNA GET YOU

Tiffany and Charlie caught up to the rest of the gang just as they reached the front of the art studio. It was a square wooden building with a short concrete ramp leading to the front door. The blue paint on the wood had flecked off or peeled up, giving it the shore-worn look Block Island tourists loved to see.

In the window, paintings of seashells and foamy surfs stood on displays. Tiffany and Chrissy snickered at the sight.

Angela turned to her brother with wide eyes exploding with anxiety and excitement. "You ready for this?"

Charlie glanced at Tiffany. "Ready."

Chrissy took a deep breath and opened the door. A bell dinged as the screen door shot open. Charlie followed with Angela at his side.

Behind him, Tiffany said, "Stay out here with me, Doug."

As Doug protested, Charlie walked into the incense-filled studio. All the paintings on display were as Tiffany joked they'd be. Seashells and "Beach Life." Lighthouses, shores, shorebirds, waves.

A woman sat behind a glass counter, playing on her phone. She was cute. Her hair was frazzled, and she wore glasses with thick black frames, the dorky-chic kind. She put her phone down and stood, revealing her loose floral dress.

"How are you guys today?" She smiled.

Chrissy smiled back and nodded while Charlie examined the objects on the glass counter: painted shells, pins, buttons, stickers.

He rubbed his hand along the counter's edge. "Are you the artist?"

She smiled. "Yep. I did all these."

Charlie had imagined the woman would be older, but this lady was in her early twenties.

Chrissy feigned interest in the beach paintings, strolling the perimeter, rubbing her chin as she checked them out. "Is this all you have?"

The artist lady stood on tiptoe to talk to Charlie. "Everything I have for sale."

Angela, lacking subtlety, approached the counter and tapped her fingers on the glass. "We were looking for paintings of monsters."

The artist maintained her cordial smile, but her eyes flickered. "Ah, so you've read the Block Island folklore book?"

Chrissy found her way to the counter, and Charlie stepped back, figuring it best not to crowd her as they interrogated.

"Yeah, we wanted to know where you got the inspiration for that creature," Chrissy said.

The artist stared, thinking of how to answer. Chrissy made a smile where she hid her lips, and her cheeks offered big dimples. She put her hand out. "I'm sorry. I'm Chrissy. I was just a big fan of the artwork. I'm a huge horror nerd."

The artist took her hand. "Milicent. I'm also a horror nerd. I think the inspiration was just based on seeing lots of horror movies."

There was a lie there, a very obvious change in pitch when she said those last words.

Charlie stepped in. As he reapproached the counter, his nerves kicked up a notch, his pulse throbbing in his neck. He cleared his throat, unwilling to allow his social awkwardness to ruin his opportunity for answers. "Listen, my sister is lying. I mean, she is a big horror nerd, but that's not why we're here."

Milicent's eyes grew to the size of silver dollars. "Oh my god. I know who you are. I can't believe I didn't recognize you immediately."

Chrissy and Charlie lowered their faces toward their chests. Angela didn't seem to mind.

"I've always wanted to talk to you guys."

Chrissy perked up, but her eyes turned to thin slits. "Why?"

Milicent came around the corner. "Come with me."

They followed her into a back room. It was a kitchen area with a small bathroom. She waved her hand, telling them to sit at the long picnic table in the center of the room. While they all got seated, she fished for something in a cabinet.

Chrissy leaned into Charlie. "Do you think she got the picture ideas from us? Was this all just her drawing what she read about in the papers?"

"Maybe we came all this way just to meet a stupid fan. Some kind of weirdo who read about us and became obsessed with the story?" Charlie whispered.

Without turning from the cabinets, Milicent said. "Have any of you heard of Molly Mix?"

They all looked at each other to see if any of them had. Chrissy shook her head. Angela frowned. Charlie said, "No. Never heard of her."

She dropped the binder on the table with a thud. "Pretty much what I suspected. If you had, and if you knew the entire story, you'd know why your monster story isn't much of a stretch."

She pried the book open, her fingers moving erratically. Flip, Flip, Flip. Pages of newspaper articles, book pages ripped from the spine, printed documents from the internet. "I don't have any of the monster paintings here. I keep those at home. But I have some photos of my artwork along with some other drawings people on the island made. But I want to show you something else first."

She landed on a news article. The headline read, "Block Island Teen Disappears in the Middle of the Night."

Chrissy snatched it, eyes darting left to right as she devoured the article. Luckily for Charlie, Milicent dictated the highlights for him.

"Molly was my best friend in elementary school and junior high. I mean, we did everything together. Block Island is small, and the folks who opt to live here in the fall and winter are few and far between."

"And rich," Angela added.

Milicent nodded reluctantly, as if she weren't proud to have money. "And that, yeah. Not all, by the way, but a lot of them, sure. Molly and I both had well-off families, but that's beside the point. Here's the thing: Molly started getting terrible headaches when we were in junior high. They were so bad she'd bend over in pain and sometimes scream like someone was stabbing her. It was intense.

"They sent her for brain scans, worried it could be a symptom of aneurisms or something. I'm not sure. I don't know medical stuff, but the headaches were more than just migraines, is all I'm saying. Then, she started having these weird dreams at night. She'd call me and leave these voicemails where I could hear the raw fear in her voice. She'd ramble on about shorebirds. Always shorebirds. She said in the dreams, she'd be lying on the sand, frozen, unable to move, and the birds would peck at her. Nibble her flesh. Poke her eyes. She'd go into detail about them cutting through her flesh, ripping out muscles. She'd describe little thin strands of gore hanging from their beaks. I remember her telling me one time, in the dream, they plucked out both her eyes, and she couldn't see the world turning deep white, but she could picture the birds chewing on them."

"Jesus," Charlie said, pretending not to lose patience but hoping she'd hurry and explain the connection.

Milicent pulled her phone from her pocket and tapped the screen a few times. "So anyway, one day we're walking down the hall from one class to another, and Molly just drops to the floor and has a seizure."

All eyes went to Milicent's face. Chrissy dropped the article. But no one said anything, too eager for the story to continue.

Milicent didn't notice the attention she'd drawn because she scrolled through her phone, talking while she searched for something. "I freaked out. I'd never seen someone have a seizure before. It scared the shit out of me. Teachers ran over, and someone called an ambulance. She stayed home from school for three days.

"When she came back, she looked like a different person. Her eyes were all glossy, her hair frazzled. She'd jolt in fear over every little sound. When I came up to her to talk to her, she just stared at me for a minute, like it took that long to remember who I was. Once she did, she got all weird and rambled to me about how she kept having seizures, and while she was having them, she saw a monster, and he kept getting closer and closer to her.

"Because she knew I liked to draw, she asked me to make a sketch."

Milicent placed the phone down on the table and slid it to Charlie. On the screen was a crudely drawn version of the monster. Their monster. It didn't scare him, not this particular drawing. In fact, it made him excited. Someone else had seen it. It wasn't just a creature that *looked* like the one they'd seen, it was the same exact monster. And not just that, but the girl had seizures, just like Wreath did as a child. There were connections, ones written in bold lettering. **Seizures. Block Island. Monsters.**

Chrissy and Angela stared at the drawing. Angela's eyes filled with water. "That's it."

Milicent nodded. "A few months later, Molly looked like she was wilting away. She wasn't eating or sleeping. She told me it was getting closer and closer. And then one day, she disappeared."

Chrissy sat forward. "Disappeared in what way? Where was she last seen?"

Milicent took her phone back and scrolled some more. "Depends on who you ask. Her father said she was last seen getting ready for school. I had last seen her the day before in class. But her brother, well, he said on the way to school, it was super foggy and out of nowhere, he heard his sister scream. When he ran toward her cries, within the dense fog, he glimpsed a monster chewing on Molly. Then, poof, the monster and Molly were gone."

Charlie eyed Chrissy to gauge her reaction. He trusted her to make sense of this story more than he could. Chrissy opened her mouth to say something, but before she could, Milicent said, "Of course everyone thought he was nuts, but I asked him what the monster looked like, and I drew it how he described it."

She slid the phone back again, and landing right in front of Charlie was another drawing of the monster, this one with more detail. His black swirls for eyes, red lightning streaks bolting away from the dark pools. The long, slender claws. The pale, gray skin tightened like shrink wrap around the bones. Daggers for teeth. There were other details, too, ones he hadn't remembered. Its ears were crooked, the left one higher than the right, and they triangled out like little arrows moving away from the face. Its chest was covered in red lines, which Charlie couldn't be sure from the drawing whether they were cuts or part of the thing's features.

"I went to the police and showed them the comparisons between what Molly said she saw in her dream and what her brother described seeing. They didn't seem to care much, but they brought her brother in for questioning. My guess is they thought maybe someone kidnapped Molly, and her brother witnessed it. Maybe some psychopath wearing a mask. I don't know. But Molly never came back. And once I read your story, I went to the police again, just to remind them that you weren't the first people to make claims a monster went after a teenage girl. They again, ignored the shit out of me. But I'm guessing since that Block Island book brought you here, we're looking at the same monster."

Charlie nodded. Chrissy said, "Yeah, exactly the same. And our sister had seizures when she was young. I don't know how that connection works yet because she didn't have them when she got older, and she never mentioned anything about seeing a monster, but I'm sure the connection matters somehow. It's too similar."

Angela put her hand on Milicent's arm. "Can we speak to him? Molly's brother?"

Milicent frowned. "No. He disappeared too. About six months later. He became obsessed with finding Molly and proving he wasn't crazy. One night, he went out and never came back. Most people around here think he killed himself. George Stephens saw him last. He's kind of a local myth himself. A weird dude. Anyway, he said he saw Molly's brother wandering the woods, rambling to himself."

CHAPTER 14

SOMEONE ELSE'S HORROR SHOW

Tiffany leaned on an outdoor table full of Block Island sweatshirts while Doug played hacky sack with himself. She eyed the artist's studio across the street, hoping Charlie would come out soon, partially because she was bored but mainly because she was worried about him. The kid was a weathered and leaning gravestone, stuck in the place where his sister lay and ready to crumble from a gentle breeze.

Doug kicked the hacky sack all the way across the street, onto a small pocket of grass in front of the artist's studio. She came with him to retrieve it. As Doug scooped it up, Tiffany eyed the door, which Charlie had left slightly ajar.

She looked in both directions, as if someone outside would get mad at her for contemplating going inside an open business. A man crossed the road, not even looking in their direction, and even if he were, he was a salmon pantser, so no one worth worrying about.

Tiffany scrunched her brow and tilted her chin toward the door. Doug caught her drift. "You sure?"

"It's been a while. Maybe just a look-see."

Doug peeked in through the glass. After a few seconds, he turned

367

to Tiffany and whispered, "I don't see anyone in there. Is there a back room or something?"

Tiffany screwed up her face. "How the fuck would I know? Let's sneak in."

"Oh sure, when I said we should do that, you said it was spying. Now, suddenly, it's your idea, and it's awesome?"

She rolled her eyes. "Get the fuck over it. Let's go." She slid past him and gently pressed the door open. Once she was inside, Doug crept in behind her and reached up, holding the clapper of the bell in place. Tiffany gripped the door handle and closed it slowly. She didn't know why she sneaked instead of just announcing her presence. Probably because she wanted to overhear something before it could be censored.

Voices came from a side room. Doug crept in front of her and peeked around the corner.

"Door is closed," he whispered.

She rolled her eyes again. "Thanks, James Bond."

He shrugged. "What? What kind of businessperson hides out in the back room and leaves the front door unlocked?"

Tiffany scanned the walls. "One with cameras."

Doug straightened and joined her in scanning the walls. "I don't see anything. I think she just sucks at her job."

She nudged him with her elbow. "I don't think there's a lot of worry for anyone to steal this shit."

He smiled but held in his chuckle.

She knew Charlie would feel betrayed if he caught her spying, but something itched at her brain, sending her on high alert, and she felt a need to check on him.

She took slow steps down the thin hall and leaned her ear toward the door. Angela was speaking, but Tiffany couldn't make out the words.

An unfamiliar voice came in, a female, probably the artist lady. "I've sketched it about a thousand times now. It's like a mini obsession."

Tiffany leaned in a little closer, and when her hand touched the door, it creaked open an inch. She hadn't realized it wasn't clicked shut. Her face turned hot with embarrassment.

"Idiot," Doug whispered. "I got you."

He pushed her out of the way and pulled the door open. Everyone looked at them at the threshold. "Uh, sorry to bother you all. Tiffany and I are going to Ben and Jerry's, and we just wanted to give you a heads-up so you didn't think you lost us.

Tiffany knew nothing about seizures, but from having seen them on television, she just assumed a person was unaware when it was happening, but at that moment, she knew. She knew she was having a seizure, or at least knew it came on. A weird pressure drove from belly to throat, and at the same time, a wave of dizziness, numbness in her limbs, and tingling washed over her. Then, she was falling, and as she drove toward the floor, she caught one last thing before she succumbed to the seizure. Everyone else was experiencing the same thing. All of them. They were all having a seizure. Was that possible? Had that ever happened in the history of the world? A room full of people all having simultaneous seizures?

Her surroundings turned foggy, but not the dreamscape sort of blurred lines, more like an actual fog crawling toward her.

As the mist circled around her head, she smelled it. It reeked like sulfur, which made her think it was more smoke than mist, but it also had a briny scent to it. Sea water. And not the good kind. More like dead fish, as if the mist carried with it a spoiled ocean.

I'm going to die, she thought. A newfound love of life making her regret every poor decision she had made up to this point. One last gulp of clean air. She sucked it in and spit it out before the mist swallowed her whole.

Silence.

Emptiness.

She no longer heard the cacophony of panic from her friends. Her brother's hand left her arm, leaving a cold spot where his fingers once gripped. She lost all sensory capabilities. Instead, she hovered in the darkness.

Nothingness. Floating.

Her vision returned first, revealing a pale white world.

Her hearing came next. Someone giggled.

She spun. It was herself.

Her as a child.

Was this Heaven? she thought with zero belief in such a thing. The kid version of herself came into view, crossing a clearing like a shadow through a blinding light. Young Tiffany skipped and giggled toward her, coming closer. Another shadowy figure passed through the invisible threshold. Tiffany blinked, tears bubbling on the surface because she knew before the figure fully materialized who it would be. Because this wasn't Heaven. It was Hell. It had to be.

Her uncle.

The fear of it all, the mist, losing her senses, the idea she might be dead, and that her brother and friends were granted the same fate, none of it scared her down to the marrow of her bones quite like the sight of her uncle approaching the child version of herself. She needed to save the little girl. She ran, her feet touching nothing but still bending at the arch enough to propel herself forward.

"Look out!" she yelled.

Her younger version ignored her warnings.

Her uncle crept up behind young Tiffany, wrapping his arms around her, and with a swift upward motion, lifted her to his chest.

"No!" Tiffany charged forward, ready to connect, ready to smash, ready to let her bones snap in the name of destroying not only her uncle, but any memory of him. She wanted to pulverize him out of existence.

As she neared her uncle, he squeezed the little girl until she evaporated into a puff of mist. Tiffany tried to stop herself at that point, suddenly recognizing her stupidity, that she was trying to accomplish something with human actions in a world that defied the natural order of things.

Her uncle peered up at her, a crooked smile sliding up one side of his face.

She tried her hardest to stop, to even slow down, but her fucking feet kept running forward. The closer she came, the more her uncle changed. His stubbly chin smoothed out. His skin turned gray and leathery. His mouth ripped at the corners, spreading, and growing. His teeth sharpened and elongated. And her stupid fucking feet ran on.

The bones in her uncle's body cracked, expanded. His flesh too. He grew abnormally tall, and his chubby shape caved in, skin wrapping taut around the bone.

As the transformation unfolded, Tiffany knew where it was headed. Her uncle was turning into Charlie's monster.

"Please, fucking stop," she yelled to herself, tears barreling down her cheeks. "Please."

The monster's arms extended, catching Tiffany in mid-run and lifting her body in the air. For a moment, her feet kept running, just two legs flailing back and forth. The monster's arms were too long for her to use that momentum to kick the fucker in the teeth.

God, she had been so wrong, assuming nothing could be more terrifying than her uncle. She closed her eyes, slammed them shut, unable to look at the monster. Jesus, if Charlie and his siblings had to witness this as children, she couldn't imagine the PTSD they must have. Its hot breath smacked her cheeks as it pulled her closer. She punched and kicked, finding purchase with various parts of the creature but doing zero damage. Its lack of reaction didn't stop her from attacking, but it stole the oomph from her shots.

Its breath smelled like the mist, a sulfuric ocean graveyard.

When it spoke, two voices spewed from its throat. One female, one male. What it said broke her. The wind of the words ripped her body from its roots, pulled her from the soil, and slammed her spirit right back into the dirt. The sentence echoed in her skull, rattling like an unanswered cell phone on an end table. A phrase vibrated through her bones, bobbed, and made waves in the marrow, plucked her veins with discordant notes.

"Wash up, Scumbag."

Scumbag. Her uncle's nickname for her. Scumbag. There was a time before he had kidnapped her when the name was endearing, a cute, jokey name for her. Meant as a ribbing, not sincerely. But when he dragged her across the East Coast, it came to her that a person who can't be nice without being cruel was a bad person. The kind of person who had to diminish everyone, hiding behind "it's just a joke" to get there, was both lacking in self-esteem and courage. Weak. A weak fucking villain, who despite his pathetic nature still sent a tremor of panic through her limbs, because even the weak could evoke horror. In fact, they usually did.

Whenever he had dragged her into a new motel, he'd push her on the shoulder and say, "Wash up, Scumbag," with a shitty smile on his face, as if he were trying to make her laugh. But his playful mannerisms had turned to poison by then, and she'd found nothing endearing about it.

She'd been too young to recognize the man's compulsion for insult. She thought when he told her to wash up, that he just wanted to act like a parent, but it was really another way to make her feel gross, lesser. Always a dig with him.

She still woke up some nights, sweat dripping down her back, and those three fucking words ping-ponging in her mind. When he said those words to her during their cross-country trek, they seemed so unimportant in the scope of things, but after it ended, that three-word mantra stayed with her, a tattoo branded deeper than flesh, seared into the sinew under her skin. They were the motto for the worst time in her life, the whole story wrapped in a horrific, night-marish bow. *Wash up, Scumbag.*

Tiffany dropped from the memories, literally plummeted as the creature's grip left her throat. Her stomach lurched into her lungs. Free falling.

She never landed, just reappeared in her body on Earth, right where she had left it in the art studio. The mist had vanished. Doug stared at her, trails of tears drying on his cheeks. She slowly turned toward the back room. Chrissy, Angela, and the artist lady all stared off, complete and utter terror drenching their faces. She understood. They'd all just received the same warning, and she wondered what words the beast whispered to each of them. What sentence haunted their lives, or was it more than a few words? Maybe other people needed more than one expression to summarize their worst nightmare.

The next few moments were a blur of action. People were brushing past her, bumping into her as they ran into the shop. Chrissy pulled Angela. She had her fists clenched and her teeth gritted.

Doug put his face in front of his sister, horror in his wide eyes, the always stoic and strong brother, bleeding panic from his facial features. He grabbed Tiffany, and the world came back. She heard the screams, and horror.

Chrissy shouted, "We have to go! We have to go!"

The artist ran to Chrissy. "You need to get out of here. Run. Go home."

"What is even happening?" Angela asked, covering her face with his hands.

"You don't get it, do you? That was it telling you to back the fuck off. All of us. Go home and never think of that thing again. Never. I'm going to do the same thing. Don't call me. Don't talk to me. Get out. I'm sorry," the artist lady shouted.

The next thing Tiffany knew, she was running down the road with Doug, following Angela and Chrissy.

Angela ran with her arms clutched around her torso, mumbling to herself. Her face was pale and her lips, blue. She looked destroyed, but she was alive, and all things considered, that was the best one could hope for.

The world kept fading out for Tiffany; one moment, she was there, her heart pounding, her mind racing, trying to piece together everything she'd just witnessed, and the next, it was a blurred landscape in front of her, her mind homing in on ridiculous things like the bell on the door of the artist's studio, and the Block Island sweatshirts on the table.

The world no longer made sense, and her mind refused to settle on that fact, unwilling to accept it.

They reached the ferry, and everyone went into hysterics, Chrissy a frazzled mess, Angela literally pulling at her hair, still mumbling to herself, and Doug nearly hyperventilating.

"What the fuck?! What the fucking fuck?!" he shouted.

Angela wiped the snot from her nose. "What the hell do we do now?"

Chrissy screwed up her face. "We go home. We do exactly what Milicent said. We try to move on and forget it."

Tiffany looked up. Her eyes burned, but she didn't cry. She probably would tonight when her mind worked again. "We can never forget this."

"What other choice do we have?" Chrissy asked

"Exactly. We have no choice. Forgetting it is impossible," Tiffany said.

A few years back, Tiffany had a phase where she read a lot of true crime books. In one of them, she read a story about a man who witnessed a mob hit. Eventually, they found him and killed him. She wasn't bothered about the witness dying. It was the chapters in between that haunted her. When the man couldn't sleep, couldn't close his eyes, because he knew once he crossed the threshold into the darkness, he was a prisoner there. He'd stumbled into the wrong world, and once he entered, the only escape was death.

Tiffany, having been kidnapped as a child and knowing very well the feeling of being prisoner to someone else's horror show, read those chapters with a tight chest and a wind stuck in her lungs. And as someone who had lived as a prisoner, she also knew when that threshold had been crossed, when a person was trapped in a horror they couldn't escape.

She was there now. So was Doug. Her heart raced again. She could feel it in her temples.

And then she remembered another book about a prisoner. Bobby Sands, a member of the provisional Irish Republican Army, who died in prison during a hunger strike after sixty-six days of not eating. While in prison, he wrote a diary, and he, too, knew his only escape would come from death. He wrote, "I am standing on the threshold of another trembling world. May God have mercy on my soul."

Tiffany didn't believe in God, but her world was trembling, and her soul was about to leave Block Island on a ferry toward Tanner's Switch, where she knew it would never rest again until a monster clawed it from her fucking body.

Then Chrissy asked, "Wait. Where's Charlie?"

CHAPTER 15
CHOKECHERRIES

Charlie watched as his siblings and friends fell, convulsed on the floor, and he, too, fell into a seizure of some sort. A strange mist surrounded him, wrapped itself around him, and pulled tightly, squeezing the air from his lungs. His world turned to bright white and then fizzled back, and he was there on the ground, watching his friends and family continue their horrifying seizures.

He stood up, terrified, unsure what to do. But his feet reacted without his mind, and they moved him forward, yanking him past the people he needed to help. His mouth opened, and a gentle whisper dripped from his mouth, "No. Wait." But his body did not wait.

He left.

As he exited the studio, he scanned the waving flags draped in front of the shops, and each felt like fingers drawing near, ready to gouge his eyes out. The people, too, moving from storefront to storefront, all eyed him, and Charlie wondered if the creature used their sight as his own. The wind was the devil's breath, hitting his face like hot exhales.

His throat closed up, and his ribs pressed in.

When was the next ferry out of here? Would his loved ones awaken in time to flee the island before the night approached?

He wrapped his arms around his torso and turned back to the art shop, staring at the front façade. It looked unchanged, the pastel oceans and colorful boats on canvas hanging in the windows were a faux smiley face, hiding the trauma and horror quaking within.

Charlie battled with himself, screamed internally to go back in, to save the people he loved. But he marched away despite himself, slowly at first, almost floating. And his feet argued with his brain, pushing a little faster, a little faster, until he was speed walking down a long winding road to God knows where. He followed it past beautiful houses, vast empty spaces, and untouched woods between them.

Where the fuck was he and why was he going this way? He didn't know, but he kept walking. A man possessed, he marched down neighborhood streets, houses unfamiliar to him, even from his short time living on the island. Not that he had a lot of time to see the other habitats, but still, his internal GPS was spinning in circles, drunk and confused. His mother's voice echoed in his skull, *Keep marching*. The fear left him, dripped from his pores like sweat. Everything would be okay. This was supposed to happen. No more battling an internal monologue that fought against action. The old Charlie would go back, shake his family free from their prison, and run them to the docks. Away from the terror. Forever.

But the new Charlie, the brave Charlie, the one with his mother's spirit inside him, knew his friends and family were okay, that they'd wake up like he had, and they'd go to the boats and go home, and when Charlie finished this journey, he'd learn something new, something to help them all move on. His mother guided him. And she never steered him wrong.

With no sidewalks, Charlie had to keep hopping on lawns or into the woods to avoid fast-moving cars unconcerned about the bends. After a while, the roads looked the same, the houses too. Old Town

Road, Center Road, Cooneymus, Lewis Farm. They were all named, marked as different from one another, but to Charlie, they were one and the same, a bizarre melding of slithering worms, intertwining, wrapping around the island, suffocating, choking the heart, squeezing.

Or maybe he had it wrong. Maybe it was a bloodstream, the island's lifeblood, and Charlie was a free radical, a rogue cell coursing through and clogging it.

He didn't know, wasn't even sure whether he was awake or dreaming all of this as he shook uncontrollably on the floor of the studio. All he knew was that a ghost spoke to him, and his feet followed a plan. But most importantly, he knew to obey because the spirit was his mother, and she led him from the darkness toward the truth, toward hope.

He'd left the comfort of the wide asphalt streets a while ago, traveling on uneven dirt roads. The houses were still regular, but the spaces between were thicker with woods, more ominous.

His legs ached, not used to this level of walking, but his will to proceed, to see this through, kept his feet moving. But where the fuck was he going?

He shooed thoughts of the monster from his mind, not wanting it to scare him from whatever it was his feet forced him into. This trek, like going to the island in the first place, was necessary, a fate assigned to him that he tried to fight against until he knew better.

Still, when he hit those isolated stretches of road, his heart punched his ribs, and he winced at the idea of the monster storming from the white oaks.

He escaped the roads, down a thin stretch of dirt made just for walking. The trees around the path bent over, their branches hovering like hands in supplication. Charlie's palm stung, and he gasped as he saw red dripping through the cracks between his fingers. He flipped his hand and opened it. Chokecherries. Their bodies mushed and gunked, and the juices flowed down his fingers and wrist. He had no memory of picking them, no idea how they ended up in his grasp.

Suddenly, the journey felt wrong, poisoned. A shroud of safety had hovered over him, as if Charlie operated under the influence of a higher power—his mother guiding him. He'd been entranced, like when an athlete claimed to be in the zone. But the chokecherries violently shook him from his hypnosis, awakening him to his surroundings. He was nowhere, and he was alone.

He took his phone out of his pocket and checked the time. It was 7:15 p.m. He'd been walking for hours. Jesus. Seven of them? It seemed impossible. The walk felt like an hour, tops. Hell, a walk around the shore, covering the entire island probably wouldn't take seven hours. If the timing was accurate somehow, he wouldn't be back to the studio until two in the morning. But he believed that was wrong, maybe he'd been unconscious for hours and only walking for an hour or two? Nothing made sense. Panic set in. The sun hung low on the horizon, threatening to vanish. He had minutes to burn before it left him alone in the dark.

He clammed up, rooted to his spot, unwilling to step forward, too far gone to return to where he had started. Had the monster lulled him off into isolated territory?

Something had to give, a move to be made. The world fell silent, and Charlie heard the blood coursing through his veins, and his heart—an obedient workhorse—pumped it through, but it knocked hard on the door. "Hey, I need a break here. I need a fucking break," it told Charlie.

"Going to the graves?" a voice asked through a throat full of marbles.

Charlie jumped and let out a childlike screech. He turned to see a man with a yellow-stained beard smiling at him. The man had no shoes on, and his pants were worn thin, barely holding on to their stitching. But his shirt was a clean, crisp, blue button-down.

"The *Palatine*? Going to their graves?"

Charlie shook his head. His mouth turned to chalk and speaking felt like coughing up dust, "No."

The man let a smile crawl up one cheek. "Then what the hell you doing out here?"

Charlie snapped out of it, now as equally concerned about murderous humans as monsters. "No. I mean, yes. I am. I guess. I think I got kind of lost."

The man's eyes turned to slits. "Uh-huh. You're going the right way." He pointed toward a thin, unkempt path shrouded by long blades of grass with towering oaks flanking both sides. "It's right there. Not more than about ten minutes down that path."

Charlie stared, unsure what to say. He didn't want to proceed down the dark path without seeing the man go in the other direction. Hell, he didn't want to go down the dark path at all, but he knew he would, knew he was called here for some reason. If he were being honest with himself, this whole trip to Block Island was more than just for his sisters, bigger than a talk from his older brother, it was an invisible force pulling his puppet strings, urging him back. He argued as well as he could, but he knew his destiny beckoned with a louder voice than his own could speak. His only concern now was figuring out if the entity pulling the strings was on his side or luring him toward death.

The man gave up waiting for Charlie to respond. "The *Palatine* Light is chock full of bullshit, though. Ship didn't even sink around here. It went to Pennsylvania or some shit. I don't know what you're hoping to find at those graves, especially this late in the evening. They ain't anything special to look at."

Charlie moved his tongue around, hoping to bring some saliva to his mouth. "Yeah, maybe I'll just turn around."

The man tilted his head, staring with blatant suspicion in his eyes. "You on something, kid?"

Charlie felt guilty for a crime he hadn't committed. *Why yes, sir, I am currently drugged up by either a monster or a ghost, and they happen to be very much in control right now. Better watch out. They might eat you for getting in the way.*

Charlie wiped his sweaty palms on his pants. "No, sir."

The man's stony face altered, and the tides turned. Suddenly, he looked terrified of Charlie instead of the other way around. It was as if he read Charlie's thoughts, or worse, saw whatever haunted Charlie.

"Be on your way then," the man said, turned around, and walked away.

What had he seen? What had scared him?

And suddenly Charlie didn't want the man to leave because it meant he'd be alone. He opened his mouth to shout, to beg the man to stay with him, but what good would it do? The man wouldn't listen, and even if he did, could that gentleman save him from a monster?

Charlie's feet moved again, not toward houses, or the man, or town, but into the thick woods where the man told him the *Palatine* graves were. A thought occurred to him that gave him a sliver of relief. If the monster wanted him dead, it could have slipped into the art studio and eaten him in front of everyone with no repercussions. Charlie knew this because it had done just that with his sister at their old house on the island. This wasn't the monster calling him. It was his mother. It had to be. The man said Charlie neared the *Palatine* graves, and Chrissy had told him the story of the *Palatine* ship when she ranted about all she'd learned at the library. It was all connected.

He headed toward answers. And maybe that meant the monster was scared, angry, and maybe it was hovering around, wanting to attack, but it hadn't yet, which Charlie thought meant maybe it couldn't. Maybe Charlie's mother protected him.

It wasn't enough to strip him of his fear, but it tempered it. The path opened to a small field, and there stood the *Palatine* graves. The weird man had spoken the truth. They weren't much to look at. As unassuming as Charlie in a school hallway. One large rectangular stone had *Palatine Graves* etched in it and drove up from the earth like a tree root. There were no other graves, just a plot of land where Charlie supposed the few sick passengers who passed away on the island were buried. There was another small path moving away from the gravesite and spilling into the yard of a large property with a massive house looming in the center of it. It would have made Charlie more settled, knowing people were around, but all of the house lights were off, and the yard was nearly charcoal in the evening light.

"What now?" he asked the ghost. His mother. The monster. An angel or a devil. It didn't matter anymore. Here he was, a prisoner of his own fate. The concept of the next few minutes terrified him, an ethereal aura of possibility. An endless expanse of prospect or danger hovered over time itself. He could learn the secrets of the world, magically transport back to the studio with only mere minutes having passed, or he could find the teeth of a rabid creature.

The trees around him shook.

Charlie turned back to the dark path, and as his eyes landed on it, noises broke through the woody maw. At first, it sounded like choral birds, but as the noises came together, conforming with each other to produce a melody, he understood what he was hearing. Laughing. The woods laughed at him.

Dread filled his soul. "No," he said. "No."

"Welcome home," it said from behind the thicket. Both voices conjoined, so screechy and painful. It dribbled down his spine like ice water.

He turned to see the creature coming through the tree line. Tears filled Charlie's eyes. Horror. He hadn't experienced horror like this since he witnessed this monster in his house four years ago.

"Welcome home," came the song from behind him. He shot around to see another monster, exactly the same. Two times his size, it bent low to clear the tree branches.

"Welcome home," a third voice sang out from his side.

They crept toward him in three directions. They sang with their double voices, "Welcome home."

"No!" Charlie screamed. "It's not fair."

One of the things gripped Charlie's upper arm, digging its sharp claws into his muscle. He screamed again, "Please!"

The one in front of him dropped to its knees and crawled to him, head tilted. A grotesque smile fissured up its cheeks.

"Please. I finally made friends. My sisters and I just reconnected. I need them. They need me. Please."

The one on Charlie's side drove its talon through Charlie's stomach. The foreign object grinded into his insides. It burned, searing his lungs.

"Please!" he yelled into the hollow night air, then whispered, "I finally have friends."

The creature in front of him leaned in and licked his cheek.

With its touch, Charlie's mind jolted to half a dozen places at once, as if the creature was showing him what it envisioned.

A dense fog traveling from Block Island to the coast.

Gore splashing the street signs.

Charlie's sisters running through what looked like a hallway.

Tiffany barricaded in a closet.

Dead people everywhere.

The creature's tongue left his skin, and it opened its mouth. Hot air hit Charlie's ear.

"Please. Let me see my sisters. I need them. I need them. I don't want to be alone anymore."

The monster bit into his neck. From behind, the other bit into his shoulder. The third dropped to the ground and dug into the meaty portion of his calf.

"I don't want to die. I'm not ready for this. Please. I finally have people."

The bites came more ferociously. Burning, ripping, tearing. Pain went from localized to one central agonizing beat flowing through his entire body, increasing as if he sat in a frying pan and someone cranked the heat.

The monster in front of him pulled away, strands of gore dangling from its mouth, crimson dripping off its chin, and he snarled. "Welcome home," it screeched before opening its mouth so wide it covered Charlie's face. He felt the daggers digging into the space between his chin and neck and the top of his head. And then it all faded away.

CHAPTER 16
ALL IS LOST

The ferry had already boarded, and it would depart in about ten minutes. Chrissy panicked. She tried to keep it together but knew when she spoke, she yelled, the words unable to come out any softer than the ferry's horn.

"We have to go back and find him," she said.

Doug stood behind Tiffany, wild-eyed and bursting with energy. "The ferry's about to leave. It's the last one for the night. How long were we out?" He turned toward the boat and slammed his foot down. "What the fuck is going on?"

Chrissy realized as crazy as the preceding events were for her and Angela, they must have been ten times as nuts for Tiffany and Doug, who hadn't the faintest idea what any of this meant. Of course, knowing might have only made it worse.

Tiffany grabbed Chrissy's arm. "I love Charlie, but we lost like seven hours of time, and this shit is terrifying. He'll be okay. Maybe he's already on the boat. We know how he is. He gets scared and retreats."

Tiffany lecturing about Chrissy's own brother made Chrissy furious. "Are you seriously fucking Charlie-splaining to me? I know my brother. No matter how scared he was, he wouldn't leave us behind. Never."

Tiffany pulled her hair back. "I know. You're right. But as much as I adore Charlie, I can't stay here. I can't. I have a family too."

Angela came between them. "No one expects you to stay, but you can't expect us to leave. You and Doug go back. Chrissy and I are going to find him."

Doug grabbed his sister's shoulder, trying to pull her toward the boat. "Come on. Let's go."

Tiffany yanked her arm away. "Wait. I have to leave, but I really don't like the idea of just letting you guys go. Whatever we just saw, it was fucking real. I know it was. And it's here. On this island. And it's nighttime. Even if you find Charlie, none of you will have a place to stay, nowhere to go."

Chrissy shook her head. "I'll call my dad and force him to pay for a room for us at a hotel."

"I thought you didn't talk to your dad? And Charlie said he was broke."

Chrissy stepped back. "Yeah. That's not entirely accurate. Now get on the boat."

Tiffany's lips quivered. "I really don't like the idea of leaving you on the island with that thing."

Angela pushed Chrissy back toward the main road. "You don't have a choice."

As soon as Chrissy's feet left the curb into the now desolate road, the strands between her and Tiffany broke. She liked Charlie's new friends and thought they had his best interests at heart, and she also didn't blame them for leaving. Friendship is powerful, but so is perseverance, and they had their own bonds, not unlike Charlie and Chrissy's, and those bonds needed protecting too. But every second Chrissy waited was a second Charlie could be moving farther away, and she didn't have time to argue.

"Take my number. Call me if he's on there."

Tiffany handed Chrissy her phone and she quickly plugged her number in.

With Angela at her side, they ran away from the boarding station, crossed the road, and charged down Main Street back toward Milicent's studio. With the last ferry shipping out, most of the tourists had cleared, and it being fall meant there weren't many to begin with. Half of the businesses had already closed down for the night.

A bottomless pit of dread filled Chrissy's guts. Anxiety swirled with regret. How could she have traveled from the studio to the docks without recognizing her brother's absence? He never would have left without her, would have noticed instantly if she weren't there.

They turned the corner by the studio as Milicent stood at the stoop, locking the front door. Panic streaked her face.

"Milicent!" Angela yelled.

The woman startled and jerked her head toward them. Her face dropped as if it had turned to stone. "I told you to get away from here."

"It's Charlie. Have you seen him? We ran in a panic and realized he wasn't with us," Chrissy said. She hoped she kept her voice even, not trying to freak Milicent out even more.

"Shit. I don't remember seeing him either. It's like he had already left the room before I snapped out of it." She shook her head violently. "I'm sorry. I can't help you. Go to the police, but please leave me alone."

She stormed off in the opposite direction, squeezing her arms around her chest.

Chrissy and Angela stood there, dumbfounded.

"What do we do now?" Angela asked.

Chrissy put her head down, hopelessness wetting her eyes. She wanted to scream, but she had to keep her head straight. "We have no other option. We go to the police station."

Angela gave a look like she chewed on a lemon, but she didn't argue. What other choice did they have?

The police department was less than a ten-minute walk, just a straight shot down Ocean Avenue, before one right turn onto Beach Avenue. The small building looked more like a summer cottage than a police station. It sat next door to the local volunteer fire department station.

Chrissy slammed through the door, surprising the middle-aged woman behind the desk. "I need to speak to Officer Duplass."

Even as a child, when her family had called the police after the attack on Wreath, Chrissy knew no one would believe them. Who would? What happened to them was insanity personified, or monsterfied, rather. She didn't blame the police the way her family did for looking toward alternative answers, for questioning her father, her, and her siblings until they were blue in the face.

These weren't yokel police officers, and the state detectives they brought in were thorough and helpful.

But Officer Duplass stood out because he *did* take their stories seriously. Sure, not seriously enough that he dropped his concerns over their father or the possibility of an intruder, but he entertained them, showed concern and care.

The woman said, "Duplass isn't on tonight."

Chrissy shouted, "Call him!"

The door behind the woman opened, and an officer in his forties stepped into the room. "What's going on out—" He stared at the two girls standing in the doorway. "Chrissy and Angela Keating?"

Four years. It had been four years since they'd seen or talked to anyone in this department, yet this officer remembered them, recognized them through all the changes they'd gone through during that time. And Chrissy recognized him back. "Officer Carmen!"

Words spewed from her mouth, and at the same time, Angela ranted too. They both explained what happened with different tones: Chrissy pleading and Angela hostile.

Officer Carmen put his hand up to stop them. "Hold on. Hold on.

We can get to the other stuff later. Your brother being gone is the important part. Are you sure he didn't get on the boat?"

"Our friend got on and said she'd call us, but I'll call her just in case," Chrissy said.

As she dialed, Officer Carmen said to Angela, "And have you called him? See if he just decided to take a stroll and lost track of time?"

Angela huffed, but her eyes gave away her embarrassment that through all of this, she hadn't considered just calling her brother. She took her cell out and dialed.

Chrissy hung up on Tiffany. All she needed to hear were the words, "He's not here." Tiffany had kept talking, apologizing again for leaving, but Chrissy didn't have time for it.

"He's not on the boat."

They all turned to Angela, who clicked the phone off. "Voicemail after one ring."

Officer Carmen's face dropped, realizing his night wouldn't go as calmly as planned. "Okay, come here. You two sit in the back office."

"You have to do something!" Angela shouted.

Carmen's voice rose, but not in a way where he was yelling. "I am going to do something. We're gonna find your brother, but for now, I need you out of the way while I make some calls."

He ushered them into the back room, a room they'd both sat in before. It had a few round tables, a snack machine, a water cooler, and a coffee pot.

Chrissy and Angela sat across from one another, neither saying anything but both becoming balls of energy. Chrissy's feet tapped and Angela rolled her neck around, checking out every inch of the room.

"Why are you always looking in the corners? I see you doing that all the time," Chrissy said, distracting herself.

"Well, maybe you should have asked me about it."

"I just did."

"I know. Now that our little boat trip turned us into best pals, right?" She rolled her eyes and looked away.

"Never mind then. I forgot how much of an asshole you can be."

"Go read a book, bitch."

"I'd tell you to do the same, but I'm not sure you know how."

"And there's the Chrissy I know, always better than everyone else just because she likes shitty books."

"I don't think I'm better than anyone, other than you, and it has nothing to do with reading books, and everything to do with how incredibly cruel you are to everyone you meet."

Angela pounded her fist on the table. "I stare at the corners because that's where I see it. It hovers there. All the time. It's just fucking mocking me. I've seen it every single day since Wreath died. Oh, and by the way, Wreath was my sister, too, and Mom was my mom. And I sat through so many bullshit days where you and Charlie hung out and tried to understand each other, and you talked about your problems and acted like a bunch of douchey sad losers. And the entire time you were talking, there was a monster hovering in the corner above you both, licking its lips.

"You want to know the truth? If anything happened to Charlie, I'll be devastated, but it doesn't change the fact that I don't really like him, and I don't really like you either. Why should I? You both might as well have been two more monsters in the room."

She crossed her arms. "In other words—" She slowly lifted her middle finger.

CHAPTER 17

SPILL IT

After Tiffany scoured the ferry for Charlie, she went to the top deck and stared out at Block Island as it shrunk into the distance. Doug tailed her the whole time, and now that she'd stopped running from seating section to seating section, he settled in behind her. Tiffany's hands shook, from the foggy nightmare she'd experienced, and the worry over Charlie, and now the freezing cold breeze from the ferry's trek.

She pulled out her phone to text Chrissy and let her know she hadn't seen Charlie, but before she could dial, Doug put his hand on her shoulder. All he said was, "Spill it."

It was all he needed to say.

She turned to him and huffed. She wanted to tell him everything, but the nerves firing through her made it difficult to speak, let alone rant.

"When I first met Charlie, I wondered about him. He seemed cool, but he seemed, I don't know, messed up. So, I looked him up. Remember how I got all of his information when he passed out in Beth's car? Anyway, I found out a lot."

Doug's eyes softened, but a nervous curiosity twitched his top lip. "What did you find?"

"When he was little, like four years ago, his family lived on Block Island. He had an older sister and she disappeared in their house when they were all there. The police found no trace of her. Just gone. And never found again."

"Jeez. That sucks, but what does it have to do with what's happening?"

"The police questioned Charlie's father, and seemed to think he had something to do with it. But the family, all of them, right down to Angela who was super little at the time, all held on to the same story. And that's true to this day."

Now an undercurrent of fear flooded his eyes. "What was their story?"

Tiffany glanced back at the island, worried to say this part, thinking of how ludicrous it would sound even to someone who probably just envisioned the same entity she had when they collapsed at the art studio. "That they were all playing a game when they heard their sister making horrible noises in her room. When they bashed her door in, they saw—"

Doug shook his head. "What?"

"—A monster eating her." She stood up firm, not feeling as weird about it as she thought she would. "They all say they saw a monster eating their sister."

Doug put his hands over his face and rubbed hard at it, as if he wanted to scrub his damned face off. When he pulled his hands away, his eyes were bloodshot, fiery little storms. "And I'm assuming that's what I saw in my little fucked-up foggy dream?"

She shrugged. "I assume. It's what I saw."

"What happened in yours?" he asked.

"Uncle Billy."

He nodded. "I'm sorry."

"Which turned into a giant weird-ass monster. What about you?"

"You getting dragged out of the house by Uncle Billy. This time, I chased after you, but when Uncle Billy turned around—"

"—He was the monster?" she finished for him.

"Yeah."

"Yeah."

They both stared off in different directions, Tiffany toward the island and Doug into the sea. Eventually, Doug broke the silence. "So, I still don't get it. Was the monster thing the reason we came here? Why didn't you tell me?"

"I didn't know," she said. "I mean, I assumed their trip here had something to do with it, but I didn't know what. It's not like I believed there was a fucking monster on the island. I just assumed they were coming here for some sort of closure. Maybe to talk to a friend or relative about it. I'm still not sure what they were doing. I mean, I know they were going to see the artist lady because she paints pictures of it or something, but that's all I know, and I just found that out five minutes before we got there."

Doug gripped the railing hard, his fingers turning ghostly white with the pressure. "So, do you believe there really was a monster?"

She looked away from him and bit hard on her lip. "I do now. Yeah. You?"

"Yeah," he said softly. "Yeah, I do. So what now? Where do you think Charlie went?"

She shook her head. "No idea. To either question."

"Because if the monster did something to him, we never should have left."

"I know," Tiffany said more sternly than she meant to. "I know we shouldn't have left. But I was scared."

"I'm still scared," Doug said.

Tiffany saw something from the far side of the island, away from the docks they'd pulled out of. "What's that?" She pointed.

Doug leaned forward, squinting his eyes. "What is that?"

It looked like a light fog, thin and hollow, at the bottom, but as it rose up, it grew thicker, like the raging smoke of a fire.

Tiffany turned away, unable to keep staring at it, thinking of only horrors. "Jesus, I hope they're all okay."

She turned and went inside, Doug following. They sat in silence inside the boat for the remainder of the trip. Chrissy called to ask if Tiffany had seen Charlie on board. She said she hadn't. Before she could finish apologizing for leaving, Chrissy hung up on her, which only exacerbated Tiffany's guilt. When they landed in Point Judith, they hurried to the stairs and exited as quickly as possible, as if the boat contained the noxious odors of their day, the poisonous air of all they'd just witnessed.

As they came out into the square parking lot, a figure ran toward them. Tiffany flinched, seeing creatures in everything, but as the figure closed in, she recognized Beth. Her girlfriend. Beth wrapped herself around Tiffany and kissed her cheek.

"You're back!"

Tiffany furrowed her brow. "What are you doing here?"

"Sorry, I just missed you today and wanted to surprise you."

"Color me surprised," Tiffany said, pushing past her girlfriend, heading toward the parking lot down the road where Doug parked their car. "How did you know which boat I was taking?"

Beth put her head down, following on Tiffany's side. Her cheeks turned speckled with pink. "I may have been waiting here for a few hours."

Tiffany gave her a double take, not slowing down in her walk. "That's a little weird, isn't it?"

Beth's mouth curved down and hurt flashed in her eyes. "I know. But I missed you."

Tiffany stopped in her tracks and faced Beth. She noticed Doug lagging behind, smart enough to stay away from this conversation. "It's weird. It's too much. I just wanted a fucking day with my brother and friends. This is too much. All of it." She didn't mean it. Sure, it was a bit much, but on a normal day, she wouldn't have held it against Beth, would have maybe cracked a joke and smiled, because the gesture was nice.

"What? I'm sorry. I didn't mean to like, invade on your shit. I thought it would be cute and make you happy."

"Well it didn't. I think you should leave."

"I'm sorry," Beth's voice cracked a little.

"Just go the fuck home, Beth," she yelled the words so loudly a couple across the street stopped and turned to see the commotion. Beth's pink-speckled cheeks turned to beets. She opened her mouth like she wanted to respond, but nothing came out of her other than a thin wisp of air. Not even loud enough to be a squeak.

Tiffany wanted to apologize right then and there, wanted to hug the poor girl, but she had no strength for it. She was ugly and mean, and she knew it, but she couldn't stop now. All of these horrible emotions were bubbling inside her, and she felt so weak, but yelling and being angry and kicking at whatever stood in front of her took some of that away, made her feel in control again. Jesus, she was her own monster. A villain. And worse than most, because she KNEW she was one, had the self-awareness to know how she acted really sucked. But she carried on anyway.

"Leave. Go home. Stop embarrassing yourself."

Tiffany stormed off, unwilling to witness the damage she'd created on her girlfriend's face. When she reached Doug's car, she finally turned back again. Beth was nowhere in sight. Doug reached the car a few seconds later and said nothing as he started the Camry and drove them home, but his eyes showed worry for Tiffany. He wouldn't lecture her, wouldn't pass judgment, but those eyes. Those eyes showed concern.

CHAPTER 18

LANGBLASS NEBELBEWOHNER

Chrissy and Angela sat up straight as Officer Carmen stepped in. He sighed and pulled up a chair at their table, sitting on it backward.

"All right, here's what's going to happen. We have state police coming in, and we're going to turn this island upside down trying to find your brother. We already have every officer on the island awake and preparing for the search. In the meantime, I suggest you keep trying his cell. We will too. The Coast Guard is sending some guys to pick you both up and bring you back to the mainland."

"What?" Chrissy asked.

"No, they fucking aren't," Angela said.

Officer Carmen put his hand up to stop them. "It's not a conversation. I know you've both been through a lot, and I know you're worried about your brother, but there's nothing you can do here but be in the way. Listen, normally if a teenager didn't show up to meet his family at the docks, we wouldn't have state police rolling in to begin a search. This is different because of . . . Well, you know. But that means YOU two need to be safe and sound too. At your home. With your family. I'm sure you both have schoolwork to get to this weekend, and I know your dad will be worried sick if you don't get back."

Chrissy prepared to let the comment go, unlike her sister, who broke out into laughter.

"Our dad has no clue where we are and hasn't for years."

Officer Carmen pursed his lips. "Then who do you live with?"

Again, Chrissy saw no point in indulging this conversation. It didn't matter. Charlie mattered. But again, Angela had a different mindset.

"We live with our aunt. My father's sister. She also doesn't give much of a shit about us, but she at least feeds us and gives us a place to sleep, although that place usually changes on the regular." She leaned forward. "See, after you all berated him for months on end and made this entire island think he was some kind of murderer, he sort of snapped, gave away all of our money. Literally! He gave it away. Didn't consider giving it to us! He gave it to charity. Then he pushed us on his sister, moved into a little shitty house in Westerly, and spends his days drinking and sobbing like a little bitch."

Officer Carmen slumped. "I'm sorry to hear that."

"Yeah, well, maybe it wouldn't have happened if the police decided to look into everything we *told* them happened instead of going with their gut. And Milicent even came to you *before* we told you pretty much the same thing. Two different families, two different times, both with the same story, and you just fucking ignored us."

Officer Carmen grinned. Chrissy saw the way he held in his anger, how he tried to smile and take it all, but it ate at him. He leaned in, keeping his voice calm. "You think we didn't look into your story? You think we didn't take it seriously? You have no idea. Yes, we checked out your father. We also looked at some neighbors. I'm sorry it bothers you that we were thorough." He sat up now, confidence kicking into his voice. "And for what it's worth, no, I don't believe you saw a monster that night, but I do believe you saw something that resembled one. Someone in a mask, a distortion of some sort. I don't know. And yes, Milicent came to us about her friend Molly and Molly's brother. And yes, when you all described the monster to us, we put all of that together, and we've operated ever since—which, by the way, means to this day—under the assumption we are dealing with some kind of serial killer. But we don't just bring that information to the local newspapers unless we have something really strong to show them."

Chrissy put her hand on top of his, her forehead wrinkling. She wasn't Angela and had no interest in antagonistic approaches, but what Officer Carmen said offended her on a deep level, words like shovels digging through her bones. "But we didn't see someone in a mask. I know you're trying to rationalize it, and I get that, but what we saw was a giant monster. It was ridiculously tall, and its body shape, the way it moved, the way it spoke, those weren't things humans can just do. And we watched it eat our sister. It ate her. Not like a cannibal, but it chewed on her until she was gone.

"And we saw it again tonight. Not in person, but it infiltrated all of our minds at the same time. We all fell to the ground like we were having a seizure. All of us. At the same time. That isn't normal, and you can't explain it away. I need you to understand this because Charlie—" Her voice broke, and a rush of sadness sloshed in her throat. "Charlie is gone, and I need you, absolutely *need* you to believe us. He didn't just skip off for ice cream. He didn't go for a leisurely walk. He disappeared while we all, simultaneously, lost control of ourselves and fell into a nightmare."

Angela's eyes darted back and forth between Chrissy and Officer Carmen. He pushed his head forward, closer to Chrissy. "And I need you to understand it's possible for me to not believe in monsters, but to fully believe you. I, and the state police, are not going to dismiss anything. That means we'll follow through as if a damned demon stole your brother, and we'll operate as if it's possible your brother decided things got too heavy and he needed a scoop of Ben and Jerry's. Checking into one doesn't dismiss another. We'll check on everything."

The door to the back room opened, and Officer Duplass stepped in. He had bags under his eyes and a few more grays than the last time they'd seen him. He wore sweatpants and a hoodie, and Chrissy guessed he'd just rolled out of bed, probably awoken by a phone call from the woman out front. What surprised Chrissy, though, was that an elderly woman came in right behind him.

Officer Carmen turned to the sound and gave a brief smile at his fellow officer. "Mark," Officer Carmen said.

Duplass nodded. "John. You mind if I talk to them?"

Officer Carmen stood up and shook Duplass's hand. "Go for it. I need to head to the docks and meet up with the state police when they get here. We got the rest of the gang dividing up the island and preparing search party routes. When you finish up with them, drive them down to the docks to meet with the Coast Guard. Don't let them out of your sight. We don't need them running out there, making us have to search for more kids."

As Officer Carmen exited the room, Duplass spun the chair around so he could sit on it the correct way. The old woman sat across from him.

Officer Duplass wasted no time cutting to the chase. "Just want to make sure I heard all this correctly. You two, Charlie, and a couple of friends went to Milicent's shop because you saw her drawings of your monster. Then, you all collapsed, somehow lost track of time, woke up, and fled to the docks only to realize Charlie was missing. Do I have that all right?"

Chrissy and Angela nodded.

"And why do you believe this has to do with your monster?"

Angela chimed in, an impatient frustration guiding her. "Because we all had a seizure at the same time, and I guess I don't know what everyone envisioned, but I saw the monster chewing on Wreath, and then it whispered a secret in my ear."

Chrissy jumped in, realizing they hadn't shared their nightmares with each other, they only assumed each of them saw the creature. "I also saw the monster, but it was crawling out from a book, lying on my bedroom floor. And it screamed at me. It said, 'Welcome home,' which is what it always says, but this time it pointed out the window to the street, and when I looked out the window, it was the street in front of our house. The one we live in now. What secret did it tell you, Angela?"

"It told me that it had all the blood it needed to be free. Whatever that means."

Everyone turned quiet for a moment until Chrissy looked at Officer Duplass. "I think it was all a threat. Look, I'm not stupid, I know you don't believe any of this. But it's true. I swear. And I know you know there's more to our story. Milicent told me how she came to you guys with the pictures from Molly and her brother."

The old woman took a cell phone from her pocket. "Hi. I'm sorry to interrupt. My name is Cathy Bogner, and I work for the historical society. It's nice to meet you both. I wanted to ask you a question." She opened her phone with a few finger swipes and placed it down on the table. Her finger clicked the photos app, and a picture opened up. Chrissy didn't see it at first, too busy eyeing her sister to see if she was as confused as Chrissy over why a member of the Block Island Historical Society would be there.

"Does this resemble your monster?"

Angela's eyes widened. Chrissy looked down. It was a crude drawing, old fashioned, and without detail, just an outline of the creature's shape. It was on a yellowed background, as if it came from an old book.

"That looks like it, yes. What is that?"

Dimples appeared on the woman's cheeks as she gave a pleasant smile. "This is Langblass Nebelbewohner. Silly name for such a frightening creature, I know. The picture comes from a book on German lore."

Chrissy was tired, too tired to hear about German lore, even if it was closely related to her own nightmares. What did it matter? She just wanted her brother back.

"What's a Langblass Whatchacallit?" Angela asked.

Officer Duplass rubbed his hand over his mouth and turned around, checking the door. "Look, I brought Cathy here because she's been following your case for a long time. Along with Molly Mix's. She provided us with a lot of information that, sadly, our police department didn't have. Stuff from before computers stored everything.

"For the record, and I'm not saying this to be a jerk, but I want you to understand where I'm at: I don't believe in monsters. But all the stuff Cathy's gathered paints a pretty crazy picture. And I think it's a picture you deserve to understand. It's a lot of folklore and weird stuff, but somehow it all correlates to what happened to your family. How? Why? That's what we're trying to figure out."

They all stared at him, waiting for his speech to end. Chrissy felt a small wave of relief. Sure, they didn't believe the monster stories, but they had investigated it and in some way, knew it all played into something more than a family going crazy together. If only the newspapers had the information the police did.

Cathy took her phone back and put it in her pocket. "Langblasses were tall, pale beasts that lived in the Black Forest in Germany. It was believed that they infected people's minds, showing them their worst nightmares before devouring them. I never found anything that mentioned seizures like you said you had today, but I did find a story from 1837 where a man talked about his family 'falling into a spell' in the Black Forest, and when he awoke, his children were gone, and a Langblass was eating his wife. You can find tons of silly stories about them on the internet. And they are all so wildly different from one another that it's hard to parse what's real and what's nonsense. Assuming any of it is real, of course. But there are commonalities. Having a foggy brain, seeing visions of the beasts, that sort of thing. Now, that's what I found researching Langblasses, but there was another story that *did* involve a seizure and a monster."

Chrissy sat back and pinched her nose. A headache was building in her skull. She already knew the Vanderline story and didn't need this woman reiterating it. "This is all really interesting, and I especially love research and wanting to know more about things, but I'm so tired, and my mind just keeps going back to my brother, so I just don't know that I have the patience for this right now. I'm not trying to be mean. I truly need to know all of this stuff, but I just can't process it right now."

Cathy put her arms up in defeat. "I understand, dear. Let me cut to the chase. Do you know anything about the *Palatine*?"

Chrissy nodded, still pinching her nose with her eyes shut tight. "Yes. I just read all about it."

"Well, if you did your research, I'm sure you've heard the conflicting accounts where some believe Block Islanders raided the ship, killed the immigrants on board, and robbed them blind, and the other account where they kindly housed the ailing passengers until they left for Pennsylvania."

Chrissy opened her eyes. "Yes."

Cathy smiled again, a polite little stream drawing up her cheeks. "Well, there's another account, and it's a juicy one. So juicy in fact, when I brought the letters to numerous historians, I was dismissed and mocked. Most believe I forged the documents. In these letters, all from the first mate on the *Palatine*, he claims the boat only housed two immigrants. A couple. And the trip wasn't to bring them to America. The crew and the immigrants were working together to bring something else to Block Island specifically."

Chrissy sat up, getting it. Angela looked at her sister. "What? I don't get it."

"They had captured three Langblasses from the Black Forest and were bringing them to Block Island for examination by a demonologist who promised she and her husband knew how to contain the creatures."

Chrissy's eyes filled with tears. Beads of excitement. "Apparently, they failed?"

Cathy frowned. "I'm not so sure. Well, surely the beasts aren't locked in a cellar somewhere, but they seem to only appear on this island, as if they can't leave it. And they aren't marching around killing people left and right. There must be something stopping them from that, from turning this place into their new Black Forest."

Angela was nearly hyperventilating. "So, you think it's real? You think it took Charlie?"

Cathy raised a hand. "There's one interesting thing, and that thing pokes a big hole in the theory that Langblasses had anything to do with what happened to your family."

"What?" Chrissy asked.

"The demonologists, their surname was Mix. And the immigrants, they were the Vanderlines, sometimes spelled as all one word, sometimes separated after the *N* and *R*. Van. Der. Line."

"I don't get it. I mean, I understand Molly Mix. There's a connection there, probably some distant relative. But what does that mean?" Chrissy asked.

"Molly Mix wasn't the first Mix to disappear mysteriously. In fact, it happened quite regularly in their family. Once a generation. Always to the oldest child. Whether or not that happened with *every* generation, I couldn't confirm, but it happened to Molly, and it happened at least three other times in their family line."

Chrissy's shoulders slumped. "And it happened to the Vanderline family too. I read about Mary Vanderline who had a seizure in her uncle's bathroom."

Cathy nodded. "Indeed. Outside of your sister's story, it's the only time I've heard a direct mention of seizures in relation to the monster. But so far as I can tell, the Vanderline family tree ended there."

Chrissy had drawn herself into the mystery, growing more and more interested as the dots connected closer to her sister's death, but now it all pulled apart again. "Still, there's clearly something there."

Officer Duplass sat forward. "Yes. Obviously. What that something is, we don't know."

Cathy tsk-tsked. "Oh, I think we do, even if we don't know how to connect them yet."

Duplass rolled his eyes. "Okay, yes, we know it has something to do with what you saw. While Cathy may be more willing to believe in old German folk tales, I am not. But clearly there are a lot of similarities and happenstances here. And we aren't ignoring that."

His phone buzzed. "Duplass. Go ahead." He nodded as if the person on the other end could see him. "Got it."

He stood up. "Come on. Your boat awaits."

Officer Duplass drove them to the docks, and the Coast Guard helped them onto the boat, handing them life vests. As Chrissy put hers on, she looked to Duplass, who stood by the boat, watching them get aboard and to safety. "Thank you for having Cathy explain all that to us. It doesn't really help, but it also kind of helps a lot. It at least makes us feel like we've been taken seriously."

Duplass nodded. "You have."

"I don't care if it's three in the morning. Please call me when you find anything out."

Duplass nodded again. "I'm going to call your aunt and father too. And just so you're prepared, I'm pretty sure Officer Carmen already has."

Angela frowned. "Doesn't matter. They won't answer. They won't care."

The small boat took off, engine buzzing. Unlike the large ferry, Chrissy could feel the bouncing of the boat against the sea. It made her already upset stomach turn. Despite the tragedies she'd lived through, her mother, her sister, her drunken father, she couldn't accept a doomed fate, couldn't help but think Charlie was safe out there somewhere, that he'd return home soon. While she still battled the nervousness, that hope clung to her and kept her from losing it. If

Duplass called her with a somber tone later that night, she didn't know what would happen to her, if she could survive it. Charlie was the one thing in her life that felt unbreakable. Ironic, considering how fragile he was.

As the boat reached the midway point to the mainland, nearing the rock wall that arched around the docks at Point Judith, Chrissy turned back to the island. "What the hell is that?"

Angela and a coastguardsman turned to see what she noticed.

"Looks like fog," the guardsman said, but he squinted to get a better view, unsure of his own answer.

"Why does it look like smoke?" Angela asked. "It's all super thick at the top."

The fog or smoke or whatever it was wrapped around the far side of the island, away from the places they'd visited for the day. The way it moved, slithered, crept, had an eerie lifelike quality to it, not a product of nature, but something guided and maneuvered like a marionette. Thin and scrim on the bottom, but it puffed up and bloated at the top. A mushroom. And it crept along the shore, enveloping one side of the island.

Chrissy tried to make sense of it, to see it as something she could understand, and when she placed it, she had to sit down, too overwhelmed by the strong sensations at play. Something was wrong. Something bad was happening.

The fog was a mouth, and it was swallowing the island. Worse, it spread in their direction, chomping slowly away at the ocean.

ON A CLEAR NIGHT

Jackson woke with a start. Something had pulled him from his dreams, but he was too out of sorts to figure it out. He spent a minute gathering himself. His head felt okay. Usually, he woke with a splitting headache from grinding his teeth all night. His chest, too, didn't ache the way it normally did, where he felt sharp pains and a thrumming heart. Some nights were luckier than others, where he woke up without the hardcore detoxing symptoms. Was detoxing the right word? It had certainly moved beyond hangovers.

He sat up and looked at the clock, which read 11:27 p.m. Oh fuck. Well, that explained the lack of symptoms. He had only been asleep for an hour and a half, which meant he was pretty much still drunk. Dragging his feet, he went to the fridge and cracked open a beer. He wanted something harder, but his head was swimming enough already. He just needed something to soften the inevitable pain.

Sipping off the can, he slid back to the bedroom and noticed his phone had two missed calls. The vibrating was probably what woke him up.

The same number had called both times. He played the only message.

"Hello, Mr. Keating. My name is Officer Carmen of the New Shoreham Police Department. Could you give me a call at—"

Jackson quickly opened the nightstand drawer and pulled out a piece of paper and a pen. He jotted the number down.

"—It's in regard to your son, Charlie, and your daughters, Chrissy and Angela."

Jesus. New Shoreham? Why were the kids anywhere near that fucking place? And all three of them? His stomach dropped. A hysterical, helpless cry bubbled in his throat and filled his eyes before he even heard what had happened. For all he knew the kids just got in trouble. Had a fight with some locals. Stole something.

As he went to dial, a gentle knock came from the front door. Despite the soft nature, Jackson nearly fell off the bed. He rushed to answer it, shoulders bumping into the walls as he went. He could hardly stand up straight. He really wanted a long pull on his drink before opening the door, but he'd forgotten the can on the end table.

When he saw the somber police officer on the doorstep, he cried, unleashing those tears that had built in his gut.

The officer had his hands at his chest, holding his hat, and he stood tall. A man and a woman stood behind him, a step down. The officer in front wore a state uniform, and the woman had what looked like a Westerly Police Department uniform. The man in the back wore civilian clothes.

"Sorry to bother you, sir. Are you Mr. Keating?" the statie asked.

Jackson nodded.

"I'm Officer Barrett. May we come in for a moment?"

Jackson floated. Just as he had when he found his mother dead as a child, and when he received the call about his wife. He hovered above the scene, watching the actors play out their roles, watching himself, too, seeing himself open the door for the group, guiding them to the couch, and sitting next to them in an armchair.

The female cop stopped before sitting and shook his hand. "I'm Officer Burns. Or you can just call me Meghan."

Too many names. Cops on the phone. Cops at the door. It was too much.

"We have some bad news," Officer Barrett said, and just like that, Jackson was sucked back into his body, no longer floating. In fact, he hardly had the strength to sit. If he could flop over and die, he would.

"Your son, Brian, died earlier this evening from a drug overdose."

Jackson never questioned whether he was a bad parent or not. He knew he sucked. But his thoughts in the first few seconds after he heard the officer's words solidified it. Because after hearing the voicemail about Charlie, Chrissy, and Angela and then seeing these officers, he assumed something had happened to one or all of them. When he discovered it was Brian, his immediate thought was, *Phew*.

But then memories of Brian as a child, teaching Charlie to play *Mario Kart*, laughing with Jackson while watching *The Princess Bride*, all of those happy little glimmers came back. Memory was a lie, though, because most of their lives they butted heads, and those happy moments were so fleeting and desperate that they only acted as a mirage, something to cling to, something to break Jackson's heart at the end.

Brian was such a good kid, so caring about his family, so overprotective. He loved his siblings more than he loved anything, even his parents. When Jackson had to yell at Angela for coloring on the walls, Brian stood between them, talking Jackson down, reminding him how little kids behave and of the beauty in their creativity.

Jackson continuously saw Brian as himself, which made their relationship hard because the boy reflected the worst aspects of his father, projecting them for all to see. When he'd left home, dropped out of school, became a drug addict, disappeared, yelled and shouted, it was all Jackson. Jackson's Frankenstein. But worse, because he'd built this monster from his own parts. He fostered it, practically driving the boy to those dark corners. He'd failed on every front, and now Brian died so young, too fucking young. And Jackson only had himself to blame.

He bent over, head to his knees, and bawled. Sounds of anguish flew out of him—pained groans, yells, grunts.

The officers sat there, still and calm.

"Was he alone? That's all I want to know."

The man in plain clothes sat forward. "Hello, Mr. Keating. I'm Officer Long of the Providence Police. I'm the one who responded to the call and found your son. He was at someone's house, and he had a friend there with him. But he asked to use the restroom, where he proceeded to take a large amount of pills."

Jackson cocked his head. "You mean it was on purpose? Suicide?"

Officer Long nodded his head. "It appears that way. Yes."

Jackson stood up. "Oh my god. Just before you got here, I had a message from the New Shoreham police about my other children. I need to call them."

He ran into his bedroom and grabbed his cell phone and the unfinished beer. When he came into the living room, all three officers were still sitting on the couch. As he dialed the number he'd written down, none of them said anything. Probably not trained to handle a situation where a man just lost his son and also needed to call a different police department about his other three children.

The officer he dialed picked up. "Officer Carmen."

"Hello, this is Jackson Keating. You left me a message?"

There was silence on the other end. Jackson glanced at the officers on the couch, all staring up at him, and he turned toward the kitchen. As the officer on the other end spoke, Jackson made his way out the side door into his yard. The cool, fresh air hit his dry lungs. He killed the rest of his beer and tossed the can on the lawn.

"Hey, I would much rather have this conversation in person, but we're running thin here. Your children came to the island today, Chrissy, Angela, and Charlie. Apparently, they're all claiming they had a group episode—"

Jackson's heart banged hard. He stared off beyond his yard,

where the ocean lapped against the shore. "A group episode? What does that mean?"

"Well, according to them it means they, and a group of their friends, all fell into a seizure. And they lost a good chunk of time. They say around seven hours."

Jackson shook his head. "They say" were good words to hear. It meant they were okay now. "I'm not sure I'm understanding. They said they *ALL* had a seizure for seven hours?" He held in a scream of frustration. "That doesn't make sense. Are they okay? Just tell me my fucking kids are okay."

Even having seen what he'd witnessed, Jackson couldn't comprehend a group of kids having a seizure at the same time, and worse, for it to last for such an absurd amount of time. It would have destroyed their brain, right?

He continued to stare out at the ocean, and then he noticed something he'd never seen before. To be fair, he almost never went in the yard. But now he noticed a series of blinking lights in the distance. It was Block Island. He had no idea he could see it from here.

"Yes." Officer Carmen gave a big sigh as if dreading the words to come. "They said they saw the monster. In a vision. All of them. But Mr. Keating, that's not why I'm calling. When they woke up, Charlie was missing."

"What?" Slowly the blinking lights dimmed as if something covered them. "Did you find him?"

"We have the state police here, and we're currently operating a full search of the island. Meanwhile, the Coast Guard took your daughters back to the mainland, and a Narragansett officer is driving them home to your sister's house."

"So, you haven't found Charlie? Do you have anything to go on? Any idea where he could have gone?" His knees buckled under him, head swimming. He leaned against a tree. The dimmed blinking lights vanished altogether.

"We don't have much to go on outside of where he was at the

time they last saw him, but I assure you we have teams of folks here helping us search for your son, and we won't rest until we find him."

"Really? You have a full team? Seems like half the team is in my living room right now."

"Huh?"

The last blinking light visible faded as something covered it. The phone made a screeching sound, horribly high-pitched, and then the call went silent.

"Officer? Are you there? What's happening?"

The side door slapped against the wooden rail as the three officers came out into the yard. "Everything all right, Mr. Keating?" one of them asked.

Jackson fell to his knees. It was hard to breathe. "I've got to get to my daughters."

"Would you like us to call them? Do you have anyone else that can stay with you right now?" Officer Barrett asked.

"No. It's just them. I need to get to them."

The officers looked at each other. Barrett said, "I'm not sure you should be driving. We can collect your daughters and bring them to you if they aren't old enough to drive themselves."

He almost argued until he realized how stupid that would be. First, getting into a car in front of three cops with a blood alcohol level of, well, vodka, wouldn't work out well. But even if they did let him go, how foolish would he be to let his children into a car with him behind the wheel?

"Yeah, okay. I'll give you the address. That would be great." He squinted, eyes focused on the island. In the dark, he couldn't make out what covered it, but something appeared to be moving, clouding the entire land mass. Then it became clearer. It was a mist, and it was growing, expanding, and headed straight toward them.

"Does that look normal to you?"

The officers all turned to where he pointed.

"What?" Burns asked.

"That fog or smoke or whatever that is. It looks all wrong."

Officer Long leaned forward. "What the hell is that?"

Officer Barrett stepped in, putting his hand on Jackson's shoulder. "Come on. Let's get you inside and get that address."

He followed them into the house, but before he entered, he gave the growing sheath one last look. It was just fog. It had to be. But he swore it moved like it was alive, and worse, he felt it was staring at him.

CHAPTER 20

YOU CAN FEEL BLOCK ISLAND

As soon as the police car parked in front of Chrissy and Angela's house, another police car pulled onto the road and parked behind them. The officer who drove them home hopped out and opened the back door.

"Teddy Barrett? What are you doing here?" he yelled to the other car.

The second officer got out of his cruiser. "I'm here to pick up Chrissy and Angela Keating."

The sisters looked at each other. Angela felt a tightening knot in her gut.

"Did you find something out about Charlie?" Chrissy asked, scuttling out of the vehicle.

Officer Barrett looked confused, seeing his pick up exit a different police car, but he shook it off, clearly with bigger matters at hand. "Are you Chrissy and Angela?"

Angela stepped out of the car behind Chrissy. "Yes. Did you find Charlie?"

"I'm sorry, but I don't know anything about that. I was sent here to pick you up and bring you to your father's house."

Angela nearly laughed. "My father's house? You couldn't pay me."

"What's going on?" Chrissy asked.

Officer Barrett rubbed his eyes. "We have some things to discuss with you both, and your father shouldn't be alone right now, so he asked us to pick you up. There's a lot going on that we need to talk to you about, but I can't discuss it here."

Chrissy looked at Angela, and for the first time since Angela could remember, it appeared her big sister wanted her younger sibling's opinion, or at least for her to say something.

"We're not on good terms with our father. Can you just explain what this is about?"

The officer took his hat off and rubbed his forehead. "Not out here. But I was unaware you had a strained relationship with your father. If you're not safe or comfortable going over there, can we go inside so I can talk to you? And maybe you have a recommendation for someone else who might be willing to stay with your father for the night?"

"Come on," Chrissy said, heading toward the house. "But good luck finding someone who'll stay with my dad. He's not exactly pleasant company."

Angela waved goodbye to their escort and followed Chrissy and the officer inside. She worried about waking her auntie up. As soon as they entered the kitchen, Angela noticed the blinking light on the voicemail machine. Chrissy and the officer sat at the kitchen table, but Angela checked the message. As eager as she was to find out what this policeman had to say, she worried the missed call involved news on Charlie.

An automated voice told her the time and date of the voicemail. Late last night. So, it wasn't about Charlie. How'd they all go through this morning without noticing a message?

When Brian's voice kicked in, Angela grew angry until she picked up his somber tone. Her hostility toward yet another family member who abandoned her dissipated, and she realized all at once that

Brian was just an older version of her, scared and alone. Hateful of everything.

"Hey, Charlie . . . Hey, Charlie. Listen, I'm not gonna make the trip with you guys tomorrow. I just wanted to tell you something important. Not everyone is made to be a hero. Some of us don't have redemption arcs, you know what I mean? This isn't the movies, and sometimes some of us don't repair, don't come in at the last second and save the day. But you, Charlie. You are a fucking hero. I know you have anxiety and all this other bullshit fucking up your brain, so it's hard to see, but kid, you're a fucking badass. Take care of Chrissy and Angela. Y'all deserved better than me and Dad."

Tears formed in Angela's eyes, not just from the sadness in Brian's voice, but that he called Charlie a hero, and now the hero was missing, disappeared, and while everyone else went full force into finding him, Angela knew deep down that something horrible had happened, that Charlie wasn't coming back. Up until this point, she'd held it together, but the message from a night prior felt like one from the future, a delivery of bad news. The family hero had vanished for good.

Who would be the hero then? It wouldn't be her. Angela knew her place. She kicked and screamed and bit. To those around her, Angela was the monster in the corner, the entity they all feared would one day chomp them down.

And Angela lived with that because she had Charlie. Sure, she hated him most of the time, despised how much he ignored her, but she knew from the depths of her soul that when push came to shove, Charlie would die to protect her. Brian was right. Charlie was a hero. But the hero had left the story.

Chrissy ran to her, wrapping her arms around her little sister as Angela leaned against the wall and cried. Officer Barrett remained seated and said nothing, letting the girls have their emotions. Knowing there was more news to come, Angela fought against the tears long enough to ask, "What do you have to tell us?"

The officer's eyes filled with water. He wiped at them. "Was that your brother Brian?" He pointed to the voicemail machine.

Chrissy nodded.

"Is there an adult at home who can be here for this conversation?"

Angela went to point to the bedroom, but Chrissy put her hand around her sister's arm to stop her. "We live with our aunt, but she's out for the weekend."

"She just leaves you alone for the whole weekend?"

The officer's reaction was exactly why Angela hadn't wanted to lie. Chrissy's fib, probably meant to avoid waking the wrath of their aunt, would only instigate curiosity in the officer. Surely, their living situation would get a future investigation. More problems to pile on another day.

Chrissy shook her head. "No. She never has before. She just—"

Angela held in a smirk. Everything sucked right now, but seeing her sister fumble gave her an ounce of pleasure. "Our aunt is very overprotective of us, but she had a business opportunity, and she originally turned it down, but we all talked her into it and promised her we'd be fine to take care of ourselves for a few days. She left us some money for pizza and the cupboards are full. We're good kids. Not really troublemakers. And Charlie was old enough to watch us." Angela caught her use of past tense a second too late.

The officer ran his fingers along the edge of his hat. "I'm not supposed to have this conversation with children when an adult isn't present, but under the circumstances, I'm going to break the rules a little." He sighed, and the pause was enough to tell a whole story. "Your brother Brian died earlier tonight from an apparent drug overdose."

Chrissy immediately sat down, almost as if her legs couldn't carry the weight of the news. Angela stood frozen, wholly unexpecting what she'd just heard, even after the voicemail, which now became much clearer. It was basically a suicide note. Anger flowed through her. And sadness too. But she didn't break down, didn't fall to the floor in hysterics the way she would if it were Charlie, or Chrissy, or even Auntie. Brian was her brother, and she loved him to some degree, but she hadn't seen him in so long, making him more of a stranger than a relative. He was someone she knew of but didn't know.

Of course, the lack of sadness for him made her sadder *for* him because grief was a mysterious lump on your flesh, a foreign body growing on you. You see it, and know it, and recognize it, and you worry about it. One minute, you can convince yourself it's benign, just an ugly little thing you can learn to deal with, and the next, you're certain it's the start of something bigger, the kind of thing that will eat away at your flesh, devour your bones, crumble you.

It didn't matter how little she knew Brian, how far away he had appeared, because she knew *of* Brian. And while she couldn't agree with his choices, she understood them. The guy hydroplaned, and if anyone understood surviving on the inertia of PTSD, it was Angela. None of them were in control. Never had been. They all spiraled in different directions, but in the end, they all had to meet the fucking wall. One explosion after the next. It was their destiny, a tale set in stone the moment their father opened the door and revealed to them a creature who fed on their sister.

They were doomed.

Chrissy sniffled with her hands over her face. Angela stayed statuesque, not only unsure how to react but worried that if she did react, if she chose her path, whether it be an angry response, an uncaring one, or a sad one, that it would alter the fabric of reality, change not only the future but the past. Whatever movement she made would violate time and space. So she did nothing. Said nothing.

Chrissy lifted her head. "I think I actually would like to go to my dad's if that's okay."

Angela didn't want to go, and of course, no one asked for her opinion, but she'd be damned if she were staying in their house essentially alone thanks to Auntie C's sound sleeping. Chrissy followed the policeman out the door, and Angela trekked behind. As soon as they exited the house, something felt off. When they hopped in the back seat of the cruiser, Angela looked out the back window and saw a dense fog rolling in from the shore.

The car crept forward down their dark side street, and within seconds, the fog had overtaken them, slithering along both sides of the car. It wasn't ordinary fog, grayer, like smoke. And it hadn't come in like an act of nature, but with a purpose. When it had reached the front of the car, it turned on both sides, wrapping around the headlights like two sets of fingers gripping a toy.

"What's happening?" Chrissy asked.

"Bad visibility tonight," Officer Barrett said.

"No. Look. It's changing things."

At first, Angela didn't understand what her sister had meant, but then she noticed it. The houses had changed. She'd sat in the passenger seat of her brother's car and her aunt's car numerous times, staring at the neighborhood houses, and these were not the same ones she remembered seeing. They were older, more decrepit. The paint flecked off the siding, weatherworn, and damaged by time. Even the lawns had lost their green, which was normally natural for the fall, except they had been green. Just this morning. The fall had been unseasonably warm, keeping a lot of the color on most lawns and trees. But beyond the scrim fog, they'd turned yellow, brown, dead, and it had happened in a matter of seconds.

"Something isn't right," Angela said.

"Geez, this fog is something else." Officer Barrett chuckled a nervous little noise. "I can see okay, but it looks like it's swirling around us. Never seen anything like this."

He slammed on the brakes. "What the fuck?"

Chrissy and Angela turned to the front, wondering what caused Officer Barrett to stop the car short.

Angela gripped her sister's arm so tightly her fingernails may have drawn blood. The Langblass stood in front of the car, staring at them.

CHAPTER 21

WHEN THE STORM STOPS

As soon as she and Doug arrived back at their house, Tiffany ran upstairs to her room, pulled out her cell, and dialed Charlie's number. Instead of ringing, it screeched at her, a deafening wail in her ears.

She hung up and tried again, and it did the same thing.

"What the hell?"

She hung up and dialed Beth. It rang like normal, which proved whatever glitch had happened wasn't an error from Tiffany's phone, but Charlie's.

Beth didn't answer, though, and that sent Tiffany's stomach spinning with worry and guilt.

She cried, not really at any one thing. Charlie. Chrissy. The shrieking response from Charlie's phone. The monster in her dreams and the one from her past. Could anything go back to normal? Ever. She couldn't see how.

She felt a need to do something but couldn't think of what that something could be. It made her feel small, weak, helpless. Poor Charlie. Was he lost? Scared? Dead?

Something banged down the hall, and she flinched. This was her life now, flinching at every sound, sensing a crawling dread from every shadow. She'd lived through these symptoms before, struggled with them for years before her uncle died. She didn't know if she had the strength for a second go-around, though. A person can only fray for so long before they become nothing but loose strands.

Doug knocked on her door.

"Come in," she said.

He opened the door slowly. "Just checking in."

"We literally got home a minute ago."

He took a big breath and slowly crept toward the rolling office chair in the corner of the room. "Okay. Maybe I just didn't want to be alone."

"Maybe we should just fall asleep watching movies in the living room."

He nodded absently, staring off into the corner of the room. "I don't know how to deal with this, Tiff. Everything that happened today was beyond fucked, and I have a feeling—" He stopped himself, unwilling to finish the sentence.

"—It's about to get a lot worse?"

He put his head down. "I'm terrified. For you. For me. For Charlie."

Tiffany stood up. "When we were little, before all the shit with Uncle Billy, I overheard Dad talking to Mom, and he said Tanner's Switch was a doomed town. I was too little to know that he was talking about economics and shit, but later I asked him what 'doomed' meant. He told me, not realizing I'd overheard the word from him. And for years, I felt like this black cloud hung over all of us. No, not a black cloud, a giant stone, something too heavy for all of us to carry, and one day, our arms would tire out, and we'd be crushed under it. As I got older, I realized how silly that was, but I feel it again now."

He stood up to meet her face-to-face. "What happened to us was screwed up. It wasn't normal."

She nodded her head toward the door and walked out. Doug

followed. They made their way to the living room and sat on the couch.

"What should we watch?" Tiffany asked.

Doug rubbed his eyes. The exercise in distraction would most likely be a failure, but after running away from the island, Tiffany felt the need to try. To try at not trying.

"Something light, I guess."

"*Requiem for a Dream,* then?"

Doug chuckled. "Fuck you. Find a comedy. I'm going to get some chips."

He left for the kitchen, and Tiffany pulled out her cell phone. She dialed Charlie's phone, and again, a shrieking noise broke through. Even when prepared for it, she startled at the sheer volume and pitch of the sound.

She hung up and tried Chrissy, hoping for an update. The horrid sound came again. Maybe it *was* Tiffany's phone after all.

She called Doug's cell to test it. It rang on her receiver, and she heard his cell buzzing on the kitchen table in the next room over.

"Why are you calling me, idiot?" Doug yelled from the kitchen.

"I'm just making sure my phone is working," she yelled back.

"Tiffany? What the fuck?" Doug said with a shivering voice.

Something crashed, like he dropped a dish.

Tiffany stood up to check on him, still holding the phone to her ear. The ringing stopped, and the shrieking took its place. It scared her so much she dropped the phone. "Doug?"

She ran to the kitchen, where potato chips and a shattered bowl decorated the tiling. Doug stood with his back to the fridge, staring out the side door. Tiffany turned to what held his attention. Smoke plumed in from the gap between the bottom of the door and the sill. But it wasn't acting like fire smoke, or even mist. It slithered up and down, snaking in. Tiffany stepped back, worried it was toxic. She looked out the kitchen window and saw the scrim mist breezing past the window.

The foggy fingers crawling into the kitchen were pulsing. Pulsing as if they needed to breathe in and out.

She'd already inhaled fog today, fallen into a spell and lost hours of her life, and now it was back.

"Doug, we need to get out of here."

Doug stood wide-eyed, frozen in place.

"DOUG!"

He snapped out of it just as the living room window shattered. Tiffany screamed. A giant arm swung in through the newly created opening. Giant, pale gray, and bony. Sharp-tipped fingers slashed, ripping into the couch.

"Go!" Tiffany grabbed Doug's arm and led him toward the side door, where the fog crawled in. Before they reached it, the knob of the door collapsed to the floor as a sharp claw smashed the wood around it to bits.

Doug pulled his sister back. "Upstairs."

She followed him, making a big arch around the monster smashing its way through the window. As they ran up the stairs, she said, "This is the dumb thing everyone does in horror movies. Why are we going up?"

"Where else are we going to go? They're everywhere down there."

"Why aren't Mom and Dad waking up?"

"MOM! DAD!" Doug yelled, and then to Chrissy, he said, "I thought there was only one of those things."

"I'm not an expert, Doug."

They ran into Tiffany's room and Doug slammed the door behind them.

He put his hands on her shoulder. Below them, the sounds of crunching and banging persisted. "Listen. I'm going to hide behind your bed. You hide in the closet. When they come in, I'll stand up and yell at them to get their attention away from you. Then, I'll climb onto the roof and jump down to get away. Once they follow me, you need to get the hell out of here."

She shook her head, then nodded, then shook her head again. "No. That's a dumb plan. It's so dumb. We just fight. Why do we keep treating these things like they're invincible? I'm sure we can hurt them. And what are we going to do, leave Mom and Dad to fend these fucking things off?"

One of the creatures screeched. By the sound, Tiffany guessed it had fully entered the living room.

"Just get in the closet!"

She listened, not sure if she had another choice. But why weren't her parents waking up? Hopefully the monsters just wanted the kids from the island and wouldn't bother going into their parent's room.

Once she closed the bifold doors, she sat in the corner. Like a child playing hide-and-seek, she took the loose clothes lying on the closet floor and covered herself with them. The door had slats, which provided a way to see out into the bedroom, but only if she were close to the door. Squeezed into the corner, Tiffany was *not* close enough.

She couldn't hear the creatures anymore and wondered if they had left. She nearly yelped out loud when her phone vibrated in her pocket. Luckily, she kept it together. She slowly slid the phone out, worried even the vibrating sound could catch the ear of the creatures. But her heart sank at the sight on her phone screen. Charlie's face slouched in the back seat of Beth's car. A picture Tiffany had taken while Charlie drunkenly slept on his way home. She'd used it as his contact photo. *Charlie calling*, the phone screen read.

Charlie.

Calling.

She didn't know what to do. Monsters were in her house. She couldn't talk without risking the creatures finding her, and she couldn't let the phone keep buzzing either. But it was Charlie calling. Right now, police were probably scouring the island searching for him. Everyone would want to know he was okay. *She* needed to know he was okay.

She slid the bar across the bottom of the screen and slowly

brought it to her ear. With the thinnest whisper she could muster, she said, "Charlie?"

Nothing.

Silence.

She didn't dare whisper his name again.

The wood floors in the upstairs hallway creaked. A gentle sound.

She pressed the phone tighter to her ear, as if doing so would make his voice squeeze out of the phone.

Then, the voice came, that same double voice she'd heard in her seizure dream. Male and female wrapping around each other into one singular voice. "Wash up, Scumbag." She dropped the phone and bit back a scream.

The door to her bedroom crashed open, slamming into the wall.

Tiffany pushed her legs tighter into her torso, trying to make herself smaller. Maybe she could press so tightly she'd flatten into a 2D image, a thin strip of paper that could blow with the wind, get carried away with a storm.

The monster wailed, a deafening war cry blasting through the world. There were no words in its scream, but it said plenty. *I am here to kill. I will find you, and I will rip you to shreds.*

"Come get me, motherfucker," her brother yelled from the far side of the room. The monster hissed and stomped toward the voice. Doug said, "Oh shit," and from there, Tiffany couldn't make out what happened.

Grunting, wailing, Doug swearing, a bang, a crash.

Tiffany slowly crawled to the door and cracked it open. The monster leaned out the window, slashing toward the roof. She didn't know what to do. Save her brother was the obvious choice, but there had been *two* creatures downstairs. One at the front door and one at the window. But now, only one stood in her room. If she left the closet, would the sharp talons of the second monster gore her the second she stepped out? She couldn't see into the hallway, had no idea if the other creature lingered in waiting.

Fog crept in from the hall, quickly filling her room. As it crawled across the walls, it changed the environment, yellowing her white ornate wallpaper. It peeled and flaked as if timeworn. Tiffany flinched as it slipped between the slats in the closet door, wrapping itself around her. It crawled into her nose. She did everything she could to hold her breath, but she was already shaky and near hyperventilating from fear.

Fuck it. If she was going out, she might as well fight for her brother in the process. She stood up and pushed the closet door open. Time for war.

CHAPTER 22
THE HARDEST NIGHT

Jackson stood in the living room in a general haze. His wife, burned to death in a factory fire. His oldest daughter, dead at the hands of a monster. His oldest son, dead at the hands of Jackson's neglect. His other son, missing after going back to the island that housed the start of their horror, presumably to find answers or closure, to find some hidden meaning, and that, too, stemmed from Jackson's neglect.

Maybe it all did. Could going through life purposeless spark a fire in a factory twenty miles away? Could it burn up the ones you love?

A headlight flashed through the window as a car turned the corner, snapping Jackson out of his self-loathing funk. But it wasn't the police bringing his two daughters to him. Just a random car passing by. Someone living their life. Maybe going to work or to a girlfriend's house. Maybe to see their children. Who knew? But he guessed whoever drove that vehicle did better than Jackson. It wouldn't take much. The odds were in his favor on that bet.

A high-pitched screech came from Officer Burns' walkie-talkie. It made the same squeal Jackson heard on the phone when he lost touch with the Block Island cop. The abrupt sound gave everyone a jolt. The cop grabbed the walkie from her belt and turned a nob, but it refused to stop screeching. This wasn't the normal obnoxious chirps and burps the police radios usually let out.

"What the hell is wrong with this thing?" she asked.

"Just turn it off," Officer Long said.

"I can't turn my radio off. I'm on the clock."

"It's obviously not working anyway. Just turn it off for a minute and see what happens when you turn it back on."

She relented, turning the switch **<OFF>** and powering the walkie down. It went silent. Everyone took a breath as she placed it on the coffee table.

"That was the loudest I've heard a radio go," Officer Long said.

She nodded. Without her touching it, the walkie came back to life. It played a low static, just a soft crinkling sound. Then, something whispered into it. They all looked at each other.

"How the hell is it picking anything up when it's not even on?" Long asked.

"Do they still like, kind of work when they're off? Do you need to take the batteries out or something?" Jackson asked.

"No," Burns said. "It's off. Like off off. Same as when you click your television off. It doesn't still *kind of* play something. It's off."

They all leaned in, trying to hear the whisper, but it turned out they didn't need to. The voice grew louder and clearer.

"Please. I finally have friends," the voice said, and then it screamed a pained and agonized yell.

Jackson stumbled to his seat, heart beating in his ears. "Give me that."

He grabbed the radio, holding it to his mouth. "Charlie? Charlie?" But he knew deep down it wasn't Charlie at all, just something mimicking his voice. Yet, he couldn't accept it. Wouldn't. Because the implications were too horrid to handle. If it were Charlie speaking and screaming, there was time to save him. If not, well . . .

The two officers gave each other a strange look.

"You have to hit the button to talk, but it's not on," Burns reminded him.

He pressed the button. "Charlie? What's wrong?"

"No! It's not fair. Please!"

"What's not fair, Charlie?"

The walkie went dead again. No sound.

"Come on. Talk to me."

Heavy breathing came through the speaker.

"What? What is it? Charlie, is that you?"

"Welcome home."

The two officers jolted back at the horrific voice, but Jackson turned to stone, frozen in place. That voice hadn't left his ears in four years, but hearing it again in real life made it clear how much memory can wash over our senses, dulling the sounds and feelings behind things. He'd heard those two words every single day, playing out in his brain, but he hadn't remembered just how well that voice cut through his blood, chilling his heart. The way it sharply drove into his spine. How his skin frosted over at the sound.

He gripped the walkie-talkie tightly. "You motherfucker. What did you do? I never should have let this go. I never should have walked away. I should have hunted you down and fucked you up. And that's what I'm going to do. You hear me? If you touched a hair on my kid's head, I will fuck you up. I'm coming for you. You hear me? I am coming for you."

He threw the walkie on the floor and stood up. A tsunami of blood rushed to his skull and speckles of black decorated his vision.

Officer Long stood up and gripped Jackson's arm. "Sir, are you okay? What were those voices? Can you tell us what's going on?"

Jackson pulled away from him, fighting the dizzy spell. He went to the kitchen and opened the fridge. He needed to get out there and save his children, but once the detoxing took hold, he'd be useless, which meant he needed to drink. He knew how ridiculous it sounded, and it probably was, but with a throbbing pain growing in his chest and his heart slamming against his rib cage, he also knew there was some truth in it this time.

He placed a bottle of vodka on the kitchen counter and a two-liter of soda. For a moment, he stared at them, debating if he really needed them or if he was just being an alcoholic asshole. Maybe both answers were correct.

As he took two giant travel tumblers out of the cabinet, Officers Long and Burns whispered in the living room, probably trying to figure out how to approach the madman who spoke to voices on a turned-off radio.

Jackson poured. First, the vodka, filling each tumbler about a third of the way full. Then he used the soda to fill them the rest of the way. The fog rolled past the kitchen window as Jackson shook the tumblers, mixing the poor man's medicinal concoction. He wasn't even just an alcoholic, he was a frat boy dude bro alcoholic.

He took a sip as a shadow passed the window. The detoxing was no longer responsible for his crazed heart rhythms.

"It's here," he whispered.

Burns said, "What the hell is happening outside?"

Officer Long stepped into the kitchen with his cell phone to his ear. He yelped and dropped the phone. Jackson could hear the loud wailing screech coming from the other end of the line from all the way across the kitchen. He kept his eyes looking out the window, waiting for the shadow to return, to make its move.

"I'm going to turn my radio back on and try to get in touch with the station," Burns said from the living room.

Officer Long turned back to her. "Don't do that. Use your cell. Mine isn't working. It's doing the same thing your radio is."

A few seconds later, Jackson heard the high-pitched screech coming from her phone in the living room.

"What the hell is happening?" Officer Long asked. "Is this some kind of weather thing?"

Burns came into the kitchen. "I don't know. Where's Barrett? He should be back by now."

Of course, Jackson knew what they didn't. The monster was here, off the island and hunting for his family. Charlie and his sisters conjured something there tonight and let it loose. And now it was here, and it was going to kill them all.

But Jackson wouldn't let that happen. He'd save his daughters, and together, they'd find Charlie. The monster won once, but never again. He couldn't convince the cops of that, though. They'd never agree to leave until Officer Barrett returned with the kids, and they'd talk in circles about not wanting to miss him on the road, or how they needed to wait until communications were back up before going anywhere.

He'd need to steal their keys, which he didn't believe he could accomplish. He wasn't a professional thief on his best of days, and this was not his best of days. He took a swig from the tumbler, a big one. The vodka hadn't mixed well with the soda yet, despite his half-hearted shaking of the tumbler, so the sip hit hard. Just as he hoped it would. The throbbing in his chest quelled.

He tried to be patient, think up a plan, but time was not on his side. Every second wasted was a chance for the monster to kill his children. No matter what he did, he risked failing them. Robbing cops of their vehicle was a surefire way to spend the night in hand-cuffs while the creature hunted down his flesh and blood.

But the monster was here. At his house. So it wanted him first. He could fight it. He could kill it. Or at the least, he could escape it and get to his daughters.

He turned to the cops, who stood in the kitchen, talking about the communication problem. With no concern for their unimportant conversation, he interrupted them. "Either of you ever have to fire your weapon in the line of duty."

The woman smiled. "In Westerly? No. Almost a few times, but no."

Officer Long frowned. "Hell, I'm in Providence, and I haven't had to fire it yet either. Surprising, I know."

Jackson sipped his drink. He knew how crazed he must look to the two police officers. His eyes were probably glossy and red, his hair a frazzled mess. Was he slurring yet? He didn't know. A nearly empty bottle of vodka sat behind him. He discovered his child had died, and he mixed himself not one but two late-night drinks. But maybe it was good for them to worry about Jackson. He needed them on edge. On edge meant prepared for something to happen. And something *was* going to fucking happen. Any minute. He knew it because he'd seen it. And no one believed him. But they were about to.

"Well, I'd be prepared to break your cherries tonight, friends."

"What does that mean?" Officer Long asked.

Jackson gulped his drink down. "You'll see."

Burns stepped in front of Long. "Why don't you sit down and take a breather? I know this has been the hardest night for you. We understand."

The officers were probably worried Jackson planned to off himself, maybe try to take them out first. "The hardest night?" He took both cups off the counter and sat down as instructed. "No. Not the hardest. It's up there, that's for sure. But do you want to hear about the toughest night?"

They both stared at him. Long crossed his arms around his chest. Burns placed her hands on her hips, one hand close to her firearm. Jackson liked her. She was smart.

"Four years ago, I got a call from Freedell Industries. You know them?"

Long shook his head, while Burns shrugged.

"Yeah, probably not something you'd know offhand. Yet, they're one of the biggest companies in the world. In. The. World. My wife worked for them. She sat in a factory running semiconductors through a machine. Pass or fail. All day long, dropping these computerized bug-looking things through a robot that spat them back out as either a pass or a fail. And she tubed the good ones up and sent them along. The bad ones went in for a closer look to see if they could get fixed and make it through to the other side on the next go-around. Those semiconductors power the world. Cars. Video games. Televisions. Any electronic you can think of. Semiconductors. If my wife made a mistake and packaged up the bad ones in the 'pass' tubes, well that could be a hundred-thousand-dollar mistake. Maybe a whole line of cars might need to be torn into because all of the automatic windows don't roll up or down. Or maybe the latest PlayStation doesn't start up. Who knows?" He took a long sip.

The officers said nothing. Did nothing. They probably had no interest in talks about semiconductors, but they also knew better than to interrupt a man dying of grief.

"Anyway, one day, my wife goes in, sits in her little sphere, surrounded by three or four machines. See, one person ran multiple machines, dropping chips into them one after the next. As she's bundling up packs of chips, a fire spreads behind her. It managed to devour the entire room in seconds. She didn't have a chance." Another swig.

"I'm so sorry," Burns said.

"They assumed one of the machines overheated and caught fire, despite the things having mechanisms to avoid that happening. Wasn't that, though. Corporate had just installed security cameras because they'd rather spend the big bucks monitoring the employees instead of paying them. Maybe if they paid their fucking staff enough to feed their families, they wouldn't have needed to worry about people stealing their fucking semiconductors. Who would steal them anyway? Is there a market for that?" He looked at the officers as if waiting for them to answer his rhetorical question.

The officers shrugged. Long said, "I've never even heard of a semiconductor."

"There's apparently a lot of rules and regulations on electricity, which makes sense, but the company didn't comply with them when they installed this new security system. Wiring was all messed up. Something about wattage and shit. I don't know. Electricity isn't my thing. But apparently, it was a gross violation. Twelve people were in that room. Three died. A few more were severely burned. The rest were lucky."

"Jesus. I'm so sorry," said Burns.

"I can see why that was the worst day of your life." Long shook his head.

Jackson chuckled and sipped his drink. Something smashed against the outside wall. "That wasn't the worst day of my life either."

It smashed again. Burns gripped the butt of her gun. *Good,* Jackson thought. *Smart.*

"What was that?" Long asked.

"The worst day of my life was two months later. After the Freedell company gave us millions of dollars to shut up about their mishap, we moved to Block Island. Quiet as can be. That's when a monster chewed up my daughter right in front of my family."

They both looked at him with confused glances but were too distracted by the loud bangs on the side of the house to make more of it. The window in the living room shattered, and both officers ran to see what it was.

"What the fuck?" Long yelled.

Burns drew her gun. "What the hell is that?"

The creature wailed. Loud whooshing sounds came from the room where it had just broken through. Banging. Crashing. It was probably using those giant fucking claws to destroy everything in its path.

Burns fired, once, twice, before retreating.

Long ran around her, getting to the side door first. "Come on, let's go," he shouted.

Burns stopped and grabbed Jackson. "Let's move," she said. Her eyes were wild, darting everywhere. He saw in her the pure panic that drove through his children the night Wreath died, and it made him happy. Not that he wanted her to suffer as they did, but because finally, someone else knew. Someone else got it.

He grabbed his tumblers and ran with her.

As they exited the house, the fog felt like plastic wrap on his skin, not just a moist mist, but a tangible, material object floating through the atmosphere and clinging to him. They ran down the driveway toward the police cars in the street. Long got to the front of the house first, but just as he reached the end of the lawn, the creature jumped through the window back outside. It charged, driving its claws into Long. The off-duty cop's body hung high above his car, gored by the talons of the monster.

Burns screamed. Jackson grabbed her and pulled her toward her vehicle. "Come on. I need you to help me save my children."

She ran with him. The car beeped as she unlocked the door. He hopped in the shotgun seat as she jumped in the driver's seat. With the press of a button, the car started. Thank God for updates like that. The officer's hands were shaking too much to turn a key properly.

"I guess you believe me now," Jackson said as they peeled out down the road. In the rearview, Jackson kept his eyes on the beast as it chomped into Long just as it had Jackson's daughter four years ago.

CHAPTER 23
METAPHORS

Chrissy grabbed Angela and yanked her toward the door as the monster smashed through the windshield with its long arms. Its claws slashed across Officer Barrett's face. Blood splashed onto the back seat as the officer screamed away his last breaths.

Chrissy and Angela screamed too. There were no handles on the back doors, so they couldn't get out. Meanwhile, the monster ducked his head into the front seat and slammed his claws into the plastic partition between the front seat and back. The claws poked through the plastic, separating the entire wall from its base, but the monster's fingers got stuck in it.

As the monster pulled the plastic toward the gaping hole in the front of the car where the windshield had been, Chrissy planned her exit. The Langblass struggled to remove its talons from the partition and, subsequently, remove the partition from the car. The large piece of hard plastic slammed against the dashboard as the monster used its feet on the front of the car to pull itself out.

"Come on." Chrissy jumped into the front seat, thinking she could handle the sight of the dead officer, but she was wrong. His face leaked blood and ooze, no longer recognizable. "Oh Jesus," she said and held in a gag.

The plastic piece smashed against the dashboard, and as the monster pulled back to try again, the piece hit Chrissy in the head. It didn't hurt, but it made her plans difficult. She touched the officer and grimaced. His body bobbed to the side but otherwise stayed in place. "Ew. This is fucking gross."

Slowly, she reached over him and unbuckled his dead body. "Oh shit. Oh shit. Oh shit."

The plastic piece kept rebounding off the dashboard and hitting her.

"Oh, move," Angela said with a huff. She climbed into the front seat, accidentally putting her foot in her sister's face. "Get out of the way."

Chrissy scootched until her back hit the passenger side door. Angela basically sat on her lap. She reached over and opened the driver's side door. With the door open, she pushed the officer out of his seat into the foggy night. The mist had already crept into the police car, but now it barreled in, and Chrissy could taste it. Rotten fish.

"Switch with me," Chrissy said. As Angela slid over Chrissy's body, while Chrissy slipped under her sister's, someone's knee hit a button because the siren wailed into the otherwise hollow night. It echoed into the new, dark world.

Not only did the abrupt wailing set off Chrissy's already frayed nerves, but the reaction the monster had to the sound made it even worse. The Langblass screamed in pain and anger, kicking the front of the car so hard the headlights smashed to bits. It pulled and yanked, trying to free its claws. In the process, it snapped the plastic in half, which allowed the beast to pull the two pieces outside of the car.

"Oh fuck," Chrissy said.

"Start the car, idiot. Go!" Angela yelled. Meanwhile, Angela messed with the buttons until the siren turned off.

Chrissy looked all over, trying to get the lay of the land inside the car, hoping she could learn to drive it. She'd watched Charlie do it, so she had a basic understanding, but the police car had so many more buttons and doohickeys that made any previous knowledge null and void. Doing a ten-piece puzzle was easy, but harder when you drop a million other pieces on top of it.

"Do I have to do everything?" Angela snarked as she reached over and hit a button by the steering wheel. Nothing happened. "What the fuck? Why didn't that work? That's how Auntie starts her car."

The creature stepped on the plastic partition and pulled his arm upward. Its claws slowly slid out of their prison.

Chrissy stepped on the brake and hit the button. She had remembered Charlie always starting the car and forgetting to do that. He'd always giggle and say, "Oops. I forgot to hit the brake."

The engine kicked on. "Okay. Fuck. No time to figure this out."

Chrissy pushed the center stick thing to the *R* and slammed on the gas just as the creature finished the job of releasing its sharp nails. The car blasted backward much faster than Chrissy expected, and as a reaction, she jerked the wheel, which sent the car nearly toppling over. The back of the car crashed hard into a house. Meanwhile, the monster charged from the front.

In the crash, Angela's head hit the dashboard because she wasn't wearing a seat belt. Luckily, Chrissy didn't crash the car too hard, or the airbags would have deployed, which probably would have broken her sister's neck.

"Ow. You're terrible at this," Angela said.

"Put your damn seat belt on!" Chrissy switched the stick to *D*. Thank God she'd paid some attention when Charlie drove.

Again, she went too heavy on the gas, but this time it panned out because she drove straight into the monster, who flopped from hood to trunk before flying off the car onto the lawn. Chrissy and Angela screamed and bounced as the state police cruiser flew off the curb onto the road. Angela finally put her belt on.

"Will you slow down?" Angela shouted.

"What don't you understand about I don't know how to drive?" Chrissy yelled over the whipping wind coming in through the gaping hole where the windshield once existed.

Angela put her hands on the dashboard, trying to keep herself stable through all the wild driving. "Which is exactly why you should be going slower."

"If you haven't noticed, there's a giant monster chasing us." She checked the rearview and saw the creature getting up from its fall.

"Yes, I did notice that." And then she added a scream that appeared aimed at no one. "What even is this life?"

Chrissy jerked the wheel then jerked it back in the other direction, zigzagging the car until she corrected herself and the cruiser went straight down the road. "I know, right? Can anything just be normal?"

"It's so goddamned stupid."

"So fucking stupid."

"Like, who else has to deal with this shit? Monsters. Poverty. Moving all the time. A drunk dad. A dead mom. A dead sister. A dead brother." Angela's knuckles turned white as she clutched the dashboard.

Chrissy looked in the rearview where the monster took to a full-on run, chasing after them at an impossible speed. She whipped the wheel, and the tires screeched as they turned onto Route 91. The good thing about 91 was that it went largely straight for a while. Good for speeding. "It's way too much. We shouldn't have to deal with all of this crap. Normal kids just worry about running out of vape juice."

Chrissy hit the gas a little harder, and while she felt more confident driving fast on 91, the fog worried her. What if another car drove from the other direction? What if she slightly veered, steering them straight into a giant tree?

"Charlie was the only normal thing in our lives."

As soon as Angela uttered his name, their venting ended. Nothing else mattered. Charlie. What had happened to him? The monsters found their way off Block Island, hunted them all down. And Charlie remained across that small stretch of ocean, on the plot of land where the Langblass had lived for more than 200 years, according to the woman they spoke to at the station. If the Langblasses were free, what had they done to break from their prison, and what did Charlie's disappearance have to do with it?

She checked the rearview again. Through the mist, she saw the outline of the giant pale creature. It gained on them. How fast was this thing? She stepped on the gas a little harder.

Angela tightened. "Please slow down."

The wind whipped through the opening, smacking them in the face.

"I can't. It's catching up to us."

"Just dodge it, but slow down. You can't drive this fast."

"I have no choice, Angela. Now shut up, you're distracting me."

"You're going to fucking kill us."

"The thing chasing us is going to kill us."

"It'll catch us a lot easier if you crash."

"Shut up and let me concentrate."

She pushed down a little harder on the gas, and as the trees on each side of the road zoomed by, she panicked. She was in over her head, had no idea how to slow down naturally and without skidding out. The car moved too quickly for her to take a turn. And no matter how much speed she put into it, the creature gained. All she could do was keep pushing down until she lost control.

"I don't know what to do," she said, and then repeated, "I don't know what to do." And maybe she wasn't just talking about the driving. If she were reading this in one of her books, she would recognize the metaphor. Not knowing what to do. Spinning out of control. Running from demons. Everything catching up all at once until it crashed. She would crash. It was how this had to play out. And she'd probably die in the process.

"When I say to, hit the brake," Angela yelled.

The monster was so close now it almost touched the trunk with its outstretched hand.

"What? No. We're going too fast."

"Just do it."

Chrissy shook her head. "We'll spin out and probably flip over."

"Just listen to me for once. One."

"No."

"Two."

Chrissy scrunched her face. "No. No. No."

"Three."

She hit the brake, and at the same time, Angela switched the stick to *P*. The car tires screeched, and the car turned hard left until it was sideways on the road. It may have gone up on two tires, but it didn't flip. Both Chrissy and Angela's bodies jerked hard against the seat belts, whipping their heads forward.

The Langblass, still running full force, slammed into the side of the car, rolled over the top, and landed hard on the asphalt, where it continued to roll.

Angela flipped the stick to *D* again. "Take your foot off the brake and go."

Chrissy turned the wheel in the opposite direction they'd been going and hit the gas.

"Now turn down this road."

Chrissy listened, turning down Switch Road, which was another path that went practically straight for a distance while it passed Chariho High School, but a few miles down, it turned into a winding disaster.

"When we get past the school, turn right onto Dawn Lane."

"What's Dawn Lane?"

"Mom used to drive down it all the time when we were kids. The houses always had cool decorations at Christmas and Halloween."

Chrissy shook her head. "I don't remember. Just tell me when."

"Okay."

"Is this a good idea? Shouldn't I be going fast? I don't want to keep having to turn."

"Ugh. Watch a movie once in a while, you fucking book nerd."

As they drove past Chariho High, Chrissy obsessively checked the rearview until Route 91 was out of sight. She thought they may have lost the creature, until she caught a glimpse of it way back beyond the gray mist. For a moment, she had high hopes she'd get away from it, but the bubble burst. It would never stop hunting them. They were going to die. Fighting was only delaying the inevitable.

"Turn right coming up," Angela said.

Chrissy listened. Dawn Lane curved to the left and popped out onto Wood River Junction.

"Turn left here."

"That's going to bring us back to Switch Road. You're just having us do a big *U*."

"Stop arguing."

Chrissy sighed and turned left. Wood River Junction ended at Switch Road, which was the last place Chrissy saw the monster. "Now what? Drive right toward the fucking thing?"

"Do you see it?"

"No."

"Because it saw us go down Dawn Lane, and that's where it is, now go right. Fast. Before it catches up and sees us."

Chrissy turned onto Switch Road again. She drove slower now because they were heading toward the twisty part. The more she drove, the more confident she felt in her ability to do so. But she still panicked at the idea of seeing the creature return in the rearview. So far, so good.

"Jesus, one minute you're Speed Racer, and the next you're a sloth. Hit the gas a little. There's a fucking monster chasing us."

"I'm nervous. This road is too windy."

Once Switch Road ended, they took some more side streets, until they were eventually heading back to Tanner's Switch. As each minute passed, and one road became the next, Chrissy felt confident they'd lost the monster. At least for now. Her fingers still trembled against the steering wheel because a monster had found its way from Block Island to the mainland with the sole mission of killing them, but at least they were safe temporarily.

"I don't want to do this anymore," Angela said.

"I know. Me neither." Tears brewed in her eyes. "Do you think Charlie is dead?"

As soon as Chrissy asked the question, Angela broke down in sobs. "Honestly? Probably. And Brian is. Dad might as well be."

Chrissy put her hand on Angela's back as the girl curled forward and wept into her hands.

"Please keep both hands on the wheel. You aren't a pro yet," Angela muttered through her fingers.

Chrissy chuckled, and that made Angela laugh, until they were both laughing way too hard at what wasn't that funny of a joke.

After wiping her nose on her sleeve, Angela settled down. "Sometimes I really hate you, but I also really love you, and you're all I have left, so please don't die, okay?"

"I'm not planning on it."

An animal ran into the road. Thinking it was the monster, Chrissy screamed, which caused Angela to scream. In an attempt to dodge the creature, Chrissy veered right but cut the wheel too hard, and the car went off the road into a grassy embankment before smashing head-on into a tree. The airbags deployed and hit both girls in the face.

Angela growled an angry hiss. "You're an idiot."

"Some kind of animal ran right out into the road. I thought it was the monster." Chrissy could barely speak, too shaken and frazzled.

"What are we going to do now?"

Chrissy opened her door and pushed herself out. "I don't know. Find another car."

Angela got out of her side and moaned as she stepped onto her feet. "My whole back hurts. I changed my mind, I hope you do die."

Chrissy looked around at the street. "I just realized something."

"What?" Angela reached her arms behind her back to rub it.

"Do you remember seeing another car the entire time we've been on the road?"

"No. But it's after midnight."

"One? You'd think we would have seen at least one. Especially on 91. I can't even remember seeing any other cars parked anywhere."

"What are you saying?"

Chrissy waved her hand around the mist floating all around them. "I don't know. I'm not sure we're home."

"I don't know what you mean."

"I mean, I'm not sure this is the real world."

CHAPTER 24
SPIDERWEBS

Tiffany ran from the closet while the monster was leaning out of the bedroom window, focused on her brother. She prayed the second creature wasn't in the hall, ready to impale her from behind. The monster at the window craned its neck, catching Tiffany barreling toward it.

She jumped on her bed and dove, smashing her left shoulder into the thing's back before it had a chance to turn and defend itself.

It hissed and slashed as it toppled forward, falling right off the small sliver of roof outside the dormer window and onto the ground below. It landed with a satisfying thud. The fall barely hurt the thing, though, because it rose to its feet rather quickly.

Tiffany found Doug clinging to the thin strip of roof by his bedroom window. "Okay. All right. We need to get the hell out of here."

He nodded to her. "Yeah. I think I pissed my pants."

The creature growled and jumped, trying to reach them, but Tiffany and Doug stood too high. Thank God for tall houses.

Behind Tiffany, something hissed. She turned quickly to see the second monster in the doorway.

"Oh fuck." She stepped onto the roof, wanting to move slowly out of fear of falling, but lacked the time with the creature in the doorway. Terror shot up her spine. One foot. Two. She made it onto the roof. The monster slashed at the bed, lifting it off the floor and slamming it into the wall. It barreled toward her. She dropped to her knees and used her hands and feet to crawl toward her brother. "It's coming. The other one is coming!" she yelled.

Doug's mouth dropped. "Okay, shit. What do we do?"

She reached him. "We crawl all the way around."

"Why?"

"I don't fucking know, Doug, because what else do we do? Sit here and wait?"

The upstairs monster bent through the window, slashing at the air, just showing aggression for the sake of it.

"Okay, go. Now."

The monster on the ground continued to jump up and down trying to reach them. Its talons hit the roof, but the creature couldn't get the height to bring its arms in and hit them. It didn't matter, though. It followed, and that was threatening enough. It meant they couldn't hide, couldn't sneak away, couldn't jump down, and run into the woods.

Doug got on all fours and crawled in front of Tiffany. He yelled back to her, "Do we just crawl around until we get to Mom and Dad's room?"

"Yeah. We need to get them out of the house too. Do you think they really slept through all this shit?" She hoped so, because the alternative was they barged downstairs to find out the source of all the ruckus, at which point, they surely would have met their end.

Tiffany and Doug crawled around until they reached their parents' room. Tiffany noticed the second-floor monster wasn't on the roof chasing them. The ground-level monster stayed below them, though.

The master bedroom light was off, so Tiffany couldn't see

anything inside. As Doug reached the window, he put his hand on the sill to open it.

The window shattered and a giant claw came out. Doug put his hand up defensively, and the claw went right through his palm. He screamed and fell backward off the roof.

"NO!" Tiffany dove, trying to reach him, to grab him, but she wasn't close enough. Doug's limbs flailed as he plummeted. His back hit a giant white oak trunk, and his body flopped forward from the impact. After that, it was all ground. *Thud.*

He lay lifeless on the cold lawn below. Tiffany's eyes filled with water, but she had no time to mourn. Besides her brother, she'd probably lost her parents too. If the monster just smashed through their window, she doubted they stayed sleeping in their bed.

With Doug's blood on its hand, the monster crawled out onto the roof, chasing Tiffany. She only had one place to go. Up. She climbed, headed for the attic window. The second-floor monster realized what she went for and headed back inside. Once she reached the window, the ground-level monster smashed back into the house. They were going to meet her up there.

Which is exactly why she only went in enough to make them think that's where she ran to. These creatures weren't the smartest. She hopped in, waited three or four seconds, and went right back to the roof. Sliding down on her butt, she reached the edge, feet touching the gutter.

Doug lay in the same place. She thought about jumping now that the first monster wasn't right below her, but she didn't think she could make the jump without injury, so she scooted sideways until she reached the wraparound porch on the side of the house. From there, she slid down the porch roof until it lowered close enough to the ground where she felt comfortable jumping. If she were smart, she would have headed right into the woods or the family car, but she didn't. She ran to Doug.

He couldn't have survived the fall, but she had to check. If for no other reason, she couldn't carry on without him.

When she reached him, she dropped to her knees and shook him relentlessly. "Doug. Wake up. Come on, dude. We don't have time for you to nap."

Doug let out a low groan. Tiffany laughed, exhilaration pouring from her lungs. "You're alive. Thank God. Come on, then. Wake up."

She glanced at the house, back at Doug, at the house, back at Doug. She slapped him. "We don't have time, dude. I'm sorry."

He lifted his head a little. "Ohhhh. Oh God. Everything hurts."

"Yeah, perfect. That's fine. Hurting is good. It means you're alive. Let's go. Now."

She put her arm around his back and helped him sit up. He breathed hard, clutching his ribs. "Oh no. I think something's broken."

The attic window smashed open. Glass shards rained down from the roof.

"Yeah, sorry, but we don't have time for you to heal. Please tell me you have the car keys in your pocket."

He grimaced. "I do."

"Good, let's fucking go."

The monster leaned out the window and screamed. She had no idea where the second creature had gone.

She helped Doug to his feet, and he moaned a whole lot more. "Give me the keys."

The monster stepped out on the roof.

Doug fumbled around in his pocket. "Here."

She grabbed the keys from him. "I'll go get the car. Stay here."

She didn't want to leave him alone, but he was going to hobble and slow them both down. It would be smarter to grab the car and drive it through the yard. Besides, they couldn't fight back against these giant fucking things, but a car might be able to.

She ran to the front of the house and jumped in Doug's Camry. As soon as she started it, the second monster lunged through the living room window.

"Oh shit." She reversed a little then put it in drive. With her foot on the gas, the car blasted forward, and the Camry slammed into the creature, pinning it to the house. It bellowed a horrid sound. Its giant mouth opened wide. Now that Tiffany sat so close to it, she realized its massive jaws could swallow her face in a single bite. It had teeth as big as her lower arm, and they were dagger-sharp.

She reversed, and the thing crumbled to the ground. Its legs were nearly flattened, and thin strips of bone protruded from the creature's legs. She didn't have time to make sure it stayed down. The car bumped hard against the lawn as it drove around the house. As she pulled into the backyard, the top of the car dented in as something slammed hard on top of it. The monster must have jumped from the roof. Doug leaned against a tree, holding his chest.

She hit the gas again, flying forward, zooming past Doug, and just before the Camry hit the fence between her house and the neighbors, she slammed on the brakes. The monster flew off the roof, but it dug its sharp claws through the metal, so its body bounced onto the hood, face pressed against the windshield.

Tiffany screamed. The thing opened its mouth and bit the glass. Bit it! Its teeth slid down, putting a hairline slice in the windshield. The slick sound it made sent a nails-on-a-chalkboard shiver up Tiffany's spine.

The creature drew its head back and slammed its forehead into the glass. A spiderweb crack spread across the middle. What could Tiffany do? She was too close to the fence to drive forward. If she reversed, she'd risk running over Doug. Staying in the car meant waiting for the monster to break through and eat her. No matter what she did, she was fucked.

She was back in those shitty motels with her uncle, frozen, incapable of deciding, just letting life pass through her like a soft breeze. She could only stay in place and hope for a *deus ex machina* to swoop in and change her fate.

The monster's forehead smacked against the glass again, and the spiderweb spread.

Tiffany put her hand to the glass, feeling the fissures. She wasn't trying to stop the incoming explosion that would surely come with one more strike. She just wanted to feel it happen. If this was her end, she should at least get as close as possible to every second leading up to it.

The creature drew its head back once more. Tiffany squinted, wanting to protect her eyes from the shards of glass that would come, but also not wanting to completely shut herself off from seeing the destruction.

Time moved slowly. She had the chance, through those nearly closed eyelids, to see the monster's features. Its slick and slimy skin had more cracks and bumps than she had ever noticed before. Somehow, those imperfections made it feel more human, more real. Its ribs poked out from its frame. The creature's neck was thin and long, which made it hard to understand how it was capable of holding the weight of its head.

The monster's forehead flew down, slamming into the windshield. A storm of glass showered onto Tiffany. It cut into her, little lacerations all over her arms, hands, and face. Blood trickled down her cheeks, warm and peaceful. That was how she felt in the moment. If it were time to die, she refused to give the monster her fear. Not in the final seconds. She accepted her fate. Her only hope was that Doug found a way to escape while the creature chewed Tiffany to the bone.

"Before you kill me, can you tell me your story?" Tiffany whispered. "I just need to know why."

The monster hissed and opened its giant mouth. A blast of sea stench hit Tiffany as the creature breathed out. Splashes of warm, slimy saliva slapped against her, mixing with her blood.

"Can't you just feed my curiosity before you end this?"

It turned its head. For a second, Tiffany thought she might have gotten through to the thing, tempered it with her concern. But she realized it only turned its head so it could fit its giant shitty face through the hole it had created in the windshield.

It drove her insane that she wouldn't know anything about the creatures before she died, wouldn't understand why all this happened. Like her first day meeting Charlie, getting half-stories, or no stories at all, made her crazy. That absolute need for answers broke through the calm façade she'd built, and a panic set in. She was about to die. Holy shit. She was going to die.

As the creature dug its head into the car and snapped its jaw, Doug yelled, "Hey, fucker. Over here!"

"No!" Tiffany yelled, but it was too late. The creature ripped its head out from the hole in the windshield and snarled at Doug. Tiffany turned to see her brother standing up behind the car, still clutching his ribs.

"Kill me, you asshole."

"NO!"

The monster leaped over the hood and dove toward Doug. They fell to the ground, out of view. Something crunched, blood splashed, and Doug screamed.

CHAPTER 25
GOOD PARENTS

Officer Burns sped down the road, and the monster chased close behind. Officer Long's blood stained the creature's gray skin. As she neared the end of the road, she turned on the sirens and took a sharp left toward the Watch Hill area of Westerly. Jackson could have lived there, could have chosen it as a home for his children instead of Block Island. Stubbornness made a different choice for him.

Taylor Swift lived in Watch Hill, as did Conan O'Brien and a few other celebrities. It would have been a good life for his kids. They'd all be alive.

"Why are you going this way? My daughters are in Tanner's Switch."

Jackson turned and caught the monster falling behind. It was twitching and had its hands over the sides of its head.

"Sorry, I've got my own family."

Jackson shot her an angry look. "What? You're a police officer. On duty. Take me to my children or pull over."

She scoffed. "And you'll what? Walk there?"

"Yes! If I have to!"

The tires screeched as she swerved hard right to turn down a side road. "Look, I don't know what the hell is happening, but this is end-of-the-world shit, so I'm going to get my family and protect them. I'll take you to your daughters after I gather my daughter and husband, and we can all run away and hide together."

"Let me out." He reached for his door handle.

She leaned over and grabbed his arm, stopping him. "Settle down. Think it through. We'll get to your daughters much faster, even after getting my family first, than you would on foot. Don't be an idiot. And are you just going to run through that monster?"

"You're an asshole."

"For caring about my family?"

He put his head down, not having any rebuttal for that, but he wanted to scream, grab her shoulders, and push her out the door. If he thought he stood a chance against her, he might.

"Fuck!" He took a long pull from one of the travel mugs.

She did a double take at him. "Look, I can tell you're a good father—"

Before she could finish whatever sentiment she had planned, Jackson broke out into hysterics. His face turned red as he laughed so hard he thought he might throw up.

"What's so funny?" Burns asked as she turned again, no longer bringing them to Watch Hill but toward the downtown area of Westerly.

"You called me a good father." He held up his two tumblers. "Do I really look like a good parent? Son dies of a drug overdose, another one is missing, and I'm having a drink. If I don't drink, I'll shake, get dizzy, see black spots out of the corners of my eyes, and from what I've read, I could have a seizure, all sorts of dangerous health risks that should require me to go to a detox center. I'd love to be one of those alcoholics in the movies or books that just puts the drink down and ten seconds later becomes an action star, but sadly, if I want to be of any use, I actually have a good excuse to drink for once."

She sighed and clicked the siren off. "You look like you're struggling, but you also seem to care. Now tell me what I'm dealing with. You obviously have experience. What the hell is that thing? I want to protect my family and you, too, but I need to know what that thing is."

He found it remarkable how cool she kept her temperament. He could see the fear in her eyes and the trembling in her fingers, but she talked evenly and thought logically. And she managed to pull that off just a few minutes after seeing her first taste of the creature. Jackson saw it four years ago, and he still hadn't cooled.

Jackson didn't have much he could tell her about the creature, other than he'd seen it in his mind day in and day out for four years, waiting until his marbles spilled off the table again and the thing showed up back in his life. "You know I was a terrible dad long before my wife died. Not terrible. That's the wrong word. I loved my kids, and I spent time with them here and there. But I kept myself busy so I could avoid the frustrating games kids play. And I ignored them a lot while I pursued stupid dream projects.

"I was always trying to make money. Not 'get by' money, 'get rich' money. I always figured if I made enough, I could provide them with all they needed so they wouldn't need it from me. And of course, if I had a lot of money, I'd have more freedom to do things with them on my own terms."

She spun the wheel and turned onto Broad Street, driving past the library and post office, two large, looming buildings. "You sound like most parents, to be honest. I'm guilty of some of those same things with my daughter. You're avoiding my question, though."

He shook his head. "I'm not. This is all answering your question. I promise."

The strips of shops zoomed by on each side. ReReads bookstore, The Brazen Hen, the United Theater.

"My wife, she had a big thing about never going to Block Island. Her family was from there, and I guess they had a lot of tragedy in their past. She didn't even know what those tragedies were, just that they existed. Her father took her off the island against her mother's wishes. He had their names changed, moved them around a lot. When she told me this, she insisted he hadn't kidnapped her, but it sure sounded like it. He made her promise never to go to Block Island, and she kept her word on that.

"I tried to talk her into a vacation there because my parents used to bring me to Block Island all the time as a kid. I loved it. Always had a dream of living on that fucking tiny little island. When she passed away, Freedell gave us a lot of money to shut up about her death, and all those dreams I had of being rich and living on Block Island seemed possible. And I thought maybe I could even find my wife's mother and introduce her to her grandkids."

Burns pulled over by a series of saltbox houses. Most of them looked as if they'd been transformed into apartments.

"Something's wrong here," she said.

"What do you mean?"

She opened the car door and drew her gun. Jackson wasn't sure if he should get out or not. He decided he should. When he stepped out, he followed her eyes as they scanned the neighborhood.

"At first, I thought it was the fog messing with my vision, but that's my apartment." She pointed to a brown saltbox with flecking paint. The steps leading to the porch were crooked, in serious danger of collapsing.

"Okay?" Jackson said. Unsure where she was going with this.

"The landlord just painted it a month ago. And he rebuilt the porch a year and a half ago."

She walked past him, slowly going up the steps. Jackson noticed how shaky her breath had gotten.

Again, he wasn't sure if he should follow, but since she had the gun and he had tumblers, he opted to follow closely.

She used her key on the front door and guided them through a thin hallway toward a door numbered *#1*. With the gun at her side, she unlocked the door to her apartment and stepped in. "Charlotte? Kingston?" She didn't yell, but she wasn't whispering either.

The fog ran through the house too. A gray, thin cloud wisping through the kitchen and living room.

She glanced at Jackson and pointed to the kitchen walls. "We don't have yellow wallpaper. It was white."

"What exactly are you saying?" Jackson asked, following her into the living room.

She moved faster now, nearly running to the two doors on the other side of the living room. She pushed the first door open. "Charlotte?" Now she yelled.

Boom, right to the second door. "Kingston?"

She turned to Jackson, breathing hard, eyes wild and shining like marbles. "They aren't here."

"Are you sure this is your apartment? I mean, if the wallpaper is a different color?"

She pushed him. Not hard, but definitely filled with emotion. "I know my fucking apartment. My daughter's toys are in there."

She pushed past him and opened another door. A small bathroom. She looked all around. "They aren't here."

Again, she rushed past him and out into the hallway. She darted up a flight of stairs and pounded on door #2, and then she kept climbing until she pounded on #3. "Hey. Anyone here?"

Jackson stayed on the bottom step, sipping on his tumbler. Burns climbed back down to the second level, terror in her eyes. She leaned against the door of apartment #2, breathing hard.

"They probably just got freaked by the weird fog and went to stay somewhere else," he said.

She shook her head, tears dribbling down her cheeks. "You don't get it, do you?"

He shrugged. "What?"

Boom. Before he could process what happened, Officer Burns turned and kicked the second apartment's door open.

"What are you, crazy?"

She stormed in. "Hello? Anyone home?" She ran from room to room, slamming doors open.

"No one here either."

"Okay. What does that mean?"

"Jackson. There wasn't a single fucking car on the road. All communications are gone. My family is gone. My neighbors are gone. I've been yelling in an apartment building where the neighbors freak out if my kid farts."

"Are you saying everyone disappeared?"

She ran past him again, going out the front door. "No. I'm saying we did. This isn't my apartment. Did you see the post office? The stone columns looked cracked. They weren't like that. This isn't real. We're in a dream or something."

He remembered the Block Island cop's words on the phone. "Holy shit."

"What?" She turned to him. "What do you know?"

He shook his head. "I don't know. The cop on Block Island that I called. He told me my kids told him they had slipped into a seven-hour seizure. And they all saw the monster."

She rubbed her face. "Are you telling me that we're having a seizure right now? And this is like some kind of dream world we're experiencing while our bodies—"

"I don't know." He waved his hands in the air, alcohol sloshing in his tumblers. "Do you think I'm an expert at this or something? I don't know a fucking thing."

She grabbed his arm. "Come on. Let's see if your kids are in this weird seizure world." She jumped back in the car, and Jackson followed suit.

As they drove off, she said, "Finish telling me what you *do* know."

"You're going to want to get on Franklin Street until you get to 91."

She nodded.

"We weren't on Block Island long. That's when we saw the monster. It killed my oldest. She was sixteen. Wreath."

"I'm sorry for your loss."

"You've said that a lot tonight."

"You've had a lot of loss."

He glanced out the window, not wanting to make eye contact, ashamed of the amount of death surrounding him. "How could I know Elaina's father warned her away from the island because of monsters? Elaina, she was my wife. Elaina Hempfield. Well, I guess her real name was Mary Vanderline, but her father changed it to Elaina Hempfield. She was a beauty." He lost his train of thought, thinking about his wife smiling in her cheerleader outfit when they were in high school. Always happy, no matter what. Meanwhile, Jackson had swam in a sea of anxiety, always worried they didn't have enough for their family. Elaina never worried about it. She always wanted to put on her best face, even on the worst of days.

He took another swig.

"I'm sorry. And I don't want to be insensitive, but I really need you to focus on telling me what you know about this monster because I need to get back to my family. I'm bringing you to your daughters, and then I'm finding this thing and killing it so I can get back to the normal world. "

"After Wreath died, the police investigated me. I don't know if I was ever a prime suspect. They leaned on me, but not as hard as I expected, honestly. I think they were just exploring all angles. But the media had a field day. And they weren't just cruel to me, but to my kids. We were laughingstocks. The family who said, 'A monster did it!'

"True crime podcasts, websites, they either mocked us or used our story to tell scary real-life tales of terror. It's all over TikTok. But my daughter was dead. It wasn't funny. I blamed myself, but I didn't know where I had fucked up, couldn't place which part of my thinking was responsible for it. I just knew I had somehow poisoned everyone around me. The first finger pointed at the island itself. My dream of moving there. So I took us off the island. I blamed my desire for money, so I gave most of it away. Bought myself a shit little house, sent the kids to live with my sister, saved enough for each of them to go to college, and enough to keep me drinking and fed. I figured, I grew up poor, and you know what? I was happy. As a kid, I was happy. Maybe that 'money is the root of all evil' bullshit was true."

As Officer Burns turned onto Franklin Street, she gave Jackson a suspicious glance. "You don't believe that, do you?"

He shook his head and squeezed off the last drops from the first tumbler. One more to go. "Of course not. But I had just lost my wife and my daughter. I needed something to hate, and money was the answer because the other option was a monster, and that didn't go down easy. Even after seeing it."

"What does this have to do with what you know about it? How does all this help me?"

"I started drinking so I could sleep at night. But I soon realized I was terrified during the day too. So, I just drank all the time. Why not?"

"Because you had children who needed you."

"I had children who needed to stay away from me. I took the island away because it was deadly. I took money away because it brought them the biggest horror of their lives. And I took me away because I was just as much a monster as the thing that ate their sister. Me, Officer Burns. Me. I was poison. The police weren't wrong about that. It doesn't fucking matter if I actually killed my daughter because my decisions did. My thinking. It killed Brian too. 'I didn't mean for it to happen,' is what children say to escape blame. But adults? We should know better.

"So, you want to know about that monster? Here's what I think. It's here because it wants to kill my children. It wants to kill me. I somehow tied it to my family. We're bound now, all of us. My family and the monster. It won't stop until it kills us all. And you had the shit fucking luck of landing on my doorstep the same night the thing figured out how to cross a small slice of ocean, which means you're dead now too. Add it to the fucking tally. Sorry, but I killed you."

He took a long pull from the second tumbler. His head swam. "I killed everyone."

Officer Burns slammed on her brakes. Down the road something moved across the street. It turned toward them, a towering silhouette in the headlights.

A roaring bellow echoed into the tenebrous night, and the beast charged for its prey.

CHAPTER 26
VINX

Chrissy and Angela walked away from the car. They were able to start it, but the tires spun out in the mud, and the bent hood wouldn't unwrap from the tree. Angela thought about her sister's comment about them not being in the real world, but she had trouble fully getting it.

The world had changed, certainly wasn't the place they knew, and it sure did seem desolate. But there was that animal that ran into the road.

"Do you think we are in a seizure again?"

"No," Chrissy said, marching ahead of her sister.

"Cool. Nice chat. Where are we going?"

"I don't know. I don't have a playbook. I'm just moving farther away from where we last saw the Langblass."

"Langblass. What a stupid name." Angela jogged to catch up to her sister. "Why aren't you talking to me?"

Chrissy rolled her eyes. "I'm trying to concentrate and think up a plan."

Angela clenched her teeth. She nearly punched a tree as they passed it but thought better of it at the last second. Why punish her knuckles for her sister's bitchy attitude? "Stop talking to me like I'm a nuisance. Last I checked, I'm the one who saved us. You'd be dead if I didn't stop you from speeding down 91."

"You can be helpful and annoying."

"Yeah, and *you* can be smart and an asshole." It wasn't the time for arguing, and after everything they'd endured that night, Angela should remind her sister how much she appreciated her, but she couldn't. Brian was dead. Probably Charlie too. And even with all that loss, Chrissy couldn't change her attitude toward her younger sister? Couldn't be nice for ten minutes? Why did Angela have to be the one to rise above? "You know, you of all people shouldn't act better than anyone. Remember, I know who you are. You're just a dumbass book nerd."

Chrissy didn't miss a beat. "Says the girl who pissed her pants in school."

"Fuck you, how's your dumb jock boyfriend?"

"Fuck you, how's your nonexistent boyfriend?"

"Fuck you, how's your folded up Kevin Bacon poster in your top drawer?"

Chrissy stopped, probably wanting to yell at her sister for snooping but too invested in the one-upping battle. "Fuck you, how's your secret TikTok account where you post minutes-long videos of random cats you see throughout your day?"

"Fuck you, how's your butt? Seriously, I'm concerned because you take a book into the bathroom and sit on the toilet for forty-five minutes. Do you really have that much poop?"

Something barked.

Chrissy screamed and Angela jumped.

"What was that?" Angela wanted to know.

A jingling noise broke through the fog. At first, it was a distant noise, but it grew louder by the second. Both girls looked everywhere, trying to pinpoint where the noise came from.

"What the hell is that?" Chrissy asked.

They both tensed up and reached out for one another. Somehow, they ended up holding hands, bracing for impact from whatever ran their way. The jingling grew louder and louder, and out from the mist, a beast broke through. Tendrils of gray steam pulled away from it as it came into view.

It jumped on Angela, tail wagging, tongue hanging out. She laughed.

"Jesus, that scared me," Chrissy said.

Angela bent down to pet the dog's brown fur. She couldn't make out the breed. He kind of looked like a basset, but she saw a lot of boxer mixed in there. He spun in a circle with excitement and licked her face, jumping on her with his white paws. Yup, he had a lot of boxer in there. "Oh my God. I don't know where you came from, but I love you already."

Chrissy came over to the dog and grabbed its collar, spinning it until she held the tags. "His name is Vinx."

Angela hugged Vinx, and he licked her neck in response. "Vinx. I wonder what it means. Do you want to be my best friend, buddy?"

"You can't keep the dog, Angela."

Angela stood up. "The fuck I can't."

Chrissy muttered something under her breath.

"What?"

"You can't keep the dog, idiot. There's a fucking creature in that mist hunting for us. How well can we hide with a dog that jingles when he walks?"

Angela bent and removed the collar from Vinx's neck.

"Dummy. He's a dog. He'll bark and flip out if the monster comes back."

"Good. He'll protect me."

"He'll get you killed."

Angela tossed the collar into the woods. "Come on, Vinx." She walked around her sister, heading into Tanner's Switch. Vinx followed by her side, and she scratched his head as they walked together.

Chrissy huffed behind them. "Angela, stop being an idiot. This isn't some fun little sibling argument. Your decision here could get us killed, and probably the dog too. Think it through."

Angela put her head down, ignoring her sister. Vinx looked up at her. The dog loved her. Instantly. And she loved him too.

"Angela, stop. Think about it, even if we survive the night—which we probably won't—do you truly believe Auntie will let you keep the dog? Be responsible. You can't feed it. We can all barely feed ourselves. Keeping that dog would be cruel."

Angela snapped around and stormed into her sister's face. "No. You listen. You're an asshole. I'm not trying to be mean, but you are. Charlie, God—" She scrunched her face, unwilling to cry in front of her sister right now. "I'm so worried about him, but you know, he was an asshole too. Brian's dead, and he was an asshole. Dad's an asshole. Wreath, she was the nicest person in the world to everyone in our house except me. When I was like five years old, she was so goddamn mean to me. All the time. Auntie took us in, and she works hard to make sure we have some food in the cupboards, but you think I don't see how much she hates me. This dog has been with me for two seconds and he's already been nicer to me than any of you have. Ever. I'm keeping the fucking dog. I don't give a shit."

Vinx stared up at the conversation, eyes droopy, tongue sticking out. "Come on, Vinx. Let's go through the woods."

She dipped off the road toward the stretch of white oaks and pines, but Vinx stopped short. "What's up, buddy?"

Chrissy stayed rooted in her spot as well. "You're right."

Angela sighed and came back to the dog. "Don't do that, Chrissy. Come on, Vinx." She snapped her fingers and bobbed her head toward the woods. "This way."

Vinx let out a high whine.

"Do what? I'm admitting you're right. I'm an asshole to you, and I'm sorry. And if you want to keep the dog, you should keep the dog."

Angela shook her head and laughed. "I already decided I was keeping the dog. I didn't need your permission for that." She petted

Vinx's head. "You okay, bud. Why don't you want to follow me anymore?"

"Why do you do that? I'm trying to be nice. I'm admitting I suck."

Angela grew frustrated and wondered if the dog had turned on her too. Maybe she couldn't even keep a dog happy. "You don't get to treat me like shit for years and then shrug it off with an apology. I'm sorry. I'm not just going to play nice with you. I did that on Block Island. That's all you get from me."

Chrissy crossed her arms around her chest. "Fine. But there's a monster hunting us down somewhere, so can we at least play nice until this is all over? It's not going to help us to fight the whole time."

"Fine." She gave Vinx a gentle nudge toward the woods. "Buddy? What's wrong?"

Chrissy came up to Angela. She put her hand out. Angela stared at it for a second, not understanding. Then it clicked. She gave her sister a handshake. Before she could pull away, Chrissy pulled her forward and hugged her. Before she knew it, her sister was crying into her neck, and that made her cry too.

It felt so good to be hugged. To be touched at all. To be noticed.

Chrissy said through sobs, "I'm not going to make some stupid proclamation or whatever. Just, I know I was always a jerk to you, but I do love you. That's it. That's all I'll say."

Angela peeled herself away. "Okay. We should keep moving. I don't know why Vinx won't come, though."

Chrissy wiped her face. "Because he doesn't like grass."

Angela chuckled. "What?"

Chrissy laughed too. "He doesn't. I was watching him walk next to you, and every once in a while, his paw would touch the grass on the side of the road, and he'd shake it off and you could see he was upset about it."

"You're kidding."

"I swear. Walk down the road, he'll follow you. But he won't go into the woods."

Angela tested it, walking forward on the asphalt, and sure

enough, Vinx followed, but when she veered toward the woods, the dog stopped.

"Do you not like grass?" She fell over laughing, couldn't hold it in.

Chrissy caught the contagious nature of it and bent over, tears streaming down her face, laughing.

The two of them sat on the side of the road in a fit of laughter. Angela might have cracked up about the dog's aversion to grass on any day of the week, but tonight it was especially potent. Grief did that sometimes, muddled the emotions. It could make you so depressed you can't stop smiling, so anxious you can't stop laughing, and so desperate you bury yourself in a new obsession. Grief was the ultimate detonation. It was a bomb buried deep in the intestines. Mixed with fear, it changed you, removed you from your skin and sucked the meat from your bones until you became nothing but a gaseous ball of dangerous chemicals spewing out in hysterics.

Grief was the kind of laugh that strained your muscles. It hurt to be happy. It hurt to live.

CHAPTER 27
PUNK ROCK ANTHEM

As Doug screamed, Tiffany jumped out of the car. Her elbow hit the horn and a loud honk echoed into the foggy night. The monster stood up at the sound and screamed, covering its ears.

"Oh. You hate that?" She slammed on the horn. A continuous, obnoxious honking played, and the monster stumbled backward, screeching in pain. Tiffany laid on the horn until the monster had fallen back a bit.

When she felt she had enough space, she stopped and ran to Doug, but the creature instantly corrected itself and ran to her. "Shit," she said as she ran back to the car and hit the horn again. Once more, the creature fell back and screamed.

She was stuck. The horn separated the beast from her brother, who may or may not be dead already, but if she didn't keep her hand on the horn, it came right back. She needed to get to Doug, to help him into the car.

Looking around, she couldn't find anything she could wedge between the seat and the horn to keep it blaring while she got out and helped Doug. At one point, Doug had an ice scraper lying around on the floor of the car, but she didn't see it now.

"Figure it out, Tiff."

The monster fell back against a tree on the far side of the backyard.

"One, two, three." She ran from the car to Doug. "Come on. No time to talk."

Doug mumbled, which meant he was alive, but his leg had a giant open wound where the monster must have bitten him. It bled hard. Mixed with the broken bones he surely received on the fall off the roof, her brother was in danger of dying very soon. She grabbed his hands and dragged him. He screamed in pain but used his legs (including the chewed-up one) to shimmy himself forward, helping her drag him. Thank God because she'd never have the strength to carry her older brother as dead weight.

"Sorry, I don't have time to do this proper."

The monster charged.

Tiffany dropped Doug, ran back to the car, and hit the horn again. The monster screamed and stumbled back.

"Oh God," she said, letting out a deep breath. "This is too much."

She held her hand on the horn until the monster fell back a ways and then she ran to Doug. He moaned as she pulled him by the arms, getting him all the way to the side of the car. The monster charged again. She took her chances, not wanting to keep doing this over and over again, and knowing she didn't have much time to get Doug somewhere safe, she waited until the last possible second before running back to the horn. The creature's claws whooshed by her face.

She jumped back in the car and hit the horn again. "Idiot," she yelled at herself. She'd let the monster get too close. If it hadn't aimed at her, it would have taken another bite of her brother and most definitely would have killed him in the process. She had to be more careful, and even though Doug didn't have much time, she had to show patience.

Doug was almost to the back door, where she'd have a whole new struggle of getting him into the car.

Two deep breaths and Tiffany steeled herself. She let go of the horn, spun out of the car, and grabbed her brother's arms. This time, she didn't even get a second to pull him. The monster was quick and on to her strategy. She jumped back in the car and hit the horn. The creature bent over and hollered.

Tiffany leaned out of the car with her hand still on the horn. "Doug, I know you don't have the strength, but I really fucking need you to crawl into the back seat.

She pushed her foot up and stepped on the horn, freeing her hand. Twisting around, she extended her body into the back seat, and with her foot planted on the horn, she fumbled with the door handle, hoping to open it enough to help Doug have clearance into the car.

The door opened, but her foot slipped off the horn, and the monster wasn't far behind the car. It let go of its ears and charged, mouth opened wide, and eyes storming with rage.

"No." She turned to hit the horn. Just as her hand landed on the steering wheel, the creature's claws dug into her arm and threw her from the car. "NO!"

The creature turned its head toward Doug. It knew. It knew it could destroy her by killing him, that all of her actions were in service of her brother's safety, that it could kill two birds with one stone.

"NO!" She charged the monster, clutching her injured arm. It raised its huge limb into the air and swiped down, ready to shred Doug to pieces.

Tiffany dove, connecting shoulder and head into the beast's midsection, slamming the thing into the side of the car, which unfortunately closed the back door. Before it had a chance to attack, she slid into the driver's seat and hit the horn again. Blood coated her arm from the open wound the claw left, but otherwise, she was surprised how much it didn't hurt.

The creature screamed and flailed, falling over Doug. Its body slammed into the hard earth. Its foot had landed squarely on Doug's stomach before it fell, and Tiffany worried one last injury from the full weight of the creature might have been enough to kill her brother. Doug hollered in pain. At least he was alive.

With one hand, she pressed on the horn, and with the other, she punched the dashboard. How could she get out of this? Doug could hardly move. The monster, while clearly incapacitated by the loud noise, knew how to recuperate too quickly.

She yelled, "I'll hit this horn forever, asshole. I'm not letting you kill my brother."

The monster rolled on the ground, agonizing over the horn.

"One step at a time," Tiffany said. She jumped out of the car, opened the back door, and jumped back in to hit the horn again. She was quick, and the monster didn't even get the chance to stand up.

"Okay. Good job, Tiff. One more time." She ran from her seat and hoisted Doug up so his upper body leaned against the back of the car, right by the ajar back door. And once again, she jumped right into the driver's side and hit the horn.

The monster had gotten itself on all fours, and even while it screeched in pain and plunged its palms around its ears, it stared at her with contempt. Its snarling lips told her what it planned to do to her if she ever gave it the chance.

"Okay, okay, okay, okay, okay." Boom, she jumped out of the seat and hoisted Doug up. He helped, using his legs to lift himself. She dropped him half on the back seat, his legs still dangling from the car, and she ran back to the front to hit the horn again.

She'd officially given the monster enough time to land on its feet, but it still had a small distance to clear before reaching the car again. Doug was almost in. She could do this. Maybe Doug could help.

"Doug. Can you hear me?" she yelled over the car horn. "Can you just bring your feet in? All you need to do is bring your feet in and stay lying down. Can you do that?"

Doug didn't respond, just mumbled to himself. She wondered if he'd gone delusional from loss of blood.

"Doug, please, I need you to pay attention. You think I'm wailing on this horn for fun?"

"I thought you were writing a punk rock anthem." His sentence came out clear and crisp, enough for her to hear him over the horn, but there was a wetness in his voice, which made her worried he had blood in his lungs. It didn't matter, though. She'd never been so happy to hear him talk.

She couldn't help but laugh at his stupid joke. "Shut the fuck up and get in the car."

Slowly, he shifted until his dangling feet were on the back seat. His body stretched from one side of the car to the other with his knees bent.

"One, two, three, go." She ran out of the car and slammed the back door shut. Then went to jump back in the front, but before she could, the creature dug its claw into her arm again.

CHAPTER 28

REDEMPTION

Officer Burns put the car in park right in the middle of Franklin Street. The creature ran, and with its long, lanky legs, it approached them fast.

"What are you doing? Drive," Jackson yelled.

Officer Burns took her gun out. "No. I'm killing this thing. Let's end this."

"Get me to my children first."

She glared at him. "I need to get back to my daughter. If I kill the thing, your kids will be safe too."

She stepped out of the car, but before she could train her gun, the creature had already reached the vehicle. It slashed at the door she used as a shield, and the force of it knocked her flat on her back.

Jackson jumped out of the car and ran around to her side. Halfway across, as he passed the trunk, he nearly stopped and retreated. He wasn't a hero and didn't want to be one. He just wanted to keep his daughters safe. But he also knew he could hardly walk straight, let alone drive, and his best chance at keeping his children safe was with the officer's help.

When he reached her side of the car, the monster stood above her with its claw lodged into her palm. The gun she had held was a few feet behind her. The creature raised its arm, ready for a blow across the woman's face. Jackson didn't have time to grab the gun.

"Hey, fucker! You killed my daughter. You owe me a life."

The creature slowly raised its head and eyed Jackson. As it stared, it tilted its head, sending shivers down Jackson's spine. Seeing the creature this close and having the time to get a good look at it brought a new level of terror. It wasn't just a fleeting thing anymore, a nightmare closing in. It was a real, material object, moving through the world with an intent to kill. Its eyes were hollow gulfs, giant black globes with a celestial sea of red galaxies swimming in the abyss.

Jesus. It was demonic. A hell creature. An alien. A demon from the dark woods.

"Welcome home," it sang in its taunting double voice.

The monster released its talon from Officer Burns' hand and stepped toward Jackson. "Welcome home?" This time it sounded like a question. Jackson understood. It was remembering him.

And those words helped Jackson remember, too, how it taunted him with his own sentence from what he'd meant to be a game played with his children. They had meant to have fun together, God damn it, and this creature turned their lives into a nightmare. Jackson tightened his fists. "Welcome to *my* home. This is where you die."

The creature jumped, slashing its claws at Jackson. Before it could make impact, Jackson fell backward, landing hard on the back of his head. His ears rang. The monster put a palm on Jackson's face, and its claws wrapped around Jackson's head. It squeezed. Jackson couldn't breathe through the thing's tight grip.

The pressure built around his skull. He wondered if he'd suffocate or die from his head exploding like a Gallagher watermelon.

A gunshot went off and the creature screamed. Blood splashed all over Jackson. With his face free again, he saw the creature hold its chest and stumble forward, away from the car, until it fell over hard on the cement.

Jackson stood up, out of breath. Officer Burns stared with her gun still raised, aimed where the creature had been standing before falling over.

"You saved my life," Jackson said.

"And you saved mine. Thank you."

"We should get the fuck out of here."

"GET OUT OF THE WAY!"

Jackson turned to see the monster rising. He ran around the car, back toward his side, and the creature pursued. A few more gunshots went off, but they must not have hit because the creature hadn't slowed.

Officer Burns ran around from the front of the car, trying to get a clear shot of the monster without her police cruiser getting in the way. "DUCK!" she yelled.

Jackson bent low as he ran. The blood rushed to his head, and he felt dizzy. He stumbled into the cruiser. Something sharp hit his side, just below the ribs. It burned. Like a bee sting.

He fell, landing on his knees. His hand touched the wound, and as he pulled away, he saw the blood. So much of it. He looked up at the creature hovering over him.

Boom.

The monster's face exploded. Its blood splattered the car, the cement, and Jackson's face. A loud thump echoed in the night as its body hit the ground.

Officer Burns ran to Jackson's side. "Are you okay? Jesus. We need to get that bandaged."

Jackson went to speak, but he choked instead. Blood cascaded from his mouth, down his chin.

"Oh shit. Oh shit. We need to get you to the hospital."

Jackson bent over, hacking up liquid. He spat and wiped his face. A final cough left his throat. "There is no hospital. We aren't in the real world, remember."

The exertion from talking was bigger than he realized. He couldn't breathe again.

"But I killed it. Shouldn't we go back now? Shouldn't this clear up?"

He didn't answer her, couldn't if he wanted to, but if he had to guess, they were stuck in this in-between world forever, or there were more monsters out there. In which case, his daughters weren't safe.

Since he couldn't speak, he used his blood-soaked hands to write on the side of the car.

GO. He wrote.

If he had the energy he would have written more. "Go save my daughters and quit wasting time with me." But he didn't have that kind of energy or that kind of time.

He fell on his side, right on the injury. A wave of pain throbbed up his spine and into his brain.

Six years ago, Elaina convinced Jackson to pack up the kids for a trip to Vermont. Jackson had protested because they didn't have a lot of disposable income to afford a trip. Elaina's work friend had a cabin up there that she'd inherited from her parents, and she offered to let them stay there for a week in the fall, but trips still cost money in gas, food, and whatever else they might need for a week.

In the end, she won, as she always did because Jackson couldn't resist her excitement. It was infectious. They stuffed the kids into the SUV and drove up for what turned out to be a long week. The kids fought with each other the entire time. Brian bitched about the hikes they took because he just wanted to stay home and play video games. Wreath complained about the lack of cell service. Chrissy never wanted to leave her bed. Angela was only five and needed constant attention and care, which was tough to give because so did the other kids. Charlie was the only well-behaved one, but only because his high anxiety kept him in the corners, and for that, Jackson just felt terrible.

They hardly left the cabin all week. Too much work to get the kids ready to go anywhere. After arguing, getting them prepared and packed, there wasn't much excitement left to go around.

On the last night, Jackson had lain in bed with Elaina, exhausted and frustrated. On top of that, he dreaded having to wake up early to ensure the cabin was properly cleaned and everything was packed up, only to spend the next four hours driving back. Long drives brought him Charlie-level anxiety.

As he tossed and huffed under his blanket, Elaina put her arm around him and whispered, "What's wrong?"

"I knew this trip would be a disaster."

Elaina laughed. "Disaster? It was perfect."

"How can you say that? The kids were miserable the entire time."

"Jackson, kids are always miserable. All we can do is set a good example, show them how happy we can be, and enjoy our time with them."

"It's hard to enjoy our time with them when they're yelling at each other all day."

"Yes, it is. But we're still with them. And one day, you'll be sitting there dying for that opportunity again. Take the worst of what you love because one day, they won't want to see us at all."

"I don't think half of them want to see us now."

Elaina kissed his shoulder. "True. Do you remember the time we went hiking in Acadia in Connecticut? And we somehow got lost. The longer we went trying to find our way out, the more frustrated you got. And you never were mean to me, but I could see the grumpiness setting in, and you were really short. And it just got worse and worse until we finally found the car."

He rolled over to her. "Did I really? I remember getting lost, but I don't remember being grumpy. I do remember us laughing when we found the car, though, because we were never very far from it. I felt like such a doofus."

She chuckled. "Oh, you were fuming mad. Steam out the ears. But you don't remember that, huh? Only the laughing?"

Jackson put his hands behind his head. "All right. I get it. The kids won't remember being miserable, only that they had a family trip. Memory is selective and all that jazz."

She kissed his cheek. "Yes, but more than that, the kids were just like you that day. They're small, Jackson, even Wreath and Brian. When they walk the halls at school, they're small. And they're lost. All the time. And they'll lash out at us. They'll be little jerks sometimes. But when they get older, they'll remember that no matter how much they pushed us, we were always there. We wanted to spend time with them, even at their worst."

Jackson lost the memory as his vision doubled on the asphalt. Officer Burns talked to him, but he couldn't make out the words.

When the monster came back, Jackson almost felt excited, as if it were his opportunity to save his children, to redeem himself. He thought of his wife's words as his breathing grew more ragged and the pain in his chest sharpened.

He would die here. Alone. And he deserved it because he let his children wander the world alone, without a guide, without someone to fall back on. Even now, as his last seconds ticked by, he wasted it feeling sorry for himself. And he spent every day prior to this convincing himself he wasn't capable of being a good father, and he let that be a self-fulling prophecy. He could have just stopped. Just worked at improving. Worked for anything. God, if he'd only just worked.

"I didn't mean for it to happen" was a child's excuse. And it was his excuse as well. The last one, he thought, as the world faded away from him.

I didn't mean for it to happen. Any of it.

CHAPTER 29

BATTLEGROUNDS

After their bout of laughter, Angela and Chrissy walked the road again. Angela refused to go without Vinx, and since the dog wouldn't touch grass, they couldn't go into the woods. Chrissy hated being so exposed, but then again, the Langblass probably knew exactly where they were and how to find them. They were prisoners in its world, and it most likely had the keys to every inch.

But the monster also ran as fast as the police cruiser, so if it could find them so easily, why hadn't it?

After half an hour of walking, they reached an intersection that Chrissy recognized. The road crossing led to Tanner's Switch Middle and High School. Exhausted both mentally and physically, Chrissy stopped. Angela sensed it and turned back to her.

"What's up?"

"I can't walk anymore. Everything hurts."

Vinx walked up to her and put his mouth in her palm, sniffing.

"Do we have a choice? We can't just stay here."

Chrissy nodded to the right. "My school is right over there."

Angela shook her head. "No. This place is already my nightmare."

Chrissy closed her eyes. "It's not real school, Angela. No teachers. It'll actually be cool because you can vandalize the place."

Angela shrugged and turned down the road. "All right. Sold. Let's go."

When they arrived at the school, Chrissy prepared to break a window to get in, but it turned out they didn't need to. They were in some kind of rot world, and that meant the school wasn't locked. In fact, the doors were so damaged, Chrissy couldn't keep them closed no matter how hard she tried. But that also meant the Langblass could get in just as easily.

Vinx ran down the hall, excited over something. Angela chased after him, and Chrissy after her.

"Wait, don't just go running. We don't know if the Langblass is in here," Chrissy said. But like always, her sister didn't listen.

The dog made his way to the gym, where he grabbed a softball. Angela laughed. "He just wants to play, I think."

"I don't know if we have time for that."

"Of course we do." Angela chased the dog, who refused to let the ball go. He ran away from her, back out into the corridor. The dog led them both through a set of double doors, where he flew up a staircase until he reached a landing. He turned and dropped the ball, letting it bounce down the steps.

Angela chuckled and tossed the ball back. With his tail going berserk, Vinx caught it and dropped it down the steps again.

"Angela, I'm so tired. I'm super happy you made a friend, and I'm sorry I gave you a hard time about it, but we should fortify this place or something. The monster's going to come for us. We should be prepared."

Angela tossed her head back. "Ugh." She turned to her sister, eyelids drooping. "You just don't get it. I told you, I haven't had a friend in a long time. This is the single best interaction I've had in, I don't know . . . Forever? I don't care if the monster comes. This is me planning my battleground. He can show up and he can kill me. It doesn't matter. Because I'm going to die happy. I spent every fucking day afraid of that thing, hiding in the light. It took my whole life away."

She threw the ball up the steps. "This is me kicking its ass."

Chrissy nodded her head. She'd never felt so alone. She understood Angela's reasoning, but she wanted to live. She wanted to fight. And her sister had planted her feet and taken her stance. Chrissy had to fight alone.

She charged out of the room, back through the double doors, and down the hall. First, she'd need to find something to blockade the front door. She went into the classroom nearest the entrance, looking for a big piece of furniture. She didn't know the room because this was the high school side of the building. She still had classes in the middle school.

There wasn't much. She'd hoped to find a big bookshelf, like in her English class, but all the room housed was student desks and the teacher's desk. While the teacher's desk wasn't much, it would have to do. But she knew the monster could push it with ease.

She put her back against the desk and pushed. It scraped hard on the white, gray, and blue vinyl tile floor. Her muscles ached too much for this. Her strength had been depleted by the most insane day of her life.

After getting it halfway across the room, she gave up. Not just on moving the desk, but on everything. Maybe her sister had it right. This thing had taken Wreath and most likely Charlie. Its reverberating effects took out Brian too. Chrissy slowly lost everything. It took and it took, depriving her of any will to carry on.

She slid to the floor and put her head between her knees. She almost cried, but she lacked the emotional energy.

Behind her, something creaked.

She sat up straight, back against the desk, and peeked around the corner. Footsteps moved down the hall. Slow, but loud. And big. Monster sized.

She got on all fours and crawled across the room, too scared to make a noise. When she reached the classroom door, she slowly pushed it closed, terrified. Her muscles tightened. She was afraid to breathe, too worried her nose might whistle or her mouth might click.

She peeked out. Sure enough, the monster walked down the hall. Chrissy could hear Angela giggling by the stairwell, which meant the monster could, too, and that's where it headed.

She scratched at her neck, trying to summon the gall needed for what she wanted to do. As the monster moved closer to the stair-well's door, Angela didn't quiet down. Her sister had no idea how close death loomed. And maybe Angela had told the truth and didn't care, but Chrissy didn't believe that. It's easy to say those kinds of things.

Chrissy stepped into the hallway. As the monster closed in, she yelled, "HEY!"

It turned and snarled. Then walked toward her. A woozy spell came over her.

Her heartbeat went insane.

Angela must have heard her because she came out of the double doors behind the monster. Chrissy shook her head at her sister.

As the creature stomped toward Chrissy, Angela yelled, "No. Hey. This way."

The monster turned again. "No. Here. Come kill me. Leave her alone," Chrissy yelled.

"After all these years of being an asshole, you don't get to be my hero now. Hey, Banglass or whatever the fuck you're called. Come get me." Angela stomped her feet.

The monster growled and turned toward her, making up its mind. It changed stances, ready to run. Chrissy hurried and slipped her shoe off. Without thought, she picked it up and threw it at the monster, hitting it in the back of the head.

The monster turned and bolted for her like a freight train. Nothing would change its mind now. No matter how much yelling

Angela did, it was going to kill Chrissy first. And Angela did yell, but not at the monster. At Chrissy.

When the creature got close, Chrissy dipped back into the room where she'd moved the teacher's desk and slammed the door shut.

"Oh my God. What did I do?" She ran to the other side of the room and twisted the handle on the window until it was fully open. A fully opened school window meant it angled out about forty-five degrees. Chrissy climbed and got halfway out before getting properly stuck. The door crashed open, and Chrissy's nerves fired like a Fourth of July grand finale. Her body operated on its own, muscles tensing, limbs flailing.

"Get me out of here," she yelled into the night.

The teacher's desk screeched across the floor as the Langblass tossed it like a rag doll.

Chrissy slid down a little further, getting past her hips. Just as her legs snaked out the window, the Langblass swatted at her feet. It hit her one sneakered foot and tore through it, but thankfully the cushion stopped the claw from doing much damage. As she landed hard on her butt, the monster smashed the window. Chunks of plexiglass rained down on her. Thank goodness for safety windows, otherwise she'd be covered in dangerous shards.

She ran toward the back of the school, which she instantly regretted. First, she knew the front door was open, but not the back. Plus, the back of the school was shrouded in darkness. She skirted the wall and swung her arms forward, in hopes they'd touch anything in the way before she ran face-first into it. Her shoeless foot felt the rough gravel on the path, little sharp stones jutting into her soles.

The monster growled behind her, and from the proximity, she could tell it was fully outside and on the move. If it kept pace with a speeding car, she had no shot of outrunning it.

Something ahead squeaked, metal on metal, and light poured out from a newly opened door. Angela leaned on it, back against the panic bar. "Hurry up," she said.

Chrissy ran into the building and Angela slammed the door shut behind her. The Langblass smashed and kicked outside, creating a parade of bangs.

Vinx stood at the landing, ball in his mouth. He dropped it down to them. Angela grabbed it and ran up the stairs. "Come on."

Chrissy followed her. "What are we doing?"

"Killing this fucking thing once and for all," Angela said as she petted Vinx's head. "I changed my mind. If it kills me, so be it, but I'm going out punching."

"Now you're talking. Do you have a plan?"

Angela led them into the school library on the second floor. It was dark and cold. Big swaths of metal shelves housed hundreds of books that emitted a distinct dusty book smell.

"Your favorite place in the world," Angela said.

"You know I haven't even been in this one yet? Why do you think this is a good place to be?" Chrissy kicked her other shoe off. She might as well be even until she got the other one back.

"I don't. I didn't even know I was walking into the library. I'm just checking everything out and looking for weapons." She walked to the front desk and reached over. "See!" She held up a pair of scissors.

Chrissy cringed. "Scissors are probably the best we're going to find, huh?"

"I don't know. Do you guys have a wood shop or anything? My school doesn't have anything that's not wrapped in rubber, so we don't hurt ourselves or the staff."

"Really?"

Angela chuckled. "No, you idiot. I was exaggerating." She went behind the desk and lifted up a keyboard. "You want this? I'll bet you could smash it on the Banglass's face or something."

"It's Langblass, and I hope we can do a little better than a keyboard."

Something crashed down the hall and Vinx barked.

"I think we're out of time," Angela said.

"Yeah."

"Don't die, okay?"

Chrissy nodded. "Yeah, you too."

"I think we're out of time," Angela said.

"Yeah."

"Don't die, okay?"

CHAPTER 30
BLOOD LOSS

"I think we're out of time," Angela said.
"Yeah."
"Don't die, okay?"
Chrissy nodded. "Yeah, you too."

BLOOD LOSS

While the monster dug its claw into her right arm, Tiffany turned the car on with her left hand, hit the gas, and turned into the side yard. The creature stayed attached to her, running along the side of the car. She tried to pull her arm from its talon, but it wouldn't dislodge.

With one hand on the wheel, she had limited ways to fight it off. She moved her arm, the one attached to the creature, and grabbed the door handle. As the car pulled onto the road in front of their house, she attempted to shut the car door, hoping to slam it on the monster's arm, but she couldn't get a good grasp, and the angle was all wrong.

Instead, she pressed on the gas. The creature kept up for as long as it could, but after a short distance, its sharp nail slid out of Tiffany's arm and the monster fell behind. It managed to stay along-side the car, keeping the same speed as the vehicle, but it couldn't manage to stay attached to her. Her arm radiated heat and pain as she reached over and pulled the door shut.

"Wwwwooooooooooooooooo," she yelled. "Holy shit. Holy shit. I can't believe we made it out of there. Hang on, Doug. We're going to the hospital."

She zipped down road after road, turning as much as possible in an attempt to lose the monster. Whenever she saw a road to slip down, she hit the horn, which slowed the creature down. She also hoped it would draw attention, but no one came to her rescue. Eventually, she did lose the monster, but she knew it wouldn't last long. The beast ran faster than Doug's Camry could drive, but as long as she had the horn to slow it down, she could give herself some breathing room. Once she drove Doug to the hospital, she'd have their armed security to keep them safe.

"Doug, you doing okay back there?"

He didn't respond, but she could see his chest moving up and down.

She sped down 91 until it hit Post Road. At one point, she saw some strange things lying in the road around where Post turned into Franklin Street, but she ignored them. They were maybe big garbage bags or piles of clothing. It didn't matter. Not then. She made it to the hospital in record time. It had a small drop-off lane going to the front door where they typically had a valet, but she didn't see anyone. It probably wasn't something they offered this late at night.

"Stay here for one second, Doug," she said, as she ran out of the car.

The front lobby was desolate. She ran to the admissions area and rang the bell on each desk. Where were they? Shouldn't someone be on duty?

"Hello?" she yelled. Panicked, she ran to the double doors, which she knew from past experience would be locked. A security officer had to buzz people in, or a nurse could use her key card. She slammed on the door, pounding her fist into it, just needing to get someone's attention, but to her surprise, the door opened upon impact. Since when were they unlocked?

She ran in. "Hello?"

There was no one. The nurses' station was empty.

"What the fuck?"

She ran around the stations, peeking into every room. They were all empty. No nurses. No patients. No doctors. No security. No janitors. No one.

"What the fuck?" she repeated.

She stood frozen for a moment, lost and out of ideas. Her arm dripped blood onto the floor.

"Okay. I have to do this myself." She ran to the nurses' station and looked around. There wasn't much. In a back room, she found basic supplies and grabbed as much gauze as she could. Without time or patience, she did a slipshod job of wrapping her wound just to get it covered. She didn't worry about the tiny cuts on her other arm or face. Those weren't bleeding much.

She found some bottles of rubbing alcohol and antibacterial ointment and ran back to the car. Doug made a grumbling sound as she opened the back door. She couldn't do anything for his rib, which she prayed hadn't caused any internal bleeding, but she could at least clean his leg and hand and wrap them up. Just like her arm, Doug's injuries would need stitches, but the gauze was better than nothing.

"Okay, Doug. Listen to me. There's no one here to protect us, so I'm just going to do my best to slow your bleeding and then we gotta get the fuck out of here before the monster comes back. You need to be your strong badass self, okay?"

She poured the alcohol on his leg. It sizzled and foamed. Doug didn't react at all. Using some Dunkin' Donuts napkins Doug had left in the center console, she dried it off, and gooped as much antibacterial ointment as she could on the bite marks, then wrapped the gauze around his leg. Every tiny noise, a whistle from the wind, a leaf rolling by, made Tiffany jolt, ruining her concentration. The wrapping wouldn't do much, and she could already see the blood leaking through, but she didn't know what else to do. Medicine wasn't her field of expertise. She didn't even know the difference between Tylenol and Advil.

After finishing his leg, she repeated the process on his hand.

Back in the driver's seat, she contemplated where to go. "Where the hell is everyone? This is crazy."

Doug made a crackling noise like he was trying to talk, but nothing came out.

"*Shhhh.* You just rest."

She started the car and headed out of the Westerly Hospital parking lot, unsure where she planned to go. Once she got back on Post Road, she formulated a plan. She again passed the two strange lumps in the road, getting a better look this time, and nearly fell out of her own skin. She stopped the car. It was foolish to get out, but she couldn't stop herself. She needed a better look.

A monster lay dead in the middle of the road, and next to it, a man lay equally as dead. Blood pooled around their bodies. How many monsters were there? But the scene told her something else. The monsters could be killed.

She jumped back in the car and drove off, unhappy to head in this direction, toward where her monster would be coming from, but she had no choice. As soon as she could, she dipped off the main road and took side streets until she reached the place she wanted to go, making sure to bypass roads she'd taken on her way to the hospital.

All the lights were off in Charlie's house, but Tiffany didn't care. She would wake Chrissy and Angela up if she had to. As she exited the car, she got an uncontrollable shiver. It was so dark. So quiet. No one anywhere. She noticed a police cruiser parked across the way, but she assumed the officer who drove it probably went wherever the nurses and doctors went.

She locked the car, which made a loud honk. She winced at her mistake. Hopefully she didn't just alert a nearby monster. She couldn't just leave Doug in there with the doors unlocked, though.

She gently tapped on the front door first. Not wanting to make more noise if she didn't have to. To her surprise, just like at the hospital, the door opened. When someone's front door opened without needing the handle turned, it felt pretty ominous. Especially this late at night.

Tiffany's options were in short supply, so she went into the kitchen. She knew they lived with an aunt, and from what Charlie had explained, she sounded grumpy. But again, as her brother potentially died in the back seat, she didn't much care.

"Hello?"

"HEY!"

Tiffany jumped and her heart shot into her lungs. Someone had shouted to her from outside. She shot around to see a female police officer running toward her.

"I wasn't breaking in."

"Are you Chrissy or the other one?"

Tiffany put her hand on the door handle, getting a little nervous. "Ah, I'm Tiffany."

"Tiffany? Who the hell is Tiffany?" The cop spread her fingers out and pinched the sides of her eyes. She had a bandage around her hand, and blood dripped out of it, much like Doug's careless wound covering.

"I'm Tiffany. What's going on?"

"You're here. How are you here?"

"I drove here. My brother's in the back seat. He's really injured. Can you help?"

"I mean, how are you here? In this world?"

Tiffany stepped back. "What?"

"Have you not noticed there's no one out here? The whole world is just gone."

She relaxed, getting it now. "Yes. I tried taking my brother to the hospital, and no one's there. Can you help him?"

The woman shook her head like she was rattling out marbles. "Jesus. Yeah. Where is he?"

Tiffany pointed and walked to the car. "He fell off our roof and he kept holding his chest. I think he might have broken a rib or something." She stopped, which made the police officer do the same. "And I don't know how to say this, but something bit him in the leg."

The cop put her hand on Tiffany's shoulder. "A monster. I got it."

"You've seen them too?" She held up her wounded hand as she walked to the car and opened the back door.

"Yes. I thought there was only one. I killed it. I assumed once I did, this fog would clear up and I'd be back in the real world, but that doesn't seem to be happening. If you had a monster, too, there must be more of them. I've heard some fucking stories tonight, man." She bent into the car for a few seconds, assessing, and popped back out.

"So, where's your monster?" the officer asked.

"What?"

"Was it chasing you? Is it close? Did you kill it?"

Tiffany looked down the road. "There were two. I don't know if I killed the first one. I hit it with my car and pinned its legs to my house. I definitely broke those legs, but I don't know if it died from it. The second one chased us, but I lost him on some back roads on the border between Tanner's Switch and Richmond, but then I drove all the way to Westerly Hospital and back here. So I have no idea where it is."

The cop moved around her, heading toward her car. "Okay, so we have no idea how much time we have. We'll have to make do." She opened the trunk and pulled out a large first aid kit. "Your brother's wound needs better wrapping, but you did a good job getting something on there. The bad news is if he does have a broken rib, there's not much I can do for it, but I doubt he does. In my experience, broken ribs are usually very painful when you lie down. People with broken ribs want to sit up. It feels better."

As the officer moved away from her cruiser, Tiffany noticed the word GO written on the side in what looked like blood. "What's that?"

"I told you, it's been a night."

Tiffany followed her back to the Camry. "That's good, then, right? That my brother's able to lie down? So he should be okay?"

"Well, from what I can see, sure. I don't know what other injuries he might have. He could be bleeding internally, or who knows? But if I had to guess, I think he's probably got a bruised rib cage and lots of bleeding from that wound. Also, from the black and blue on his temple and the goose egg on his hairline, probably a concussion."

"Okay," Tiffany said as she hopped into the front seat, going in backward, so she could watch the police officer tend to her brother.

"No. No. You stay out there and keep an eye out for the monster. Yell as loud as you can if you see it. There's no neighborhood to wake up."

Tiffany nodded her head. The advice made sense. It was good. She had something to do, something important, something to keep her mind occupied, focused. And the news on her brother sounded promising too.

She stood outside the car and worked to wrap her head around the evening. The thin veil of fog slithered and rolled around her. A gentle breeze felt nice on her skin. Yesterday, she was a normal teen. She had friends, a girlfriend, a nice family. Then she went to Block Island. She wished she could call Beth, apologize, cry to her, beg her for help on all the upcoming sleepless nights.

She hoped Beth slept sweetly in the real world, the one outside all the fog, and she hoped when Beth woke up, she would wear her forgiveness shoes. Tiffany owed her a hell of an apology.

The ocean was somewhere behind her, way too far away to see from here, but she smelled its briny breath and felt its breeze between her fingers. She prayed to it, asking it to return Charlie to her.

The officer, still in the car bandaging her brother, interrupted Tiffany's thinking. "Do you have any idea where Chrissy and the other one would go if they weren't home?"

"Angela."

"Yes, Angela. Chrissy and Angela. Do you know where they could be?"

Tiffany shook her head. "No. If not here, I have no idea. Unless they went back to Block Island to find Charlie."

The officer huffed. "Well, you came down the opposite side of the road, so you didn't see the gruesome scene on the other end. A state police officer came to their house tonight to deliver them to their father. His name was Officer Barrett. He never made it back. I know why, now. His body is at the end of the road. Monster got him good. No sign of the girls, though, or his car. Lots of glass. And the partition was removed. My guess is the girls have that car. Unless you think the monster drove it away."

Tiffany shrugged. "I don't think so."

"Which gives me high hopes they're okay. So I say we drive around a little bit and see if we can't find that car."

"I guess that sounds like a plan. What about my brother?"

"Well, I got his leg wrapped. Looks like he sprained his ankle too. I want to check on his ribs and head really quickly, but after that, we can get him into the back of the cruiser."

"Okay," Tiffany said.

"On the drive, I'd love it if you could give me some backstory here."

"What do you mean?"

"I mean, we're in some weird fog world created by monsters set on killing this family." She pointed to the house. "I'm stuck in it because I happened to be at their father's house when it all went down. So why are you and your brother here?"

Tiffany nodded. "Yeah. That's gonna be a long story."

"Uh-huh." The officer went into the back seat.

Tiffany thought about Charlie again, how their visit to the art studio was the catalyst for all of this. She wondered if Milicent made it home okay. If there was a cop dead at the end of the road, it meant a lot of collateral damage related to their trip.

She tensed. "Officer?"

"It's Burns. Or you can call me Meghan." The officer sat half in the car, doing something in the back seat.

"Fine. Meghan."

"Yeah?"

"The monster is here."

CHAPTER 31

KINGDOM COME

Chrissy ran behind the librarian's desk. "Quick. Find me something better than a keyboard."

They both opened drawers. Angela eyed Vinx staring at the door with his hackles raised and teeth snarling. The monster moved closer, and she'd be damned if she let the Banglass thingy hurt her dog.

Chrissy tossed stuff from the desk drawers. "Aha. Another pair of scissors."

"How many pairs of scissors does the librarian need in your school? What the hell are they cutting?"

Angela tapped Chrissy's arm and bobbed her head toward the shelves. Chrissy nodded and they snuck over, hiding behind the stacks. Of course, this was a high school library, so the stacks were only four shelves deep, but that should be enough for bobbing and weaving around.

"Vinx. Come here," Angela whispered. The dog didn't listen. He continued to snarl by the door.

"Vinx!" she whispered again, but a little louder.

"Fuck." She put the scissors down and ran to the dog. Her sister objected behind her, but she ignored it.

When she reached Vinx, she wrapped her arms around his body and waddled back to the shelves with him. "You need to be quiet. I know you want to fight, but you can't. Not with this thing."

Chrissy pointed to a door behind the librarian's desk. "Maybe you should put him in there until this is over, so he doesn't get hurt."

"Good idea." She lifted the dog again and waddled with him toward the door. Halfway there and she was out of breath. When she finally got to the door, she brought the dog all the way to the handle so she could twist it while keeping him in her arms. The door popped open, revealing a small, square room filled with supplies and books. She walked the dog in about halfway and ran to the door, but the dog followed.

"No. Vinx. Stay in here." She slid through the narrow opening and shut the door. Meanwhile, the doors at the main entrance crashed open, and without a second wasted, the monster came at her.

She didn't have time to think, and she didn't even have her scissors to use on it. The creature moved like a bullet, but before it reached her, Chrissy lunged at it, scissors in hand, and drove them into the creature's arm.

It slashed its injured arm, backhanding Chrissy so hard in the face, she flew backward into a shelf. The scissors fell out of the creature's skin. Books tumbled to the floor. Blood dripped down Chrissy's nose. Angela took the keyboard off the librarian's desk and smashed it across the monster's face. It snapped in half, and the monster barely blinked.

"Well, you were right, Chrissy."

The monster swatted at her. She dodged it by jumping backward, barely escaping the thing's sharp claws, and she pulled a muscle in her calf.

Chrissy ran at it again, jumping on its back. While it struggled to remove her, Angela hobbled toward the shelves and grabbed the scissors she had left on the floor. Chrissy wrapped her hands around the monster's neck, and it extended its arms back to try to claw at her. Angela ran as best she could, ignoring the pain in her leg, and plunged the scissors wherever they landed. They hit the creature in its upper torso.

It roared again and slashed at Angela. Luckily, she was too close and only felt the brute force of its forearm instead of its dagger-shaped fingers. The blow knocked her into the wall, which hurt. She flopped to the floor upon impact.

From all the creature's flailing, Chrissy's grip loosened. As the Langblass shook itself, Chrissy rocked from side to side, her legs flying in each direction.

Angela stood up, a little dizzy. Vinx barked up a storm behind the door. Chrissy hung on by a thread.

Angela stumbled, looking for the scissors that had fallen from the creature's arm. She only had a few seconds. Chrissy wouldn't last much longer. She turned around the desk and accidentally kicked them. The scissors slid across the floor, landing back by the book-shelves. She hobbled for them, and on the way, her sister screamed behind her. Something thudded.

She picked up the scissors and turned to see her sister on top of a computer desk, curled up in a fetal position. The monster made its way toward Chrissy. Angela ran with the scissors raised above her head, ready to plunge them into the monster's heart, but it predicted her movements and turned in time to grab Angela by the top of the head. It lifted her in the air, squeezing her skull. She swatted at it, trying to stab, but the thing's arms were too long. The creature opened its giant mouth and moved in for a bite. Angela kicked her leg up, landing it right on the thing's forehead. With all the force she had in her, she used her leg to keep it back. The creature lifted its face, trying to bite the foot on its forehead. Angela drove the scissors up and into the monster's lower arm.

It screamed and dropped her, then with a forceful rage, swatted her in the head, knocking her down. This hit hurt a lot more than the first, and it took a second to snap back to reality. She felt out of sorts, not quite there. Her vision blurred.

Chrissy ran from the table she'd been laid out on, a vague shape running across the library. The monster, a fuzzy, tall white entity in front of Angela, screeched. Her sister smashed into the monster's leg, and the beast fell to the floor with a loud smash.

"C'MON!" Chrissy's voice was low and distorted, a demonic sound.

Angela looked at her, confused. The ringing in her ears faded and her vision coalesced.

"C'MON!"

Angela tried to stand but almost fell over, as though her legs had turned to seaweed in a current.

"C'MON!"

The white shape returned, rising above her sister.

"C'MON!"

What was it? What was that thing?

"COOOMMMEEE OOONNN!"

"Welcome home." The two voices came together and infiltrated Angela's muddled brain, bringing reality back to her. The library. Her sister. The monster.

The monster! It stood behind Chrissy.

"COME ON!"

"CHRISSY!" Angela yelled.

The monster's claw drove into Chrissy's back and the tip protruded through the other side. Blood shot out of Chrissy's stomach, spraying Angela's pants. Chrissy's face turned to shock, pale white. Her eyes grew two sizes bigger. Her mouth dropped.

"Run," she whispered, then the monster ripped its claw free. Chrissy flopped to the floor.

Angela listened. She ran faster than she ever had.

CHAPTER 32
LOST AND FOUND

Tiffany shivered at the sight of the monster. She'd faced it already—two of them, in fact—but she'd run out of steam, and Doug was immobile and unconscious in the back seat of his car. She had nothing left to give.

The officer stepped in front of her. "Get in the car and protect your brother. I'll take care of this thing."

Tiffany had no interest in arguing the cop's points. She was happy to let the lady do all the heavy lifting. To Tiffany's surprise, Doug was awake in the back seat.

"DOUG!" She almost jumped on him for a hug but stopped herself before she injured him further. "You're alive."

Outside the car, the monster let out its intimidating screech. Two gunshots fired.

"Ugh," Doug said.

Tiffany teared up. "You don't need to talk. I just can't tell you how good it is to see you with your eyes opened."

"It fucking hurts." He chuckled, which turned into a cough, and as he hacked up a lung, his face turned red and he grimaced, clutching his chest.

"Dude, stop. Rest. Don't talk. Just let me rant about how much I love my brother while you chill the fuck out."

The monster growled.

"Oh fuck. What's going on now?" Doug's eyes were glossy and red.

"Don't worry. There's a cop now. She's got a gun."

Doug rested his head on the back door. "That's good. I didn't want to have to kick its ass myself."

Now it was Tiffany's turn to laugh.

Another gunshot went off. Tiffany got nervous. If the gun could take the thing down, why was it taking so long?

Something banged against the car with so much force, the whole vehicle shifted. Doug's head slammed hard on the car door. "Ow, fuck."

The creature ran by the back of the car. Tiffany's heart sped up, and she prayed the cop could finish this. Doug closed his eyes.

The monster stood by the door where Doug rested. A single slash from the creature's powerful claws could kill her brother right now, but the creature didn't notice them in the vehicle, or at least didn't care. The policewoman stood on the other side of the car with her gun raised, but Tiffany guessed she refrained from firing out of fear she might accidentally hit one of the siblings.

Maybe the monster had known they were in the car and used them as a human shield. She hated the idea of it, but she had to do something. Or maybe not. Could she help the officer, or would she just make the scene more difficult?

The creature jumped on top of the car and in one swift motion smashed into the cop. The woman crumbled to the asphalt and her gun skidded across the road. Within a second, the creature spun around and bent low, its face at the driver's side window where Tiffany sat backward, facing her brother.

The monster's hot breath hit the window and a blast of steam came between them.

Tiffany froze, terrified.

"Wash up, Scumbag," it sang.

Anger flared inside Tiffany's guts. The taunting nature of the creature's tone made her furious.

"Oh, fuck you." She shoved the car door open, smashing the creature in the face. It hadn't expected that, and a look of shock landed in its wide, black eyes.

If she weren't so horrified and scared, she would have gained great satisfaction from that face. But the monster was huge and supernaturally strong, so while the door shot might have hurt, it didn't slow it down. The creature thrashed and the door slammed in Tiffany's face. With a second thrash, it had broken through the window and reached in for her.

Why hadn't she considered using the horn? She was too tired, too out of it, and wasn't thinking straight. When she'd hopped in the car, her brother had awoken, stealing her thinking, and she'd accepted that an adult—one with a weapon—had things under control. Now, it was too late. The monster's arm swatted around the driver's seat.

Tiffany shimmied into the passenger seat, opened the door, and spilled out onto the sidewalk in front of Charlie's house. Her only objective was to move the fight away from her brother. The creature jumped on top of the hood and over to Tiffany's side. Before the thing could land, Tiffany made her way to the back of the car. Cat and mouse.

The policewoman sat up, groggy and out of it. Tiffany ran past her, hoping to reach the gun before the monster killed her. Her arm throbbed from her wound, and as she ran and her heartbeat increased, it became more noticeable. It shot pain into her shoulder, and she worried she might be having a heart attack.

The monster growled behind her, letting Tiffany know it wasn't far behind. The thing could keep pace with cars for a short distance, so she had no shot of outrunning it.

A loud crash went off behind her. She knew peeking would potentially slow her down, but she had to look. The monster had fallen but was on the way back up. The officer had her arms wrapped around its lower leg.

Tiffany had to hurry and get the gun before the creature retaliated on the cop. She'd seen the weapon sliding but missed exactly where it landed, and in the dead of night on a dimly lit street with fog rolling around, it proved difficult to see.

"Come on. Where are you?"

She quickly glanced back at the cop, who held the monster's wrists while it tried to slash at her. Burns had impressive strength if she could hold the monster back as well as she did.

Tiffany examined the street, searching for the weapon, when she noticed a glint under the police cruiser. "Oh no." She tilted her head to get a better view and saw the gun resting midway between both front tires.

"Fuck." She had no choice, so she dropped down and crawled under the car. As she reached for it, she gave another look toward the ensuing fight. The cop still clung to the monster's wrists, but it held both arms up high, dangling her in the air. She tried to kick at him, but with its long arms, she didn't have the range. The monster slammed her into Doug's car, and she lost her grip, falling to the ground.

Without hesitation, the monster turned and ran toward Tiffany.

"Fuck. Fuck. Fuck." She scooted out from under the car with the gun. She needed room to maneuver her hands. Wiggling out, she watched as the monster came closer and closer.

It grabbed her ankle and opened its jaws wide. Tiffany pulled her arm out from under the car and fired directly into the creature's mouth.

Its lifeless body collapsed on top of her. She lay there, shaken to her core, trembling. Blood and gore slipped out of its mouth onto her clothes. She didn't move. Couldn't.

She'd once been lost, stolen by a family member, forced to travel the East Coast. She'd once been found, brought home to a caring family, introduced to new friends who loved her and kept her safe.

And now she was lost again, and no amount of love could save her, could shine a light on the scared girl tucked into the dark corner. This would break her. Today ended her in some way. If she survived, she'd go on, but she'd never be the same Tiffany again. The whole night stretched her thin, pulling and pulling, barely giving her a second to comprehend the mess she'd fallen into, but this final shot, the blast of the gun, and the body falling on top of her snapped her. Stretched too far. She had once been lost. Then found. And now she was gone for good.

The policewoman groaned across the street. She sat upright on the side of Doug's car, holding her arm.

Tiffany rolled out from under the monster. "Are you all right?"

The cop nodded. "I'll be fine. You?"

Tiffany stood up. "No. I'll never be fine again."

The cop looked around. "Either that wasn't the last of them, or we're fucked for life."

Tiffany handed the gun back to the cop. The officer had a much sturdier hand than she did. "Well, let's go find the rest and kill them because I'd like to get my brother to a hospital, and my arm is starting to really hurt."

The cop stood up, wincing and groaning as she did. "Okay. Let's get your brother to my car and see if we can't find Chrissy and Angela."

CHAPTER 33
ANGELA'S WORLD

Angela ran out of the library and down the second-floor hallway, hating herself for leaving Chrissy and Vinx behind. She had faith the monster wouldn't hurt the dog, and she doubted her sister survived the attack, but she needed to find a way back into the library to check. Her leg still ached, but it improved as the minutes ticked by.

She turned into the first door she came across, hoping to hide before the monster left the library and spotted her. As soon as the automatic lights turned on, she lost her breath.

"Of course," she whispered.

The girls' bathroom.

She ran into a stall, hoisted herself on top of the toilet, and removed the tank lid, brandishing it at nothing, just waiting for the thing to appear.

She knew the monster would find her, that it could somehow sense her location, otherwise it never would have found her and Chrissy at the school after they'd lost it in Richmond.

It didn't take long.

The door to the bathroom opened, banging hard on the wall.

Angela flinched. The monster was taller than the stall walls, so she could see its head, and once it moved closer, it would see her without needing to open the door.

She stepped off the toilet as the monster crept closer. She realized that inside the stall, she wouldn't have enough room to pull the tank lid back and get a good strike. As she considered how to correct this, the monster stepped in front of her stall.

Boom.

His claw drove through the metal door and ripped it open. She'd never get a good hit from inside, so she held the tank lid with both hands and charged, using all her force to slam it into the thing's body. It stumbled backward until she had it pinned to the wall.

She stayed as close to its body as she could, so it wouldn't have the opportunity to slash her with its incredibly long claws. The monster screeched and fell sideways, causing Angela to slip too. It hit the ground and she landed on top of it with the tank lid between them. Their faces touched, and the monster's slick skin left an oily residue on her cheek.

And then she fell into a dream, seeing the monster's life in quick flashes.

A thick forest. Screaming women. A boat. Block Island. Murder. Murder. Murder. Always young men or women, dying by the Langblasses. Chomp chomp chomp.

A group of people in a circle in the middle of the woods.

The monsters were with them. With them. Not attacking. Not eating. With them.

As soon as Angela pulled her head back, she lost the visions.

"I don't give a fuck about your world," she said, as she stood up and jumped on the tank lid in one swift motion.

The monster heaved as her full weight landed on its chest. The tank lid slipped off the monster, and Angela crashed onto the hard linoleum floor. She crawled forward, slowly rising to her feet, and dashed out of the bathroom, knowing it wouldn't take the Langblass much time to recover.

But as she entered the hallway, she changed her mind, turning back into the girls' bathroom. The monster rolled on the ground. Angela walked around it, grabbed the tank lid, lifted it high above her head, and yelled, "This is my world." She drove the tank lid down onto the monster's head. It screamed and held up its lanky arms.

She lifted the lid and did it again. And again. Blood oozed from the creature's head.

The tank lid hit the linoleum with a loud bang, and Angela dashed out of the bathroom and back to her sister in the library. Chrissy lay on the floor, shivering. Blood pooled around her.

Vinx continued to bark behind the door. "Come on, Chrissy. I killed the monster. You need to stay alive."

Chrissy's skin had turned porcelain white, lips purple. She shook uncontrollably.

"I told you not to die. Why don't you ever listen to me?"

Chrissy eked out a small laugh and blood shot from her mouth.

Angela stroked Chrissy's hair. "Fuck. I don't know what to do."

She ran to the phone, wondering if the world would have righted itself now that the monster had died. But there was no dial tone, just a wailing screech.

"Fuck!' she yelled at nothing.

The library door crashed open, and the monster, now covered in its own blood, stood at the threshold.

CHAPTER 34
SEARCH PARTY

After Tiffany and Officer Burns brought Doug to the back seat of the cruiser, they drove around a series of Tanner's Switch neighborhoods, looking for Barrett's police cruiser. Tiffany remained shaken from the last monster attack, a feeling that would probably never subside. On top of that, her worry for Doug kept her stomach in knots.

"Nice area over here," Burns said absently.

Tiffany snorted. "Don't lie. Tanner's Switch is a shithole. It's one of the poorest towns in the state."

Burns frowned. "Yeah, but it's still scenic. Lots of beautiful woods. Plus, it's an anomaly. Typically, crime rates and low income correlate, but Tanner's Switch has very low crime rates despite its economic challenges."

Tiffany smirked. "You've been very helpful, and I'm so glad I ran into you, but if you don't mind, what a shitty thing to say. First, you sound like a textbook. Second, crime rates correlate to poverty but also to population density, and Tanner's Switch has a low population rate. But yes, thank you for saying it in the kindest way possible: Y'all broke asses aren't a bunch of heathens. Remarkable!"

Burns' face turned red. "That's not what I meant. I'm sorry."

"I know you didn't, and I'm sorry. I'm just on edge. But let me tell you something about Tanner's Switch. Did you ever hear the story of the girl who found a dead body behind the old Wellman's house?"

"No."

"Within the next week, her coworkers and family all wound up dead. Not all of them in The Switch, but still. No one ever found out what happened to those people, but everyone around here knows. How about the two girls at the abandoned amusement park?"

Burns shook her head.

"They were teens when I was just a kid. Both of them were mean assholes. One of them was like a major criminal. Violent. The other pushed her friend off an abandoned Ferris wheel. She was arrested for it. And her defense claimed—and I am not making this up—that she was possessed by the evil spirit of a dead bird."

"Wow."

"Yep. Then there was the woman who was obsessed with Carli Long, the internet star. I don't think I need to get into that one. I know you've heard the story. Everyone in the world has. You have the alien sightings in the seventies, the nuclear reactor accident in Richmond, which led to a bunch of folks in Tanner's Switch claiming they saw glowing objects in their yards despite being miles and miles from where the reactor killed that dude. I could go on and on all day."

"With the exception of the Carli Long one, I hadn't heard about any of those."

"No? How about the one where a family moved to Tanner's Switch from Block Island after claiming their sibling was eaten by a monster, only to have the entire town turn into a creepy fog land filled with monsters picking them off one by one and taking out every person associated with them on the way?"

Burns glared at her. "Yeah. Yeah, I know that one."

"Makes all the urban legends and fairy tales about this shithole feel a little more real." Tiffany put her feet on the glovebox door.

"So what are you saying? Tanner's Switch is really unsafe, despite the numbers?"

Tiffany looked in the rearview to get a peek at Doug. He slept soundly. "Did you know we have over twenty sightings a year of lamppost monsters? LAMPPOSTS! The goofiest, fakest monsters in the history of television. Folks around here see them all the time."

"Do you believe people really see lamppost monsters?"

"After today? I believe anything. I believe everything. You want to know the truth about Tanner's Switch? It's been rotting since the tracks stopped rolling through. Economically, the town died and then, poof, so did the people. We've all been dead since we were born. Tanner's Switch is doomed. It always has been. It's decay. It's death. It just fucking festers and bubbles and slowly it eats away at all of us. If we don't get killed by monsters, we find another way to die young. Do you know what the life expectancy in Tanner's Switch is? First, do you know what the life expectancy in America is?"

Burns shrugged.

"In America, it's seventy-seven years. In the best states, like Hawaii, it can go as high as eighty. In the worst state, it's like, seventy-one. I think that award goes to Mississippi. In Rhode Island, it's seventy-eight. So we're ahead of the national average. But Tanner's Switch? Luckily, we have a low population because our life expectancy is sixty-eight. Sixty-eight! Do you know how many tragically young deaths have to occur to bring the entire town's population that low?"

"Shit, that's bleak."

"Try living here."

Tiffany stared out the window. Trees zipped by. She'd lived in Tanner's Switch her entire life. Watched as the income levels flatlined, but the cost of living skyrocketed. She saw the small shops close down as more and more folks opted for a trip to Walmart in Westerly. She watched the few wealthy people who lived in the area use their influence to avoid paying their fair share of taxes. She witnessed the old lady at the gas station get older until she passed away and her daughter took over ringing people up for their cigarettes and sodas. She watched new houses go up, only to have them dropped into the hands of rich assholes who rented the houses out as vacation properties—*Just five short miles from the ocean!*—instead of letting people move to the area. She watched the rot seep in, take hold of them, and the townspeople argued about cleaning it up because it meant they'd have to adapt.

The monsters came in and out. The apparitions, the death, the chemicals, the smells, the demons. They came in and out. And the whole town died on their hills.

"There!" Tiffany shouted. Burns slammed on the brakes. Hidden by an embankment and wrapped around a tree, Barrett's car rested.

They ran out of the car, checking the abandoned police cruiser.

"They aren't here. They must have taken off on foot," Tiffany said.

"Unless the monster ate them."

Tiffany ignored her, pointing down the road. "If I were them, I'd head that way. Back toward their house. And our high school is just down a side road a little ways up."

"Okay. See if Barrett's car starts."

Tiffany hopped in and hit the button under the steering wheel. Despite the damage done, it started right up.

"Can you back it out?"

Tiffany put it in reverse and gave it gas, but the wheels spun in the mud, and the car stayed put.

"Let me try," Burns said.

Tiffany went back into the road, standing by the other cruiser. She checked in on her brother while Burns tinkered with Barrett's. The engine roared, and the wheels moved a few centimeters back and forth. Finally, with a loud shattering sound, the car released from the tree and mud. Burns brought the car up to the road, and Tiffany again admired the cop's ability to accomplish.

Burns kept the car running but stepped out. "All right. You drive Barrett's car. It's in terrible shape and may not run for long, but it's the best we got. If we find Chrissy and Angela, we're going to need both cars, though, especially with your brother out in the back seat.

Tiffany nodded. She wondered if the cop knew she didn't have a license. It probably didn't matter under the circumstances.

Burns drove slowly down the road, allowing Tiffany to keep up in the beat-up cruiser and probably to keep an eye out for the girls too.

After a few minutes, they drove past the road Tanner's Switch High School resided on. Tiffany glanced at it as they drove by. She could make out small fragments of the front façade from her angle.

They continued to crawl toward Chrissy's house.

"Wait!" Tiffany shouted as if Burns could hear her. Realizing her error, she clicked her high beams on and off and stopped the car.

Burns hit the brakes and yelled out the window, "What's up?"

"The lights are on at the school," Tiffany yelled to her.

CHAPTER 35

HOW IT ENDS

Angela's fear turned to anger. She'd had more than enough. The monster snarled in the doorway, and she never wanted to smash a head in as badly as she did now, which was saying something because she often wanted to smash people's heads in.

"Welcome home," it sang.

"No. Shut up. You don't get to say that ever again. Fuck you."

It ran toward her, slower than typical. She'd messed it up good with the tank lid. She ran toward the bookshelves, wanting to keep the action away from her sister. The monster followed her path, and while she had slowed it down, it still kept a good pace thanks to its long legs. She dipped down one aisle and then the next.

"I've been running from you all my life. You think you can wear me down now? I'll never slow down."

As she reached one side of a shelf where the monster moved on the opposite side, she pushed the shelves. It wasn't enough to knock the whole structure down as she'd hoped, but it did manage to drop some books on the creature.

"I never want to hear your shitty song again. I want to go to the bathroom in peace." She ran around an endcap into another aisle, and the monster pursued. It gained on her.

As she ran out of the aisle, the monster walked only a few steps behind. She stopped to push the last shelving unit over, hoping to knock it down on the creature behind her, but again, it didn't topple, only dropped some books on the Langblass's head.

She turned to run into the next aisle when the monster slashed at her. She thought she had the clearance, but she was wrong. The claws whipped across her back, tearing her shirt and skimming her skin. She fell to the ground and slid across the linoleum.

"You'll never win. I saw you every time I closed my eyes. I hid from you. I hid from my life because of you. You already killed me. You can't win."

The Langblass tilted its head, confusion washing over it. "Welcome home?"

"AAAAAAHHHHHHHH!" She jumped up and tackled the monster, punching it in the face. While she managed to knock it over, it quickly recovered. Even with the major head damage, it outpowered her. Within seconds, it had rolled over and got on top of her.

Angela and the Langblass engaged in a power struggle, her pushing its giant hands away from her face while it pushed hard to bring its claws down.

A pair of scissors sailed across the linoleum, landing next to Angela. Her sister stared, still lying on the floor, bleeding out. Angela wanted to reach for them but doing so meant letting go of the creature's hand.

The Langblass opened its huge mouth, drool dripping on Angela's face. The foul scent of dead ocean overtook her. She cringed and turned away from it.

The school intercom crackled to life, and a high-pitched whine played over the speakers. Feedback. The monster flopped off Angela, gripping its ears, roaring with rage. Angela rolled over and grabbed the scissors.

As the monster screamed in agony, she got on her knees by the Langblass's head and plunged the scissors into its eye, and then ripped them right out.

It screamed and flailed even more. Its legs kicked a shelving unit, knocking the whole aisle over. One set of shelves collapsed onto the next, a series of dominoes, until the entire middle section of the library was on the floor.

She drove the scissors into the creature's neck. It gurgled and whined. She did it again, this time to its chest.

Its claws latched onto her wrist, and she fell into one of its dreams again.

Three Langblasses tied up in the cabin of a boat. They rocked with the rumbling waves. A man and woman sat in front of the creatures, old-fashioned guns at their side. They held contempt in their eyes. The creatures, on the other hand, were steel-faced. They had no reaction to the humans. The man looked ready to shoot them. The woman had tears dribbling down her face.

Angela pulled away and stuck the scissors into the Langblass's neck once more. Blood coated her hand.

"Welcome home?" the creature asked.

Angela fell over, exhausted. "No," she said. "Never."

Someone shouted, "Hello?" from the hallway.

Until Angela heard the voice, it hadn't clicked that someone else must have been in the school to turn the intercom on.

"Hello?" they asked again.

The library doors kicked in.

"Oh my god." A female officer immediately ran to Chrissy. "Oh my God, she's lost a lot of blood."

"Angela?' Tiffany ran to her.

Angela sat up and leaned against the wreckage of the shelves the monster had created. "Hey, Tiff. How was your day?"

Tiffany wrapped her arms around Angela and hugged her. Angela noticed the bloody gashes on Tiffany's arms and realized she must have seen the monster too. "We have to get Chrissy to the hospital," Angela said.

Tiffany pulled away and examined the room. "The mist hasn't cleared. There's no one left."

"What?"

"The mist. We aren't in the real world anymore. We hoped when the monsters all died, the mist would clear and we'd return home, but the mist isn't clearing, which means there's either more monsters somewhere, or we're stuck here forever."

Tiffany's words ran through Angela's mind in a confused and jumbled mess.

"Wait. There's more than one of those things?"

Tiffany eyed the dead creature next to them. "I'm up to a four count."

Angela stood up on unstable legs. Her stomach whirlpooled. "I can't do more of these things."

The officer stood up. "She needs help I can't provide here. We need to get her to the hospital. I'm not a doctor, but at least they have supplies and I can do something for her. I used a lot of my supplies on your brother. This girl could die soon."

Angela brushed past Tiffany. "Let's move then." She unlocked Vinx from the back room and he barged out with his tail going insane.

The officer moved fast. They found blankets in the nurse's office and used them to build a makeshift stretcher for Chrissy. With Doug in the back of the officer's car, they had to put Chrissy in the back of the wrecked cruiser. Burns drove that car with Angela riding shotgun, while Tiffany drove behind, escorting her brother with Vinx in shotty.

Burns drove the cruiser as if racing in a high-speed chase, with the lights and sirens raising hell.

"The sirens will keep the monster back. Tiffany figured that out. She said the horn really upset one of those things at her house. It was her idea to make feedback on the intercom. When we reached the school, Tiffany caught that the lights were on, so we stopped to see if you ended up there. As soon as we entered, we heard the monster roar. Tiffany remembered the noise thing and figured it would mess the creature up until we found you. I planned to shoot it, but thanks to you, I didn't need to."

Angela slowly turned to her. "I'm sorry. Who are you?"

"Long story. I've been looking for you all night, though."

Angela turned back to her sister. Chrissy looked worse than before, her skin a weird waxy color. Her breath came out in sharp, harsh bursts. It was the only way Angela could tell she wasn't looking at a dead body. "Is she gonna make it?"

The officer shook her head. "I don't know. I hope so. It would be really helpful if we had doctors."

"So, you think the fog means there's more of those things out there?"

"Yeah, because the other option is we're stuck here forever, and I refuse to accept that."

Angela rested her head back and crossed her arms. "I kind of refuse to accept that I have to deal with another one of those things, too, though."

CHAPTER 36
PRIVY

Officer Carmen walked through some woods on the north side of the island, feet crunching on leaves. The fog made the search for Charlie even more difficult. His flashlight beam scanned the perimeter, back and forth, as he kept up his march.

Some of the local help had already called it a night, giving up on the search, but Carmen refused to stop just yet. The state officers stayed on the island, but they were losing steam. The whole search was unorthodox, and if it weren't for Carmen's fervency, it never would have happened as quickly as it did. Charlie's disappearance was connected to his sister's and Molly Mix's disappearance, and although Carmen didn't believe in the supernatural, even he was a little spooked by the constant similarities of the monster claims. Because he hadn't solved Wreath's disappearance, Carmen felt personally indebted to Charlie and the rest of the Keating family.

"Officer Carmen," someone said. A figure walked toward him from his left flank.

He turned the flashlight, and the man put his arm over his eyes. "Carmen, it's me, George Stephens."

George stepped closer. His gray hair was disheveled, eyes drowning in dark bags. He was barefoot, but that wasn't unusual for the old weirdo.

"George, what are you doing out here? If you're helping with the search, you need to check in at the station. Don't need you going missing too."

George moved closer. "No, sir. I don't need to join the search. I know exactly what happened to that boy. I saw him early today walking down the road over there."

Carmen stood up straight. "Why didn't you tell us earlier?"

As George took another step, Carmen could see his bloodshot eyes, not the victims of alcohol as they usually were, but of sadness. "Officer, you're a good man. You're going to learn a lot about this island tonight, and I'm sorry for that. I'm sorry for it all. I think I may be responsible for everything that's happening, and I figured it was high time to end it."

"George? What are you talking about?" Carmen slid his hand around his waist, nearing his gun.

"I could have stopped that boy from going into the cemetery. I should have. I debated on it when I was talking to him. I knew what those monsters were doing and what the result would be, but I also knew if this shit was ever going to end, this was how."

"I need you to speak a little clearer. I'm not following."

George sniffled. Tears rolled down his face. "The deal was always the firstborn. Those were the terms. Both families agreed to it. The Mixes and the Vanderlines. They gave up their firstborn to the monsters to keep those beasts trapped on the island. Not just on the island but in their own little worlds. But how could that last? How could it, Officer?" He stopped as if waiting for Carmen to actually answer a question that made no sense.

Carmen said nothing.

"We all had a job. Generations of us, God damn it. We all made sure the Mixes and Vanderlines kept their word. Until we didn't. These things get passed down, year after year, and when you haven't witnessed it yourself, you stop believing. No one cared anymore because who thought it was real? Of course, part of that *helped* keep it going. If you ain't afraid of monsters, you don't hide from them. But Mary's dad, he knew, and he ruined everything. Left the island before the monsters could get her. And none of us stopped him." He openly wept now, his words coming out in a whimper, "We should have stopped him, but gosh, we didn't want the blood on our hands either, even if it meant opening the world to so much more of it later on. And then tonight, I let them take that boy so I could wash my hands clean."

Carmen pinned the light right in George's eyes. "You're rambling. This isn't making any sense. Is Charlie in the graveyard?"

George looked up, his weak, sad face changing to one of anger. "Once Mary died off the island, and those things didn't have their firstborn as promised, they just had to spill the blood of any one person from each family in the graveyard. Don't you get it? They're free now. They're in both worlds. Theirs and ours. You know you can only kill them in their world, right? 'Course, other than when they'd come here for the firstborns, they can only kill us in their world too. But that's what they do. They bring you in with the mist."

"Okay, I've had enough of this. Are you saying the boy was in the graveyard?" Carmen walked quickly toward the graves but kept his sight on George.

"You're going toward them, Carmen. You'll get all of your answers soon. I'm sorry. I'm so sorry."

Carmen left the woods and entered the small field where the *Palatine* graves lay. He shined his flashlight all over. "Charlie?" While the fog made it hard to see, Carmen didn't notice any signs of struggle.

As he stepped into the center of the gravesite, the fog changed, moving like a snake around his ankles. It poofed around him, then dissipated, and when he could see again, everything had changed. He wasn't sure how, exactly, but the landscape looked off, tilted on its axis, rotten. The tree roots were darker, the leaves not the beautiful colors of fall but a crisp dead brown. The gravestones them-selves came out of the ground at an angle, crooked little cutting teeth emerging from the gums of the earth.

Something breathed loudly, a deep exhale, and the woods crunched with the sound of movement in front of him.

"Charlie?"

As a figure emerged from the shrouded forest, Carmen gasped. It was huge with long, lanky limbs. Its face housed a gaping mouth with black orbs for eyes.

"You're real," was all Carmen could spill from his lips.

It stepped closer to him.

"You're in its world now," a voice said from behind.

Officer Carmen snapped his head around to see George standing on the outskirts of the field with his hands in his pockets, cool as can be.

"That fog, it takes us to the thin space just outside our world. It's where they live most of the time. But they can bounce back and forth easily. You're lucky. Before they freed themselves, when they didn't have much power, it would cause you quite the seizure to get in between. Now you're vulnerable, though. Now they can hurt you."

Carmen turned back to the monster as it walked closer, tilting its head left and right, examining him.

"What are you?"

George laughed behind him. "And this one's just a youngin'. Used to just be three of them. They had a couple of offspring over the centuries. Not sure why they don't reproduce more than that."

The creature leaped forward, landing right in front of Carmen. The officer flinched. The monster sniffed him, snarled, and lifted its massive, clawed hand. Carmen closed his eyes, waiting for impact, too shocked to react otherwise.

"Don't kill him yet, little guy. Show 'em. Officer Carmen's a good man. He deserves to know the truth before he departs," George said.

Carmen opened his eyes as the creature opened its hand and slowly moved its palm toward the officer. Carmen squinted, squishing up his face, waiting for the slimy creature's hand to hit his skin.

"Welcome home," the creature said in a gentle voice, but the tone of it, the way it came out as two voices instead of one, sent a shock wave down Carmen's spine.

As soon as the creature's palm made contact, Carmen fell into a series of visions, whooshing through not only his mind but flowing through his bloodstream, as if it truly transported him to the world of the past.

The monsters lined up on the outskirts of the forest, all with their hands tied behind them.

"Those ropes really gonna keep them there?" a large man with a fisherman's beard asked.

"Honestly, the ropes are more symbolic. Molly's got them roped up in their minds. That's what matters," a man in a rain jacket said. He stood tall, sucking on a pipe.

The large man with the beard looked over at a woman sitting by a contained fire. She slouched and rubbed her fingers together. "Mary, come over and meet Mr. Mix."

The woman either hadn't heard him or chose to ignore him.

The bearded man turned to Mr. Mix and said, "Don't mind her, she's more than willing to do what must be done to keep these things from getting free, but the price is haunting her."

Mr. Mix put his hand on the man's shoulder. "Well, let her know we aren't happy about it either, but it's the way these things work. Molly is a woman of great power, but nothing comes without a price, and when she has to create something as large as binds between worlds, the price comes heavy."

"I understand. We understand. We wouldn't have made the trip otherwise."

Mr. Mix took a puff from his pipe. "These creatures had their day in the Black Forest and could have kept having it, but they overstepped. They've enough power to turn our world into theirs, rotting it from the soil to the sky. Someone had to be brave enough to pay the toll."

"Yessir," the bearded man said.

"Trust me, if our family could have made the sacrifice alone, we would have accepted to keep you from bearing the cross, but one can't feed three."

A woman walked into the field from the woods, wearing a black cloak. She pulled her hood off, revealing long, slick black hair. When she looked up, the bearded man gasped. Her eyes were glowing red.

Mr. Mix said, "Molly, our guests have arrived."

"I see that."

The woman by the fire noticed the new arrival and ran to her husband's side.

Molly said, "Mr. and Mrs. Vanderline, it's a pleasure to make your acquaintance. I apologize it has to happen under these circumstances."

Mrs. Vanderline stepped forward. "I'm sorry. It's been a long trip. I agreed to this with good intentions, but I've had time to think about it, and I just don't know that I understand. What does firstborn mean? If I have twelve children, will all eleven survivors have to feed their firstborn to these demons?"

Molly smiled. She had an ethereal quality to her face, the way her eyes glowed, and her smile stretched like a galaxy. "Your second born will always be responsible for the next generation's sacrifice. And it's imperative you have a second born, as it is equally imperative they do as well. If the line ends, so does the compromise."

The woman nodded, tears filling her eyes. "I'm sorry. It's hard to accept I'm poisoning my bloodline for generations to keep these awful beasts appeased."

Molly puffed out her chest. "You're not. You're giving to the greater good and not allowing these things to turn our world into theirs. You're saving all life as we know it. If they're ever set free, given free rein to release their veil, they'll first take out their viciousness on our families, and once they've gotten their revenge, they'll devour everyone else.

"What I'm going to cast will keep them on this island, and it will keep them in their realm, stuck forever, only to come out to feed once every generation. The world will never know of their existence from this point forward. Some with great vision will see the Langblasses out of the corner *of their eyes, but it'll be nothing more than a scary story for them to pass on to their children."*

Mr. Vanderline hugged his wife. "She's just tired."

Molly tilted her head. "I know what they did to your child in those woods. And I know it seemed easy to promise your firstborn when you'd already lost her. But now you're realizing the reverberating effects of your choice. It's not just the child you've already lost. But remember, it isn't just you that will be sacrificing. My husband and I will also be poisoning our bloodline, as you so eloquently put it, and this isn't our first sacrifice in the name of protecting our world from others. This is what we do. This is who we are."

Something cracked. A fissure broke through the vision until Carmen was in a different place. A fog world.

The creatures walked the shoreline. They looked defeated, broken. A woman stood on the shore. She turned, revealing her face. Mrs. Vanderline. She was much older than in the last vision, probably by decades. Her cheeks were wet and red. She pulled out a small blade and brought it to her neck. With a swift motion, the blade danced across her flesh, and her neck spilled crimson on the soft beach sand.

The monsters stopped and watched as the woman twitched to her death. Within a few minutes, shorebirds came and picked at her corpse. One of them plucked out the woman's eye.

Another crack. Another fissure in the vision.

The monsters stood within the fog, walking throughout the island. People walked all around them, tourists visiting the island, shopping, laughing. Modern times. And the monsters watched. The people surrounding them were completely unaware of the creatures' existence.

One of the beasts slashed at a person, and his claws went right through them, unable to connect. It hollered a sorrowful cry.

Another fissure came, cracking through the foundation of the vision.

A monster lay on the ground, screaming in pain, as a little monster came out of her.

Another fissure.

The monsters stood on the shoreline, the same three from the first vision and now two others. Smaller ones. As boats drifted by in the distance, the creatures pounded on an invisible wall, screaming and crying, doing everything in their power to break through.

The monster removed his palm from Officer Carmen's forehead. "All this time," Carmen said.

Behind him, George cleared his throat. "All this time. We've been dripping blood into the ocean since before your daddy's daddy was born."

The monster pointed to the side, aiming his finger toward some unknown destination shrouded in the night's charcoal sky, made even more impossible to see thanks to the gray fog. "Welcome home," it cried. "Welcome home."

George stepped over to Officer Carmen's side.

"I'm ready," George said.

The monster snarled and slashed George's neck. Blood sprayed on Carmen's face.

"Jesus," Carmen said and drew his gun, but before he could use it, the creature drove his claw through the officer's chest.

Carmen went to scream, but only a low whistle left his throat. As his body slid off the creature's massive talon, he lifted his arm, putting the muzzle to the monster's mouth.

A gunshot fired.

And two bodies fell to the earth.

CHAPTER 37

CLOWN FISH

Burns drove down Franklin Street, and Angela noticed two lumps lying in the road. One of them was a monster, the other harder to distinguish. As they neared the lumps, they disappeared. Completely vanished. The fog thinned.

Headlights shined ahead of them in the distance. Lights flickered on from the streetlamps.

The farther they drove, the more the fog dissipated until fully gone.

"Holy shit," Burns said.

"Is it clearing?" Angela could barely contain her excitement. If they were back in the real world, her sister stood a chance of surviving.

She turned to look out the back window to see if Tiffany stayed behind. The rules of crossing in and out of the real world were a weird-ass mystery, and she had no idea if Tiffany would exit it the same way they just had. Sure enough, the second cruiser sped behind them.

When they reached the hospital, Burns ran out of the car. Angela wept at the sight of a man smoking a butt by the entrance, and through the large front windows, two women worked behind desks. Did that mean the monsters were gone for good? That her sister would survive?

Teams of people rushed around her. A stretcher—a real one—carried Chrissy into the hospital. Another came for Doug. Angela didn't know what to do. Was she allowed past the double doors? No one seemed to notice her. No one asked. She had claw marks down her back. Surely nothing more than scratches. Maybe she should ask to get them checked, but she didn't.

With both cars abandoned, she walked over to the second cruiser and found what she worried she might find. Vinx was gone.

Burns came out shortly after, phone at her ear. She had tears in her eyes as she hung up. She smiled at Angela. "I just woke my husband up and made him check that our daughter was asleep in her bed. He thought I was crazy. I need to get home to her, but I gotta talk to you and Tiffany first."

"How's my sister?"

"I'm not sure. I think it'll be a while until they have answers for you, to be honest."

Angela nodded.

"Where's the dog?" Burns asked.

"Gone. With the mist."

"Shit. I'm sorry."

Angela threw her hands up in the air. "The dog had two tags. Two."

"Huh?"

"My sister checked the tag. That's how we found out his name was Vinx. But there was a second tag. It said, *If lost, please return to Kendall O'Connor.* Then it had an address. He was never my dog."

Burns bit her bottom lip, clearly unsure what to say. "Still sucks. I'm sorry."

"It doesn't. We don't own something just because we need it. It never belonged to me. Sometimes a girl and a dog meet, and it's not destiny or the beginning of a lifelong friendship. It's just a whole lot of luck that they were both there for each other when they needed that for a little bit."

"I think I get it. You're way too smart for your age."

"Officer, my mother died when I was nine. My oldest sister too. Last night, I found out my oldest brother died. My other brother disappeared, and I'm pretty sure he's dead too. Who knows what will happen to Chrissy—"

The officer opened her mouth to say something but thought better of it. Angela decided not to pursue it.

"The point is, I'm used to relationships being short-lived."

Tiffany came out of the hospital with her hands wrapped around her abdomen.

"How are you holding up?" Burns asked her.

Tiffany offered a small smile. "Okay. My arm's fine. They got it all stitched up and gave me antibiotics."

"And your brother?"

"He'll be fine. How's Chrissy?"

Angela stepped in. "Don't know yet."

Burns grabbed them both by the shoulder. "When you were in there? What did you tell them happened?"

Tiffany pulled her arm away. "I didn't. I avoided giving answers, and they weren't happy about it. They called my parents, who are on their way to pick me up. I have no idea what kind of story to tell."

"Yeah, that's what I want to talk to you both about. We need a story. I have no idea how to make one stick. From the eyes of the people who didn't get sucked into a different world, here's what they'll piece together. Doug's injured from a fall. Tiffany has multiple stab wounds, as does Chrissy, but not from any kind of weapon they'd recognize. Charlie disappeared. Two police officers and Mr. Keating are also gone. And we drove to the hospital in one of those officer's cars."

"Wait. What?" Angela asked.

Burns caught her mistake and mouthed the word, "Fuck." She rubbed her temples. "I'm sorry, Angela. I wanted you to find out a better way than this."

She had no response, but Tiffany and Burns waited for her to say something. To divert the conversation and to keep her brain from wrapping around the new revelation, Angela said, "We either tell the truth and look like crazy people, or we say there was a serial killer. We'll create our own *Friday the 13th* story and use what happened to my sister as part of it. It'll make the media feel like shit for what they did to us four years ago. 'Serial killer dresses as a monster and terrorizes family, comes back four years later for murder spree.'"

Burns pulled at her ponytail. "There's probably a million reasons why that story wouldn't work, but I'm too exhausted to think of them. Stick with that, don't give any details. In fact, fucking flat out refuse to answer anything. You're both suffering right now, and the police will be sensitive to that. But they will want a story. Just tell them you were terrorized by a man in a mask, and you can't talk about it. Cry a lot. Say you can't remember. Too traumatized. Details equals screwing up our story. Got it?"

They both nodded.

"Good. Eventually, we'll need to give them a lot more, but we can meet up and clean up the details another time. For now, go be with your families. I'm sorry for everything you've had to go through."

Angela flinched when the cop awkwardly jumped forward and hugged them. Once in the embrace, though, she didn't want Burns to let go. Tiffany's hand wrapped around Angela's back, and the three were locked in a group hug. When it ended, the cool autumn air hit Angela's skin, making her feel naked. Exposed.

Shortly after, Burns drove off to be with her family. Tiffany's parents came and took her inside to visit Doug. Angela sat alone in the waiting room. In the center of the Westerly Hospital waiting area, a fish tank housed a half dozen beautiful, colorful fish. A clown fish swam from one end to the other, and she stared at it until her eyes blurred. One end to the other. One end to the other. One end to the other. Over and over.

After a few hours, she had to pee. And she did. She peed alone in the public restroom and felt nothing. Not anger, not grief, not even fear. For a few minutes, she'd run dry of emotions.

CHAPTER 38

CORNERS

A FEW MONTHS LATER

Chrissy stood at the bottom of the steps leading to Tanner's Switch Middle School. Kids brushed past her on both sides. When a student brushed shoulders with her, her heart spun into overdrive. Each step in front of her stretched in her mind, growing impossibly long.

Almost two months had passed since she last attended school. The isolation during recovery only exaggerated her already growing anxiety and terror of her surroundings.

She closed her eyes and breathed in deep. She could run away from this, fly home, and not a single person would blame her. No one would stop her from taking more time. But if she did, if she didn't fight her instinct to run, she'd retreat further and further into her shell, and she'd end up just another victim of the Langblass.

Her breath caught in her throat as she ascended the stairs. A student pulled on one of the double doors, and it banged hard against the outside railing. Chrissy flinched.

The thin strips of hallways inside the school sharpened the

cacophony of teenage chatter, focusing it and pushing it on Chrissy. Her chest caved in, strangling her heart. Lockers slammed. Hastings opened his locker about fifteen feet away, pulling out some texts and shoving them into his bookbag. Luckily, he hadn't seen her yet.

He'd called numerous times and visited the hospital with flowers. She always refused the company, too terrified of showing anyone her scars.

The bell rang and she flinched, jolting backward and banging the back of her skull on the wall. The pressure in her chest grew, tightening. She couldn't breathe. Her limbs trembled and her teeth chattered.

People looked at her as they passed, unsure what to make of the full-blown panic attack happening in front of them.

She turned and ran, heading straight into the girls' bathroom. A few students walked out, giggling to each other.

She flew into a stall and shut the door, locking herself in. Outside of a gentle drip from the sink, it was quiet.

She sat on the toilet seat and rested her head against the back wall. With her eyes shut, she let air come into her lungs and out through her nose. Her hand went to her chest, so she could feel her heart rate simmering.

She opened her eyes. Maybe she wasn't ready for this, but if she could escape to the bathroom when needed, then maybe she could use it as a crutch to get through the day. At least within the confines of a stall, she could be alone.

Alone.

Her heart sped back up, beating hard against her ribs.

Alone.

Tears formed in the corners of her eyes. Slowly, she turned her head toward the far corner of the bathroom.

Alone.

The Langblass did not hover in the corner as it had for so many years with Angela. But if Chrissy looked away, would it appear, forming from her fear? Would it coalesce, recreate itself and finish the job on her family? What if more of them existed? How could they ever be sure? Would she forever be trapped in a revenge cycle?

She stared at the empty corner.

How could she look away?

How?

How could she ever?

Her eyes blurred. She glanced away, bringing her eyes to another corner, then another, and then the last before bringing herself back to the first again.

She wiped snot from her nose and cried.

Jesus. She could never look away. Not for long. The corners owned her.

CHAPTER 39
LEFTOVERS

The microwaved dinged. Angela carried the plate of spaghetti to the kitchen table. It looked like shit. They were out of sauce, so the only flavor on the plate was the dried sauce caked to the noodles from when her aunt cooked it a few days ago.

As soon as she sat, someone knocked at the door. She left her plate and answered it.

"Hi," Tiffany said. Angela found her delivery too friendly for someone she hadn't seen or talked to in months.

Nonetheless, she waved Tiffany in as she went back to her plate. "Sorry, I'm just about to eat. I don't have anything to offer. Do you want something to drink, at least?"

Tiffany rubbed her arm. "Ah, I could go for a glass of water, but I don't want you to have to get up. Just tell me where the cups are."

Angela pointed to the cupboard to the left of the sink. Tiffany opened it and grabbed a plastic cup.

"I didn't expect to see you when I opened the door."

Tiffany turned the sink on and filled her cup. "Yeah. I'm sorry I haven't been by. I wanted to. And Burns kept calling about the story, and the police, and the fucking news. We've already given our story a thousand times, and she keeps nagging me to make sure I still have all the details. I just kind of sunk into myself, and then when I felt like I really wanted to connect with you guys, I didn't know how. Ya know? It felt like this open wound and the more I ignored it, the bigger it grew. And then today, I figured I should do something about it."

Angela took a bite of her hard noodles. "What have you been up to? I mean, besides all that."

Tiffany shook her head as she grabbed a chair from the table and sat across from Angela. "Avoidance, mostly. I try to spend time with my girlfriend so I can feel normal, but she grills me as much as the police. It's really hard to hang out with people who don't have a fucking clue."

Angela swallowed another bite down. "I get it. How's Doug?"

"Physically? Fine. Mentally? Fucked-up. How about you? How are you holding up?"

Angela laughed and shook her head.

"Fair enough. How's Chrissy? I don't see her in school."

"After surgery, she got sepsis. She's just getting back on her feet. Her boyfriend or ex-boyfriend or whatever he is keeps calling. I think she might be practicing the avoidance thing you talked about too. She keeps to herself mostly."

Tiffany sipped her water. "How about you two? Do you get along better?"

Angela frowned. "Not really. I mean, I guess. I think we're less mean to each other, but we're still totally different people. It's not like we're going to magically become best buds because of everything that happened."

Tiffany stared at her. At first, it made Angela uncomfortable, but then she realized Tiffany's eyes were filling with water. "I just thought once it was over, we'd all end up okay, but I'm not okay," she said.

Angela nodded. "Why would you think it would be okay?" She

sighed and put her fork down. "I guess that's not fair to you. I've done this before. It just gets worse. You asked how I'm doing. Well, both of my brothers are dead, and I can only outwardly mourn one. The other I'm supposed to pretend to hold out hope for. We can't even have a funeral for him. My father's dead, and I have to pretend I don't know that either. And for whatever reason, even though I hated that man for so long, his death really hurts."

She choked up, cleared her throat.

"I always hoped he'd show up at the door one day all sobered up and we'd fix everything, like our family would somehow just get back together. And he had some money squirreled away for us, at least some of it, but who knows when we'll see it, if ever. For now, he's just 'missing.'"

She picked her fork up again and stabbed at her spaghetti.

"The one thing I did think would get better is the way I was always scared, but it didn't. It might even be worse. I can pee alone now, so there's that, but every loud noise makes my chest ache until I can't breathe, and I feel like I'm going to pass out. Kids at school were talking about how they're building a pop-up escape room nearby based on original Caleb Jones stories. You know, the old horror director guy, and all I could think was, *I'll never be able to do normal shit.* If I tried to do an escape room, I'd end up curled in a ball in the bathroom hyperventilating and bawling my eyes out."

The fork stabbed harder.

"I wake up screaming in the middle of the night. So does Chrissy, who needs the rest more than anyone. And I worry about her because she's all I have left."

Stab. Stab. Stab.

"And I'm still eating leftover spaghetti, and I'll be poor forever. Like, I can't even function in school, so I have no hopes of using my brain to get some big degree that'll buy me a nice house one day. I'll be this fucked-up adult who can't hold a steady job, moving from one shit place to another, and I'll be eating the same shitty leftovers in kitchens just like this one for the rest of my life."

She slammed the fork down and tossed it across the table.

"Welcome home, right? Welcome home."

Tiffany put her hand on Angela's. "Hey, it's okay. I mean, it's not, but it is."

"I'm sorry I just dumped that on you." Angela's hands trembled, and she couldn't make them stop.

Tiffany chuckled. "Don't be. It feels good to know I'm not the only one who's fucked-up." She sighed. "Angela?"

"Yeah."

"I could use a friend."

Angela put her head down and sobbed. "Me too." She looked up and hugged Tiffany. "I hate these two words, but I kind of want to own them. Welcome home."

Tiffany sobbed in her ear. "Welcome home."

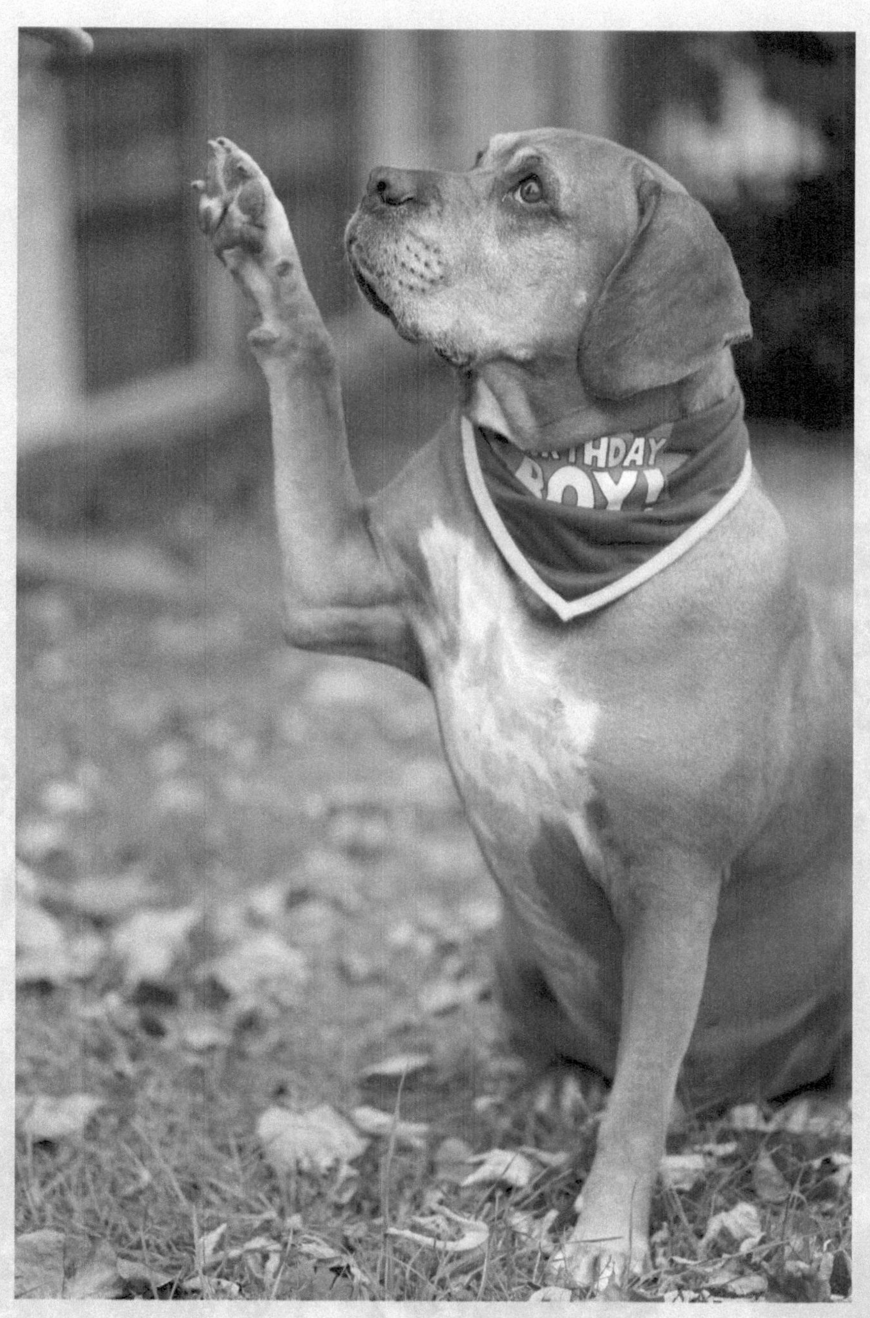

Long live Vinx!

Notes on *On a Clear Day You Can See Block Island*

One day I was watching a horror movie that solidified a belief I've had about horror for a long time. In the movie, a mother and daughter moved into an apartment. It was clear they were struggling financially, and times were tough. Throughout the movie, they faced a ghost that haunted and tormented them. In the end, after they nearly died numerous times, they defeated the spirit and came home happy to an apartment free from hauntings.

I felt so underwhelmed by this ending that I literally said out loud, "That's it?" It proved my point that horror stories can't have happy endings. I don't mean that I am opposed to a solid ending where the characters win. What I mean is that the story isn't over when the movie rolls the credits, or the book ends. There would have to be more. Trauma, grief, PTSD, for example. A little girl faced a malevolent spirit that wanted to kill her! She would never sleep soundly again. How could she?

I was also frustrated the movie never addressed the poverty. Yay, they defeated a ghost, but they still didn't know how they'll eat tomorrow.

When I conceptualized On a Clear Day, I wanted to open with

a scene where a family defeated a monster, and the rest of the book would be the aftermath. In other words, I wanted to show what happened during the credits. Because horror never ends. Eventually, I decided to let the monster live through the first scene.

The opening scene came from a short story I'd written eight years prior. It was a story of a family whose children died mysteriously one by one until all that remained was a grieving father. The story lacked a cohesive point, and essentially ended up being a disjointed series of deaths. But the telephone game through the walls always stayed with me as a cool scene. Imagine the horror of expecting to hear your child's voice on the other side of a wall, only to hear an otherworldly monster and some crunching.

I rewrote the scene and used it as a launching pad for On a Clear Day You Can See Block Island, a story about the never-ending cycle of horror.

I didn't want to leave the book with a cliffhanger, and unlike in Bunker Dogs, I wanted the reader to have all of the information. But I didn't want the characters to have it. I gave each of them a little of something but deprived them with the big picture. This, to me, was especially cruel for Tiffany, who expressed from the beginning that she needed to know things. She couldn't handle a stranger keeping information from her on the beaches of Charlestown, and in the end, she doesn't know why the world turned to fog and tried to eat her alive.

The ending was my attempt to put a final stamp on the story, something that lets the reader know it won't continue on, but that also expresses the continuity of the horror. That we the audience can leave the story, but the characters must keep going, must keep suffering, and will never see their way out of it.

The title "On a Clear Day, You Can See Block Island" came eight years before the story. Freshly sober, I met my girlfriend, a grad student working at the marine biology department of our local university. At night, I would drive with her to the labs, and we'd spend hours setting up trials for her lobsters. When it was over, we'd stop and appreciate the view of Block Island.

One night she said to me, "I always thought On a Clear Day You Can See Block Island would be a cool title for a short story." I agreed and the next day I set to write one. The finished product was a story about our lives at the time, me working through my sobriety and finding purpose helping someone else with their doctoral work. Watching lobsters mate and fight proved a weird way to find inner peace, yet there I was.

The world is a scary place when you're freshly sober, and anything you can latch onto to claw your way out is worthy of exploring.

Ultimately, at the time, I couldn't find a purpose to the story, a meaning, a destination, and that's because the story was about myself. It would take a long time before I found some purpose.

I tried three or four other times to write a short story with that title, and all of them hit road blocks.

Then came this book, which was so perfect for the title, I had no option but to use it.

There's a scene in the book that I bet makes readers laugh. When Jackson leaves with the police officer but takes two thermoses of alcohol with him. It feels cartoonish and silly, but, as a recovering alcoholic, I can assure you it is more real than you'd think. I always scoff at books where an alcoholic tosses the drink to the side, cleans up, and saves the day. Detoxing is no joke my friends. I spent weeks on a friend's living room floor, aching, seeing weird shapes out the corner of my eyes, feeling like I would have a heart attack any minute. I'm nearly certain I had a seizure or two. I couldn't have fought monsters no matter how hard I tried.

During my alcoholism, I didn't go anywhere without a drink handy unless our destination was close and/or served alcohol.

A few months before I published the book, I made a post on Facebook where I said, "People are going to hate the dialogue in this next one," and boy was I right. There's plenty of reviews that complain about the eye-rolly dialogue between the kids in the book, but that was all by design.

I wanted to show that these kids are not kids at all, and never had the chance to be them. They say this directly. Charlie criticizes his sister and tells her, "No one talks like that."

In one scene Angela makes commentary about how kids her age are supposed to be worried about normal things like vaping. I wanted her to sound like an out of touch adult, and how they would view kids today. I was half-tempted to have her make a Tide Pods joke, and only didn't because I worried they'd sue me. The point was that these kids are so out of touch with their own age group, they not only speak differently than them, but can't even view them normally.

I've met a lot of people with extreme trauma, myself included, and one thing I've noticed in some of them is that they are incredible at self-assessing and recognizing their own flaws with a rich philosophical nature most can't keep up with. And then they can also revert to the thinking of children, screaming about how unfair life is treating them.

That's how the kids in this book act. One minute, they're talking way above their age range, and the next, they're talking way below it. What they're never doing is acting their own age.

Speaking of, what is their age? Throughout the book, we learn the ages of the children in chapters where Jackson is driving the narrative. If you pay close attention, those ages don't always match up. I may have been a little too abstract with this one, but I wanted to show how little Jackson really knew his children. And because I wanted to express that their ages really didn't matter, because none of them knew or understood what it was like to be that age, I had him get it wrong often. We can guestimate, but the exact details of their ages is lost to the mind of an alcoholic father who loved his children, but also wasn't a very good dad.

All this to say, their ages were not important to me, because it wasn't important to them or their family. In a lot of ways, the children were treated a bit like the monsters, sent to live in their own foggy world, left to deal with themselves. Neglected. And when living creatures are neglected, they come together and find their own families, their own ways to survive. And they fight for their freedom.

The infamous chapter in this book is the one where Charlie dies. I hadn't planned for that to happen. In fact, I had an entire ending planned out where Charlie was the only one left alive. As I wrote the chapter where Charlie walks away from the art studio in a daze, I kind of stepped back from the story and let Charlie lead. I wanted him to find out some information, much like the police officer at the graveyard, but then I just kept typing and the next thing I knew, he was dead. I immediately took a break, went outside for a cigarette, and considered whether his death would be good or bad for the story. I found a lot of pros and cons in either direction, and decided to let things play out how they wanted to.

Sometimes you don't write the story. The story writes itself and makes you deal with the consequences.

Since I was telling a story about the never-ending cycles of horror, I thought the only way to make Charlie's death truly impactful was to ensure the siblings (and Tiffany) never discovered if he really died or not. Just like the themes in Bunker Dogs, the not knowing is a terrifying reality to life.

Have you ever watched the news after a major tragedy, and one of the victims is screaming and crying? So often, they're yelling, "WHY?" And the fact that so many of those victims will never find a satisfying answer to that terrifies me. The happiest a horror ending can get is when it gives the answers to the trauma. A true tragedy leaves any survivors in the dark.

That's one of my favorite parts of the title. The surviving character were never granted a clear day, and they'll never see the truth of Block Island.

- Gage

Join my Patreon to get new writing, behind the scenes fun, and bonus content: www.patreon.com/gagegreenwood

And don't forget to sign up for my newsletter to get the latest news and updates! www.substack.com/@gagegreenwood

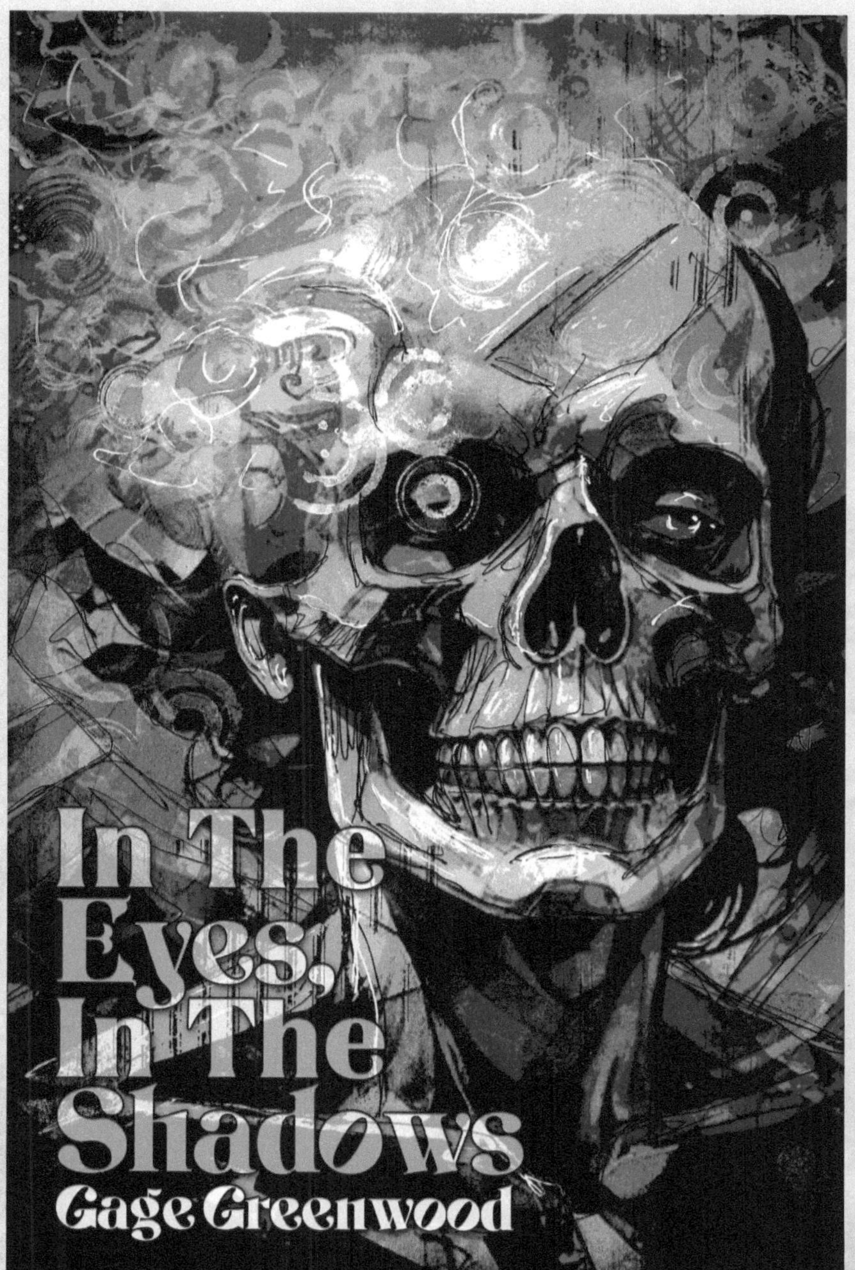

In The Eyes,
In The Shadows
Gage Greenwood

FOREWORD BY FELIX BLACKWELL

Somewhere in the vague Northeast, adrift in the ocean of teenagers at a Taylor Swift concert, is a man. At first glance he seems menacingly out of place: he presents as a middle-aged, curiously wet-lipped goon leering through corpse eyes at the spectacle. What the Tiktok vampires around him don't realize is that beneath this stranger's surface is a depth impenetrable by gaze alone, and the secrets it hides are even more horrifying than his visage. He is Gage Greenwood - *and he is angry.*

There may be some writers in that ocean of kids, and they might be inspired by the horrific encounter with Gage enough to pen a scary story. They could describe a creature who lurks in the darkness and pursues human prey with relentless glee. They could weave a tale of a Peeping Tom slipping from window to window on a moonless night. They could write a slasher about a lunatic driven over the edge when TayTay failed to perform his favorite song.

Though there are many horror novels about strangers and shadows and monsters, few of them accomplish what Gage's do. Other writers so often focus on the antagonist, the danger, the terror. They carefully construct their eerie scenes and heap on the gore and adjectives in hopes of tormenting the reader. Meanwhile, their viewpoint characters, often the targets of that horror, are little more than floating cameras who exist only to witness the scary stuff. In my early days as a writer, this was a major flaw of mine.

What always struck me about Gage's stories was the space devoted to emotion. His tales contain the ghosts and ghouls horror fans love, but the true terror lies in the naked humanity of his protagonists. Gage isn't content to reveal a monster and note how it made a character's heart race. Instead, he delves the uttermost depth of pain, shining a light into the unexplored parts of the heart and soul. His novels brim with page upon page of broken people feeling dreadful things and trying to understand those feelings. They do not always succeed - but Gage does, ever delivering to readers an uncanny realism uncommon in modern horror stories. Truly, his works are examinations of our psychosomatic reactions to death, in all their darkness and complexity. His protagonists are high-strung, tightly woven, and thickly layered. When his monsters cut them, they don't just bleed. They unfurl.

Textured and contradictory characters do not make for simple writing. Their nuance speaks to the mind from which they spring. It makes sense that Gage Greenwood should write people in this way; he dredges them up out of his own hideous depth, where all his personal monsters lurk. The untimely death of his mother sent him on a dark quest for the substances that nearly destroyed him, and in his effort to clean himself up, he developed an uncontrollable compulsion for cleaning and scrubbing. In his own words, however, his life was still "a cluttered mess" until he began writing.

Though she had passed on, Gage's mother left behind a trove of poetry she'd penned over the course of her life. It was through these works Gage came to realize that drugs and booze were methods of avoiding pain, whereas writing could be a means of confronting it. He studied his own demons and sculpted people they could haunt. He etched his agony onto the bones of these protagonists and cast his many shadows over them, forcing them to react in rich and complex ways unconceived by less-experienced writers. These characters fill with unpredictable energy in the face of death: they reach for cigarettes they haven't carried in decades. They drum their fingers and tap their toes while ruminating over a fresh corpse. They hallucinate during emergencies, splintering off from reality in a subconscious act of self-defense. Gage's characters are so neurotic and utterly swallowed into themselves they barely exist in the world, like baffled aliens visiting our dimension for fleeting moments.

As a person with a lifelong anxiety disorder, Gage's humans feel like kin to me. They are a reminder of my own tendency to fill my world with the terror of the unknown and the inevitable. While other authors spend their page space fashioning the scariest monsters and serial killers they can, Gage writes stories about how everyday people are filled with even scarier things, gnawing and scraping to burst out at the first sight of trauma. *Depth* is the true horror of his books, and the expertise with which he can reach into it and drag out those things we hide from ourselves. The brooding soul and its many anxieties define his work, and if pop princesses and their Starbucks-chugging admirers provide inspiration, I say *let the goon leer*.

Sincerely,

Felix Blackwell

CHAPTER 1
THE HOUSE GUEST

Jackson woke to a streak of sun slicing across his face and, for a moment, he forgot cancer was killing a man a few feet behind his head. Only three-and-a-half-inch studs and gypsum board separated him from his father's slow, heaving breaths, his pale, waxy skin, and his deteriorating body.

The walls grew thinner at the thought.

He just wanted to get through the day, go to work, come home, maybe finish reading *The Once and Future King,* and watch the Sox on replay. Sometimes he wished for his father to pass, to let the suffering end, but the idea of that also terrified him. So, every day where nothing happened felt like a blessing. He was living in a constant state of inertia, waiting for the car to slam into a wall.

He propped himself up and leaned his head against the wall, listening for signs of life on the other side of the barrier. At first, all he heard was the incessant chirping of the morning sparrows and grackles screeching from the front lawn. He pressed his ear tight against the wall, and still nothing came.

In his chest, a truck hit a corner too quickly, tottered up on two wheels, and hung there.

If his father had died while he slept, he didn't know if he could handle it. Sure, he'd wished for it from time to time. It might have been easier for his father's pain to slip away while they both slept comfortably in their beds, but he had also stupidly hoped for one of those cathartic movie moments where he would be able to say his final piece and let his father pass away with a full understanding of how much his son loved him.

Finally, his ears adjusted and he picked up the faint, raspy, wet breaths on the other side of the wall. His father had lived through the night; maybe today wouldn't be so bad. Instead of dying, Jackson Senior continued suffering. Fuck.

Jackson took a short shower, brushed his teeth, and dressed for work, letting the mundane daily routines take his mind away from the pain going on in the other room. After he finished, he still had time before his neighbor, Marybeth, would arrive to play caretaker for the day, which meant he could spend a few minutes with his dad before he left.

When he opened the door to Senior's room, a damp, thick air poured out into the hallway. Everything was all wrong in there, as if the cancer had metastasized beyond his father's body and rotted the oxygen around him.

Jackson pulled his father's rolling office chair up to the bed. As he sat, Senior's throaty wheezes lost their rhythm and melded into a low, droning gurgle.

He put his palm against his father's arm. It was burning hot, moist with sweat, and covered with raised bruises patterned like the shadows of the moon. Senior's muscles had deteriorated, leaving his skin to stretch around the bone like plastic wrap.

Jackson remembered being twelve years old, shooting baskets in the driveway on a crooked hoop his father had installed. Jackson Senior came outside wearing his khaki shorts too high and his tee shirt a size too tight.

"Throw your Pops the ball," he said with outstretched arms.

Jackson tossed him the ball, and as soon as it reached his dad's hands, the man launched it toward the hoop. The faded Spalding arced nicely and went in after a messy bounce on the rim. Jackson grabbed the ball on its way down and returned it to his father, who shot it again. This time the ball made a clean wisp sound as it passed through the hoop.

"Ha! Your Pops is like Michael Jordan."

"More like Sam Bowie. You wanna play a one-on-one?" Jackson tossed him the ball for a third time.

His father planted his feet, bent his knees, and extended. His hand released the ball with perfect follow-through. The ball flew at the hoop and rattled as it fell in. "I would just kick your ass again."

"Yeah, yeah. You're just scared you'll lose."

He walked over to Jackson and put his arm on his shoulder, pulling his son's scrawny body toward him and squeezing. "If there's one thing you can count on from your Pops, I don't lose. Never have, never will."

When Jackson was a kid, it seemed true. He never noticed his father losing. As he grew older, he recognized it happening more and more often. Senior lost with his wife, with his dreams, with his drinking, until finally, he started losing the big one. Now, Jackson looked upon his father playing the final minutes of his last game.

He brushed a rogue clump of hair off his father's sweaty forehead. "I'm gonna go make my lunch for work and then I'll come right back and hang with you, Pops." He walked out of the room, pretending his father could hear and understand what he had said.

As soon as he entered the hallway, he shut the door, placed his back against it, slid down to the floor, and began to cry. It had built up in him since he put his hand on his father's skinny frame, but he had bottled it up, not wanting to cry in front of his dad. He didn't believe his father's subconscious could hear him anyway, but just in case, he wanted to give the impression he had stayed strong.

As he let the last of the tears seep out, a noise came from behind his head. A brushing. *Swoosh Swoosh Swoosh.* He wiped his cheeks, turned his ear toward the door, and listened for it again. Footsteps.

The sounds of feet sliding against the rug penetrated through the door.

"Jesus. Dad?"

He jolted up and shot the door open. Senior remained unmoved. He knew his father couldn't walk even if he wanted to, but the hospice workers did mention that sometimes a cancer patient will start crawling or trying to walk, usually in such a drug-induced daze that they don't know where they are, let alone why they shouldn't attempt to go anywhere. If his father did get up and try it, he could fall instantly and his fragile body, with cancer-eaten bones, could shatter.

Jackson's heart settled at the sight of his sleeping father. He let out a long sigh and turned to leave the room, but he did a double take at the closet, where a coat hanger, hooked around the closet doorknob, swayed.

A second passed where panic returned to his chest, but then he laughed at himself. He'd opened the bedroom door in a frenzy, which must have caused a breeze in the direction of the closet. "Settle down, Jackie," he said to himself with a whisper. The stress of watching over his father had made him paranoid.

He went into the kitchen to make his lunch but left his father's bedroom door open. As he made a peanut butter and jelly sandwich, he let his gaze drift toward the room.

He was being ridiculous. His father could barely lift his fingers, let alone take himself out of bed, make it to the other side of the room, and do something by the closet door that would cause the hanger to sway, or get back into bed and fall into his half-comatose state, for that matter. "The breeze from the door moved it," he kept telling himself, but it didn't feel right. And what about those foot-steps? Had he imagined them?

After he packed the sandwich in a bag with chips and a can of soda, he moved to the hallway. He wanted to explore the room further, but his legs betrayed him, and he stopped short of entering. Yes, everything was all wrong in there.

He pushed forward, sliding his hands against the stucco walls, feeling the plaster bumps under his palms. When he crossed the threshold, everything was how it should be, except nothing was. The shadows defied the direction of the sun, the air pressed down, and there was a soft, whining sound. The whine was thin and ringing, like the noise electronics made so softly and so often you'd never notice it, but every once in a while, you'd hear it, and then you couldn't stop hearing it. It came from everywhere, pulsing towards him from all directions and bringing with it an overwhelming miasma of dread.

He clutched at his chest. An all too familiar feeling washed over him.

When Jackson was a teenager, he suffered from severe panic attacks. Well, they weren't panic attacks at all, but for lack of a better word, that's what everyone called them. They had all the symptoms of a common panic attack: chills, nausea, heart palpitations, hyper-ventilation, numbness, dizziness, trembling. You name it, and it showed up at some point. But those symptoms were usually the *start* of something much larger, a floodgate. It all lead to things like audi-tory and visual hallucinations, blackouts, or fainting. When he'd come to, he'd often be clenching his fists and screaming at nothing.

Now, thousands of pins pricked his fingers and moved up his lower arms. Years ago, he'd taught himself how to quell the attacks before they could settle in, but it had been so long. This one crashed into him while his guard was rusty.

The floor below him rocked. He tried to hold on, but his legs buckled. He knew what came next but had no time to prevent it. The world began to tunnel, and the floor sailed toward his face.

BOOM!

He opened his eyes. His cheek tickled from how it pressed against the rough fur of the rug. A blurry black circle orbited his vision. It was as if he were looking through an out-of-focus telescope. He saw the skeletal metal frame of his father's bed—Hospice's gift: a sterile hospital bed, to be returned upon death. On the other side of the bed, a set of feet appeared.

Maybe they were feet. They were blocks of mist, with squiggly black streams rising from their base.

They moved like feet. They arched and a set of—knees? Yes, those were knees—planted in front of them. Whatever this shape was, it crouched by his father's side, as if it were examining him closely.

Jesus, someone had broken in. Someone stood by his father. He yelled at the intruder, "Get away from him," but only a garbled groan worked its way out of his lungs.

The shape whispered in a feminine tone, pretty and calming, like a mother lullabying her child to sleep. Mmmmmmm Hmmmmmm Hmmmmmm.

Like Jackson's mother, who loved him once, who sang to him and gave him peace with a gentle touch and a soft voice.

Jackson attempted to move, but he had not returned to a conscious state yet. His mind and body were not connected. He could only watch this invader do whatever he, she, or it planned to do.

His vision opened, the telescope turning into binoculars. The figure stood and walked around the bed. As it walked away, Jackson breathed a heavy sigh, but then tensed further at the notion he no longer had a visual on the trespasser. It had moved behind him, but he couldn't be sure it continued to move. For all he knew, it hovered over him.

He yelled at his mind, telling it to hurry up and get straight, to get those limbs of his moving again. He rotated his hands. You can do this, he reassured himself. He started to feel a throbbing in his temple where it had met the floor. It hurt, but it meant he was gaining control of his body again. He opened his mouth, and shifted his jaw back and forth, exercising the muscles.

Toes. Feet. Fingers. Forearm. Shoulders. Stomach. And it all flooded back. His body was his again.

He rose to his feet and put his arms out, ready to defend himself. Everything turned normal. Not normal; the air was still dense, and the shadows still seemed off-kilter. He quickly rotated toward the closet, where he thought he'd heard the intruder go.

The area was bare, which meant Jackson's hallucinations had

returned, which meant an added stress to his already complicated and crumbling life. He had no time for visits to the doctor, for examinations and tests and more, "We just don't see anything wrong" diagnoses.

He continued to stare at the closet. Someone was watching him from that corner of the room. There were eyes burning a hole into him. He couldn't see them, but he could *feel* them.

A shiver wormed up his body.

The doorway out of the room stood less than ten feet in front of him but moved away from him every second. His consciousness threatened to slip away from him again, too. He didn't want to leave his father alone with whatever lingered in there, but he wouldn't do much good passed out on the floor.

Like a coward, he fled the room. Behind him, the rumbling of his father's breath quieted into melodic purrs.

He'd been awake for less than an hour and already his day had gone straight to hell. He splashed cold water on his face, trying to shock the grogginess away, the insanity, the returning illness in his brain. When he pushed his hair out of his eyes, he winced at his own face. Months of worry collected in black pools under his eyes, his skin had turned the pukey white color of the stucco walls, and red lightning bolts crashed toward his pupils.

After a moment, he sat down on the living room couch with a granola bar and a bottle of water, letting the food and drink calm his nerves. He worried another attack would strike and he'd end up collapsing at the wheel on the way to work. Luckily, Marybeth seemed to be running late, giving him some time to recover. He leaned back and let a gulp of cold water moisten his throat.

These hallucinations were different from the ones he'd had as a teenager. The effects of them lingered. The physical embodiment of the hallucination ended, but the presence, somehow, remained. *Whatever I saw was still there. It was still watching.* He shook the idea away.

His last bout of attacks had destroyed him. It tore his life to shreds and stopped only when it took away one of his greatest joys. Basketball. He hoped this one was an isolated incident, a one-time visit while Jackson learned to cope with his father's looming death.

Thinking about the attacks made his heart speed up. He was bringing them on by worrying about them, a self-fulfilling prophecy. He needed to relax, to take deep breaths—inhale, hold it, exhale— like he was in a Lamaze class, or practicing deep meditation. He felt stupid doing it, but it worked. With the breathing, his mind traveled to the tranquility of the quiet morning.

In the silence, he picked up the sounds his mind usually toned out: the refrigerator's ice maker rumbling, the clock ticking, the trees rustling with the morning's ocean breeze.

And then he heard another noise in the room with him. Right behind him, in fact.

Breathing.

CHAPTER 2
SHINY NEW THINGS

The breath blew against his ear and moved the hair around it like leaves swaying in the fall breeze. He couldn't turn, too terrified at what he might see, but also iced over at not having the visual.

There was a second reason he couldn't turn. Doing so would allow him to jump into the hallucinations, take them seriously. He *knew* this fault in his brain, remembered the horrific shadows and creeping phantoms that haunted long stretches of his life. And with that, he knew to disobey them, to turn away and refuse to accept them.

A normal person would call out of work—he'd had a panic attack and collapsed, for Christ's sake, and on top of that, he was hallucinating—but it was possible that going to work would be just what he needed. Maybe his mind would fix itself once it had some time outside of the house, away from death, away from cancer, away from the emaciated creature his father had become.

Marybeth walked by the living room window, heading toward the front door. The sight of her snapped him out of it, and he raced to meet her, told her he was running late, and headed right for his car, forgetting his lunch.

Half an hour later, he pulled into the Valiant Video parking lot and lit a cigarette while he waited for Ray. The canvas awning on the front façade flapped with the morning breeze. On the other side of the lot, Simon swept the sidewalk in front of PizzAmore. With his tall, lanky body hunched over, he looked like an old lamppost.

PizzAmore and Valiant Video shared a rectangular building made of brick piers whose reds had faded to pinks and oranges years ago. The brick wall jutted inward where the video store ended, leaving an open space, allowing the PizzAmore patio area to spill onto the parking lot.

In the summers, the patio would fill up with out-of-towners, especially after the beaches in Charlestown and Narragansett closed on Friday and Saturday nights. The seasonal folks could be messy, obnoxious jerks, but they liked to eat, and they had money to spend. Of the two businesses in the building, one of them did well. On weekend nights, it looked strange seeing the busy parking lot and the bustling PizzAmore patio next to the flapping "Going Out of Business Sale" sign in front of Valiant Video's dim lights.

Ray's walnut-colored Cadillac clunked into the lot. Jackson stubbed his cigarette and got out of the car. The nicotine eased him, transported him away from his growing worries.

He and Ray exchanged good mornings as they pulled the security grilles up from the large picture window and the four-paneled folding doors.

Ray looked like Comic Book Guy from *The Simpsons*. His plain shirts always fit too tightly, and never fully covered his belly. His hairline had drifted a few inches away from the top of his forehead, but his brown hair remained full and thick in the back. Sometimes he had a goatee, although not at the moment. Where he differed from Comic Book Guy was in his attitude. He had none of the snobby cynicism, always keeping positive and happy, even now when his business was closing in little over a month. Still, every so often Jackson would convince him to say, "Worst. Movie. Ever." and the two of them would have a big laugh about it.

While Ray punched in the alarm code, Jackson checked the drop box.

Two months ago, it would have been full, but today, only two DVDs rested on the drop box floor. No one wanted to rent now that the going out-of-business sale made it cheaper to buy the movies.

Ray counted the cash registers and prepped the deposit bag, while Jackson put the movies back on the shelves, straightening as he went. The sale gutted huge chunks of the inventory, exposing the store's wire rack bones. The empty spaces reminded him of his father, and he had to push his mind away from it, focusing solely on organizing and alphabetizing.

The last remnants of the panic attack—twitchy fingers, fuzzy brain—stuck around, but he knew the morning routine so well that he pressed through it in a habitual fashion.

As he worked his way through the comedy section, he heard a mumbled whisper and looked around, thinking Ray had opened the doors early. The store was empty, and Ray continued to count cash in front.

He inhaled sharply and went back to shifting movies, refusing to accept the disease in his mind had followed him here. Valiant, for all its failings, had been a fortress for Jackson. His safety zone.

The whirring of the air conditioner grew louder, or maybe he was just noticing it more.

He felt the familiar drum of his heart against his chest, the rising tempo.

Slowly, like an intermittent plunk in a sink basin from a dripping faucet, a song came into his mind. One drop at a time. It was too low and too short to mean anything, but as he worked his way around the shelves, it grew louder and stayed a little longer.

It was the same song the misty shape sang at his father's bedside. And now that he heard it with more clarity, he realized he knew the tune. But he couldn't place it. "Mmmmmmm Hmmmmmm Hmmmmmm."

If not a sign of his brain breaking, it would have been soothing.

The humming grew louder, more defined. Where did he know the song from? Just as he thought he might place it, it went away. For all the hallucinations he'd experienced, a gentle song in his ear wasn't the worst problem to have. He tried not to freak out. This he could handle.

It came back again and left just as quickly. *If this is the worst you can do, I think I'll be alright,* he said to himself.

"She is waiting."

He stood up stiffly. As a teenager, when his mental disorder was at its worst, he always hated the auditory hallucinations more than the visual ones. His visual delusions were always bent reality. He never saw something that could be real, and therefore, he knew what was real and what wasn't. Black humanoid shapes did not really happen. When the walls melted around him, he knew to dismiss it. But the auditory hallucinations often came in the voices of people he knew, saying things they might actually say, and sometimes it happened when they were in the room with him, making it difficult to determine what someone actually said to him and what was a delusion.

And now, with only Ray in the building with him, and a woman whispering, "She is waiting," in his ear, he knew they were coming back.

"Mmmmmmm Hmmmmmm Hmmmmmm."

"She went there for you."

He jolted backward, stumbling into the shelves behind him, almost knocking their contents to the floor. Ray turned his attention to Jackson, twisting his mouth and wrinkling his brow.

"Mmmmmmm Hmmmmmm Hmmmmmm."

"The blood, it turns pink."

"Mmmmmmm Hmmmmmm Hmmmmmm."

"Find her."

"Mmmmmmm Hmmmmmm Hmmmmmm."

He waved to Ray, pretending he was okay. Ray spoke to him; his mouth moved, but Jackson couldn't hear him over the singing and whispering. A chorus of voices filled his head like helium in a balloon, and his mind threatened to burst.

"Mmmmmmm Hmmmmmm Hmmmmmm."

"She shines."

"Mmmmmm Hmmmmmm Hmmmmmm."

"Find her. Find her. Find her."

The whispers turned to talking, angling towards shouts, as if they were moving from suggestion to demand. The hums lost their comforting melody, ratcheting up to the rupturing feedback of an electric guitar.

"Mmmmmmm Hmmmmmm Hmmmmmm."

"You're going under."

"Mmmmmmm Hmmmmmm Hmmmmmm."

"They're no good for you."

"Mmmmmmm Hmmmmmm Hmmmmm."

"Did you clean the fucking sink?"

Ray had turned the corner of the front counter and bounded toward him. Jackson attempted to play cool, but he knew he was failing. He was nearly hyperventilating.

"Mmmmmmm Hmmmmmm Hmmmmm."

"She has a story. She tells her story."

"Mmmmmmm Hmmmmmm Hmmmmmm."

"You need help."

That last one was Amanda. If he knew the voice of one in a chorus of a thousand, it would be hers. Her gentle, earthy voice—a shy Etta James—would have been a comfort, if not for the words she spoke. *You need help.*

Yes, Amanda, I think you are right.

"Mmmmmmm Hmmmmmm Hmmmmmm."

"Finish what she started."

The chorus of voices yelled now. They ripped into his ears with their high-pitched wails, and now they came from inside his skull. He couldn't hide it anymore, falling to his knees and plunging his palms over his ears. He thought he might pass out again.

"Mmmmmmm Hmmmmmm Hmmmmmm."

"FIRE IN THE AISLES."

"Mmmmmmm Hmmmmmm Hmmmmmm."

"GIMME THE EYES. GIMME THE EYES."

"Mmmmmmm Hmmmmmm Hmmmmmm."

"We're going under, buddy."

We're going under, buddy. The one male voice in the chorus. His father.

And the assault ended with that final blow. Tears poured out of Jackson's eyes. Ray crouched over him, rubbing his shoulder. Jackson could hear him now.

"You alright, pal?"

He tried to push words through the weeping.

"Okay. Okay. Let's sit you down and get you some water."

He stood up and followed Ray, and they sat down on metal folding chairs in the back hall. Ray brought him a bottle of water from the front cooler.

"What the hell happened, buddy?"

A brain tumor, he said to himself. What else could it be?

"I don't know. Just stress, I guess." He reached into his pocket and pulled out his cellphone. "Gimme one second."

He called his house. Marybeth answered on the third ring. "Hello?"

"Is my father okay?"

"Sleeping like a baby."

"You're sure? You see him in front of you?"

"I'm sitting by his bed, reading a book."

"Okay, thanks."

"Is everything okay?"

"Yeah, I just had a bad feeling. Thanks, bye."

He hung up but kept the phone in his hand. Amanda's voice had said he needed help, and if he did, she would be the one to give it. With his father dying, the store closing, and now his faculties leaning toward insanity, Amanda stood as the one constant and stable thing he had left.

"Oh, I understand, but like, what literally was just happening to you?"

He ignored Ray while he typed, his fingers stuttering against the keyboard.

> Can I see you tonight?

Ray sat patiently, waiting for him to respond.

"I just. I got weak. I felt like I was going to collapse."

They sat in silence for a few seconds. His phone buzzed.

> Of course. I'm off at five. Is everything okay?

> Having a bad day.

He knew he shouldn't go to Amanda's. If anything happened to his father while he was away, he would never forgive himself.

But Marybeth wouldn't mind staying for an extra hour or so. Hell, she loved taking care of Senior. She would stay all night if Jackson asked, not that he ever would. No, one hour, that was all he needed. Maybe an hour and a half, depending on how things went.

"You're going crazy taking care of your dad."

Jackson took a gulp of water. "Definitely."

Ray sighed. "It was six months after my mother died when I opened this place. Six months. In the time between, I'm not sure I ever got an ounce of sleep. Just couldn't do it knowing my mother's room was ten feet away from mine. I was a walkin', talkin' zombie straight out of a Romero flick. When I opened the store, I started sleeping in the back room. You know where those metal shelves are where I put the damaged DVDs and the old paperwork?"

Jackson nodded, letting his old friend lick his own wounds.

"Yeah, I put a crappy mattress right in front of that and slept in the backroom. Slept like a log, too. For two years, I did that. The only time I used my house was to store stuff or take a shower. I hated being there, Jackie. It felt so empty and sad. I let those feelings break me down for a while. I thought I might lose my marbles. Eventually, I went and found myself someone to talk to. A professional someone. I don't tell people about that, and I know you won't tell anyone, either. Thing is, I didn't have any friends like you back then. If I did, I would have had a helping hand from the get-go and I might not have needed the professional."

Jackson smiled at this. He and Ray had years of friendship under their belt, but he didn't know just how highly Ray thought of him.

"Point I'm trying to make is you do have a friend like that, and his name is Raymond Shanley. He happens to be the sexy man standing in front of you. Don't let yourself go crazy. You need someone to talk to, I'm here for ya, buddy." He patted Jackson on the shoulder.

Don't let yourself go crazy. It might be too late for that.

"Thanks, Ray."

"Come here, asshole." Ray wrapped his hefty arms around Jackson and squeezed.

Jackson felt his phone buzz and pulled away from Ray. He opened it and smiled.

I'll come right home. I have stuff to tell you about, too.

Jackson clocked out at 5:00 and headed right for Amanda's house. Usually, he took Route 138 to 2 and rode that all the way to Charlestown, but time mattered today, so he took the shortcut down Almeda Road.

Normally, when he took Almeda, he drove slowly and carefully, playing defense, but again, time mattered today, so he took his 2004 Honda Civic well above his comfort speed.

Almeda was a wide two-lane road walled in by thick black oak forests on both sides. About ten feet of dirt and slash separated its edge from the first line of trees. The narrow space didn't leave a lot of room for error.

The road ran straight and wide for miles, tempting drivers to press down a little harder on the gas. Thirty-five miles per hour speed limit be damned. Abruptly, the road gave way to a series of hairpins, the sign announcing the change to 10 mph poorly positioned just one turn too late. Almeda's virgins, unprepared for this serpentine shift, often veered off-road, spinning onto the strip, if lucky, or colliding with a firm oak, if not. Flower bunches and stuffed animals adorned some of the trees, serving as constant reminders of Almeda's danger.

He approached the dangerous section of Almeda and slowed down. On the left side of the road, a sole house broke the tree line. Residents of Tanner's Switch called it the Milner House, and everyone had a story about it.

Jackson peered at it as he passed. Its sad saltbox frame, strangled by ivy, wept lichen down its sides. The porch slanted to the left toward the unkempt yard, shrugging apologetically. *Sorry for the mess.*

Dead leaves, twigs, and sprouts of knotweed blended along the clearing between the house and the woods. A barrier of thick rhododendron bushes mingled with patches of overgrown boneset, ironweed, and sedge, masking the back portions of the yard.

From behind the rhododendrons, a sharp light shot into Jackson's eyes and the world disappeared into an ocean of white.

His eyelids disobeyed him and slammed shut, protecting his eyes. The tires screeched against the pavement before he even realized he had hit the brakes.

As his vision returned, a car whizzed by on the other side of the road. *Shoooooom.*

He jumped in his seat, bracing for an impact that never came.

"Wooooooooooo." He spewed the sound out of his throat and laughed nervously.

His heart knocked on his chest like a jealous lover at the door, and his mouth turned to cotton. While these symptoms were usually sure signs of an approaching panic attack, it did not come. In its place, a smooth humming slid into his ears.

It was the humming he had heard when he'd collapsed and again when the voices came, but this time it carried no dissonance.

It spoke without lyrics and stole from him the worry and the fear. He relaxed and fell into the rhythm. It was as if this singular voice with its familiar song was there to help him, to help him fight his anxiety. A saintly hallucination battling the demonic ones.

Despite how much he hated her, the humming reminded him of his mother again, and the way she had sang to him when he was sick as a child. She'd scratch his back, and drip cold water on his fevered flesh. *Mmmmmmm Hmmmmmm Hmmmmmm*, starting with a muh, a quick exhale, before the long, drawn out em, whirring and droning like an air conditioner on a humid day.

Afterwards, she would lean down and kiss the nape of his neck and her hair would tickle his ears as it cascaded by them. He would keep his face pressed deep into the folds of his pillow, but he would wholly envision her—the brown of her roots streaming into blonde waves, the intensity with which her pupils darted left to right, and her thin lips never rising into a full teeth-exposing smile, but always expressing contentment regardless.

A car horn blasted him back to reality. He jolted and almost flipped the driver off, but realized his Honda was stationary in the middle of Almeda. The tires began moving, and he waved to the person behind him, feeling more embarrassed than sorry.

Having the memory of his mother made him hate her more. How pathetic of her to come back into his head after all this time. How selfish.

The humming had put him in a daze, and he struggled to stay

alert. It had hypnotized him, and now his body acted as if it had just awoken from a hibernation. He yawned and stretched. The blood pumped and his wits blossomed back on earth.

He turned onto Route 1, and the world opened up. The sun escaped Almeda's hovering oak limbs. There was safety in the sky, in the wide lanes of Route 1, in the signs for Ninigret Park Beach and Dunkin' Donuts and Cumberland Farms. Something had whispered a song in his ear, but at least he could drink some coffee.

He picked up a frozen caramel coffee for himself and a frozen mocha for Amanda. As he drove toward the breachway, he sipped on the coffee and enjoyed Charlestown's beachy atmosphere.

He thought about the flash of light that had blinded him on Almeda, probably also a figment of his melting mind. But as a teenager, his hallucinations were a mish-mash of nonsense. A collage of insanity. Now, they all felt connected. Like they were all trying to tell him a story.

He would have to get himself checked out and deal with it at some point, but first, he had other people to take care of. His father. Ray. And Amanda.

He pulled into her driveway, tiny pieces of gravel crinkling under the tires. Her small one-story ranch hung back from the rest of the houses, shyly hiding behind two large white oaks that bookended the driveway. The unpainted wooden porch looked like an afterthought against the red paneling of the house. Strokes of neglected ryegrass crawled up the base.

The cool breachway wind danced along the sticky skin on his arms and neck as soon as he exited the car. The air tasted like brine and smelled like sunscreen. It brought with it memories of devil's purses and sand in the crevices of his feet. Then he thought about his father on a bed that smelled like a hospital, in a room that smelled like urine, and Jackson felt guilty for having enjoyed the senses around him.

Amanda emerged from the front door and bounded down the porch steps toward him, her sandy hair flopping around her ears. She bobbed her hips around the car door and wrapped herself around him, almost making him spill her coffee. Her embrace contained a lovingness that was foreign on a day so dark. Her touch acted as an anti-anxiety pill.

He handed her the coffee, and she thanked him, giving an appreciative smile.

"What's wrong, honey?" She pushed his hair behind his ear, caressing her fingers along his lobe.

He smiled. "I'm just stressed. I wanted to see you. You make it better. Tell me about your day?" Now that she stood in front of him, he lost his courage to tell her what had happened throughout the day. He wasn't ready to divulge his loss of mind.

"Do you want to have a cigarette with me on the porch swing? I have good and bad news: lots to discuss." Her voice sounded playful. Her smile rose and the freckles on her cheeks sunk into her dimples. She bit her bottom lip, an action that normally meant they were about to have sex. On this day, it meant something else, but something still alluring, sexy, and fun.

They sat on the porch swing, its old, wooden frame complaining against their weight. Jackson put two cigarettes in his mouth, lit them, and handed one to Amanda. She moved her right leg across his left, letting her foot dangle between his legs.

It wasn't that he forgot about the voices, about the figure in his father's room, about his father, about anything outside of this moment, it was just that they all became a collective force that he refused to let penetrate this porch. Amanda had that power. She captured him wholly.

"Okay, I'm just going to start with the bad news, to get it out of the way." She inhaled on her cigarette, either to give herself a second to decide how to say it, or just to keep him waiting. "In two weeks, I have to go to Syracuse for a while."

He had a moment of panic. Was she leaving him? Did she want the relationship to end? A lull had occurred recently, sure, but that had to do with his father dying and her job requiring more time for the summer basketball camps. They still loved each other, and Amanda was never shy in showing it. She always messaged him, checking up and making sure he wasn't slipping back into his old problems while dealing with his father.

He *was* slipping back into his old problems, but that remained a secret for the time.

He should feel safe about their bond, but with everything else falling apart around him, he had to wonder if this relationship would follow the trend, too.

"You're not breaking up with me, are you?" He said it with a sarcastic tone, playing it off as a joke.

She jerked her head in his direction, eyes bulging. "What? No! Why?"

"So, the bad news is just that you have to leave for a while? How long?"

She took another drag and talked as she exhaled. "Three weeks, give or take."

His relief came out of him in a laugh. "This is for a job?"

She nodded and her smile grew. A small giggle wafted into the air.

"Are you talking Syracuse, as in the school? As in Syracuse College? Division 1 big-time college?"

Her nodding increased in speed.

"New York? Syracuse?"

"Yes. Friggin' Syracuse!" The excitement burst out of her. She wrapped her hands around Jackson's arms and shook them.

"Wait. Tell me everything. Backtrack and give me the whole story." His emotions fluctuated. Her energy was infectious, and his excitement grew with hers, but he still clung to the nervousness and concern, waiting for the moment her story took a turn. *When someone tells you they have good and bad news, and the bad news turns out not to be so bad, there's a good chance the good news ain't so good.*

"There's not much to tell. They called me today, right before I texted you. Their summer camps have started up, and they're looking for a new assistant coach. Jenny's working for them. Do you remember Jenny Tremont? I coached her about seven years ago?" She didn't wait for him to respond, which was good because he didn't remember her. "So, she gave them a good word about me. They want me to come down and I guess they'll probably test me out and see how I do training the girls during practices, and I can see how I like the school. If it's a good fit for me and I'm a good fit for them, I'll have a new job as assistant coach for Syracuse College."

"That's amazing." He hugged her. Her arms dangled loosely at his side while he squeezed. Then it hit him. "I don't want to kill the excitement. I really am so happy for you, but I need to know, what does this mean for us?"

"If I get the job? Well, that's where the good news would come in. I would hope you would move to New York with me. I figured you could probably use a fresh start somewhere. With the store closing and your dad. . . " Her voice trailed off as she considered how to continue. "It seems like a good time for you to start over. I mean, if you wanted to."

"I do." He wanted to play it cool, but his tone gave away his excitement.

The idea of moving with her thrilled him, but also terrified him. His mental state was a major question right now, and he worried by the time she needed to move, he would be tied to Rhode Island with a straight jacket in a rubber room. He would have to figure these hallucinations out, and he would have to do it alone. Getting help meant letting the cat out of the bag, and that could ruin the one good thing he had to look forward to.

At least she wasn't leaving him. A fresh start with Amanda: he finally received some positive news.

He had misunderstood the methodology of life. While all of the good things around him died, his relationship welcomed new beginnings: life's little balancing act.

Before he left, she kissed him like she did the night Tanner's Switch had won the state championships, and he was brought there, the hardwood court under his feet, the crowd moshing in excitement, and her, wrapped around him, kissing him with pride on her tongue and hope on her lips.

He had spent more time at Amanda's than he should have, so he risked driving Almeda again on the way home. He called Marybeth, letting her know he would be home soon. She told him not to worry and he thought that was a great idea.

When he passed the Milner house, his attention was brought to the rhododendrons. Behind it, an object reflected the last remnants of the evening sun. He hadn't hallucinated a blinding light. He had actually seen one when the shiny—thing?—acted as a magnifying glass and concentrated the sun's energy directly into his eyes. He laughed. Even the worst days can have their good moments.

LIFE AND DEATH, CLASPING HANDS

Jackson came home and Marybeth left, reluctantly. After her husband had died, she enjoyed the opportunity to take care of someone else. Caring for Senior presented her with the satisfaction of feeling important, of mattering. "You make sure you come right over and get me if you need anything. Wake me up in the middle of the night, for cripes' sakes, I don't mind."

Jackson felt the same heavy air as soon as he came through the door. Death was looming and his father's cancer killed the oxygen around them. While he'd spent the day away from the house, he'd convinced himself that what he had witnessed after he collapsed, what he had heard and felt all around the house, were just delusions brought on by the panic attack and the stress. Now that he was home and he felt the dead air, the absence of hope, he questioned that idea.

The drugs in his father's system put a thick sound barrier between his sleeping state and the real world. Still, Jackson considered it appropriate to walk with slow, quiet steps. His father's chest rose and fell in dramatic fashion. His exhales sloshed phlegm. No matter how many times he saw his father this way, no matter how much he prepared himself for it, the sight of his deteriorated body and the sounds of suffering he created made Jackson want to break down.

He kissed Senior's forehead and stood up, hovering over him, as if staring might morph him into a healthy man again. After a few minutes, tears built in his eyes, and he left the room.

Sometimes, he wondered if the doctors were right. When they had discovered his father's cancer, they had put him in a hospital room for a few weeks. They wanted to keep him there longer, but Jackson, after promising his father he would get him home, fought with the doctors.

They expressed their concerns, telling him that monitoring his father on his own would lead to unnecessary stress and pain. He ignored them, demanding his father would die at home, just as promised. Senior deserved to die in the place he felt most at peace: tucked away in his room.

Once the medication took hold and his father's behavior turned erratic, Jackson realized the weight of his decision. He slept minimally, waking to every creak, worried his father had attempted to move around on his own. He viewed the disintegration of Senior's body, watching it get worse every day.

He measured out liquid medications, organized a multitude of different pills, kept track of which ones his father needed more of and which ones he was unable to keep down. He fed him, bathed him, held him, shifted him, fixed his pillows, placed cool rags on his forehead, and systematically flipped them over every few minutes.

He did this because his father wanted to die at home. No amount of stress or grief deterred him from giving his father his wish to die where he wanted. No matter how much he questioned himself, doubted his decision, he kept his word. Jackson would always have that.

After he released some stress in a sobbing fit, he sat on the couch with an ice water and watched television. NESN aired a rerun of the

Sox/Mariners game from the afternoon. Buckholz made quick of the inning, getting the Sox back at the bat in twelve pitches. *Yes, the worst days can have their good moments.*

His phone vibrated in his pocket.

I love you. I'm glad I got to see you today.

A wide, stupid grin crashed up his cheeks. He thought about how to reply when he heard a loud, painful groan coming from the other room.

"Dad!" He charged down the hall.

"Dad!" Jackson kicked at the bathroom door. "Open the fucking door, Dad."

"Leave your Pops alone, Jackson. Just leave me alone."

"I'm not leaving until you open this door! You understand me? I won't leave. Never. Open the fucking door."

Jackson slammed the bedroom door open. His father lay stiff as a board, clenched, grinding his teeth. His eyes bugged, darting back and forth. His breathing blasted out in semi-automatic rapid fire. Inhale. Exhale. InhaleExhale. InhaExha. InEx. InExInExInEx. Jackson ran to him, scooping his arm around his father's head, and putting his other hand on Senior's arm.

"Pops, you have two seconds or I'm kicking the goddamned thing down."

"Stop it, Jackson. Get out of here."

He took four steps back, giving himself plenty of room to charge. "I'm coming in."

"Listen to me, Dad. I know you're in pain. You don't have to be in pain anymore." He patted his father's sweaty mop.

Jackson charged. Right before he reached the door, he lifted his leg and kicked. The wood around the handle snapped. Shards of wood splintered all over the floor. The rest of the door slammed against the bathtub.

"I know you're hanging on for me. I know that. Everything's gonna be all right. I'm gonna be alright." He put his hand in Senior's palm. His father gripped it with a fist. It was the first coherent movement his father made in weeks. It was a small gesture with a mighty impact, a final indication of love.

He looked at the pink swirls dancing in the water. "What the fuck is wrong with you?" He grabbed his phone and dialed 911.

"You don't have to hang on anymore."

"Just let me go."

"You can let go."

"No."

"You can leave."

"I'll never leave you, Pops."

"Let go, Pops. Let go." His father's eyes flickered and his pupils danced back and forth, back and forth, back and forth. "I love you so much, Dad. Please, stop being in pain." For months, he avoided crying in the presence of his father; now, the tears flooded on Jackson Senior's arm, shirt, and blanket.

The pink water spilled out of the tub, splashing against the white and blue tiled floor. He bent down to his father and hugged him. "You don't get to leave."

Something locked around Jackson's fingers and touched his palms. It held his hand, clutching it firmly. It didn't scare him, but instead calmed the waves in his stomach. It gave him the sense that the words he spoke were true. Everything would be all right.

His father turned his head, showing more animation than he had in weeks. Adding to the surprise, he spoke. He put together his first sentence since the medication stole his coherence. "You promised me I could die at home. Why did you lie to me?"

God's final cruel joke: his father spoke. After all of the hard work and struggle, his father's last thought on this earth was that he lay in a hospital and his son failed to fulfill the promise.

Senior's sharp breathing stopped. Silence eroded the atmosphere. The dense air cooled. The *whooshing* of footsteps against the rug shuttled across the room, toward the closet. Jackson held his father's lifeless body in his arms. Death had come. Death had gone.

Jackson held his father as he shook.

"I'm so sorry, Jackie."

"It's you and me, Pops. It will always be you and me. You can't leave me."

EMTs came through the door, rushing to the bathroom where Jackson held his father's pale body in a sea of blood.

WHERE DO WE GO FROM HERE?

A stratus veil crept over the world. He had things to do, but no concept of how to do them, in which order to do them, or even what exactly they were. Hospice gave him steps to take. They wrote them down, they recited them, they gave him papers, but when your father is dying, you try not to think about the appropriate actions to take after he is gone, so you let them speak and write and hand out pamphlets, and then you forget about it. If you focus on the things you have to do after he passes, then you are allowing the idea that he *will* pass into the world, and in doing so, you might just make it happen.

But, of course, it happened anyway. His father's body lay in front of him. The suffering was over. On its way out, it peroxided the air, cleansing the gunk and humid death from its atoms. A calm drifted in, carried by a light breeze from the window. Whatever presence he had felt in the house, it had abandoned its post and left the place feeling empty. The shadows righted themselves.

He could breathe again but had to remind himself to do so. Nothing worked correctly. Nothing made sense. Life had lied to him. Its promises of fairness and justice were all a lie. His father's last words caused a rift between Jackson and life. If God existed, he and Jackson were at enmity.

His thoughts oscillated between the last few weeks and the last few years. Between life and death. Between his father's cancer and all of the suffering that came before it. It went everywhere but here and now, because as bad as things were before, they were better than here and now.

Here and now was fictitious. It was an imaginary place where God let a good man suffer and dangled death in front of him like a treat. Oh, and just when the man reached for the treat, God gave him one more compensatory payment for good behavior in the form of a delusion that the man was betrayed in the end by the only person he relied on.

His father's agape mouth and wide eyes aimed at Jackson. His face was devoid of life, yet it spoke with its contortions, letting linger his accusatory last thoughts. His eyes. His betrayed eyes smacked Jackson's soul like a gavel. *Guilty. Guilty. Guilty.* And while Jackson pled innocence on these charges, he knew he was guilty. Guilty of not doing more. *I'm sorry, Your Honor, I am innocent of what I am being accused of, but shall I list my various other failures?*

He deserved the guilt, and he punished himself by keeping in front of Senior's face. He let his father act as judge, jury, and executioner. He accepted the stare, letting it chip away at his soul, letting it throttle him, wanting nothing more than to suffer for his sins. Unlike his father, he would have deserved it.

He stood up and walked to the bedroom door, turned around, and sat back down. His fingers tapped against his palm. His feet tapped against the rug. Every part of him wanted to act, react, or do *something*. His limbs moved, jittered, and shook. Energy built up in his veins, starting at his dancing appendages, spreading to his arms and legs, gathering in his chest. He sucked in a gulp, trying to bottle up the mass building inside of him. He screamed.

"Fuck you." He spoke to no one and to everyone. He spoke to God, to his mother, to streaming movies for destroying his job, to Syracuse for offering him an alternative to the place where his father raised him, to his father, to himself.

"I hate you. Why did you do this to us?"

He stood up again, this time making it all the way out of the room. He went into the bathroom and turned the shower handle to one degree below scalding. The water bit at his flesh and the steam clogged his throat. The water swirled down the drain. Either the burnt color of the fading incandescent merged with the white-washed tub, or his memories took control, but the water seemed to drain pink.

It didn't shake him. He watched it swirl and dance around the drain without fear or concern. He wiped at his nose to make sure it wasn't bleeding into the water, otherwise, he didn't care if he was hallucinating or being haunted. It didn't matter anymore. Nothing did. Bring on the ghosts. Bring on the brain tumor. Bring on anything to change the current paradigm. His concepts of life crumbled, and while it pushed him into unknown territory, he jumped with the push, diving full force into it. *Let there be chaos. If the world wanted to stop making sense, it needed to go all the way with it. Change gravity. Change love. Either we have laws, or we have nothing. Make your choice universe.*

After his shower, Jackson smoked a cigarette. Senior had had a rule, "We both smoke, but we do it outside." That rule died with his father. The smoke rose and clustered around the ceiling, and he watched it twist in on itself. The cigarette tasted different, sharper, more intense. It pricked his throat and the back of his mouth.

On one of Jackson Senior's many attempts to quit drinking, he had told his son that the hardest part was learning how to be normal without alcohol. The drinking had become such a big part of who he was that normalcy meant drunk, and sobriety made things distorted and askew. Ray probably felt the same way seeing his business close down after it had captured his focus for decades. Amanda would surely gain the same unstable thoughts if she took the job in Syracuse and had to leave her team in Rhode Island behind. It was how Jackson felt now.

It was over. Everything that conquered his mind, stole his focus for months, gone. He had checked on his father every few minutes, had thought about him constantly while at work, soaking in the drama of it, drowning in it. He wasn't sure what to do with himself now that it had ended.

He called Marybeth. She would know what to do now, or at the very least would provide him with some comfort in knowing his sadness had company.

"Hello?" Her voice sounded groggy and half-awake.

"He died."

Silence traveled through the line. He considered hanging up.

"Oh dear. Would you like me to come over, hon?" Her tone perked up. She sounded almost excited.

"If you wouldn't mind. I'm sorry to have woken you."

"I'll be right there."

He decided to look at Senior one last time before they took him away. He didn't have any special desire to do so, but thought, in a few days, when his father's absence sunk in, he might regret not taking the available opportunity. Now that he had removed himself from the view of his father's accusatory face, he shivered at the thought of seeing it again.

Jackson Senior's plastic expression lay before him, glossed eyes, paled lips, absent of spirit. Jackson fell into his father's eyes, and in the emptiness, he saw something magnificent. He saw it and forgot it at the same time, watching it as it erased from his memory. He could not describe it as anything other than a swirling ball of life and death. He fell into it, and then it disappeared.

He instinctively pushed a clump of hair off his father's face, without recognizing the action's inanity. When his hand touched Senior's forehead, the universe apologized to him: a feeling of fingers sliding up his spine and wrapping around his trapezius. His muscles eased, and he leaned back. Tears streamed down his face, releasing the pain, cleansing him. Everything turned perfect. The colors changed, turning sharper, more vibrant. His senses intensified. His skin tingled, as if he stood in the center of a plasma globe. He could taste the air, with the juicy intensity of a cool, crisp apple, could feel the tartness of death and decay, and it was beautiful and sapid. The shadows shifted again, and the air tightened, but this time, it didn't carry dread, or fear, or worry. It offered peace. He could stay here forever.

The doorbell rang and the peace removed itself from Jackson, ripping away from him. A sadness sank into his belly. A sense of loss struck, for his father, but also for the sensation he had just felt. He wanted it back. As he walked to the door, he bit back an urge to scream in frustration.

Marybeth, true to her word, strode in just minutes after their phone conversation. She walked in like a ballerina, graceful and exuberant, but dizzying and obtrusive. She paced around the living room, listing all of the things that needed to be done, stopping for brief periods to lament. *We'll need to arrange to have the body picked up. —Oh, your poor, poor father.—Is he being cremated or buried?*

She dialed a number, made a call, hung up, and continued pacing and jabbering. Watching her made Jackson feel like a canoe in a maelstrom. It went on this way for another half hour.

As the storm began to settle, he saw lights flash in the driveway and he pried himself from his seat. He opened the front door for the —body removal guys? He didn't know who they were, or even with whom they associated. He knew Marybeth had called hospice, and they called someone else, and that someone else was here. Actually, the someone else turned out to be two someones else. Both broad-shouldered men exited the anonymous white van and nodded to Jackson, showing sympathy with their scrunched brows.

Marybeth hovered over Jackson's shoulder. The action made him regret asking her to come by. He yearned to be alone, wanting to tell the men to take her instead and leave him in peace with his father. Why had he been in such a rush to have his father's body removed?

Let him stay. He always stood by his father's side, even at his most ugly. Drunk. Depressed. Suicidal. It didn't matter. Jackson had remained unwavering. He desperately wanted to continue that trend now, even with his father's cancer-devoured corpse.

In the past twenty-four hours, he had witnessed and heard all sorts of oddities, but these normal men, in their normal van, following a normal procedure, made Jackson feel like he was in an episode of *The X-Files*. Why didn't they say a word? Why didn't their van have some distinguishing name on it? Why did they look like ridiculous professional wrestlers? He laughed. It slipped out of him, but once it escaped his mouth, it brought all of its friends. He bent over in a fit of hysterics.

He couldn't stop. What was so funny? He didn't know. He didn't care. It was a wonderful feeling to laugh, but feeling wonderful made him feel guilty, and feeling guilty made him feel angry, and the whole cycle of emotions made him laugh even stronger.

Marybeth looked at him with concerned eyes and the men shrugged in confusion. His laughter fell into a hysterical bout of snorts and giggles. He released them unapologetically, exaggerating them in an attempt to spit in the scrunched faces that surrounded him.

A bizarre desire brewed, and he wanted to grab one of the men and say, "Who are you men, and where are you taking my father?" and laugh at them when they didn't know how to react. He wanted to confuse them, scare them, anger them. Why not add Marybeth to the mix, too? Fuck them all. He hated this world, and he hated all of them for being a part of it. And the hatred was hilarious.

He guided them to the cusp of the bedroom, showing them in, but unwilling to let himself go with them. He didn't want to watch these two strangers lift his father out of bed. What they were doing, albeit necessary, felt like some sort of violation. He imagined his dad reacting to it, saying, "Don't you let those wannabe Fabios go into my room, invade my privacy, and put their stinking hands on my body." Picturing his father uttering these words was funny, but

Jackson had no desire to laugh at it. The abderian fits were behind him.

Marybeth remained a step behind Jackson, clinging to the wall like plastic wrap. She kept her arms straight down and her hands planted along the wall, trying to show her ability to stay out of the way, but Jackson thought she very much was in the way. He wanted to throw her out the window and roll her into the woods, wrap her up in a box made from twigs, and mail her to Zimbabwe. When she arrived, he would mail her a letter that said: Now you are out of the way.

The men walked out, carrying his father on a stretcher. They had the legs of the stretcher up, navigating the body like they were moving a couch. Jackson wondered why they didn't wheel the body, but had no desire to ask; instead, he just watched his father bounce like rubbish, undignified and violated.

"Wait, wait, can I just say goodbye one last time?"

"Yeah, we can bring him back to the bed and leave you alone for a few minutes," one of the men said. They probably dealt with this sort of thing a lot.

"No, you don't have to do that. I just want to see his face one more time." He lifted the sheet, exposing his father's head, and realized the absurdity of the situation unfolding in front of him. He should have let the men put the body down. They made awkward expressions at each other, unsure how to handle it, but continued to hold the body in place while Jackson said his last goodbye.

Marybeth turned around, unwilling to look at the deceased face of his father. She cupped her hands around her mouth as she turned, as if she needed to make it clear how upsetting she found the whole thing.

Senior's face held on to its horrific expression, absent of life, but there was also something beautiful about it. Jackson didn't understand yet what he found so captivating about it, but he had trouble looking away. He knew he should hurry, but he needed to touch his father's face again, hoping to recreate the sensation that washed over him last time. He brushed the outside of his fingers along his father's jawline. "Goodbye, Pops." Nothing happened. He felt no peace. His gaze darted toward both of the men, who continued to stare awkwardly, the faces of people who accidentally walked in on someone else in the bathroom. He couldn't keep them waiting any longer. He brushed his hand on his father's forehead. Nothing. One of the men sighed.

"Okay. It's okay." He placed the sheet back over Jackson Senior's vacant face.

The men carried the body to the van; afterward, they came back in and collapsed the bed, taking that with them too. Jackson watched as his father left for the last time. He wondered, would he ever feel those ghostly hands and the tranquility they delivered again, or had they just gone out the door with his father?

CHAPTER 5

COMMUNION

Jackson woke up on the couch, his neck throbbing from how it slanted in his sleep. He lit a cigarette from where he lay, not wanting to move just yet. The smoke slithered upward, becoming prominent in the ray of sun that invaded the living room. It merged with the floating dust motes, highlighting a microcosmic meteor shower.

He wanted nothing to happen, to stay on the couch and let the day disappear, the motes his only company. The craziest day of his life came and went, and now he wanted to let the sunlight paint the room while he remained as unmoving as he could be.

The television continued to play from last night. Jackson had wanted to sleep to the flickering of the screen. An infomercial for fishing rods played, reiterating the same boring facts ad nauseam. Boring worked. Boring, he liked.

He finished his cigarette and considered what he was supposed to do now. His father insisted there should be no funeral or memorial service. He wanted to go quietly, unnoticed. He chose cremation over burial, blaming a fear of enclosed spaces, but Jackson thought it was more than that. He believed his father wanted to wipe out all remnants of himself from the world, destroying any proof he had ever been there.

In a way, his father's wishes made him thankful. It left him with little to figure out. He thought about whom he should inform but couldn't think of anyone. Other than Jackson, his father affected no one. He left no mark on the world. The sun came in today, just as it had yesterday.

It tickled him to consider telling his mother. He would love to call her and tell her the man she had abandoned had passed away, and she was too busy being a selfish asshole to know it had happened. Of course, to do so, he would need to know how to contact her. As far as he knew, she was dead, too.

He messaged Amanda and Ray. They would care, for Jackson's sake anyway. He sent them both the same text:

> He died last night.

Amanda responded first.

> I'm so sorry. I'll be over right after work.
> Okay? I love you.

Ray's came in seconds later.

> Sorry friend. Beers on me tonight?

He responded to both with the same message.

> Okay

With those four letters sent twice, he tossed the phone to the other side of the couch. He heard it buzz again, but there was nothing else to say and nothing else to hear.

He pried himself off the couch and made a bowl of Cheerios. As he slurped a spoonful, the emptiness of the house swept over him.

His father would not be coming in to talk about the Sox, or *Law & Order*, or work. Those conversations would never happen again. The finality of it, the absoluteness, pressed down on him. A spasm flumed from his stomach to his chest, and he bawled. It flooded out of him, tears, loud wails, swearing at the ceiling. He pushed the bowl to the side; his hunger had abandoned him.

"I can't do this without you. I can't do it." He heaved, his lungs trying to take a full gulp of air. "I'm so sorry, Pops. You didn't deserve to die that way. You didn't deserve to live the way you did, either. You deserved a better life. I wish I could have made it better. I wish you could have been happy."

He kicked the table, and the contents of the bowl splashed onto the table cover. He left it that way and walked into Jackson Senior's room. He stood by the empty spot where the hospital bed had stiffly cradled his father a few hours earlier. Four divots outlined the ghost of the bed where the legs had once smooshed into the rug. Inside the dotted corners of the square, the cranberry color of the rug looked lighter. Jackson couldn't tell if it was just an illusion, a trick of the eye making sense of the outlined shape, or if the fibers on that portion of the rug had a fresher, brighter color from avoiding weeks of treading.

He sat in the square, curling his knees into his chest and wrapping his hands around his legs. The last of his tears drained from his eyes and dripped toward the top of his lip. He took in a large chuck of air and spoke to his father again, this time slower, and with more clarity. "I'm sorry. I'm sorry I wasn't better to you."

His mind flew through every disappointment, every letdown that he brought to his father. He pictured Senior's face every time Jackson told him he didn't feel like going to the package store with him, every time he turned down eating dinner at the table, every date, or practice, or night out with friends that could have been better spent hanging with his father. Jackson was all he had, the only thing that could have saved him from his loneliness and depression, and he had failed.

He needed to get out of his head and out of this house. He had hours before Amanda would be coming over, so he decided to take a walk. Behind his house, a bike path bent along the line of his backyard, passing through on its journey from the now-defunct Tanner's Switch Train Station to the beach area of Charlestown. The path crossed the Bass Rock Trail, which led to Tanner's Switch Park. Jackson's father had vowed he would walk the trail one day, but like most of Senior's ideas, it never came to fruition.

Never one for nature, Jackson had avoided walking the trail, too. When he wanted exercise, he preferred the hard cement or wood paneling of a basketball court. Today, for his father, he would walk the trail, hoping that in some mystical way, he was lugging Senior with him, fulfilling at least one of the man's goals.

He walked the path with his head down, managing to ignore the open greens and browns surrounding him. Dead leaves and twigs crackled under his feet, and he imagined hearing the sounds echoing behind him, his father's legacy stepping toward a second chance. Occasionally, he shouted something to his pretend shadow. "See, this isn't so bad."

"Come on, Pops. Pick it up."

"Some big stones over here, we could take a seat and rest your feet."

"It's only like five miles, quit being a baby."

"Hey, Dad, we should of done this sooner."

When the trail met Tanner's Switch Park, it shed its walls made of trees and brush and opened into a field of maintained, fresh green grass. A cement path looped around the park lawn, and older women power-walked it, listening to their headphones, ignoring the world around them. A large gazebo protruded from the center of the lawn where, in the summers, middle-aged men got together with their bandmates and gave their version of "rocking out," the power walkers hooting and hollering around them.

Jackson sat on the gazebo admiring his accomplishment, despite how little of an accomplishment it was. The path was short, and the land stayed mostly level. He felt sad for his father, missing such an attainable aspiration. Sometimes in life, it's the smaller goals that become the easiest to dodge. Maybe on another day he would stray from the path's yellow markers and follow one of the other trails that collided with it, but for today, this journey satisfied.

As he walked back to the house, he opened his field of vision and paid mind to the forest. Rows of skinny white pines shot out of the ground like lightning bolts. Hemlocks, beech trees, and oaks mingled with the white pines, their leaves caressing. The gray and patchy skin of the oaks, the lichen-covered stones, patches of deadfalls, it all came to life around him.

The tree branches extended upward and entwined at the tips, creating a triangular ceiling. Up ahead, an outcropping protruded into a pulpit. Branches snapped and dropped deep in the woods, echoing like footsteps in a church nave. The brushing of slash at his feet reverberated through the massive, cave-like space.

He felt small inside of the aisle.

Below him, the treading of those who walked this path for every turn in their lives, from baptism to wedded bliss to mourning, and finally as they were carried out in maple boxes. With it came the dusty, archaic smells of incense and hope, of guilt and shame, of lies and community.

He hit a corner where the path bent and distorted. Edging from the forest and lining with the pathway, a raccoon's corpse lay on a lichen-green stone. He stopped to examine the carcass, grossed out by it but unable to look away.

He crouched to get a closer look and found himself face to face with the creature, its black marble eyes pleading to him for life. "I'm sorry, buddy," he said to the dead thing.

He picked up a stick and used it to move the body, looking for wounds, curious as to what brought about its demise. He didn't find any noticeable damage, but its body peeled off the stone, stiff and rough. It must have died days ago. He pushed it with the stick again, making its face easier to see. Moving it the way he did made him wince with regret. He had disturbed the dead, raped it of peace.

He contemplated getting up and walking away, but his body stayed put. He saw in the raccoon's lifeless mug the same beautiful absence of spirit that he saw in his father's, and he wanted it to stay with him, to watch it until it melted away. He took out his phone and snapped a picture, hoping a photographic image would capture the ambiance of death lingering around it.

"I need you." The words left him. He didn't know why he said them, or to whom he was speaking, but they came out definitive and clear. The world seemed to hear because, in that moment, a slight wind came and went. It drifted off his back like the fingertips he felt one night ago. The white pines waved their arms while whispering psalms from their pews.

CHAPTER 6

SHARDS

Amanda stood at the doorstep, garlanded by the last remnants of the day's sun. Her bright orange coach's polo did its best to unflatter, but Jackson knew what was underneath, and he recognized her curves despite the flat, straight edges of the shirt that tried to conceal them. She stayed in place, staring at him, her eyebrows arching, her lips curling inward as if she were trying to hide them.

He could tell she was unsure what to do, how to treat the situation, so he saved her from having to figure it out by pulling her toward him. She wrapped her arms around his neck, pushing herself on tiptoe to be level with him. He pressed his forearms tightly against the small of her back, wishing if he squeezed hard enough, she might become a part of him.

They stayed this way for a few minutes, wrapped around each other on the front door saddle. He was reluctant to separate because he didn't know where to go from there, unsure if it could get better. Succumbing to her embrace took away the past, erasing the pain and death that hovered behind him. It fogged the future, taking away the fear of what loomed ahead. All that mattered was this, and separating from it would be reintroducing himself to all of the possibilities of horror that the world could produce.

Eventually, she released her grip and leaned back. His neck relaxed as her hands separated. Their eyes met and neither knew what to do next. This time Amanda broke through the awkwardness.

"I'm so sorry." She started crying.

He wanted to cry with her, but he had drained all of the tears a few hours ago, and he held onto a belief that crying for his father was a private matter, not to be shared with anyone else.

He rubbed her shoulder. After a few seconds, he took her hand, leading her into the house. They sat in the living room in silence, while she looked around. The last time she had stood in this house, it must have been ten years earlier, maybe longer. She scanned everything with exploratory eyes, the way a child does when they're introduced to new stimuli.

If eyes could frown, hers were doing it. He wondered what made her so sad. Was it Senior's things or Jackson's lack of things? Embarrassment warmed his cheeks. She had her own house, a nice beach house filled with her personality. Jackson only had Senior's scraps.

The living room was decorated with remnants of a time when Senior cared about himself, when he collected things that documented his life or reminded him of who he was, because at one time, he had liked that person.

She stood up and walked over to two paintings by the living room table. They were both impressionist paintings—Monet rip-offs —one of Pawtuxet Village, where Senior grew up, and the other of St. Paul's church in Cranston, where Senior had gone to elementary school. The neo-gothic stone church looked weird against the colorful, thin brush strokes, but the impressionist style did wonders to encapsulate the movements of the Pawtuxet River's low falls.

When Senior had looked at those paintings, he had seen his youth. When Jackson looked at them, he saw the happiness Senior once had. He didn't know what Amanda saw while she examined them, but the way her lips curved and her cheeks lowered, he knew it upset her.

He came up behind her and put his hands on her forearms. Her focus stayed on the pictures, deeply invested in them, as if she saw herself as one of the children playing in front of the church.

"Do you ever think about your father as a kid, playing with other kids, still hopeful, still thinking life will be an adventure?" She touched the picture, running her fingers along the church's arched wooden doors.

"It's hard to."

She turned abruptly; he almost fell back from it.

"I'm so sorry, Jackie." His name crackled when she said it.

He grabbed her and brought her into him. Her eyelashes flickered against his neck and droplets tickled his skin. "It's okay."

She had come here to comfort him, but life has a way of getting twisted.

"It's not just him. It's you," she said in a whisper.

They separated and he lifted her chin so they were eye to eye. "I don't know what that means."

Her eyes spoke for her as her brow scrunched, and she looked even more sad that he didn't know what it meant, like that, above everything else, was the real tragedy. "I know," she finally said and then she kissed him gently, quietly, slowly, her tongue brushing against his lips, meeting his tongue, reading his mouth.

When they stopped, she brushed her hand against the scraggle that had built along his jawline. "I really do love you."

He smiled and lied, "I know."

Normally, he did know it, but after his father's last words, nothing seemed sure. Everything had turned unsteady.

She gripped his hand tightly and guided him into the bedroom without another word. He followed without question and dropped onto the bed. After that, they reacted. They had something that needed to happen, and it needed to happen now.

Her shirt flew to the floor. He leaned up onto the edge of the bed and kissed her defined abs, while she unhooked her bra.

All of this was new. Their relationship didn't lack sex, but it occurred infrequently as of late. With Jackson's father and her job, they hadn't had much time for lust. Hunger flashed in her eyes. She wanted him. His hands shook because, Jesus, he wanted her too.

Emotions are strange little things. You think you know which ones go together. You know that anger connects to disgust and that happiness shares a space with laughter, but it's hard to understand that sadness can leave you starving, and grief can be goddamned sexual. Sometimes you're just so depressed you want to fuck. Sometimes you just want to cry until you cum.

Her breasts were small and muscular. He rubbed her nipple between his index and middle fingers while kissing along the constellation of freckles on her ribs. Moving upward with his mouth, kissing her clavicle, neck, cheek, mouth, he slid his hands around her waist and grabbed her butt. He lifted her, spun, and collapsed on top of her on the bed.

She giggled as she bounced against the mattress. The cuteness of her laugh proved infectious, and he chuckled with her. She worked on his pants, using her feet to push them down when they dropped below her arm's reach, but she struggled with them at his ankles. He laughed again and helped her get them off his feet. Somehow, she had made her way on top of him, kissing his neck and chest. There was a smile; then, it crawled up her face with devious charm, and she wrapped her hands around his penis and put it inside of her.

Just as he entered and felt her warmth, there was a loud crash outside of the room, an explosion of glass. They both jolted and looked toward the door.

"What the hell was that?" Amanda asked.

"I have no idea."

"Do you want to go check?"

A sarcastic laugh burst out of him. "No, no I don't."

He rolled over, putting himself on top of her, taking the lead, letting the strange noise join the rest of the world somewhere else, anywhere else. They had sex for a long time, hard, fast, and passionate. Their hands clenched each other's skin, their legs tangled. Sweat streamed down his chest onto her breasts. She gasped and moaned, the sounds of her pleasure turning him on, instigating him to slam into her harder.

He went to another place. The sex brought him to a fairer, more worthwhile Earth, a place God hadn't abandoned. There was something beautiful still left in this derelict universe. There was something beautiful still left between them. There was something beautiful and as long as there was *something,* he could face the rest.

Afterward, they lay on the bed, looking up at the ceiling, catching their breaths. She rested her head on the edge of his chest, rubbing her fingertips along his ribs. This reminder of what he still had settled in him, relaxing him, and creating peace in his frenzied body and weathered mind.

"What do you think that noise was?" she asked.

"I dunno. I should check, but moving from this position with you right now would be a sin."

"Yeah, I think we should stay this way for a while. Maybe if we don't move, the world will stop moving too and we can stay this way, infinitely."

"Now that's a plan; although I'm not sure it's scientifically accurate."

"Let's test it out. See what happens." She kissed his chest.

"Seriously, that was amazing."

"Yeah, it was." She turned her head and placed her gaze directly on his, making sure he saw the smile that grew on her face.

"I love you," he said.

"I love you too, but seriously, go check what that crash was."

He sighed and pushed her head off him as he sat up. "I'm sure it was just a glass falling off the counter or something."

He shimmied his boxers and jeans up his legs and opened the bedroom door. He thought the noise had come from the kitchen, but across the hall from his room, he saw the glimmering of glass shards crowding on the bathroom floor. He guessed it came from the bathroom mirror, but when he clicked on the light, he could see it was clouded glass. He looked up at the sliding shower door, which was now a set of empty metal frames.

"What the fuck?"

"How did that happen?" Amanda said.

He tensed at the sound of her voice, unaware that she had come up behind him.

"I have no idea."

He examined the shower and the frames, looking for some sign of what caused the damage. He found nothing, but his best guess was that The Hulk ran through it. He glanced over at Amanda, checking to see if her face looked as baffled as his must have. It did, but his attention immediately went toward the shimmers behind her. The glass had blown fully across the bathroom, and dusty pieces powdered the top of the sink counter.

He walked to them, careful not to press his bare feet on the clusters. He felt tiny tickles where granular specks stuck into his skin, but continued to the sink without pause. Amanda, draped in a bed sheet, followed him with her gaze, and when he reached the counter, she saw what had captured his attention.

"No way."

He touched the countertop with his fingertip, letting some grainy pieces cling to his skin. "It's like something smashed the glass with a sledgehammer." As soon as he said it, he recognized that he used the word "some-*thing*." Amanda didn't seem to notice.

He was scared. If this had been a solitary act of weirdness, he would have thought some bizarre freak incident occurred that had a logical explanation hidden somewhere. It was easy to chalk it all up as delusions, exhausted bewilderment. Stress makes crazy things happen to people. But now that he was looking at the blown-out structure of the glass shower door, he couldn't simply shrug off the oddities as figments of his imagination. If one occurrence could defy reason, then it was possible that all of them were real, and having all of those past events become truth horrified him.

"Let's get out of here. I'll clean this up later."

She backed out of the room. He clicked the light off and closed the door, shutting the insanity in, locking it away from him. He didn't want to deal with it. Amanda was here and their night had gone fantastically. Whatever was happening around him, he would figure it out later. Right now, he wanted to focus on her, on them.

"That was weird."

"I know," he said as he leaned in to kiss her. She stopped him.

"I should go."

Of course she had to leave; she had to get up early for work, but the concept had never crossed his mind. He had let the temporary magic of the night trick him into thinking it would stay that way indefinitely. She would stay the night, and call out of work tomorrow, not ready to separate herself from him. It was completely illogical, now that he let it sink in.

"I'm sorry, Jackson. I just have to get up early. You can call me if you need me, though." She grabbed his arm. "I love you so much. Do you want to come stay at my house?"

Now that he had let the foolishness out, he remembered he had told Ray he would meet up with him for drinks. However, he made that plan before he knew Amanda would offer an invitation to her bed for the night. Nothing could be more important than time with her.

He wasn't considering her feelings, though. She invited him, yes, but it was probably more out of respect and maybe a little worry for his mental state after losing his father. She was showing love, and it was sincere, but he should let her get a good night's rest. She had a lot going on, too.

"Ugh. I wish I knew that invitation was coming. I told Ray I would meet him for drinks tonight."

She put her palm on his chest and like a mystical healer, sucked the stress from his bones. "I'll see you tomorrow, though?"

"Yes," he said, but what he meant was, *my God, yes.*

She put her clothes on, and he walked her out. She kissed him goodbye and they said they loved each other. After he watched her car reverse out of the driveway, the headlights vanishing down the road, he regretted every decision he had just made. It wasn't the desire to sleep at her house. He knew that opportunity would come again soon; maybe they'd even be living together in just a few months. No, what made him regret his decision was realizing that he was now all alone. He stood in the driveway, surrounded by the purple tint of evening, looking at the house where he saw a shadowy figure and where glass violently blew out of the shower door. He had never felt so lonely.

CHAPTER 7

COMING BACK

Jackson walked the few miles to the bar, predicting he would drink enough to make it unsafe to drive. When Ray mentioned meeting for beers, they didn't need to determine the logistics of the drinking session. They only met for drinks at one place, and it was always right after Ray closed up the store.

The Knotwood defined the term "dive bar." Jackson's father used to say, "You know why it's called The Knotwood? Because when you see the girls in there, what do you leave with? NOT wood." He always had a big laugh at that one, despite having been a regular patron. Before the agoraphobia took hold, before he only left the house to buy beer, Senior used to go to The Knotwood five or six times a week, spending hundreds of dollars. If anyone in the godforsaken town of Tanner's Switch liked Senior, it was the crowd at The Knotwood.

Mackey Mills, a retired sheriff and the proud owner of the bar, preferred to keep the place low-key. He never attempted to bring in karaoke DJs, or weekend comedy shows, or local bands, believing that a cold drink amongst friends deserved peace and quiet. Because of the lack of entertainment, the patronage leaned toward the AARP crowd, and that was why Jackson and Ray liked to meet there. They didn't have to deal with the amateurs, the rowdy, those that felt the volume of your voice directly correlated to how many drinks you've had. Instead, they could relax, have a good conversation, and enjoy the warm feeling of a fresh draft.

Jackson showed up around half an hour before Valiant would be closing, which meant he had a good hour before Ray would arrive. While he waited, he played a few games of Keno and took out the frustrations of the last few days on a frosty mug.

"Heard about your Pops," Mackey said as he handed him a Coors on draft. "I'll miss that son of a bitch."

Even though over a decade had passed since the last time Mackey saw Senior, Jackson knew he meant it, and the fact that he called him a son of a bitch made it even more endearing.

By the time Ray showed up, Jackson had already taken down four drafts and had a fifth one fresh and waiting for him on the reclaimed heart pine counter.

"How many mortgages do I have to take out?" Ray said, patting Jackson on the shoulder as he sat next to him.

"I've been paying as I go. If I let you pay for the drinks tonight, you'd have to sell your house along with your inventory."

"Ouch," he said as he put his hand up to get Mackey's attention. Mackey brought him a Guinness, no need to ask what he was drinking.

"You gettin' anything else, Ray?"

"Yeah, chicken wings. We need chicken wings," he said and then turned to Jackson. "You'll have some wings too, right buddy?" He didn't wait for an answer; he wasn't really asking. "Twenty wings, bossman."

Now that he took care of the food business, Ray turned his attention to Jackson. "How ya' holding up, friend?"

"I dunno. The last few days have been a clusterfuck. I'm all over the place."

"I think that's to be expected." He thought about it for a second, and added, "When my mom died, I thought about her quirks and told people about them. It got folks laughing, which got me laughing, and sometimes getting all that out, it helps you deal with it."

Jackson only talked about the surface part of his father. He didn't like to discuss the inner workings, or the personality Jackson Senior presented to him. In life, Jackson was the only person who truly knew his father, and he wanted to keep it that way in death as well. For more than fifteen years, his father kept himself a secret, and the secret lingered in Jackson's ear. He promised himself he would keep it there, a reward for his years of service and dedication to the man, never to be uttered or shared with anyone else.

"Mackey, is it a smoking night?" Jackson asked.

Rhode Island passed a law banning cigarette smoking in public places, but Mackey was an ex-sheriff and a pack-a-dayer, so he often allowed smoking inside, knowing his pals wouldn't fine him. He nodded to Jackson, letting him know this was one of those nights. Jackson lit one, letting the first drag sit in his lungs. He didn't want to talk about his father, but Ray was a good person to talk to about his problems. They were piling up lately, so he just had to decide which one to start with.

"What the hell am I gonna do when you close up, Ray?"

Ray used his fingers to rotate the glass. "Well, you know I'll give you a great recommendation."

Jackson recognized the question's stupidity. Ray had made it clear that he didn't even know what he would do when the store closed. Why would he have the answer for Jackson?

"This is the only job I've had since high school. It's all I know."

"You're preaching to the choir, friend."

Mackey brought over a bowl of wings and a stack of napkins.

"Enjoy." Mackey's verbosity was on full display.

Ray grabbed a wing and chomped. He used his finger to pull the bone out of his mouth, sucking the meat off on its way out. "What do you wanna do, ideally?" The meat danced in his mouth as he asked the question.

Jackson put his cigarette out in an empty peanut bowl and

immediately lit another one. "I have no idea. I don't really think about it. I guess I just wanna work, doesn't matter where." He didn't want to mention that he might need to find a job out of state. Until he knew that for sure, he didn't want to announce any moving plans.

Ray licked his fingers and grabbed another wing, waving it as he talked. "Do you know who my hero is?"

"Roger Ebert?"

Ray's eyelids pulled away from each other and he stopped short of shoving another wing in his mouth. "It's scary how well you know me."

"Well, Valiant has been a second home to both of us, so I guess that means we've been roomies."

"Whoa, then I guess you owe me a lot of back rent." Ray cleaned off another set of bones. "Anyway, do you know why I love Ebert so much?"

Jackson shrugged.

"Because he wrote film reviews that were often more powerful than the movies they examined."

Jackson inhaled on his cigarette and waved for another beer. Was he on six now? Or seven? He couldn't remember.

"I mean, if you ask someone with a lot of knowledge on Hollywood to talk to you about the history of movies, they'll bring up Hitchcock, Wilder, Gene Kelly, Monroe, the list goes on and on, but I guarantee you Ebert makes the list almost every single time. Think about that. With the exception of his involvement in the Dolls movies and the Sex Pistols thing, he wasn't around the camera. He didn't direct, act, or produce. He wrote about what other people did, and he did it so awesomely that he became as synonymous with film as the industry's greats. Seriously, consider this for a minute. The man became an integral part of Hollywood just by talking about it."

Jackson sucked the head off his beer and a wave of liquid charged below his belly and into his groin. He tapped his feet, trying to bounce the urine back up.

Ray continued. "He basically did what we do every single day with the customers, but he did it with truly beautiful writing. You could feel his passion in his words, his insight, his intelligence, his emotions."

"Before you have an orgasm, what are you getting at?"

Ray let out a giant roar. The older men on the other side of the bar took notice before turning their attention back toward their own conversations. Before Ray could start again, Jackson decided to interject; he couldn't hold it anymore. "Wait; finish the story in a minute. I have to piss."

He jogged into the bathroom and let the urine blast out while he used his elbow to hold himself steady against the urinal. The misty yellow walls closed in, and the smell of the urinal cake made him want to gag. The alcohol rocked and sloshed in his stomach, but he wanted more.

He appreciated Ray's speech, but as soon as it started, Jackson knew he wasn't in the mood for it. He didn't want to be rude to his friend, who was only trying to be helpful, but he wanted to tell him to shut up.

There was another reason he didn't stop Ray from talking. If he did, Ray would have an excuse to leave. Talking kept him busy, and Jackson didn't want to go home. So, he had to put up with Ray's speech; it put a blockade between Jackson and whatever waited for him at his house. Eventually, he would have to go back there, he knew, but he needed a lot more liquid courage before he did.

He made his way back to his seat, fondling the edge of the bar as he went, using it to keep him straight. Ray must have realized his talk had lost its momentum because he wrapped it up, short and to the point.

"The point I was making was, you love sports. You lived and breathed basketball. Things happened, you couldn't play anymore; chances are you wouldn't have made it to the NBA anyway, even if the panic attacks didn't mess you up. Not trying to be rude, just realistic. Sure, you would have had a good college career out of it, but things like that, they end. Doesn't mean you had to walk away from it entirely. Write about it. Referee. Announce at games. Coach it, for crying out loud. Isn't that what your girlfriend does with cheer-leading?"

"Basketball."

"Huh?"

"She coaches basketball."

"I thought she was a cheerleader in high school?"

"She was. She was also a basketball player, soccer player, she ran track, the list goes on." He didn't know why he needed to point out her accomplishments, but he received great pride in bragging about her.

"Jesus, when did she sleep?"

"Yeah, her free time was limited. Still is. She still keeps just as busy."

"Well, there you go. Be like her. Coach it. There has to be a ton of kid's leagues that need coaches or JV teams or something. Build up your reputation and go from there. When she started coaching, why didn't you think of following in her footsteps?"

He had never considered it before, but now that the question presented itself, he knew the answer instantly. "The panic attacks told me to stay away from basketball. I listened. When I stopped playing, they stopped visiting." *Until now*, he thought.

"You think that would still be the case? It's been a long time. You got rid of the attacks years ago. You should try it, friend. I think you should give it a shot."

Jackson gulped the last of the beer and waved to Mackey. "Yeah, maybe," he said, not really considering it.

"Anyone can make a comeback," Ray said, still trying to inspire.

You should have told that to my father, Jackson thought.

They sat for a while longer, turning the conversation over to lighter fare: movies, books, customers at the store. Jackson pounded down three or four more beers while they finished the rest of the chicken wings. Ray never asked him if he planned on coming in tomorrow; he didn't need to.

He offered Jackson a ride home, which Jackson refused; walking would swallow up more time. Ray's mouth opened, as if he were going to put up a fight about it, but chose against it, and for that, Jackson was relieved. He already spent a good portion of the night biting his tongue, holding back hostility he knew was unwarranted.

Jackson stumbled down his street, pacing himself, still wanting to avoid his home. In front of his neighbor's house, a squirrel carcass rested on a sewer grate by the curb. He went to it, looking for something to move it with as he approached. Unlike the raccoon, the squirrel's cause of death was obvious. Its squished hind and distorted shape stuck to the metal grate; the weight of a car had ground its body into the street.

The thin moon produced limited light, so Jackson snapped a picture with the flash on, trying to capture the critter's face, especially its eyes. He hoped the creature would still be smooshed in this spot tomorrow, so he could examine it in the light of day, but just in case, he would settle for a grainy cellphone picture.

The accumulation of odd events from the past few days terrified him, but somewhere within the madness came the calming hands along his back and the peace that those hands held. The shattered glass, the blurry figure, the humming, all of these things scared him in a way he had never been scared before, but that moment by his father's side brought a sensation of peace that he yearned for. He had no idea what caused it, or how it came to him, but he wanted to understand it, to feel it again.

He knew he'd seen something in his father's eyes. He couldn't remember what it was, but he knew he had touched his father and looked him directly in his dead eyes when he felt the sensation. What was it about those eyes? They were different. They lacked life, but they possessed something else, some kind of spirit or... it was lost to him, now. He couldn't remember. The whole experience was hazy, which was why he was looking at a piece of roadkill. It made little sense, but it was better than anything else he could come up with.

He knew that an animal wouldn't be as adequate as a human would, but he did sense something in the wind when he looked upon the raccoon, so that had to count for something. Not to mention, he didn't have access to human corpses. Animal carcasses would have to suffice. He could study them, and eventually, the answer would come to him. He would find that peace again, someday.

CHAPTER 8
SLINGING MUD

Jackson woke up with a dull headache and a scratchy throat but was otherwise unscathed by the night of drinking. He guzzled a few glasses of water and took some vitamins anyway, because sometimes hangovers had a way of creeping in on you as the day progressed. He didn't want to count his blessings yet.

After he took a shower—draping towels as a makeshift curtain—he smoked a cigarette while reviewing the pictures of the squirrel and the raccoon. He wished he had taken one of his father so he could search for the common denominator. Something existed in all of their faces, something that didn't occur on the faces of the living.

The picture of the squirrel was useless. He'd zoomed in too much, turning the picture into a grainy mess, and the flash masked the squirrel's eyes with a pool of white.

He closed out the photo app and noticed he had four missed text messages, three from Amanda and one from Ray. All four were check-ins, asking if he was alive, Amanda's increasing in intensity each time. He sent them both a message letting them know he was, indeed, alive, adding an "I love you" for Amanda.

He vaguely remembered hearing his father's breathing during the night. He could have been making it up, his mind coalescing various events in an attempt to defog his drunken stupor, or maybe having to hear his father's horrid breathing for weeks forced it to come out in a subconscious manifestation, as if those sounds had burned into his brain, permanently etched there, coming to haunt him while he slept. The other option, of course, was that the breathing really happened, and he could add it to the growing list of weird occurrences.

He went outside to see if the squirrel carcass was in the same place. He was surprised to see that not only did it remain, but he also had a new friend just a few feet away. Another squirrel, this one slightly more intact, lay against the curb, positioned as if he were staring at his fallen comrade. Apparently, the road in front of his neighbor's house was a death trap for squirrels.

He crouched down next to the first one. Its face had changed overnight, having dealt with a few more car tires in the process. Its features pulped into a mangled, crushed mess, making it useless. Jackson turned his attention to the new carcass. If this one died from a car, its body disguised the wounds. It seemed full and unharmed, so much so that Jackson worried it might still be alive, ready to bite him.

He found a nearby twig and used it to poke the critter. When it didn't jump up and claw him or scurry away, he knew he could move in for a closer look. He lay down, placing his head against the cement road, gravel pressing into the skin on his temple and cheek. The white fur around the animal's askew, brown nose had smudges of earth in it. No matter how close he breached the dead's personal space, nothing changed in or around him. With his father, the sensation was powerful; with the raccoon, it happened lightly, just a teaser. Now, with the squirrel, he found nothing. Had he used it all up, whatever it was?

He propped himself up and snapped a picture of its face. He decided he should go online and look up pictures of dead people and animals, comparing those to his photos. When he stood, he noticed his neighbor looking out the window at him. He should have known; the woman always looked out the window, judging every soul that passed, condemning them all. She'd probably call the police about it. To her, everything was a crime. She'd probably rant and rave in local Facebook groups about the weird neighbor examining roadkill.

The internet provided him with pages of dead faces, morbid and hideous. Some of them were clearly fake, others harder to determine. He saved the decent ones in a file and cycled through them repeatedly, zooming in, zooming out, staring blankly, looking for something undetermined.

He uploaded the pictures from his phone and pulled them up, putting them side by side with the ones he took from the internet. The difference was obvious, but he couldn't determine what that difference was. His pictures had something more to them. An unknown anomaly existed on the faces of the dead he encountered, and whatever it was, it was absent from the internet photos.

Maybe there was no difference. Maybe he was going crazy. If you stared at anything too long, you could make it turn into whatever you wanted. Like your own personal Magic Eye, you could make shapes pop out of tile patterns, or smiley faces with the back lights of a car, or in this case, unknown *things* in the eyes of dead animals. He had to call them things because he didn't even really see anything definable. At least with the tile patterns or the Magic Eye, you actually had objects to morph in your mind. In this case, he looked at two sets of eyes that appeared *exactly* the same, and he decided one was different from the other.

He needed a bigger sample size. The more he could add to the folder, the greater his chances of figuring it all out.

He drove around, keeping to high-speed roads near woodsy

areas. He knew the ridiculousness of his actions, scouring the streets looking for roadkill, taking pictures of dead animals, poking them with sticks, leaning close to them, chasing a feeling that he couldn't be sure was anything more than a bodily reaction to the end of his father's suffering. Still, he had no intentions of stopping now that he was traveling down this road. He had to play it out, see where it took him, and if he never found what he was looking for, at least he found something to do while the rest of his world collapsed around him.

He found more dead animals than he had expected, surprised by how many met their demise in the streets. Of course, he had never kept an eye out for them before, either. After four hours of driving, he added seventeen new pictures to the folder, and that's not including the ones too unrecognizable to shoot. Overall, he saw about twenty-five dead animals in the short time he was looking for them.

Each time he came across a new one, he pulled his car over, moved the carcass to the side of the road—if it wasn't there already—and put his face as close to it as possible, waiting to see if anything happened. After each disappointment, he took the picture and moved on, looking for his next sample.

He went home and uploaded the pictures to his computer, shuffling through them, happy with the day's work.

His phone vibrated against the computer desk, sounding like a power drill, and he jolted back, almost falling off his chair. Amanda's text told him she'd be out of work in an hour if he wanted to come over. He did. The pictures could wait.

He drove down Almeda, having a new appreciation for high-speed roads with woodsy surroundings. When he passed the Milner House, he noticed the flashy object again. Curiosity brewed in him to find out what it was, but a dead fox on his side of the road stole his attention. So far, he had only come across smaller animals: raccoons, squirrels, cats. There may not be a difference between bigger and smaller animals, but he guessed that the larger the animal, the clearer he could examine them, the better chance he would have of finding the mystery in their dead mugs.

He pulled over in front of the fox, attempting to get his car as far off the road as he could. The driver's side wheels stayed on the edge of the asphalt and the passenger side of the car angled downward onto the dirt and slash.

He stopped himself from lying down in front of the creature, reminding himself that he just showered and cleaned up so he could look nice for Amanda. Instead, he bent his knees and crouched down, legs spread, like a baseball catcher, putting his phone inches from the fox's face. Just as he attempted to snap the picture, a car sped around the curve, hugging too close to the side, barely missing both Jackson and his car. The wind force and the sound of the wheels screeching against the turn made an already skittish Jackson fall on his side.

He cried out in surprise.

He stood up and looked at the side of his shirt and pants, both covered in gravel, shredded sticks, and dead pine needles. Now that he'd managed to get himself dirty, he figured he could lay down in front of the fox and get a better picture, but he should hurry before another idiot drove by, bringing him closer to the fox than he wanted to be.

His head pressed against the dirt, and a pebble stuck to his lobe. He positioned his phone to get a good angle, and a vibration tickled his ear through the soil below him. It was that humming again, the same one he heard when he drove by this spot two days ago. Mmmmmmmm Hmmmmmmm Hmmmmmm. It rumbled in the dirt and quaked against his skull. The pebble danced under his ear.

He snapped the picture and rose to his feet in one swift motion. The humming kept going, muffled now that he moved away from it. As he scurried to the driver's side door, the noise opened up, getting louder and clearer, as if it exited the ground and fused with the air, floating toward him.

He lost his train of thought, forgetting that he was standing in a very dangerous spot, where a passing motorist could easily annihilate him. He turned his head, following the sound. It drifted away from him, floating across the street, toward the Milner House.

The humming was nice, gentle, and sweet, but something about it terrified him.

He almost followed it, putting a foot forward while he thought about those hands on his back. God, it was a beautiful feeling. But as he stepped, another thought came to mind: the shattered glass all over his bathroom.

The sun hid behind the oaks, and the lavender sky prepared for night. He chickened out. The difference between the gentle touch he had felt next to his father and the violent shattering of glass in the bathroom was a mystery, and whatever hummed those luring sounds could offer either side of the spectrum. Even worse, there was the distinct possibility that he was going completely mad, and none of it, including the humming, really existed. If he had imagined all of this, following his madness toward that house would be the worst thing he could do. He might as well go check himself into a rubber room.

He hopped into his car and drove away, unsure if he regretted it, longing for how the air tasted when he had sat by his father's side.

At Amanda's, they sat and talked about her day, and the night he'd had with Ray. If she noticed the dirt on his side, she neglected to mention it. She looked him in the eyes while he spoke, laughing at all the right times, really paying attention to him.

He pulled out his phone to see if Hulu had added any new shows, but when he opened his phone, the picture of the fox glared back at them.

"What the heck is that?"

He closed the camera roll in a hurry. "Nothing."

"No, what was that?"

He moved the phone to his side, opposite her. "Nothing. It's a fox."

"Was it dead?"

"Yeah."

She released an unsteady laugh, unsure if he was kidding or not. "Why do you have a picture of a dead fox?"

"I just saw it and... wanted to take a picture of it."

She arched her eyebrows. "Let me see it."

He moved the phone back in her direction but hesitated before opening it. "No. You think I'm weird."

"Yeah, I do, but I already did, so just show me." She smiled, letting the discomfort escape her features. She put her hands around his wrist and moved it closer to her.

He sighed. "Fine."

He opened up the camera roll and showed her the picture. He chewed on the inside of his lip while she studied it, every second taking its time to pass by. She moved his phone closer to her, and then her finger darted across the screen, swiping to the picture before it. The fox turned into an opossum.

"What the hell, Jackson?"

He panicked and tried to pull the phone from her, but she snatched it. He reached over, trying to get it back. She moved her arm away so that he had to lean over her to reach for it.

"Give me the phone back."

"No."

"Give it to me. Seriously."

She turned her head away from him and began flicking. Picture after picture of dead animals took over the screen. "Jesus Christ,

Jackson." She dropped the phone on his lap like it was diseased. "What the hell is this?"

"It's a long story."

"Well, tell it. Are you killing animals?"

His head jerked back. She might as well have punched him. He knew the pictures looked crazy. What kind of person goes around taking pictures of dead animals? But he didn't expect her to think he killed them. Now that she made the accusation, it made sense that she would think it. The kind of person who would take pictures of dead animals would probably be the kind of person who killed them. Still, she knew him. Better than anyone else, she knew him. The only living person that knew him, truly thought he killed animals and took trophy pictures of them.

"Of course not. They're roadkill." *Oh, much saner.*

"Why do you have pictures of roadkill?" She inched away from him.

He tried to force a story into his brain, something that made sense, something that seemed normal. Nothing was coming, and the longer he waited to respond, the more impatient she grew, tapping one foot against the hardwood floor, bulging her eyes, sighing. She appeared to be a step away from a seizure. He forfeited.

"I watched Pops die. I saw his face afterward. It was, you know, vacant. Dead." He put his head down, embarrassed. "There was something about it. Mysterious, I guess. It made me curious. I don't know how else to explain it." He did know how to explain it, but he was skating on a thin line, trying to reveal as little crazy as he could.

"Jackson," she always used his full name when she was upset, "this is really weird."

"I know."

"You have to stop doing this. I mean, it's like the kind of thing serial killers do."

"I know. Yeah, I'll stop. It was just a weird thing I did today. Just a one-time thing. My Pops just died. I'm not sure how to react to it, I guess. I just did some weird shit to pass the time." He was placating her, and she knew it.

"Okay." She didn't mean it. He had seen her have many different emotions toward him, love, anger, sadness, but he had never seen this before, the way she was angling her body away from him, the way her eyes drifted around his face, not wanting to look at him directly; she was afraid of him.

He put his hand on hers. She let him, but her body stiffened up. He wanted to fix this. He *needed* to fix this.

When Jackson was thirteen years old, there was a rainy day where he spent the entire morning and afternoon practicing in the driveway, soaking wet, but having a blast. His father had marched through the rain and joined him in the driveway, where Jackson had moved from shooting hoops to throwing chunks of mud against the garage door. Senior ignored the rain, and came right up to his son, putting his hand around Jackson's shoulder. Jackson held a piece of mud in his hands, letting the pressure of his father's fingers on his shoulder sink in. His father leaned down so he could look up to Jackson while he talked.

"You know you're a good kid, right buddy?"

Jackson launched the mud. "Yeah."

"You know you mean the world to your mother and me, right?"

He took a step away from his father. "What's wrong, Pops?"

His father leaned his head toward the ground and sighed. "There's no easy way to say this, so I'm just going to spit it out. Your mother is going to be moving."

"What?"

"She and I have been having problems and she's going to go stay with your aunt in Maryland. At least for a little while."

Jackson picked up a chunk of mud from the lawn and threw it with all his strength.

The wad of mud broke apart in the air, leading to a series of *pings* against the garage door. The fury that blasted through him left him confused. He wanted to punch and kick and scream. He wanted to walk away. He wanted to charge at his mother and yell every obscenity he knew. If he was being honest with himself, he shouldn't be surprised. His mom hadn't been his mom in a long time. She'd come into a room and smile at him, but her eyes were always somewhere else. It was like she'd checked out a long time ago.

"So, she's just gonna quit? I don't even see you guys argue."

"You don't see us talk much, either, though, do you?"

"Well, what about me? She's not just leaving you, she's leaving me too!"

"Son, you can't look at it that way. Try to understand where she's coming from."

"No. I wanna talk to her." He started to charge toward the house, but his father latched his hand around Jackson's arm.

"Stop, Jackie. Calm down first. Cool down for a bit."

Jackson struggled to free himself from his father's grasp. He saw his mother's face in the upstairs bedroom window, watching her husband talk to her son, hiding like a coward.

"You couldn't come tell me yourself?" he yelled. It just blurted out of him, the rage building up.

"Jackson, stop."

"No, I won't stop," he said to his father and then quickly turned back to his mother's face in the glass. "Go. We don't need you, anyway. Just get out of here! We're better off without you."

He stormed away from his father and picked up a clump of mud. He chucked it with all of the force in his body, as if the mud might connect with the garage and right all the wrongs, keeping his mother at home.

Senior came up to him again. He sighed, looking for the right words, but there were no right words, so instead he crouched down and hugged his son. Jackson gripped his arms around his father and leaned his mouth toward his father's head. "We don't need her anyway."

"Thank you, buddy," Senior said. "You're all I need."

He knew his father had lied when he said that. Jackson had seen the effects of that lie in the years to come, but not until this moment did he understand it. He felt Amanda's hand against his, so close to him, yet she might as well have been on the other side of a window, two stories up, looking down at him with wandering eyes and a traveling heart, and all he had to offer was clumps of mud.

CHAPTER 9

FADING OUT

The next morning, he woke up angry and confused. The rest of the night at Amanda's had increased in discomfort. She stayed quiet, letting the pictures spoil their evening. He tried too hard to fix it, pressing her about it. Every fifteen minutes or so, he would ask her if she was okay, instead of letting her breathe and calm down.

His shift started at Valiant in an hour, so he'd have to figure out how to fix his relationship later. For now, he needed a shower. While he washed his body, he remembered hearing his father's wheezes in his sleep again. This was the problem, all of this crazy nonsense happening all around him, dragging him into these insane thoughts.

He thought about the way he felt when Amanda hugged him, the way he felt when they had sex, the way she smiled when she first saw him. Those sensations were real. Those feelings were the ones worth chasing because they had substance. The ones he experienced by his father's side were fake or, at the very least, unattainable. The taste in the air, the way the colors changed, the massaging tingles on his back, they were dreams, desires, but nothing that he could experience again.

He drove to work; on the way, he noticed at least three dead animals. Granted, he didn't have time to stop anyway, but even if he had, he had no desire to do so. At least, that's what he told himself.

He and Ray droned through the opening procedures, and he felt good to be back at work. While he straightened the shelves, he sent a text to Amanda, wishing her a good morning.

A line of customers congregated around the front entrance, and by opening time, it had stretched to the side of the building. Ray opened the doors and the horde swarmed in. Jackson stood by him, watching the mob crowd the aisles, trying to find the best deals, taking advantage of Ray's failures. They pick-pocketed the dying, a bunch of zombies ripping the meat off the bone, and the day the store closed, all Ray would have left would be the skeletal remains of his only love.

Like a man in prayer, Jackson lowered his head, finding the massacre in front of him too depressing to watch. Ray turned and looked out the front window, probably feeling the same way. It must have been tough for him to go through this every day, watching decades of hard work turn into a yard sale. And that's all this was, a yard sale, making as much cash as he could before he threw everything out.

Most of the customers walked out without buying anything, the sales not satisfying enough. They would rather wait until the final few days, when the prices really plummeted, robbing Ray of his inventory, plundering his store, giving as little as possible in return.

The crowd fizzled down to a few wanderers, the types who read the back descriptions of every movie, debating if they wanted to own the new Jack Black comedy or wait until it showed up on Netflix. Ray took advantage of the lull and ran to grab lunch at Pizz-Amore. Jackson gave him some money and wrote down what he wanted.

As Ray left, Mrs. Belmont crept in, her tiny steps and underwhelming figure easily dismissed. She walked past Jackson and rotated her hunched back, looking back and forth at the half-empty shelves. She turned to Jackson, taking many steps to do so. They locked gazes, her eyes beginning to well.

"Hi, Mrs. Belmont." When he spoke to her, his voice turned childish, like he spoke to a baby or a pet.

"No more video store, Jackie?" Her voice broke.

"No more video store." He walked around the counter, moving in closer.

"What am I gonna do for movies?" She said it as if she were talking about losing a child.

"I guess you could try Netflix."

"I don't use computers, Jackie. I don't understand that stuff."

"Well, you don't need one. You just have to make an account, and you can stream movies right on your TV."

"Oh, those things. They don't ever have my movies. I like the old ones; you know that. James Cagney." She said his name, and it was a revelation; she saw the end of times. "How will I ever see one of my Cagneys again?" Tears started trailing down her cheeks, swaying along the wrinkly waves.

"I'm so sorry, Mrs. Belmont."

"I read that they want to put the libraries on the computer now, too, and everyone's got those computer phones. Doesn't anyone want to hold anything anymore?"

Jackson saw now that she wasn't upset about the movie store closing, or even the loss of her Cagneys. Technology changed rapidly, making the past obsolete. Records, cassette tapes, VHS, 8-track, they all disappeared, and DVDs and books were on their way out. Every time one vanished, it took away another thing she understood. Newer stuff came in and replaced it, a little more out of her reach every time. She wasn't worried about things becoming obsolete. *She* was becoming obsolete. The world moved forward and left people like Mrs. Belmont behind. He hugged her, gripping her tightly.

"I understand, Mrs. Belmont." He wished there was more that he could do.

Ray came back a little while later, tossing Jackson's chicken parmesan sub on the counter. He scanned the store, but quickly jerked his head back toward Jackson.

"Are you alright?"

Jackson tilted his head. "Yeah, why?"

"Your eyes are all puffy."

Jackson burst out laughing, trying to disguise the embarrassment in it. "Mrs. Belmont came in."

"Say no more."

"That poor woman."

"She's a sweet lady. I had Thanksgiving with her last year."

"What? You never told me that." He unwrapped his sub. Grease had made the white wrapping translucent.

"She came in one day, started crying about having no one to cook for. I figured, why should we both eat alone? She made the turkey and vegetables; I brought sweet potatoes and rolls. I had a nice time." Ray examined his slice of pizza, debating where to take the first bite.

"You're probably the nicest person on this planet," Jackson said and then dug into his sub.

"We live in a weird time." His eyes fixated on the customers digging through DVDs, but they glossed over as if they were looking into a different world entirely. "Humans are social creatures; by nature, we like to interact. But we're changing, becoming more solo. We don't need each other anymore. The world will keep moving that way and it'll be fine. We'll adapt, become more independent, interacting less and less. People like Mrs. Belmont, though, they lived their whole lives being social, learning from an early age that the better you are at social interaction, the more successful you'll be. I mean, that generation trained to learn proper etiquette. They had parties where they learned how to be polite. She couldn't adapt to this way of living if she wanted to. It's in her blood. It's who she is. There's an emotional investment in conversation. She needs to talk to someone. It's how she feels valuable." He faced Jackson, looking him dead in the eyes. "Your conversation with her today probably added minutes to her life. You have no idea what it means to a lady like her."

Jackson thought of his father, the way he locked himself away for years, keeping his head down when he did go out, avoiding people at all costs. He wondered if his father liked the privacy, or secretly wished to interact, wanting to feel human again, to be a part of the community, but just knew he didn't belong, knew he couldn't entwine with regular society the way he once had.

About four months before his father passed away, when the medication had diminished a good portion of his faculties, Jackson had brought Senior outside for a cigarette. They sat on the back patio and his father brought the cigarette to his lips, struggling to aim it with his trembling hands.

"We should go to Alaska." He exhaled wind, never having lit the cigarette.

"Alaska, huh?"

"We can build a cabin. Me and you, and you can bring Amanda." His shaky hand brought the cigarette back to his lips. He inhaled and exhaled and flicked the unlit cigarette into the ashtray. Jackson knew he should get him back to bed.

"That sounds like a great idea, Pops. Alaska."

"We'll build a cabin. That's what we'll do." He mashed the cigarette into the tray. It crumbled and broke apart.

"That sounds great."

"Me and you and all of our friends. We'll build a cabin."

Jackson glanced over at Ray, who sorted through a stack of returns from the drop box. He pictured him sitting at a table with Mrs. Belmont, eating turkey, and talking about old film noirs. He imagined how Mrs. Belmont must have felt, having a friend for the day. He wondered if he brought that to his father, gave him all he needed for friendship. Was he enough? When he came home from work, tired and stressed, did his father's face exude disappointment as Jackson walked past him and went straight to his room? Was he always waiting for Alaska?

CHAPTER 10

HER HANDS, HER HEART, HER FACE

Jackson drove down Almeda. He had grown to love the road, even the dangerous parts. The shimmer still existed behind the bushes next to the Milner House, and with it, Jackson's curiosity. He noticed a flock of birds swarming the area. Which kind of birds, he wasn't sure, but the scavenger type: crows, maybe.

Amanda had never responded to his good morning text, which could have meant she was still upset, or it could just have been that she had a busy day at work. During the day, she rarely responded. Either way, he had mending to do.

He pulled into the driveway a few minutes after she did. She closed the back door on the driver's side of her car, holding a white rectangular box in her hand. She looked at his car pulling in and gave a wide, phony grin. She put the box on the trunk of her car and waited for him.

He opened his car door enough to stick his head out. "Hey, can you hang out for a bit?"

She nodded and crossed her arms, not aggressively, just trying to wrap herself up. He moved toward her, looking at the white box. "Whatcha got there?"

"Oh, look at this." She opened it, revealing a half-eaten cake. The writing on it said, "Congr Amand." He filled in the blanks. "The team gave it to me. I have about forty cards in my purse, too."

"That was sweet of them."

"Yeah."

They both hovered over the cake for a minute too long, hoping the uncomfortable atmosphere would let up before they had to face each other. She broke first.

"I'm sorry I got so upset last night. I have no idea how I would handle someone I love dying. Especially the way your pops did."

"It's okay. I understand. It would have freaked me out, too."

"Let's just go inside."

The rest of the night they spent on the couch, watching whatever they could find, flipping channels, cuddling. They were good at that, spending time together without having to speak or do much else. There was enjoyment just being near each other.

She stretched her arms. "It's getting late. I'm gonna go to bed."

They walked to the front door together and kissed goodbye. Before he left, he asked, "So, we're okay, right?"

She nodded.

"I'd do anything for you," he said.

She leaned in and kissed the side of his head. As she did, she whispered, "Do anything for yourself, first."

He wanted to ask what that meant, but instead, he nodded and left. Maybe Ray had been right. Once Jackson left for Syracuse with Amanda, he might look for some kind of basketball-adjacent job. He'd spent a lot of time stalling out, and he should probably do something about that.

On the way home, he saw the shimmering thing again.

At his house, a deep loneliness crept over him. Where Amanda had once been his girlfriend, he found her growing into an obsession, something to cling to when all else went off the rails, and he didn't like the feeling. It wasn't good for either of them. He sat on the couch dissecting their entire encounter, trying to find problems, things to fix, contemplating ways to make it better. Their night had been completely normal outside of the ending whisper, yet he couldn't help but worry himself over it all.

A glass of water stood on an end table next to the couch. He grabbed it and launched it across the room. It shattered and splashed against the wall by his father's paintings in a satisfying display.

"Look, I can smash glass too," he said to the hollow house. "Do you want to hum, or break things, or screech, or whatever the hell else you do?" His house responded with silence, and it was too much to bear. He screamed, "Give me my father back!"

He stormed into his father's room and faced the empty cranberry square. "Wake up! Wake up. I need you. Pops, please."

When they had moved into this house, after his father had depleted most of his savings and had to sell off the old house, Jackson lied to his father about how much he liked the place, not wanting to rub salt into a wound by letting him know how small it felt. Now, he couldn't imagine feeling that way. The house loomed around him, taunting him with its size. He needed to leave. He needed to get away from this overbearing place.

It was time to find out what that shimmering was.

He pulled the car back out and sped off. By the time he reached the Milner House, it was nearly one in the morning, and he let the car idle with the blinker on for a good minute before deciding to pull in, worried that an excursion this late at night was asking for trouble.

He sighed. It was high time he grew some balls and took some action. Amanda said he should do something for himself, and she was right. His car rocked and crunched as it pulled into the dirt clearing in front of the house.

The Milner House was a place of legend in Tanner's Switch. Children whispered many different variations of lore involving the maniac who built it. Either he built it to house his victims, or he killed his family and buried them in the basement, or Jackson's favorite, the owner believed the house to be hungry and fed it the bodies of children from Tanner's Switch. The true story was a lot less scary, but far more depressing.

James Milner, a dentist, lived in Newport with his wife and two sons during World War I. Both sons volunteered for service and shipped off to war, one in the Army, the other, the Navy. James, proud of his boys, decided to buy some land in Tanner's Switch, build two neighboring houses, and gift them to his sons when they returned from war.

After long days in the office, he left work and drove to the land, working on the house until the early hours of the morning. On good days, he slept for three hours before having to head back to his dentist's office. The house came together quickly, but James deteriorated in the process. After finishing the frame and walls of the first house, he suffered a heart attack at his office, collapsing on a patient.

His work went unfinished. He left two cavities unfilled, one in his patient's mouth and the other within the hollow structure for his older boy, Troy.

Troy never made it home from the war to see the half-built gift his father toiled over for the better part of a year. A landmine fragment blasted into his throat. He wasn't even the one who stepped on it.

His little brother, Walter, returned home with only a mother remaining. She showed him the house and explained what happened in the process. She urged him to take it, to finish building it, and start a family. His father's hard work should have some positive outcome, after all. Walter simply replied, "That's Troy's house."

Jackson didn't know who owned the land or the house at this time, but whoever it was, they showed no signs of repairing it.

Jackson edged toward the wall of rhododendrons, stepping slowly and carefully, afraid of running into a fisher cat or some other vicious creature. The trees rustled with a cool night wind and he heard the sounds of snapping twigs nearby. He followed the sounds with his gaze, hoping to catch sight of the critter behind them. A fat silhouette waddled by, and he figured it to be an opossum. He released the air he held in his chest and continued forward.

He crossed a bend and stepped along a footpath until he could finally see the object. It came into view, and he scoffed at the cause of his curiosity: a silver Ford Focus parked crookedly along the other side of the bushes.

It all seemed perfectly normal until a question popped into his mind. How did it get back there? He had trouble finding room for his feet, let alone a car. He inched closer and noticed a yellow mist of pollen had accumulated on the car's body.

Teenagers frequented the Milner house, bringing their buddies, and goading them to go in to face the ghosts. It could have belonged to one of them, but why would it have been there long enough to gather pollen? Maybe someone was squatting in the Milner House after losing their own home. It would explain why the owner of the vehicle went out of their way to hide the car.

He crept forward, despite every instinct telling him not to. As he reached the back end of the Focus, his eyes adjusted and recognized a shape by the steering wheel. He leaned his head forward and squinted. The shape fixed and he realized he was staring at a person slumped over, head leaning between the driver's side door and the steering wheel.

He froze. Moving forward or backward would create noise. He could wake the person up, and who knew what kind of person sat in there?

His heart drummed against his ribs.

The person wasn't sleeping, though; he knew this no matter how much he preferred it to the alternative. Someone was dead in that car. Someone had been dead in that car for days, and he drove past it repeatedly, noticing the silver paint and backlights as they shimmered against the sun and the moon.

He shivered.

With a sudden blast of courage, he stepped forward and knocked against the back passenger side door. The figure—dead person—didn't move. It didn't move because it was dead, not sleeping.

His breath turned heavy. He had no idea what to do, so he stood there, staring, frozen.

He moved his left foot forward, forcing himself to keep exploring. As he walked around to the driver's side, the slumped figure stayed in place. He acted without thought, leaning forward and knocking on the door, and then he leapt back, waiting for a reaction. Again, it didn't move.

Something about all of this felt dirty, and dangerous, and terrifying.

He could make out the figure a little better now. It was a woman's body. Long blonde hair cascaded from the back of her head to the center of her arched back.

Sometimes, people can lose track of themselves. They start doing irrational things because they are in irrational moments. His fight-or-flight response disappeared, and instead, a voice told him, *Go on. Check it out. Have a peeksie.*

He pulled on the latch and the door opened, but he kept it ajar, making sure the body wouldn't fall to the ground if he opened it all the way. The body stayed against the dashboard, locked in by a seatbelt.

He opened it wide, leaving nothing between him and this dead woman, unprepared for the smell. A horrendous odor seeped out and poisoned the air: gaseous and rotten. It smelled like a truckload of rotten eggs collided into a sewage treatment plant. It assaulted his nose, lungs, and eyes.

He gagged and heaved. Streams of saliva poured out of his mouth, and he struggled to bring his lungs back to functioning organs.

The saliva wasn't enough. He ran away from the door, having the forethought not to soil the scene, and puked all over the rotted wood siding of the Milner House. The parmesan sub left him like a waterfall, but the disgusting odor remained in his throat, turning his insides. He yakked again, and a sharp pain throbbed in his temples from the force in which his body shot everything out of him. His stomach refused to settle, and he suddenly felt weak, like he might pass out.

He leaned his back against the house and tried to catch his breath. The heaving and coughing wouldn't let up. Another wave of puke shot out of him.

He spent the next fifteen minutes getting himself back to working order: breathing in fresh air away from the car, taking long, slow inhales, rubbing his stomach.

When he felt confident that he could hold off on throwing up again, he called 911 and told them he found a body by the Milner House on Almeda.

He grew restless as he waited for them to arrive, and curiosity bubbled. Going to that car would be foolish, but when again would he have the opportunity to examine death in the face of a human? It would be stupid, absolutely stupid to go back to the car.

He put his shirt over his mouth and nose like a surgical mask and decided to be stupid.

He crouched down by the driver's side seat and held his breath, the shirt barely masking the smell. He thought for a moment and decided to take the stupidity to a whole new level. More than that, he was about to do something insane, something totally and ridiculously illogical. And why not? The whole scene, no, the whole night, warranted it, like it was some abstract foreign film where the dead girl might jolt up, start dancing, and offer him an omelet.

His chest felt like an alien was about to burst out of it as he leaned forward.

He touched the girl's pink tee shirt in the center of her torso, under her neck, and lifted her head. So much for not soiling the scene. Her body flopped back onto the seat, and her head tilted to the right.

"Oh my God."

Nothing could have prepared him for it. Seeing his father,

photographing countless carcasses, nothing. Her lips were blue. Streams of blood vessels mapped across her blistered skin. Her eyes protruded and her tongue, swollen and discolored, stuck out of her mouth. A black liquid stained the skin under her lips. He was no longer in an abstract film, this was a straight-to-the-point horror flick.

He tried to look away. With all he had, he tried, but her face was so beautifully wretched.

He knew what he had to do. He reached into his pocket and struggled to get his phone out, afraid to look away from the girl. The screen lit up and he tilted it horizontally. He held it close to his eyes, viewing her through the screen, seeing her face in all its spectacular megapixeled glory.

The front light blared, and the picture snapped. For the briefest moment, the night washed into a brilliant white.

The screen returned. And there was the dead girl, looking at him, right in front of the camera.

He dropped the phone and yelled. The noise ripped out of his lungs, a howl almost.

Now that he had dropped the phone, nothing stood between him and the dead-but-not-dead girl.

She grabbed his wrist and let out a scream that could have peeled the lichen off the Milner House. He felt it up his spine, in his ears, in his brain. It sounded like a warning siren, *This message is brought to you by the Emergency Broadcast System. The world as you know it has been destroyed, welcome to a place where dead girls can touch you.*

He ripped his hand away and fell backwards from his own force, hitting his head on the door, slamming his back into the hard soil. He felt a tear on the small of his back, and he yelped, like a dog when you accidentally stepped on its paw. *"Yyyyooowwwwttttt."*

It burned and shot bursts of sharp pain into his upper back, his stomach, and his ribs. For a second, he couldn't move, and he couldn't see the girl.

"Fuck. Fuck. Fuck."

She could be making her way right on top of him.

He finally forced his feet to kick, and his hands dug into the dirt, pushing backward with all of his strength. Every movement hurt. He didn't care. He had to move. As he crab-walked backward, he was able to crane his neck so he could see where the girl had been. She was slouched in the seat again, exactly as she was when he took the photo.

He managed to get himself back on his feet and almost ran, but remembered he had dropped his phone by the car. He saw the white shell of the phone in the dirt right by where she'd grabbed him.

All of the symptoms came at once. Full-on panic attack. Unless this time, it was actually a heart attack. His vision tunneled. A grand piano sat on his chest. He just had to fight the attack long enough to grab his phone, and then run to his car. He could work out the symptoms when he got there.

He inched forward, seeing the maps of death on the dead girl's face come into clear view as he approached. He looked down to assess where his proximity to the phone was, and quickly brought his eyes back to the girl.

His fingers tingled, like he had slept on his arms wrong.

He was close now. Too close. The disgusting smell oozed into his nostrils. Luckily, the panic attack had closed up his throat, so he didn't get the entire flavor of the smell.

One more foot forward, one more quick look at where the phone was in relation to him, and he went for it. He bent down, his arm swung like a crane, his fingers snatched the phone, and he was off and running, ignoring the intense pain in his lower back.

He whizzed past the rhododendrons, the footpath, into the dirt clearing, and he threw up once again, this time in front of his car. The world closed in around him. All of his limbs turned cold and numb. He couldn't breathe.

He gasped for air, gulped for it, pushed it down his dry, tight throat as best he could.

He wanted to drive away, but he couldn't leave. He had called 911.

They would easily find out who called them, and they would come to his house. They would have all sorts of questions about why he managed to soil the scene with his fingerprints and vomit before deciding to flee. The claustrophobia kicked back in. The Milner House towered over him, and the trees around it bent, their branches closing in like giant fingers, their shadows enveloping him.

He turned back toward the site of the dead girl, making sure she didn't follow him. He pictured her walking with stiff limbs like a zombie. The bushes did not move, and the sticks and twigs that carpeted the ground stayed silent. He kept his eyes facing that area until he saw the flashing reds and blues in his peripheral vision.

CHAPTER 11

STICKS AND STONES

"The one part I'm not getting is why you stopped here in the first place," Assistant Sheriff Carvallo said while tugging his pants over the bulge in his belly.

Jackson sat in the backseat of the cruiser with the door open, his legs extended outside of the vehicle, his head tucked into his hands. "I just kept noticing something shining back there and it made me curious. It was a weird thing to do, I know."

The strobing lights from the cruisers and the ambulance made Jackson feel like he was going to have a stroke. He didn't know why they needed an ambulance anyway. The EMTs weren't going to be reviving anyone tonight. Right now, they weren't doing much of anything, other than talking to Deputy Vassar about the Red Sox.

"I've seen weirder," Carvallo said. "All right, you just relax while I go talk to my guys." He patted Jackson's knee and turned away, but then turned back again, having one more important question to ask. "You still shoot around? Ya' know, you still got the three-point record."

Jackson looked at the ground. "Yeah, I still play a little," he lied.

Carvallo obsessed over high school basketball, attending every

639

Tanner's Switch game as if it were Sunday mass. Jackson's father once said, "Any man who loves high school sports that much has a wife that sleeps in a separate bed." In Jackson's junior year, he broke the Rhode Island high school record for three-pointers, leading his team to a state championship; for that, Carvallo would always look at Jackson as a hero. In his senior year, Jackson quit midway through the season, and for that, Carvallo would always look at Jackson as a disappointment.

Carvallo approached Vassar and the EMT guys, saying something to them that put them all into a fit of laughter.

Jackson's mind spun, and the Earth tilt-a-whirled around him. He pushed back whatever was fighting its way up his esophagus. All that shimmers is not gold; sometimes it's a Ford Focus with a dead girl inside.

The EMTs walked the footpath to the other side of the rhododendrons and the horror show behind them. Carvallo and Vassar paced in the direction of the house. Jackson listened to them talk, picking up parts of the conversation.

"Girl's been dead for days."

"His father just died."

"No way she touched him."

Deputy Vassar and Jackson also had a history that went back to high school basketball. Vassar was a year younger and a bit shorter, and not nearly as talented as Jackson had been. Jackson suspected Vassar always hated him, but then again, Jackson thought everyone did.

Carvallo ran his hand through the slivers of hair that striped across his bald top. He sighed and walked back to Jackson.

"Everything alright with you, son?"

My father called me son, not you, he thought. "I just saw a dead body. Other than that, yeah, I'm fine."

"I mean, other than this whole mess. You been okay?"

Jackson looked up at him, confused by the line of questioning. "I'm not sure what you're asking. It's been a bad few days."

"That's what I mean. I'm sorry about your dad, by the way. You handling everything okay?"

In Jackson's junior year, his father came to one of his games, back when he still left the house on occasion. During the game, his father drank vodka from a sports mug. At some point during the second half, the alcohol got the best of him, and he decided he couldn't stand Carvallo's incessant yelling anymore, so he walked up to him and, right there in the stands, punched him in the face.

Carvallo handled it like a gentleman, dragging Senior outside before he could embarrass himself any further, sending him on his way. He didn't have him arrested and never made much of a deal about it, but the two men avoided each other like the plague afterward.

"I guess so, why?"

Carvallo pulled his pants up, making the high-waters even higher, and crouched down like he wanted to whisper what he was about to say, as if the rest of the crew didn't already know whatever it was. "I didn't want to bring this up before; you were clearly shaken about the body you just saw, but you calling us tonight was a hell of a coincidence."

"Why's that?"

"We had just come from your house. Neighbor of yours, Mrs. Barlow, called us, said you had a bit of a ruckus going on in there. Screaming, smashing, she said it sounded like a war was going on. We knocked, but your car wasn't there, and we knew you were gone. Turns out you were finding yourself a dead body."

"I threw a glass. That lady makes a big deal out of everything."

"She said she saw you looking at dead animals the other day."

"She's fucking nuts."

Carvallo patted him on the shoulder. "We can agree on that. I believe ya' son. You'd be amazed at the nonsense she calls us for. I just wanted to check and make sure you were okay."

"It's been a weird few days," he reiterated.

A few more cars pulled up, regular cars, bland sedans, not emergency vehicles. A tall redheaded woman exited the first one, and a skinny old man with glasses stepped out of the second. Vassar jogged toward them, pointing in the direction of the Focus. Carvallo remained crouched in front of Jackson but turned his attention in their direction.

"Looks like it's going to be a weird few days for me too." He nodded his head in the direction of the new people. "Forensics."

Jackson loved procedurals; he had already assumed who they were. Carvallo patted his knee. "All right, let me go deal with these clowns. I'll be back. I'll drive you home in a bit, unless you're feeling okay to drive? Either way, expect more questions. We'll probably have a lot of them."

He wanted nothing more than to say he was okay to drive. For the first time since his father's death, he couldn't wait to go home. The thought of his bed made his muscles yearn for rest. Everything inside him groaned for sleep. His eyelids gained fifteen pounds over the last few hours. Unfortunately, the thought of standing up made him afraid for his safety. The world continued to sway, and his legs felt removed of their bones.

"I'll stick around. Do you mind if I lie down on the back seat?"

"Of course," Carvallo said as he stood up, the bones in his knees cracking.

Carvallo waddled his elephant trunks toward the bushes, and stopped himself once more, turning to Jackson. "You still with Amanda Canter?"

Jackson nodded.

"No shit. Still with your high school sweetheart, huh? She was a catch. Her field goal percentage was in the six hundreds, if I remember correctly." Carvallo liked girls' basketball, too.

Jackson dropped backward, landing on the cruiser's hard back-seats. He worked on keeping his breath steady while he looked at the ceiling. After seeing the body, he assumed he wouldn't be able to sleep for days, haunted by the images, but within a few minutes of staring up, the metallic shell darkened, and he drifted into sleep.

The sounds of the trees rustling, the flashing reds and blues, the crinkling of leaves and twigs, all disappeared, and Jackson was at sea. His father yelled from the stern, *Hold on, son!* The waves crashed against the side of the boat, shoving it at an angle, dangerously close to capsizing it. His father looked back at him with a devilish grin. *That was a doozy. The next one's gonna be a real treat. We're going under, buddy. Haha.*

And then he was on the Bass Rock Trail, following the path, surrounded by dead animals hanging from the trees. Their ropes swayed against the branches. Behind the tree line, Amanda moved sideways, keeping pace with Jackson. She tried to push past the wall of trees, but an invisible shield kept her locked amongst the forestry, the dead animals acting as swaying pendulums between them. *Let me in, Jackie. Let me in.*

A thin stream crossed the trail and gathered along a dam of sticks, pooling until it was a bathtub, his father's body floating and bobbing at the top. Pink streams poured out in waterfalls, landing on a tiled floor. There, Jackson saw something floating in the water, something he hadn't noticed before. A dark silhouette reflected and rippled in the turmoil of the tub. His father's eyes opened. *We're going under, buddy. Haha.*

He woke up, confused by the world in front of him. His mind slowly grasped the real world that surrounded him: the police car, the dirt clearing, sticks and stones, the Milner house, the dead girl. He sat up and leaned his head against the back seat, giving himself a minute to absorb everything.

When he stood, he felt the bones in his legs again, his strength returning. He walked along the path toward the voices, toward the dead girl. Carvallo walked around the clearing, and Jackson was relieved to know he didn't have to go near the Focus again. Carvallo was surprised to see him up and moving.

"I'm feeling better. I have to work soon. I'm gonna drive home and get some sleep."

Carvallo stuck his fingers into Jackson's shoulder; it was like he stole Senior's playbook. "You sure you're okay to drive? Because if I let you go and you get banged up, or worse, I'm gonna get in a lot of trouble for letting you take off."

"I promise. I'm fine. Just tired."

Carvallo's tongue slid across his teeth while he considered it. "All right. Get some rest. I'll be in touch soon."

Jackson sat in his car and turned the key, hoping it wouldn't take long for the heat to kick on. The cool night breeze had blown away the summer warmth. He turned the volume up on the radio so it would keep him from dozing at the wheel, and he chain-smoked as he drove; the cigarettes kept him busy and helped him stay awake.

He pulled into his driveway and looked up at the house. Its menacing size shrunk Jackson's courage. The car door squeaked as it opened. Jackson stood face-to-face with the house, the place he lived, and his heart sped up. He felt weak again. He tapped his fingers against his jeans, took a deep breath, and headed toward the front door. *We're going under, buddy. Haha.*

CHAPTER 12
GOING HOME

Jackson woke up in a fog. His alarm abruptly swept him from a deep sleep into the morning light. He jolted up, carrying the dream world with him. He was surprised he slept at all, surprised his eyes weighed down on him in the police car, and again when his head crashed into his bed. He grabbed his wrist. It wa achy and tender. Purple circles formed along the bone. A dead girl had latched onto it. A dead girl who died days ago, really, really dead, grabbed his wrist. Either she defied all laws of nature, breaking apart the foundations of everything we know about dying, or his brain tumor theory rang true. Both options should have been enough to keep him wide awake, yet he had slept more soundly than he had in weeks.

Horrific dreams had hounded him, but not the kinds of dreams that judder a person awake with heart palpitations. These were the types of dreams that slow your heart, dragging your subconscious deeper into the REM world, capturing you, forcing you to stay with them, so when you awaken, they follow you and you spend the rest of the day wondering if the nightmares are right around the corner.

The bloated face belched noxious, rotten gas, and the dead girl crawled toward him, carrying the stench closer and closer. His father's chest quivered as pockets of air machine-gunned out of his throat. Amanda's eyes bled and she clawed the skin off her cheeks, screaming for Jackson to die. Stacks of deadfalls surrounded him, each pile of decayed forest containing decomposed animal corpses.

He lugged his heavy feet to the kitchen, dragging his toes against the carpet. The sun wasn't bright enough, and the lights didn't destroy enough shadows. The refrigerator whirred as it made ice and the sudden change in sound made Jackson jerk. His mind worked to separate reality from the seeping remnants of his nightmares. He drank a glass of water, letting it wash over his arid throat.

His phone vibrated on the nightstand by his bed, and he thanked himself for leaving it in the bedroom. If it vibrated near him, it may have caused heart failure. Three sets of rattles let him know a call was coming through, not a text, so he ran to it.

The cremation people wanted to let him know he could pick up his father's ashes. He would need to bring a death certificate, proof Senior was his father, and the full payment. He didn't know how to get any of those things. He would have to ask Ray during their shift; Ray knew everything.

"Town hall for the death certificate. Birth certificate for proof of relationship. And what are you asking about his bank accounts?" Pieces of Dunkin' Donuts munchkins flew out of Ray's mouth as he spoke.

"I can't just take money from his account, right? Isn't that identity theft or something?"

"Oh, yeah, that part's a pain in the ass. You need court documents where a judge says it's cool for you to close your dad's account. Personally, I would just use an ATM and clean it out as close to the nearest dollar as you can and leave it like that. No one is gonna bust your balls. They'll probably never even figure it out. In twenty years, your dad will still have an almost empty account floating around in their systems. It'll have collected an extra dollar in interest. I hate banks, though, so maybe I shouldn't be giving you advice on that one."

"All right, thanks."

"You look like crap today, by the way."

"Thanks, pal."

On his break, Jackson sat in his car smoking a cigarette, thinking about the dead girl. He grew curious, wondering about her. What happened to her? How did the car get back there? More than those things, he wanted to know about the girl's life: who she was, what she did, what brought her to the end.

He opened his phone and checked his text messages. Nothing from Amanda yet, not even a check-in to make sure he made it home safely last night. He Googled the sheriff's department and gave them a call. They put him on hold, then connected him to Sheriff Alingon, who told him Carvallo wouldn't be in until five and he didn't have any specifics on the case Jackson asked about. That turned out to be quite all right because by the time he connected to Alingon, he needed to get back to work.

He left Valiant at five, and since he still hadn't heard from Amanda, he decided to go to the sheriff's department, hoping to catch Carvallo before he hit the road and sat in parking lots all night, like town sheriffs do.

Carvallo called him right into his office, sitting down with a fresh mug of coffee, looking excited to see him.

"What can I do you for?"

"I didn't know if you guys had more questions."

Carvallo stretched back and clasped his fingers together behind his head. "It turns out we don't. I mean, that could change, but as for now, looks like we have it all under control."

"Oh. Okay."

Now he sat up, sensing the disappointment in Jackson's tone. "We appreciate all of your help, and it's nice of you to come down here and try to help further."

"So, what did you guys find out?"

Carvallo sipped his coffee. "You know I can't tell you any of that, but you can read the papers tomorrow because a whole slew of reporters ended up at the scene last night. Parasites."

"If it's going to be in the papers, can't you just tell me?"

"Why are you so interested?" His pitch lowered a level.

"I found a dead girl in the woods. I'm curious to know who she was, or why she was there."

Carvallo stood. "Well, all I can tell you is to read the papers. Sorry kiddo, but that's the way it goes."

"Yup." Jackson nodded goodbye and walked out.

Behind him, Carvallo called out. "Come by and talk basketball anytime, though."

On the way home, Jackson sent a text to Amanda.

> Company?

He decided to head in the direction of her house while he waited for a response.

With no real reason to, he pulled into the Milner House's dirt lawn. It split the distance between his house and Amanda's, so it made a good place to wait, but that was just an excuse. He parked there because his weird curiosity took hold.

When he found the fox on the other side of the road, he distinctly heard a humming come out of the ground toward him, and then it veered to the Milner House. It tried to lead him to the dead girl. If he had imagined the noise, what a strange coincidence it would be that the imaginary sound led him right into the arms of a dead girl. Why did it want him to find her?

The girl had touched him, too. No, he wasn't losing his mind. He didn't have a brain tumor, and he wasn't imagining things. That girl really fucking touched him, and he had a bruise on his wrist to prove it.

He waited in the car, lighting up the phone screen every few seconds, just in case he didn't feel it vibrate on his leg. Outside, he heard the crinkling of sticks as they fell off their homes. *Crrinnkkk.*

He couldn't take it anymore, sitting in the car, waiting. He slammed the door and headed for the rhododendrons.

The Ford Focus remained in the same spot, and as Jackson walked around to the driver's side, he half expected to see the bloated corpse still flopped on the front seat. Whoever was in charge of such a thing removed the body but forgot to take the stench with them. It had diminished but still lingered slightly. He noticed maggots and flies clumped in spots around where the corpse no longer lay. Most of the larvae and bugs were dead themselves: tiny bodies. Jackson pictured himself taking close-ups of their little dead faces, and that made him laugh, which he felt guilty for at the site of someone else's horror.

He glanced at the backyard and the woodsy area that surrounded him, still baffled by how the dead girl managed to get her car there. Thick bushes spread across the back. Next to them, a small footpath —the one Jackson used to enter—opened into a small passageway before turning to a densely populated woods, large oaks and elms slaloming through it. No more than two feet in front of the car, a small shed jutted out into a weird angular shape, blocking the car in.

He crouched down by the driver's side and talked through the door, as if the dead girl still slouched inside, as if she listened. "I'm sorry. Whatever happened to you, I'm sorry for it." He heard the humming again, merging with the crickets' chirps, but this time he knew it wasn't there. He wanted to hear it, so he made it play in his ears, pretending to have a peaceful tune when he needed it.

Back at the car, he checked his phone. She had responded, but not with the answer he wanted.

> Not tonight. I'm tired. Maybe tomorrow!

He drove home with the radio blasting, drowning out traffic sounds, and his thoughts. At a red light, he texted Ray and asked him if he wanted to grab a beer. A few minutes later, his phone lit up:

> Nah, too tired tonight.

Seemed like an epidemic.

He *should* get to bed early. He *should* be tired, too. His sleep the night before had been deep, but short. His back still hurt, and his brain worked like mush, so his bed would be nice, but sleep meant going home, and going home meant facing the overbearing house, which was back to feeling haunted. He had nowhere to go, nowhere to feel safe.

He reluctantly drove home, scared and panicky. Agoraphobics have such a tough time with panic attacks they end up convincing themselves that their home is the only safe place to be. Jackson's father had that problem. Right now, Jackson seemed to have the opposite problem. He had no home to go to because it was the least safest place.

He cried in the driveway for a while, not knowing what he was crying about, but it felt good to do it, nonetheless. Once inside, he struggled to get comfortable on the bed; it took him three hours of tossing around before he fell asleep. He let every sound deliver chills, every change in temperature alert him into a sitting position, and every time he did drift to sleep, a slight noise would wake him in a fright.

In the morning, he woke up groggy and sad. He planned to go to the town hall for the documents he needed. He showered, threw on some jeans and a black tee shirt, and was all ready to go. It took until he opened his front door before he realized it was Sunday and the town hall wouldn't be open.

He took his phone and hooked it up to his computer. When the picture of the dead girl took up the screen, he cringed. Her face was horrific, and looking at it brought back the taste and smell of her awful decay.

He zoomed in on her eyes. They were black. It could have been from the lack of light and the terrible quality of the picture, but her irises looked like black holes. He shivered. Something was there. He didn't doubt himself this time. Her eyes had something to them that differed from any internet photo he'd seen. Swirls. They were almost invisible, but he could feel them, and now that he did, he remembered *feeling* a swirl in his father's eyes. That was why he didn't recognize them in the animals. He looked for a thing, an object, but it was not a thing, it was feeling; it was an action; it was an event.

Hours slipped away. The daylight drifted into a cool, bruised evening sky. And he looked. He stared at dead eyes for hours, and when he needed a break, he pulled up the eyes of the animals he photographed and even the ones he found on the internet, and he examined them so closely, he could point out every discoloration, every reflection, every pixel, and he could do it all by memory. His own eyes swelled and oozed tears from staring too long at the screen.

He tried to go to sleep at three in the morning. When he closed his eyes, he saw the lifeless faces of his subjects. He had found it, had pinpointed what he wanted to see in their eyes, but it led him to another brick wall. What could he do about it? Knowing what existed in their eyes didn't bring him a step closer to feeling the sensation again. He had wasted the entire day.

In the morning, he drove to the town hall and picked up the death certificate. He battled with his eyelids the entire time. Another night had passed where Jackson tossed and couldn't sleep. He paid for his documents and left, barely remembering the transaction ever happening.

On the way to the funeral home, he stopped at the ATM and drained his father's savings account. His checking had a balance that exceeded the maximum amount allowed for withdrawals from the ATM. Eventually, he would need to get the court documents so he could have that money. He could take a small amount out every day, but that felt like pushing his luck. Someone would catch on.

At the funeral home, an old man in a crisp black suit greeted him. He remembered the man from his visit here three months ago, when the hospice woman and the funeral director introduced him to all the options. He walked Jackson to a side office where Jackson showed him Senior's death certificate along with his own birth certificate—a strange juxtaposition of documents. The man glanced at them briefly, probably not even reading the necessary parts, just going through the formalities. After a sufficient number of seconds passed, he handed them back to Jackson and walked out. The whole scenario played out as if Jackson were picking up a rental. *Here's the dead guy you ordered.*

The man reentered with a shiny black urn. Jackson didn't remember picking it out; it looked like nothing he had ever seen. The base and top were flat, while the sides arched into a large center. An egg. They crammed his father's ashes into a black spaceship egg with a flat bottom and top. It must have looked better in the catalogue.

He sat in his car for a while, smoking a cigarette, his father's spaceship buckled into the passenger seat. The car engine rumbled and Jackson let a puff of smoke drizzle out of his nostrils. He inhaled another drag and put his hand on top of his father. Laughter gushed out of him. He tried to stop it, but that only made it worse. Loud, hysterical bursts turned into wheezing until his lungs couldn't keep up and he coughed. His eyes watered as his tender lungs exuded seal-like croaks. It winded down and he turned to the urn. "You look ridiculous, Pops." And the laughter started all over again.

He put the car in drive, continuing his laughing fit as he pulled away from the funeral parlor. "Come on. Let's go home."

CHAPTER 13
THEY WILL EAT YOU ALIVE

Jackson had forgotten to pick up the Sunday paper to see what news Carvallo couldn't tell him, so he stopped at the Cumberland Farms in Charlestown on his way home. The kid working the counter checked the back room and found a copy for him.

Finding out about the girl had been a top priority, yet he managed to forget to grab the paper because other important things had come up in its place. When everything had importance, nothing did. Each thing dilutes the others.

"What do you want with yesterday's news?" the cashier asked.

"Yesterday's news is today's problems." The kid got a kick out of that. Jackson didn't know what it meant, and he didn't think the kid really did either, but they both pretended it was funny anyway.

At home, he placed his father on the living room table, checked his watch, and figured as late as he was, ten more minutes wouldn't kill Ray. He wanted to read.

MISSING SHANNOCK GIRL FOUND DEAD

After four days of searching, Alexandria Lucia, 17, was found dead on Friday, from what police believe to be a suicide.

Alexandria's mother reported her missing to the Richmond Police Department at 9:55 p.m. Monday after Alexandria failed to return home from school, according to police spokesperson Mark Goggins. Since that time, the police department worked together with family, neighbors, and friends in an attempt to locate the missing teen.

Alexandria was found late Friday night in her car, parked by an abandoned house that is known to locals for its strange history. Police are unsure why the girl went to this location, but they believe she chose it specifically for her suicide.

No note was found, and police are waiting for a toxicology report before they give any further information.

"She was always smiling," Allan Casperson, a neighbor said. "Goes to show, you never know what someone's going through."

Alexandria's mother was unavailable for comment, but a neighbor described her as "distraught" and asked that she receive "respect and privacy in her time of grieving."

Jackson traced his finger along the picture that accompanied the article. It amazed him how the monstrous bloated thing he saw in that car was once such a beautiful, young girl. The haunting, distorted creature frightened him every time he closed his eyes, but the creature was a seventeen-year-old kid. She had probably listened to pop music, talked to her friends about sex and booze, and watched reality dating shows.

He drove to work, unable to think about anything else. The newspaper said the police were waiting for a toxicology report. That meant she'd probably accidentally overdosed or intentionally swallowed a bottle of pills. His fingers danced across the steering wheel while he imagined the life she had led and what brought her to the point of suicide. He filled in the blanks, designing an entire life for her in his mind.

At work, he rang up customers while he pictured her eating Sunday dinners with her mother. He cleaned up the aisles, seeing Alexandria putting on make-up before school, deciding if the darker eye shadow would look better with her rouge. He ate his lunch, and made-believe Alexandria cried into her palms, listening to sad songs while she thought about angsty teenage things, like break-ups and lost friends.

What broke Alexandria? Her mother? A boyfriend? Bullying? He doubted any of those things. It's hardly ever a *thing* that breaks a person. It's not what's there, but what's missing. If he wanted to understand what brought her to the Milner House, he needed to look past what was there and bring his attention to the empty spaces. Ghosts hide in the shadows. They lurk in the gaps. They haunt from the rafters.

After work, Jackson searched for Alexandria's Facebook page and used it as a way to get inside the girl's head. She posted often, sometimes fifteen to twenty times a day.

Her statuses were erratic, but he imagined most teenagers' social media pages would be. She posted one status claiming her day was the best ever. Within a half hour of that one, she posted a passive-aggressive status telling someone unnamed to go to hell. Good portions of them were defensive.

So what if I don't like U? Why do U care?

He looked at the pages she followed, the movies, music, and books she listed. A common thread linked all of them: they were all depressing. Some people just like to cry. Jackson understood that well.

Her classmates took over the top of her page with goodbyes. They told her they loved her and missed her and didn't know what they would do without her. Jackson wondered how many of them let her know how they felt when she was alive. He guessed most of them didn't love her, miss her, or plan to change anything about their daily routines, except maybe to take some time to cry in public for the sympathy. Even in death, they couldn't let her have the attention.

Jackson checked his phone; still nothing from Amanda. When something happened, he had always gone to her. He found a dead body, found the rotting corpse of a teenage girl who stole her own life, and the only person ready to listen to him lived in a black egg on the living room end table.

Even if he could talk to Amanda about it, he wouldn't know what to say. Certainly, not the truth. He was starting to believe he was meant to find the dead girl. All of the weirdness and strange events led to her, and that was by design. Whose design? Jackson had no idea.

He missed Amanda's voice, her logic, and her intelligence. He grabbed his phone and texted:

I miss you.

CHAPTER 14

THE COMPANY OF STRANGERS

The next morning, after another lousy night of unsleep—as Senior liked to call insomnia—Jackson woke up to an

I miss you, too

text. He decided to send her another message and test the waters.

Wanna hang out tonight?

Periodically, he looked over at the black egg, uncomfortable with the idea that his father hovered in the room. It felt like a set of eyes remained on him at all times, but worse, because maybe his father's ashes read his mind too. If a negative thought or a strange idea popped into his head, he tilted his gaze toward the egg. "What?"

He pictured those scenes in movies where the main character, drenched in rain, cries at their loved one's grave. A tinge of jealousy ran through his veins, knowing he would never have those cathartic moments. He had the egg. It hardly seemed like the proper vessel for a powerful scene of remembrance. Besides, he had decided not to keep his father in it. First, he had to figure out where to spread his ashes, and then he would let them fly.

He had asked his father once where he would like to be scattered. "Don't give a shit. I'll be dead. Hand out cups of me on Halloween." His father, always helpful.

Senior spent a lot of his time in the john. The toilet and the package store upended each other on the list of his favorite places; it depended on the day which one took the top spot. Before Jackson's mother had left, Senior still lived life and enjoyed the world. At that time, Senior loved many places, but none so much as Bar Harbor, Maine. He took Jackson there every summer and they explored the tourist attractions. They climbed a cliff and took pictures with a dangling boulder, visited the petting zoo, and stood on a dock, getting soaked from a cove that spewed water.

His father allowed himself to have fun back then. Jackson thought of his dad shaking his hand on Jackson's wet hair as they walked away from the cove, laughing as water sprayed off his son's head. His father must have laughed after his mom left, too, but Jackson struggled to think of a time.

Bar Harbor represented the old Jackson Senior, though. The sentiment was nice, but it didn't fit the person in the egg. Jackson spent a while considering the best place for his father, and the answer jumped into his head while he smoked a cigarette on the back deck, staring deeply into the trail.

The Bass Rock Trail symbolized what Senior strived to be. He had dreamed of walking the short path, and if Jackson spread his ashes there, he could live his dream, figuratively speaking. It beat the toilet, anyway.

Jackson nested the black egg between his arm and chest as he walked the path, sprinkling a small amount every twenty or thirty steps. He imagined a glass version of his father, filled with sand. Every time he poured a little, the glass man drained.

When he reached the place where the raccoon once rested, he

wondered where dead animal bodies ended up. Does someone have a job picking up corpses from trails and the sides of roads?

"There goes your beer belly, Pops," Jackson said as the sand in the glass man reached waist level. His ashes danced and trickled along the raccoon's former gravestone.

When he reached the end of the path, a good portion of his father still rested in his urn. Jackson sat on the gazebo, twisting and untwisting the black egg's flat lid, debating, deciding. He knew what he wanted to do, knew before he even started spreading his father along the trail, but talked himself out of it. It served no purpose, and everything about the idea stretched way beyond the line of peculiarity, even for Jackson. He also knew that once the idea came to him, he was going to follow through with it, and that was why he sat on the gazebo holding the urn with half of the ashes still inside of it.

When he pulled into the dirt opening in front of the Milner House, he caught the twinkling of the Focus's back lights reflecting in the sun. The police must have given up trying to figure out how to get it out of there. Eventually, Alexandria's mother would want it, and they would either find a way to move it or make her figure it out.

As he approached the car, he realized he was wrong; his idea did have a purpose.

He started from the back and walked backward around the car, pouring the ashes in a constant thin stream. He tipped the urn further as he finished his loop, letting the bottom clear out. If his father's spirit lingered with those ashes, and if a piece of Alexandria remained where she died, then they would both have some company. Hopefully, they could get along.

When he settled back into his car, his phone lit up. He had hoped the message came from Amanda, but when he saw Ray's name on the screen, his head dropped, and his fingers tapped against his jeans. "Oh, Shit."

Dude, where are you???????????

He looked at the time: 12:30 PM. "Shit, shit, shit, shit, shit, shit."
The tires of the Civic screeched and kicked dirt clouds into the air as he drove off.

Jackson's tardiness pissed Ray off, but he never said it, or even asked any questions. He just shut down, keeping to himself and the work in front of him. When he did have to speak to Jackson, he kept it short, grunting as he walked away. If Jackson told him what he had spent the morning doing, Ray would understand and his anger would turn to sympathy, but what occurred that morning was a private event between him and his father... and Alexandria.

Jackson had worked at Valiant for twelve years, and in all of that time, he had called out sick on two occasions, including the Thursday after his father passed, and he had shown up late once. Adding one more late day still gave him a solid track record. Before Jackson's shift ended at five, Ray would get over it.

At lunch, Ray strolled out to PizzAmore and came back with a sub. Jackson made a comment about the Red Sox overtaking the Yankees in the AL East, hoping to lure some conversation out of his boss. Ray munched on his sub, giving a placating nod. Jackson decided to wait a few hours, let the anger subside, and then give it another go.

He focused on work, doing his job in silence. The time dragged by and his mind kept drifting to Alexandria. He couldn't stop wondering about her.

Just before the shift change, when a couple of the second shifters showed up, ready to take his place for the night, he decided to give Ray another chance to forgive him.

"Ray, drinks tonight?"

Ray counted the cash register, keeping his attention on the bills. "Nope, I gotta get some rest. Is tomorrow your day off?"

"Yeah," Jackson said as he walked out.

He went home and sat in silence for a while. Nothing happened. His phone stayed quiet. Amanda never responded. Ray stayed cold. Not even the strange noises wanted to spend time with him. Life rotated back to normal, and normal was empty.

CHAPTER 15
WALK THE WALK

The night drifted by, and the sun crept in, breaching the living room curtains and spilling onto Jackson's face. He woke up to the bright assault, and he scanned the sun-drenched room. He checked the time on his phone, unbelieving of how deeply and how long he slept. He was glad to have rid himself of the insomnia, but one night of rest didn't make up for days without it, and he still felt exhausted.

The bright afternoon sun penetrated the room, but it did nothing to remove the austere atmosphere in the house. He shifted his groggy body, pulled himself up, and headed to the bathroom. He held his hand against the wall as he drained his bladder. Amidst the splash of pee hitting the toilet water, Jackson heard a gentle rumble coming from the living room. He'd grown quite sensitive to noises lately. The rumble increased in volume as his stream trickled down.

When he finished up, he could hear the sound in the living room a little clearer. At first, he thought it was a truck outside making the living room floor rattle, but the sound changed slightly, resembling more of a cough.

Yes, it was a cough, loud and phlegmy.

His heart turned to cement and plunged. He thought he might pass out.

He did not attempt to pretend it was anything other than what it was: his father's cough. He convinced himself to believe many things were not as they appeared, even started to find excuses for the broken shower door, but his father's coughing penetrated with a clarity that Jackson could not dismiss. If it wasn't there, then he had officially lost his mind.

He opened the bathroom door, and the coughing grew louder and clearer. What started as a hacking cough melded into a deep, painful croak. A wheezing and gasping for breath. Sounds of suffering.

He crept forward, trying to stay silent. Whatever made the noise, he didn't want it to hear him until he had a visual on it. He tapped the tips of his fingers on his boxer shorts until he caught himself doing it, reminding himself to keep silent.

His exhales poured out shaky and fast. As he approached the bend where the hallway opened up into the living room, he told himself that when he turned the corner, nothing would be there. Isn't that how these things work in the movies? You hear a sound, you investigate, nothing is there. Maybe if the movie is really cheesy, a cat will jump out.

As he approached, the coughing continued to grow stronger. He kept quiet, moving one foot and pausing before lifting the other. He kept a beat between movements, hoping to avoid a clumsy mistake. He maintained control, slow, quiet, patient control. *Don't let the fear overtake you*, he told himself, repeating it in his head over and over.

Then his phone buzzed against the end table. He jumped back, but his foot stuck to the rug. His arms swung around, and he fell backward. BANG.

"Shit." He held his breath, listening for the noise to change, come toward him, or disappear, unsure which scared him more. If he wasn't terrified, he would have laughed at himself for falling.

The noise in the other room remained constant: wheezing, hacking, guttural roars. He picked himself up and leaned his body against the wall and a dizziness set in from standing too quickly.

An unseasonable wintery breeze had turned the air snappy and painfully cold. It shocked him. He stood in place, knowing that the coldness and the coughing went together, and anything powerful enough to change the seasons had to be goddamned frightening.

He inched forward and a puff left his mouth in a thin, silvery jet stream. The sight of his breath added to his terror, but he stepped toward the living room anyway.

Guh heeeeeee Guh heeeeeee Guh heeeeeee. It was so close, and so clear, and so vivid, and it belonged to his father. He wanted to see him. His father, standing, breathing, living.

When he hit the corner, his prediction proved wrong. Something was there. Not his father, though.

This hacking fit belonged to the bloated, rotting corpse of Alexandria Lucia. *Guh heeeeeee Guh heeeeeee Guh heeeeeee.*

He'd cried a lot over the last few weeks. Sometimes he had tiny weeps, sometimes gut-wrenching bawls, but nothing like what came out of him now. He cried out of fear, plain and simple, raw horror. He was an adult man, crying like a little kid who saw the boogieman. And isn't that what he saw? The friggin' boogieman?

She stood looking at him blankly, as if she had been waiting for him to show up. Her arms hung loose at her sides, her head drooped to the left. A black liquid streamed from her mouth down onto her soiled pink shirt.

He just kept on crying. His limbs didn't work. In fact, nothing did. He couldn't even blink. The only parts of him that functioned were his tear ducts and his throat, which expelled a sort of muted scream.

Everything he knew, every piece of logic, every concept of how the world worked, shattered. It shattered, and ice coursed through him. His fingers clenched, turning his fists into stones. The tips of his fingers dug into his moist palms.

Silver puffs left his mouth with each shivery breath. She swung her arm, swatting at the tiny clouds. He stumbled back.

She coughed a violent hack, and the black liquid slapped against his shirt in small droplets. He reacted to the spittle as if it were bullets, falling from the blast, landing hard on his tailbone. The pain shot from his butt into his brain and a red cloud flashed over his vision.

Her cough turned into screaming.

Her high-pitched wailing stabbed inside of his ears.

He covered them with his hands, but the sound protruded through. "Stop it. Stop it. Stop it."

She didn't listen. In fact, she increased the volume. The pain it created surpassed unbearable. It made him feel weak, like the noise could not only shatter glass, but his bones as well. It increased in decibel with each second, and he tightened up, restricting his insides, crushing his guts, trapping the air in his lungs.

He responded with his own screams: painful, agonized yowls. He turned on his side and wrapped himself into a ball. His knees dug into his chest and his forehead clunked against them.

He forced his eyes open, and the girl bent over, dropping her palms to the rug, bouncing her feet back a few inches. She mimicked a dog, hunched and ready to pounce. Her screams turned into growls, raw and throaty, and she used all four limbs to race at him.

He tensed, preparing for the impact. She moved too quickly for him to stop her or even move out of the way.

With inhuman agility, just as she reached him, her body rose back to a standing position and then came down fast. Her face flew toward his and he couldn't keep himself from flinching. As her head dropped, the black liquid splashed dime-sized drops all over his face. His lips pursed as he held in a gag.

She put her face to the side of his, their cheeks almost touching. A light electric sensation prickled the fur on his face. Her hot breath smacked against his ear, and he twitched every time she released an exhale.

She moaned into his ear. It sounded pained. His eardrum reverberated with it.

With that, he found the power to move.

He shoved her backward and ran. His feet hit the ground before he could consider each step. They worked without him, taking over.

By the time his brain came back, his black Honda Civic sped down Almeda, heading toward Amanda's house. She would be at work, but he couldn't think of anywhere else to go. He certainly wouldn't be stopping at the Milner House today, and Ray was still pissed at him for showing up late.

He looked in the rearview mirror; the droplets on his face reassured and horrified him that what he ran from did, in fact, exist. A deep sigh escaped him, almost bubbling into a crying fit, but he stopped it, not allowing himself to break down again.

He stayed in Amanda's driveway, smoking cigarettes and talking himself down, waiting for her, waiting for something. He could spend the rest of his life waiting for Amanda.

She would be leaving in four days, and he had hardly seen her since she told him, had barely even spoken to her through text. He wasn't sure Amanda wanted to spend time with him. It didn't matter. He had just been attacked by something very fucking dead. He needed to be somewhere safe, with someone safe.

CHAPTER 16
NEVER AGAIN

Sometimes Amanda felt like a sitcom wife. She always hated that character: a woman who has her head on straight, who tries to stop her husband's idiocy, and ends up looking like the stick in the mud for it.

When she and Jackson first met, they fell in love pretty quickly. They were both athletic, both studious, and they respected each other's need to spend time on the things they loved. A lot of people who don't compete get upset when their significant other dedicates a large amount of time to their passions, but because Jackson and Amanda were both competitive, they knew time with each other would be limited, and they rooted for each other to invest as much as needed into those passions.

Which made the short bursts of time they had together sexy and wild.

When Jackson's episodes came, Amanda put a little less of herself into her athletics so she could help him navigate his struggles. He didn't ask for her to do that, but she did it anyway because she loved him. She'd spend late nights on the phone with him when he couldn't sleep and talked him down when he'd freak out about his hallucinations. Her own burnout felt like a ghost whispering.

At the bottom of his descent, just before the big basketball incident, he came over to her house one night. Amanda's parents had gone out for the evening. When he arrived, he looked disheveled, and his eyes were bloodshot. He ground into his teeth like a drug addict.

Amanda let him in and tried to distract him by talking about her day. He turned to her and interrupted her story by ranting about shadows, and how they move. While he rambled, he stood up and walked toward her, closer and closer, and a horrible thought crossed Amanda's mind. *He's going to kill me*. He didn't, of course. Jackson had never even raised his voice to her before, but in that moment, he looked... feral.

Once she realized he wasn't going to hurt her, she still hurried the night along and sent him on his way fairly quickly. When she locked the door, she slid down to her butt and breathed relief at his absence.

She promised herself she'd never let anyone make her feel that way again, especially not someone she dated. And Jackson never did make her feel that way again. Shortly after, his episodes ended, and he went back to normal. Well, not normal. He lost something to the panic attacks, something that never came back.

But he never scared her again.

After high school, Jackson worked hard for Ray at the video store. Amanda didn't mind that Jackson never had money or that he had no ambitions outside of working hard for a company that dealt in a product years beyond its heyday, but she did resent how much her role as girlfriend had shifted toward caretaker.

Jackson couldn't afford to live on his current income, and Amanda often helped out where she could, which at first felt like the right thing for a girlfriend to do, but later started to feel like an expectation. She even gave Jackson and his father money to pay their bills sometimes. Mortgage. Electricity. Groceries.

Jackson never directly asked for these things. But he'd come to her stressed about them, and she'd offer, and that happened until it became a given. So, she stopped offering to see what would happen, and Jackson would continuously bring it up, never dropping the financial difficulties he faced. It was like he wouldn't accept no for an answer without actually asking the question in the first place, which she found both deceitful and cowardly.

Yet, she loved him. Part of that was from longevity, but there was something else, too. He had moments where he'd shine, moments of brilliance where she'd see in him what she saw all those years ago. This was someone who could go far. If only he could let himself.

Jackson didn't know this, but Amanda had heard word about Syracuse a long time ago. Nothing was set in stone, which was why she hadn't brought it up to him, but she had a good feeling it would work in her favor. And in her mind, she planned to cut the relationship off if she was offered the job. It would have broken her heart, and she would have hoped it would spark in him a renewed desire to change, but she felt if she didn't end it, she'd never get to fully thrive, as if she were running a race and Jackson lay on the ground behind her, clutching her leg, hoping she could carry them both to the finish line.

Then, Jackson's father got sick, and she knew it wasn't the right time to end it. And for a while, Jackson seemed to get better. He worked hard all day and came home to focus on his dad. Amanda was no longer this thing he had to cling to, and in fact, he'd sometimes go days without texting her. She started to doubt herself and thought maybe taking Jackson with her to Syracuse might be the very thing he needed to get back to his old self.

When she went to his house after Senior died and looked at Senior's old things, she saw the possibility of Jackson becoming an exact replica of his father, but she also saw Jackson trying, and that let her know he could branch away from it, become his own man. And in their grief, they found passion that night, like nothing she'd experienced with him in years.

And that was the last she'd seen of the Jackson she knew. When he came over and she found the pictures on his phone, it wasn't the photos themselves that freaked her out. They were weird, and creepy, but it wasn't the photos that broke her. It was him. His eyes were bloodshot again, and his movements were skittery. She once again had that voice in her head.

He's going to kill me.

He was the same Jackson she met that one night at her house during the height of his episodes. And it didn't matter if he'd just lost his father. She'd promised herself she'd never let herself feel that way again.

When she pulled up to her house after another long day at work, she found Jackson pacing in her driveway, smoking a cigarette. His face was speckled in something black, as if it had rained mud on him. His eyes were darting left and right. Her heart slammed into her chest.

She had to end it. For her own good, she had to. But it's hard to let go of someone you've loved, someone you've taken care of for years. It's especially hard when you know that person is hitting their bottom and facing some of the most difficult challenges of their life. He'd just lost his father.

She was afraid to open her car door. That's where this road had taken her. She was scared to get out of the car at her own house. But she did. She opened the door. Not out of love. Not anymore. Although love still existed for him. She opened the car door because she saw a wounded dog. Sometimes wounded animals bite, and sometimes they even kill, but she couldn't let the poor thing die without offering to heal it.

And she hated herself for that. Because she'd promised herself she'd never let herself feel this way again.

CHAPTER 17

JUST LIKE IN THE MOVIES

Jackson nearly cried when Amanda came out of her car, as if she were an invisible dome that could block out all the pain and terror racing toward him.

"Come in," she said as she walked past his car toward the front door.

He hurried to catch up to her. She stopped at the door to hold it open for him and scanned his face and shirt.

"Jesus, what the hell is that?"

"That's why I'm here."

They walked inside. She threw her purse on the couch and turned to him, crossing her arms around her ribs, and released a sigh. "What is it?"

"I dunno, blood or bile or something."

"God, Jackson. I meant what's wrong, but tell me you're kidding?" She leaned back, acting disgusted by the idea of being too close to him. "You're messing with animals again?" Her eyes widened and she balanced on her tiptoes, preparing to get away from him if she needed to.

"I have so much to tell you, but I don't know how."

"You're scaring me."

Tears gushed out of him, and he fought them, angry with himself for letting them out. This wouldn't help. It would make him look pathetic.

"I have so much to tell you," he said again.

One thing that always drove Jackson nuts in horror movies was when the main character tried to explain to authorities or family the paranormal events that invaded their life. Why would any person think another rational human being would just accept their illogical claims? *Oh, you battled a werewolf ghost? Awesome, I believe you.*

What's worse was when said main character showed surprise when no one believed them. *Why don't you believe me? A killer lamp-post bit me, I swear!*

But here Jackson stood, next to the woman he loved, trying to figure out how to explain his encounters with a dead girl. He figured he might be losing her anyway. It was hard to tell. At least this way, she would hear the truth. If she wanted to assume he'd lost his sanity, she should at least make those assumptions based on what really happened.

Even though he wanted to let her in on everything, he also wanted to minimize the craziness. He needed her to understand this was real, and not a rehashing of what happened to him in high school, so he skipped over his initial panic attacks, the figure he watched approach his father, and the hands he felt on his back in his father's final moments. He began with the shower door; this she saw, so it would be a good starting point. She may be more accepting of the strangeness that followed if she witnessed its conception.

From there, he explained the animals.

At the mere mention of the photographs, she shifted her legs, angling them away from him, and she scrunched her arms around herself.

Now he had to make a big jump in the story's absurdity: the dead girl. He told her about Alexandria Lucia, starting with the information he read in the papers. She chewed on the inside of her mouth while she tried to figure out where this played into the story.

When he said he found the girl, a change came over her. Her eyes glossed and he couldn't tell if she was petrified, completely unbelieving, or both. He quickly explained the police ruled it suicide, worried she may think *he* killed the girl. How she could think such a thing, he couldn't understand, but he knew it was there, lingering in her mind.

He had dulled the story, diminished the ethereal aspects, and now that he approached the finale, he had a long jump to make. He blurted it out, best just to rip off the Band-Aid.

"I know how crazy this sounds, but I saw her today, in my house. God, you sat through all of my hallucinations, and I know it seems like this is one of those, but how do you explain this stuff on my face? You see it too! That's why I didn't wash it off before you came home. So you could see this isn't a figment of my imagination."

Her hands cupped around her mouth, and her eyes seemed to grow twice their size as they filled with water. They sat in silence, staring at each other for an uncomfortable amount of time. Jackson quaked, waiting for her to respond.

"I know you don't believe me. How could you? But it's true."

"Jackson, please, just stop for a minute. Just stop. I really hate to do this to you, but I need you to leave. I'll text you later, but for right this minute, you have to get out. "

"Wait, talk to me."

"I need to think. We can talk later."

"You can't do that. I just need you to talk to me."

She clenched her teeth. "I don't care what you need right now. I'm sorry, but I don't. Get out of my house. Right now."

He put his hands up and stepped back. He tried not to cry, but the tears overpowered him. "Can I just wash my face?"

She scoffed. "No."

"Please. Amanda. You're all I have left. I feel like the world is turning against me, and you're the only rational thing still in my life."

"Jackson, I'm not asking again."

He took another step back, eyeing the bathroom. He didn't want to argue with her, and he didn't want to upset, but he thought if he just gave her a few minutes, some time to think about things, he could win her over.

"I'm just going to wash my face really quickly." He stepped into the bathroom, not waiting for her to respond.

He splashed warm water on his face and the black spots dripped into the sink. Then, he took his shirt off and put it under the water, whirling it around, squeezing it, whirling and squeezing. He took it out, drained the sink, and wrung the shirt.

Surprised to see the dark spots completely removed from the grey cotton, he sighed at the removal of death. He grabbed a hanger from the bathroom closet and hung the shirt on the shower rod. It felt good to be clean.

Now he just had to wait a few more minutes for Amanda to calm down.

He turned toward the bathroom door and fell backward. He stumbled over the side of the tub, smacking his head against the tiled shower wall.

Alexandria Lucia stood at the door.

"No. Not now. Please, not now."

He pushed himself up, ignoring the stinging on the back of his head. Before he could get back on his feet, Alexandria landed on top of him. Her fingers grabbed his wrists, pinning him down. Her strength outmatched his. No matter how much force he used to push his arms up, she kept him restrained with the weight of a truck. It might as well have been a building collapsing on top of him.

He twisted his torso, trying to disrupt her balance. She shifted with him, and they rotated from side to side.

Amanda knocked on the door. "Did you fall? Are you okay?"

The hot, putrid breath of the corpse blasted against his face. "No, I fell. Help me. Kick the door open."

"What?"

Alexandria leaned her face against his.

"Kick it open."

Her lips, wet and cold, touched his cheek.

"I can't do that."

The corpse groaned and one of her hands released his wrist.

"Please, Amanda. Please."

Her fingernails dug into his chest. He yelped in pain.

The door banged.

"Please hurry." If Amanda just opened that door, she'd either see the proof of his claims, or Alexandria would disappear, and he'd be free of her for the time.

Alexandria moved her lips to his ear and whispered, "No."

The door crashed open.

And Alexandria was gone. Of course, she disappeared. Just like in the movies, when the character is trying to prove he isn't crazy, the paranormal vanishes before anyone else can witness it.

A part of him expected this to happen. He used that forethought when he'd told Amanda he fell, instead of saying, "A grotesque, bloated ghost is beating me up." His latest goal was to minimize his outward lunacy.

What he didn't prepare for was the scratches, which had gained Amanda's attention. He stood up and she looked at him, mouth agape, focusing on the marks across his chest.

"I scratched myself when I fell." He answered the question she didn't ask.

She nodded, not really listening. Jackson's attention left the bathroom as he heard sirens approaching. Across the hall, through the den windows, red and blue lights flashed.

"Oh."

She backed away. "I'm so sorry, Jackson. You need help."

CHAPTER 18
A MATTER OF LIES AND DEATH

Carvallo leaned his chair on its two back legs. Jackson thought he might be trying to intimidate him with the silence and the way he kept looking Jackson up and down. If so, his plan failed. Maybe if he didn't know Carvallo, he would find him intimidating, but it's hard to worry about a guy who spent his days obsessing about teenagers and their athletic abilities.

"Where did the scratches come from?"

"I scratched myself."

"Nah. The angle is all wrong."

"I don't know what else to tell you. I scratched myself."

"What about the blood you had on your face and shirt? Amanda said you were covered in it." Jackson looked down at his black tee shirt he took from Amanda's closet before going outside to meet the police and considered himself lucky for having washed his face and the grey shirt.

"There was a dead deer on Almeda. That's a dangerous road. I didn't want anyone to swerve and kill themselves. So, I moved it."

"Uh huh."

"Go check if you want. I'm sure it's still there. Someone nailed it. Must have messed up their car pretty bad."

"You've been finding a lot of dead things lately, huh?"

"Like what? My father, who I took care of while cancer ate away at him?" He hoped the sympathy would work in his favor.

Carvallo leaned forward, the chair's front legs slapping against the hard floor. "Or the teenage girl tucked away from the main road."

"Are you implying I had something to do with what happened to her? I thought you guys already had that one wrapped up?"

"I find it curious how you showed up the next day, nervously I might add, asking what we found out."

"Seriously?"

"Now your high school sweetheart is running on about how she thinks you might be harming animals. She said she wondered if you dug up the dead girl, said you've become obsessed with dead things. This is your girlfriend."

"We're going through a rough patch."

Carvallo slammed his palm against the table and laughed. "I'd say! My wife accused me of eating the last donut this morning. Not murder, though."

"Who did I kill?"

"I know you didn't kill anyone. The girl committed suicide. I also know you didn't dig her up because I happen to know where her body is, and it is very much where it's supposed to be."

"Then what the fuck am I doing here?" His eyes went to the door. He wanted it to open, wanted to walk away from here. The room's walls closed in on him.

"I just want to know what's going on. There's more to you stumbling on that corpse than you're letting on. And what's with the animals? Do you really have pictures of dead animals in your phone?"

"I promise you, everything is exactly as I've explained it. Just a lot of coincidences with the timing."

"But your girlfriend is afraid of you. What's that about?"

"The pictures. They freaked her out. I started collecting photos of roadkill. I don't know why. It seemed interesting to me. Maybe I grew a morbid curiosity after my dad died. That's also why I found the girl. Almeda has a lot of dead animals around the road. I noticed the car when I stopped to look at a fox one time. The next day I decided to check that area out, figuring there'd be a lot of animals. And I won't lie, the shimmering made me curious."

"You're an odd kid. Always were."

"Yeah."

"You're not a killer, though."

"No, sir."

"But those scratches are bothering me."

"I scratched myself. I told you this."

"You did, but that ain't right."

Jackson sighed. He was out of things to say about it.

"You should stay away from Amanda."

Jackson straightened. "What?"

"Son, she thinks you killed animals. You may want to call a cow a burger and accept that the relationship is cooked."

"No. She's just freaked about the pictures. She'll calm down."

Carvallo pushed his chair forward; if not for the table, Jackson thought he might have climbed on top of him. "I'm going to have to insist you stay away until she contacts you. If you're right, and she'll get over it, let her take the time to do so."

"Okay."

"Are we clear on that? I have to insist."

"Yeah." He pinned his eyes on Carvallo's, turning his face to stone, covering up any tells.

"I'm going to drive you home. I'll have someone bring your car back to your house. You can't go back there. That needs to be as clear as a saint's conscience. I know I have said it a few times now, but I'm gonna say it a few more. It needs to be stuck in your brain. No exceptions. You stay away until she comes to you."

Jackson stood up. "Got it. Can you get me out of here, please?"

When they left the station, the night had brought an empty blackness over the world. Carvallo changed characters as he drove, going from the concerned Assistant Sheriff to the high school basketball fan. He cracked jokes about the modern players, saying they paled in comparison to Jackson's team. Jackson remembered him saying the same when he played. The thing about guys like Carvallo, they always think yesterday was better than today.

Jackson started to feel relief until Carvallo turned down Almeda. "Let's make sure that deer you found is way outta the way."

The Assistant Sheriff returned, and he planned to check out Jackson's story. Why would Jackson say something so stupid? His biggest lie regarded the easiest thing to check up on.

"I moved it way off the road. Not easy, he was a heavy bastard." Details. Flesh the story out.

"Those things can be. I'm surprised you were able to get him over by yourself." Translation: *You were lying, and I am about to prove it.*

"I don't think it was an adult."

Carvallo turned his head back and forth, barely putting his foot on the gas. "Just let me know when we get to it."

Jackson pointed to the spot where he had found the fox. He hoped the fox's blood remained mixed in the dirt, so when no deer turned up, he could try to use that as proof it was there at one point.

Carvallo pulled the car off the road, the tires crunching in the gravel. It turned out Jackson didn't need the fox blood to cover his story. A massive deer lay mangled in the woods five feet behind where the fox had been. Blood painted the creature and pooled around its corpse.

Carvallo jammed the car in park. "Jesus, you weren't lying. That thing is huge. You didn't think that was an adult? God damn, son."

Carvallo hopped out of the car with vigor Jackson wouldn't have guessed the old man had in him. Jackson followed, masking his bewilderment. Sure, it wasn't uncommon for cars to nail deer on this road, but this coincidence served him too perfectly. Jackson and luck didn't spend much time together, but for this one, he owed it a huge thank you. Who was Jackson kidding? The luck he had experienced, both the good and the bad, went by the name Alexandria. Her hands were all over this.

The woods were alive with nighttime chirping from crickets and peepers. It was peaceful, even with the sanguinary scene in front of them.

"I can sure see how you got yourself covered in blood too. Big boy here is draining like a faucet." Carvallo leaned in front of it.

Jackson approached from behind him, wondering if the blood would mess up his story. If he found the deer hours ago, would it still be bleeding now? While he stepped, movement caught his attention across the street in front of the Milner House. He looked from the corner of his eye and Alexandria Lucia stared at him from the line of rhododendrons that hid her car.

He quickly put his attention back on the deer, hoping she would go away if he ignored her. He tensed up. *Go away. Please go away.*

Carvallo used a thick branch to prod at the deer.

"What are you doing?"

"Doesn't look like a car did this."

Carvallo had convinced himself Jackson had killed the deer, just as Amanda had assumed he killed the animals he photographed, and now Carvallo was looking for holes in Jackson's story. It didn't matter. Even if he discovered someone mutilated the deer with a carving knife, Jackson's story worked. How could he know how the thing died? He saw a deer on Almeda and assumed a car struck it. What else would you assume, unless you prodded it with a stick? Let Carvallo think what he wanted.

"Let me ask you something," Carvallo said as he lifted the deer's limb with the stick. As the leg spread, a series of slashes revealed itself. Something had cut it up, brutally.

"Yeah?"

"What happened in game one of your senior year?"

"I choked." Why was Carvallo asking such stupid questions?

Carvallo turned his head away from the deer, putting his gaze directly on Jackson's eyes.

"You choked? Well, that we know. You choked and you punched."

Jackson smiled. Carvallo didn't.

"I snapped. I've never done anything like that again."

Carvallo stood up, dusting off his hands. Jackson flicked his vision back to the Milner House. Alexandria remained in place.

"You were an animal unleashed that day, son."

"I know."

"This deer ain't got eyes."

"What?" Carvallo was all over the place. Basketball, the deer, Jackson couldn't keep up.

"Someone took the damn thing's eyes."

In his peripheral, Alexandria flailed. It was a quick motion, a gyrating of the arms, but it was a strong enough movement that he caught it clearly out of the corners of his eyes.

First came the screeching of rubber on cement. It was a violent sound, like a baby screaming with fever.

After that, it was the crash of aluminum, steel, and glass. It boomed, reverberating through the forest. It could have been a car accident, or it could have been a fault line shifting across the galaxy.

Jackson turned in time to see a shower of plastics and glass spraying the air in a rainstorm. He dove toward the woods, colliding with the hard earth between two oaks, and turned around to see the disaster unfold.

A red Chevy Tahoe had skidded off the road. The side of it had smacked into the back of the cruiser, pushing the car forward. When Jackson turned, the cruiser was still moving and the SUV was on top of it, flipping in an acrobatic display.

Carvallo was on top of the cruiser's hood. He must have jumped on it in an attempt to avoid being hit by the front end when it was pushed forward.

The Tahoe rolled off the cruiser. The top of the SUV met the windshield of the cruiser and then continued to roll right over Carvallo. His body flopped like a doll.

When the Tahoe hit the ground, it landed on the passenger side tires, almost hovering at a 75-degree angle, like it might stay that way, suspended on two wheels for eternity. With just enough luck, it could land safely on all four tires. Jackson watched it while the seconds dripped away in a slow leak.

"No," he whispered while he watched the weight of the car lose out to gravity.

It slammed into the ground, swallowing the dead deer. Clouds of dirt and debris puffed out from all sides. Glass sprayed everywhere.

Across the street, Alexandria walked away, while a stream of smoke began to pour from the Tahoe's hood.

Jackson didn't think; there was no time for that. He just reacted. First, he ran to Carvallo. The muscles in his back ached again from slamming them into the ground, but he had to ignore it for now.

Carvallo's body was soaked in blood and his mangled limbs were spread into positions limbs can't go.

"Carvallo!" He chose not to touch the body. Who knew how they would find a way to blame him? It didn't matter, anyway. Carvallo was long gone, possibly in worse shape than the deer. Jackson couldn't do anything for him.

He shot around and ran to the SUV. The smoke continued to pour out of the hood, turning thicker and blacker. The driver, if not dead already, would be soon if he didn't get away from the car.

This time he took a few seconds to think before acting. He could die too, if he didn't get the hell away from there, but he couldn't just let the driver die without seeing if he could help first.

He stood at the roof, reached his hands up to the driver's side door, and lifted himself up, climbing onto the door, which was now the top of the Tahoe. He placed his feet on the back door and leaned toward the driver's window, looking down at the panicked man trying to unbuckle himself.

Streaks of red ran across the man's grey hair and trickled down his forehead and cheek. Speckles of glass twinkled all over the man's clothes and inside the car. He slapped at the buckle. It wouldn't unclip.

Luckily, the window was down. He hoped to have more room to get the man out, but the window space was fairly big, and it would have to do.

The man looked up at him. The blood on his forehead rolled into his eyes. He reached a hand toward Jackson. "Help me."

"Okay. Okay, listen. I'm going to grab your hand and pull you up. As I do, I need you to use your other hand to unbuckle that belt. It's not opening because your weight is on it."

The man nodded, but Jackson wasn't sure he heard him. He grabbed the man's arm and yanked upward. "Now hit the belt. Hit the belt."

Jackson's arm stretched and crunched as it pulled away from the socket. If he didn't hurry, he wouldn't be able to lift the man. The man fumbled to find the buckle. His sweaty hand pulled away from Jackson. He was losing him. The man's other hand found the buckle and he clicked it. It didn't release. Panic took over and his finger pressed the button rapidly. "Come on. Come on."

Jackson gripped the man's wrist and moved his other hand to the man's arm. He pulled harder. The muscles in his arms, chest, back, and abs all clenched. His entire upper body felt like it was going to give in.

"You have to get that belt off."

The man's hands fumbled on the buckle. "I'm trying. I'm trying."

The wind took the bellows of smoke. Black, thick streams covered Jackson, making it harder for him to see. The clouds were hot. He turned his attention from the man and saw huge flames coming from the hood.

"You have to do it now."

The seatbelt snapped free and collapsed in on itself, wrapping around the man's arm. The full weight of the man pulled Jackson down. He tried lifting, but the guy was too heavy.

Jackson yelled as his muscles stretched and his socket popped. The pain burned from Jackson's shoulder down to his lower back.

"I'm sorry," the man said as he latched his hands onto Jackson's shoulders and lifted himself.

He couldn't believe the guy was apologizing. The flames grew, and the wind made them flicker and dance.

As the man pulled up, Jackson released his grip and quickly latched onto the man's underarms. From this position, he had an easier time pulling. The man separated his arm from the belt loop and lunged his upper body onto the back door with Jackson. He pressed his feet along the side of the seat and yanked the rest of his body out.

The flames blasted from the hood, dangerously close to the trees. "Come on. We gotta get away from this thing."

He jumped off, buckling as he landed. The man followed. Jackson helped him stabilize and they ran across the street. They turned back to the car and watched the flames leak from the hood. They managed a few seconds of regaining their breath before bad turned worse.

A white Buick Roadmaster with wood paneling on the side sped by, and the flames caught the driver's attention. Jackson saw it happen before it actually did, knowing how it would go, expecting disaster. The driver's drifted attention made him lose control. Like a moth, he veered his Buick directly into the fiery SUV. An explosion of metal and glass and fire erupted on the other side of the road.

YOU CAN'T BREAK A PROMISE TO A DEAD MAN

Red and blue lights swirled across the iron-black evening sky. Horns and sirens disturbed the serenity of the woods, drowning out the peepers and crickets. The firefighters had put out the fire, an ambulance drove the Tahoe driver to the hospital, and Carvallo's body headed to the morgue. Yet firetrucks, cruisers, and ambulances continued to pollute Almeda.

"It was like the car was steering itself," the Tahoe driver told the officers.

The Roadmaster's driver, AKA the moth, probably would have said the same thing, but he died on impact. His charred body was cremated like that of a citizen of Pompei. Jackson knew what caused both cars to crash. Alexandria. The first was to say, "I can help you," and the second was to say, "Or I can destroy you."

Jackson dug his thumbs into his temples, trying to massage the headache. He sat on the porch of the Milner House, watching the men and women scurry around the scene, yelling to each other, taking pictures, trying to make sense of it all.

He lit a cigarette, knowing it would only worsen the headache, but yearning for one enough not to care. The first drag filled his lungs, and he relaxed. His whole body throbbed from the workout of helping the man out of his car, and muscles he didn't know he had hurt when he moved, coughed, or even breathed too deeply.

"This is unbelievable," Sheriff Alingon said, coming up on his side.

"Been a fuck of a day." He inhaled hard, pushing the smoke toward his chest, feeling it against his sore muscles.

"Was Carvallo planning on taking you home after he checked out the deer?"

"To my car, at my girlfriend's house." It made him nervous to lie. Just before they had left the station, Carvallo had spoken privately to a few of the Deputies. If he had told them anything, Jackson might get caught in the lie. Not to mention, Alingon must have known Amanda had called them, and that's why he was in this situation to begin with.

"All right, come on. I'll take you."

Jackson's shoulders eased.

They drove in silence, disrupting it only when Jackson needed to tell Alingon where to turn. When they pulled into Amanda's driveway, he caught her peeling back a shade, furtively watching. The sight of her half-tempted him to go to the door, explain to her that the police proved him innocent, make her understand he didn't kill anyone, but it would only frighten her more if he acted so aggressively. Texting her later seemed more logical.

After everything that happened tonight, his relationship seemed almost trivial, but then again, it also felt like the crutch he needed to stay upright.

He drove home, avoiding Almeda. Taking the long way worked just fine for him. The idea of going to his house scared him, but if Amanda's bathroom and Almeda Road proved anything, no place offered safety from Alexandria.

Why did she attack him? Why did she hum for him to come to her and find her, only to try to kill him by creating a car accident? What did she mean when she said, "No more," at Amanda's house?

He became aware of the slashes on his chest again, and he rubbed his fingers against the wound. The flesh around it had raised and swelled. With his luck, probably turning toward infection. He supposed rotting, bacteria-infested nails clawing at your skin will do that.

Every time a headlight flashed in his rearview, he jerked in his seat. The list of things that frightened him grew exponentially every day. Alexandria could be behind any light, sound, sensation, or dream. She could be anywhere at any time. Until he figured it out, he would never know peace. Those hands on his shoulders were a distant memory.

He pulled into his driveway and debated sleeping in the car. That way, if she attacked again, chances were Miss Nosy next door would see it. In a way, the crabby old lady prevented him from being alone. Maybe her nosiness wasn't so bad after all.

His shift started early tomorrow, and Ray might still be pissed about Jackson's tardiness, so he needed to sleep well tonight. The car would not suffice. He also needed an alarm, and his phone battery would never survive long enough to wake him in the morning.

He paraded through the house, turning on every light in every room. He opted for the couch again. The bedrooms made him claustrophobic. He dragged a pillow and blanket over, made a bed for himself on the couch, and turned NESN on. They were replaying the Sox game. He turned the volume up, hoping it would drown out any sound anomalies that might occur while he slept.

Every time he drifted, his body jerked upright a few minutes later, protecting him from the vulnerability of sleep. He tried to calm himself, but every time he awoke, his heart made a death metal beat against his ribs. By the time he relaxed himself, an hour would waste away, and he would repeat the cycle. The night slipped away from him. The black sky turned dark blue.

His alarm blared and he slapped it silent, already in a sitting position, watching infomercials, having long ago given up on sleep. His eyes burned and his chest felt cold. He wanted to call out of work, considered it while he showered and ate breakfast, but knew Ray held a grudge about the other day, and he didn't want to further the sting.

Besides, he needed to make money.

He drove to work with every muscle aching, every ounce of his patience languished by the lack of sleep, every piece of sanity up for debate.

Ray came up to him in the parking lot before they started the morning drill. "I'm sorry about the other day. Must be getting grumpy with my old age. That or I'm just pissed to see this place go. I've been holding onto that anger for a while now. Not that I condone you showing up late, but I know it's not how you are, and I know you got a lot going on right now. Anyway, I'm sorry. That's all I got. I'm sorry."

"You wanna hug it out, old man?" Jackson put his hands up and Ray wrapped his bulbous arms around him.

"I love ya' buddy."

"You too, boss man. I'm sorry I showed up late. I had slept through my alarm. I'm having a tough time sleeping at home."

"I can tell. Your eyes look like fireballs."

"Yeah, I can't sleep. I may need pills."

"Same shit that happened to me, friend. Go see a doctor. Get a script and get yourself some rest. Do it soon. I told you before; you don't want to end up like I did."

"Yeah."

Ray sighed and thought of something else to talk about. "Hey, did you see the news today? Carvallo died. Apparently, there was a huge accident over on Almeda."

Jackson shivered. "I heard about it. I don't want to talk about it."

"Oh, yeah, you knew Carvallo, didn't you? Basketball and all that jazz. I'm sorry, buddy. I don't know what to say."

Jackson closed his eyes and took a deep breath. "I didn't. I mean, I knew him, but we weren't close. It's sad, but, to be honest..." He stopped there, unsure how to go on; *but to be honest, I have bigger things to deal with, like spiteful spirits, who, I might add, are kind of responsible for Carvallo dying?*

Jackson worked the day, keeping in his own head, thinking about Alexandria. He decided he should investigate her more. Maybe he could find answers to why she was attacking him. He wondered if he reminded her of someone negative in her life. But why then, had she hummed and called him to her?

At lunchtime, he sat in his car, smoking a cigarette, picking on a sub from PizzAmore. He hadn't messaged Amanda yet. He was eager to say something to her but had no idea what could be said at this point. Time was slipping away. She would be leaving soon, and he wanted things to work out before she did. If the tryouts went well, she may not come back.

> The police let me go because I DID NOT hurt anyone and I AM NOT crazy. Do you think they would have let me go if they even suspected it a little bit??????????

He rested his head back against the seat, debating if he should send it. He glanced in the rearview and screamed in surprise.

Alexandria gripped her hands around his cheeks. He flailed, trying to get away.

One of her fingers hooked onto his lip. He pushed himself forward, but she yanked his cheek. He was a fish on her line.

She screamed, "No!"

He twisted his head, opened the door, and stumbled out of the car. He didn't look back. He just ran.

A young couple exiting their vehicle laughed as he frantically made his way inside. He turned his run into a walk as he entered Valiant, but he still moved with speed, past Ray, past the shelves, head down, toward the back room.

"What's all over your face?" Ray yelled.

Jackson ignored him, keeping his pace. He moved straight to the bathroom. He scrubbed the muddy gunk her hands left on his cheeks. After he removed it all, he continued to splash water on his face. "Get off me. Get off me. Get off me."

His eyes had sunken into his face, and his cheeks had lost all color. His hair draped down his forehead around his eyes. He looked like shit. He felt like it, too.

"Everything all right, friend?" Ray knocked on the door.

"Yeah, yeah. I just spilled my sub all over myself and it was hot."

He sat on the toilet. A panic attack built in his chest. His heart pounded. His fingers turned numb. He was going to die. He went to his breathing. Inhale, hold it, exhale. Inhale, what the fuck, exhale. Inhale, he couldn't take it anymore, exhale.

He was sick of playing defense, sick of letting these weird things happen to him, and not being able to do anything in return. He needed to strike back. If things continued the way they were, he would never get a sound sleep. His body would never be able to keep up with the pain. He would start losing his mind. *Start?* It was time to face Alexandria head-on.

He went back to work, fighting with the attack all day, ignoring it as best he could.

After work, he drove home. "I'm going to figure out why you're doing this," he told the backseat.

It was easier to find her address than he expected. Luckily, the newspaper mentioned she lived in the Shannock part of Richmond. There was only one listing for anyone named Lucia in Shannock. The name belonged to Alaina Lucia, and in a small town like that, if she wasn't Alexandria's mother, she would know where to find her.

He found her house in Shannock. A blue station wagon straight out of an eighties movie sat on the humped sidewalk that merged into the driveway, which had a thin layer of grass cruising up the center, like it had a Mohawk. The house was a double-decker row, thin and scrunched between a series of other double-decker rows. He climbed the frail wooden steps onto the soggy porch floorboards. The blue paint on the house had chipped and peeled. The edges of the stained yellow curtains in the windows curled inward.

The screen door wailed as he opened it, and he knocked on the front door with the metal knocker. He heard footsteps walking across the old floorboards, and the door opened with a groan.

A tall woman in her fifties answered, sucking at her cigarette. Her orange hair twisted and turned in on itself: ocean waves crashing into each other. The veins on her arms and legs protruded, leaving purple roadmaps across her skin. Her knees and elbows were knobbed. They looked like car tires on tree branches.

"What the fuck do you want?"

Jackson expected to see a distressed woman, broken at the loss of her daughter. He didn't see this type of aggression coming. "Uh, I wanted to ask you about. . . "

". . . I got nothing to say about her. Quit comin' around here. Tell your friends, too."

"I've never been here?"

She started to close the door. "Might as well have. Get the fuck off my property. I ain't got nothin' to say."

He slapped his palm against the door, stopping it from closing on his face. Her eyes opened wide, and she pushed harder.

"Ma'am. I'm not a news person if that's what you think."

She used her hip to push the door. "I don't give a fuck what you are. Get off my property."

The door slammed. He yelled through it. "I'm the one who found Alexandria. I found her and her car in the woods by the Milner House."

He waited, but it didn't take long for her to reopen the door.

"Still doesn't explain what you want."

"I guess I just wanted to know about the girl I found. I've been having nightmares since I found her. I thought, maybe if I knew a little about who she was, I'd feel better. I want to know the person behind the. . . " He stopped himself.

"Behind the body." The aggression left her voice and a somberness replaced it.

He hung his head in shame. "Yeah."

She stared at him for a moment, sizing him up. "Well, fuck. Come in." She walked inside, not waiting for him to follow.

The ease with which she went from yelling at him to letting a complete stranger into her house surprised Jackson.

He caught up to her and kept pace while she went into the living room and plopped herself on a beige hamburger-cushioned couch. He imagined Alexandria plopping her bookbag on that couch after a tiring day at school. He sat on a Victorian chaise across from her mother. The dusty fabric looked like an episode of Pokémon puked all over it. Deep, bright colors splashed into each other as the fabric wrapped around the solid wood frame. He had to remind himself that the itching was psychological; he couldn't really feel the dust mites eating his flesh.

Alexandria's mother flicked her cigarette ash into a ceramic ashtray that sat on a wooden coffee table with a glass top. The glass had solidified coffee rings in multiple spots.

"Lexia's father always made her promise not to go to that place. He had some horror stories about it. Said he went there as a kid or some shit. Haunted nonsense. He made her promise, and I'll bet that's why she chose that fuckin' place. Just to shove it up his ass."

"Do you mind if I smoke?"

She nodded.

He put a cigarette between his lips. "Is her father around?"

"Oh, he's long dead. Good riddance. He was an angry man. Lexia hated his guts. I don't blame her. That's why she went there. To shove it up his ass. Break her promise to him. Not that you can break a promise to a dead man."

"Do you think that's why she did it? She was angry at him?"

"What? Kill herself? Oh no. He died years ago. She didn't give a fuck enough about him. She just chose that spot to give him a final fuck you. You know what I mean?"

He inhaled and let the smoke exit through his nose. "So why did she do it, if you don't mind me asking?"

"That's hard to explain. You gotta know Lexia. She was fragile, let stuff eat at her. She didn't like not being liked. She wanted everyone to love her, but in tryin' to get everyone to, she made it so no one did. Ya know, besides me. She was overbearin', needy. She always just wanted someone to talk to. All the time, though. Didn't stop yappin' even when she was alone in her room. She'd just yammer on to herself."

He thought he might have a guess where she got it from. Alexandria's mother went from *I don't want to talk to anyone,* to chatterbox in .02 seconds. He saw a brief glimmer of light in her eyes when she realized she had someone to talk to about her daughter. Someone who wasn't trying to cover a story in the papers anyway.

"Did Alexandria date anyone?"

"Stop callin' her that, please."

"Huh?"

"Alexandria. She didn't like that. She liked Lexia. She's dead. Least we can do is respect her wishes on that matter."

"I'm sorry, ma'am. Did she. . . "

". . . And while we're on it, stop calling me ma'am. Names Alaina. Some people call me Laney. Some call me Lain. Any of those work for me, just not ma'am. Makes me feel old."

"Okay, Alaina. I'm Jackson, by the way. Did. . . Lexia. . . date anyone?"

She took her cigarette from the ceramic ashtray, leaving a worm of ash in the dish, and used the stub to light another one. "Yeah, she dated this kid, Jason. He was a good kid. She drove the poor bastard nuts. Poor girl, she was too young to know ya can't be so clingy."

"Did they fight a lot?"

The head of her cigarette turned orange, and her lungs expanded. She held it in for a few seconds. "What are you tryin' to do?"

"Huh?"

"I get it. I do. I did the same thing at first."

"What do you mean?"

"Your wonderin' if maybe this boyfriend killed her? Tryin' to come up with any other answer. Don't want to believe she killed herself? I just don't understand why you're doing it. For me, it makes sense. I'm her mother. I *should* have doubts. Who wants to believe they fucked up so badly that their kid goes off and kills themselves? But you, you just found her. What difference does it make to you?"

"I'm not. I promise you. I'm not trying to find out anything other than why she did it. I feel like, I don't know, like I owe her that, like I had stumbled on some version of her she wouldn't have wanted anyone to see, and I have to make it right by seeing the whole picture."

Alaina's eyes turned to slits as she judged his explanation. After a few seconds, she smooshed the cigarette into the tray and stood up. "All right. Come with me."

He followed her, unsure if she was leading him to secrets or out the door. Her legs creaked with the hardwood floor as they made their way down a thin hallway. He found it odd the way she talked about her daughter, as if Alexandria was someone from a distant past, not someone who walked these halls just a few weeks ago.

She walked him into a bedroom. The small room had enough space for a twin-sized bed and an oak dresser, but not much else. Lexia had covered the dull orange walls with posters of celebrity men. Jackson recognized the brothers from *Supernatural,* but he guessed he had gotten too old to recognize the rest of them.

She had taped dozens of pictures to the dresser mirror. Most of them were of her with a boy, presumably Jason. They looked happy, but that's the point of a picture, isn't it? To pretend.

Her mother raised her arms like a carnival barker showing off the amusements. "You wanna know who she was? This was her. Just an average teenage girl. Checkin' out boys. Happy one minute, sad the next. Filled with angst and rage until she was bored of it, then she might sulk for a while before decidin' to be happy again. Just like I was. Just like they all are."

Jackson put his finger on a picture taped to the mirror. Alexandria smiled with a mouth full of braces. She looked a few years younger than in the paper's photo. The boy—presumably Jason—stood behind her, his arms latched around her, and his chin rested on her shoulder. They both cheesed huge smiles.

"She was fifteen then. Her and Jason took that at Snug Harbor."

She sat down on the corner of the twin bed, staring at the pictures like a proud mother watching her daughter's dance recital. For the first time, she showed herself as a grieving mother.

"Jackson is it?"

"Yeah."

"You swear to me you are what you say you are?"

He turned to her, wanting her to see the sincerity in his face. "I promise."

She stood up and trotted to the dresser, opening the top drawer. "I still don't understand why you're so concerned, but I'm glad someone cares besides me. Now, listen." She stopped searching for whatever she looked for in the drawer and pinned her stare right on him, drilling her gaze into him.

He nodded.

She went back to the drawer, tossing strapped tees and bras to the side. She pulled out a few notebooks. Silver marker graffitied the front cover: Lexia in big block letters, the other words he assumed were band names he had never heard of.

"These were hers. I read them once a long time ago. It's mostly nonsense. Just teenage rantin' and ravin'. I've wanted to read them again since she died, but I can't bring myself to do it. The police took them when she disappeared. They returned them when they found her. When *you* found her. Every day, I fight with myself to try and read them again. I just can't do it." Her voice cracked. "I know why she did it, but I don't know, ya know? She was impulsive and sad and emotional, but what made her do it? What was the final straw? I know she got sad." The crying took over.

Jackson understood Laney now. She was a strong woman. From the way she talked about Lexia's father, he guessed Laney raised Alexandria without much help. She grieved for her daughter like anyone else but refused to show that to other people. If you let the outside world see life beating you up, it will swarm at the sight of your blood. Life kicked your ass, and the scavengers stole your wallet while you were down.

He hugged her and she awkwardly put her arms around him. After a moment, she let go, wiping away the tears and taking a deep breath. She let herself cry and now it was behind her. She brought herself back to hard-ass Laney.

"I want to know what she had to say. I just can't read them. But there's more to it than that." She shuffled the pages in her hands. "When she was in school, sometimes I'd flip through them, ya know, bein' nosy. There was just your normal teenage nonsense, but sometimes it got really weird. Really...odd."

Jackson's eyes widened.

"She would say stuff that just wasn't right. She'd write about death a lot. She wasn't gothic or anything. Thank God. I would never tell her how to dress, but I would have been bitin' my tongue if she started wearin' black fishnet stockings and black lipstick."

Jackson wanted to snatch the notebooks from her and dive right in. His fingers tapped against his belt.

"Just weird stuff, like she was obsessed with it."

He wanted to see if he could read them but was afraid to ask. He hoped she was leading up to it, wanting him to read them since she couldn't.

"I'll make you a deal."

"Yeah," he said, trying to mask his excitement.

"You come by again. You come and talk to me about my daughter. I don't have no one to talk to about her. You do that..." Her voice trailed as she thought for a second. Her fingers continued to flip through the notebooks, fanning them. "You do that, and let me get to know you, and I'll talk to you about what's in these. God, she'd kill me if she knew I ever read them, let alone talked to some stranger about them. Anyway, maybe if you and I can get along and I can feel comfortable with you, I'll get the nerve to go through these again, and then you can get to know about her. We'll learn together. Sounds awful, I'm her friggin' mother, and I gotta learn about her by invading her privacy after she died."

He wanted to tell her he needed the books, that he would read them for her if she had trouble with it, but how do you present that? *Excuse me, ma'am, I mean, Laney, but I don't have time to wait while you "get to know me," because that daughter you love is actually quite the little psycho and her ghost keeps kicking my ass. You see, if I don't find out about her NOW, she is probably gonna break me down until she kills me.*

"That would be awesome," was all he could come up with.

"Now come have some ice cream with me before you go. I'll tell you about the time she dragged me to see some shitty pop group at The Dunk."

They sat at the kitchen island and ate caramel swirl ice cream. She had held onto the books and brought them into the kitchen, leaving them on the island as they ate. He kept glancing at them, enticed by them, wanting to tear them open and read every word. She talked about her daughter and her daughter's quirks, talking about the things she hated, but describing it with love. When facing the death of a loved one, you learn the traits you hated in them are usually the most beautiful attributes they had. What annoyed you, you end up craving. What angered you becomes what you mourn.

He almost asked her if she experienced anything paranormal, but decided that if Laney found it crazy, she may kick him right out the door, and then he'd never have a chance to look at those books. Instead, he ate his ice cream and let her do the talking. She needed it.

After they finished eating, she walked him to the door and put her hand on his arm. "Please come back and visit."

He smiled. "I will. I promise."

He sat in his car, thinking about the books, eager to know what the "odd things" were that Lexia had written about. He had noticed one thing while Laney fanned through the pages: the writing changed frequently, turning from messy to neat, big loopy letters to detailed blocky letters. The poor girl couldn't even figure out who she was in her own words.

He scanned the porch and the side of the house, wondering if it would be easy to break in. *Break in? What the hell was wrong with him? He was a cat burglar now?*

The windows on the side of the house were high off the ground. It would take too much reaching. The windows on the porch looked too secure. They would probably be locked, and he would have to smash them. Then he remembered the door. That old wooden door had one of those standard twist locks, but the wood was old and weak. He could probably unlock it by shifting a credit card through the side. He had to do that a few times when he was a teenager when he forgot his keys and stayed out too late. He'd think about it.

As excited as he was to plan his burglary, he had something more important to do first.

He had promised Carvallo he wouldn't see Amanda until she contacted him, but as Alaina said, you couldn't break a promise to a dead man.

CHAPTER 20

SO CLOSE TO HER, SO FAR AWAY

Jackson pulled into Amanda's driveway and noticed her peeking out the window as his headlights drenched the front of the house. She quickly moved away. He debated with himself whether he should follow through, but it didn't take much convincing.

He knocked on the door and listened as her feet stepped closer. The sound was slight. He pictured her on tiptoe, trying to avoid making any noise.

"You don't have to answer. I know you're scared. I'll just talk through the door."

He waited, hoping for a response. None came.

"Did you get my message?"

No response. He opened his phone and looked at his texts so he could read it to her, but realized it sat in his drafts, unsent. Alexandria had attacked him, and he had forgotten to send it. Which was good, because now that he read it, it looked crazed.

"The police let me go, Amanda. I didn't kill anyone and I'm not crazy. Would they have let me leave so quickly if they even suspected one tiny thing? I didn't tell you the whole truth, though. Let me just tell you the whole truth and I'll leave.

"I found that girl completely by accident, and when I saw her. . . it wasn't like my dad or the animals. It was awful, Amanda. She was long dead, and horrible to see, and. . . I just lost it. I haven't been able to sleep or close my eyes without seeing it. When you saw me, I hadn't slept in days. Literally, days. I was practically hallucinating from lack of sleep. Do you remember when that happened to me in high school? It was like that. I had blood all over me because there was a deer on Almeda and I moved it off the road. The blood covered me, and my mind just snapped. I am so sick of seeing blood and death. And I just felt so haunted and messed up from everything. I made up the story about the ghost because it's how it all felt. I feel like she's haunting me because I can't stop seeing her.

"You're right about one thing. I'm not okay. I'm losing it, Amanda. I need help. I need you. I just want to feel normal again. I'm not looking to find dead things in the road anymore, I'm looking to get away from it. I don't want to see death again. I don't want to see it ever again."

His voice shook as he turned the lie into truth. "I'm just alone all the time, with no one to talk to about this stuff and it's all just been weighing on me. It just keeps piling on, and I'm not handling my dad's death very well, and I don't know what to do. I just want to sit and watch movies with you and not think about it and feel okay again. I just want to forget about my dad. I just want to get a good night's sleep without having nightmares."

He waited and nothing came. "Okay. I'm going to go. I just wanted to tell you that."

He walked down the porch stairs, and the door creaked behind him. He turned and Amanda leaned on the doorframe with pitying eyes. "Come in." It came out as a whisper, and she cleared her throat.

They walked into the living room, and she turned, still keeping a small distance from him, unable to hide the fear from her wide eyes.

He moved toward her; she leaned back but didn't step away. He slowly put his arms around her. As soon as their bodies touched, she pulled back.

"Amanda, I love you."

"I love you, too, but this is all too much for me, Jackie."

He moved in again. She put her hand on his chest, half lovingly, half to keep him at a distance. Her fingers rubbed against his chest, and she gasped.

"What's wrong?" he asked.

She lifted his shirt, and her mouth fell at the sight of his chest. "Jesus Christ, Jackson."

He looked down at it. He had managed to forget all about the scratches. The lining of the wounds jutted out into raised hills. The flesh turned red around them. Outside of the bumps, red and purple lightning bolts stretched from the wound to his shoulder, across his chest, and down to his stomach. His body had endured so much damage and pain, it had just melded with all of the other aches.

"This is beyond infected. You have to go to the hospital."

"No, I don't. Let's just put some ointment on it." His cheeks turned hot with embarrassment. He looked like a fool, unable to care for himself.

"Jackson, it's near your heart. An infection could kill you. That is way past infected. You need medical attention." She linked her fingers around his. "I know things have been screwed up Jackson, and we can talk about it. I promise I will talk to you about it, but for now, you have to go get that checked. Like, now."

He put his head down, relenting. "Okay, I'll go. Can I just stay with you for a little while?" He wanted to tell her about Carvallo, how he watched another man die right in front of him, but with all of the fear she had in her right now, it might be best not to talk about anyone else dying. He had no one to talk to about all of the disasters happening to him.

She shook her head. "I'm sorry. I know you want to spend time with me, and I promise you, if you go to the hospital, tomorrow you can come over and I'll talk to you. Just go get that checked out. Please. For me."

"Okay." He had no chance of winning this argument, but he felt better knowing she let her guard down and was, at the very least, willing to hear him out. An hour ago, she had suspected he murdered things. Within a few minutes of talking, he managed to get her to let him in her house. Never underestimate the importance of history. People will deny their own rational thoughts if someone they have a history with is the one in question.

As he left, she made him promise to keep her updated. He promised, excited by the idea that she not only invited, but demanded future contact.

He sat in the car and checked the backseat, never knowing where Lexia might show up. The silver lettering on Lexia's notebooks came into his mind. He should listen to Amanda. He should go to the hospital. He pictured Lexia's erratic handwriting. The wiry letters called him. He decided to go get some rest. He had a big day tomorrow. He could go to the hospital after he broke into Laney's house to steal Lexia's journals.

He turned the key in the ignition. The car hummed. The night was quiet.

And then Alexandria grabbed his face from behind, clawing at his cheeks.

He screamed in pain, unable to control it. Hopefully, Amanda hadn't heard it.

Alexandria left scratches from his mouth to his ears on both sides. He felt the warm blood ooze down his cheeks. He pulled his head away, pressing his hands to the new wounds, trying to lean forward and away from her.

"NO!" Her voice shot up his spine.

He turned toward the back, ready to defend himself, but she had disappeared as quickly as she came.

The blood drizzled down his face. The wounds didn't matter, his heart was going to burst from fear. He felt it slamming into him. He couldn't breathe. Wheezes shot out of his throat, like he was asthmatic.

Going to the hospital served no purpose; as soon as one wound healed, she would have given him ten more. He pulled out of Amanda's driveway and drove, battling his panic attack the whole way.

"Why are you doing this to me? What do you want? I want to help you."

Minus the war going on in his chest, the rest of the ride home was quiet. Lexia didn't appear. Cars didn't flip on top of his. It was too quiet.

Once home, he ran straight to the bathroom, where he threw up. After he finished, he scrubbed his face with antibacterial soap. The scratches were thin and once he cleaned them, they looked like pen lines. He took off his shirt and examined the chest wound. These scratches were deeper and wider.

He scrubbed them with the antibacterial and the lightning bolts muted until they disappeared. He had assumed they were an infection, but they appeared to be coloration on the outside of his skin, like marker. It looked like a dark liquid exited his wound, leaving a lightning bolt trail as it drifted away from the opening.

Now that he cleaned it off, it looked much better, like a small scratch, but it was still raised and tomato-red. He gasped and sat on the toilet, trying to relax, letting his body regulate.

When he left the bathroom, something in his room caught his eye. He walked in and clicked on the light. Someone had torn all of his drawers open and splayed his clothes all over the floor. A picture of him and Amanda leaned against the baseboard. He picked it up and the shattered glass frame crumbled to the floor. He gathered up the clothes and his fingers fell inside one of the shirts. He held it out and sighed at the sight of the rips. A black stain smeared up its arm. Lexia was angry.

He knew it wouldn't stop until he stopped it. He had no idea how to do that. So, he did the only thing he could think of. He sat down on the couch and cried, wrestling with the idea of breaking in and stealing the books.

He needed results fast, but he also needed sleep. His eyelids threatened to close on him and his body ached in places he didn't know could ache. Yes, he wanted to sleep; he could figure out the burglary tomorrow.

Being honest with himself, the notion of reading her journals terrified him. How would she react? How much more violent would she become? It may help end the problems, or it may make them worse.

He closed his eyes until the growling started behind him.

No. No, not now. He froze, unsure what to do. Run? Hide? His heart spoke to him: *boom, boom, no sleep tonight.*

He wanted to turn and face her but stopped that thought. He told himself to look ahead, even when the sound of her rumbling breath loudened. He had the opposite of a staring contest going on inside of himself. How long could he keep from turning and looking her in the eyes? A ghost was behind him. A ghost that attacked him twice with her claws and once with a giant SUV. She was behind him, and he chose not to turn and look at her.

"What do you want from me?"

Her motorcycle breathing moved closer. Her hot exhales hit his neck.

"Why are you hurting me?"

Her nose touched the hair on the back of his head, her mouth so close it spilled hot air down his spine.

"Do you want my help?"

Tick. Tick. Tick. The seconds drifted by, evaporating the minutes, stealing his sleep time.

She gurgled.

"Please let me sleep."

Guhguhguhguhguhguhguhguh vibrated in his ear.

The muscles in his back tightened, causing his spine to arch in a painful bend.

He stayed this way, frozen. He watched the minutes on the clock disappear.

Tick. Tick. Tick.

She wouldn't let him sleep, but his tired mind went into a dream anyway. At four in the morning, while completely awake, he fell into the past.

He was seventeen years old, waking up in the middle of the night to go to the bathroom. As he passed his father's room, he noticed the light creeping through the crack of the door and heard clicking behind it. He cracked the door and saw his father hunched over his desk, typing on his laptop.

"Dad?"

His father turned around, his eyes swollen and red. Long black bogs pooled under his eyes. "Come in."

His father spun the chair around, swiping a beer bottle off the desk as he turned. He took a slug. "I found what I can do."

"What do you mean? You look like you need some sleep."

"Haven't done that in days."

Jackson approached, peeking over his father's shoulder to examine what he worked on. His father caught where his son's attention was headed.

"I'm writing. I can't drive anymore, son. But I need work. Our accounts are draining. I found this site. I can get paid giving legal advice. I have the expertise, so I can help people. No one has to know I stopped working in law over three years ago."

Jackson's eyebrows raised. "That's awesome."

His father lifted his hand, looking for a high-five. "Pretty cool, right?"

Jackson smacked his palm. "But why don't you do it tomorrow? You need sleep. You look terrible."

Senior threw the bottle.

Jackson curled his arms around himself and flinched. The bottle smashed in a brilliant display.

"I always need sleep! I'm tired all the time. I sleep for days and then I can't sleep for a week. Every time I close my eyes, I see her. I'm sick of seeing her fucking smug grin."

"I'm sorry, Dad."

"I'm exhausted. You know what, though?" He turned back to the computer. "This is good. People listen to me. I can help them."

"Okay, I'm going back to bed. I'm sorry you can't sleep." He headed for the door.

"Jackson?"

Jackson turned back to his father, who looked at him with pathetic, droopy eyes. "I do need sleep. You're right. Maybe soon."

A *swoosh* of hot air down Jackson's back brought him back to the living room. He stared at the wall behind the television. Another *swoosh* blasted under his shirt, down his spine. He still refused to turn around. Tick. Tick. Tick. The clock turned to five fifteen. His body begged for rest. His muscles throbbed. His throat burned. His blood felt cold. His head swam.

Frustration rocked inside of him, and he wanted to cry, but he vehemently refused. He wouldn't allow himself to show her how weak she made him. *Swoosh*. His spine tingled.

He stood up and raced toward the bathroom, listening to see if she followed. As far as he could tell, she did not. He put his hands against the wall and let the shower's hot water wash over him. The pulsating stream loosened his achy muscles. He wanted to lie down and sleep while the water spat on him. He wished he could stay here forever.

He remained in the shower until the water turned cold, and he walked to the kitchen, keeping his head down and away from the living room. While packing his lunch, he listened for her breathing but heard nothing. He finally forced himself to look in the living room, and of course, she had disappeared. Now that he had to get ready for work, she had no reason to stick around and torture him. She stole his sleep and left.

He headed out for work, thinking about how to steal her books, wanting to burn them in a fire along with any memory of Alexandria Lucia.

CHAPTER 21

THE QUIET MOMENT BEFORE YOU CRACK

As soon as Ray caught a look at Jackson, his jaw dropped. "Jesus, what the heck, friend?"

"What?" It came out more hostile than he intended.

"You look awful. Did someone scratch you? Are you still not sleeping?"

"Yes, and not really, Ray, and I don't particularly want to talk about it. Can we just work?"

Ray sighed, patted him on the shoulder, and walked away. Jackson directed his attention to organizing the shelves. The store looked half-empty a month ago and still appeared that way now. Either the movies replicated, or the sales diminished in the last week or so.

When he lowered himself to the bottom shelves, his knees cracked and the pain in his lower back turned sharp, as if a torn muscle ripped cleanly in half. His stomach reacted to the pain, closed up, and shoved the air out of his diaphragm. He winced and doubled over.

Ray walked to him. "You okay?"

Jackson grimaced as he forced himself upright. "I'm fine, just bent wrong."

"You don't look fine."

He put his hand out, telling Ray to stop. "I'm fine."

Ray sighed. "Look, I have to talk to you about something."

"Ray, please. I'm fine."

"Amanda called me."

Jackson put his arm on one of the shelves and leaned on it. "When? Why?"

"It was probably days ago. I don't check my answering machine very often."

Good ole Ray, stuck in the past. "What did she want?"

"She said she was worried about you. She said you were taking pictures of dead animals?"

Jackson closed his eyes. He wanted to slam things, throw things, punch things. He counted in his head, like a child; he counted to calm himself.

"I'm not trying to get into your business, just saying, it's a little weird."

One. Two. Three. Four. Five.

"You've been having a tough time. I know that. But you're starting to slip past the normal kind of tough time and into the kind where you may need to talk to someone. I want to help, buddy. I told you that from the get-go. Talk to me."

Six. Seven. Eight. Nine. Ten.

"Jackson, say something, brother. Let me know what's up."

He opened his eyes. The bright morning sun stunned him. His fingertips danced across the waist of his pants. "You mind if I run out for a cigarette?"

Ray tucked his lips in and nodded.

Jackson sat in his car, inhaling the cigarette. "If I read those books, are you going to attack me?"

He waited for her to show up. Nothing. "I'm asking. I won't do it if you don't want me to, but otherwise, my plan is to take them and read them tonight. I need to know if you'll be mad. Just tell me. Do you want me to read them? Do you not want me to read them? It's not fair if you don't let me know now and then later you attack me for it."

Nothing happened. He stubbed the cigarette out and headed back in.

Around noon, while he was fixing some shelves in the center of the store, an older man checked out the DVDs in the drama section behind him, and a few other customers looked around at the newer movies along the outer walls. He re-alphabetized the misplaced titles, saying the alphabet to himself to remember if SP went before SQ. His mind had officially debased itself into mush.

The man behind him coughed.

He gripped the shelves and used them to lift himself. His back pinged with pain.

The coughing behind him turned into a hack.

He rubbed the small of his back as best as he could reach it and wiped the sweat from his forehead. His whole body burned, but his veins felt cold, and his teeth chattered.

He reached into his pocket, remembering Amanda wanted him to text her and let her know how the hospital went. One simple text could have helped bring things back together—even if it was a text filled with lies—and he forgot to send it. How could he be so stupid?

The hacking from the man turned from annoying to downright frustrating.

Finally, it turned into a cough he knew too well.

Guhguhguhguhguhguhguhguhguhguh.

Shit.

He turned quickly, pulling on the injured muscle in his back. A blast of pain rode an express all the way to his brain.

The man had moved to the comedy section.

Standing behind Jackson was the ghastly, bloated dead girl.

He darted his eyes to the other customers and to Ray at the register. Did anyone else see this? No one reacted. No one else could see her. She existed only to him, his own personal demon.

He whispered, trying not to gain the attention of anyone else, "Leave me alone."

Guhguhguhguhguhguhguhguhguhguhguhguh.

"If you don't want me to read the book, I won't. Is that why you're bothering me?"

Guhguhguhguhguhguhguhguhguhguhguh.

"Leave me alone." He forgot to soften his tone. The customers glanced at him.

Lexia moved closer. He grabbed a movie and threw it at her. Everyone looked now, including Ray. She reached her arm up. He slid his hand across a shelf, tossing the DVDs on the floor. "Leave me alone!"

The customers mumbled to each other. They were watching someone have a breakdown, and they loved every second of it. Ray came around the counter.

Jackson lifted a shelf off its latches and slammed it on the floor. He swiped his arm across another shelf; movies flew everywhere. Once those hit the floor, he swiped another shelf, emptied it of its contents, unlatched it, and slammed it into the ground.

"Leave me the fuck alone."

Ray was running now. Jackson gave him a death stare, unconcerned with how crazy he looked.

"Hey, hey. Calm down. Why don't you go home and get some rest, friend? I'll cover you for the day."

The girl disappeared and Jackson laughed.

"You have to go get some sleep."

"She's gone. Boop. Just like that. Gone." His laugh turned to hysterics.

"Jackson. You need to go get some rest."

Ray was the nicest man Jackson had ever met. He deserved a happy life, good friends, maybe a beautiful woman who would love him. In that moment, Jackson wanted nothing more than to hurt him. "Why Ray, am I ruining the wonderful reputation of your store?"

"Jackson! Stop. Now. Go home and get some sleep." Ray offered every ounce of patience he had. This would be the last piece.

Jackson lost control of himself. His anger owned him, and he felt like he was watching himself talk, unable to stop. "Reputation. Give me a fucking break. You own a DVD store, Ray. You know why you lasted longer than any of the other ones? Because they were smart enough to close shop when DVDs became retro."

Ray grabbed his wrist.

It just kept pouring out of him. The more he talked the more he hated himself, but the better it felt to spit venom. "This business is the most important thing to you? It's fucking archaic. It's a joke. You're a joke. The people of this town laugh at you. A DVD store? What's your next business idea? Eight tracks?"

Ray pushed his hand off Jackson's arm, like he was disgusted to even touch him. He pointed to the door. "Get out. Don't come back. You're fired."

"Fuck you, you clown. You fucking joke." He slammed his fist into a rack of shelves, and it tumbled to the ground, shelves and movies crashing to the floor.

He walked out. Before he exited, he turned back to Ray, who stood, watching him leave. His lips pursed and forehead wrinkled. Ray had staved off depression for months, not letting the fate of his business break him down. Jackson managed to defeat him in five minutes. He doubted either one of them had ever felt worse.

As soon as he walked out into the cool summer air, his chest caved, his lungs constricted, and a panic attack punched him in the gut. He fell to his knees, gasping and wheezing. His hands trembled and he started bawling. Spittle dribbled from his mouth onto the white concrete sidewalk. He must have looked like a rabid dog.

A shadow crawled over him and a pair of feet stepped onto the cement in front of him. He looked up. "Fuck you," he said to the dead girl, and she smiled before disappearing once again.

Another set of steps came toward him. They skidded against the concrete with slow, thin movements. Jackson knew without looking up that they belonged to Simon.

"Mista Jackie, are you okay?"

He pushed the air in and out and wiped his face. "I'm okay."

Simon crouched down to Jackson's level and put his wrinkled hand on Jackson's hot arm. "You're a good boy, Jackie."

"Thank you." A trail of spittle left his mouth and hit the sidewalk.

"You're looking no good. You need something."

Jackson lifted himself up. "I need a lot."

"You need vodka. You need drink and nap, I think." Simon chuckled. Jackson couldn't help but find the man's accent charming. What was it? Greek? Italian?

"Drink fixes everything." Simon clapped.

Jackson's chest loosened up. "Drink can't fix me." He wanted Simon to leave him alone. Maybe a joke would help. "Some of Simon's pizza could help."

"Simon's pizza cures everything, Jackie," he bellowed. "Simon's pizza cures everything, except a broken soul." His face turned to solid stone. "You need to fix your soul, Mista Jackie."

Jackson put his gaze right on Simon's face.

"You fix your soul, then you come in and I give you pizza to fix the rest." He patted Jackson on the shoulder and stood up, fixed his pants where they had bunched at the knee, and walked back to work. Just like that. Problem solved. Jackson couldn't help but crack up and in some ridiculous way, it did help his panic attack disappear.

He sat in his car, smoked a cigarette, and tried to relax. He didn't know if he had it in him to drive home, so he leaned his head into the seat and closed his eyes. He just needed to sleep.

After a few minutes, the darkness came. A magnificent sleep washed over him. He fell into it, landing directly into a dream world. He enjoyed it for ten minutes before a knocking on the driver's side window jarred him back to life.

He opened his eyes and saw Deputy Vassar peering in at him,

tapping his knuckles against the glass. His heart raced from the abrupt wake-up, and the tease of sleep just made the tiredness grow. He rolled down the window.

"What?"

Vassar took his sunglasses off. "What? Is that how you talk to an officer of the law?"

If Vassar had a list of people he hated, Jackson was probably in the prime location of numero uno. When Carvallo was around, Vassar kept his hatred for Jackson in check. Their relationship was about to change.

"What do you want?"

"Someone called us, said you were causing a ruckus in the video store."

He sighed. "You have to be kidding me."

"Seems like we been hearing about you a lot lately. Finding dead girls. Scaring your girlfriend. Coincidentally being around when Carvallo gets killed. Now you're destroying property?"

"I found a dead girl, which should have been your job. I didn't scare my girlfriend. In fact, I'm going to her house tonight. She invited me over. I was with Carvallo when he died, because instead of driving me home, he made pit stops on the side of a dangerous road, and if you go into that store, you'll see nothing destroyed. Maybe a few movies on the floor, but nothing damaged."

"All right. I need you to come with me to the station and we can get your statement there."

"You gotta be fucking joking." He opened the door, and Vassar turned him around, pushing his hands together behind his back. He knew that Carvallo's death opened up a lot of possibilities for Vassar to be a dick, but he didn't expect this.

"Settle down, deputy." He said it in a yokel kind of voice. *Dee-yep-U-teeeeeee.*

"Deputy? Ah, you didn't hear. I'm Assistant Sheriff now." He emphasized this sentence by clipping the cuffs on, squeezing them around Jackson's wrists as hard as he could.

"What happened, that box of Junior Mints on Carvallo's desk turn down the job?"

Vassar slammed him against the door. "You're not real smart, you know that?"

Ray waddled out the front of the store. "Hey, what's going on here?"

"Oh, hey Ray. We got a call from one of your customers about Jackie here. I'll get your statement in a minute."

"Statement? There is no statement. Jackson didn't do anything. What are you talking about?"

Vassar took his hands off Jackson. "Someone called and said he knocked over your shelves and caused a scene."

"You can have a look at my store. Everything is in tip-top shape. Jackson's been cleaning it all day. He had a little hissy when one of the shelves accidentally fell, but nothing we all haven't done when we're frustrated."

Jackson felt the tension escape. He didn't want to spend the night in jail. He had things to do, diaries to steal, a girlfriend to win back.

Vassar unlocked the cuffs and spit on the ground. "All right, then. Guess it was a mistake." He looked at Jackson. "You're free to go, but maybe keep yourself off our radar for a while. You're pissing me off."

Jackson turned to Ray and frowned. Ray's eyes narrowed: *I could have ruined your day but chose to save your ass instead, because I am a better person than you are.*

He felt a pain in his chest and his stomach turned. How could he have been so terrible to the only person who consistently looked out for him? He mouthed the words, "I'm sorry, Ray."

Ray spun around and walked back inside his store, not bothering to respond to his apology. Vassar drove off.

Short sleeps in his car weren't enough and he needed to create a more permanent solution to his problem. Unfortunately, he had no idea how to remove a spirit hell-bent on harassing him. Maybe this

Jason character could help him. He should talk to him before trying to break into a house.

He used the Facebook app on his phone to find Alexandria's profile. From there he went to the "about" section and found the link to her boyfriend's page. Jason Sansone went to Chariho High School, but Jackson had no idea how to figure out where the kid lived.

He could ask Lexia's mother, but she told him she worked until six, and he hoped to be at Amanda's by that time. He scrolled through Jason's page, looking for any information.

"NO!"

She was back. Lexia appeared in the passenger seat and lunged at him. He attempted to dodge her but banged up against the door. She clawed and scratched, tearing into the flesh in his arm. He opened the car door and fell out onto the parking lot, slamming the back of his head onto the hard ground.

His vision blurred and a ball of red appeared in the center of his eyes. It grew and swallowed the world around him.

Waves.

Water drizzled out of the bathtub. A shadow floated across the pink tub.

Animals hung from trees. Amanda screamed.

His father laughed.

Lexia howled.

Pink water.

A misty, black figure walked toward him. It came for him. It reached for him. He lifted his hand to it.

He came to, still lying in the parking lot, one foot inside the car. He must have only been out for a minute or two. No one noticed him. He squinted, trying to adjust to the light. He stood up and realized the pain in his arm for the first time. Giant claw marks traveled from his elbow to the top of his hand. She was literally tearing him apart.

The world bobbed and weaved around him. *We're going under, buddy.*

He plopped onto the driver's seat, waiting until the world

corrected itself. His body had never suffered so severely, and his heart felt like it wanted to give up on him. But he had experienced pain like this before, hadn't he? Thirteen years ago.

Basketball camp had been especially brutal leading into the school year. Every time Jackson drove to a practice, he ended up having to pull off the road to battle an attack. Sometimes it was so bad, he had to turn the car around and head home.

On top of that, the air conditioning stopped working in his house, and the abysmal heat created an environment unsuitable for sleeping. The insomnia worked with the panic attacks, the two feeding off each other.

Jackson's inconsistent sleep pattern and the persistent panic attacks wore on him. No matter how much he had adjusted to living with them, his body struggled to recover. His faculties were sluggish, and he wrestled with the most basic school assignments. On the court, his reaction time slowed, causing weaker passes and an increase in stolen balls. When he and Amanda found time to spend together, he often fell asleep, finding her presence to be a minor cure for his sleeping problem.

He had felt himself starting to crack and found no solution to fix any of it. The first game of the season approached, and he debated on whether he should quit the team, throwing away the only goal he had ever had in life. He saw no other option. His body screamed at him with frail bones, sore muscles, and itchy skin.

The night before the game, he tossed in his bed, praying for sleep. He heard his father walk into the bathroom, and a half hour later, still awake, still struggling to sleep, he realized his father had never left the bathroom. If he had any chance of sleeping that night, it went out the window when he smashed open the door and found his father sitting in a pool of water and blood.

Now Jackson sat in the seat of his car, remembering the pain he felt that night. He thought about having to sit in the emergency room for hours, watching the clock steal time from him, knowing his school day approached, knowing his father gave his best impersonation of his mother and tried to bail on him, knowing his team counted on him to play his best, and he hated the world. He hated his father for dismantling all of the hard work and care his son provided. He hated his coaches for not recognizing he needed a break. He hated his psychiatrist for not solving it for him.

He thought about all of this while Alexandria pushed hot air onto his neck.

CHAPTER 22

THE VIRTUE IN PAYING ATTENTION

He turned the key in the ignition, unsure where he planned to drive, just knowing he needed to get somewhere, anywhere but here. Lexia continued to breathe on his neck. If he thought about it too much, he would freak out and probably have another panic attack. He couldn't worry about it. She wasn't doing anything violent, just breathing on his skin like she did last night. She was tormenting him. Tormenting he could handle, violence, not so much.

His eyes swayed back and forth as he drove, trying to overcompensate for his slowed reaction time. He jolted at every movement, trying to stay alert to any change in his peripherals. His skin itched and he scratched around the claw marks, avoiding the open wounds as best he could.

At first, he thought he could handle her annoying breaths on his skin, but he grew impatient. Every time a hot stream of air hit his flesh, his stomach turned.

Swoosh. His fingers clenched around the wheel.

Swoosh. His teeth grinded.

Swoosh. His jaw clenched.

He pulled over on a side road, unable to take it any longer. He turned to her and swung his fists. "Get out. Get out of my car!"

She curled her upper lip and released a feral hiss.

"Go ahead, make all the noises you want, just do it outside of my car. Leave me alone."

The hiss calmed into a phlegmy gurgle. She tilted her head, examining Jackson. Her hands left the driver's seat headrest and crept toward him. He flinched but didn't pull away, fighting every flight response that shot through him. *Go ahead, go ahead and do what you need to do.*

Her hand reached his face and the coldness stunned him. Her slimy fingers crawled up his cheek. He felt sick. Just from remembering it, he could taste the rotten smell that left her body the night he had found her.

Her hands slid into his hair. The wetness from her fingers moistened his neck, and he cringed. She pushed his hair back and a tingle danced down his spine. He wanted to strike her hands away, wanted to tell her to get the hell out, but he stayed statuesque, letting her molest his face and hair.

Her hands stayed on the side of his head, her fingers entwined with his hair. He looked into her dead bulging eyes. They fixated on him, and he shivered.

Her mouth opened wide. Guhguhguhguhguhguhguh. The sound grew louder. GUHGUHGUHGUHGUH.

And she screamed.

He jerked his head away and shoved his hands to his ears. The screaming stopped. He opened one eye. She had disappeared. He released the oxygen built up in his lungs. *Whoosh.*

He turned back in his seat, facing front. He looked out the windshield, pouring out deep breaths. What just happened? What the hell was that all about?

Outside, two kids ran around a parked car, playing tag, laughing as one chased the other. The oaks' branches trembled in the wind while they provided shade to suburban lawns. A woman carried groceries into her house, holding two paper bags against her chest with one arm, fumbling for her keys with the other. Jackson hated them all for their normal lives.

He drove to Richmond, still unsure what he planned to do. He went by the high school and checked the outside courts, looking for Jason. After that proved unsuccessful, he traversed through Lexia's neighborhood. If they had started dating before either one of them turned 16, they probably lived near each other.

He drove for a good hour, up and down the same streets. He saw no one. The sky changed to a dim evening blue. He would need to head to Amanda's soon.

On his final loop around—or so he told himself, but he had also told himself that on the last three loop arounds—he passed by Alexandria's house in a slow crawl. If he broke in and got caught, what would be the worst that could happen? He'd get arrested? He didn't have a police record; the punishment couldn't be that stiff. Besides, it beat letting Alexandria continue to mess with him. There was a good chance she might kill him.

He parked and went to the door. As he walked up the rickety porch steps, he looked left and right to see if anyone was around. When he got to the door, he knocked. If anyone were looking, he wanted it to seem like a normal visit. Besides, he wanted to be one hundred percent sure Laney wasn't home. There were a lot of variables. What if her car broke down, and it was in the shop while she stayed home, unable to get to work?

No one answered. He tested the doorknob. It was locked. He took his library card out of his wallet.

His heart sped up. *What the hell am I doing?*

The card curved into the crevice between the door and the frame.

He slid it up and down until it hit the latch. He twisted the card, and the lock clicked. The card slid in, and the door opened.

Holy shit, I did it.

The door flew open, and he moved, walking with quick, but small steps. His feet creaked against the hardwood floor. He didn't bother to look around; if someone was there, he was caught no matter what, so he just moved forward, straight for Lexia's room.

As he opened her top drawer and pushed her underwear around, looking for the diaries, he examined the pictures on the mirror. He hadn't noticed it the first time, but in a few of them, her eyes were swollen and bloodshot. He wondered if she had been on drugs.

After a few seconds, he realized the diaries weren't there. His heart refused to slow down, and he was twitching with nerves. He didn't have time to go scouring the house looking for them.

He almost left but remembered where Laney put them on the kitchen island.

The kitchen floor provided him with quiet footsteps, but his nerves were still frying.

The books sat on the kitchen island just as she had left them. Maybe she had built up the nerve to read them after he left. Jackson had no chance of them going unnoticed now. If they were in the drawers, it could have been weeks before she realized they were gone, but they were on the kitchen island. She would know minutes after she returned from work.

He snatched them and headed for the door, out of the kitchen into the loud, creaky hallway, to the front door, into the bright sunlight, off the porch, to his car. *Exhale.* He was safe, no attacks from Alexandria, no one stopping him, no one in the house. It went smoothly. What a change of pace.

He threw the books in the backseat and opened the driver's side door when he saw the boy from the pictures turning the corner. For a moment, they looked at each other. He was surprised to see the boy, and he guessed the boy was wondering who this man was parking in front of his now-deceased girlfriend's house.

"Jason?" he said, loudly enough for the kid to hear him three houses away.

"Who the fuck are you?" Jason said with equal volume.

Jackson moved toward him. The kid didn't run, but he put a foot forward, stretching his scrawny legs, ready to spin around and take off if need be. As Jackson moved forward, slowly, not wanting to scare the kid, it became obvious how tall Jason was. He had to be 6'3" or 6'4".

Jackson stopped a few feet back to give the kid breathing room. He wanted to appear as nonthreatening as possible. "This is going to sound weird. My name is Jackson. -I'm the one who found your girlfriend at the Milner House."

Jason's fists tightened and he stepped back.

"I met her mom the other day. We talked for a while. I came here hoping she was home so we could talk some more, but she's not. She showed me pictures of you and Lexia, though." He used the name she liked, hoping to alleviate some of Jason's concern.

His fists relaxed. "You talked to her mom?"

"Laney, yeah."

Once he heard the name Laney, he sighed. "Laney. She told you to call her Laney?"

"Yeah."

"She's a good lady. What do you want to talk about?"

Jackson offered to buy the kid a soda at the gas station down the road. They talked while they walked, but Jackson avoided the heavy topics until they could sit somewhere and have a good conversation. Instead, they talked sports. What else do you talk about to a stranger in Rhode Island?

He ran into the gas station and bought two sodas for the same price he could have bought a factory of them anywhere else. He led

Jason to a bus stop bench in front of the grimy gas station. Cars zipped by every few seconds with loud clangs and rattles against the bumpy, potholed road.

"Her mom said you were a good kid. She liked you." He handed the kid his soda.

"It's my fault."

Jackson didn't expect that to come out of the kid's mouth. He didn't know how to respond, so he let Jason keep talking.

"I play baseball and basketball. . . "

". . . You play ball? I used to play basketball for Tanner's Switch." Years later, and he still got excited to talk basketball with someone who played.

Jason gave him a double take and a smile drew up his cheeks. "Wait, you said your name's Jackson? Jackson Rathburn?"

Jackson tried not to smile but couldn't help it. "You've heard of me?"

Jason laughed, putting his hand on his gut. "Yeah. Yeah. Everyone's heard of you."

"Oh man, that doesn't sound good." He knew what the rumors would be, and they would have all been true.

"Nasty from three." He held his soda bottle out in mock cheers.

"Yeah. I was nasty from three."

"That's not what people talk about, though."

"I had a feeling."

"Are the stories true?"

"Probably."

Jason jumped out of his seat. "You seriously knocked a dude out on the court?"

"Two of them."

He clapped, enjoying it. "You get in trouble?"

"Suspended from games and school. So, no. I got a vacation."

"If you're going to take a break, that's a good way to do it."

Jason sat back down. Jackson sipped his soda. They both stared off at the sky. Jackson liked his new friend.

"So, anyway, you were talking about sports."

"I play baseball and basketball. I'm also vice-president of my class and I help my parents with their business. They own a landscaping company. I just never had time." His voice cracked. "It's not like I didn't want to have time. She was all I thought about. I loved her. I always worried she would leave me, but she worried the same thing about me. She yelled at me all the time. She just wanted someone to pay attention to her, and I never did. When I did have time, I just wanted to sleep."

Jackson wondered whom he had more in common with, Jason or Lexia.

"She needed me, and I wasn't there for her."

"Sounds like you tried."

"Not always. I loved her and I tried to spend time with her when I had it, but sometimes she yelled so much, and I was so tired, I just wanted to go somewhere to relax. This one time I worked all day, and I was just exhausted. She called and asked me to come over and I told her that I already had some of the guys from the team coming by my place. So her voice perked up, and she said, "Oh, great, I'll just come by and hang with you guys." I told her no. I told her I just wanted to relax with the guys and not have her giving me a hard time every time she didn't have my undivided attention. She bawled and bawled and begged me to cancel with the guys, just pleading for me to come over. She kept saying she needed me. At the time, all I could think was, see, this is why I don't want to see you right now. It's too much. I just want to relax. I hung up on her, but I heard her say something before I did."

He started crying but tried to act tough and not let it out. Jackson put his hand on the kid's shoulder.

He struggled to get the words out. "She said, "I just want someone to play video games with me.""

As soon as Jason said the words, he lost all of his control. He cried and sobbed. Jackson's guts twisted. He felt bad for both of them. He and Jason sat there for a while, Jackson letting him get it all out, not saying a word until Jason was ready to say something else.

"That's why she did it. She never found that person. She spent so much time pent up in that room, just waiting for the day someone walked in and wanted to play video games with her until she finally gave up."

Jackson stayed with Jason for a while, making sure the kid wasn't going to go home and follow in his late girlfriend's footsteps. He wanted to convince the kid that it wasn't his fault, but he knew there was nothing he could say to change Jason's mind. In Jason's head, he would always be the one to blame.

Jason's story matched up with Laney's. From everywhere he looked, Lexia's suicide came from loneliness. He didn't know how this would help him get her off his back. He had more information but was more confused than ever. What did she want? What could he do about her loneliness now? His last hope to understand Lexia was her diaries. The idea sickened him, excited him, and terrified him all at once.

A sense of dread filled his body. Not only had he managed to find out little to nothing new, but he might also have just pissed Alexandria off by prying into her life. Convincing the man she loved to open his wounds and spill his guts on the bus stop bench may not have been the best decision Jackson had ever made.

The world moved around him: passing cars, broken houses, rustling trees. Alexandria could be anywhere at any time, and he may have just provoked her to come at him a little stronger.

CHAPTER 23

APOLOGIES AND GOODBYES

Jason walked home, drinking his soda and eating from a small bag of potato chips he bought after Jackson left. Jackson seemed like a nice guy, albeit slightly strange. The man moved with fidgety and nervous twitches. But he had bags under his eyes and was probably just overtired.

Jason wished he had thought to ask Jackson some questions in return. What did Lexia look like when he found her? Did she look sad? But once he got talking, all he could think about was how badly he had failed her. Not that it's not what he would have been thinking about anyway.

He couldn't stop picturing her alone in her room, desperate for company, playing video games by herself. He wished he could hug her and let her know how much he loved her. He wanted to tell her it was all going to be okay, convince her to stay. It was too late for all of that.

When he had initially seen Jackson, he had been on his way to walk by her house. He did that often, torturing himself by looking at her bedroom window, reminding himself of how shitty he was by seeing her light off, knowing it would never be on again. If only he could go up there and play video games with her. He used her window as his self -flagellation.

He turned the corner onto her street. Jackson was gone and his car left an open space in front of the house.

Jason looked up at her window. The light was on. *Her* light was on.

Lexia's light was on.

He almost fell over. His first thought was to run to her, but then common sense kicked in. Lexia was dead. Maybe her mother went in there and forgot to turn the light off before she left for work. He approached, keeping his head arched upward at the window. When he closed in on her house, he noticed a movement in her room: a quick flash—a silhouette of a person.

The driveway was empty, no station wagon in sight. Her mother wasn't home, but someone definitely moved in Lexia's bedroom. He placed the empty chip bag and soda on the ledge of her porch and knocked on the door. His knuckles hit the wood, and it pushed open an inch. Her mother would never leave for work with the door unlocked, let alone partly opened. He suddenly felt weak. And scared. Something was wrong.

He stepped onto the door saddle and peeked in. He wanted to yell for someone, but if a thief had broken in, the worst thing he could do was draw the person's attention. He looked around and saw no one, but the light coming from Lexia's bedroom flickered and flashed like the television was on. Maybe Laney left Lexia's television on. That was what he saw in the window. He relaxed.

Laney must have rushed out the door this morning, leaving the light on and not closing the door securely. He couldn't imagine Laney leaving like that, especially with a television on. Why would she watch television in Lexia's room, anyway? None of it made sense. Other than texting Laney and slamming the door, he couldn't do much else. He grabbed the door to close it.

"Jason?"

His heart sank.

"Jason, is that you?"

His lungs quivered. "Yes. Lexia?"

"Come play video games with me."

He threw the door open. Was it all a cruel joke? Was she alive? He ran to her room and flung the door open. His body filled up with fear, but he ignored it.

He saw the pictures on the mirror, the posters on the wall, her pink bed sheets, and he missed her, missed her in the way you miss breathing, missed the way her legs clasped around his while they lay on that bed, her head tucked into his chest, while she talked about how she wanted to get out of Rhode Island, always wanting to get away.

The room was empty. He walked in, looking around in all directions. "Lexia, where are you?"

The channel on the television changed and the blooping sound of Xbox Live kicked in. *Bloop bloop bloop*. The menu shifted until it chose a game to play. Sadness took over the fear. Lexia was dead. She was dead and alone, and still wanted him to play games with her, because even in death she had no one to spend time with her.

At least he may be able to let her know all of the final things he never got to say, the final "I love yous" that people always regret not saying to a lost loved one.

"I love you, Lexia." He broke through the fear, pushing aside the absolute horror of the situation, reminding himself of how special it could be. Another chance.

He took a controller from the dresser and dropped down the menu to "Co-op campaign." He sat on the edge of the bed and shivered at player two's character, marching forward, shooting at an NPC. He was horrified. More than that, he was sad.

Everything in him wanted to run out of this room and pretend it never happened, but he had to play with her. It was all she ever wanted. Why couldn't he have done this while she was alive? Having her spirit this close to him made him miss her even more, like he could almost touch her, could almost feel the bumps on her skin. He wished he could hug her. He wanted to squeeze her and protect her fragile thoughts from this world and from herself.

The bed bounced and he clenched, every muscle in his body straining under a truck of emotions.

He didn't know what to do, so he smashed on the buttons, playing the game with the girl who wanted nothing more than to play it with him. His character joined player two's, shooting at computer-controlled aliens. "You don't know how badly I've wanted to play this with you."

The bed bounced harder, and a set of hands touched his neck.

He cried, so scared and so relieved. He wanted to turn but feared she might not be there. At least this way he could convince himself it was real. He didn't want to push his luck and ruin it all.

Her cold hands slid upward, and her fingers touched his cheeks. The hairs on his face stood at attention from the coldness and the absolute uncertainty of what was happening.

A horde of aliens surrounded their characters, laying on them with rapid rifle fire.

Her fingers traced the outline of his jaw.

His character crouched behind a broken rock wall, peeking out to lay pistol shots on the enemy. Her character stayed up, running in circles.

"What are you doing?"

Her fingers wrapped around his neck and squeezed. She screamed and the television flickered and turned to snow.

He started choking. Panic and confusion hit him all at once. He didn't understand what was happening.

He tried to get his fingers under hers, fighting to pry them away. They tightened and he felt the wind drain out of him. The snow on the television faded to all white, and a picture burned into the screen: Lexia popping pills in her car, alone in the woods. He tried to say something to her, but all that came out was, "HHHHHHHHH."

He lunged forward and the ghostly fingers lost their grip. He ran for the door, ran all the way outside, and kept on running down the road, past the tracks, and onto the trail he took to get home. At some point, he remembered he left his chips and soda on the porch and felt stupid for thinking about something so inane when his dead girlfriend just attacked him.

He stopped at a chain-link fence, resting on it to catch his breath. His heart punched his ribcage. He tried to make sense of it all, tried to convince himself nothing that had just happened was real, but he knew it was, knew it the same way he knew she hated him now.

"I'm so sorry."

A thick slice of moon defied the daytime light and hung in the early evening sky. Its presence made Jason frightened of the woods ahead, wondering how long he had until the sun slithered away. He should have at least two or three hours, but the navy sky made him doubt himself.

The fence rattled as if someone shook it. He looked both ways. The area was deserted. It shook again, violently rattling. He backed away from it. It shook again, and Lexia's scream echoed through the woods.

He ran along the path by Horseshoe Falls, keeping close to the falls where the dirt stayed even.

As he hit a bend, something slammed into him with the weight of a linebacker. His body flailed in the air.

Something cracked as he hit the ground, and his body twisted, crashing hard. He howled in agony as he heard a loud *snap*. A sharp pain traveled from his neck to his brain, and then he felt nothing. He tried to move his hands and feet, but nothing happened. He urged himself on, putting all of his thoughts onto his fingers and toes, trying to wiggle them. Nothing.

A shadow cast over him. Lexia stood above him, her golden hair waving like a flag. Her perky red lips smirking. He knew what she planned to do, and still, he loved her. He wished to wrap his arms around her and run his fingers through her beautiful hair.

"Lexia. I love you. I love you so much."

Her knees crashed onto his waist. He watched it happen but felt nothing. She leaned her head inches in front of his and sniffed, smelling his flesh. "Please, help me, Lexia. Let's go back to your house. We can play video games."

A weird growl exited her mouth. Guhguhguhguhguhguhgughuhguh. Her upper lip curled, and her fingers latched onto his hair and pulled. That he could feel.

The hair ripped from his skin, and she held the clump in front of his eyes, making sure he saw it.

He began to cry. Not from the pain. Not from knowing he was probably paralyzed. Not from knowing he was going to die. He cried for her. He cried that she hated him.

She leaned back, and her arm left his view toward the ground. She groped, looking for something. When she found it, she raised her arm above her head, and he saw the stone as she drove it down to his jaw.

He screamed inaudible words.

His teeth cracked and popped. Two of them shot down his throat and he choked. He gasped and wheezed trying to exude one of them from his lungs—the other, he'd already swallowed. Blood trickled down his throat, making it harder to remove the tooth. He hacked and hacked, putting so much attention on trying to reopen his airways that he failed to notice the stone coming back at his face, this time from the side.

His mandible snapped. His mouth remained open from his jaw being out of place. He couldn't move it, couldn't make it shut. He tried to scream, but only half moans came from his swollen and broken face. The pain overcame him, and Lexia blurred before fading into complete darkness.

When he came to, he looked up at the scythe moon, still relaxing in the sunny sky. He clenched his face, trying to move a muscle, any muscle. Nothing worked. He wanted to scream for help, but she had totally detached his jaw. The best he could come out with was a low "aaahhhgg." Blood drained down his throat and he had to keep swallowing it. He spit and it shot up and landed on his face.

The moon moved a few inches toward his feet. A few seconds later, it did it again. A few seconds later, it happened again. And then he caught on to what was happening. Lexia was dragging his body. He didn't feel it, but the world shifted around him. The sky moved and all he could do was watch the world slip away from him.

Something cold hit the back of his head. It took a few seconds before he figured out what it was. The falls. And then he knew what his fate was. She planned to drown him. He tried again to scream. *Aaaaahhhgggg* He choked, drops of blood falling down his throat too quickly. If she didn't drown him in the falls, he would probably drown in his own blood.

The water reached his ears. He yelled for Lexia to stop. He pleaded, telling her how much he loved her. *Aaaaahhhhgggggg*. Her hand spidered over his face, the palm squishing his nose. He breathed and made a *huff* against her hand.

His head went under the water. It gushed down his throat, his broken jaw unable to stop the flow. He gagged and choked, and more water flushed in. He exhaled as best he could, but he put up little fight. He had nothing left to fight for. He managed to twist his face enough to kiss her hand before the darkness came. She dug her fingertips into his eyes as his lungs filled with water.

The last thing he ever thought was, *This is not Lexia.*

CHAPTER 24

WHERE TO DREAM AND WHERE TO WAKE

Jackson pulled into Amanda's driveway, looking at the books in the passenger seat, eager to get into them, but more eager to spend time with Amanda. He only had two days left before she would be heading out.

Her shades were drawn, but her car was in the driveway.

His heart sank as he walked up to the front door where she had taped a bunch of folded pink notebook pages. He peeled the tape off, causing a small tear in the top of the paper. His hands couldn't be gentle, not while his spirit tore in two.

Jackson,

I am going to bed right after work. Please do not knock or wake me up. I thought about calling or emailing this to you to save you the trip, but I knew you'd come anyway, just as I know you'll still knock despite me asking you not to.

I know we made plans to see each other tonight, and I suppose I have plenty to address. I am aware that I am leaving in two days, and you really wanted to spend time with me, but there are many reasons I don't think it's a good idea. I'm sure what you're about to read would have been better served in a face-to-face conversation, but you'll (hopefully) understand why I had to do it this way.

 My day at work was ridiculously difficult, not only having to say goodbye to my team, who I love and care for, but also having to wrap up all of the final details so the next coach will be all set and can transition easily. Because I am so exhausted, I apologize if some of this letter is all over the place. There is a lot to say, and a lot of emotions attached to all of it, so I'm more than a bit flustered.

The letter already confused him, and he still had plenty of pages to go—he often made jokes to Amanda about her lack of brevity. Did she quit her job? She had explained it to him as if the Albany trip was a tryout. He flipped through the pink notebook pages, determining whether he should finish it in the car. Her loopy cursive handwriting filled up page after page. He sighed and sat down on the porch swing.

The letter read so formally, as if she were speaking to a colleague, not the boyfriend she'd dated since high school.

 Do you remember the time we went to the beach with your father? You spent weeks convincing him to go, and he shocked us both by actually taking you up on it. Getting him to leave the house seemed like a milestone. We had a great day.

She remembered it as a good day. This surprised him since he remembered it as one of his toughest. It happened right at the peak of his insomnia and panic attack period. He had labored to get through the day, trying his hardest to feign happiness for the sake of his father. This happened shortly after his father's suicide attempt, and Jackson wanted him to appreciate life again. He never thought his father would actually take him up on the offer.

At one point, he had started to hallucinate. When you deprive your body of its dream state, after a while, it forces the dreams on you. They meld with the real world, and you see them with your eyes open. Most of the time, this comes in the form of dark shapes in the corner of your eyes, or trails in movements.

That day Jackson witnessed dark figures ascending from the water: an army of black shadows marching out of an underwater world. He knew he was imagining them, so he hid any reaction, but even when you're aware it's just a hallucination, a congregation of black shadows still terrifies you.

Your father not only took to going, once he let his feet into the sand, he allowed himself to have the time of his life. I felt like I was watching someone experience the outside world for the first time, and considering how long he had locked himself away, it probably felt that way to him too. You made that happen, Jackson. You created magic that day, for your father, but also for me. It taught me to appreciate the simple things, the sand, the water, the air, and most importantly, my sanity. It made me appreciate that I didn't have to fight with myself to go outside every day, that I could experience and enjoy those things whenever I chose.

It also made me appreciate you for how much effort you put into trying to make his life better when you were struggling to keep your own together. I know how hard you were fighting at that time. I know you battled those panic attacks, trying so hard to beat your demons so you didn't end up like him. You refused to let anything stop you.

We walked the beach with your father, and when we arrived at the rock jetty, his face lit up. Do you remember that rock jetty? We went there a few times when we were young, hiding ourselves in the night, letting the water lap at our feet. Anyway, your father remembered it when he saw it. He must have gone there before the agoraphobia, because he drew his eyes on you and said, "I always wanted to jump off this jetty."

Jackson smiled at the memory, even though he knew where she planned to bring this story.

You spent the next half an hour trying to get him to do it. He didn't, but you sure made him contemplate it. On the way home, he kept telling us he would do it someday. Do you remember how often he said he would do something some-day? His bucket list must have been bigger than War and Peace. I loved your father. He was a good man. But he gave up on life.

When the panic attacks forced you to quit basketball, something changed in you. You stopped caring. You woke up and you did what you had to do, but little else. You let those panic attacks take more than basketball. You let them take part of you, part of your identity. You gave up on life, just like your pops did. I don't mean to bring him up to rub it in. I know how much his death hurts you, but you have to see the regret he faced in the end. You have to know that he wished he could have taken one of those "somedays" and made them any day.

I don't want to see you meet those same regrets. I worry

that your father's death deepened your desire not to care. I see you giving up again, even more than you already had.

I'm leaving in two days. I want you to do me a favor while I'm gone. Please do this for me. I want you to jump off the jetties. Find out what your jetties are and jump.

I'm not sure why I opened the door yesterday. I was terrified to do it. The second you walked in, my heart pounded. I'm honestly worried about you. Mainly because I worry you'll hurt yourself and that would kill me.

You're intentionally surrounding yourself with death. It's weird if nothing else. No, it's terrifying. And the scratches? You had a major infection on your chest, and you shrugged it off like it was no big deal. It's like you don't even care if you die. (You never messaged me to let me know what the doctors said by the way, but I am so done with chasing you and babying you. If you don't care, why should I?) I have to assume you never went to the hospital. And Jesus, this is what pisses me off. I say I don't care, but I do, and you know it. If nothing else comes across in this letter, let one thing: get that checked out! You could die. I won't lie, when you never texted me to let me know how it turned out, that really was a turning point for me, not that I wasn't already on the edge.

I worry about the way you're dealing with everything, or NOT dealing with everything. I worry that you haven't applied for a job, knowing Valiant is closing in a few weeks. I worry you can have an infection that could kill you, and you look at it like it's no big deal, almost like you're cool with it killing you. Something is wrong with you, Jackson. You need help. You need to get a lot of things fixed because you *are going down fast, and I'm sorry, but I can't go down with you. I tried to help you. I did everything I could for years. It's too much now. I need to move forward.*

I do love you. I do wish you the best. I pray you'll get it together. I'll think about you constantly. Good luck. Find the jetty and jump in the water.

Love,

Amanda

He crumpled the letter, turning the pages into a ball, and dropped it on the porch swing. He drove away, letting the wheels screech on the pavement, hoping the sound would wake her up. A few minutes later, he pulled into the Breachway Grille parking lot and kicked the car's old CD player until electronic bits peppered the floor of his car.

Halfway home he decided to turn around. Amanda expressed how she felt in the letter; he needed to do the same. If it brought her discomfort to end it face-to-face, he would write a letter for her and leave it on her windshield.

At the next intersection, he pulled a U and pushed the pedal until the speedometer hit sixty. As soon as the needle touched the sixty line, the windshield fogged up. Like a spreading infection, the condensation draped over the side windows. He glanced into the rearview just as the rear window joined the rest in fog. The murkiness turned the entire car into a blind spot, but a light shone through it. A car moved toward him, and he had no idea on which side of the road he maneuvered.

He pushed his arm forward to wipe the windshield, but the seatbelt strangled him. He fumbled to unclick the belt and as it zipped free, he regretted the decision. If the car barreling in his direction slammed into him, he had just sealed his fate. He used his sleeve to wipe at the window, but it remained misty, so he clicked the wipers on, hoping they cleared the outside before he swallowed the other car's front grill. Nothing happened. The fog acted as if it existed in the middle of the glass.

His fingers slid against the door, searching for the power window switch. Despite his occluded vision, he kept his attention on the windshield. His finger found the button and pressed it down. The window made the *whirring* sound as if it were dropping, but it stayed in place.

The light came closer, and even through the foggy window, blinded Jackson. The other car's engine grew louder. His body tensed, preparing for impact. The other car's horn blared. The sound caused Jackson to jump in his seat and survival instincts kicked in. He turned the wheel to the right.

The car bumped and bounced, clunking against the uneven ground. His head smashed against the doorframe. The fog dissipated, revealing the earth around him as it rocked and shook. Tree branches smacked against the car. *Twick. Twick. Twick.* The windshield fully cleared.

The car barreled toward a giant oak tree. He stomped the brake, but the car kept on bouncing forward. *Twick. Twick. Twick. SLAM.*

The front end's bits showered the earth. His head met the windshield. The night came.

CHAPTER 25

THE NATURE OF THINGS

Jackson woke up to a foggy world. Either a mist spread through the woods, or he had rattled his brain too hard when the impact drove his head into the windshield. Whichever turned out to be true, he blamed Alexandria. A red blob crossed his view, and he wiped it away, smearing blood onto his wrist.

He stayed still, trying to piece the world together in his mind. He had crashed. The front of his car had wrapped around a giant oak. The windshield had shattered; pieces of it shimmered along the mangled hood and the ground in front of it. His head swam.

He bent his fingertips as if he were wrapping them around a weight, testing their ability to work. Next, he rotated his wrists. He went all in after that and bent his upper body forward, arching his back to stretch it. It took a second for the pain to enter, but once it did, it charged through him.

He opened the car door and put a foot onto the ground but fell right over. He lay there, giving himself some time to accept the pain, to acclimate to it.

A chorus of chirps surrounded him: birds, locusts, crickets. Leaves rustled. His vision returned to normal.

The dead girl laughed.

At first, he assumed she was mocking him, but he decided she was playfully enjoying her work. She was proud of herself. She planned to break him down bit by bit, and unless he figured out why or how to stop her, she would succeed.

He gripped his hand on the door's map pocket, using it as leverage to lift himself. His bones cracked as he put himself on two feet. The girl continued to chuckle, but she remained out of sight. He punched the door, wanting her to shut up, but only managed to invite a burning pain into his lower back muscles as he jerked his arm forward. He ignored it, kicking the car repeatedly. "Fuck. Fuck. Fuck. Fuck. Fuck."

His dad, his job, his girlfriend, and now his car, all gone. He managed to lose everything in two weeks. Without the job, he would lose his house next. Even his body stood on the verge of falling apart. "Fuck. Fuck. Fuck. Fuck. Fuck."

He looked back toward the road and then turned toward the woods. This area was unfamiliar to him. He thought it might lead toward Switch Falls—a shallow stream, good for fishing trout, popular for its miniature rapids, not so much for nighttime strolls—but he could be wrong. His house was east. Amanda's house was west. He limped forward, heading north. He had nothing waiting for him in the other directions anyway.

He made it about twenty feet before he dizzied. The blood continued to drain from above his eyes. He grabbed a leaf and pressed it against the fault line in his forehead. It turned red in seconds. He took his tee shirt off and wrapped it around his forehead, tying it tight. The pressure made the top of his head feel like it might explode.

An urge to fall asleep grew in him, but with his head in its current condition, he thought better of taking a nap.

The colors of evening tinted the foliage a crimson red, leaving everything bright enough to see, but dark enough to lose definition.

His mouth and throat felt like they were filled with thick insulation. He ventured forward, hoping to find water. When he stepped, twigs and slash rustled under him, but they echoed. He paused and listened.

Just as he had thought, the rustling continued. It came from behind him.

The crackling grew louder. Whatever followed him moved faster than he did. He sped up, but it still closed in. *Crickcrickcrickcrick*. He picked up speed, going from a walk, to a stride, to a jog. His left knee buckled each time his foot hit the ground. A lightning bolt of pain shot through him, pleading for him to slow down.

More rustling came from his left, and another set of steps joined in from the right. They flanked him and closed in fast. As he hobbled, he flashed his gaze to his sides, trying to catch sight of his pursuers. He lost his footing but corrected himself before falling on his ass. The stumble slowed him enough to allow his hunters to catch him.

Something slammed into his back. He crashed.

His body skidded against the ground. Dirt, gravel, and twigs scraped against his arms and stomach. He almost laughed. One more collision with *anything* had a good chance of ending him. If a leaf fell from a tree and landed on him, his bones might shatter.

The anxiety of not knowing what hit him sent a chill throughout his body, but he stayed put, face to the ground. Whatever chased him had him. If it planned to do him harm, it faced little resistance. The fight had escaped him on impact. But the idea of seeing whatever wanted to hurt him made him more terrified than not seeing it. So, he would die blinded.

It snarled and its wet nose touched his bare back. He cringed. The causes of the crinkling from his left and right approached, closing in on both sides of his head. He squeezed his eyes shut and started saying his goodbyes.

"I'm sorry, Pops. I should have done more for you." Wet snot rubbed against his skin.

"I'm sorry, Amanda. You deserved a better version of me." A paw pressed against his upper leg.

"I'm sorry, Ray. I didn't mean any of it." An animal growled on top of him.

"I'm sorry, Alexandria. I can't help you." Something pressed against his cheek.

The pressure against his face startled him. He opened his eyes. A raccoon pushed its nose into his face. He pushed back. A raccoon? He turned his head in the other direction. An orange cat. He spun himself around. Before he had a chance to laugh at himself for running from small animals, he saw the medium-sized coyote— mouth curled, fangs showing—nearly on top of him.

It growled, saliva dripping onto Jackson. The cat screeched. He used his elbows to shift away from the coyote. It moved forward with him.

He cracked up, laughing out loud, alone in the woods. He could do something about this. He could survive.

Yes, the coyote's size made his fear rational, but he could fight it off. All he had to worry about was rabies.

The coyote's matted fur rubbed against his stomach. Red smears decorated the coat, and it felt wet against Jackson's skin. The raccoon's fur had the same sanguinary smudges.

He caught on.

These animals were dead. Alexandria brought them here to torment him.

As the revelation struck him, a deer crossed onto the path.

It dripped blood, leaking from it in quarter-sized drops, pooling into each other on the ground. The deer's face lacked the peaceful aura that most deer possessed, and in its place, black eyes and a sneering mouth emitted a miasma of death.

Jackson used his elbows again, scooting away from the animals. He pushed back slowly, trying to keep his panic in check. The deer bucked. Her back legs kicked high into the air in fast, sharp motions. If it struck him with those legs, it could take his head off.

Then the front legs jumped forward. It repeated this, spinning in circles. The raccoon and the cat backed up, afraid of the wild animal. The coyote used the ruckus as an invitation to attack. It jolted forward, and Jackson put his forearm out, using it as a shield. It bit, clenching its teeth deep into his flesh.

He bellowed in pain and his arm shook in a reactionary jerk. The coyote fell to its side, keeping its teeth locked into the moving snack. He struggled to his feet. The coyote stuck to him. He couldn't shake it off. He was holding the coyote up, its body in a straight line, feet toward the ground, head held high, gnawing into him.

The deer's frantic kicking moved close. He could feel the wind from the force of its gyrating legs.

He ran, taking the coyote with him. Its teeth, stained pink with his blood, dug in deeper as he moved. He smacked it. Even now, while it chomped into him, he wrestled with his conscience when it came to hitting an animal. Even a dead one. He clenched his fist and swung fast, but before his knuckles clashed with its fur, he slowed and hit it gentler than he initially planned. He tried again, but again gave it no follow-through.

The deer charged him. Jackson ran along the path, slowed by his feral accessory. The pain it caused in his arm made the aches in the rest of his body disappear. At least one positive came from the bite. The deer moved too quickly for Jackson. Its head brushed against his back. Thank God it wasn't a buck; he would have been punctured by its antlers.

He turned, veering off into the woods. The deer followed but fell behind with the turn. Jackson slalomed around the thick oaks, slowing the deer with each turn.

He slammed his arm into a tree trunk, crushing the coyote between him and the tree. Bark flew off the tree in chunks. The coyote yelped and kicked and released his bite.

The air on his new wound made it throb with pain, but he felt lighter having knocked the beast off him. It scampered away, but the deer maintained the chase.

Freeing himself from the coyote renewed his spirit, and he used that momentum as he ran north, increasing the gap between him and the deer each time he curved around an oak. It was amazing what adrenaline could do. Moments ago, he could barely walk without limping.

The burst of energy lasted all of two minutes before his lungs began to burn. He needed to slow down. He needed to catch his breath. The shuffling of brush sounded too close. He had to keep moving despite the pain, despite the pounding in his chest, despite the inability to breathe.

The uneven landscape sloped upward. He pressed on, digging his feet into the dirt, battling the incline. It slowed him down. The pain in his muscles returned and the strain of the climb increased it tenfold. He reached the top and considered letting the deer kill him. Any ounce of energy he had escaped him on the climb.

He dropped to his knees and wheezed. He coughed seal-like hacks, streams of saliva draining out of him.

He assumed the deer must have breached the hill by now, readying to devour him in whatever way a dead deer does that sort of thing. The pounding of his heart boomed in his ears, mixing with his coughing, blocking him from hearing the sounds of his pursuer.

He looked back and saw the empty woods. He darted his gaze back and forth, trying to find the deer. His heavy breathing made the only sound. He relaxed a little, but recognized he dealt with dead animals, and who knew the laws of physics when it came to such things. The deer could reappear at any moment, from any direction, with any temperament.

He still needed water. After the run, he needed it more than ever. He dusted himself off and walked, listening for the trickling sounds of a stream. He knew Switch Falls was around here somewhere.

His legs begged for mercy, but he plugged a foot into the ground and moved forward, refusing to stop. Blood continued to stream from his arm. How the hell was he still moving?

It took about a mile of hiking through thick forest before he picked up the sounds of running water. A gentle bubbling came from somewhere but could easily have been miles ahead. He sighed. At least he knew he was moving in the right direction.

His throat felt like he had swallowed liquid cement, and it slowly hardened. He questioned his strength, doubting he had much more in him.

To keep from quitting, he forced his mind to shift from the pain and concentrate on distractions: the trees, basketball, memories of his father and Amanda. No matter what, it came back to pain. Any path his mind took, it led to places he didn't want to go.

Up ahead, the land bent upward again, and he braced himself for another climb. The summer heat drained the sweat out of him. It leaked out and rained down his face and body.

He reached the top of the incline, and the ground leveled for around twenty yards and ended. He limped toward it, praying for a small drop. If he stood atop a cliff and had a long climb down, he might just call it quits and throw himself off.

He looked down from the edge. Clear water traveled through a rocky pathway. The cliff looked down on it from about twenty feet up. He was so close he could almost taste the water on his wallpaper tongue.

A snarl gurgled behind him, followed by a hiss.

He kept his view on the water, pushing his feet to the edge. Stones reflected under the stream. It was too shallow to jump into.

He turned to face his attackers. A menagerie of dead surrounded him. It had to be every dead animal he'd ever photographed. Most of them were too small to be dangerous. He could kick them, punch them, fight them off. A few larger ones had the potential to kill him. All of them combined definitely would destroy him, especially since he was already beaten to near death. They growled, howled, and barked, hissed, moaned, and screeched. His legs jelled. Even if he attempted to run, they would catch him with ease.

Alexandria appeared from behind the deer. She patted its blood-soaked fur and hummed. The humming. She hummed the lullaby Jackson had chased after his father died. He shouldn't be surprised, but he was. Still, what was that song? He knew it from somewhere, but he still couldn't place it.

When she made her way to the front of the deer, she tapped her fingers on its head and snickered.

Jackson's feet slid backward, his heels dangling off the edge. If he stayed, the animals would eat him. If he jumped, he could die, but by his own making. Either way, he faced a potential for death. He inhaled a large gulp of air, appreciating what could be his last taste of it, and he made his decision.

CHAPTER 26
KISS TOMORROW GOODBYE

R ay clunked his feet up his front stairs, his tired old bones creaking with each step. A brown envelope leaned against the door, and he picked it up on his way in. He knew what the package was and opened it with excitement. Three DVDs fell out onto the dining room table.

He went to his room and grabbed the three DVDs he took from Valiant and put them with the new three. He smiled at the makeshift box set. He picked the perfect six Cagney movies to give to Mrs. Belmont.

He placed the movies in a gift bag and shoved some blue paper inside. His mother's skill for wrapping had never washed off on him. Even something as simple as a gift bag looked bad when he put it together. It was like the bag was throwing up the paper. It didn't matter, of course. He could give Mrs. Belmont an empty bag with rips in it and she would consider it the greatest gift of all time.

He cracked his knuckles and made himself a bowl of microwavable spaghetti. As he slurped the noodles into his mouth, he dialed Mrs. Belmont and put the phone on speaker. He worried about calling her so late—seven thirty at night was late to Mrs. Belmont.

She picked up after three rings, saying hello in her confused, soft voice. He always felt the need to yell when speaking to her.

"Hello. Mrs. Belmont? This is Ray."

"Hello?"

"Hi. Mrs. Belmont. It's Ray from Valiant."

"Oh, Ray. Hi."

The phone picked up static. "Hi. I was wondering if I could stop by in a while. I have something I want to give you." He smiled, waiting for her excited reaction.

"Hello?" The phone fuzzed again.

"Mrs. Belmont? Are you there?"

"Ray? I'm having trouble hearing you, honey."

"There's static. Do you mind if I stop by?"

Silence.

"Mrs. Belmont? Mrs. Belmont?"

"Did you clean the fucking sink?" his mother's voice cackled.

He dropped the phone and the bowl on the floor. Spaghetti splattered on the rug. His hands shook.

"Did you clean the fucking sink?"

He hollered and kicked the phone.

The voice turned to a high-pitched shrill. "Did you clean the fucking sink?"

"Stop it, Mom."

Did you clean the fucking sink: the last words his mother had ever spoken. In every movie or television show, when a character dies, they have one final conversation with their loved ones. They say their peace and give each other a beautiful catharsis. In real life, his mother asked him if he cleaned the fucking sink, slammed her door, closed her eyes, and never opened them again.

He hadn't cleaned the sink, and she wasn't really asking. She had seen the clumps of old Chinese food gathered in the drain catcher. At that point, he had probably told her he would take care of it five or six times.

After they carried her body out, he cleaned the fucking sink. He scrubbed it and wore away the metallic surface until his upper arms throbbed and his clenched fingers cramped.

"Ray? Ray, are you there? I think something is wrong with my phone." The phone call screen closed as Mrs. Belmont hung up.

He picked up the phone and the bowl and went to the sink, letting the sound of rushing water slow his shaking hands and quiet his pounding heart. The death of Jackson's father must have reawakened Ray's inability to cope with his mother's death. Her death had haunted him for many years, but time eventually softened the pain. Since Jackson's father had passed, and Ray found out about Jackson's dead animal hobby, he found his mind drawing toward his mother again.

He wiped the bowl clean and took a wet rag to the carpet. He pressed down, scrubbing with more vigor than he meant to. His teeth were clenching.

He forced out a laugh, trying to make light of his delusions, but the chuckle turned to weeping.

His phone buzzed and he jumped. This time he laughed without having to force it. Mrs. Belmont's name appeared on the screen, and he swiped to pick it up.

"Hello."

"Ray?"

"Yes, Mrs. Belmont. Can you hear me now?"

"Why did you do that?"

"Why did I do what? I called you to ask if I could stop by and... "

". . . Why did you pretend to be my husband?"

He scrunched his eyebrows. "What?"

"Did you clean the fucking sink?"

He threw the phone. It hit the wall and cracked. He had heard what he thought he'd heard. There was nothing delusional about it.

The door at the end of the hall slammed open. The door that he had kept shut since his mother had passed. It had belonged to her, and he refused to open it, putting that room to rest with his mother.

It opened, and he looked into the dark abyss he had avoided for decades.

His skin crawled and itched. "Aaaaaffffffff," was all that he could say. Tears poured down his cheeks.

A creak came from the darkness, and then another. They kept coming until a silhouette protruded from the room. His mother. She moved toward him with the same crooked old woman limp she had when she had lived. His mouth dropped.

He pictured himself running, heading for his car, and driving to Valiant, but his body stayed put. He tried to peel his eyes off her, but they refused to look away. She limped.

His head turned up to keep his eyes locked on hers as she stepped closer. She hovered above him.

"Did you clean the fucking sink?"

He ran. His body and mind joined forces, and he made his way to the door. His heartbeat shook his eardrums. He jerked and jiggled the doorknob, but it acted as if someone had glued it shut. He yanked, pulled, and twisted, but it stayed put.

The footsteps creaked behind him. He ran the other way, toward the stairs.

What kind of idiot runs into the attic? He said it so many times while watching horror movies. Now, here he was, lugging his fat ass up the wooden steps into the dank, dusty attic while his dead mother chased him.

He pushed the door shut and locked the bolt. *What makes you think the dead follow the laws of physics? A door isn't going to stop her.* Right on cue, the wood-paneled floor creaked in the attic corner.

He opened the door and ran out. He would play back and forth all night if he had to. Maybe he and ole mama could have a rousing Benny Hill chase through the bedroom doors. He chugged his way to the bedroom.

He reached under his bed and pulled out a baseball bat: a replica from the movie *The Natural*. He gripped his hands around it and waited.

The creaks moved through the hallway.

He leaned forward, placing his left foot out, readying to make a move.

Creak.

He put the bat above his shoulder.

Creak.

He leapt out and swung so hard he heard a rip in his arm. The bat made contact with the wall and flopped out of his hands. His mother ran at him.

He grabbed the bat and pushed it at her, like shooing a mouse.

"You dirty, double-crossing rat." His dead mother looked him in the eyes, and he was quoting movies. What the heck was wrong with him?

Why not? He always had movies going through his head, and that line he dedicated to poor Mrs. Belmont, who he suspected was facing a similar battle at this very moment. *Why did you pretend to be my husband?* Yes, he and Mrs. Belmont both faced their ghosts tonight.

His mother growled and slapped at the bat. He kept prodding it in her direction while moving backward. She swatted it and inched toward him, pushing him further down the hall.

He scuffed his feet until he stood in the doorframe of his mother's room. She was luring him in there. What other choice did he have? He pulled Wonderboy over his shoulder again. When he crossed the threshold into the dark room, he found the clearance he needed and swung. The bat cracked against his mother's skull and blasted into pieces.

He leaned down to her. "Red, my mom wanted me to get out of this game. She begged me. But she died before I could." He laughed. Screw it. He loved his mother, but this wasn't her. He'd seen too many movies where a good guy dies because he tries to reason with a zombie or a ghost of a loved one.

"Hey, Mom, I cleaned the fucking sink." He laughed and walked to the kitchen, not sure what the hell to do. He'd gone completely insane.

A creaking moved down the hallway, and his heart stopped pounding. In fact, it seemed to disappear completely.

He loved horror movies, but he always knew what would happen next, because they only went a few different ways, and he knew that to be true tonight, too.

He could have knocked his mother's ghost to hell and ended the day enjoying a beer. The other option walked down the hall now. The ghost kept coming. No matter what he threw her way, she would find a way to devour him. His death was the only way to end it.

He sighed, opened the fridge, and grabbed a beer.

The cap popped off and the bottle made a satisfying hiss as his mother lumbered into the kitchen.

Ray gulped down the last beer of his life, and boy, did it taste sweet.

She dug her fingernails into his eyes and plucked them out.

He screamed.

CHAPTER 27
THE PINK WATERFALL

Find your jetty and jump in the water. Jackson turned and bent his knees. The animals reacted and moved their semi-circle in, turning their formation into a messy mob.

Alexandria screamed, and the animals went ballistic. They whined, screeched, kicked, and raced after him.

He jumped. The ground flew at him fast. On impact, his knees buckled, and he flopped forward, but he lived. The important thing was he lived.

The blood from the coyote bite dripped into the water: a pink cloud moving upstream.

The pink turned into the waterfall pouring out of the bathtub. His father looked at him with apologetic eyes. Something moved in the rippling water, the shadow of something moving in the bathroom. A black fog formed into the shape of a person, and then he heard the humming, the beautiful humming. The shape noticed it had been seen, and it reacted by curling into a ball and reforming in front of him, whispering and humming simultaneously, telling him to forget, telling him to go back to his life. He brought himself into the present. He'd have to think about it later.

The animals took turns jumping off the cliff. It would have been comical if not for the horrendous *thud* their bodies made as they slammed into the ground below.

One after the other, the animals lunged from twenty feet above, following him like lemmings. *Thud, thud, thud.* Their bodies slapped against the water and splattered, blood and entrails mixing with the otherwise clear stream.

The deer was the most awful to watch. Its body flailed and bucked as it fell, and it slammed into the ground with a thunderous crash.

The squirrel launched itself off the cliff. Jackson was still in shock and didn't have enough time to react. It landed on his chest and clawed at him. He stumbled backwards, onto his ass.

Coyotes. Deer. No, it was a fucking squirrel that brought him down. A fucking squirrel.

He let go of his apprehension to hurt the animals and grabbed the creature. Its body snapped, first in his tight fist, and again as he pounded it into the stones. It died on the first impact—or died again, anyway—but he kept going.

Slam. The EMTs came in and lifted his father out of the water. One of them scurried to wrap tourniquets around his arms.

Slam. Jackson sat in the back of the ambulance while they worked on his pops.

Slam. Sweat poured from his father, but his lips turned blue.

Slam. His father opened his eyes in his hospital bed.

Slam. "I'm sorry, Jackie. I'm just not strong enough."

Slam. "You don't get to do that again. You're not allowed to give up. I'm in charge. You listen to me now."

Slam. He had seen the figure in that bathroom all those years ago, had heard the humming. And that's why the song rang familiar.

Slam.

The squirrel's body transformed into mush in his hand. He released the soupy guts into the water and raised his head toward the cliff. "Are there any more of you? Come get me!"

The woods fell silent. He rinsed his hands in the stream and wiped them on his jeans. Somewhere in the chase, he had lost the shirt he'd tied around his head. He cupped his hands, collected water, and slurped it up. He was too thirsty to care if the water may be polluted, if his hands were filled with dead animal bacteria, if the guts of the dead infested his drink. The cool water trickled down his throat. The burning in his lungs cleared up. He bent over, put his face into the water, and splashed it on his head.

Every part of him hurt, but the water made it acceptable. In a series of losses, the water represented a win. He lay down in it, letting it soak him. A few feet over, a graveyard of animals oozed blood into the stream. It didn't matter.

He was glad he had never stopped to photograph any dead birds. They wouldn't have slammed into the ground; instead, they would have flown right into his face. Alfred Hitchcock, no thank you.

He lay in the water for ten minutes, enjoying the silence of the forest. If only Amanda's arms could be wrapped around him. If only they lay in this water together, letting it wash away all of the bad. He missed her more at this moment than ever. He wanted to feel her skin against his, to wrap himself around her body.

As he lay there, he realized he had left the diaries in his car. Dread washed over him. His last chance to figure Alexandria out and he left it behind.

He sat up, contemplating his next move. He wondered if she planned to give him enough of a break for him to catch some sleep. He doubted it. Sleep deprivation appeared to be a part of her plan.

He walked along the riverbank. Ahead, the water deepened and meandered, and the current gained momentum. The sounds of gushing water brought him a strong desire to urinate, so he stopped and pissed on the rocky cliffs that lined the banks. The urine streamed out of him, and he listened to the splash against the flowing of the river until there was no flowing, only the sound of his piss hitting the cliffside. The silence was eerie. The river's bubbling and streaming had completely stopped, like the river had frozen in place.

He finished draining his bladder, zipped up, and spun around.

The river had stopped moving, but that wasn't what scared him the most.

Along the edges of the water, figures rose out onto the banks. A series of black shadows marched toward him.

They had horrified him when he saw them at the beach with his father and Amanda all those years ago, and they hadn't lost their touch to do so. If hell had opened up onto earth and unleashed its poisoned souls, they would look like this.

At first, all he could do was watch them. His fear was met with awe and fascination. Black smoke twisted into their forms, evil and beautiful.

He gripped a rock, tightened his fist around it, and ran, ready to attack if he needed to. The banks turned from loose gravel into large, sharp stones. He navigated with speed but had to maintain caution on the uneven earth.

The water pushed forward again, getting angrier and more volatile as he moved further upstream.

Up ahead, the waterway dropped off. From his position, it was impossible to see how far down it was, but he knew that he had to jump and he prayed for the second time tonight.

The last of the day's sun had drifted, and he could barely see two feet in front of him. When he glanced back, he couldn't see the shadows anymore, but knew they still chased him.

He picked up speed, disregarding caution. His sore ankles pulsed every time his feet dug into the stones' pointed tops. As he reached the end of the level ground, he looked back upon the shadows. They were close enough for him to see now, traveling across the choppy earth with grace and balance. He leapt. *Find your jetty and jump in the water.*

The falls splashed and thundered as he dropped with them. *We're going under, buddy.*

He crashed into the water. It smacked against his skin, stinging his belly and chest. He went under, deep into the river.

He jogged onto the court with his team, but he felt like he moved underwater. The crowd moaned; everything around him moved in slow motion. His eyes turned to weights.

On the jump ball, the center tipped it in his direction. He caught it, dropping his arms back, pulling the ball to his side.

A player from the other squad reached for it. His nail scraped Jackson's arm. It was an honest mistake. He was reaching for the ball.

Jackson saw the kid turn into a shadow, his molecules changing into dark mist. The bleachers dripped pink water, spilling waterfalls onto the court. He swung. His knuckles connected with the player's nose, and the kid dropped.

The pink water rippled and waved, penetrating the court. He found himself surrounded. The benches cleared and the entire gym erupted. A combination of people and shadows bounced into each other like they were in a mosh pit.

A player charged from his left. Jackson turned and bashed him in the eye. Another one dropped. This one wore the same colors as Jackson.

He bobbed and jerked with the current of the crowd. A man knocked into him, and Jackson reacted, wrapping his hands around his throat. He leaned on top of the man, holding him on the ground, squeezing his neck. The guy's face turned bright red, and there was such satisfaction in seeing him struggle. This man was his panic, his insomnia, his father's suicide attempt, his mother. Squeeze. Do you like that? Do you feel that fear?

Someone wrapped their arms around Jackson.

Whoever grabbed him dragged him through the crowd, out of the gym, and into the locker room. Once they were alone, he released Jackson from his grip. "You could have killed that man," Carvallo said.

"What?"

"Jesus son, are you here?" He snapped his fingers in front of Jackson's eyes.

"Why are we in the locker room?"

"All right, listen to me. You just hurt someone. I can't cover you on

those punches you threw. Everyone saw you do that. I'll gladly say I saw that boy hit you first, but you're probably gonna get suspended from some games. I'll say that after the crowd rushed the court, you were with me the whole time. You following?" Jackson nodded, although he didn't know if he followed. "You never touched that guy. You and I rushed back here to get to safety. Now you stay back here. I gotta go break that crowd up. Then I'm gonna take you home and you're gonna get some fucking sleep. Okay?"

Something grabbed Jackson's leg, and the surface of the water pulled away from him. He tried to kick his leg away, but the figure continued to drag him down, down, down, deeper into the river. He squirmed and pushed up against the weight on his foot. He put his sole on the figure's forehead and saw Carvallo holding him down. He watched that man die, and now that man was going to return the favor.

Whispers reverberated in the water.

Let go.

Be free.

Swim.

The air in his lungs pushed into his mouth, wanting to escape. His face felt like it may explode, along with his heart. The distance between him and the surface grew.

Just when he thought he was dead for sure, Carvallo let go.

Let go.

Be free.

Swim.

Swim with us.

He swam. His arms and legs flapped. The surface raced toward him.

When he emerged, he inhaled too quickly, sucking in a gulp of water. He choked and gagged on it. Water mixed with saliva dribbled out of his mouth. The river was shrouded in blackness, making it impossible to see beneath the surface. Carvallo could be right behind or under him, ready to grab him again.

His arms flailed as he propelled himself toward the riverbank.

Something slid against the skin on his ankle. He twitched, praying it was a fish.

When he reached the bank, he pulled himself up, crawling against the stones. He heaved, spitting out water, gagging, begging for oxygen.

He expelled the last bits of water, puking away its invasion on his lungs, gasping in the fresh air.

In front of him, a shadow man swelled out of the river, an army of shadow men behind him. Jackson tried to stand up but fell right back down. A sharp, stabbing pain grew in his chest. He was going to die.

No, he was going to run. He would run forever. Amanda had said he had given up on life. He hadn't. Twice tonight, he had jumped off his jetty and he fought with every ounce of his energy. He would continue to do that until Alexandria and her platoon of dead things left him alone. He cared about his life.

He cared.

His eyes began to shut.

He would fight.

His arms lost their strength, and he couldn't prop himself up any longer.

He would never give up.

The shadows closed in around him as he drifted into the blackness.

CHAPTER 28

LONG TIME COMING

Vassar sucked on a lollipop while the MEs checked on the body in the kitchen. His partner—no, his underling—Deputy Sheriff Morgan sat next to him with his legs spread out and his arms around his chest. Vassar stared at the cute redheaded ME's butt as she bent over the body.

"You watch the Sox last night?" Morgan said.

"Nah." He twirled the pop in his mouth.

His radio chirped. *"This is Murph, responding from the 10-42 down at 480 Woodbine. We have a body. Looks like a 187. We need a bus and some MEs over here."*

The MEs looked up from the body. "Did I hear that right?" the pretty redhead said.

"Sounds like it." Vassar pulled the walkie to his mouth. "Murph, can you repeat?"

Murph repeated the same information. The redhead wiped her brow with her forearm, avoiding touching it with her stained glove.

"We still got a lot to do over here," she said. "Ask him if he can sit on it for a bit."

"Murph, I have them over here, right now. Gonna be a little bit. Can you hang?"

"Yeah, I got nothing else to do. This lady has a record collection."

Vassar laughed. The redhead and her old man partner snapped some pictures.

Morgan kicked Vassar's leg. "Two 187s in one day? About a block apart, too. Seems odd."

Vassar thought it was odd, too, but didn't want to say anything. He hoped they weren't related, but if a dolt like Morgan wondered about it, he had to at least check. He pulled the pop out of his mouth and hit the button on his walkie. "Murph, anything weird with your vic's eyes?"

"You mean, like, are they missing? They sure are. You know she has these things alphabetized by artist and then put in chronological order?"

"No shit? Two vics, no eyes?" the redhead said while she snapped a picture.

Vassar leaned forward. "Needs to be one more for us to call 'em a serial killer, but we definitely got someone on a roll."

"Actually, I think that would be called a spree killing. Serial killers have cooling off periods."

Vassar shrugged.

The redhead continued to look at the bulbous body, snapping pictures from all angles. "My guess is you'll have your third one show up soon enough."

Vassar sat up. "I'm gonna go out for a smoke, leave you two to your job. Morgan, why don't you head down the road and meet up with Murph. Walkie me and let me know anything I need to know."

Vassar sat on the front steps, letting the morning sun saturate him. His eyes squinted, adjusting to it. He lit a smoke and tried to piece together what he suspected happened in this house. He had an idea. He had a damn good idea, but like most of his damn good ideas, people second-guessed him. He needed to make sure he pieced this thing together perfectly, so no one could doubt him.

The new victim messed with his theory, but it didn't stop him from trying to connect the dots. Once Morgan reported back, he'd pull it together.

The ambulance guys sat in the back of their bus, chatting with each other, waiting for the MEs to let them take the body away.

The door opened behind him and the redhead came out. She had taken her gloves off and held a cigarette in her hands.

"You mind if I join you?"

"Sure. What you got going on in there, besides what I already know?"

She lit the cigarette and puffed a clump of smoke into the air. "Looks like he put up a fight. Nailed someone with that bat. Some kind of black gunk on the bat and on the floor around it. No idea what it is. It isn't blood, though. We'll test it at the lab. After that, we don't have much. Whoever got him did it pretty easily. Plucked his eyes out with their thumbs and then slit his throat. It's all nice and clean. Not finding any prints yet, but we still got a lot to check over. I may just finish it on my own and send Ron over to the second call. Gonna be a long fucking Sunday."

"And on the seventh day. . ."

"The lord rested." She puffed a hard drag on the butt, sucking it down quickly.

"It's a messy scene. If the other one's the same way, you guys got your work, that's for sure." Vassar wasn't in a rush to get back inside, so he took his drag nice and slowly.

"Wonderboy," she said.

"Huh?"

"That's what the bat said. Wonderboy."

"It's from *The Natural.* Good movie. Ray was a movie buff. Owned Valiant Video."

"Ah, no shit? I never cared much for movies. I like television better." She flicked her cigarette onto the sidewalk and headed back in.

Vassar stayed outside, waiting for Morgan to radio.

"Same thing over here, Vas. No eyes, slit throat. Hanging in the

kitchen. Damn near same positioning, too. Almost identical scene, 'cept her house looks about fifty years in the past."

"All right. Do me a favor. Check her purse or whatever she has for a billfold. Lemme know if she has a Valiant card."

He lit another cigarette while he waited for a response. Across from Ray's house, a stretch of woods spread around Switch Falls. A rabbit dashed through the bushes. Birds fluttered from branch to branch chirping their obnoxious songs. Everything over there felt so alive.

"Yeah, she's got one."

"Do me another favor. Get in touch with Margie Bastille. She works there a couple nights a week. Find out how often your vic rented."

"You want me to call the store? They can check their computers or something."

"Store won't be open, dumbass. Ray opened the store. If you haven't noticed, he's in no position."

"What about Jackson? I can call him. He'll know for sure."

He gripped the walkie hard, pretending it was Morgan's throat. "I said call Margie. Do not call Jackson. Clear?"

"Got it."

"When you find out, get back over here."

He squinted across the street. The rabbit hopped along the roadside growth. Vassar walked toward it, keeping his movements slow and quiet. He made it halfway across the street before the rabbit saw him and ran straight into the woods. It scurried into the thick green forest floor. In the distance, the falls ran deep and loud. Beyond the bushes and trees, he could barely make out the showering waterway. He moved his head forward. The water moved oddly, almost pouring down the falls in slow motion.

"You gonna try and catch us a rabbit for lunch?" one of the EMTs said.

Vassar turned around and walked over to the ambulance.

"Woulda had him if you guys coulda just shut the fuck up for five minutes."

They laughed.

"Some fuckin' day, huh boys?" Vassar said.

"Better than that night we had the suicide. Jesus, the sun sitting on her for days. Ack. I've seen a lot of shit. That one was rough," one of them said.

"Oh yeah, speaking of which, I worked a shift over in Richmond yesterday, found a dude who drowned; someone popped his eyes out for good measure. It was a mess. Anyway, turned out to be the suicide's boyfriend. Her mom was at the scene when we got there. She was a fucking wreck," the other EMT said.

Vassar leaned forward. "Wait, the suicide girl's boyfriend got murdered?"

"Yup."

"Eyes gone?"

"Yup."

"Why the fuck didn't you tell me?" He smacked the guy on the side of the head, hard enough to let him know he meant it, but light enough so as not to start a fistfight.

"Why does it matter?"

"The body we got in this house has its eyes popped out, you dipshit."

"How the hell was I supposed to know that? ME has us waiting out here."

Vassar stormed to the cruiser. *That makes three*, he thought. *That makes a serial killer*. And just for added punctuation: *I got you now, fucker*. He pulled his cell out of the glove box and cycled through his contacts looking for Richard Massen.

"Yellow."

"Richie?"

"Hey, buddy. I was just about to call you."

"Hold up. Did you work the case the other day where a kid drowned, had his eyes removed?"

"That's what I was just about to call you for."

"You find the body of a kid who dated a girl we found dead over here and you decided not to call me for a day?"

"Whoa. Slow it down. I called your Sheriff last night. He said the dead girl was an open and shut suicide."

"It was. Might not be anymore. Why were you gonna call me then?"

"Ah, I'm looking for someone who was last seen with our vic. He's a Switch guy. A witness said he saw them together at a gas station, knew the guy because, and I quote, 'Everybody knows him, he's famous.' Of course, the wiseass doesn't have a name for this supposedly famous character, only that he knew who he was, because the guy is infamous."

"Who?"

"Witness said he's the guy who played for the Tanner's Switch basketball team some ten to twelve years ago and knocked a Chariho player out on the court. Says it was all over the local yokel news for weeks. I personally flip the channel when sports are on, so I don't have a fucking clue what this guy is talking about. Anyway, I'm looking for a name. Can you check out any basketball fights, help me figure out who this guy is?"

A smile crawled up Vassar's face. "No need. It's common knowledge, you're just an idiot."

"So, who is it?"

"His name is Jackson."

What Vassar decided to keep to himself, was that after Jackson knocked out one of Chariho's players, he knocked out one of his own. He'd cold-cocked a sophomore small forward, number 17, named Frankie Vassar.

"You're kidding? Jackson what?"

"Jackson Rathburn."

"Oh shit." There was silence after that.

"What?"

"Hey, I gotta go."

"No, tell me what you just figured out, Richie."

"The mother of your suicide was at the scene when we got to this kid. She kept telling us someone stole her daughter's diaries and swears it was that name you just said. Jackson whatever. At the time, we were like, lady, we got a murder here, we don't have time to find missing diaries, but if this all ties to your suicide, maybe we got something here."

Vassar smiled so wide it hurt his cheeks. "Do me a favor, Richie?"

"Sure, what's up?"

"Let me apprehend this kid. You can have the arrest. Just let me bring him to you."

"You wanna do the legwork, go for it. But the questioning happens here."

"Whatever, I just wanna see his face when I cuff the fucker," Vassar said as he looked up at the glorious sun.

CHAPTER 29

THE BURNING OF THE GASPEE

Simon prepped the veggies, cutting onions in half-slices, putting the peppers in containers and wrapping them in plastic, slicing, dicing, keeping a tempo with the knife as it knocked onto the cutting board. PizzAmore had opened an hour ago, but he started late, unable to get himself in gear. Luckily, customers usually didn't come in until noon.

He placed everything in the walk-in cooler when a soft giggle floated through the air.

He could have explained it away. Maybe some customers had come in, maybe the buzzing from the walk-in freezer made him imagine the sound. Simon was too smart for that. He knew what it was, and he knew what it meant.

"Hello, Bunny," he said as he walked out and shut the cooler door.

The giggling continued. It came from the back hallway, which led into the backroom of Valiant Video.

The girl ran by the threshold, and he had about one second to process the figure in his mind, but he didn't even need that second;

he could have envisioned her with his eyes closed.

"Bunny."

She wore the beige dress with the ruffles at the bottom. Pictures of chirping birds fluttered in the wrinkles on the straps and the waist. Her chestnut hair blew back like a windsock. Oh boy, could she run. Her legs were little sticks, hardly bending at the knee, extending back and forth. Zip. Zip. Zip. Simon would laugh. So would Charissa. Little Petrina, their Bunny, would run and run, and he and Charissa would crack up as she chased the wind.

Charissa died last year. Old age stopped her ticker. Petrina died in 1997. It wasn't her who ran through the hallway, nor was it her ghost. Simon knew better than that. He had seen the face of death in the dark pools under Jackson's eyes. He approached the boy when he fell to the ground in front of the video store, just to make sure. Those pools were genetic, carried from his father right on down. But death visited no man solely. Death visited all who knew the man. Simon's turn had arrived, and he would have to accept that.

Petrina ran by again. She dragged a yo-yo. It lit up and flashed neon colors as it hopped and spun against the hallway tiles.

She had bought the yo-yo at the Gaspee Day's arts and crafts festival in Pawtuxet Village. She had dragged Simon's hand, leading him to every booth. "Pop-Pop, can we buy this?" Her pouty lips and wide eyes played against him.

Two weeks later, Simon took Charissa and Petrina to the Burning of the Gaspee reenactment. The Pawtuxet Rangers sprang to action, setting the boat ablaze. The crowd cheered as if the revolution began anew. Simon wrapped his arm around Charissa as the boat flapped its flames into the air.

Behind him, Petrina ran with the other children, dragging the yo-yo. A small red-headed boy chased her with a handful of bang snaps, tossing them at her feet. She laughed and screamed, pretending the pops were dynamite.

When she slipped, her head cracked against the front grille of a smoky blue doughboy truck. The accident could have happened to a thousand children; each would have walked away with a different injury, some more serious than others, but only one in a thousand would have died instantly. Petrina was that one. The wrong angle met the wrong velocity met the wrong time. Run, run, little girl, run. Run until you can't run no more. And so Petrina did.

Simon and Charissa never had another child, never considered it. PizzAmore took the place of childcare, and they worshipped it with the same magnitude a person would adore their young. It kept them busy. It left them no time to consider what would have happened if they had watched more vigilantly, or if Simon hadn't bought her the yo-yo whose string tripped her up, or if they had told the little red-headed boy to stop throwing crackers at their daughter.

"Catch me, Daddy." Her footsteps echoed down the hall.

Simon walked with slow, plodding steps, no longer at an age to catch her, too old for that even when she was alive.

"Where are you, little Bunny?"

He turned the corner into the hall and an unseasonably cold draft whipped the skin on his face and arms. The cement brick walls exuded coldness even in the thickest parts of summer, but what it produced to Simon while he pressed toward his pretend daughter was not cold stone, but winter breeze. It snapped and bit his flesh.

Petrina skipped toward the back entrance of Valiant. She opened the door, turned to her father, let a smile worm up one side of her face, and entered. The half-smile, with all of its malicious intentions, sent a shiver up Simon's spine in a way that even the faux winter breeze could not. If he had any question on whether this figure was his daughter, that smile was the tell he needed. Petrina's soul contained no evil and, thus, could not produce such horrifying glee.

He followed her into the video store. Valiant had a grimness to it when the lights were off and the shelves were half-vacant.

She giggled.

He turned his head, scanning the store, the abandoned shelves, the empty spaces, the thin aisles. She hid from him, playing a game before the fun turned ugly.

"Find me, Daddy."

Three of four movies fell from a shelf down one of the aisles.

He moved toward them. "Where are you hiding little Bunny?"

"Hahahaha."

He knew he would die, knew this evil presence would kill him. He knew this was not his little girl, nor her spirit. Yet, he had to find her, let his arms wrap around her one last time. Is it okay to hug away your sadness before that very sadness strangles the life from you? He thought so.

He turned down the aisle where the movies had fallen. Nothing. What did he expect?

This evil spirit may not have been Petrina, but to imitate her, it must know her, must know her truths. He should use that to find some comfort.

"Petrina?"

"Hahahaha."

Movies fell from the other side of the store.

"Petrina, what do you remember best about your father?"

An entire rack of shelves fell forward, landing on his back. Simon tumbled to the floor. The shelves were light, so it didn't hurt him too badly, but his fragile bones clapped into the ground.

"Petrina? What do you remember best about your father?"

"The stories." Her feet pitter-pattered toward the back door. It swung open. She had gone back into the hallway.

The stories. Every night, he would tuck her into bed and pull out a children's story. After he had read a few pages, he'd toss the book to the side and say, "I have a better story for you." She would smile and laugh, and he would tell her a story from his childhood, adding in as much embellishment as needed to make the story fun. Superpowers, monsters, aliens, whatever made his life sound more exciting, whatever helped her sleep.

It took him a while to get back to PizzAmore. His knees hurt from the fall, and it's not like his legs carried a lot of speed before the injury.

When he opened the backdoor to his restaurant, he nearly fell over in fright. Petrina stood in front of the grease trap, pouring something into it. He smelled it. Some kind of gas. A stream of it slicked the floor from the door he'd just entered to the grease trap.

"No. Not this way. Please. Not the restaurant. Just me. Please. Please."

She dropped a match and laughed. "Bye-bye, Daddy."

The flames whooshed into the sky, bursting upward, then driving toward him. He had no chance. The fire would spread before he could escape.

"Please, Bunny. Let me hug you."

The flames came at him; he moved out of the way and walked toward her. The line of fire screamed and grew on his right. Petrina stood in front of it, smiling.

"Let me hug you." He extended his hands.

She giggled and put her arms out.

Flames extended to the grills. The propane would explode any minute.

"Come to me, Bunny." Flames spat at his face. The skin on his arm burned from the heat.

He reached her, bent down, and hugged her. She hugged him back, wrapping her arms around his head. He squeezed tightly.

"I love you, Bunny."

"I love you too, Pop-Pop."

She pulled his hair back. His head jerked into the flame. "AAAAH-HHHHHHH!"

"HAHAHAHAHAHA."

He fell backward into the flame. She landed on top of him. The fire immersed them. His flesh melted and he screamed.

The last thing he heard on this planet was Petrina's malicious laughter and the vulgar popping sound his eyes made as Bunny ripped them from his face.

"HAHAHAHAHAHA."

CHAPTER 30
HEADING HOME

Jackson woke up to a streak of sun slicing across his face, and, for a minute, forgot that his father was no longer dying two feet behind his head. He sat up, trying to figure out where he was and how he got there.

Stones jutted into his legs, and his back hurt from where it had rested against them. It all came to him. The animals. The running. The shadows. The figure in the bedroom with his father. The voices in the water.

He had passed out or collapsed or just straight fell asleep. Either way, he felt refreshed in a way he hadn't in weeks. He must have been out for hours. He guessed it was afternoon by the way the sun beat down, bright and hot.

Why hadn't the shadows killed him? First, one of them let him go when it was drowning him, and then they let him sleep? Maybe they couldn't kill him yet. Maybe there was more damage to be done. It didn't matter. He was tired of trying to figure out something that defied logic.

He stood up and stretched. The aches in his muscles returned, but it was nice to stretch them, almost good to feel the pain.

The scratches that had accumulated on his body itched.

He went to the water. In the daylight, he could see the bottom, crystal clear. He splashed some on his arms and face to wash the wounds. The coolness invigorated him, the fountain of youth.

He dove in, giving up his fear, giving up his worry. Life came back to him. The water took away the pain. It was cool and fresh and numbing.

After his dip, he walked along a narrow pathway. Patches of tufted hairgrass smacked against his ankles and lower legs, making them itchy. The humid air dried the water from his flesh and made it sticky with sweat.

Up ahead, a neighborhood came into view. Alexandria's wrath could happen anywhere, but the street ahead felt like a better place to be. The woods kept him alone, made him prey. The open street emitted a sense of security. It promised, if nothing else, witnesses to whatever insanity came his way.

As the street came closer, he recognized Ray's house. He had been there a few times over the years, mainly in the evenings to have a movie marathon. He knew where he was, and that was good. Ray only lived about ten blocks from him.

After dashing past some of the large oaks, through some more patches of prickly grass, he saw the ambulance, the EMTs, and Vassar talking to someone on the phone. He couldn't hear Vassar, but the EMTs were loud.

"So, who is gonna open the video store tomorrow because that's my day off, and I wanna buy some goin' outta business movies?"

"Go get the keys off the vic. We can go shopping tonight." They laughed.

Jackson cringed, jaw dropping.

Ray was dead. Someone had killed Ray. Not someone, Alexandria had killed Ray. He knew it. In his heart, he knew it. His friend was dead, and the last time he had spoken to him, he had verbally torn the man to shreds. He had never felt so low in his life.

This changed everything. If Alexandria killed Ray, she did it for a reason. She did it to destroy everything Jackson loved.

He also knew that the police would blame him for it. Alexandria had surely made it look like he did it, and that wouldn't have been difficult. Despite Ray having covered for Jackson when Vassar tried to arrest him, there were plenty of witnesses to Jackson's breakdown, and word would have gotten out that Ray had fired him. Alexandria was hell-bent on breaking him, not just physically, but emotionally. She would destroy his bones and his reputation. She would make the world cheer for his destruction as she wrung the life out of him.

Amanda. If Alexandria was going after the people in his life, Amanda could already be dead. He had to get to her. Maybe there was time. Unfortunately, his car was wrapped around a tree, and her house was nowhere near Ray's neighborhood.

He would rush to his house, call a taxi, call Amanda, and pray she answered. Whether she did or not, he would take the cab to her house. Nothing else mattered at this point, just her.

He took a sharp turn left and rushed through a spread of ferns, masking himself behind the lines of oaks. He dashed toward Woodbine.

He leapt over a series of bushes onto the sidewalk where Ray's street met with Woodbine. Down the road, Vassar and the EMTs kept each other preoccupied, while Jackson darted across the street and out of their view.

He must have looked like a lunatic. A shirtless man, covered in gashes and cuts, traversed through a quaint neighborhood, running like he just robbed a house. The police presence in the area probably had everyone up in arms already. Once they saw him, it seemed likely that 911 would receive more than a few calls.

He needed to get out of this neighborhood.

Two cruisers sat in front of a house on Woodbine. More cops. To get out of the area, he had to run right past them. If the cops came outside, at the very least, they would question him. If these cops had already spoken to the cops down the road, they would cuff him before he had a chance to say a word.

He came to a house on his left, a gaudy, pink colonial with a short vinyl fence wrapping around the yard. The driveway was empty, the lights were off, and the fence could provide a decent cover. With strength he thought left him days ago, he pushed himself over, rolling off into the yard.

Of course, there was a god-damned dog. At least it was a living dog. It shouted guttural woofs: *Police, hey, police, weird guy with no shirt on over here!*

"Shh Shh Shh Shh."

The brown boxer stayed back, barking at this stranger in its yard, but showing no signs of attacking. In fact, as Jackson hunched forward, the dog skipped backward. Jackson reached toward it. He glanced toward the cruisers, able to see them through the spaces between fence boards, which meant if the police came out to their cars, they could see him, too. He needed to shut this dog up fast.

He lay down on the lawn, trying to make himself look less intimidating, and extended his arms. "Come here, pup."

The dog reduced his barks, hesitating for a few beats before letting out another roar. It looked at him, unsure what to do. He opened his palm, and the dog slapped it with his paw. Its owner must have taught him the trick. High five.

He pet the dog's head. It shot him a confused look and let out one last half-bark. It came out like a question. "Rrrruufff?"

He continued to pet the dog's head, and with each stroke, the dog calmed. Within a few minutes, the boxer sprawled onto the grass with his tail wagging. Jackson had a new friend, and he loved that his new pal had life in his eyes.

He took the opportunity to book it across the yard. The dog chased him playfully. He hopped the fence on the other side, into another yard on another street. He had about a twenty-minute walk before he reached his house.

On Spindle Street, he saw the tail end of a bus. Its metal bones let out a series of violent belches as it bobbled along a minefield of potholes, and it hissed as it turned a corner and rode away from him. He wished he had gotten here two minutes earlier so he could have jumped on. His insane appearance would have fit right in on Rhode Island's public transportation.

He jogged. He jogged, and he ran, and he stopped, and he limped. Amanda. He needed to get to Amanda. This is what she had wanted out of him. She wanted action, and God damn it, he acted. He would save her. He had to. This was his purpose. He couldn't save his father from cancer, but he could save her.

A cruiser flew down the road, its sirens blaring.

He jumped, gripped his chest, and almost booked it into someone's yard, but the cruiser just rolled right on ahead, going in the direction he went. He needed to get to his house and off these streets.

More sirens blared in the distance. Something major went down. Jesus. Maybe there was death all over Tanner's Switch. Maybe the focal point of the world's end spread from Jackson, through the streets, through the town, through the universe, blood spilling everywhere.

The sun beat down on him. He grew tired and worn by the time he reached his street.

Panic flushed through him as he turned the corner. He trembled, looking at three cruisers, lights flashing on his road. The officers headed into Marybeth's house.

At first, he sighed a breath of relief. They weren't after him. Then it hit him. Shit. Alexandria got to Marybeth, too. The only crime Marybeth committed was helping Jackson's father die in peace. Jackson shouldn't have wished those mean thoughts about her.

Alexandria went after inconsequential people in Jackson's life. Amanda was probably dead already.

He ran past Marybeth's, past Miss Nosy's, and up his lawn to the front door. He unlocked it, struggling to get the key to work. The door opened and he charged in until he saw something that outdid every odd occurrence he had dealt with over the past few weeks.

He stopped running. He stopped moving. He may have even stopped breathing.

He had taken pictures of dead animals, and those dead animals came to life in the woods and attacked him. He had stared into the face of a dead teenage girl, and she came back to haunt him, torturing him. Carvallo had met his end when an SUV rolled on top of him. Yet, he came back and snatched Jackson's leg underwater. Jackson had seen the living versions of every dead thing he had come across. All but one. All but the one he wanted to see, the one who haunted him the most without having to appear in front of him.

Of all of the dead eyes he had looked at, only one set had failed to reappear. Until now.

"Hello, Buddy."

CHAPTER 31
BELIEVE WHAT YOU WILL

Amanda rolled up her spaghetti straps and added them to the Samsonite luggage bag. After she squished them in with the rest of her clothes, she took a picture of her and Jackson out of its frame and placed it in a zipper compartment. In the picture, she and Jackson were smiling and holding hands while sitting on a giant stone along the walkways of Purgatory Chasm.

She zipped the bag, pulled out the retractable handle, and propped it on its wheels, ready to take it to the car. The picture awakened a sadness that prodded her chest, and she needed to sit.

She hated herself for ending it the way she had, hated leaving a note, hated having to say the things she did, but she needed him to experience a rude awakening.

She hadn't told him that the job was set now. The coach for Syracuse had surprised her and had come down while she coached the Tanner's Switch girls. Mrs. Randolph, head coach of the Syracuse College women's basketball team, liked what she saw and hired her on the spot. Amanda asked her if she had the power to make that decision or if it needed to go through the Dean or the athletic department, honestly unaware of how college basketball leadership worked. Mrs. Randolph winked at her with a rambunctious grin and said, "There's formalities, but you'll soon learn, I get what I want."

This proved to be true. Within a few days, Amanda received a letter welcoming her to the team. Now, she was off to work the summer camps and look for a place to live. She would come back to Tanner's Switch, of course. She still had to sell her house—although a house near the Breachway could be on fire and still sell for above its asking price—and take care of some minor details, maybe even see Jackson and... Well, who knows?

Crash.

The shattering sound startled her. She leapt up and ran toward it. It reminded her of when Jackson's shower door exploded. When she entered the kitchen, she saw it was shattered glass, but the source of what caused it was not a mystery the way it had been at Jackson's house.

A dead raccoon lay on the kitchen floor, adorned with shiny pieces of glass from the window it had smashed through. Someone had thrown a dead raccoon through her window, and for a moment, she couldn't lie to herself; she thought it was Jackson.

Her mind changed a few seconds later.

She screamed as every window in the house smashed. The one behind her in the living room and the ten sliding picture windows from the sunroom on her left exploded glass pieces all over her.

She kept screaming, thinking someone had set off a bomb, or that something had exploded outside. Her arms formed an arc over her head, protecting her as best they could from the shards. Pieces stuck into her arms and, despite the cover, into her face and hair.

She looked up, panicking. She didn't know what to do.

It wasn't a bomb. A cat. An opossum. A fox. Dead animals lay all over the floor. Someone had thrown carcasses through every single window. No one could have done that. It had to be a group of people, but she knew it wasn't. She knew what it was but refused to believe it. It couldn't be.

Guhguhguhguhguhguhguhguhguhguhguhguh.

She squeezed her eyes shut, not wanting to turn to the sound that came from her bedroom.

Guhguhguhguhguhguhguhguhguhguhguhguhguhguh.

"Please, God, no."

The noise was getting closer. She had to either turn and see it or run and never look back.

Guhguhguhguhguhguhguhguhguhguhguhguhguhguh.

She turned.

If she had to explain what happened next, she would have said her soul left her body. The world froze. Her heart, her breath, her blood, her skin, all went somewhere else. It was just her mind wrapping around what she faced.

Jackson truly had been haunted. He'd tried to let her know her in his own way, telling her without saying it directly, hoping she'd piece it together.

The dead *thing* moved toward her, its face covered in broken blood vessels and decay.

It would kill her. That's what it wanted to do. It wanted to kill her.

"Jackson," Amanda said.

Guhguhguhguhguhguhguhguhguhguhguhguhguhguh.

Amanda came back into her body again, and she ran. The ghost creature stood between her and the front door, so she went out the back, running across the patio, into the backyard where her neighbors had all gathered to see what caused the smashing sounds, through the side gate, and into her car.

Poor Jackson. She just kept thinking it over and over again. Poor Jackson. She wasn't wrong to have thought his ramblings were crazy. They were. This was crazy. Her windows smashing in due to the impact of dead animal corpses, a dead girl walking out of her bedroom, this shit was crazy.

She turned the car on and sped out of the driveway.

"Jackson."

LIAR, LIAR, STORES ON FIRE

Vassar almost exploded with joy. Another person murdered, this time Jackson's neighbor. This kid had lost his shit. He was going to kill everyone. Luckily for Vassar, no one in The Switch had picked up on the Jackson thing, yet. So, he had time to make this arrest exactly how he wanted it.

Marybeth, the newest victim, lived a few doors down. Vassar could head there, make an appearance at the scene, stroll a few doors down, and make a beautiful arrest on this beautiful day.

Tanner's Switch had an inordinate number of unsolved deaths within its confines, many mysteries, but not this one. Vassar would wrap this one up in a nice, neat bow.

As he drove toward Marybeth's, information came through dispatch that a raging fire had broken out at some local businesses. Vassar had more important things to do than sit and watch some firefighters do their jobs. Someone else could handle it.

A minute or two later, Murph chirped through on the walkie. *"Vass, ain't that Valiant Video's address? Seems weird after we just left Ray's and all."*

Holy shit, the kid had burned down the video store. He was on a roll. Vassar laughed. Maybe Jackson wasn't home, after all. It depended on whether he set the fire before or after he killed Marybeth. He should call some officers to check out Jackson's home, bring him in if he was there, but he wanted to, HAD to, catch Jackson himself.

"Nance, I'm gonna head over to that Valiant Video fire."

"Okay, Vass."

He spun the car around, heading toward the sirens. When he turned onto Valiant's street, he couldn't believe his eyes. Valiant and PizzAmore were engulfed. Sirens blared from everywhere. Firefighters rushed around the building, spraying the fire, yelling to each other. Jackson really outdid himself.

He parked across the street and ran across the four lanes between him and the raging flames. Something popped and a ball of fire shot out from the side of PizzAmore.

"Shit."

"Jesus Christ."

"There's more propane in there."

Vassar walked around, creating a large loop, keeping a safe distance, but wanting to get a view from the back. He had to assess where Jackson might have run. A killing spree happened in Tanner's Switch this morning, and the only other person who knew the culprit was a Richmond cop. The other dolts in the office could say what they wanted about Vassar, but he figured it out before any of them. The rest of them would get it eventually—the clues were pretty glaring—but Vassar caught it first.

The back of the store had flames shooting out the doors. The dumpster sitting against the brick wall had caught on fire, too. Firefighters worked on it. Vassar sidestepped into the woodsy area beyond the back asphalt lot. Jackson could have come out this way, using the woods as cover as he made his way to his next killing location.

Vassar edged the woods, looking for clues, anything to tell him where Jackson went.

An explosion blasted through the front of the building. The ground shook. The men out front screamed, glass shattered, a car alarm beeped.

The firefighters in the back ran toward the front. Vassar saw movement in the back door. Someone laughed. A little girl appeared, wearing a beige sundress.

His heart sank.

"Hey, get over here. It's dangerous in there."

"Help me. My daddy is in here."

He moved toward her. "I can't go in there. The firefighters will help. Come here. They will save your daddy. For now, I need you to come to me."

She stood in the door.

"Someone come back here. I need your help. We got a survivor," he yelled.

He doubted anyone could hear through the loud rumblings of flame.

He reached his arm out, unwilling to go much further. He saw how far those flames could blast out. He wouldn't take any risks.

"Come on little girl. Let's go."

She laughed.

"I'm serious. Get out here."

"Okay."

She reached for something inside the hall.

"Little girl, don't do that. Just come out."

She turned to him. A dirty, grotesque smile crawled up her cheeks, sending a chill down his spine.

"Bye-bye."

"What?"

She threw something. At first, he couldn't tell what it was, but it appeared way too heavy for a little girl to throw. It flew at him, though, barreling at a speed Nolan Ryan would have been impressed with.

He didn't have time to dodge, or run, or even figure out what it was until it was in his face. First, he saw the flames wavering in the air, coming from a nozzle. Then it all clicked. It was a propane canister.

"Bye-bye, Vassar. Bye-bye, scumbag. HAHAHAHAHA."
BOOOOOOM.

CHAPTER 33

FAMILY REUNION

"You're not really my father."

"Come with me, buddy. We'll go to Alaska and build a cabin."

His father stood at the front of the couch. Jackson moved in closer, using the couch as a shield. He needed to see the man up close, had to know if this imposter had the right features. His mind screamed for Jackson to touch him, to hug him, to know the feel of his father again, but he couldn't do it. He had to be smart, not let emotion dictate what happened now. Emotions would lead him to mistakes.

The father he looked at was not the man who shriveled away from cancer. This father carried muscle and a little bit of a beer belly. His eyes were alive, on fire almost. The crevices on his tired face soared across his cheeks, under his mouth, and along his forehead.

Jackson's fists clenched and tears dribbled down his face. He didn't wipe them but kept his fists at his sides. He loved this man. He knew this wasn't his father, though. He had to keep reminding himself. Life does not give you second chances with death. It's a period, end of statement.

"I watched you die." Jackson moved along the back of the couch.

"If there's one thing you can count on from your father, I don't lose. Never have. Never will." He moved along the front of the couch, approaching the side.

When Jackson was a child, they played tag this way. Senior would chase him, and Jackson would find a piece of furniture to use as a blockade. They would rotate around it until Jackson was too tired and too dizzy to continue.

"You did lose. You always lost."

"We'll build a cabin, that's what we'll do."

Jackson was in front of the couch now, and his father was behind it. Their eyes locked onto each other. If one changed speeds, so did the other. If Jackson tried to run, his father would be right on his tail.

"Oh, yeah? We'll build a cabin in Alaska? Another pipe dream, Dad. We can't go to Alaska because you can barely get out of bed and smoke a cigarette." Jackson lost himself in the memory, unable to see his father as anything but *dying*. "You lost, Dad. Don't you get that? You lost over and over and over, and you made me lose with you."

Tears roared out of his eyes. "Why did you always do that to me, put your problems on my shoulders? I was a teenager, a kid. I deserved a life, too. I deserved to live, but you never let me. Why did you do that to me? Why?"

"Son, it's beautiful here. Come with me."

"Yup, Dad. We'll build a cabin. And I can bring Amanda too, right?"

His father's eyes widened. "You have to."

Jackson began to weep. He had handled the ghost of the girl, the ghosts of the animals. This was too much. Whatever haunted him played a cheap trick this time. It was unfair. It knew his weakness. It knew he would die for this man, even for the lookalike of him.

"Don't you understand, Son, what this is all about? Don't you get it?"

He shook his head.

"It's always been about you."

Jackson looked up at him, not understanding what he meant. "Just leave me alone. Dad, please, please. I miss you so much, but please, you can go. Just go."

"Alexandria Lucia."

"What?"

"For you. The animals in the woods."

"What do you mean?"

"For you. Having the panic attacks come back."

"Oh, that was for me, huh? Getting attacked by some girl, and some animals, getting thrown off a fucking cliff, not sleeping, not being able to breathe, that was all for me? Well, I hate to be rude, but your presents suck. You can return them." He put his hands on the back of the couch. They shook.

"Son, give your Pops a hug. You're all I need, buddy. It will be me and you." He pepped up. "And you can bring Amanda. You should. You should bring Amanda. We'll build a cabin."

He could hug this man. He could let his father strangle the life out of him. It would be a great way to go. "Did you try to kill yourself for me, too? Was that for me, Dad?"

His father paused, tilted his head as if he considered it. "No. That was for me. That was selfish, but man, oh man, look at the outcome. That's what made all of this possible for you. A misfortunate happenstance, with a fortunate outcome." He smiled a delightful grin that in another life would have made Jackson happy to see, but in this life made him want to punch his father square in the jaw.

"How fucking pleasant. Where's Alexandria? Oh, sorry, wouldn't want to piss her off, Lexia."

"She's at the cabin. You have to see it."

"No, Dad. I don't. I won't."

They had traveled around the couch three times, but now Senior stopped. "But, I love you. You're all I need, buddy." It came out pleading, as if he hadn't even considered the possibility that Jackson would turn the offer down.

Jackson didn't understand what the offer was. Nothing made

sense, but his father's sad plea made Jackson's heart wilt away. Could he turn the man down? He'd done that before, said no when his father asked to hang out, said no when his dad wanted someone to watch the game with him. Jackson had gone out with Amanda instead, gone to bed, gone to be alone. Wasn't that fair, though? Hadn't he done enough? He'd cared for his father his entire life, gave Senior so much of himself. Still, could he turn him down again? He'd regretted every time he did. Could he bear one last regret?

Jackson's stomach dropped in that way a stomach does when you see an injured puppy. He wanted to take away Senior's pain.

But he couldn't. He had tried so many times. He had done everything there was to do, and it was never enough. His father continued to suffer.

What if this actually was his father? What if, in death, Senior suffered even more than in life?

He wanted to throw up, keel over, and bawl. The idea that death does not ease the suffering, but only drags it on, was too much to bear. One life of misery was enough. An eternity of it was an injustice. "Dad, I'm so sorry. I am so sorry. I tried so hard for you. I wanted you to be happy."

His father's eyes scrunched. "I know."

Jackson wiped his eyes now. His father stood on the side of the couch, leaning his hands into the arm. Behind Senior were the stucco walls of the hallway where Jackson ran his fingers before entering that dungeon of a bedroom where Senior died.

"You know."

A laugh shot out of Senior so loudly that Jackson flinched. "Of course."

And he turned and walked toward his room.

"No!" Jackson hopped onto the couch and ran after his father. He didn't want him to leave. He changed his mind. His pops had already left him once.

Senior turned to his son as he closed the bedroom door. He put a finger over his lips and said, "Shh," with a smile as the gap between them closed.

"No, Dad. Please. Don't go."

Jackson jiggled the handle, but the door wouldn't open. His foot kicked and his hands punched, and his head butted into it. "Come back. Please."

He slid to the floor like a bullet had just blasted through his head. Screams and wails left his tongue, startling his own heart. The door wouldn't open.

Clunk. Clunk.

The noise came from inside the room.

"Dad? Open the door."

Something slid under the door. He knew what it was from the silvery lettering on the cover: Lexia's diaries, which he had left in his car, which a tree currently possessed.

He took them.

"Please, Dad. I don't want to kick the door in again. Fine. We *will* do this again." He stood up. A fire burned into his fists. He pounded on the door. "Ten seconds, Pops, or I kick the door in."

The door creaked. It opened just a sliver. His anger mixed with the draft coming from his father's room. He opened the door. The daylight disappeared in the room's darkness. A hollow draft slipped past his feet.

He walked in. His father had disappeared. Gone again.

He sat at his father's computer desk and turned the lamp on.

The words on the front of the diary flickered and glowed. He opened to a random page.

I need him here with me, but he doesn't understand. I can't tell him why only that I need him. Only that if I close my eyes, and he isn't around, I see my father. I see the shadows. I hear the humming, and I know it's bad. It's always bad.

He flipped to another page, somewhere in the middle. A sharp pain landed in his throat. Was it wrong to read the desperate words of a girl who had ended her life? He read, anyway.

I haven't slept in weeks. Two maybe. The girls at school make fun of me because my face is saggy. But it's like, why should I care? I have something they'll never have. I have those sssssongs. . . .

Every page changed. Some of the writing had the tone of normal teenage gibberish. Movies. Music. Complaints. Some of the writing turned erratic and nonsensical.

The way I see what they can't see, it makes me better than anyone. I'm in love with two. ttttwwwoooo. You and me. Me and you. Jason and the songs. I want to talk to someone about them. They. Are. So. Beautiful. But only I can understand it.

Jackson cried, more than a few times, mainly from knowing his father left, but also from Lexia's words. The poor girl had gone through what he now faced, and he knew her outcome. He knew where it led her. He wished he had met her before his father passed. Maybe they could have saved each other.

I have chosen a place for us to meet. My father did, actually. He told it to me in a dream. He told me it would be a special place for me and you, where you and I can finally be happy together, where we can finally touch. Will you like how I feel?

A sickness bubbled in his guts. Bile rode up his esophagus. He read her plans to kill herself. He ran to the kitchen and grabbed a bottle of water, washing down the acidic fluid.

He shouldn't read anymore. It was wrong. He had to. How else could he understand this?

After a few minutes, he went back to the book, unable to stop, despite every piece of his mind wanting him to.

You have asked a request of me that I will not do. I won't, but I am still coming to meet you. Please don't hate me for not following through. I will give you me, but no one else. Let that be enough.

Jackson turned to the creak coming from the direction of the living room. His eyes opened wide.

Please be my father.

On the threshold of his father's room, Alexandria Lucia stood, snarling and caked in blood.

"This is my father's room. You're not welcome here. This place is sacred. I know who you are now." He held the books up. "I understand you. I know what's happening. We both fell in love the same way, didn't we?"

He stood up. She stayed in place, growling like a mad dog. For the first time, he wanted her to come toward him. He wanted to hurt her. "What do you want from me?" He yelled it so loudly, his voice scratched his lungs.

She ran faster than a human should be allowed to run and slammed into him. He flew against the wall where his father once put a picture of Jackson's mother, where his father would fall into a gaze, wishing for a life that would never come because it had already driven past.

She was on top of him, snarling. He fought her, punching and slashing at her with all he had. She fought back with the strength of a God until he lost his energy.

Defeated, he asked one more time. "What the fuck do you want from me?"

She leaned into him like she wanted to whisper a secret, but when her lips touched his ear, she screamed, "YOU."

It echoed in his skull, and he closed his eyes. She screamed the word again and again. "YOU." Each time, it shot into him and pulsed through his veins. It burned as much as it was frigid.

The television screen smashed to bits.

"YOU."

The mirror in his father's bathroom shattered to the floor.

"YOU."

All of the windows exploded out into the lawn.

"YOU."

And then it stopped.

He opened his eyes, and Lexia hovered over him until she folded in on herself the way a newspaper does when you haphazardly turn the page. She crinkled and morphed until she was his father.

He reached for his pops, but before his hand could touch the man's face, it was no longer his father.

Now it was a shadow, and then Ray, and then his mother.

Despite the hate he had for her, a pang hit his belly at the sight of her, knowing she must have died too if the shape had become her.

The figure turned into a ball of mist floating over him, steaming and pouring into itself. Finally, it turned into him.

Jackson.

It seemed weird to look at himself, more alien than all the rest.

And he breathed it in. The mist poured into his nostrils, into his mouth, down into his lungs. It seeped into his eyes and his ears.

Inside of him, it traveled through his bloodstream and into his brain. It turned into a swirling ball of life and death, and he knew what the swirling ball meant. He knew what it stood for. He knew the purpose of everything that had happened.

He knew everything.

He had been a child in a room with a ball and four white walls, and he had thought that was the world. Now, he viewed the galaxy from a plane yet unknown to humanity, and he saw the way a star becomes an ocean, and a mountain becomes a freckle. He saw himself, but now from every angle. He could see the pores on the back of his neck. He saw what lingered in every room. He saw it all and wept for humankind because people could only see in front of them. They would never know that entire lives are born and killed behind their heads. He saw it all, and he no longer felt lonely. All of the emptiness disappeared, the gaps were filled in, the shadows righted themselves once more.

The doorbell rang. He couldn't wait to answer it. Nothing could be more perfect.

He just had to grab something first.

CHAPTER 34

OF ALL OF THE PLACES I COULD TAKE YOU, I CHOOSE EVERYWHERE

He opened the door, and Amanda's face, chiseled with fear, stood in front of him.

"Jackson, I am so…"

"…I am so glad you're here."

He grabbed her. As he plunged her toward him, she frowned, and her eyes opened wide. He waited for more, but nothing came, just a small gasp, a tiny release of air from her mouth.

"It all makes sense now. I need to tell you about it. I need you to understand. I'm so happy you're here. You can come with me."

She gasped again. It sounded like steam from a teapot before it really got going.

"Do you remember when my father tried to kill himself?" He didn't wait for an answer. There was no time for conversation. "I had had those panic attacks for a while, and I couldn't sleep. I had really bad insomnia, remember? Anyway, that night in the bathroom, I saw it. It was the panic attacks that made me see it.

"All of the stuff that's been happening recently, it's not new. I saw it back then. I saw death. No, that's a terrible way to put it. It's not death. When you hear that term, you picture the guy with the scythe. It's not death. It does appear as a figure, but that's only how we understand it because we're human." He laughed. "I know, this sounds so weird, right?

"We shouldn't call it death; we should call it dying because it's not a noun. It's a verb. It's an action. Isn't that so beautiful? It's an action, and I can see it. I can see it happening. You can't see a kick. You can see the boot, and you can see it move in the motion of a kick, but you can't see a kick because a kick isn't a thing, it's a verb. It's like that word we learned in high school. What was it?" He paused to think about it. Amanda did not speak. Did not move. He was surprised by her lack of response to what was happening.

"A gerund. Yes, a gerund. A verb acting as a noun. I can see dying. I can see the actual substance that creates death. I saw it that night in the bathtub, and I heard it hum. But it knew I saw it, and it was afraid. It made me forget." He sighed and squeezed her tighter. His teeth clenched as he brought her into him.

"It could have all ended there. I could have gone on living my life the way I wanted to, but dying felt vulnerable when I saw it, and it loved me for making it feel that way." He laughed again, the laughter of someone who just discovered a cavern filled with treasure.

"But I still had too much stake in life at that point. It tested me, though. It made my insomnia and panic attacks worse to see if I would sacrifice for it. It made me hallucinate those shadows. And I did. I showed it that I was willing to sacrifice for it. I quit basketball. But there was still my pops and there was still you." His right hand pressed hard on her shoulder.

"My pops might have seen it, too. I think that's why he tried to kill himself, but in the same way I had you, he had me, so after the suicide attempt, he didn't try it again. Anyway, I still had you, and that love was strong, so death, dying, I mean, left me alone. Then it came for my pops, and it hovered in that room, and it saw me day in and day out feeding and caring for my dad, and it wanted me. It longed for me." He stopped to think.

"Did you ever long for me? I never felt longed for." He paused to let her consider this. Another small gasp left her mouth, a radiator in winter.

"It purposefully gave me a panic attack so I could see it again. And I did, and I heard it sing so beautifully. It has a wonderful song. I had the same thing happen after my dad's suicide attempt, but I forgot about it, considered it a symptom of the insomnia. Anyway, it showed itself again in my dad's eyes when he died. I felt it. I felt dying. It was so perfect. So, I started looking for it on the faces of dead animals. I was so stupid. I honestly thought there were that many dead animals out on the roads. There weren't. Death, dying I mean, put them there. It gave them to me as a present. That's why so many of them weren't killed by cars. Their bodies were perfectly intact." He paused.

"Are you following me?" She didn't respond.

"The last gift it gave me was Alexandria. See, she had also seen dying. She had also experienced it and was haunted by it in the same way I was, until she realized, just like I did, that it was nothing to be afraid of. So, dying told her where to meet it, and lured me toward her. It was pulling us all together. Don't you see?

"I thought Alexandria was torturing me, but she wasn't. Do you know why she kept attacking me? She was dying. Dying was her. They had turned into each other, and they were jealous. . . Of you. Every time she attacked me, it was because I was coming to you, or texting you, or thinking about you. 'No,' she kept saying to me. Or 'No more.' She meant no, stay away from you. Dying thought you were no good for me. It thought you didn't care as much as it did. The other times Lexia came to me, she didn't attack me. She just wanted me to see her." He paused again, thinking. He learned it as he said it, and sometimes it took him a second to keep up with himself.

"Except in the woods. That was something else. In the woods, dying needed to break me down. Oh, and in the video store. That was also out of jealousy, I think, because I was attached to the place and to Ray. She took care of that, though. Took care of Ray, too."

Amanda gasped again, this time with a hint of sadness.

"In the woods, it needed to detach me from the rest of it all, to separate me from this world, to let me know the world had nothing to offer me but pain and shitty consequences. And then I was free. I am free. Now, I am. Once and for all. I have someone who truly loves me."

Amanda sobbed when he said it.

"But there was still you. I still loved you. Dying, Lexia, whatever you want to call it, took care of everyone else in my life, but it refused to take care of you. Do you know why?"

He pulled away from her, sliding the knife out of her ribcage. "Because I had to do that myself."

Amanda flopped to the ground on her knees. Blood dripped from her mouth. She looked up at him wide-eyed and reached to him. He took her hand in his. "I had to prove to it that I would sacrifice for it."

She never screamed. She just listened. As he walked away, he heard her body slap against the rug. He said to her, "Don't worry. We'll all be together soon."

He went to the bathtub and drew the water piping hot. By the time he heard the sirens coming, it was too late. He was swimming in a sea of pink, a swirling ball of life and death. *We're going under, buddy. Haha.*

Join my Patreon to get new writing, behind the scenes fun, and bonus content: www.patreon.com/gagegreenwood

And don't forget to sign up for my newsletter to get the latest news and updates! www.substack.com/@gagegreenwood

Notes on *In the Eyes, In the Shadows*

In the Eyes was the fifth novel I published, sixth book if you include the short story collection Levitating, and eighth publication if you count the two short stories I published individually (Grackles on the Feeder, and Through Flickering Lights, a Silhouette). However, it was very close to being the first.

See, of all the things I've sent out into the world, In the Eyes was the first one I wrote. Almost ten years before I released it, I sent it out to small publishers and got a bite instantly. I signed a contract with this company, and we went to work on getting it ready for release. Unfortunately, it didn't take long for us to realize we had two entirely different ideals for what we wanted the book to say.

After we parted ways, I grew frustrated and shoved the book in a file, expecting it to never see the light of day again. Eight years later, my author journey took flight with the launching of Winter's Myths, and a few years later, I decided to release that old book I had thrown in a dusty folder.

It's important to know where I was when I wrote In the Eyes. I was a vastly different person from the one who wrote everything else you've read, including the two other novels in this omnibus.

The first sentence of this novel took form about two months after I sobered up. I was on extremely rocky ground, feeling unsure, desperate, angry, embarrassed, and useless. My outlook on life was bleak.

If you've read Grackles on the Feeder, I wrote that story around the same time as this novel, and you can see the utter despair in both stories. There's threads of hopelessness, existential dread, and pure hatred for life's methodologies. I hated the world. Or, well, I hated myself and that reflected on the world.

It's true that there's a dollop of antinatalism and misanthropy in all my works, but I think there's more slivers of hope and even a little love for life in the more recent stuff. The difference, of course, is that I have a child now, and I don't prescribe to that level of thinking anymore. I still like to explore it, dabble in the themes, but in the end, I do not believe in the net negative effect of life the way I once did.

It's that change in personality that made me hesitant to publish In the Eyes. I don't think it really reflects who I am.

When I finally hit publish on it, I was ten years sober. I had a family and my dream career. Things were relatively okay in my world. I still had my share of problems that my therapist helps me work through, but I am not crippled with self-loathing, and I don't live in a world of negativity anymore.

In the Eyes does not have a positive message, and it wasn't meant to. The whole point I wanted to make at the time of writing it was that the longer you live, the more you witness the death of everything you love. Hope exists in the book, but it is used as a weapon, something to smash in the character's faces.

The running commentary about living in Alaska is a real one. My mother always dreamed of moving to Alaska and living in a cabin. She used to watch documentaries of folks who lived there, built their own cabins, started a new life in the wilderness. It was a dream of hers, and when she faced her final days and rambled in a drug-addled daze, she often talked about going there. It broke my heart, and even thirteen years later, as I write these author's notes, I have a hard time not crying.

My mother's ashes rest in a ceramic cabin that sits on a shelf in my room. It was our way of getting her to the Alaskan wilderness.

While I'd been an alcoholic and drug addict before she died, it wasn't until she was gone that I made it a daily routine. I used it all as a way to avoid facing those final months. I couldn't think about them, couldn't see her face withering away. I am still haunted by the soft gasps of pain she delivered in regular intervals in her final weeks.

Sobering up scared the shit out of me. I had to strain my mind to stay exactly in the moment I lived in. I couldn't look back without shame and embarrassment, and I couldn't look forward without being terrified.

I was nearing 40 and starting over from scratch. I had no discernible skills, hadn't made any headway toward my dreams, and knew I'd wasted a huge chunk of life getting fucked up instead of doing anything of value.

You can see that theme running through In the Eyes. From Jackson's missed opportunity of walking the path behind his house to the jetties. Then, of course, there's Alaska. I have always had a tough time thinking about how much folks leave behind as nothing more than an idea in their mind. That's why I so often chased whatever I wanted. I didn't mind giving up a real-world lifestyle to become a stand-up comedian. I didn't mind packing up my shit and moving across the country on a whim. If there was something I wanted to do, I just did it, because the alternative was leaving this little monster of creativity stuck inside me.

And I think that's why I published In the Eyes, despite my reservations about the content. The monster needed to come out.

In that way, I sort of look at novels like tattoos. I can get artwork of something I love now without worrying if I will still like the thing years later, because it doesn't matter how I feel about it later. I'm getting the tattoo because it matters to me now. It's a timestamp, and the collective of the artwork tells a story. My story. Where I once was and where I will be.

I hope someday my novels do the same thing. You can see the different Gages that exist throughout the timeline of my books. And this one? The Gage who wrote In the Eyes? Well, he was choking in grief.

I hope you can forgive him.

- Gage

FAN ART

I want to thank all of the amazing fans who have created art of my books. I wouldn't be able to put them all in here, even if I wanted to, but here are a few of my favorites. I hope you enjoy them as much as I do. Please note, almost all of these had some color in them, but because the book was printed in black and white, you won't see that here. I encourage everyone to look up the artists and see their full color illustrations. Each of them will be worth following!

Artwork by Jaime Stearns @the_macabre_bibliophile

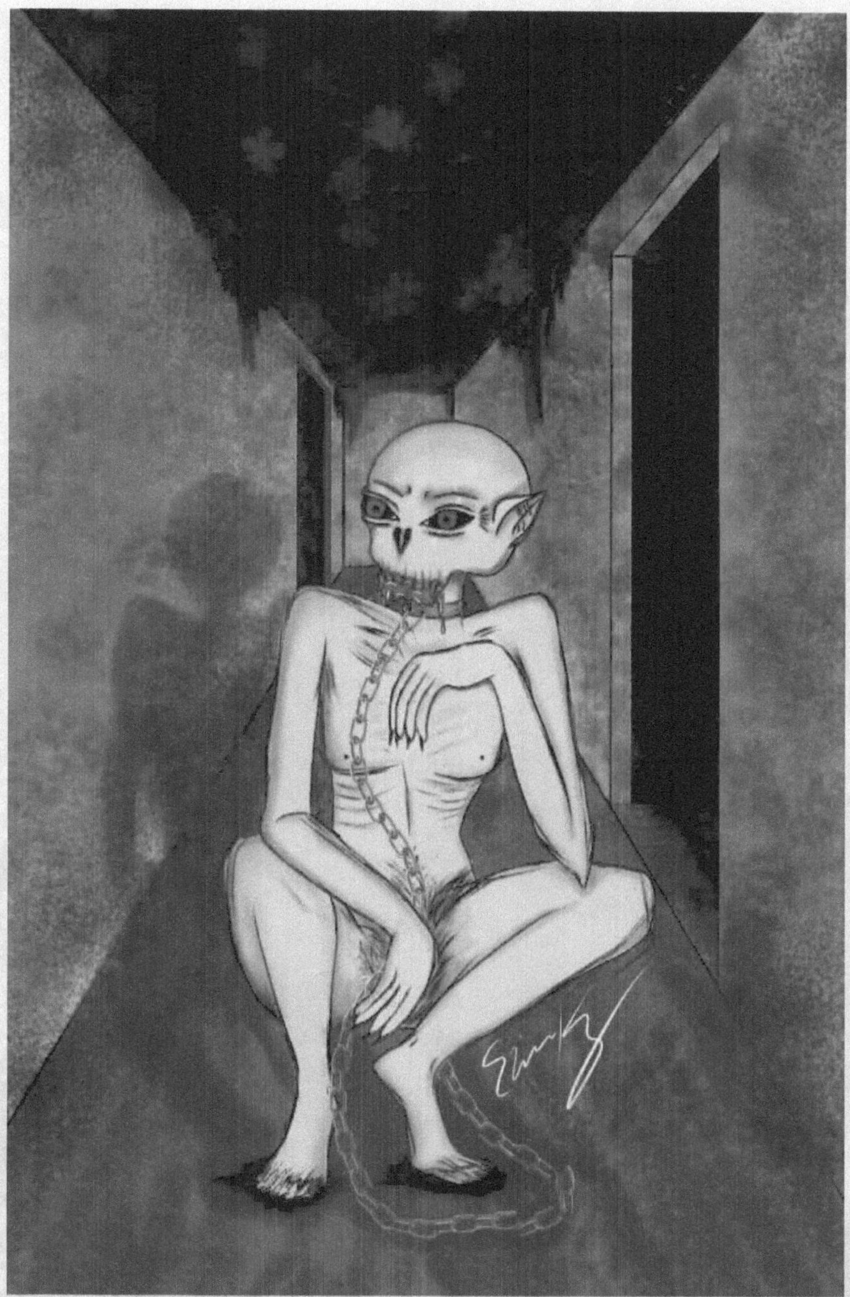

Artwork by Erica Kennedy @erica.kennedy.horror

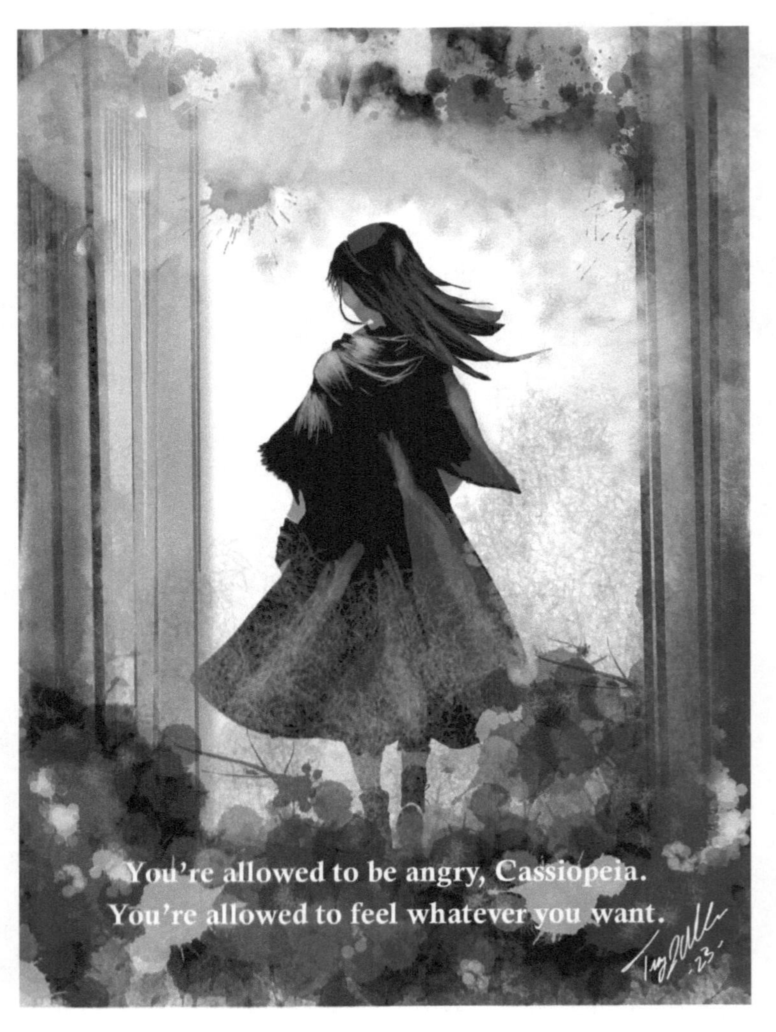

Artwork by Tracy Allen @violin.and.candlestick.design

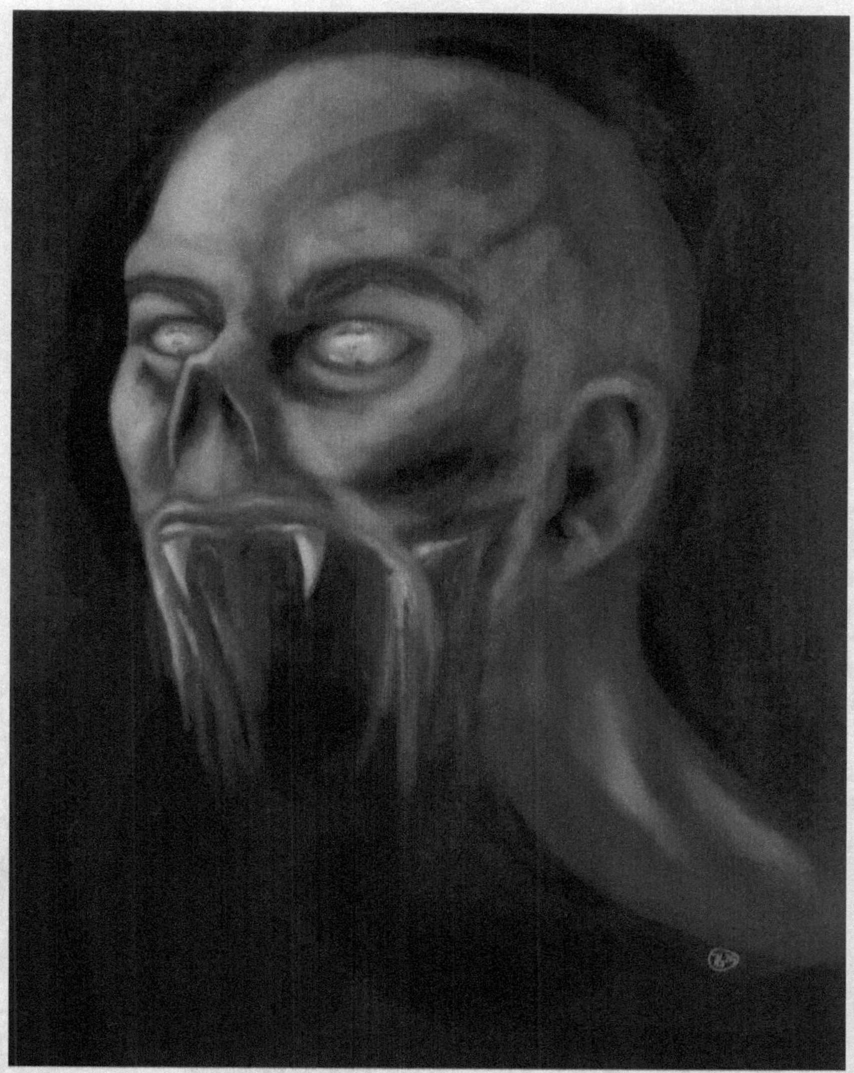

Artwork by Taylor Gibbs @teabeegibbs

A HOLE IN THE SWITCH

octor's waiting rooms always looked so drab and uninviting, at least from what Roth remembered of them. It was a long time since he last sat in one, but if Dr. Renard's waiting room were any indication, psychiatrists followed the pattern of wanting their patients to experience deep depression before entering the office.

He couldn't complain, though. Not many doctors were willing to see their patients long after hours, especially at 11:00 at night. Of course, the time of the appointment proved the least unusual aspect of this visit. First, Renard booked him. Not the other way around. She waltzed right up to him at Cuddy's and said, "You're lonely, and your life is repetitive. You're ready to snap from the cyclic and boring lifestyle." She slid a card across the bar, unconcerned that a beer glass ringlet wet the edges. "Call my receptionist and book an appointment." Then she did something no one had done to Roth in many years. She touched him, putting her hand on top of his. "I specialize in the strange."

With a playful wink, she stepped backward and walked away before Roth could gather enough wits to respond. He searched for her later in the bar amongst the sea of drunks but couldn't find her. It was as if she came there solely to drop that card in front of him while he sipped his Sam Adams. And maybe she had. *"I specialize in the strange,"* she'd said.

She couldn't have meant... But obviously, she did.

Probably a good thing she gave him no time to speak because, as a reflex, he probably would have told her to fuck off. In fact, he spent the entire night boiling from the encounter. How dare she? She didn't know him. He had a good life, better than most! The "I specialize in the strange" stuck out to him, and he knew he'd have to dig into that, but all the shrink talk about his feelings was a swing and a miss.

But the next night, he found himself drawn back to the conversation repeatedly. No matter what he did, her words cut into his brain like razor blades. Maybe she knew him better than he knew himself, because if she hadn't said it, he never would have recognized just how fucking miserable he was.

So, four days later, he sat in her office, scoffing at the beige walls and sickly yellow lighting. A receptionist sat at her desk clicking away at a computer keyboard. A receptionist! At 11:00 pm. What kind of doctor's office was this?

Each minute he waited for his session, he doubted coming here. What value could he possibly gain from it? He certainly couldn't be honest, unless the doctor *really* meant she specialized in the strange, which he doubted.

The office doors swung open, and Dr. Renard smiled at Roth. "Ready?"

He rolled his tongue over his top teeth and said, "Yup."

He stopped short of entering when he saw a teenage girl sitting on a couch in the office. He'd never seen a head doctor before, but he'd watched enough movies to know how the sessions went, and as far as he knew, there wasn't supposed to be a third party with the patient and doctor.

Dr. Renard put her hand on the small of his back. Another unex-

pected touch. It sent shivers up his body. "Don't worry. It'll all make sense soon. I promise."

He stepped in and moved out of the doctor's way, but otherwise stood in place, waiting for directions on where to sit. He'd have guessed the couch, but someone else sat there. In movies, the patient always lied down, crossed their arms, and stared at the ceiling. He couldn't do that with some teenage girl sitting in his spot.

Dr. Renard waved her hand toward the other side of the couch. "Have a seat."

So, he wouldn't get to lie down like in the movies. He found this disappointing.

He sat next to the girl. They shot each other a quick glance and an awkward smile before returning their attention to Dr. Renard, who sat across from them.

Roth had an atypical sense of smell. It wasn't just that it was strong, but that it was *smart*. He could isolate and separate different odors, pushing aside the most noticeable ones to sniff out the hidden. The girl sitting next to him wore Love Spell perfume from Victoria's Secret. But Roth focused on her mouth, where the scent of chokecherries reigned supreme. He knew a man who lost four horses in one night thanks to a chokecherry shrub. Supposedly they weren't deadly for humans, and people even put them in their jams, but Roth had never smelled them so prominently, as if the girl sat at a chokecherry tree and plucked it bare.

Dr. Renard crossed her legs. "Roth, thank you for coming in. I do things a little differently than other psychiatrists, as you can probably guess from your near midnight appointment. It'll seem strange at first, but I promise you'll find it worth it in the end, because the other thing I am outside of unorthodox is effective."

He had a lot to unpack from her introduction. First, she thanked *him* for coming in, reaffirming that she planned his appointment, not him seeking professional help. And then the woman who told him she specialized in the strange, presumably *knowing* what that meant to Roth, said *he* would find things strange in the appointment. If she worried that an oddity like Roth would find the session peculiar, he had to admit, it piqued his curiosity.

She continued, "While this isn't a group session, per say, it will be a session between the both of you. Molly will go first, and you'll host the second half of the hour. I know you may not feel comfortable sharing with another patient present, but I promise by the time Molly's half hour is up, you'll feel better about it." She gave him a large, faux smile. "For now, all you need to do is relax and give Molly your attention."

The idea of listening to a teenage girl whine about her high school woes made him want to punch himself in the skull, but he'd play along. This whole visit was an exercise in playing along. Curiosity killed the cat, but Roth had lived through enough lifetimes that he sometimes thought curiosity was the only thing keeping him alive.

No longer focusing on him, Dr. Renard said, "So, Molly, you've mentioned having bad dreams again."

Dreams. Jesus Christ this was going to be a long hour.

Molly slipped her flip flops off and put her feet on the couch as she crossed her legs. She looked like a Buddha statue minus the wisdom. And she dressed like an idiot. Fluorescents. It reminded Roth of late 80s / early 90s cornball hip-hop videos. She had a neon green muscle shirt that gave away her white bra on the sides, blindingly bright pink spandex style shorts, and a rainbow of colors dyed into her long, otherwise blonde hair. He knew her hair was blonde because the dye job was too shoddy to cover the roots or ends.

He presumed her *dreams* would be as vapid as her appearance. At least he'd learn who the newest heartthrobs were. NSYNC? Were they still popular? Or did they fall out with the last century? How long ago was Y2K? Roth couldn't remember. Three years, he guessed.

Molly tucked her hair behind her ears and smiled. "Yeah, the dreams are getting more intense, so I had to investigate."

Dr. Renard's forehead scrunched, and she scooted forward in her seat. "What do you mean you investigated? You know you're not supposed to do that kind of thing without guidance."

"I know, but it was calling me."

Dr. Renard shook her hands violently. "Exactly. And what if the thing calling you was bad?"

Roth leaned back, taking this all in. Maybe he misjudged the situation. Was Molly... like him?

Molly crossed her arms across her chest like a grumpy child. "I knew it wasn't."

Dr. Renard gave her scolding eyes. "Tell me about the dream and where it led you."

"Ever since I left the island and moved to Tanner's Switch, I've been hearing a heartbeat. Sometimes it's soft and sometimes it's really loud. At first, I thought it was different based on the time of day, but then I realized it was all about location. As soon as I determined that, I tried traveling to it."

"Physically traveling to it or mentally? Not that I approve of either."

"Mentally. At first. But every time I got so close I could *feel* the heartbeat as if it were in my own chest, it would soften, and I'd be back to square one. I decided I was wrong. That it wasn't a location thing, and I went back to studying the times. Maybe it happened at noon one day, midnight the next, and five on Friday, but I guess there could have been a pattern."

What the fuck were these people talking about?

"Was there?" Dr. Renard asked.

Molly shook her head. "No. But I was right when I thought the heartbeat had a location. I just didn't realize it was moving. One day, it just clicked in my mind, and that's when I knew I needed to physically go to the beat."

"What did you find?"

"I found a hole in Tanner's Switch. It's always moving, but it's always around. I found the heartbeat in a parking lot by the boat launch on 91. When I stepped on the center of the dirt lot, my foot went through the Earth as if the ground were made of paper."

Roth stepped in now, utterly confused. "In the middle of a parking lot? Wouldn't other people have fallen into it?"

Dr. Renard lifted a finger, telling him to shush. "I don't think the hole she's speaking of is the kind of thing that affects normal people." She moved her eyes back to Molly. "Where did it lead? Were you able to see or did you just get the hell out of there?"

Molly smiled. "Oh, I dove right in." This admission led to a giggle.

"What did you find?" Roth asked, somehow invested in something he wholly didn't understand.

Did her eyes turn red? He couldn't tell.

"I saw Tanner's Switch."

Dr. Renard tilted her head. "What do you mean?"

Molly sat up. "I saw Tanner's Switch on fire, and people screaming into cameras. I saw dead birds and lampposts. I saw mist. I saw people moving around and living their lives with no idea what's to come, what's about to happen to all of us. And it terrified me, seeing the faces who don't know. It was a mistake to jump in." Her eyes filled with water. "Because now I have the burden of carrying this secret forever." She turned her head to Roth, and back to Dr. Renard. "Because none of you can ever know the truth. You'd snap."

Dr. Renard stood up and slashed her arm across the room like she was karate chopping imaginary wood. "That's enough. You can *never* speak about this to anyone. Not even a hint at the heartbeat. Okay? Not even to me. And I'll probably try to get answers from you in moments of weakness, but you can never, ever tell me anything about it."

Molly nodded.

Roth eyed them both, unable to hide how ridiculous he found them both. "Is this some kind of skit? What the fuck are you all going on about?"

Dr. Renard slid her hand down her skirt as she sat down, fully back to normal. "Your turn Roth."

He laughed. "I thought you said I would change my mind after her time was up. All I saw was ten minutes of jibber jabber. Nonsense."

"Yes, Molly's meeting today was not what I expected. It's normally a little showier. I'll demonstrate. See, you probably think her talking about weird dreams is no big deal, but Molly's dreams are not like ours. She hasn't slept in over a decade."

Roth laughed again.

"Molly, show him how you sleep."

She slowly turned her head to him. Yes, her eyes were indeed red. Her neck snapped back and her whole body left the couch. It shot up to the ceiling like a bullet and smashed hard into the stucco. The whole room shook. Meanwhile, Molly's body slid from one side of the room to the other before dropping back to the floor. Breeze escaped her like her skin was a fan, blowing cool air on Roth.

And then she was up, completely back to normal. She giggled. "Cool, huh?"

Dr. Renard said, "Convinced? Do you want to send her a message in the black mist?"

Roth said, "Huh?"

"Don't play coy. How many people have you killed, Roth?"

He blinked, a nervous tic. "What?"

Her eyebrows went up. "Ever kill a demon?"

He laughed. "You have the wrong guy."

Dr. Renard pointed to Molly. "She's not like you, but she can still read your black mist. Send it to her."

"No."

"NOW!" She slammed her fist on the table.

He opened his mouth and a cloud of black steam twirled out of him. It floated across the room and Molly swallowed it.

She licked her lips. "Oh, he's a bad one." Her nose scrunched cutely. "It tastes good. He's mean to the ones he's killed. It's not just for the need. He gets his fill and then toys with them."

"Fuck you," Roth said and jumped across the table, teeth out, ready to rip into the doctor, his curiosity not thick enough to coat his rage. Halfway between the couch and the doctor's chair, his body froze in midair. He couldn't move, not even to open or close his eyes.

Molly walked in front of him and placed a finger on his forehead. "He's never tasted a demon, so he's pretty weak. I mean, he finished off a human yesterday, so he's normal strong, but he's only ever eaten people. Nothing that could make him super strong."

"What's his name?"

"Roth Fischer."

"No, I mean, check the files and see what the name of our next subject will be."

"Oh!" Molly skipped to a file cabinet in the corner and flipped through some manilla folders. She took the folder over to Roth and slapped it on his forehead. "You, mister, will now be William Henry Harrison."

For the first time in over a century, Roth's heart raced. The one thing in his body that moved. In a way, he was thankful. It felt good to feel something again.

Renard hit a button, and the receptionist walked in.

"Take him to the tunnels. Molly has him frozen. He won't be moving for a long time."

The receptionist did as she was told.

ALSO BY GAGE GREENWOOD

NOVELS:

Winter's Myths

Winter's Legacy

Bunker Dogs

On a Clear Day, You Can See Block Island

In the Eyes, In the Shadows

We Are All Dead Anyway

SHORT STORY COLLECTION:

Levitating: Stories

SHORT STORIES:

Through Flickering Lights, a Silhouette

Grackles on the Feeder

ABOUT THE AUTHOR

Gage Greenwood is the award winning author of *Bunker Dogs*, *On a Clear Day, You Can See Block Island*, and *Levitating: Stories*.

He's been an actor, comedian, podcaster, and even the Vice President of an escape room company. Since childhood, he's been a big fan of comic books, horror movies, and depressing music that fills him with existential dread.

He lives in New England with his girlfriend and son, and he spends his time writing, hiking, and decorating for various holidays.

Find out more, or contact him: www.gagegreenwood.com